THE FAMILY IN 1870

Alexandria "Alex"
(1800–)
m.
St. John "Sinje" Carrington (2nd Marriage)
(1789–1829)

Christiana
(1816–1819)

Morgan (Son of Rane)
(1817–)
m.
Samantha "Sam" Elisa Seldon Burke
(1818–)

Nigel
(1819–1845)
m.
Piety Thurgood
(1814–1863)

Seth
(1841–1863)

Adam
(1844–)

Nigel
(1845–)

Virginia "Gincie"
(1842–)
m.
Travis Culhane
(1835–)

Alexandria Abigail "Lexy"
(1865–)

Kendrick Carrington "K.C." "Kace"
(1868–)

Taylor Falconer "Tay"
(1868–)

2nd marriage for Alex & for Rane

Alexandria
(1800–)
m.
Rane Falconer
(1795–)

See Morgan under Alex's first marriage

Gweneth "Gwenny"
(1832–)
m.
Christopher Bettingdon
(1829–)

Hugh
(1854–)

Nicholas
(1854–)

Eveline
(1858–)

A Season of Swans

with fire and grace. But in two cases, I feel obliged to note the true winners. The 1888 Futurity at Coney Island was won by Proctor Knott, and the victory in the 1889 Kentucky Derby went to Spokane.

The writing of a book as intricate as this one takes a great deal of time and concentration, and for me, it means letting the characters possess my life. I hope that makes me a better writer, but I know it makes me a difficult friend or relative. I am enormously grateful to both friends and relatives who have treated me so generously during the creation of this last *Swan*. According to their individual talents, they have offered me moral support, fine meals, companionship, commiseration, and laughter—always according to what my writing schedule would allow. For their patience, kindness, and love, for all their gifts, I thank the people hereafter listed as well as those I have, despite my good intentions, undoubtedly forgotten: Eric Auest, Terry Burchell, Barbara Caldwell, Craig and Laura Campbell, Joseph and Donna Campbell, Craig Corder, Clint and Susan Dailey, Jean De Blasis, Gary and Marcia De Vaul, Michael Edgar, Jon Goodwill, Dorothy and Leonard Henderson, Glee and Hike Heikes, Michael Lowe, Fred and Mae Nassif, Nancy Nielsen, Pat and Eddie O'Brien, Jim O'Donnell, Alice Sauls, Tony and Ernie Sgro, Patty Short, Anna Slavick, Austin Stockdale, Katie Taylor, Jean Wells, Susan Wells, and Sandy Winberry.

There is one additional person I wish I could thank once again, but "Big Pete" McRae died last summer. I miss him dreadfully. He was like a father to me, always open in his love and pride. But it was not he alone who gave me those gifts. His wife Bonnie and his children, Marcia and Peter, shared him with me for all of those years, and they are still a very special part of my life.

Celeste N. De Blasis
June 1988

as for poisoning, I needed to know how much would be lethal for a
horse. Two local veterinarians, Allen F. Hawley (with his office
assistant Marie Follis) and Ronald Johnson, obligingly did the com-
putation for me. Others willingly shared their expertise, too. Buck
Abbott, William H. Anderson of The Jockey Club, and Mrs. Russ
Cullen shared their knowledge of races, Thoroughbreds, and jumping horses. Mary Carey, reference librarian for the New York Historical Society, found the record of Tattersals in New York. Kent Crosby
checked the Spanish nomenclature of the California ranch. Madeleine
Fabby made inquiries about nineteenth-century medical schools in
France and Switzerland. Elaine E. Mann, director of the National
Museum of Racing at Saratoga Springs, New York, recommended
source material. Antoinette Paris Powell and her staff of the Agricultural Library at the University of Kentucky loaned me original sporting and agricultural gazettes that I could not obtain anywhere else.
Meg Ruley helped me track down various books. Ellen Schwartz,
librarian at the State Railroad Museum in Sacramento, California,
supplied me with nineteeth-century train schedules.

I discovered that there is a separate bookselling world that deals
in sporting and equestrian titles. Most of these booksellers know
each other, and if one dealer didn't have the volume I wanted, he or
she was quick to refer me to another. My thanks to the following,
who cooperated with each other and with me: Barbara Cole, James
Cummins, Jim di Marco, Harris Books, Mr. Hooper, Edward Johnson, Neil E. Nelson, and Cim Smith.

In the final weeks of finishing this novel, I remained passably
sane, but my office equipment didn't. I'm grateful to my "pit crew"
for keeping things chugging along. Ray F. Beckwith is the only
reason I still use an IBM typewriter. Howard, Vicki, and Wendy
Kack made copies of the manuscript for me when my copier wouldn't,
and Ed Laube kept after my copier until it would.

Because the historical framework of this story has been constructed from so many original and secondary sources, I hesitate to
single out a few for fear of slighting the others, but three books were
particularly helpful in very specialized areas: *Abortion in America: The
Origins and Evolution of National Policy, 1800–1900,* by James C.
Mohr; *The History of Thoroughbred Racing in America,* by William
H. P. Robertson; and *Racing in America, 1866–1921,* by W. S. Vosburgh.

The horses of Wild Swan and Sunrise are as real to me as if I
could look out of my window and see them running down the
pasture, but they are, of course, fictional. However, the contests
they entered and the horses that lost to them or defeated them
existed all those years ago. For the most part, I stole races with a
clear conscience, giving my mythical beasts the chance to compete

Acknowledgments

In order to establish historical accuracy for the background of this novel, I consulted hundreds of primary and secondary sources. However, this time, the quest for information was more difficult than ever before.

Part of the difficulty concerns the materials. Much of the printed matter of the post–Civil War period was a product of the industrial age, done on mass-produced paper with a high acid content. The paper is consuming itself in its own fire; the pages crumble at a touch. So much material is being lost, and the loss is not confined to original pages. Where microfilming was done years ago, the film itself is decaying. To me, it is a tragedy that libraries across the country lack the funds to preserve what they have.

In some cases, libraries also lack the means to make loans, even on the formal level of entrusting the material to another library. The result is that sources of knowledge about our past may be preserved, but they are locked away, rendered increasingly inaccessible and thus useless.

But by far the most frustrating aspect of the search for history came from the bureaucracy of many library systems, which ignored, misplaced, or mishandled requests for information. Some books and reels of microfilm showed up a year and a half late; some items, though labeled available at the time of the request, have yet to arrive. Had I not had the assistance and perseverance of local librarians, much of the material I did use would never have reached me; these librarians battled with headquarters and with outside libraries in order to push the requests through. I owe special thanks to Nancy Nielsen, who was endlessly patient with my demands and my temper, and to Roberta Bradford, Willow Brown, Joyce Burke, Alice Christiansen, and Esther Empey.

Often I needed odd bits of arcane information. For instance, I read an old account of dosing horses with arsenic in order to tamper with a race, but no details were given beyond the fact that several of the horses died. Since arsenic has long been used medicinally as well

With thanks once again to the Tribe.

Some are gone;
some are new to the magic meeting place;
all of us have aged and changed;
but the essential way remains the same.

Blessed be.

A SEASON OF SWANS
A Bantam Book / June 1989

Library of Congress Cataloging-in-Publication Data

De Blasis, Celeste.
  A season of swans / Celeste De Blasis.
    p. cm.
  ISBN 0-553-05362-0
  I. Title.
PS3554.E11144S44   1989   88-37614
813'.54—dc19   CIP

Published simultaneously in the United States and Canada

Bantam Books are published by Bantam Books, a division of Bantam
Doubleday Dell Publishing Group, Inc. Its trademark, consisting of the
words "Bantam Books" and the portrayal of a rooster, is Registered
in U.S. Patent and Trademark Office and in other countries. Marca
Registrada. Bantam Books, 666 Fifth Avenue, New York, New York 10103.

PRINTED IN THE UNITED STATES OF AMERICA

DC   0 9 8 7 6 5 4 3 2 1

A Season
of Swans

Celeste De Blasis

BANTAM BOOKS

NEW YORK • TORONTO • LONDON • SYDNEY • AUCKLAND

To every thing there is a season,
and a time to every purpose under heaven.

Ecclesiastes 3:1

Book One

TRAVIS
AND GINCIE

Chapter 1

Stockton, California, May 1870.

Travis Culhane heard the exuberant whoop of excitement and stopped speaking in midsentence, grinning as he turned to gaze across the crowd at his wife.

Though none of their horses was running in this race, Gincie appreciated the beauty and form of the filly that had just won, and her face was alight with approval.

She felt Travis's gaze as if he had touched her, and she smiled back at him before focusing her attention on the horses once again.

Boston Thaine, Gincie's great-uncle, observed the exchange between the two fondly. Gincie and Travis had been through so much, caught in the maelstrom of the civil war that had destroyed so many lives. Though they had met when they were both working on the Underground Railroad, guiding runaway slaves northward, when the war came, Travis, a Virginian, had felt honor bound to fight for his home and thus the rebels. His years in gray had left him with a rare maturity in a man who was only thirty-five and with a limp, vestige of the wound that had nearly killed him at Gettysburg.

Boston was enormously proud of Gincie and of his sister Alexandria Carrington Falconer, for it was Alex and her husband, Rane Falconer, Gincie's grandparents, who had raised the child to be the entrancing woman she was now. But Gincie burned with her own special fire that went beyond anything that could be taught.

Her hat covered most of her golden brown hair and shaded her face, and she was too far away in any case for his aging vision to perceive her features clearly, but he knew her grass green eyes were luminous, her finely etched features alive with the enjoyment of the day.

"We are fortunate to be so besotted with our wives," Boston said, and he wished Rachel, his own wife of thirty-four years, were with him today.

When someone moved to stand close to her, Gincie started to turn, thinking it was Boston or Travis, but the words stopped her.

"Don't turn around, just keep watching the track, Gincie, sister mine."

Gincie's first reaction was total shock. She could not have moved if she had had to. It was impossible, unthinkable, but he had called her by name and by their relationship. It was his voice.

"Mark?" His name came out as a mere whisper of sound.

"The very same, and so pleased to see you after all these years."

Five years it had been since the marauders had come to Wild Swan, the farm in Maryland where Gincie had been raised by her grandparents, five years since Mark had shot Samson, the runaway slave who had found refuge at Wild Swan and had become the guardian not only of the Thoroughbreds bred there, but of generations of children. The war had been drawing to a close, and the invaders had been no part of the military operations, just thieves and murderers scavenging the vulnerable land while the men were gone to war. And Mark had led the raiders to Wild Swan.

Travis, she needed Travis. Her paralysis broke, but before she could utter a sound or take a step, Mark gripped her arm to restrain her. "Do you want your pretty husband alive or dead?"

That was enough to freeze her in place again. "What do you want?" She hated the fear she heard in her voice.

"To share your good fortune," he said. "I've kept my eye on you for some time now. Such a happy chance that brought us both to California after the war, and happier yet for me that you and your husband are so industrious and well connected. What I want is little enough to ensure the continued good health of little Lexy, the twins, and their father, not to mention Boston Thaine and his family."

A shudder of horror went through her at his specific mentions of her family, and Mark felt it. "Oh, yes, I've watched them all," he said. "It would be impossible to keep them all safe." Then with sudden urgency, he rapped out his instructions. "Two weeks from today, before the noon hour, at the Russ House in San Francisco. Five thousand dollars. Come alone. Watch the race for proof of what I can do."

As quickly as he had appeared at her side, he was gone. She caught only a glimpse of him as he melted into the crowd that was surging forward to have a closer look at the race about to begin.

It seemed to be happening very slowly, the horses leaping forward to run the first mile heat for the three out of five that would win the race. She saw their own three-year-old colt, Gold Fire, gleaming bright chestnut. He seemed to get off to a good start, but then he swerved madly, causing one of the other horses to jump and stumble in its attempt to get out of the way before it regained its footing and went on. But Gold Fire was totally out of control and veered toward the inside rail, crashing through it and going down with a high-pitched scream that sounded over the shocked gasps of the spectators.

"Oh, Christ!" Only at the sound of his voice did Gincie realize that Travis had appeared at her side, and then he was crossing the railings, running toward the fallen horse and rider.

Gincie stood absolutely still. Mark had done this, or caused it to be done. Gold Fire had been drugged; she was sure of it. She felt cold seeping into the marrow of her bones. It was murderous proof of what Mark could do to her family.

Boston gave Gincie's arm a little shake. He had been right behind Travis, moving toward the rail when the accident happened, and he had expected Gincie to follow Travis when the horse and rider had gone over. Gincie had been trained to help in emergencies since her earliest childhood; her immobility was wholly unlike her. "Gincie! Your jockey might need help!"

The unusual sharpness in her great-uncle's voice pierced Gincie's consciousness, and she went with him, trying to banish the specter of Mark and concentrate on the disaster before them.

Tommy, the jockey, was shaken and bruised but otherwise all right physically. But he was distraught over the colt and kept murmuring, "I couldn't hold 'im, just couldn't hold 'im."

There was no question of saving the colt. His right foreleg was badly broken, and he was screaming and struggling to get up. As soon as the track was cleared, Travis put a bullet through Gold Fire's brain.

Their head trainer, Malachi, did not try to hide the tears in his eyes. "He was excited before the race, but he always was. I should have known this was different."

"You couldn't have known," Gincie said, thinking that Mark was too clever to be found out but feeling compelled to ask anyway. "Was anyone near Gold Fire right before the race, any stranger?"

Malachi shook his head. "Only the usual, but the usual means a lot of people—jockeys, trainers, owners, some of the crowd. You think that . . ." His question trailed away as he contemplated the idea of someone tampering with the horse. It was not unheard of, but it was rare, usually involved heavy betting, and was a method despised by every honest horseman. Malachi was as honest as his father had been. And his father had been Samson, shot dead by Mark.

Travis studied Gincie's set face. He did not reject her intimation that someone had interfered with Gold Fire, but, like Malachi, he could think of no reason it might have been done. "The bettin' on these races just isn't that great," he said. "It doesn't make sense that anyone would go to such lengths to stop Gold Fire."

Gincie wished she had not wanted to know how Mark had committed the crime; she didn't want Travis or the others to suspect that she knew it had been done and who was behind it. The evidence of Mark's continued savagery lay before her. Although the colt had only been dead for minutes, already it seemed as if the red fire in his coat was fading. And the victim could have been Travis, or one of the children, or Boston, or Rachel, or the Thaines' son Caton, or . . . the list of people Gincie loved was too long.

The days of dissembling had begun. Mark was her curse, hers to deal with.

"I suspect I just want a reason for this," she said, her voice trembling. "Gold Fire was too fine to die this way. But at least none of the riders and none of their horses was killed." With effort, she put more strength into her words. "Tommy, Malachi, neither of you is to blame yourself. We all know this is a dangerous sport, despite all of our efforts to make it safe. Gold Fire was hot-blooded; no one could have held him." Lies upon lies.

When Travis put his arm around her to comfort her, she hardly felt it, and when other horse owners began to gather to shake their heads and commiserate with the Culhanes, she perceived their words as nothing more than a swirl of noise. Two weeks, she had two weeks to decide what to do about Mark.

When they returned to La Salida del Sol, their ranch in the Sonoma Valley north of San Francisco, it was all Gincie could do to control her panic until the three children came out to greet them, Lexy holding her twin brothers by the hands.

Gincie's eyes filled with tears as she watched them come toward her, three matching heads of golden brown hair: Alexandria Abigail—"Lexy"—wiry and tall for her five years, green eyes dancing with happiness at having her parents home again; Kendrick Carrington—"K. C."—and Taylor Falconer—"Tay"—sturdy little boys of two with the turquoise eyes of their father, though they were not identical twins.

Gincie hugged each in turn, so compulsively that K. C. squirmed and protested, "Mama, too tight!" before he gave her a smacking kiss on the cheek.

"Why are you crying?" Lexy asked, always direct.

Gincie swiped at her eyes. "I'm not crying, not really. I'm just so glad to see all of you!" To see all of you safe, she added silently, and a chill went through her as she wondered how often and where Mark had observed the children.

It didn't take long for Lexy to notice that the red colt was not with the returning stock. "Where's Gold Fire?" she asked.

Travis and Gincie exchanged a look; the temptation to lie, to say that the colt had been sold, was great, but both of them knew the truth would leak out one way or another.

Travis hoisted Lexy in his arms, and the drawl in his voice was more pronounced in tenderness. "Well, little darlin', Gold Fire had an accident at the races. He bolted and broke his leg. We had to put him out of his misery."

Travis loved all three of the children fiercely, but Lexy pulled at his heart for special reasons. She was his first born, conceived in the last dark year of the war; she looked so much like her mother; and she was such an intelligent, responsible child. It broke his heart to see the sorrow dawn in her eyes before she hid her face against his shoulder with a little sob. She had been raised around Thorough-breds and other livestock since her birth at Wild Swan in Maryland, and she cared passionately about each animal on the ranch and mourned each loss. But she also had the acceptance that comes to children who live close to the land. Lexy already knew the cycles of life and death.

"We couldn't let him be in pain, crippled so that he would never run or even walk again. He could not have lived long like that." Travis rocked her in his arms.

"Go' Fi' go 'way?" K. C. asked, and Tay looked around as if he thought the horse would appear out of thin air.

At first Travis thought the loss of Gold Fire and having to tell the children were the cause of Gincie's abstraction, but he soon doubted that judgment. The ranch had been a place of productivity and solace for both himself and Gincie from the day they had purchased the acres. Because of the diverse nature of their various businesses, coupled with the enterprises they shared with Boston and Rachel Thaine, the Culhanes traveled about the state a good deal, but Rancho de Salida del Sol was always waiting to welcome them home to well-tended livestock and crops.

The spell wasn't working for Gincie this time. Travis caught her staring off into space, her hands stilled in the midst of some task, and more than once he saw her start as if in fright at the mere calling of her name by himself or one of the staff.

And it was worst of all in their moments alone. They had always loved each other well and kindly, the pleasure of one being the pleasure of the other. But now when Travis touched Gincie in what had been a casual, constant pattern of mutual reassurance, he could feel her stiffen before she made an obvious effort to relax. And though they had always slept intertwined, that was changed, too.

Even on their first night home, when Travis was so tired he could hardly keep his eyes open and assumed Gincie must surely feel the same, he was awakened several times during the night by her restless tossing and turning. When he called her name softly, she didn't answer, but he suspected she was awake nonetheless. And though by morning she was sleeping soundly, she was across the bed from him, huddled in her own little space.

He leaned over her and kissed her gently. "It's time to get up, love."

Her eyes opened wide, and a little shudder ran through her before she focused on him.

He stroked her hair back from her forehead. "What is it? What's troublin' you so? I know it was hard to lose Gold Fire that way, but I don't think that's it. Unless you truly do think someone tampered with him before the race?"

He waited for her to answer, and the silence stretched out between them.

She wanted to tell him. She wanted to share the burden. She heard Mark's smooth threats as if he were standing beside her again, and she saw Gold Fire plunging out of control on the track. She saw Samson dying from Mark's bullet. Mark would stop at nothing to have his way. It was a terrifyingly small step of the imagination to see Travis dying as Samson had.

She looked up at him with eyes that glittered strangely, a feral green looking more like cat's eyes than Travis had ever seen them. Very deliberately she pulled his head down and kissed him. "Nothing is wrong." She vowed to make it true.

Distracted by the seduction of her kiss and the flexing of her body against his, Travis did not notice that she had not answered his questions.

She raked her nails lightly over his shoulders and back, her hands asking her own question as they drifted lower to test the readiness of his sex, teasing him sweetly until he forgot the long list of chores that awaited them both.

Gincie wanted him with a ferocity that stunned her, wanted him safe, warm, and hidden inside of her.

It was going much too fast, even as his own passion compelled him to follow Gincie's lead, Travis registered that, and when he entered her, her body clasped him so tightly, the pleasure was near pain and brought him to a swift, wrenching climax as if he were a green boy.

He lay over her, panting hard, knowing she had not taken her own pleasure, but when he started to stroke her into completion, she pushed his hand away. "No, I don't need . . . it is enough."

He rolled off of her and knelt beside her, staring down at her. "What was that about?"

"About loving you and about needing to be up and about before the children come in search of us." Her eyes did not meet his, and she slipped out of bed and began her morning ritual of washing and dressing as if nothing untoward had happened.

Despite the fact that they had just been as physically close as a man and woman could be, Travis felt abandoned and wanted to demand that she tell him what in the hell was going on. But he restrained himself with the reminder that marriage did not mean full possession of the other person physically or mentally. It meant accepting what the other offered and making one's own offerings in return. The war had taught him that. There were things he'd seen and things he'd done that he would never share with Gincie.

"Whatever it is, I'm here for you," he said, dropping a kiss on her shoulder as she sat brushing her hair, clad in her shift. Her slender body suddenly appeared very fragile to him, and he wanted to wrap her in his arms and slay all of her dragons, but he went on with his own preparations to greet the day.

For a moment, Gincie watched him in the mirror, his hard nakedness beautiful to her in every line, even to the savage scar of Gettysburg that ran from his right hipbone down his thigh nearly to his knee. He had been so hurt then, he had nearly died. As long as she could prevent it, no one would ever hurt him again.

The days passed in a strange haze for Gincie. She endeavored to fulfill the multitude of roles she normally played—wife, mother, and equal partner in the running of the ranch—but all the while, her mind worked frantically to find an acceptable way out of the trap Mark had set.

And in spite of her best efforts, she knew she was betraying her agitation. She caught herself being overly protective of the children, warning them not to wander too far, not to do this or that unless she or one of the ranch hands was with them, until Lexy protested, "I always take care of the twins!"

"I know you do, sweetheart," Gincie said, holding back tears. "It's just that I love you all so much, I worry even when I shouldn't. Mothers do that sometimes."

But it was obvious that Lexy did not find this a satisfactory explanation, for she too often regarded her mother with a troubled little frown and went out of her way to be so well behaved that it was as if she were taking the blame for the change in her parent.

It was the same with the hands at the ranch. Nervous, short-tempered, and abstracted—this was not the normal behavior of their employer, and the ranch hands began to tread as carefully as Lexy.

Even the horses behaved differently, showing the whites of their eyes and stomping nervously when Gincie's disquiet communicated itself to them.

And through it all, Travis endured her moods, his eyes so full of patience and love that she thought it would be easier if he railed at her. At night he held her when she wanted him to and let her curl away from him when she could not bear to be touched.

She could not fool herself into believing that Mark would somehow disappear without getting what he wanted. He made sure her feeling of being stalked never lessened. A message arrived with supplies a week after the Culhanes had come home:

Being acquainted with your family in Maryland, it would be my pleasure to call upon you one day soon.

M. Stockton.

Seeming innocuous, it was wholly vicious. Even had Travis read it, he would have been no wiser. But to Gincie, it said plainly that the secret, the bond, was between herself and Mark.

At Wild Swan, little distinction was made regarding the degree of consanguinity. Alexandria had raised her dead sister's twins, Blaine and Flora, as if they were her own, as she had later raised her granddaughter Gincie. But Gincie had always minded being the daughter of Piety Thurgood Carrington, a woman devoid of kindness. After she had gone to live permanently at Wild Swan at age two, while her half brothers, Mark and Matthew, Piety's sons by her first marriage had remained with their mother. Gincie had seen her mother only once more. She had been just seven years old at the time, but she remembered overhearing the woman demanding money from Alex and, in turn, being warned away.

Alex had assured her granddaughter that she did not and never would resemble her mother, but Gincie had never been fully convinced. It was her mother who had set the fire in the stallion barn, the fire that had caused the death of the prize horse, Wild Swan, the fire that had persuaded her father, Nigel, to leave the daughter he loved with her grandparents. The feeling of tainted blood flowing in her veins had been heightened by Mark's treachery at Wild Swan. Now it seemed she would never be free of the curse, certainly never while Mark lived.

It was there constantly, its tentacles slithering into her mind even while she denied it—she would be better off, her family would be better off, if Mark no longer existed, if Mark were dead.

She searched desperately for other options, but nothing served.

And thrown back on herself, she wondered if she could do it. To hire it done was out of the question, an invitation to further blackmail.

Death was not an abstract image to Gincie. She had seen it firsthand in Virginia and in all its grotesque power at Gettysburg. More than the sight of it, the smell came to her again, a smell so strong that it became a taste and texture, metal and oil in the mouth, enough to make her stomach heave when she tried to eat.

Travis watched with growing concern, and then with the dawning of an idea that led him off on the wrong track entirely. He did not think she had skipped her last monthly course, but he could not be sure. It was a natural part of her woman's body and did not disgust him save in the sense that he was sorry when it made her feel unwell. Perhaps he had lost track. Perhaps she was pregnant. In light of that, her sudden aversion to food and her mood changes were explicable.

Gincie had had such a hard time giving birth to the twins, he had not wanted her to bear another child too soon, if at all. He was more than satisfied with the three children they had. He and Gincie had both done what they could to prevent conception in the past two years, but he knew of no method except abstinence that worked all the time, and abstinence was not part of their marriage.

Though he wished more than ever that she would confide in him, he could not blame her for keeping her secret until she was sure, until she had time to adjust to the idea. He began to see her strange behavior in light of that adjustment. She would have to face going through another pregnancy and birth in the midst of her busy and demanding life. And they would both have another lively child to care for, if not two more. He sincerely hoped that another pair of twins was not in the offing. K. C. and Tay were enough of a handful.

His mistaken belief made him even more patient and tender with Gincie, and that, paradoxically, made it harder for her. Sometimes she felt so violent inside, she wanted to scream at him and force him to match her own aggression. And then she would feel overwhelmed with remorse, fearful that Mark's poison was seeping through her to those she most wanted to protect from it.

"I do love you, Travis, more than anyone else in the world. Please, don't ever forget that."

She whispered the words in the darkness of the night as he held her, and his arms tightened around her. "How could I forget when I love you no less than that?" he asked, but it was all he could do not to demand that she tell him whether or not she was pregnant. A sudden sharp current of fear shot through him as he wondered if she'd had some premonition, some horrible early sense that she would die this time in giving birth.

"Don't ever leave me!" The words were harsher than he intended, and his need for comfort penetrated the thick fog of Gincie's own despair.

"Never, never, never." She punctuated the words with soft kisses against the hollow of his throat and settled against him so that she could be cradled in his warmth. But even here there was no longer any escape for her. Even here she could feel Mark's evil, could see his eyes watching them, could sense him gloating over the misery he had already brought to their lives.

Chapter 2

There was nothing unusual in Gincie's announcement that she was going to San Francisco; she and Travis spent a good deal of time there, and Boston and Rachel were always happy to welcome them, so much so that a part of their house was kept in continual readiness for the Culhanes.

Travis was relieved at Gincie's plan. He had business to attend to in the city but had been afraid to leave Gincie or to suggest she accompany him while he was so unsure of her moods. And he hoped that the faster pace of the city would brighten her spirits.

It was hard for Gincie to let the children out of her sight, but there was no question of taking them to San Francisco; Mark was going to be there. And Travis did not press her to take them, even though he knew the Thaines would have been delighted to see them.

The trip to the city and the first two days there passed in a blur for Gincie, and then, after all the mindless terror, she suddenly felt utterly calm, as if everything were already resolved. She would not let Mark touch her family—not Travis, not Lexy, not the twins, and not Boston's family. Mark should have died that day at Wild Swan. Instead, Samson had fallen. That image remained as sharp in her mind as if it were happening over and over before her. She could hear her grandmother and Della, Samson's wife, keening, could see Samson's blood seeping into the earth of Wild Swan.

She knew what Mark was capable of; she doubted he knew as much about her.

She studied the little pistol as if it were an elegant piece of jewelry. Travis had given it to her when they had first come to California. She had never wanted anything to do with firearms, but her grandfather Rane had insisted she learn how to shoot and to carry a weapon on her missions for the Underground Railroad. She was more thankful for that training now than she had ever been.

When Gincie told her that she had to go out for a short while, Rachel immediately offered to accompany her, the men having already departed for the office where much of their joint business was centered.

Having been able to convince Travis that he was to go along without her, Gincie was not about to let Rachel impede her. "No, thank you," she said. Her voice was polite, but implacable, and her eyes were steady as she looked at Rachel.

Rachel watched with a puzzled frown as Gincie left the house. She could not be offended. She was certain Gincie's refusal of her company was nothing personal. Something was troubling the younger woman. The Culhane children were flourishing; Travis and Gincie seemed to be as much in love as ever; and all was well with the various business enterprises. The vital things all seemed in perfect order. It was sad that the prize colt had had to be destroyed after the accident at the races, but despite her tender heart, Gincie was not the sort to brood about the accident for this long.

Rachel considered other possibilities, and a slow smile curved her mouth as she came to the same conclusion Travis had. Perhaps Gincie was pregnant. Rachel could understand how distracting that could be. The birth of the twins had been so difficult. It would be no wonder if she had reservations about another pregnancy, but Rachel was confident that she would welcome the knowledge soon. It was likely Gincie had come to the city to consult a physician about her condition. It explained her strange mood and the fact she looked hollow-cheeked and pale and was eating little. Nor had Rachel missed the concern in Travis's eyes.

Rachel and Boston had only one child, their son Caton, who lived with his wife, Muirne, and their three children on a ranch in Grass Valley at the foothills of the Sierras. Rachel had always wished she could have borne Boston at least one more child. She doted on her grandchildren—before long there would surely be great-grandchildren to spoil—and she looked forward to spoiling the new Culhane, having now convinced herself that one was on the way.

Creating a new life was the furthest thing from Gincie's mind. All of her concentration was on whether or not she would be able to end one.

Fleetingly, she wished Mark had chosen a more obscure hotel

than the Russ House, but at least it was not the usual haunt of any of the social sets, such as the Virginia City Bonanza Kings and their wives or the railroad magnates, whose members might recognize her. But that was the least of her concerns. She found that she most dreaded that Mark would not be there for their meeting. She could not bear the unresolved threat hanging over her family any longer.

It was repellent to have to ask the desk clerk for Mark Carrington's room number, obscene to have Mark connected to the Carrington name. She wished he were using "Stockton" as he had in the note he had sent to her at the ranch, but she had known he would feel no need to continue the jest. In his arrogance he was sure everything was going to go as planned for Mark Carrington.

She ignored the clerk's avid stare and his offer to escort her to Mr. Carrington's room.

Right to the moment when Mark bid her enter, she feared she would not have her chance, but once she heard his voice, the almost mystical sense of purpose descended on her again.

"My sweet sister, so glad you could attend this little meeting," Mark said as she entered. He did not rise from his chair.

She took careful inventory of the room before she looked at Mark. "You seem to be able to afford fine accommodations. Have you other schemes, other victims?"

Mark was taken aback by the aggressive contempt in her voice; he expected her to be fearful and compliant, and he spoke quickly to reestablish the dominance he had felt at the races. "You will do quite nicely. Have you brought the money? The more I've discovered about the enterprises of Culhane and Thaine, the more I've realized how easily you can share the profits with me. Travis, beautiful little Lexy, K. C., and Tay—five thousand dollars, that's little enough to protect your family."

"Too little," Gincie said, fighting the wave of rage that he should dare speak the names of the people she loved above all others. "Too little in my mind, and I'm sure too little in yours. You will never stop this. You are a greedy, evil man. It makes me ill that we share blood. You brought death to Wild Swan. You killed Samson." She needed to state the charges aloud.

She hated him for the blank look and more for the dawning of memory that made him say, "Oh, that big buck. Your grandmother always was a nigger lover, wasn't she? So was your father."

Gincie had thought that if there was the slightest chance she could rid her family of the threat of Mark without violence, she would take it. She had harbored a faint hope that, faced with her determination, he would change his course. Now she realized he was as malevolent in reality as she had known him in memory. There was no bargain possible, no half measure that would suffice.

"There are things you don't know about me," she said. "I once killed a man for raping me; I killed him with my bare hands. You are a thousandfold worse than he; you threaten my husband and my children. I cannot allow that."

As she spoke, she drew the pistol and held it steadily pointed at him. At first he was too stunned to react. He had played this scene over and over in his mind, and not once had Gincie strayed from her role of helpless victim. Now it was like watching a mouse turn into a viper, and he could scarcely comprehend it. But the transformation assumed a terrible truth for him as he was caught in the pitiless stare of the slitted green eyes, as he saw that the pistol did not waver.

"Come now, sister mine, you can't mean to . . ." He stood as he spoke and started toward her, and in the split second before she fired, Gincie saw the pure terror in his eyes.

It was a clean shot to the heart. Mark crumpled to the floor. Gincie knew he was dead even before she felt the last faint pulse of life in his neck.

She put the pistol back into her bag and left the room, carefully closing the door behind her. Doors were beginning to open in the corridor, and fragmented voices were asking what had happened, had there been a shot?

She didn't run. She simply walked out through the growing curiosity and confusion. No one paid her much attention, but she knew that would not last. The clerk would remember the woman who had come to visit Mr. Carrington, and though her hat had a short veil, it was not heavy enough for full concealment.

By the time she returned to the house, Travis was there with Boston and Rachel.

"I have something to tell all of you," Gincie said, and the light in Travis's eyes died as he studied her white, set face. Surely this could have nothing to do with another child?

Gincie put down her purse and took off her hat and cloak. "I just shot and killed Mark Carrington, my half brother." She made the announcement very calmly, and then her eyes closed, and she would have crumpled to the floor had not Travis caught her.

For Travis, Boston, and Rachel the immediate concern was Gincie, but her claim that she had killed her half brother seemed to echo in the room as if it were being voiced over and over again.

Rachel whispered the echoes in Travis's own mind. "I thought she was with child again, not this, never this."

When Gincie came to, she began to tremble violently, and her words were jagged, hard to decipher. But Travis understood enough to know that this was no mental lapse or hallucination; Mark had stalked her, and she had turned on him and made him her prey.

"My God! Why didn't you tell me? To have let it come to this!" He was sorry as soon as he said the words, but the consequences of his wife's act were beginning to occur to him with terrible clarity.

Gincie bit her lower lip until it bled, struggling to gain control of herself. "He was evil, so evil! He would have killed you or the children! It was my responsibility. He was my half brother, not yours. And he was a murderer, a cold-blooded killer. He should have died that day at Wild Swan. He should have died! Not Samson!"

Travis had known about his wife's struggles with her background since the beginning, since she had been shot by the slave catchers and had raved in the fever about her fear of her mother coming for her. Before he had married her, he had asked her grandmother Alexandria and had learned about Piety. And he had known how deeply hurt Gincie had been by the death of Samson at Mark's hands, how she had taken undeserved blame, convinced that Mark had come to Wild Swan with the raiders because he had known she was there.

He had known, and yet he had been unaware. He had known she had killed before, but that had been during the war, in self-defense against a man who had raped her and might well have killed her. By her own account, her shooting of Mark had been an execution.

From the beginning, Travis had loved Gincie's fierce dedication to those she cared for, but he had not known her capable of this ferocity. And something inside of him cringed from the knowledge that when she had been most threatened, most in need, she had not come to him. All of his patience and love had come to this.

He held her in his arms, but he felt distant from her, as if she were a stranger.

Boston was as stunned as his wife and Travis, but he made himself concentrate on the practicalities. Gincie had killed Mark Carrington; there was a body and sure discovery of it.

"Gincie, my dear, there are things we need to know. Did anyone recognize you at the hotel?"

Gincie pushed herself out of Travis's arms. "I don't think so, but the veil on my hat isn't very thick."

All the eyes in the room went to the discarded hat as if it contained some special property.

"I didn't think about disguising myself, only about confronting Mark," Gincie admitted.

"Unless someone did recognize you, it will take some time for the authorities to connect the . . . the . . . to connect Mark with you, but they probably will in the end. I doubt that Mark told anyone here the exact nature of his business, but that doesn't mean he hasn't spoken about his ties to us. He was obviously obsessed with Wild Swan and its people." Boston could not bring himself to name Gincie as Mark's sister and main obsession. "Was Mark armed?"

"No, not that I could see," Gincie said. "He didn't think he had to use a gun or a knife. He thought the threats against my family would be enough."

Boston sought a way around what he saw as the only course and found none. There was infinite sorrow in his voice when he spoke again. "Gincie, you must leave California. I do not blame you for what you have done. I know it was the only way you could see to defend yourself and your family. But the court can scarcely find less than premeditated murder. You went to the hotel to meet him; you were armed, while as far as we know, he was not. And an old agony from the war, particularly one that concerns the death of a black man, would not be likely to sway a judge or jury in your favor."

"The children?" Gincie's question was faint, dull. On one level, she understood what was being said in the room, but on another, she was lost. The rush of energy and purpose that had enabled her to kill Mark was gone, leaving her dazed, as if everything were happening to someone else.

"We will all go," Travis said. It was not a choice. He recognized the truth of Boston's words. He honestly did not know how he felt about Gincie at this moment, but he knew he could not let her leave without him and the children.

"I'll have the children here by tomorrow," Boston said. "The train east from Sacramento should see you safely away on the following day."

He and Travis exchanged a look, silently acknowledging that it was possible the connection between Gincie and Mark would be made by then. It was a chance they would have to take. Neither of them could imagine Gincie fleeing from one point to the next in California, hounded by the authorities. She needed to be gotten entirely away, and the transcontinental railroad was the best and fastest way out.

Rachel wrapped her arms around Boston and hugged him tightly before he left. He tipped her head up and kissed her. "This family has survived difficulties before; we will do so again."

Rachel had to smile; his British accent was suddenly very pronounced, and his calm in the face of emergency was the same strength that had helped her and others on the Trail of Tears so many years before.

Part Cherokee, part white, Rachel had lived as a white woman for years, but she understood the fierce ties of kinship and still mourned those she had lost when the Cherokees had been forced from their eastern lands to territory chosen in the West by the government. Families were to be protected at all costs, even at the cost of dealing with a blood tie who threatened the others, as Mark had done. She understood perfectly what had driven Gincie. And she understood that her own role was to support the Culhanes now, to do everything she could to make their departure as efficient as possible.

Though it was Boston who had thought of details to be attended to, it was Rachel who purchased the train tickets and cashed the bank draft to provide the Culhanes with funds for traveling. She nodded to acquaintances and spoke to those she could not avoid, exchanging pleasantries in her usual calm manner while her heart pounded in fear that she would somehow betray Gincie. She found herself more than willing to bore her friends with tales of the grandchildren's activities, the safest subject she could imagine.

Travis stayed with Gincie. He had no option. The link between her and the murder might be made at any time, and the Thaines' house would be the first place the authorities would check. He had to be with her in case that happened. And he had to be with her for her own protection against herself. He had no idea what her next mood would be, whether the calm that had followed the violent trembling would last.

He knew all the reasons he had to remain at her side, and still he felt like a prisoner, felt as if his nerves and muscles were trying to jump through his skin. He hated the idea that Rachel and Boston were having to do so much for the Culhanes, taking risks that would surely make them accomplices to harboring a fugitive, if not to the murder itself.

The murder itself. Everything came back to that, and he continued to have a very hard time facing it head-on. Every time he tried to imagine Gincie shooting Mark, the image dissolved into fragments.

"I should have asked." Gincie's voice was as startling as a scream in the silence.

"Should have asked what?" Travis responded with a calm he didn't feel.

"I should have asked about my mother and about my other half brother, about Matthew. What if they are part of this? What if they are waiting for Mark to bring the money? What if they try to harm you?"

Travis wrapped his arms around her against the rising hysteria. "Gincie, Gincie! We're not talkin' about a conspiracy, we're talkin' about one man, Mark Carrington, and he's dead. He would have told you if anyone else were involved. He would have threatened you with that; you know he would! What possible reason could he have had to hide the fact that he had people who could make things worse than he could alone?"

The dark, primitive fear was still with her, but she had no rational answer for his arguments, and she subsided from sheer exhaustion.

The day seemed never ending to Travis, but he was careful to thank Rachel for taking such good care of them and for making all of their travel arrangements.

"We are family," Rachel replied, and then she added, "I don't think anyone suspected anything. I have never been more grateful that people come and go so frequently in this city."

Neither of them admitted it aloud, but both of them were waiting for the knock on the door from authorities searching for Gincie. Travis wondered what he would do if it happened, wondered if he were a good enough liar to swear that she had been with him, though there were witnesses who could testify that they had seen him without his wife that morning.

Finally the day had passed without intrusion, and Travis longed for sleep for himself and for Gincie, just a few hours of oblivion, but he found it impossible. Gincie was curled away from him, lying very still, but he didn't believe she was sleeping either. He started to reach for her to hold her close and then decided against it. Awake or asleep, she was clearly not in the mood to be touched.

He left the bed and stood at the window, gazing at the moon on the bay. He had loved this place from the day of arrival. California had meant a new life after the years of slaughter, a new inheritance after he had sold Hawthorn, the once beloved acres in Virginia, to the relatives who had grown fat on the war while others starved.

California had indeed been a golden land for him and for his family. He and Gincie had worked hard since their arrival four years before, but this land offered ample reward for those who believed in her. Travis thought of the Thoroughbred racehorses, the saddle horses, and the beasts trained to harness; little by little they were achieving the same fame as the horses of Wild Swan in Maryland. He and Gincie had bought, traded, and sold animals from California, from the eastern United States, and from as far away as Australia and England, always searching for the best combination of blood, bone, sinew, and heart.

He considered the land, the acres of the ranch, and the city lots in Oakland and San Francisco, purchased because he believed that, despite currently falling land prices, this city by the bay would flourish. And there were silver mining shares in Nevada, shares apt to fluctuate widely in value and validity if the owner did not keep careful watch on the operations.

Most of all, he thought of the children. California was a fine place to raise them, away from the most vivid scars of the war, in a place where many had come to escape the legacy of killing.

It had been hard to put life back together again, but California had helped to make it possible. To have to go east once more was bitter agony. He tried to tell himself that the murder would never be solved, but it was no use. Gincie was a tall, striking woman, and her relationship to Alexandria Carrington Falconer was well known. The Carrington Falconer name had its own fame in the racing world.

Gincie and the children were all that mattered. He would manage, whatever the circumstances, even returning to the East Coast, as long as they were with him. He bowed his head, trying to relinquish his dream of life in the Far West, trying to accept the change Gincie's nightmare of Mark's power had wrought. He was not aware of the tears streaking his lean cheeks.

Gincie watched from the shadows of their bed and saw the moonlight catch in his tears. She had not seen him weep since the day the twins had been delivered at last, and he had welcomed them with tears of relief and tenderness.

Before, she would have gone to him immediately and wrapped him in her warmth and love, but now she simply watched, knowing she was the cause of his sorrow, not the solace for it.

Chapter 3

Boston returned with the children the following day, bringing Malachi and Conchita, "Conchee," one of the ranch hands' wives, a woman of whom the children were particularly fond, who had helped with the journey to the city. As he and Travis had decided, the story Boston told the employees was that the Culhanes had been summoned east by the family at Wild Swan. It was a credible lie.

Travis was particularly conscious of that when he bid farewell to Malachi before Malachi and Conchita returned to Sonoma.

Though Malachi asked no questions aloud, his eyes betrayed his worry. His concern went beyond the fact that his livelihood depended on the Culhanes. One of Samson and Della's two sons, his loyalty to the Culhanes had it roots clear back in his birth at Wild Swan, and thus, what happened there concerned him directly. And it worried him that Gincie was not in evidence for this interview.

Travis could not bear to vex Malachi further by manufacturing a lie about illness, and instead found himself weaving an elaborate fiction about bloodline decisions to be made about the horses in the East and in California. "And it seems a good time for the Falconers to see Lexy again and to meet the twins . . . ," Travis's voice trailed away in face of the steady concern in Malachi's dark eyes.

He cleared his throat and handed him the list of instructions he had written. "You will be in charge of the ranch while we're gone. Boston will be available should you need help solvin' problems, but Gincie and I know that there is no one more suited to the job than you are."

"I'll do my best," Malachi said, his own throat tight with emotion. "May you and Gincie and the children travel safely to Wild Swan. Please tell my mother that I, my wife, and our children send her our love and to my brother Jotham, too."

The handshake between the two men was firm, and spoke as much of friendship as it did of an agreement between employer and employee.

The children were glad to see Boston and Rachel and excited when they were told they were going to ride on the train, but they were also uneasy about the sudden disruption of their lives. Heretofore, trips of any sort had always been heralded by planning and anticipation, and as young as they were, the children sensed the difference.

Lexy, told that she was going to visit the place where she had been born, kept asking, "But how far is it really? Longer than it took us to get from here to the ranch?"

The children's demands for attention made the time speed faster and even served to dilute the sorrow of leavetaking the next morning. The Thaines went with the Culhanes to see them off on the ferry to Oakland, and suddenly there was no more time, just a flurry of embraces, handshakes between the two men, and last-minute fragments.

"We'll send anything that you need, once we receive word from you," Rachel said.

"Don't worry about anything," Boston instructed. "Everything will be taken care of here; just see yourselves safely to Wild Swan."

"We'll miss you, and we'll look forward to your return." Rachel's voice wasn't steady any longer, and Gincie's own eyes filled with tears as she saw how close the other woman was to weeping.

She watched the figures of Boston and Rachel grow smaller as the ferry pulled away, and she dug her fingernails into the palms of her hands to refocus the pain, refusing to consider that this might be the last time she would see the Thaines, refusing to accept that California and La Salida del Sol were lost to her, perhaps forever.

At Oakland, they boarded the train to Sacramento. The Western Pacific Railroad stopped at nearly every town in between, but was called an "express" because it met the eastern connection on the same day, unlike the afternoon run, which necessitated an overnight stay in Sacramento.

San Jose, San Jose Junction, Pleasanton, Midway, Vanta's, San Joaquin Bridge, Stockton, Gault, Elk Grove, Brighton—at every stop, Gincie expected someone to grab her and announce the apprehension of a murderess. She was finally too numb to feel horrified by the prospect, but she was sorry for the embarrassment Travis would surely suffer, and she wondered how the children would react.

She was also too numb to feel jubilant when they had traveled the one hundred and thirty-five miles without hindrance, arriving in Sacramento just before two P.M., in time to catch the eastbound Central Pacific a scant twenty minutes later.

Being caught for shooting Mark no longer seemed like the worse possibility. It was surely worse to think that Travis's face might always look so defeated. She had caused this, she had caused the dimming of the light in his vivid turquoise eyes, the line-bracketed set to his mouth. The numbness cracked into terrible pain when she thought of that, so she made herself creep back into the great blank space of her mind where she was safe.

They had Pacific Hotel Express accommodations, the newly introduced weekly service designed to spare first-class passengers the rigors of travel. The plush seats converted into berths at night; steam heat and fresh linen daily added to the comfort. Meals equal to those in a fine restaurant were offered on board, allowing passengers to avoid the plain, often indigestible dishes served to less fortunate travelers at the stops where the train took on water and fuel.

Early on, Travis reflected grimly that while the luxurious accommodations would surely make their trip more comfortable than it would have been in the more spartan confines provided for cheaper fares, nothing could make this journey easy. The children, even Lexy, who was generally very well behaved and responsible, were too young truly to enjoy an experience that became monotonous for them very soon. And though Lexy informed anyone who asked where she was going that she was going to visit her *great*-grandmother and *great*-grandfather and their horses, her little face in repose had a sad, watchful expression, as if she were well aware that this excursion was not for pleasure.

In normal times, Travis knew Gincie would have been amused by Lexy's emphasis on the "great," clear indication that she was imagining the word meant something quite different from familial relationships. But instead, Gincie seemed detached from all of them even while she tried to see to their physical needs. She tried to keep the children clean despite the dust that even luxury could not keep out and to coax them to eat when the novelty of dining aboard the train had worn off. But it was more as if she were a paid nursemaid than their mother—or Travis's wife. He felt as if her spirit had not boarded the train at all, but was back in California living her brief moments with Mark over and over. He could see it in her eyes, could see it in the sudden flare of memory that was always followed by the shutting down of the light.

From Ogden, Utah, they changed to the Union Pacific line and were in Omaha, Nebraska, two thousand miles from California, in less than a week, crossing the "Big Muddy," the Missouri River, by ferry because there was, as yet, no rail bridge from Council Bluffs to Omaha. There they changed rail lines again to continue east. Though the country was now crossed in a time unimaginably short compared to the era before the completion of the transcontinental railroad just the year before, the journey heightened rather than diminished the feeling of the vastness of the United States. Mile after mile of empty or sparsely settled land rolled by. Some of the emptiness was not promise, but sorrow. They saw a few scattered herds of buffalo, but the dark expanse of uncountable animals was gone from the land bordering the tracks.

Travis wanted his children to remember that they had seen the survivors.

"Buffles," K. C. called them when Travis told the children what they were.

"There used to be so many no one could count them all," Travis told them.

"What happened to 'em?" Lexy asked.

"The men who built the railroad had to be fed, and the buffalo were hunted for that, and many, many were wasted."

"Why?" Taylor asked, because that was his favorite word, though he was not interested in the answer most of the time.

Because men are greedy and shortsighted, because they destroy even what they need, because no one gives a damn about the Indians who have lived on the buffalo forever. The silent answer ran through Travis's mind, and he was glad that Tay didn't really want to know.

It was not so easy with Lexy and the Indians. Her Aunt Rachel was proud of her Cherokee heritage, and Lexy had never been taught to disdain those of different color. Differences in skin color were not differences at all to Lexy. And while passengers spoke nervously of the hazards of crossing lands still inhabited by Indians, the reality was that most Indians were already aware that attacking the "big wagons that go on metal roads" was futile.

The Indians the passengers saw on this trip were far more pathetic than threatening, some of them no more than hirelings who haunted stops along the way to be objects of curiosity in return for what they could beg, plus a small stipend from the railroad or wayside facility. The others, whether on horseback or on foot, were only small groups that kept their distance.

When she heard one of the women passengers fearfully pointing out a filthy, blanket-wrapped old man as "one of those savages, a real Indian!" Lexy took immediate exception.

"Is not!" she told the woman. "My Auntie Rachel is one, and she doesn't look like that."

Though Rachel was also one of the "great" relatives, being a great-great-aunt to Lexy, Lexy did not know of that distinction and adored her aunt as one of the very special people in her life. She wasn't quite sure what this woman meant by "those savages," but the tone of voice told her it wasn't nice.

Travis groaned inwardly at the attention Lexy had attracted; everyone who had heard her pronouncement was now eyeing the family as if the Culhanes would suddenly don war paint.

"That old man *is* an Indian," he told Lexy, his voice gentle. "There are different sorts of Indians who lead different lives, just as there are different sorts of white people. Do you understand?"

Lexy regarded him for a long moment before she nodded in reluctant affirmation and mumbled, "Well, somebody oughta give him some better clothes."

"Someone should stop taking everything the Indians have." The angry words were so low, Travis barely heard them, but for an instant, he saw the familiar fire in Gincie's eyes before it was extinguished.

Somewhere inside, the Gincie he loved still existed, but there was very little sign of her for most of the trip. By the time they arrived in New York and then traveled south to Baltimore, they were all exhausted, and the children had gotten to the stage of perpetual whining, asking repeatedly for Conchee and for various other people, pets, and even the horses left behind.

Travis caught sight of them first—Alexandria Carrington Falconer and her husband, Rane Falconer, both of them tall and straight in spite of their respective ages of seventy and seventy-five. And for the first time, Travis realized that it was not just Gincie who needed shelter; he needed it as well, at least for a while, needed Alex and Rane to help him heal Gincie, to help both himself and Gincie to find a way to repair their disrupted lives.

The Falconers didn't know what had caused the Culhanes' flight from California; neither Boston nor Travis had dared transmit such volatile news by telegraph. But they were not long in doubt. As Gincie went to her grandmother, she said, "I shot and killed Mark Carrington. I did it deliberately."

It was as if she needed to put it as baldly as possible, as if she were testing the person who had been her refuge since she was a tiny child. But though Alex's face paled, her voice was steady as she asked, "Why did you do it?"

"Because he threatened my family," Gincie answered. "And because he was too evil to stop any other way."

"Then it was well done."

No hesitation, no stuttering in shock, no string of questions, just that simple acceptance. With a little sigh, Gincie let herself be cradled in her grandmother's arms.

It was left to Rane to address the others.

"Welcome," he said to Travis, who held Tay in his arms, and then he squatted down so that he would be nearer the level of Lexy, who held K. C. by the hand. "And welcome to you, too. I am your great-grandfather and am very glad you could come to visit us."

Lexy studied him carefully before announcing, "Your eyes are green like Mama's an' mine."

"Indeed they are. We have quite a few people in the family who have green eyes." Though Rane could see the inheritance of Travis in the little girl, it was even easier for him to see Gincie and Alex, and that touched him deeply. Gincie was Nigel's daughter, and Nigel had been Alex and St. John Carrington's son, not Rane's. It didn't matter; it never had. Before St. John had died, Rane had come to respect him very much, despite the fact that both of them had loved the same woman. And with his own marriage to Alex, Rane had become father to all of the children. Looking at Lexy and the twins now, he could not have felt any more connected to them had he been their great-grandfather by blood.

Emboldened by the warmth and the lack of condescension she felt from this tall old man, Lexy asked him, "Why do they call you 'great'?"

Rane controlled his laughter with difficulty, giving the matter the serious mien Lexy obviously expected. "Actually, not many people call me great, and you don't have to either. It's a rather silly way of sorting out families so that one doesn't become confused. If you have a little girl someday, your father will be her grandfather. And if your little girl has her own daughter someday, then your father will be her great-grandfather."

Lexy digested this information, and then gave Rane a big smile. "I 'spect I'll know all about that when I'm a big girl. For now, I'll just call you 'Grandpa'." Trustingly she put her hand in his, and Rane heard K. C. echo the "Gwandpa."

"You better pick him up," Lexy informed Rane with the long-suffering knowledge of an older sister. "He walks slow!"

Rane did as he was bid, hoisting the sturdy little boy in one arm so that he could still hold Lexy's hand. And then he met Travis's eyes. "You have beautiful children," Rane said, and Travis felt the warmth touch him.

It was too dark to see by the time the carriage reached Wild Swan, but Gincie felt the land wrapping around her, shielding her from the outside world. She felt safer than she had since Mark had found her at the races, and she felt that Wild Swan and its people could give Travis and the children the nurturing she seemed incapable of giving them now.

"It's so good to be home." She whispered, but Travis heard her. Gincie did not see the look of pain in his eyes.

Chapter 4

Nearly equidistant from Baltimore and Washington City, in Prince George's County, the acres of Wild Swan boasted plenty of sweet water, grazing, woodlands, and well-kept buildings that spread out from the red brick, five-part Georgian main house. Vegetables, fruit, and flowers flourished in their seasons; Devon Red cattle grew fat, and pigs, chickens, and geese added to the larders of plenty. But the main business of the farm was to breed, raise, race, and sell the Thoroughbred horses that were among the best in the country. The practice track, the training rings, the various barns, the immaculately tended paddocks and pastures were all designed for the horses' comfort.

Despite his weariness, Travis awakened at first light out of long habit. He propped himself on an elbow and watched Gincie's sleeping face, seeing her stir as the waking calls of the horses and other livestock filtered into the room. A smile curved her mouth, but she did not awaken, and noting the shadows beneath her eyes, Travis took great care not to disturb her as he dressed.

When he checked on the children, he found that they, too, were still asleep. He was relieved because he wanted a chance to speak to the Falconers without Gincie or the children there.

He found Alex and Rane sharing a pot of tea before beginning the business of the day, and they were as anxious for information as he was to give it.

He stated the facts calmly as he recounted Gincie's story from the meeting at the Stockton racetrack to the shooting in San Francisco, but whatever the lack of passion in his narrative, his emotions showed in his eyes.

"It has been very hard for you," Alex said. "Please don't deny that or feel guilty about it. Perhaps there was no other way to dispose of that creature. I have good cause to know how dangerous he was; he would have killed me that day had not Samson moved to protect me, to die in my stead. But the fact remains that Gincie made a decision and committed an act that has changed your life as much as it changed hers."

"The most difficult part is waiting to discover if Gincie will be identified," Rane said. "Boston is a good man; he will handle it as well as possible from his end, but I suggest we consult Blaine in the meantime. He's a fine lawyer and may be able to shed light where we see none."

Travis marveled at the choir of their voices, still touched with the British accents of their origins, rather than at the sensible things they were saying. Alex and Rane had been together for so long, not only physically, but in their hearts and minds, that while they remained separate individuals, they also had a shared presence that radiated a tangible power. And though their only bond by blood was far in the past with a great-great-great-great-grandfather, they were both marked so strongly with the green eyes and dark hair of the Thaines, they appeared to Travis to be eerily like the female and male side of the same entity.

Travis drew comfort from them. They had what he wanted to have with Gincie until the end of their days. And he knew the Falconers' history, knew that what they had now had not come easily to them.

Though she had been only thirteen at the time, Alex Thaine had known that a marriage between her sister Florence and St. John

Carrington would be a disaster. Eleven years older than she, St. John, "Sinje," had always been kind to her, and she regarded him as a friend and deserving of a better life than the one he would have were he to marry Florence. But when Alex warned him, Florence overheard, and the weaving of the tapestry of Alex's life with Rane's had begun.

In her immediate family, Alex had two people who loved her, her father and Boston, one of her brothers. But her mother was more powerful than either of these and had no use for Alex at all. Florence in her blond, blue-eyed prettiness was all the daughter Margaret Thaine needed; she regarded girls as generally useless offspring, and Alex was too much a throwback to the strong-willed, unconventional Thaines. The minimal tolerance she had had for Alex was destroyed by the girl's meddling. Though St. John Carrington was a younger son with no prospects, still he was of the nobility, his father having a minor title, and Margaret saw Florence's marriage to him as a way to elevate her own status from the merchant class.

The house where Alex lived, never much of a home, became a nightmare of cold silence interspersed with screaming recriminations. She turned to the one source of love and acceptance that had been sure for as long as she could remember, to her paternal grandmother, Virginia Thaine, who lived close by.

At first, Virginia's response seemed nothing more than another punishment. Virginia took Alex clear across England from Kent to Devon, to distant relatives named Falconer. But what had seemed exile to Alex quickly proved enchantment. The Falconers welcomed her as if she were one of their own and loved her without measure, giving her a sense of family she had never experienced before. And Rane Falconer was part of it, the two of them such mirror images that everyone marveled that blood so distantly shared could be strong enough to produce such a match.

Rane was more hampered by that than helped. The five years between them then seemed like an enormous gap because he was eighteen and she only thirteen. And because she had come to live under his family's roof, he tried to regard her as the sister he had never had even when he realized he did not feel fraternal toward her as he watched her blossom daily in the warmth of his family's love. Nor had it helped him that she was overly mature in some ways while being totally unaware of her own feminine charms. As far as Alex was concerned, her sister Florence was alluring, but she herself, being totally unlike Florence, could not possibly appeal to a young man. Even when he acknowledged his love for her to himself, Rane resolved to wait until she was older before burdening her with the truth of it.

Their world changed forever in Alex's fifteenth year. St. John and Florence had married, and it had proved even more disastrous than Alex had predicted. Bitter and discontented in her marriage, Florence had died after giving birth to the twins, Flora and Blaine, and Sinje had gone off to fight against Napoleon's daring return to power, leaving the twins in Margaret Thaine's reluctant care. Alex could not abandon two helpless infants to such a cold place, and she had harbored the dream that when she went home to care for the children, her mother would somehow be changed, would discover that she loved her younger daughter after all.

But Margaret and Alex had never become friends, let alone sharing a loving bond of mother and daughter. And at fifteen, the last of Alex's childhood was over. She became mother to the twins. When Sinje was brought home from Waterloo more dead than alive and needing his right arm amputated if he were to survive, Alex took responsibility for him, too, giving him a reason to live, becoming mistress of the little rented cottage where St. John's small household was established, and then becoming his mistress as well.

He offered her marriage, but they discovered that the law in England forbade the marriage of a man to his dead wife's sister. The law had been designed to prevent women from being forced into marriage simply to care for orphaned children, but Alex did not need the sanction of the Church of England to know where her duty lay. The twins were like her own children, and she loved Sinje, too, and could not abandon him as he struggled to reestablish his image of himself as a man, though his once perfect body was maimed. It was also a struggle to find a way to provide for his family; he had never been trained for useful work, and now his parents and brothers would have nothing to do with him. His marriage to Florence Thaine had been enough of an insult to them; his liaison with Alexandria Thaine was unforgivable.

St. John did have one area of expertise: he knew fine horse-flesh, particularly Thoroughbred racing stock. While Alex worked with her grandmother as a "wise-woman," a practitioner of the healing arts, Sinje began to spend more and more time away from home as he attended race meetings at various courses in England, winning more wagers than he lost, dreaming of his own racing stable, and rejoining the world of his own aristocratic set. And gradually he lost sight of all that Alex meant to him, treating her as nothing more than a light-skirt and allowing his less savory sporting acquaintances to treat her the same way.

Then, without warning, Rane Falconer came to Kent to claim Alex. He had waited for her to grow up, but instead of finding a young girl on the verge of womanhood, he found a sad, overburdened young matron who was mother not only to her dead sister's children, but to her own small daughter by St. John.

He did not know at the time that the marriage was not official. He only knew that Alex was frail, tired, and unloved. He was ruthlessly tender in his courting, willing to do anything to insure that she would come away with him, even with the children. He loved her unbearably and believed she had a right to be loved and protected.

But when he left, he left without her. Alex was sure Sinje wouldn't want her or the children with him for much longer, but she could not take them from him until he bid her to go.

It never happened. Sinje returned from the races a changed man. Lord Bettingdon, a friend who cared about both Alex and St. John, had taken the most direct route to make St. John aware of his cruelty to Alex. The duke had made an offer for Alex, calmly telling St. John that he would like to make Alex his mistress or perhaps even his duchess, since her current protector so obviously had no further interest in her.

It was a rude awakening for Sinje. Suddenly he faced what life without Alex would be like, faced how much he loved her and depended on her.

Rane was everything wild and tender about being young and in love, but Alex relinquished the dream in face of St. John's remorse and need. From that day, despite the precarious beginning, the marriage between Alex and Sinje had grown strong in love and understanding. It had seen them through the tragedy of losing their little girl in England and of leaving everything that was familiar to begin life anew in Maryland in the United States. And it had not faltered when Alex discovered that Rane Falconer had emigrated to Maryland before her, having remembered, as she had, the descriptions of that state by Caleb Jennings, an American prisoner of war whom Alex and Rane had helped to escape back to his homeland.

Nor had Sinje, after meeting Rane for the first time in Maryland, ever questioned Alex about the paternity of Morgan, Rane's son, the result of the brief time Rane and Alex had had together in England. St. John had never treated Morgan as less than his own child in spite of the fact that Morgan was the precise image of the two strains of Thaine blood coming together.

Alex and Rane loved each other no less; they simply could not indulge that love, Alex because now she cared too much about Sinje to so betray him again, and Rane because he would not harm her by tempting her more. Morgan, beautiful and bright child though he was, was proof enough of the cost of infidelity. And Rane had his own marriage to weigh down his spirit. His American wife, Claire, was a woman who had grown more violently mad with each year's passing. And Rane's guilt was never-ending because, though he knew that Claire had never been stable, still he felt that if he were able to love Claire instead of Alex, Claire might somehow be cured.

Rane dedicated his energy to his partnership with Caleb Jennings, and they prospered in the building of ships and a shipping line, while Alex and Sinje merged her dream of a new life in a new land with his of a racing stable in the establishment of Wild Swan as a premier breeding farm for Thoroughbred horses that combined the best of English and American bloodlines.

And then the Carringtons' marriage succumbed to the only thing that could end it. St. John was thrown and trampled by a rogue horse he had insisted on riding. St. John had never walked again, and the slow death began, though Alex fought it at every turn, caring for her husband through all the infections and fevers until he was too weak to go on.

Alex went on without him because she had no choice. She had the children, the horses, and the land to care for. And even when she was not consciously aware of it, she had Rane in her world, encouraging her, serving as a patient cousin to the children, his enduring love sustaining Alex even as he tried to cope as humanely as possible with his wife, Claire, who grew more demonically mad as the years passed until the best Rane could do for her was to keep her a pampered prisoner with a staff to look after her in his Baltimore house. But in spite of the depths of her insanity, Claire sensed when Rane and Alex became lovers again, sensed it not because she knew anything about it, but because Rane committed the unpardonable sin of being happy again. Claire could not bear to feel the joy in him, and she punished him in the one way her shadowed mind knew could not fail to break that joy; she freed herself from her own devils and made them his by taking her own life.

Alex and Rane nearly lost everything with that death. Rane went back to England, his guilt pursuing him, and Alex used the speed and danger of the racehorses to counter her despair, paying no heed to the risks she took, until finally she pushed her luck over the edge.

The horse had been showing an occasional irregularity in his gait, sometimes running smoothly, while at other times seeming to hesitate, though there was no clear indication of a problem. Alex insisted on taking him out on the track to test him, rather than letting one of the exercise boys do it.

Rane was there in time to see the horse's leg give way, to watch the horse crash over the rail and onto Alex. Rane's family had sent him back to her, bidding him not to be so foolish as to lose the one woman who had had the power to make him happy since he was a boy. But it was Rane's own sense of impending disaster that had sent him rushing to Wild Swan that day; it was Rane's will that kept Alex alive.

They had never forgotten how close they had come to losing each other. This year would mark their thirty-ninth year of marriage, their fifty-seventh year of knowing each other, and because of them and St. John Carrington, generations of lives were interwoven—children, grandchildren, great-grandchildren, and likewise the generations of families, black and white, who had lived and worked at Wild Swan, and beyond, to all the people affected by the various pursuits of the Carringtons and Falconers.

Even Boston Thaine, whom Travis knew as an independent and adventuresome man, had come to America because he had had his own sorrows in England and had been infected by his sister Alex's dream of a new beginning in America. He had accompanied the Carringtons on the voyage and had worked with them for some time before setting off to explore the vast wonders of his new country and so finding a new life with Rachel.

Travis himself had had his whole world changed on the night he had met the young agent for the Underground Railroad, the agent who turned out not to be a stripling boy, but rather Gincie Carrington.

Travis thought of all that the Falconers had weathered—financial reverses that would have ruined less determined people and losses of the heart that would always be mourned. Though Gincie's father, Nigel, born in England before the emigration, had been Alex's only surviving child by St. John, Rane had felt his untimely death twenty-five years before no less than if Nigel had been of his own flesh. And during the war that had engulfed the country, the Falconers had learned that losing a grandchild was no easier.

Alex and Rane had not asked for quarter, and life had not granted it. With rare courage and love, they had endured everything life brought. They continued to do so. Travis believed that he and Gincie had at least a fighting chance to persevere as well if they could only survive this upheaval in their lives without losing each other in the process.

Now, Alex's calm voice brought him out of his reflections. "We will, of course, defer to your wishes regarding how soon and how much you want the rest of the family and the people of Wild Swan to know," Alex said, "but we are so closely bound to each other's lives, it will be difficult to keep it secret for long."

"Gincie must decide what she wants, but for my part, I would just as soon that the truth be told immediately," Travis said. "Blaine will have to know if we are to ask his advice, and I think Gincie will be happier if she feels free to confide in her family."

He hoped that was true, but as the day wore on, he wondered if her retreat into herself would allow support from any source. The children were up and lively, seeming to have recovered fully from the rigors of the journey, but Gincie did not awaken.

"Let her sleep," Alex suggested. "It will do no harm, and she will have to face everything soon enough."

Travis complied, and he had his hands full keeping watch over the children as they explored their new surroundings. The Falconers and everyone else at the farm were delighted by their presence, but while Lexy and the twins responded well to the friendly overtures, they didn't want their father out of their sight.

For all his doubts about returning to Wild Swan, Travis discovered that seeing the people who had treated him so kindly despite the fact that he had fought for the Confederacy was an experience that brought a lump to his throat more than once. The people of Wild Swan had wished the Culhanes well when they had left for California, and though no one asked a question aloud, now Travis could see the concern and puzzlement in their eyes. They knew there must be some pressing matter that had brought the Culhanes east with no more warning than a couple of telegrams, and they wondered when Gincie would appear.

Padraic Joyce had been at Wild Swan for more than a quarter of a century and had more invested in the place than his years of training horses. His wife, Katy, an Irish immigrant, shot by slave catchers before the war, was buried here, her grave carefully tended and decked with flowers in season by Padraic. Slender, of medium height, with dark hair going gray, and dark blue eyes, his fair skin deeply weathered, Padraic was probably sixty or so, though it was hard to tell. At one moment his eyes were ancient, yet in the next, when he smiled, he looked like a young man.

"If yer as foine a hand with the horses as yer mama an' yer papa, I'll be countin' on yer help with the beasties here," Padraic told Lexy after they had been introduced.

Lexy regarded him solemnly and then smiled back at him. "I like the way you talk. It's like singing. An' I like the horses too." Suddenly her face clouded. "Gold Fire didn't come home. He hurt himself."

She gazed at Padraic as if he might have the answer, and the Irishman looked helplessly at Travis.

"We lost a good animal at the Stockton races a few weeks ago. He bolted through the rail and broke his leg," Travis explained, but he remembered too well Gincie's first frantic questions about whether or not anyone had been around the horse right before the race, and he wondered for the thousandth time whether anything would have been different had he pursued the suspicion she had betrayed in those first moments of trauma.

"Well, little Lexy, 'tis a sad truth that sometimes bad things happen to horses an' to people, too. The best we can do is to be takin' good care a' them, an' Wild Swan's a grand place fer that."

Pedraic's words, Travis knew, were directed as much at himself as at his daughter, a special welcome and a promise that Padraic would do all he could to ease the Culhanes' troubles, no matter what they were.

He found it particularly difficult to face Della without telling her everything on the spot. Della was Samson's widow, and as such, it seemed she had more right than anyone to know that her husband's killer was dead. Beyond that, Della was an intrinsic part of the heart of Wild Swan. She deserved to know both the good and the bad.

Like Alex, Della was a beauty even in her seventies, her pale brown skin scarcely wrinkled over the proud bones inherited from her white father and her slave mother, who had been freed upon her master's death. Della had gone to work for the Carringtons when they established their first business in America, the Wild Swan tavern in Annapolis, and when they had moved to the farm, she had come with them. Not fully part of either the white or the black world, well educated and more than a little contemptuous of the ignorance of slaves, the last thing on earth Della Johnson had meant to do was to fall in love with the fugitive slave Samson. But the huge man, so scarred on the outside, had possessed a heart and soul that utterly captivated Della.

Theirs had been a marriage that produced two fine sons and years of loving that Mark Carrington's bullet had ended.

At least Travis felt he had something to give Della, though not the truth of why the Culhanes were back at Wild Swan. While Della's son Jotham and his wife and children were part of Wild Swan, Travis was able to give firsthand reports of Malachi and his family, whom Della had never met.

"They're a fine family," he said, "and I know you would like your daughter-in-law very much and your grandsons. They all send their love. They seem very content in California; it is a good place to raise a family."

Though she only voiced questions about her son, her eyes asked Travis why, if California was such a good place, were the Culhanes three thousand miles away from it. She confined herself to saying, "The Falconers will be so much happier for your visit. They are very proud of what you are accomplishing in California, but I know how much they have longed to see you and the children."

Travis hoped that "visit" was the proper word.

Gincie slept until late afternoon. When she awakened, she had
no idea where she was. She missed the swaying and clacking of the
trains without knowing what was absent. But the awful panic waiting
at the edge of her mind was real enough. Her eyes searched the
room and found Travis sitting in a chair by the window, his face
touched by the light and shadow of dusk. And she remembered
where they were and why.

She wished she could retreat into sleep again, but when she
closed her eyes, she saw Mark's face, his leer changing to terror as
she pulled the trigger, the blood gushing out. It was as if now that
the flight from California was complete, her mind had time to dwell
on exactly what had caused it. It was horrifying to consider that it
might be like this every time she awakened henceforth, and her
voice was urgent when she spoke Travis's name.

He was beside her in the instant. "Well, darlin', you nearly
slept the clock around." He leaned over to kiss her. "But the
children and I had a good day. Lexy is quite pleased that she was
'borned' here, even if she doesn't remember. Everyone is being very
patient with havin' the three underfoot." He went on speaking
calmly until the fear in her eyes eased.

"Does everyone know?" she asked.

Travis shook his head. "I felt it was up to you, so only Alex and
Rane know the whole story, but . . ."

"But everyone will have to know soon." She finished the sen-
tence for him. She understood that it was a tribute to his belief in her
as an independent adult, but part of her wished he would take all
responsibility, even her own for herself, from her, wished he had
told everyone after all. But even as she considered it, she knew she
would have been angry had he done so.

She sat up and buried her head against his shoulder for a
moment. "I hope you can continue to bear with me. I don't seem to
be coping very well with anything."

Travis thought of the Falconers again. "As long as we're together, everything else will take care of itself."

She clung to the strength of him for an instant longer, and then
she pulled away. Della. Della above all the others deserved the truth
from her.

She had to reassure the children that she wasn't going to sleep
forever and to listen patiently to their discoveries of the day before
she was free to go to Della. It did not surprise her to find her
grandmother with the housekeeper. In spite of their formal relationship of employer and employee, the two old women were friends,
bound together by decades upon decades of sharing each other's

lives. It was Alex who had taken Samson in and given him shelter in defiance of the law against harboring fugitive slaves, and it was Alex for whom Samson had given his life. Once Della had forgiven that circumstance, there existed nothing on earth that could threaten the bond between the two women.

Though Alex had for years been trying to lighten Della's work by providing her with extra help, Della considered the kitchen her domain and retained firm control over it and anyone who stepped foot therein. Alex had no defense when Della asked, "Would you like to have someone else take charge of the horses?"

It was a telling point. There were trainers, jockeys, and stable hands, but Alex remained the ultimate authority regarding the horses of Wild Swan.

As she approached the kitchen, Gincie heard Alex saying, "First I thought my children were the most beautiful in the world, and then I thought my grandchildren were incomparable, but now I find my great-grandchildren are surely the most clever, most wonderfully fashioned children on earth. Gincie and Travis's three simply confirm it. There are more than a few things I detest about growing old, but seeing the new generation is not among them."

Gincie smiled sadly to herself; at least her action had allowed her grandmother to see the children. No matter the brave face Alex had put on, Gincie had known how hard it had been for her to see baby Lexy leaving four years before.

She squared her shoulders and went into the kitchen. Conversation ceased immediately, and then Alex said, "Della, you and Gincie will have more privacy in the library," before she turned back to the task at hand.

Della didn't hesitate. She had been desperate to know the truth behind the Culhanes' visit ever since Alex had told her they were on their way to Wild Swan, and more since she had seen Gincie's pale, strained face when they had arrived the night before.

The kitchen was in one of the two "dependencies" of the house, which were connected to the main block by the covered halls of the two "hyphens." Gincie tried to use the time it took them to walk to the library to decide how she would tell Della, but once they were in the book-lined room, all subtlety deserted her. The gleam of silver was rich in the room, trophies won over the years by the horses. In most cases, Samson had trained the horses that had won.

The words poured out, compulsive and graphic, until there was no more to tell. And then silence fell between them. A clock ticked on the mantel and a fire crackled in the grate, throwing its warmth into the room against the chill that still came in the evenings, though it was spring.

Gincie could see it all come back to Della, could see her remembering Samson's death as if he were dying in her arms again. Her face was the face of mourning shared by every woman who had ever lost her cherished mate. And then in the instant, the grief was transformed into something so ancient and powerful it took Gincie a moment to recognize it.

Della's dark eyes glowed, and her skin seemed to pull more tautly over the bones of her face while her mouth stretched wide, part smile, part snarl, all of it fierce exultation.

"He deserved it! He should have died five years ago. He should have died even before that. He should have died before he ever had a chance to murder my husband! I'm sorry for all the trouble it has brought to you and Travis, but I am glad you did it, glad! I feel as if I've been waiting to hear this news since that day. Now it is complete."

The silence was between them again, and then very softly Gincie said, "Before I killed Mark, I should have found out about his brother, my half brother Matthew, and about my mother. I didn't. They could be part of this. We are all part of the same blood."

"No!" Della's denial was instantaneous. "I didn't like your mother any more than anyone else here did. But it was Mark Carrington who brought death to Wild Swan, and it was Mark Carrington you killed. And there's an end to it. If you don't let it end there, then he has won after all."

Gincie wanted to be convinced by the words, but failing that, she clung to the image of Della's savage joy and gathered the courage to face the rest of the family and the people of Wild Swan.

Chapter 5

Of Gincie's own generation, only her cousin Larissa and Larissa's husband, Reid Tratnor, were at the family meeting, the other cousins and their spouses either living too far away or, in the case of Adam Falconer, away from Baltimore on business for the Jennings-Falconer shipping company. But the second generation was fully represented by Morgan and Samantha "Sam" Falconer, Blaine and Philomena "Philly" Carrington, and Blaine's twin, Flora Jennings.

In some ways, it seemed to Gincie that it had only been short days ago that she and Travis and baby Lexy had taken leave of these people, but in others, there was visible proof that four years had passed. The proof was not only in her own children, in Lexy now being an active five-year-old and the twins providing evidence of the passage of years in their own lively ways, but in the marks time had left on her aunts and uncles.

It was beyond normal aging, for these people were, like her own generation, marked by the war, marked by years of violence and loss. Not only had Seth, the oldest of Morgan and Sam's sons, died at Gettysburg, but Morgan himself had nearly perished of malaria and neglect at the Confederate prison at Andersonville, Georgia.

In his fifty-third year, Morgan was the image of Rane and Alex, but his excessive leanness was legacy of the bouts of fever he still suffered when he overworked. And though Sam, a year younger than Morgan, was still a lovely woman, there was a lot of silver in the red-and-gold-touched brown of her hair, and her hazel eyes held the shadows of sorrow despite the fact that the first acute pain of loss had dulled enough so that she could speak quite easily of Seth and could laugh in memory of how quick-witted he had been in boyish escapades with his brothers.

Though Blaine and Philly had three daughters rather than sons, they had found that no proof against the terror of war as their daughters had gone one by one to serve—Larissa and Anthea to nurse the wounded, and Phoebe to teach the newly liberated slaves in the South. And though the war was five years over, Phoebe and her husband were still teaching with missionary zeal in a climate where whites who believed in equal rights for blacks were facing increasing resentment.

Blaine and Philly, both in their fifties, were a study in contrasts, Blaine tall, gilt-haired, blue-eyed, and rather reserved, as befitted his nature and his work, while Philly was short, a bit rounder with the years, and as irrepressible as she had always been. Blaine's sense of humor was quiet and dry; Philly's was never far from the surface, betrayed by the sparkle in her bright blue eyes. Her black hair had yet to show any gray, and her small stature made it easy to forget that she had a formidable mind, well trained in the classics by the elderly uncle who had raised her, and that she had raised three daughters to think independently.

Philly taught with Flora, Blaine's twin, at the school Flora had established years before. The school was still based on radical principles, in that it was open to both blacks and whites, to all ethnic backgrounds, and to boys and girls, as well as providing instruction for a growing number of adults who needed basic education to have any hope of prospering.

Of all of them, Flora was the most changed. Her hair was silver now, she was so thin she looked ethereal, and her blue eyes had a sad, faraway look in them that was very unlike her, or had been before she lost her husband.

Flora had made a foolish marriage to a foolish man when she was quite young. The marriage had ended disastrously when her husband had been killed in a duel over another man's mistress. Her second marriage had been unlikely and perfect.

When Flora had married Caleb Jennings, he had been a widower whose oldest child was twenty-one years old. He had married his first wife in the same year that Flora was born. Flora was only two years older than Caleb's eldest child and had grown up in close contact with the Jennings's children. At first glance, it seemed a recipe for further disaster, as if Flora were exchanging one extreme for another. But in fact, Flora had begun the process of maturing into a forceful, compassionate woman as her father, St. John, had been dying.

Her first marriage had been a last attempt to hold on to the part of her that had wanted nothing more than to be a pretty butterfly. By the time she married Caleb, the season of the butterfly was long over, and in each other they found the perfect match. He never ceased to celebrate her beauty inside and out, and he supported her causes, be they equal rights for women and nonwhites, equal education regardless of financial status, or simply helping to feed and clothe the hungry in Baltimore. And though Flora had often thought the gifts of their marriage were all given by him to her, she had admired and loved him deeply throughout their years together, thus giving him all he desired from her.

Flora had had only two regrets about their marriage. One was that she was never able to give Caleb children, and the other was that, given the span of years between them, it had always been likely that he would die before she did.

The war had added the extra weight to those years. Caleb had overworked as the shipyard produced for the navy, and the loss of a grandson, his namesake, had been a hard blow. Caleb's heart had begun to fail him before the war was ended, and it had been a struggle for him to remain alive as long as he had, a struggle he had waged only because, no matter how weary he was, he did not want to leave Flora. But on a January night of the previous year, he had gone to sleep beside her and had not awakened when morning came.

Flora could have asked for no kinder death for him, but that did not prevent her from missing him constantly. They had been married for thirty-one years, and though she knew the truth of his death, she found it nearly impossible to accept that he was no longer part of her days and nights.

Gincie found it difficult to accept as well. Her grandmother had sent news of Caleb's passing as soon as it had happened, but death at a distance was difficult to believe.

There had been other losses in the past four years. Timothy and Mavis Bates, who had come to America with the Carringtons and who had stayed in Annapolis to run the tavern after the family moved out to the farm, had died within a year of each other, Mavis of pneumonia and then Timothy because, Alex said, he simply had no reason to go on.

Gincie glanced at her grandparents, and gratitude swept over her. Life was precarious at best. Caleb, Mavis, and Timothy were gone; suddenly it seemed miraculous that Alex and Rane had survived the passage of years. They had served not only as her grandparents, but as her parents, too, and they were here for her still.

She held Travis's hand tightly, but she did not find it as difficult as she had thought it would be to tell the family why it had been necessary for the Culhanes to leave California.

They had all been prepared in the sense that they knew only some dire circumstance would have caused the precipitous flight. They had speculated variously on illness in one of the children, financial reverses, a gradual disenchantment with life in the Far West, or even, as unthinkable as it seemed to all of them, trouble in the Culhanes' marriage. But not one of them had considered anything like the reappearance of Mark Carrington or Gincie's solution to the problem.

Gincie was growing accustomed to the shocked silence that inevitably followed her revelation, and she could almost see how each mind was considering it, but it was Philly who spoke first. Her expression was abstracted, her voice musing as she inadvertently spoke her thoughts aloud.

"Isn't it too bad it couldn't have been done during the war. If Mark Carrington had been killed then, it would be just another casualty, so tidy, with no repercussions."

The focus of the room shifted from Gincie to Philly, and feeling it, Philly looked up, blinking. "Oh, I suppose that does sound rather bloodthirsty, but surely you must all be thinking the same thing. Mark Carrington was an evil man."

Blaine studied his wife for a moment more, and then he laughed aloud because he was helpless against the impulse. "Trust you, my dear, to go right to the heart of the matter. I sometimes forget that the heart of a lion can be found in someone as small as a mouse."

Philly made a face at him. "You forget because this is a family of giants."

Blaine's laughter was echoed in a nervous ripple that ran through the room, breaking the tension, and suddenly everyone was talking at once, offering opinions and suggestions as if the trouble were no more out of the ordinary than a problem with spring planting or a business venture. And for the first time, Gincie believed there might be a solution.

Blaine reluctantly interjected a note of sanity into the proceedings. "There really aren't any plans we can make until we hear from Boston. Much depends on what the authorities in California discover. They may never connect Mark's death with Gincie, or even if they do, it may be that Mark will be no more lamented there than he is here."

Blaine's words were comforting to Gincie. She felt the power and support of her relatives so strongly, it was as if she could wrap herself in the protective cloak they provided.

She glanced at Travis, but she could not tell if he shared the feeling. His expression was pleasant enough, but guarded, as if he were reserving judgment.

The conversation swept on to other subjects, to questions about Boston and his family and about life in California. There was no reserve in Travis when he spoke of that.

"It is truly a place for new beginnings. There is still good ranch land available all over the state, much of it from old ranchos that are being broken up and sold." He qualified his enthusiasm by adding, "There is more than a little injustice in the land policy in that the old grants and agreements haven't been upheld in the courts in many cases. But there is land to be purchased and worked honestly. It's such vast and varied country, it would be hard to be bored there in a lifetime."

It was no surprise to anyone that Travis was so fond of his adopted state; he had gone there to establish a new life for himself and his family, and he had done it very well. Only Gincie heard the note of desperation in his voice, but she could think of nothing to say to ease it.

The room became a babble of noise when the children were admitted, not only the Culhanes' three, but also Larissa and Reid's four-year-old Benjamin and their two-year-old Gillian. The cousins seemed to be getting along quite well, with all of the younger ones deferring to Lexy's authority as she marshaled them like a hen with a brood of chicks.

"I may borrow your daughter now and then," Larissa told Gincie. "She seems to be managing my children better than I do."

"She's wonderful with the twins," Gincie said proudly. "Things might change when they're older, but for now, the boys consider her word law. She's very good about keeping them out of trouble. I'm glad she was born first."

Gincie had grown up with her Carrington and Falconer cousins. She felt comfortable in Larissa's presence and was fond of Reid, too. Larissa, five years older than Gincie, was the eldest of Blaine and Philly's three daughters and the most striking. Tall and slender with a cloud of dark hair and silvery gray eyes, Larissa had inherited her grandfather St. John's aristocratic bone structure and could appear aloof when, in fact, she was warm natured.

On the eve of the war, she had married a kind man, Luke Carstairs, whom she liked more than loved. But he had courted her for years, and she was fond enough of him to think that by marrying him, she could keep him from marching off to battle. Instead, he died in the first engagement, at Bull Run. Larissa blamed herself for not loving him enough and had certainly not intended to become involved with another man. Reid Tratnor, the blue-eyed, black-haired newspaperman from New York, had changed all of that by sheer force of will. He took one look at Larissa and decided that he had found the woman he wanted. Alex abetted Reid in his pursuit, and Larissa stood little chance against that alliance. It was a failure of resistance for which Larissa gave constant thanks.

Although Reid's goal had been to spend his life with Larissa, he gained the added benefit of sharing her family. The death of his parents when he was very young had left him to be raised by an overburdened older sister who had little time and little idea of how to handle the wild young man he had been, and Reid had grown up without much experience of familial warmth. To be enfolded by Larissa and her family as if he had always been part of their lives was an unlooked-for gift to Reid. Larissa would have moved to New York with him after the war, but he had not hesitated to put down roots where they could be close to her family.

They lived in Georgetown, and Reid worked for a Washington newspaper as well as sending occasional pieces to his old New York paper and other publications. His parents had left him enough of an inheritance so that he could provide a comfortable, if not lavish, life for Larissa and the children. But he was well paid now on his own merits, having established a name for himself as a war correspondent who had witnessed the battles rather than getting his copy from Washington gossip, and he fully intended to own and publish his own newspaper before too many more years had passed.

Larissa watched him answering a question from Ben, the two faces so intense and so alike that her heart turned over. She shifted her attention back to Gincie. "I would have done the same thing you did," she said, "the very same thing. There is nothing I would not do to protect Reid, Ben, and Jilly."

Nothing was settled. Everything still depended on events in California, but Gincie allowed the warmth of her family to surround her, a protective barrier against the world.

"I'm so glad we came back to Wild Swan!" she said to Travis as they got ready for bed. When he didn't answer, her hand stilled, and she put down her hairbrush and turned so she could see him. His face wore the same guarded look she had noted earlier.

"You aren't glad to be here at all, are you?" she asked reluctantly, not wanting to hear the answer but needing to anyway.

Travis rubbed his eyes wearily, trying to find the words that would explain without wounding. "I love your family. I am as grateful as you are that we've found shelter here. I know we need to be here. But this is not my home. My home was in Virginia, and now it is in California. Everythin' we have is invested there. I know that Malachi and Boston will watch over everythin' for us, but I'm anxious to return as soon as we can."

The most difficult question lay unvoiced between them—whether or not they would be able to go back. Only events in California could answer that.

Gincie began to see that though she felt safe behind the wall of her family's support, Travis felt that he was on the outside. She could think of no way to bring him inside if this were not where he wanted to be. Even when she curled into his arms to sleep, she felt as if they were worlds apart, and it was her fault. Their lives were suspended until word came from Boston, and Gincie both dreaded and wanted his report to come.

When the packet did arrive, her hands shook too much for her to open it. Wordlessly, she handed it to Travis.

Boston's flowing script was in stark contrast to the words:

I wish we had better news. But there is no way around what has happened here. The authorities do suspect Gincie in the death of Mark Carrington.

The man had a wife, and I suspect she knew what he was about, though she protests that he only wished to contact his half sister, with whom he had lost contact during the war. I suspect other things about her. I suspect her husband was less than kind to her and that his death may be as welcome to her as it is to us. She has the sly, beaten look of someone who has learned to survive in the harshest way and now sees a way to profit by circumstance. She came to this city to obtain death money, not to mourn her husband. There are no children.

*We have, of course, denied all knowledge of the incident. I was so proud
of Rachel, who, when questioned about Mark Carrington, appeared
completely innocent and asked, "Oh, is he a relative of my husband's
family? I'm afraid I have only met a few Carringtons, and that was
long ago in Maryland."*

*We decided that to acknowledge Mark's crimes, past or present, would
be to give motive to his being shot. Instead, we maintain ignorance of
the man. I have admitted having heard of him, but have pointed out
that I never met him and that as far as I know, Gincie has not seen her
half brother since she was a tiny child. Further, both Rachel and I have
said that it was family business that called you back east—as you know,
the fame of Wild Swan is well known here—and we added a small lie,
saying that Gincie has been homesick for the green country of Maryland
for some time.*

*We have tried to keep all of our statements, denials, and, yes, lies as
simple as possible. And I think we have managed to make the idea of
Gincie as a murderess preposterous in the authorities' eyes. But I do not
believe it is safe for you, Gincie, to return as yet. "Out of sight, out of
mind" is too appropriate in this case.*

*Do not fear for us. There is nothing to connect us directly with the
shooting of Mark.*

*We will take good care of your properties here until you decide what is to
be done.*

We send our deepest love.

Boston's account was restrained compared to the newspaper
clippings that fluttered out of the letter. "Mystery Woman Shoots
Man at Russ House!" "Was This Love Denied or Love Avenged?"
"Connection with Prominent Citizens Investigated!" "Widow Grieves,
Demands Justice."

The only good thing was that neither the Culhanes nor the
Thaines were identified by name, though enough references were
made to shipping and horse racing for many to suspect. Travis could
imagine the effort Boston must have made to keep their names out
of the papers, and it was a mark of the power as well as the respect
accorded Boston that he had been able to do it at all, particularly since
Mark's widow had undoubtedly been vociferous in her accusations.

"There's an end to it," Travis said, and his voice was flat, dead.

That night, Gincie dreamed she was shooting Mark over and
over again, but when he finally fell, it was Travis who lay bleeding to
death.

Her violent thrashing awakened Travis before she began to cry
out. He wrapped his arms around her. "Wake up, darlin', wake up
now! You're havin' a nightmare. That's all, just a nightmare."

She stilled against him, and then her voice came in the darkness, as if from a long way off. "But it isn't a nightmare at all. It's the same whether I am awake or asleep. I'm killing you as surely as I killed Mark!"

"No, love, no! You and I and the children, we are alive and well because of you. Mark Carrington might well have carried out his threats. If not you or me, he might have harmed the children!" He kept all doubt from his voice.

She had believed it enough to kill a man. She wanted to continue to believe it. But it was growing more difficult to remember how terrified she had been of Mark and too easy to see how terrified he had been of her at the end.

She clung to Travis all night, but the cold inside of her never lessened.

Chapter 6

Gincie was hiding. If strangers came to Wild Swan, she was not to be seen. When Travis suggested they visit Baltimore, she had a host of excuses, and her response was the same when he mentioned Washington. He knew if he pushed hard enough, he could make her go, but the frightened look in her eyes made it impossible.

Gincie was perfectly safe at the farm, but nonetheless, Travis felt guilty for leaving her there. Yet he had to spend time away. He was beginning to feel more and more a prisoner, a useless one at that. He was accustomed to days full of purpose and work, and his enforced idleness grew increasingly odious.

He took Lexy with him on his excursions, not only because she was overly sensitive to her mother's distress, but also because he enjoyed her company. She was comfortable now with Rane and Morgan, so a visit to the shipping offices of Jennings-Falconer was a treat, and she was a special favorite there with Adam Falconer, the elder of Morgan and Sam's two remaining sons. He had come out to Wild Swan immediately on his return to Baltimore and had met the children.

At twenty-six, Adam was broadly built with chestnut hair, strong features, and bright green eyes that were already framed by fine lines from the time he spent aboard ship. He had served with the Union blockade fleet during the war, and not even that often boring duty had tempered his love for the sea.

Though Adam had no family of his own yet, he was at ease with children because he was genuinely interested in them. He was delighted to show Lexy maps of various shipping routes and to tell her what the cargoes were.

He traced the line from the woodlands of Pennsylvania to the forests of the Carolinas. "Lumber comes in to be made into everything from furniture to houses to ships.

"Trains come to Baltimore from other parts of Maryland, from Pennsylvania, North Carolina, and states quite a ways west of here, and they bring wheat, corn, oats, rye, and barley. Some is milled into flour, and some is left just as it is. Then the grain and flour are loaded onto steamships and taken down south and even clear across the Atlantic Ocean to Europe, to countries that can't grow enough for their people.

"Oranges and lemons come from Florida and Sicily, almonds and raisins from Malaga, Canton ginger from China, and all sorts of other good things to make candies and conserves. Spices come from all over the world to make your food taste better. Molasses to make sugar comes from New Orleans, Cuba, and other warm places. And fish, oysters, fruits, and vegetables are packed here to be sent to more places than you can count. Leather shoes, cotton cloth, soap, candles, pottery, paints, and chemicals are made here and sent out . . ." his finger skipped faster and faster until both he and Lexy were laughing. "And our ships carry a lot of these cargoes."

Listening to his daughter, Travis realized how little he had heard her laughter lately and was resolved that no matter what happened to himself and Gincie, the children would not suffer for it.

He showed Lexy the statues that gave Baltimore the title of "City of Monuments," and he took her to Druid Hill Park, which was particularly lovely in the early summer with its lake, deer herd, abundance of flowers and trees, and the view of the city from Reservoir Hill, the highest point in the park.

And he took her to Washington, where Reid gave her a tour of the newspaper office. Though Lexy was shy of the scurrying bustle and held tightly to her father's hand, she was immediately fascinated by the printing process.

The tradition of early reading lessons was part of both Gincie's and Travis's families, and so Lexy could scarcely remember a time when she had not known how to read at least a few words. She loved books, and the newspaper office was a revelation to her.

"What you say gets made into real pages for everybody to read?" she asked.

"That's right," Reid said, and with a grin, he added softly to Travis, "I wish my own children treated my work with such awe."

Though Lexy was interested in the shipyard in Baltimore and in the various activities on the farm, the newspaper held even more fascination for her.

"The ink smells good," she said, sniffing audibly, and she stated firmly, "I am gonna write things for newspapers when I get big."

"Perhaps by then I'll have my own newspaper, and I can hire you as a reporter," Reid told her.

"She'll probably hold you to it," Travis murmured.

The men took Lexy to dine at a restaurant, treating her as if she were a mature young woman, and she responded by behaving with her best party manners, though her eyes remained huge and wondering throughout as Reid identified various government officials and told her what they did.

"I wish Mama and the twins could be here, but Mama doesn't want to leave the farm," Lexy observed at one point, and Travis was grateful that her attention was fixed on her plate, for he knew his expression betrayed him.

He swallowed hard. "We'll bring them all for a visit someday soon, and then you'll be able to tell them about the capital."

This plan contented Lexy, but Travis caught Reid's look of sympathy and realized everyone in the family was aware of Gincie's behavior.

Though the twins were too young to enjoy the outings in the cities, he tried to make up for it by spending long hours with them at the farm.

He did not fully acknowledge it even to himself, but he knew sooner or later he had to go back to California to decide what to do about the properties there, and that that would mean leaving Gincie and the children for an unknown length of time. It was difficult enough to contemplate leaving Gincie, but he was determined that at least the children would feel comfortable in their Maryland life before he had to go.

Travis was grateful that in many ways the children, particularly the twins, were adjusting better than their parents. They were young and resilient, and they had found security and interesting things to do at Wild Swan. Lexy still asked when she could again see Conchee and various others, including Uncle Boston and Aunt Rachel, but now there was less anxiety in the asking. However, there was no way Travis could undertake a long journey while Gincie was still so vulnerable.

Alex, like Travis, kept hoping Gincie would regain her courage by herself. She was pleased to see that her granddaughter seemed to be showing more interest in the daily life of the farm, and Alex began to give her various tasks. As Alex's grandmother had taught her how to heal the sick with a combination of practical skill and herbal medicines, so had Alex taught Gincie. And Gincie had learned to work with the horses and to do myriad other jobs that were a constant part of life in the country.

But the illusion of normalcy was shattered when Dr. Cameron came to visit.

Alastair Cameron's life had been intertwined with the lives of the Carringtons and Falconers for so long, they were very much like family to him. Though he had been born in America of Scottish parents, he had taken his medical training in Edinburgh, and that, coupled with the way his parents had spoken, had left him with a slight but permanent burr in his speech.

Alastair and Alex shared mutual respect and long years of friendship, and he was so much a part of the landscape of their lives, it never occurred to Alex that Gincie would regard him as a threat. But when he rode in, Gincie fled.

There was no subtlety about it—one moment she was with Travis and the children, all of them perched on a fence watching the schooling of a colt, and in the next, she had disappeared into the house.

Alastair greeted Alex calmly and approached Travis and the children with a smile, but his eyes looked so baffled and sad, Alex could not bear it. Before she could decide what to do about it, Travis said, "Children, mind your grandmother. I'll be right back."

"Please, it's not necessary," Alastair protested.

"Oh, yes, it is!" Travis retorted without slackening his stride.

"I never meant . . ." Alastair began, but Alex forestalled him.

"You are part of this family," she said firmly. "And Gincie loves you. This sort of behavior is as harmful for her as it is for you. You know why she's here, don't you?"

Alastair nodded. "Word does travel, even to a backwater such as Annapolis. And having business in Baltimore, I paid a visit to Rane yesterday." He was careful about what he said, his attention fixed on the children.

"Gwandpa Wane," Tay said with a big smile, and Lexy asked, "You know Grandpa?" She, like her brothers, accepted that relationship as cause enough to treat the newcomer cordially.

"I don't know how he does it," Alex said in mock despair, as Alastair produced a stick of candy for each of the children and listened patiently to their chatter as they told him everything they'd done so far this day. "I think my husband's charm grows more lethal by the year."

Travis found Gincie in their bedroom, and his temper, so long under control, flared hotly at the sight of her. "That was inexcusable!" he roared. "Dr. Cameron has been part of this place since long before you were born! He was your father's mentor when your father decided to be a doctor. For God's sake! It was through Alastair that you began to work for the Underground Railroad, through him that we met! What you did out there was cruel. Are you so concerned with yourself that you no longer care how other people feel?"

She stared at him, her green eyes magnified by the tears filling them and spilling over to run down her cheeks. "I can't face him, I just can't! All of his life, he has worked to save lives. He taught me, as Grandmother did, how to save lives. He knows, now he knows that I executed Mark!"

Travis's anger broke on her tears. "Oh, darlin', you've got to keep rememberin' what Mark threatened to do, what he would have done if you hadn't stopped him. It's done, Gincie, it's done! If you go on like this, Mark has destroyed us. I can't make you go to Dr. Cameron, but I beg that you do."

He opened his arms, and she nestled against him, trying desperately to draw strength into the lonely place where she was. She pulled away and started to wipe at her eyes. Travis gently batted her hands away and used his handkerchief to blot her tears. And then he offered his hand. "Come with me?"

She clung to him until she was facing Alastair, and then she let go of Travis's hand and approached the doctor. He had looked rumpled and weathered for as long as she could remember, his face a map of wrinkles over craggy bones, the reddish blond of his hair faded to white over the years. But now he looked truly old to her, and in the instant she understood why.

Alastair was a man of certainty. While he might wish others would share his convictions, his main concern was that he himself abide by them. And despite his sometimes gruff manner, he took nothing to heart so much as the stipulation of the Hippocratic Oath, that he do no harm. He applied it not only to medicine, but to every aspect of his life. When his wife had run off with another man years before, he had been the first to say that the fault was his own for having neglected the woman, for having seen to the needs of his patients while ignoring the needs of his wife completely.

Now standing before Gincie, he judged that his visit had already done her harm, and therefore, he should never have come. His body seemed to be trying to shrink inside of his rumpled clothes, and his blue eyes, usually so alert and penetrating, were hazed with apology.

Gincie didn't notice that Alex and Travis were shepherding the children away; she was overwhelmed with remorse.

"Gincie, I am sorry, I . . . I . . ." he stammered, and that was as far as he got as she closed the distance between them, put her arms around him, and buried her head against his coat.

"No! I am the one who is sorry!" she sobbed. "You are as close to my heart as my grandparents. Please, please, forgive me!" She didn't try to explain; she trusted him to understand, and she was not disappointed.

He patted her back and cradled her as if she were no older than Lexy. "Ah, Gincie, my girl, there is nothing to forgive between such old friends, and old friends do not judge each other." He was relieved she did not ask him about the rumors; it was difficult enough to repeat them later to Alex.

"The truth is that Mark Carrington threatened Gincie and her family, and she did something about it," Alastair said. "And though I know it is impossible, I wish that could be told, just the bare facts of the matter. The rumors are so much worse. One has it that she murdered someone for an inheritance, another that it was a love triangle, yet another that it was over a horse race—stupid, vicious lies that have made their way across the country. It makes me regret the ease of travel these days."

"It would be as well to regret all the success we have had at Wild Swan," Alex pointed out. "If this family hadn't gained prominence in racing and shipping, no one would give tuppence for news of our affairs. Unfortunately, Gincie's determination to hide here is surely making everything worse. I meant to give her all the time she needs, but . . ." Her voice trailed away as she considered a different tack.

Alastair felt his spirits lift; he had seen that look before. When Alexandria Carrington Falconer looked this determined, there was little that could stand in her way. He did not ask what her plan was, but he left Wild Swan convinced that he would not have to listen to attacks on Gincie for much longer.

Alex spoke to Travis first, telling him what she had in mind, but adding, "I will not demand it if you do not agree."

Travis considered all that her plan entailed and the risks, and then he nodded. "We'll do it. In my own way, I've been hidin' as much as Gincie has. I've been pretendin' we could simply wait this out. But it isn't helpin' Gincie. I don't understand all of what she's feelin', but I've begun to realize her guilt's gettin' worse, not less, as the days pass. I think she's forgotten what Mark was like; I think she can remember no more than that she killed him."

Because he believed it was for her own good, Travis was relentless in his arguments, and he had the added weapon of truth on his side. "You know your grandmother seldom sends her horses to major race meetings without goin' herself, and yet, her concern for you, for us, has kept her away from Jerome Park. She wants us to go to Saratoga Springs with her, and I think it is the least we can do. Our lives are part of Wild Swan now and perhaps for a long time to come. And that must surely mean doin' what we can to help."

Gincie knew she was being manipulated, and the idea of appearing before the racing world at Saratoga was terrifying, but she was helpless against Travis. Their relationship was based on recognizing their individual needs and working toward mutual decisions. The last time he had focused his will on her to try to make her do something she did not want to do was when he had tried to convince her that they were mad to consider marriage on the eve of the war. He had been trying to protect her then, though in the wrong way; he was trying to protect her now. And this time, he was right. She could not go on the way she was. Running away from Alastair Cameron had shown her that.

"I'll go," she said.

Her acquiescence came so swiftly in the low whisper of sound, and she looked so much like a chastened child, that Travis, braced for a fight, had to cling fast to his own courage. "We'll be there with you," he promised, and suddenly he looked so fierce, Gincie thought she might be able to face the world at Saratoga as long as he was beside her.

Chapter 7

Nothing in Gincie's previous experience of racing had prepared her for the wealth and splendor of the gathering at Saratoga Springs. Though long noted for its mineral springs, the addition of horse racing in 1863 and the opening of a new track in 1864 had transformed the sleepy health spa. New hotels were still being built and old ones expanded, and yet so many people came during the races that every spare room in the town would be let to boarders.

The rail station was the scene of wild confusion, with "Saratoga trunks" containing the wardrobes of the fashionable forming small mountain ranges and disembarking passengers impatiently hailing porters. It was the day before the races were to begin, and Gincie was glad the horses had been shipped ahead in the care of Padraic and his men; at least they should be settled in and calm by now. For her part, as she got her first look at Saratoga, she discovered that not even her dread was as strong as her fascination.

The architecture alone was astonishing and extravagant, with no expense spared in the production of bays, balconies, cupolas, turrets, towers, and miles of fretwork on the buildings along the elm-shaded streets.

"It looks as if the architects went a little mad," Gincie said.

"Or perhaps the water here has more than minerals in it," Travis speculated, with a grin that grew wider when Gincie laughed.

Though many people stayed at the huge Union Hotel or at the slightly smaller Congress Hall, which nonetheless also boasted impressive piazzas, the Falconers preferred the Clarendon. With its white woodwork and green shades, it was inviting and restful, and though it did not embrace modernization with the same fervor as other hotels, it remained a favorite among its elite clientele, who demanded a quiet refuge with good service.

The day was warm and sunny, and Broadway and every shady spot along it seemed crowded with people who had one thing in mind—determining which horses had the best chance of winning in each race on the program.

Never had Gincie been more aware of her grandmother's reputation in the racing world. The memberships in the various jockey clubs were in Rane's name, but nearly everyone knew it was Alexandria Carrington Falconer who raised the horses and made the decisions about them, just as Rane did in his shipping business. Alex had been known as the "Englishwoman" for decades. It was a tribute, and now it had added luster because she was one of the old guard whose stable had survived the war because she had shipped the racers to Canada and England on the eve of the conflict.

So many of the prize animals in the South had been ridden into battle and died there or had been driven off by raiders such as the ones who had come several times to Wild Swan. Horses in Kentucky had fared somewhat better, though there had been depredation there as well because Kentucky, like Maryland, was a border state. There had also been horses brought by grooms from southern plantations in the dark of night and left at Kentucky farms to be taken care of. They presented a unique problem since many, while clearly of the best blood, had arrived at their havens without papers proving their bloodlines. Before the war, racing had been a southern sport; now it belonged to the North.

H. Price McGrath and Daniel Swigert, both of Kentucky, were part of the old world of racing, and they too were at Saratoga. But the new kings of the turf were clearly the Northerners, such as William R. Travers, M. H. Sanford, and August Belmont, a German-Jewish immigrant who had come to the United States in 1837 as banker for the Rothschilds and had then established his own business.

In his late fifties, Belmont looked the part of a prosperous man of Wall Street with his side-whiskers and balding pate, but the slightly gutteral edge to his speech and his courtly demeanor were reminders of his Old World background. He walked with a limp, legacy of a duel over a lady's honor nearly thirty years before, but that had happened in the United States, as had his marriage to Caroline Slidell Perry, a daughter of Commodore Matthew C. Perry, in 1849, and he had, for years, been passionately involved in the affairs of his adopted country.

He and Rane shared a special bond, for they had met in England during the war when both had been there to work against the recognition of the Confederacy as a separate nation by the British. And in recent years when there had been nasty rumors that cast doubt on Belmont's loyalty to the Union, rumors that stemmed from prejudice against his Jewish heritage, Rane had defended him publicly.

Mr. Belmont was visibly pleased to see the Falconers, and after the pleasantries were over, he said to Alex, "Your Swan's Sailor looks very fine for the Travers Stakes tomorrow. I think he will give my Telegram a good race."

"I hope he will," Alex replied. "But I fear another may put us both in our places." She meant it. Although Sailor was a promising three-year-old, even Padraic, who was always loath to relinquish his loyalty to Wild Swan's horses, felt that Mr. Swigert's Kingfisher, a colt by Lexington out of an imported mare, would have the edge in the race.

Mr. Belmont took the comment with good grace, appreciating her honesty. "Then I shall just have to buy him," he said.

It was no idle boast. His Nursery Stable, located in Babylon, Long Island, was constantly being improved by his purchases of winning stock.

Oden Bowie, governor of Maryland, was attending the races, too, and his racing stable was as notable as his politics. Though a sympathizer with the South and a Democrat, he had opposed secession, and he wanted the wounds of the war healed.

He greeted the Falconers with a wide smile. "There may not be many Marylanders in the horse racing business anymore, but with your fine animals, we'll uphold the honor of our state."

"We're looking forward to the resumption of racing in Baltimore this October," Alex said. "And the credit for that is surely yours."

The decision to reestablish racing in Baltimore had been made among the racing elite at Saratoga two years before, and Alex, through Rane, was among the original subscribers to the forthcoming "Dinner Party Stakes." The name was quite literal since the race had been planned at a congenial gathering of turfmen, the sort of function Rane attended for the benefit of his wife's business. But if horses were not his passion, he was very knowledgeable about them; otherwise, the horsemen would never have allowed him within their ranks.

Although forty-one years had passed since the death of St. John Carrington and thirty-nine since Rane's marriage to Alex, he never lost sight of the fact that the service he did for Alex with the jockey clubs was nothing more nor less than taking Sinje's place. He had once found it difficult to live with the knowledge that Alex had had a full life with another man, but the years had burned away the last of that jealousy, leaving only gratitude for the children and grandchildren St. John had added to his life.

Gincie noted the warm look her grandfather gave her grandmother as the conversation about the horses continued, and she eased closer to Travis, feeling her heart lift as he glanced at her with the same sort of love she had just observed.

Gincie observed something else, too. Some of the older horsemen had met her when she was a young girl at Wild Swan; some knew of her and Travis because of their involvement in racing in the Far West. Suddenly, she was quite sure that they were aware that trouble in California had caused the Culhanes' return to Maryland. Yet, no one asked uncomfortable questions or treated them with anything but courtesy. The knot of misery Gincie had thought would never leave her began to ease.

The next day, Thursday, July 14, marked the opening day, and though the races would not begin until noon, the Falconers and Culhanes left early, taking a huge picnic hamper provided by the hotel so that they could share breakfast with Padraic and the men. Even at this unfashionable hour, the road was well trafficked with splendid equipages.

The sun was soon bright, and the track appeared to be in excellent condition, but Padraic refused to be cheered.

"I feel it in me bones," he declared. "There's rain not far off, an' Sailor's no mudder, game lad that he is."

"Despite all evidence to the contrary, I hesitate to contradict him," Alex confided to Gincie. "If he says it's going to rain, it probably will, and he's right about Sailor, too. Speed and heart and everything one could wish as long as the track stays dry, but when it rains, I vow that horse wants to go home and put his hooves up by the fire."

By the time the races were due to begin, there were close to five thousand people in attendance, women and men dressed in their finest, trying to ignore the dark clouds rolling up from the south and the thunder beginning to boom. At least Padraic had the satisfaction of being able to mutter, "I knew it, I knew it!"

As if on the signal of the bugle call to the horses for the Travers Stakes, the sprinkling of rain increased to a downpour, quickly turning the course into a bog sure to slow down the race.

Since the race was one and three-quarter miles, the seven entries were started from the extra quarter stretch, which began at the rear of the judges' stand and intersected the main course at the half-mile pole. Two false starts prolonged the agony, but finally the flag fell. For a moment, it looked as if Sailor would overcome his distaste for the mud as he jumped away first, with Kingfisher following hard on his heels. Then Telegram passed Kingfisher and began forcing the running.

Sailor quit running, it was as simple as that. He began to mince along as if reluctant to get his feet wet, all his flash and fire extinguished by the mud. The rest of the race was a contest among three horses—Kingfisher, Telegram, and Chillicothe—with Kingfisher winning as the betting had predicted.

"A taste of the whip would have kept Sailor moving," one disgusted spectator mumbled. Alex's lips thinned in distaste, but she didn't bother to dispute the man. Her jockey had followed instructions. Neither she nor Padraic thought there was anything to be gained from beating Sailor for something that was as much a part of him as the ground-eating stride he displayed on a dry course. No horse could be expected to run well in every circumstance.

Mr. Belmont agreed with Alex, and he made a handsome offer for Sailor, honoring Alex's position as the true owner and breeder by making the offer directly to her.

"I'm flattered that you see the potential in him," she told Mr. Belmont, "and your offer is generous, but I must decline. I have plans for him to continue to race for us and then to stand at the farm. As you know, he's Lady Sailaway's last foal, as well as one of Swan's Chance's last sons."

That was precisely the reason August Belmont saw such promise in the stallion. Lady Sailaway had been imported from England and had impeccable bloodlines, while Swan's Chance also had English connections through his sire, Fortune, and in the grandsire and granddam on his maternal side. Mr. Belmont, with his own ties to England, appreciated those bloodlines.

From England, Alex and St. John had brought the lame mare Leda with her foal, Wild Swan, at her side and had continued their association with English stables through Hugh Bettingdon, the Duke of Almont, the man who had awakened St. John to the idiocy of mistreating Alex. The bond between the two families had grown stronger over the years, with Hugh's marriage producing two children, a son and a daughter, and Alex and Rane's marriage producing a daughter, Gweneth, born in 1832. When Hugh and Angelica's son, Christopher, had come to visit America in 1852, he had left with Gweneth as his wife.

In addition to the benefits of friendship and kinship, the relationship with the Bettingdons had given Alex a direct line to the most elite of the racing world in England. The duke had a notable stable which included Derby winners.

After a period of disdain of all things English following the War of 1812, the 1830s had seen the resumption of the importation of English racehorses, and that had fit perfectly with the pattern already established at Wild Swan of breeding the best of England with the best of America, particularly with Sir Archy, who had been foaled in 1805 and had died in 1833, and whose blood continued to produce endurance and speed typical of the country's best racers.

All Thoroughbred horses, English and American, traced back to the same three sires, Matchem, born 1748, Herod, born 1758, and Eclipse, born 1764, who were descended from the three Eastern sires, the Godolphin Barb, the Byerly Turk, and the Darley Arabian, themselves imported into England in the late seventeenth and early eighteenth centuries to be bred with native stock. But for a hundred and fifty years, Americans had been breeding horses to sustain speed over long distances, such as the four-mile heat races, while for nearly a hundred years, the English had been perfecting animals who could run very fast at shorter distances and at a younger age.

To blend these two types into an even better animal than either of the roots was as much a matter of luck as it was of agricultural science, and Wild Swan was known for having a good combination of luck and skill. When there was a yearling sale at the farm, there was never a lack of buyers. And each year, mares were sent from all over to be bred to the stallions standing for the season.

But if Mr. Belmont failed to secure Swan's Sailor, he kept his word about Kingfisher, purchasing the horse from Mr. Swigert for fifteen thousand dollars. Mr. Swigert hesitated when Mr. Belmont insisted that, for an additional five hundred dollars, the deal must include the winner's piece of plate, a large silver punch bowl lined with gold and decorated with two horseshoes in a wreath of flowers and two jockeys in full costume. As soon as Mr. Swigert had agreed to sell the punch bowl with the horse, Mr. Belmont requested Mr. Swigert to do him the favor of presenting the silver piece to Mrs. Swigert with his compliments.

All in all, it was a good day for the generous Mr. Belmont as his horse, Glenelg, won the second race, a sweepstakes for all ages.

However, Alex's attention was focused on the Flash Stakes, a half-mile dash for two-year-olds. Wild Swan's entry was Lady Lex, a filly by Swan's Legacy out of a Lexington daughter Alex had purchased after the war. Alex and Padraic had done their best to see that as few people as possible had witnessed her speed. The filly had been exercised in the early morning hours and had been started at various points on the track so that most observers would be confused by the time and distance involved.

Of twenty youngsters originally entered, seven appeared for the race, including two horses from the stable of Leonard T. Jerome, a financier respected for his brilliance as well as his genial manner and known for being an astute judge of horseflesh.

The betting men had been shy of this race, unsure of which horse to play for a winner, so that only four pools had been sold on the race, one the night before, the other three just before the race. Lady Lex was a long shot in the public and the private betting. That was fine with Alex; it meant that if the filly won, it would be so much the better for anyone who had had faith in her.

When the bugle called the horses to race, Lady Lex took the field quite calmly, her chestnut coat gleaming. Standing fourteen and three-quarter hands high, the symmetry and beauty of her was undeniable. Her sweet head and neck, her good shoulders, short, stout back and loins, good hips and stifles, her long elastic pasterns, all promised that if she had the heart to go with her conformation, she would be a threat to any two-year-old on the track.

Though her grandmother looked very calm, Gincie found that her own palms were damp with nervousness, and she groaned when one false start was followed by another.

"She's doin' fine," Travis said. "She hasn't worn herself out yet." False starts were always a risk because some horses expended so much energy and ran so far before they could be brought back to the starting line, they lost the race before it began.

Finally they were off, bunched together, but they hadn't gone far before Lady Lex rushed to the front. From then on, it was her race, and coming up the homestretch, she opened a gap of several lengths to stride home an easy winner in fifty-four seconds, a good time given the condition of the track.

"Well done, Lady Lex, well done!" Alex exclaimed while Gincie expressed herself with less restraint, throwing her arms around Travis and crowing, "She did it! She was glorious!"

Over her head, Travis's eyes met Rane's, and they exchanged a look acknowledging their shared pleasure in Gincie's joy. It was a reaction they had not seen often enough in the past weeks.

When they congratulated Padraic and the jockey, the Irishman was understated in word, observing only that "the lass did a foine job," but his grin stretched ear to ear.

The next day saw perfect weather, complete with a gentle breeze that mitigated the heat of the sun. Gincie and Travis walked to the track since it was less than a mile away.

Though Wild Swan had no entries in it, Travis was particularly interested in the first event, which was a steeplechase for all ages. The danger and beauty of the sport was riveting. There were thirty-six leaps over fences, stone walls, hedges, and ditches, and the spectators were enthusiastic. Ladies waved handkerchiefs and gloves and wagered with their escorts on favorite horses.

Gincie put her hand out and announced gleefully, "You owe me a dollar!" when Oysterman won.

"Anyone who bets against a gambler trained by your grandmother is a fool," Travis complained good-naturedly as he handed over the money.

Alex had an entry, a four-year-old stallion, in the third and final race of the day, and she and Rane were there in time to witness it. This time, Alex was not calm because she didn't like the size of the field. With thirteen horses running, there was more danger in the jockeys' maneuvering for better positions than in a race with fewer horses. And the horse Alex had entered didn't like being crowded. Up to post time there had been the chance of entries being scratched, but the number didn't decrease.

"You can still forfeit," Rane reminded her.

Alex did not withdraw her entry, but she gave the jockey clear instructions. "Don't pull him. I want a fair race, but I also want him and you alive at the end of it. Don't push to win if it's too tight."

Padraic was beside her, agreeing completely. He, no more than she, wanted to see his charges injured, particularly needlessly.

Her instructions were hardly necessary. Five false starts had Wild Swan's entry in a lather before the race finally got off; he had exhausted himself so completely that he was never in contention for a place in the finish.

Much of the race was observable only as a boiling cloud of dust. When it was over, it took both officials and the crowd a moment to realize that one horse was missing. The spectators' eyes were drawn to an object lying on the extra stretch. Metairie, a six-year-old chestnut, had stepped into a gopher hole and fallen on his rider. The horse had broken his back and was shot; the boy was pronounced severely but not mortally injured with a broken rib.

Travis was sorry about the horse, concerned about the jockey, and terrified for Gincie. He feared the accident would bring back the loss of Gold Fire all too vividly.

Gincie saw his fear. "It is not the same," she said. "This is a dangerous sport, and what happened is very sad. But no madman caused Metairie's death. It was an accident."

That night, before pool selling began for the next day's races, money was contributed for the jockey who had been injured, and Travis and Rane were among the subscribers.

Saturday, the third day of the meeting, was an important one for Wild Swan, and indeed for all racegoers, because both the Saratoga Stakes for two-year-olds and the Saratoga Cup for all ages were to be run, as well as a third but less important contest. The crowd was larger than on the two previous days, and the women in bright finery with parasols blossoming against the sun made the grandstand look like a flower garden.

Alex had a two-year-old filly, Chance's Lass, entered in the stakes race and no entry in the cup, so all her attention was focused on the first race. Of forty-seven entries, nine horses made it to the race.

The distance was three-quarters of a mile, and the horses were started from the quarter pole instead of the cross stretch, which was not used because of the accident of the previous day, the hole in the track not being filled in yet. Alex doubted anyone would have trusted prized animals on that ground so soon anyway.

Two-year-olds were always less predictable than older horses, most of them flighty with youth and energy even if they would someday emerge as steady, dependable beasts, and Alex really didn't know Chance's Lass's potential for winning. The black filly was classically built, bred out of Irish Lass by Lady's Chance, and had shown astonishing bursts of speed even as a yearling. But she was also quixotic—fast and businesslike one day, playful and wholly undependable on the next, even more temperamental than most two-year-olds.

The race was twenty minutes delayed, and then the flag fell to a wretched start, with Mr. Jerome's filly rushing away in the lead by a length, closely followed by another while the rest straggled in the rear.

Gincie closed her eyes, but then she heard her grandmother saying very softly, "She's going to do it; she means to win this race!"

Gincie opened her eyes in time to see Chance's Lass steadily gaining on the leader and then passing her, not slowing even then, but continuing to flow like a black shadow over the ground until she had won the race by a length.

The stake was worth $3350 to the winner, and the prestige for winning the race added its own value.

The Saratoga Cup was won by Helmbold, a four-year-old chestnut colt. Mr. Belmont's Glenelg came in third, and when Mr. Belmont made an offer for Chance's Lass, Alex suggested they trade straight across.

"Your wife, she is not easy to best!" Mr. Belmont declared.

"You'll find no argument from me on that," Rane said.

Padraic shared the celebratory supper with them, and champagne made him wax more Irish by the minute, until he gave in to Alex's urging and sang "Kitty of Coleraine," a lilting ballad that concerned the breaking of a pitcher and the kissing of a dairymaid. Padraic still had a good tenor voice, and beyond that, the song held old memories for him and for Alex, harking back to the time when he had finally known that he had found a new home at Wild Swan, leaving behind the sorrows he had known in Ireland.

Far from minding the exuberance of the Falconer party, other diners at the restaurant applauded Padraic's song, and there was a continuous stream of people coming by to offer congratulations on the Saratoga Stakes victory.

After supper, Alex drew Gincie aside. "Rane is planning a visit to the Club House, and I know he would like to take Travis with him, but he won't do it if you would rather Travis did not leave you for the evening."

Gincie was tempted to refuse—Travis was her shield—but she instantly reconsidered. He must surely feel hagridden by now, and she wanted him to have as much time with her grandfather as possible. It pleased her enormously to see how well the two men got along. "I think it would be good for both of them," she said.

Travis was flattered by Rane's invitation, but he looked immediately to Gincie, still fearful of leaving her alone, and Rane suggested that the women go also.

"I have no desire to be in a place which closes its most interesting doors to women," Alex said. But then she added, "However, I will not refuse any interesting bits of information you glean there, particularly regarding the chances of the entries for the races at Baltimore."

Travis saw that Gincie really did want him to go, and as the two men departed, Rane muttered audibly, "I believe the women are quite happy to be rid of us."

Alex ordered tea sent to the Falconers' rooms, and she and

Gincie enjoyed the luxury of relaxing with no demands being made on either of them, something that seldom happened at Wild Swan.

They spoke of the children, of the horses, and of various crops and markets for the same, and then though Alex's voice remained calm, Gincie could not mistake the fact that the tone had suddenly changed and her grandmother had a specific point in mind.

"We have had pleasant days here," Alex said, "but now I would like you to consider the people you have met. There are men here who were involved with Mr. Fisk and Mr. Gould last year when they attempted to control the gold supply, men who habitually prey on President Grant's lack of good sense regarding business affairs. By the time 'Black Friday' came and the president realized he had to release government gold after all, many people were already ruined, not only speculators, but legitimate businessmen who needed gold to conduct their affairs. The country has not yet seen the end of the trouble they caused." Alex's voice was sharp with the anger she always felt when someone betrayed the virtue of her adopted country.

"There are men here who make fortunes on the bones of others again and again and never consider that their actions might be immoral. There are those who strip others of their humanity by quite direct means, working men, women, and children in their factories and mines every bit as inhumanely as slaves were worked in the fields of the South. There are women here who know what is going on, who yet enjoy the lavish lives provided by these men. There are women here who know that their lovers have wives and children at home, and yet, they will not forsake the favors or the pleasure."

With an inner shiver, Gincie considered what it would be like to be one of those women, richly dressed and pampered but, with few exceptions, desired only as long as they were young enough, beautiful enough, and generous with their sexual favors.

The anger faded from Alex's voice as she continued. "I do not wish you to think that everyone here is corrupt. There are many, many men and women who live lives of good conscience and who deal honestly in their private and their public affairs. You have met a good many of them, too. What I want you to consider is in which group you belong. I want you to ask yourself if you have ever lived a day of your adult life when you did not ask yourself how your actions affected others. I want you to ask yourself if you have ever dealt deliberate hurt to someone else without good reason or simply for your own gain. Rane, Travis, I, and the rest of the family know the answer, but it is far more important that you know it."

Gincie had to swallow hard before she found her voice. "I do know the answer. Logically, I do know it. But I have to learn to live with the knowledge that I executed Mark. There has been part of

me that has wanted Travis or you or Grandfather—*someone*—to make
it all different, to turn time back. That can't be done. And now I can
live with it. Seeing Travis and my children safe at Wild Swan—they
remind me of what I had to lose and that I did not lose them.
Nothing is more important than tat."

Gincie got up to return to her own rooms. She leaned over and
kissed Alex on the cheek. "Thank you, Gran," she said. "Thank
you for giving us shelter at Wild Swan and for taking me in so long
ago. I am not like Mark. But I might have been. If you hadn't
protected me from my mother, I might have been."

Alex watched Gincie depart. She didn't think of Piety, Gincie's
mother; she thought of Nigel, Gincie's father. "She's become a
magnificent woman, Nigel. You would be so proud of her," she
whispered. Her son had been dead for twenty-five years, but she
could see him more clearly at this moment than she had been able to
in the years immediately after his death. Now he was caught forever
in the amber of her mind, never aging.

Nothing he had heard about the Club House since coming to
Saratoga had prepared Travis for the reality. Everything was of the
finest quality, from fine wood paneling to crystal chandeliers and
plush carpeting.

John Morrissey had fashioned the Club House to be run exactly
to his specifications. Mindful of the Puritan reservations that periodically swept the Springs, he allowed no local residents to gamble at
his tables, lest losers promote some town action hostile to his interests, and though women were allowed into an exquisitely furnished
dining salon and offered ices, sweets, and the like, they were barred
from the gaming rooms. The gaming rooms themselves had their
own hierarchy: a large public room on the first floor allowed small-
sum bettors to test their luck at faro and roulette, while the heavier
action took place upstairs in private rooms where the games lasted as
long as the players' money. Cash was the only passport to the Club
House; no credit was given.

Rane had introduced Travis to Mr. Morrissey when they met on
the street, and there Mr. Morrissey had been wearing flamboyant
clothes, complete with beaver hat, cutaway coat, striped trousers,
patent leather boots, white kid gloves, and a small fortune in diamonds, but at night in his club, he wore his uniform—white linen
and black broadcloth and a singular, valuable diamond stud in his
shirt. His wife, Susie, was on hand as well, beautifully gowned, big
black eyes alive with intelligence and with obvious affection for her
husband.

"They have so much," Rane told Travis. "But the one thing

John wants for himself and, more, for his wife is the one thing they can't have—acceptance from the elite of New York society. His connections with gambling and with shady politicians is too well known, and besides, he and his wife are judged as having the wrong sort of background. It's a sad flaw because I think it taints all he has accomplished.

"John is good company and runs honest tables. I wish, for his peace of mind, that he could be satisfied with things as they are."

Travis saw the genuine warmth with which Rane and the Morrisseys greeted each other, and as the evening progressed, his respect for Rane grew as he watched the ease with which the older man moved among both the powerful and the less fortunate, currying favor with none, but treating all with polite interest. And in turn, Rane was deferred to not for Alex's horse business, but in his own right, as a man who knew a vast amount about ships and shipping.

Travis won a few hands at poker and lost a few turns of the roulette wheel, ending up slightly ahead at the end of the evening, but he, like Rane, had no real compulsion for gambling of this sort, appreciating the social opportunities instead.

It was an enjoyable evening, but Travis was relieved when they left before the hour was too late, and Rane echoed his own thoughts when he said, "I discovered long ago that I am not one of those men who finds more pleasure in the company of my fellows than of my wife, and for that, I give Alex full credit."

It occurred to Travis that he was learning lessons this night, and he wasn't sure whether Rane had intended just that or whether they were inevitable. He had met a great many men in the course of the evening, many of whom possessed enormous wealth and were far more settled in their lives than he was at present. And yet, he would not have changed places with any of them because that would mean not having Gincie and the children. When he thought of the Morrisseys, content with each other and prosperous, but still wanting something they would never be able to attain, he thought of his own longing to be living in California again; and he began to face the fact that it might be as impossible and as destructive as the Morrisseys' desires.

Gincie was asleep when he returned to their hotel rooms, but when he drew her into his arms, she murmured his name and burrowed against his warmth without ever waking fully. He took it as a good sign that she did not curl away into herself.

Because the next day was Sunday, there were no races scheduled, a fact that distressed those who would have liked no pause in the excitement. But it suited Travis exactly.

The mercury was in the nineties before the day was too old, but that did not stop several hundred people from wandering up and down Broadway, from the American to the Clarendon Hotel or on the shady walks of Congress Park.

The park was Travis's goal, and Gincie laughed as he hurried her toward it. "If you don't slow down, we will both collapse from this heat," she pointed out. "Is there something there that is going to disappear in the next ten minutes?"

He pulled her to a stop so abruptly, other pedestrians had to veer sharply to avoid bumping into the couple. He ignored the disgruntled passersby. "No, it will not disappear, not in ten minutes, not as long as we live. I want this day with you; I want every day I can have with you for the rest of my life."

Paying no more attention to the people around them than Travis had, Gincie drew his head down and kissed him soundly. "Since that sounds wonderful to me, it seems that we ought to be able to manage it."

In the park, they followed the curving walks past flower beds, fountain, pond, bandstand, and Congress Spring, the most visited spring in the village, which boasted more than a hundred and fifty in and around its environs. The cool shade of the park was welcome, and the air was sweet with fully blossoming summer.

They settled on a bench and watched the other people strolling by. Gincie took off her hat and leaned her head against Travis's shoulder. "I feel more at peace than I have in a long, long time."

"So do I," Travis said, and then after a pause, he added, "Your grandfather is a wise man who gives subtle counsel."

Gincie laughed. "Grandmother is wise too, and not so subtle."

They both caught sight of the elderly couple at the same time. It wasn't that there was any oddity in their age; the Springs, like any spa, attracted many people of advanced age who hoped the mineral-laden water would ease a variety of ills. But this couple, despite their years, moved with sprightly dignity, both smiling and nodding to acquaintances and stopping often, pointing out various sights for one another's interest and enjoyment.

"They're like Alex and Rane," Travis observed, "not in the way they look, but in the way they're sharing the day. They look as if they've done that for decades. I would like us to look just so when we're their age."

"You are special, Travis Culhane. There aren't many men who want to look well-married." There was still laughter in her voice, but Travis could hear the other note as well, the low purr of desire, and he suddenly wished they were back at the hotel.

"So do I," Gincie said, as if he had spoken aloud, and Travis thought that they were doing fairly well at sharing the day, even if they were much younger than the old couple they had been watching.

They stood to walk back to the hotel, and the voices drifted to them, freezing them in place.

". . . Alexandria Carrington Falconer, the Englishwoman, I vow I never thought to see her in person. It's quite thrilling! And that tall husband of hers. My, he's a handsome man, even if he is old. My grandfather used to talk about seeing the Englishwoman at the races, and it used to make my grandmother so angry! How can one compete with a legend?"

"Indeed," the other voice tittered. "And now the granddaughter seems to have become quite legendary in her own right. They say she killed a man in California."

"I know," the first speaker said, "but I heard she was defending her honor. You know how uncivilized it still is out there, for all the pretense to the contrary. And speaking of honor, I wouldn't have any if Travis Culhane looked my way. Have you seen his eyes? What a tragedy that he doesn't seem to use them to see beyond his wife."

Travis was angry, embarrassed, and apprehensive all at once, sure the gossip would ruin Gincie's newly discovered sense of peace and strength.

But Gincie's reaction wasn't at all what he expected. When he would have gone to the two young women they had overheard, she put a restraining hand on his arm. "It isn't necessary. I've dreaded this sort of thing since we arrived here, and now I find it is not so awful after all. In fact, I find that woman's defense of me more generous than not. And she's certainly right about your eyes."

Her mouth widened in a smile as she saw the deeper color stain his tanned cheeks.

She had spoken softly, but when they passed the two women who were sitting on a bench around the curve of the path, Travis tipped his hat and said very clearly, "Good-day, *ladies*."

Gincie didn't know either of the expensively dressed young women, but she doubted she would ever forget the identically stunned expressions they wore, complete from rounded eyes and mouths to fiery blushes. She could hardly contain her mirth, and once Travis was sure this was not delayed hysteria but genuine amusement, he began to chuckle, too.

They were still laughing when they gained the sanctuary of their rooms, but the laughter was quickly transformed into something else when Travis picked Gincie up and spun her around and then let her body slide down his own.

"We are wearing too many clothes," she said, beginning to work at the fastenings of his.

The tiny buttons on her dress took longer, but even that Travis turned into an erotic ritual, brushing the skin he could reach as he undressed her.

Travis's hands. More than his sex, more even than his eyes that still had the power to stun her with the color and life in them, his hands. Long, strong fingers, hard and lean and calloused from competence at many tasks, yet capable of great gentleness. Gincie shivered with the tantalizing pleasure his hands were creating by running over her body with the lightest pressure until it seemed as if every inch of her skin was sensitized to his touch.

He could feel her muscles rippling beneath the surface. "Like a sleek cat, purr and all," he murmured against her throat.

She ran her own hands over him, glorying in the power of his body from his broad shoulders to his taut buttocks and long muscled thighs. The raised scar tissue running down from his hipbone reminded her, as she had been reminded countless times, how very fortunate she was to have him alive and with her when so many women had been widowed, as the bullet scar on her own shoulder reminded her that she had owed him her own life before the war began.

Suddenly she was wild to have him, even though he had not yet physically touched the core of her desire. "Right here, right now!" she gasped, her hands finding his swollen readiness.

He lifted her up, and she wrapped her legs around him as he thrust into her. He held her very still, and she nestled against him, both savoring the fit of their bodies before he gripped her hips more tightly and began to move her in time to his thrusts, her throaty mews of pleasure pleasing him as much as the hot welcome of her flesh.

And then their moods, still in perfect harmony, shifted again, and they crashed on the bed laughing, still joined so that the laughter of one shivered through the other.

"Oh, if the park ladies could see us now," Gincie giggled. "They would envy me more than your eyes." In counterpoint to her mirth, her hands traced delicate patterns down his back and buttocks.

He groaned and resumed the rhythm of loving until both of them were satisfied, drifting toward sleep.

Gincie settled drowsily against Travis's chest, idly stroking the hard planes and the sprinkling of hair.

"I never thanked you," Travis said softly, tightening his arms around her. "My pride got in the way. But I thank you now, Gincie Carrington Culhane, for protectin' me and the children from Mark."

She flinched involuntarily from the mention of her half brother, but then the tension flowed out of her. She had not known until now how much she needed Travis's benediction. She would always have to live with what she had done, but with Travis's support she could live with anything.

She waited until she was sure she could speak without crying. "I know you must go back to California soon. There is so much to be taken care of there, and it's just too much to expect Boston and Rachel to do it all. I won't like being without you, but I can bear it now. You have been so patient, and I love you dearly."

Travis admitted to himself that he would never find it easy to live with a situation where others had made the decisions that determined his course. The war had provided day after agonizing day of that, and he was a man who had known long before the first battle that it was vital to him to have control of his own life. And yet, he also realized that he had shifted the center of his life when he married Gincie, shifted it to include another person and to live with her decisions as well as his own and those they made together. And nothing, not even his dream of life in California, not even the children, was more important to him than Gincie. With that in his mind and his heart, he could live with whatever decisions he had to make about the shards of their life in California.

Chapter 8

At Wild Swan, the Culhane children were happy to have their parents back again, but it was clear that they had not suffered in their absence. All three were golden brown from days in the sun and were full of chatter about adventures they'd had, the greatest of which seemed to be the new litter of kittens in one of the barns.

"They're so little!" Lexy was so enthusiastic, it was as if she had never seen kittens before, and Gincie thought that ability to see everything as new and special over and over again must surely be one of childhood's greatest gifts.

Wild Swan hummed with the rich life of summer, with crops being harvested each in its turn and the schooling of the horses being done in the early morning and in the late afternoon to avoid the hot, humid middle hours of the day.

There would be another meeting at Saratoga in late August and one at Jerome Park in early October, but Alex had no racing planned until the Baltimore schedule. Except for the intensive prerace training, which was suspended in the heat of August, the pause in the racing schedule made little difference to the tasks to be performed at the farm. All of the horses needed continual care; the youngsters needed constant handling to accustom them to willing obedience; and there were saddle horses, jumpers, and road horses to be trained, both Thoroughbred and half-bred. Though racing and horses that did it well would always be most important to Alex, she had long been increasing her business in providing other types of mounts from the same good bloodlines. There were beautiful, willing beasts born every year which were simply not racecourse material, and Alex preferred to train them for other things rather than to sell them off cheaply to doubtful treatment.

Gincie and Travis enjoyed the early morning workouts, each helping where special interest lay. Gincie liked handling the youngsters, teaching them to lead without panicking and to feel and accept weight on their backs though every primitive instinct told the animals that something on their backs could kill them, as a predator leaping upon them could. Travis was more interested in training animals to work smoothly in harness and, most of all, in schooling the horses destined for the hunting field or steeplechases and hurdle races.

His own smooth gait had been forever altered by the saber cut at Gettysburg, and while he did not allow it to interfere with his activities, only in the saddle was he capable of completely unhampered movement. He loved the feeling of following the rhythm of a horse closely enough to be able to soar over a high wall as if he were part of the animal.

Gincie was a fine enough horsewoman to handle jumps competently, too, and she enjoyed it well enough, particularly when she did it astride rather than on the perch of a sidesaddle. Still, she found it difficult to watch Travis risking his neck and had to make an effort not to caution him to greater care. However, when she could put aside her fear, there were few sights she found more stunning than Travis taking the jumps with consummate skill and grace.

Dawn at Wild Swan was golden, the first light illuminating the dust motes as the livestock began to move and the horses were taken out for exercise. The sounds of the domestic fowl and the wild birds and the animals steadily rose from the first faint notes to a full-blown chorus. The cool damp of the night warmed and released a thousand scents. Even the children liked the early hours enough to be up and about, and Travis chose to tell them of his impending trip to California one morning shortly after he and Gincie had returned to Wild Swan from Saratoga.

The children's lives had been severely disrupted by the move from California, but they had adapted well to life at Wild Swan, and Travis did not want to jeopardize that adjustment by disappearing without preparing them for his absence.

He explained it carefully as being a matter of business, and he added, "I'll be back as soon as I can. While I'm gone, I want you to obey your Mama."

The twins looked more confused than distressed, but Lexy clearly saw this as far different from the trip her parents had taken to the races. "Can we all go home to California?" she asked bluntly.

Gincie closed her eyes in a spasm of guilt, but Travis answered calmly. "No, we can't. Home is here now. Maybe someday we'll go back to California, but I don't know when that will be. And if you left Wild Swan, wouldn't you miss Grandma Alex, Grandpa Rane, Della, Padraic, and the others?"

He knew it was emotional blackmail, but he wanted Lexy to remember what she had here, not what she had lost.

She studied her father's face for a long moment before she said, "I guess I don't want to go yet, but I miss Conchee and . . ." her firm little voice listed nearly all the people and animals on the California ranch, leaving no doubt that her memory of the place was acute.

"Lexy, I promise, someday, if you want, you will go back there to visit."

Lexy was satisfied with this because a promise from her father was absolute. But that did not prevent the tears when the day came for him to leave, and when Lexy cried, so did the twins, whether they understood what was going on or not.

Gincie felt like weeping along with them, but she managed to swallow her sobs and offer a fairly convincing smile. "Travel safely and come back to me."

Travis kissed her and held her hard against him for an instant, and then he was gone, heading for Baltimore and the train. Gincie was glad he had wanted to say good-bye to his family at Wild Swan rather than at the rail station; she needed the security of the land around her to watch him out of sight.

She restrained herself until she was alone that night, and then she hugged Travis's pillow, inhaling his scent, and let the tears come.

Alex gave her little time to miss Travis. Gincie found that she was suddenly in charge of all sorts of tasks: overseeing the harvesting and marketing of fruits and vegetables, drying the herbs and brewing the simples with which Alex treated various ailments, and even participating in vital decisions regarding the horses.

The change in her status was acknowledged by the workers at the farm. Old Jed and Mabel Barlow, who had been poor tenant farmers before they had come to Wild Swan nearly fifty years before and whose sons had found a new way of life as jockeys and horse trainers; the Carter sisters, Polly and Cassie, free blacks who had married and raised their children at Wild Swan; all of the old guard was suddenly deferring to Gincie even more than they had when she had lived at Wild Swan before the war.

Gincie doubted that Alex had said anything directly to anyone; the people at the farm were so attuned to each other and most of all to Alex, that even the subtlest changes were noted by all. And Alex was not being subtle in the trust she placed in her granddaughter.

Gincie's activities were not confined to the farm. Having faced the public at Saratoga Springs, she no longer felt the need to hide, and at her grandmother's urging and when she could find the time, she visited Philly and Flora in Baltimore and Larissa in Georgetown, and they in turn spent a fair amount of time at Wild Swan.

She did not see as much of Sam as she would have liked, but she assumed Sam was coming less often to Wild Swan because of her duties at her own farm, Brookhaven. Sam, like Alex, lived a dual life because Morgan was often in Baltimore at the shipyard while the work at Brookhaven was Sam's domain. When Morgan couldn't get away from the city, Sam tried to spend as much time as she could there.

Gincie was more likely to see Sam in the city now than at Wild Swan, though Brookhaven shared a boundary with the farm. Even when Gincie made an effort to ride over to Brookhaven, she felt a strange distance between herself and her aunt. Sam was always polite, but Gincie missed the old warmth and wondered what the trouble was, lacking the courage to ask. Sam could be very self-contained when she wished, and it was then difficult to penetrate her reserve.

No matter how busy Gincie was, Travis was never far from her mind. He wrote to her often, but he was obviously taking care not to mention anything that would upset her. That alone told her that the scandal had not died in California.

It was mid-October before he returned. He was bone weary and his news was not good. He waited until he and Gincie were alone that night, and then he recited the facts as briefly as possible.

"Mark's widow will not leave it alone. I would sympathize if I believed she truly mourned her husband, but I'm sure Boston's assessment is correct—Mrs. Carrington cares far more for Mark dead than she did while he was alive. We've gathered some details of their life together, and by all available accounts, it was not a good marriage. Mark was capable of violence toward more than you; his wife often wore bruises. And now she wants money to make it all worthwhile, money from us."

"Did you speak to her directly?" Gincie asked, appalled by the thought.

Travis shook his head. "I wanted to, but Boston's good sense prevailed. The only contact I had with Mrs. Carrington was through Boston and his lawyer. They continue to deny that you had anything at all to do with Mark's death. We investigated the desk clerk at the hotel too, and for all that he has an unpleasant manner, he seems to be an honest man. He is a witness, Gincie. His description of you is accurate and would surely be refreshed by the sight of you."

Gincie studied his face, trying to match what he was saying with the expression she saw there. He seemed so calm and not in the least bit angry.

He picked up her right hand and touched it to his mouth before cradling it in his own hands, working the fine bones gently. "Darlin', I learned a lot while I was in California. The ranch is still a beautiful place, all golden now until the rains come and turn it green again. But nothing there is as important as you and the children. It just wasn't home anymore. It isn't safe for you in California, and therefore, it isn't safe for me. I found myself lookin' forward to comin' back here to Wild Swan."

He had sold the land on the Oakland waterfront to the railroad. "Boston always said they'd be hungry for it, and they are. In a few years they would probably pay more for it, but as it is, we got a good price. They aim to own all of the shippin' facilities there.

"Land in San Francisco isn't movin' as fast right now, but I sold that commercial property . . ." He went on to tell her in detail what he had kept and what he had sold or had up for sale, from land to some of the mining shares to livestock, but when he came to the ranch in Sonoma, his voice faltered.

"I didn't . . . I couldn't even look for a buyer. I thought of all the work and heart we put into that place and how much Malachi and the others have put into it. It's theirs, too. So I worked out a deal with them for shares of the profit. We'll still own it, but most of whatever they make in profits will be theirs for now. And I promised we would help in the lean years. It is the least I could offer for their continued stewardship of land they will never own."

His voice dropped until it was so low, Gincie could just barely understand. "I could not quite relinquish the ranch. Not for us—I don't think we'll live there again—but I wanted to know that the children could go west someday if they wish and that they would find a beginnin' had been made for them."

Rancho de Salida del Sol. They had named the land for the sunrise because it was golden for much of the year, because it had been a new beginning for them. Suddenly, she was fiercely glad Travis had decided not to sell it, that Mark and what she had done to him had not brought darkness on that brightest part of the dream.

She freed her hand from his so that she could frame his face. "You did exactly the right thing in each case and most of all about the ranch. I would not like to know it was gone from us forever, even if I never see it again."

Time enough to relay all the messages of love and concern from Boston and Rachel, from employees, from friends, from all the people in California who were beginning to accept the fact that Gincie was not coming back. Time enough to decide what he and Gincie would do now. Ironically, his recent dealings in the Far West had left them with enough capital to make a substantial investment in something. But for now, Travis just wanted to savor being with his wife.

The last thing he meant to do was to fall asleep, but Gincie's hands were relentlessly soporific, kneading the tight muscles of his shoulders and back, running down his arms and legs until even his fingers and toes were beyond his power of movement. He started to say something, but a long drawled "darlin' " was as far as he got before he curled on his side and sweet darkness closed over him.

For long moments, Gincie watched him sleep, glad to give him rest, glad to have him home. And then she turned down the lamps, removed her light gown, and settled against him, reveling in the familiar fit of her back against his chest, her bottom against his stomach.

They awakened together just before dawn to touch each other in wordless delight until Travis murmured, "Now I'm truly home," as her body welcomed his.

Even when the many activities of the day had captured them, Travis caught himself several times gazing at his wife like a lovesick youngster, and to his amusement, she was as transparent, a warm blush coloring her cheeks more than once.

But despite their harmony with each other, nothing was really settled in their lives, and Travis had one more journey to make before he felt he could make any decision. This time Gincie went with him.

After the war, Travis had sold Hawthorn to relatives. His home in Virginia meant a great deal to him, but the land, located not far from Fredericksburg, had been raided by both sides and by some who had no allegiance to anyone. For both the Culhanes, Hawthorn, once a haven of fertile, well-tended land and livestock, had come to symbolize all that the war had cost in lives and property. And for Travis, there had been the conviction that, if many Southerners were like his relatives, there was no resolution to build lives different from the ones they had had when slavery had existed. Hawthorn had been sacrificed to a new life in California.

Now that was over, and Gincie couldn't blame him for wanting to see how Hawthorn had fared in his absence, for considering settling there once again. But she knew as soon as they arrived, this was not where she wanted to be.

Travis's cousins had made improvements to the war-ravaged land. However, it was evident they had no real interest in farming, but, rather, in living as country gentlefolk. They could afford it. They had profited during the war by dealing in goods the blockade runners brought in and by avoiding Confederate bonds and currency. Their profits had been in hard money. They had seen some thin days in Richmond, but they had emerged with both their lives and their old way of thinking intact. They had never seen anything morally wrong with slavery, and they saw nothing wrong now in hiring blacks for as little as possible and treating them as if they were invisible. A few hours in Cousin Lucinda's company was enough to make Gincie wish she could apologize to all the servants. She was glad she saw no one who had worked there for Travis's grandmother or for herself and Travis.

A new house had been built, but Gincie could discern some of the old foundation that had not been covered by the new. The original house had been burned while Travis was away with the army and while Gincie and the servants had hidden in the woods and watched, unable to prevent the destruction wrought by looters. Gincie had stubbornly resisted going north to Maryland even after the house had been destroyed. But when Travis had stolen home to visit her and had discovered she was pregnant with her first child, he had sent her to Alex.

Now, being here again and listening to the vapid voices discussing how the South was going to be reborn in all its glory, Gincie had to work hard to repress her panic. There had been slaves in Maryland, too, but Maryland was a border state, as influenced by the North as by the South. She had almost forgotten that Virginia was so Southern.

"The poah deahs, they were surely betta off befoah they were freed. Now they jus' wanda all ovah th' place lookin' foah somebody to take care of 'em."

Gincie dug her fingernails into the palms of her hands to keep from shrieking. It was no use to protest such statements; these people truly believed this way, and nothing was going to change their minds. She risked a glance at Travis and was gratified to see that his expression was one of barely controlled disgust.

It was he who made the decision. Without guilt for the lie, he told his relatives that he, Gincie, and the children had done very well in California but had returned east due to the advancing age of Gincie's grandparents. He did not ask if his relatives would sell Hawthorn back to him. He said only that he and Gincie had wanted to see the place once more, since this was where he had brought her as a bride. He was as relieved to leave as Gincie was.

"Would you really have moved back to Hawthorn?" he asked.

"Yes," she answered. "If that had been what you wished. I kept reminding myself that the relatives would not be there."

"No, they would not, but the memories and too many ghosts would be there." Travis's voice was low and sad. "It doesn't feel like my home anymore. I guess it hasn't since the day I sold it, or maybe even a long time before that, maybe since the day Virginia seceded from the Union and I went with her. I know there are many, many humane people in Virginia and the rest of the South, but I fear theirs will not be the voices heard for years to come."

He did not have to explain to Gincie; since coming east again, they had grown increasingly aware of the efforts the southern states were making to dismantle the federal restrictions placed on them and the programs designed to make life better for the freed slaves.

Gincie and Travis were no closer to knowing what they would do next, but for both of them, there was a certain peace in knowing that Hawthorn was no longer part of their considerations.

With the Falconers, they attended the inaugural meeting of the Maryland Jockey Club at Pimlico Park, four days of racing with four races each day, including both dashes and old-style heat races, which were so well attended it seemed a clear indication that the more northerly tracks were making a mistake by not including the contests of endurance in their programs. The Dinner Party Stakes was won by Mr. Sanford's Preakness; Mr. Belmont's Glenelg captured two races, and Kingfisher, now under the Belmont colors, took another; Wild Swan's horses won one of the hurdle races and the Monumental City Handicap; but no winner was cheered more loudly than Governor Bowie's chestnut filly, My Maryland, when she was victorious in a handicap race for three-year-olds that had already run in the meeting. There were more than a few people who did not consider it proper for the governor of the state to lend his name as president of a jockey club, and the thunderous cheering was intended to put such people in their place as much as to celebrate the victory of a native son.

Though the meeting was at the end of October, the weather was fine for each of the four days. Turfmen from all over the country came to celebrate the dawn of a new era of racing in Maryland, the crowds at the track were immense, and hotels such as Barnum's hosted celebrations that lasted far into the night.

Gincie and Travis were greeted warmly by the people they had met at the Saratoga races, and the apprehension they had felt when they had gone north was completely absent now. They enjoyed the festivities start to finish, particularly because Flora, Philly and Blaine, Larissa and Reid, Morgan and Sam, and even Adam, who had little interest in horses, attended the races in order to see Wild Swan's entries run.

Alex observed Gincie and Travis carefully during the course of the Baltimore meeting, but she waited until they had returned to Wild Swan before she broached her plan to them.

There could be no mistake that this was not to be a casual conversation. Alex held her meeting in the library, and the account books of the farm were carefully stacked on the desk.

"I ask that you hear me out, and then I will answer any questions or listen to anything you have to say," she began. "I have a business proposition for you, and I want you to understand that I have considered this carefully and offer it to all our benefit, not for charity's sake.

"This farm and the horses mean a great deal to me. I have spent the greater part of my life here." Her face softened as the memories flowed through her mind. "Sinje, Seth, and good friends are buried in this earth, as are the equine champions we have raised here. But I have long accepted that this is my dream and that it loses nothing if it ends with me. The rest of the family, well, they like horses well enough, but they have no passion for them; they are not caught in the magic of dreaming that an awkward, long-legged foal will become a beast fit to race the wind. Sam comes closest to sharing that passion, but even for her, the emphasis is different. She is more interested in increasing the crops the land yields than in breeding horses. And she has the responsibilities of Brookhaven, and more, of a husband who is, like Rane, tied to ships and the sea.

"Rane and I are growing old," she said it without regret. "Before too long, it will become more difficult for us to summon the energy it requires to attend race meetings throughout the season. And for all his blessed graciousness in doing it, Rane has never truly wanted to be a turfman. You know as well as I that his memberships in the jockey clubs, his faithful attendance at the races, are all for me."

She studied the two faces before her. "Your situation is quite, quite different. You share the bond; you are both part of the magic. I propose that I gradually turn over the reins of Wild Swan to you. It would not be easy. I will not pretend that I would relinquish all interest and control; it would be foolish to try. And I am not the only one involved. As it is, what I have will be left to my children, to Flora, Blaine, and Morgan, and to you, Gincie, because your father is gone. Gweneth will receive a gift of money because she is too far away in England to be connected directly with Wild Swan anymore. She knows of my plan and agrees with it; her responsibilities in England are burden enough.

"The change I would make would be to carve an additional share from the whole to give to you, Travis, so that at my death, you and Gincie would own two-fifths of Wild Swan. I would further propose to the others that if they had no interest in their shares, you would have the first opportunity to purchase them at fair value. The financial affairs of this family are complex, with diverse businesses independent of each other but also interwoven in inheritance. The only way for such a system to function well is for everyone to be reasonable, but there is no guarantee that that will be true generation to generation, though I certainly pray it will be.

"While I live, you would share in the profits of Wild Swan, but I would not expect you to cover the losses from your own funds should some disaster overtake us. It is your time and skill I want, not your money. Nor would I expect you to confine your financial interests to this partnership. I am sure there are various enterprises which will continue to engage you as they did in California. Those would remain separate. What you chose to do after I am gone would be your business."

Her hands touched the ledgers. "If you consider this idea at all, I expect you to explore the accounts thoroughly. You would be fools if you did not. And it is most important that you believe nothing need change if you are not interested in my proposal. You and the children are welcome to remain here for as long as you wish, whether or not you are a legal part of the business of Wild Swan.

"Travis, it particularly matters to me that you believe this. This is Gincie's home, and while I would hope you regard it in the same light, I know that it may never mean as much to you as Hawthorn did."

She had not asked about their visit to Hawthorn, and they had told her little, but she was quite sure Travis had found welcome from neither the land nor the people there.

"And it may never mean as much to you as your land in California either," Alex continued. "To build on someone else's dream is not the same as beginning your own. Only you can judge whether resentment would eventually overwhelm whatever feeling of achievement you might gain here."

She smiled tenderly at their stunned expressions. "It is certainly clear that neither of you anticipated this. And it is not a decision you must make immediately."

Travis found his voice first, though it was not quite steady. "Whatever we decide, we won't forget the trust you offered us."

Alex left them there, and for a long time they sat in silence, hearing Alex's offer as if the words were suspended in the air.

Gincie was afraid to say anything. Her grandmother's offer appeared to be the answer to everything, putting within reach a varied, secure life in a place she loved. But if accepting the offer were to kill Travis's spirit and his pride in himself, it would be better if they had never returned here. She did not want to consider at all that Alex had also been speaking of a time when she and Rane would no longer be here.

Finally Travis murmured, "I don't know, I just don't know." And then he asked, "Would you ever forgive me if I declined Alex's offer?"

Gincie answered without hesitation, glad to have it out in the open, "There would be nothing to forgive! Oh, Travis, I will stay here or go anywhere you wish to go. The choice must be yours. I did not mean to make the choice for us to leave California, but I did. What we do next must be your choice; it is only just."

Travis understood how much she meant what she said, knew she would abide by his answer for all the days of her life. It did not make his decision any easier.

In the next days, Travis tried to contemplate every side of the offer as he would any business proposition, but he could never lose sight of the fact that because Gincie had been raised here, it was something much greater than that.

He inspected the ledgers and found exactly what he expected, meticulous figures reflecting a well-run, profitable enterprise. He spent long hours exploring Wild Swan, covering ground already familiar, but seeing it with new eyes as he contemplated being its steward and part owner for the rest of his life. Unlike too much land in Maryland and in the states further south where tobacco had exhausted the soil, the acres here had been nurtured with crop rotation and fertilizers so that they yielded rich harvests of grain, hay, and vegetables. And nowhere, not even at Hawthorn when he had run it or on the ranch in California, had Travis seen healthier livestock or more contented workers.

But Wild Swan was far more than the sum of these assets. It was the risks Alex and St. John had taken in the beginning, and Alex had continued to take after St. John died. It was the orchard called "Grandmother's Gift" in tribute to Alex's grandmother, Virginia Thaine, who had sold a precious oak wood in England so that Alex and St. John could emigrate to America. It was generations of Carringtons and Falconers. It was the graves of family, friends, and workers buried here. It was even the small stone markers bearing the names of the horses that had been raised and had died at Wild Swan. It was truth and legend; it was decades of love and effort and courage; it was decades of other people's dreams.

If he accepted Alex's offer, people would say and would be justified in saying that no matter what his own talents and efforts, he had achieved his position by marriage to Gincie Carrington. He would certainly not be the first or the last man to prosper by his marriage, but his pride flinched at the image. And then he reminded himself that when he had taken over Hawthorn, he had been assuming his grandparents' dreams. Had the war not come, he, Gincie, and the children would surely have stayed in Virginia.

He thought of his grandmother Abigail, of her strength and serenity. She had been a devout member of the Society of Friends, a Quaker, but she had never demanded or expected that others believe as she did, not even her husband. She had asked only that people treat each other decently. Travis knew how fortunate he had been to have been raised by his grandparents after his parents had been killed in a steamboat accident. And he had been only thirteen when his grandfather had died and his grandmother had had sole charge of him. Abigail and Alexandria were so different in many ways, so alike in the essentials.

Abigail was gone, and Alex would be too, someday. She had spoken quite openly about it, but it was something Travis, no more than Gincie, wanted to think about. He was shaken when he realized the depth of love he felt for Alex and Rane. He had loved few people so deeply in his life—his grandparents, Gincie, the children, and Alex and Rane.

He began to see that taking the position at Wild Swan would be an act of love, not only for Gincie, not only so that Alex would know her dream would not die with her, but also for himself and for the land. In the end, it did not matter who had begun the work here. The Indians were right in their belief that land could not truly be owned, but only held and cherished in trust for generations to come and for the spirit of the land itself.

Travis's grandparents had seen to it that he was well educated and well traveled, too, so that he would not suffer from the insular view that had crippled thinking in too much of the old South, but he recognized that his essential talent lay in being a good steward to the land. And this land, this way of life, were worth preserving.

He felt more peaceful and more purposeful than he had since their life in California had changed so drastically.

Gincie searched his face anxiously when he told her his decision. "You're sure you're not doing this just for me?"

"I'm doing it for you, for the children, for Alex, but most of all for myself and for this land." His eyes were blazing turquoise blue, clear of the shadows and regret she had grown accustomed to seeing.

Though they sought out Alex to tell her formally, she did not need the words; the shared joy and contentment in their faces were eloquent acceptance of her offer.

Chapter 9

Christmas and New Year's Eve had always been special at Wild Swan, and this year the celebration promised to be extraordinary because nearly the whole family would be together for the first time in years. Only Gweneth and Christopher, with their many obligations in England, would be unable to attend the reunion.

Though Rane had known from the beginning about Alex's offer to the Culhanes, Alex decided to tell the rest of the family when they were gathered for the holiday.

Gincie approved the plan; she approved everything lately, drifting in a haze of happiness she had not thought to know again. Her one reservation was about Sam, and she was not even sure there was a problem. But it bothered her enough so that she told her grandmother.

"It isn't anything she's said or done; it's more what she hasn't done. She's hardly ever here anymore. Oh, Gran, I just don't know. But I have a feeling Sam is sad about us being here."

Gincie thought of all the kindness her Aunt Sam had shown to her and Travis in the past, even to keeping watch at Travis's bedside after Gettysburg though her son Seth had been mortally wounded by Confederates in the same battle. Sam had also nursed Confederate prisoners of war as well as Union wounded. She was one of the most generous, nurturing people Gincie knew, and she hated the idea that Sam was sorry the Culhanes had returned. She hoped her grandmother would quickly dismiss the notion, but instead, after considering the idea, Alex looked as stricken as Gincie felt.

"My God, what unforgivable blindness!" Alex exclaimed, and then seeing Gincie's expression, she added, "No, my dear, not your blindness, mine. And the truth is that the person who is really responsible for Sam's vulnerability is her father, for all that he's been dead for five years."

Alex rubbed her forehead wearily. "What awful damage a bad parent can do! I longed for my mother's approval and love for years after she died; you fear the blood of yours as if it were a plague; and Sam will forever be offering proof of her usefulness that her father might love her."

Gincie knew Sam's story, but not until this moment had she considered that it had no end. Sam's father had been addicted to marriage, and after Sam's mother died, he had chosen two additional wives, one after the other, without regard to how they would treat the child of his first marriage. Mr. Sheldon-Burke had not been overtly cruel when Sam was young; he had simply ignored her most of the time.

It was that neglect which had allowed Sam to wander the countryside with little restriction, and thus, she had met the children at Wild Swan. She had been eight years old, and Morgan had been her champion from the beginning. When Alex and St. John had discovered her existence, they had welcomed her as if she were another of their children. Sam had received her early schooling at Wild Swan, and from Alex she had learned how to care for the land. She had taken those skills back to Brookhaven to make her father's acres produce as they never had under his lazy care. But in the end, even that usefulness had failed to impress him. During the war he had indulged his Southern sympathies by spying for the Confederacy, and only Sam's threat to expose him had gained his help in getting Morgan released from Andersonville prison. When Mr. Sheldon-Burke died right after the war, he left the land Sam had cared for so well to her half brother, who hadn't left the South in years.

Brookhaven belonged to Sam only because Morgan had purchased it for her from her half brother. For all her years of work and devotion, the only legacy Sam had received from her father was the hatred he had carried to the grave because she had forced him to help Morgan.

"Sam must feel as if I have taken her place here," Gincie said.

"You did not take it; I gave it to you," Alex corrected her. "And for what seemed a thousand good reasons both for you and for her."

"I can't bear to have her feel this way. Do you think it would help if I spoke to her?" Gincie asked.

"I appreciate your willingness to go to her, but this is between me and Sam," Alex answered. "Though it might not seem so, you have little to do with this. It is how I have treated Sam lately that has caused the problem."

Gincie prayed her grandmother was right. She could not bear the idea of having to tell Travis they could not remain at Wild Swan after all, particularly when she thought of the long hours he had spent coming to terms with this new plan for their lives. And yet, she could not imagine taking the position Alex offered if Sam were estranged because of it. There could be no worse beginning.

Alex rode over to Brookhaven immediately.

Sam's face lighted with pleasure when she recognized Alex, but her delight was swiftly followed by alarm. "Is something wrong? Has something happened at Wild Swan?"

"Indeed something is wrong, but not the sort of thing you imagine." Alex turned her mount over to a stableboy and gestured toward the house. "I would be grateful for a cup of tea and some privacy."

Sam eyed her nervously, but it did not occur to her to refuse her mother-in-law's demands.

When they were settled inside, Alex came right to the point. "I have been so preoccupied with Gincie and Travis, I have failed to note how seldom you have been at Wild Swan of late. Or if I did consider it, I assumed you were simply too busy with all the work that requires your attention here. But that is not it at all, is it? Gincie fears it is her presence that has driven you away. Yet it isn't quite that simple. I think it has more to do with you and me and with your place at Wild Swan."

Sam had no defense against Alex's directness. She wanted desperately to deny the truth, but instead, the tears came. "I'm so . . . so ashamed! I've been be . . . behaving like a child who has had a toy taken away. In fact, I ought to be thankful that Gincie is ba . . . back." She drew a deep breath and steadied her voice. "I have enough to do here, and every year I want more time with Morgan, not less. But . . ."

"But deep inside you still believe love is conditional for you. You love others without limit, but for you, love must be earned. If you do this job well or that job or the other, you deserve to be loved."

Alex reached out and captured one of Sam's hands in hers. "Dearest Sam, you are the beloved wife of my son Morgan; you are the mother of my grandsons; but beyond that and before those things, you are Sam, just yourself, and that is enough. It has been enough since you came to us when you were eight years old. We loved you then; we love you now; we will love you always. For every gift we have given you, you have given endlessly in return by simply being the woman you are. No one, not Gincie or anyone else, could ever take your place. I want Gincie and Travis gradually to assume the responsibility for Wild Swan, and they have agreed. I planned to tell everyone at Christmas; only Rane, Gincie, and Travis know now. The decision is not graven in stone. If you cannot bear it, then neither can I.

"I used to think that the most despicable thing your father ever did was to allow my son to rot in that prison until you forced his hand. But making you beg for love and never giving it to you was far, far worse."

The quiet, even tone of Alex's voice emphasized her savage indictment of Sam's father, and no denial rose in Sam's mind to refute it. Instead, she saw the seemingly endless images from the time she was small until she was grown, and in none of them did her father offer anything beyond the briefest, most impersonal kind of attention, designed to make sure she was causing no upset, particularly to first one stepmother and then the next. Even the comfort she and her half brother and half sister might have found amongst themselves had been denied by distance when the younger children were sent away to school in Virginia.

Sam knew about loving children, knew about loving them so that one's own heart broke when they were sad, knew that losing a child changed the world forever. She did not know how one could have a child and not love him or her, not unless there was something terribly, unimaginably wrong with the child. "Was I such a difficult child to love?"

Alex put her arms around Sam and cradled her head against her shoulder as if Sam were a small child again. "My dear, you were enchanting! Sinje and I wanted you for our own daughter from the first moment we saw you."

With startling clarity, Alex saw Sam as she had been all those years ago, a very grubby little girl with her hair in two straggling braids, a smear of dirt across her nose and one cheek, and her eyes, a luminous combination of green, brown, and gold, so big and wary. She could hear her voice saying, "My name is Samantha Elisa Sheldon-Burke, but I like just plain Sam better." And when she had been asked if her parents knew where she was, she had answered, "They don't care as long as I don't get into trouble. And I am not supposed to bother the neighbors." She had been honest and matter-of-fact; even then, neglect was an accepted part of Sam's life.

"Oh, Sam, the saddest circumstance is that some things can never be made right. Your father was not fit to be a parent, and when he remarried, he chose women who were as lacking as he. He's gone, and he won't ever be back to make things right between you." Privately she thought that if Mr. Sheldon-Burke were present, she would gladly strangle him with her own hands. "But you have the victory, if you would just recognize it. No one could be a more loving parent than you are, and where your father neglected the land, you have made it bloom."

She stroked Sam's head gently. "Don't allow your father to diminish you; he was never worth it."

Finally Sam pulled away, wiping at her eyes. "I have several fences to mend. Poor Morgan, he's been so patient with my moods lately without knowing why I have been so disagreeable. And I've failed Gincie when she most needed my support. It is the perfect solution to have Gincie and Travis at Wild Swan. There is no one else of my generation or theirs who can fit into the life of the farm so well."

Alex understood the shadow of sadness in Sam's eyes, and she voiced the thought aloud. "It would be different if Seth had survived the war. He loved Wild Swan, and I believe he could have had a good life there."

"For the short time he had, he did have a good life there," Sam said, and though Seth's grave at Wild Swan was a constant reminder that he had perished at Gettysburg, both women were seeing him as he had been before the war—a handsome young man working and playing at the farm he had loved.

Sam was as relieved as Gincie to straighten things out between them, and Gincie was being honest rather than flattering when she warned her aunt that she would undoubtedly seek her advice frequently. It was soon proved true as both Wild Swan and Brookhaven were swept by preparations for the holidays, which necessitated a flurry of cooking and planning at both farms, the whole coordinated by Sam and Gincie.

Dr. Nigel Falconer, Sam and Morgan's youngest son, and Anthea, Philly and Blaine's youngest daughter, and her husband, Dr. Maxwell Kingston, arrived together a few days before Christmas. They had held their own reunion in Baltimore the night before and were cheerfully the worse for wear. Nigel had traveled south from Philadelphia in time to meet the steamer that had brought Anthea and Max home from Europe, and the three of them, abetted by those other family members who were in Baltimore, had found that nothing less than champagne would do to toast the achievement of their goals.

Nigel and Anthea had a bond beyond being cousins because even when they had been very young, they had been determined to become doctors, but no childhood dream could compare with the knowledge that they were qualified physicians now. They also shared the experience of having served as volunteers at field hospitals during the war. That bloody baptism had given both of them strength and experience beyond almost all of the other medical students. In Anthea's case, the nightmare of the war had, ironically, provided her not only with the determination, but also with the authority, to pursue a medical career despite all the opposition to women in the field.

At twenty-five, Nigel was still slightly built, but with wiry strength. He had golden brown hair, strong, clean features, and alert green eyes that were very like his brother Adam's.

Anthea, three years older than Nigel, had her mother's bright blue eyes set in a heart-shaped face framed by dark hair. Of medium height, Anthea had a nicely rounded figure that was apt to make unwise men judge her to be decorative rather than useful.

Max Kingston had never made that mistake. He had met Anthea while they were both caring for the war wounded, and the sharp intelligence in her eyes had appealed to him every bit as much as the lovely color of them.

Nor had Anthea been superficial in her judgment of Max, for at first sight he looked more than a little like a frog. In his midthirties when Anthea met him, even then he had had no more than a thinning brown fringe around his bald pate, and now his hair was further reduced, and what there was was gray. His brow was high and round over protruding blue eyes; his nose looked as if it had been designed for someone larger; his mouth was too wide; and he was a beautiful man. His warmth was tangible, his sense of humor unfailing, and his erudition rare and wide-ranging. Max was interested in everyone and everything.

He had been born in Pennsylvania, but had taken his medical training in Edinburgh. After the war, he and Anthea had gone to Switzerland, and while Max had found much to study there, the principal reason for the years away had been to allow Anthea to take her medical training in a place that was more tolerant of women in medicine than was the United States, allowing women equal education and clinical experience rather than the limited access and questionable quality of the education available in the States.

Anthea and Max had been away for five years, and the reunion between Anthea and her sister Larissa was particularly exuberant, with the two of them speaking so quickly that sentences were seldom finished, yet neither suffered any confusion.

Anthea was thrilled with the role of aunt to Larissa and Reid's children and forthright with her sister about her own childlessness. "If Max and I are lucky enough to conceive, we'll both be glad of it. But having no children does not spoil our days . . . or our nights," she added with a laugh. She eyed Larissa speculatively, "And you needn't feel reluctant about making your announcement—that is, if you are pregnant."

Larissa smiled in rueful surrender. "It's bad enough to have a sharp-eyed sister like you, let alone one who has had medical training."

"It's more the sister than the doctor who noticed," Anthea confessed. "You're just slightly round at the edges, and you're glowing—not very scientific terms. When is the baby due?"

"May, a lovely month," Larissa said, and she looked so contented, Anthea laughed aloud.

But neither of them was as sanguine when they discussed their sister Phoebe, due to arrive with her husband and child the day before Christmas Eve.

"It's been difficult to make a fair judgment while I've been so far away and the only contact I've had with her has been letters," Anthea said. "But still, I have wondered. In the past couple of years, she's sounded so . . . so . . . ."

"Humorless?" Larissa offered, and Anthea nodded.

"Unfortunately, I fear it's true," Larissa said. "She and Aubrey didn't come for Christmas last year; they didn't come north at all. But even the year before, I noticed the change. It's not just being serious; Phoebe was always that. And God knows, what they do is serious indeed. But being humorless in this family is as serious as being a horse thief in others, and nothing is more uncomfortable than commitment turned to fanaticism."

Phoebe had started to teach at Flora and Philly's school when she was only seventeen, but in 1863, when she was twenty-four, she had found what for her was the perfect teaching position. She had gone south to Port Royal in the Sea Islands off the coast of South Carolina to educate the freed slaves who were there under the protection of Union forces. The teachers were called "Gideonites" or "Gideon's Band" by their detractors because many of them were fanatical abolitionists and evangelists, and Phoebe's moderate beliefs at the time had seemed in sharp contrast to that. But while she had agreed that many of her fellow teachers, mostly New Englanders, were dour, overly pious, and quite naive in their perceptions of the true condition of blacks in the South, she had found the work with the former slaves infinitely rewarding. Among them she had found people who agreed with her that the most powerful combination on earth was the written word and the knowledge to read and write it.

She had met Aubrey there, and in the years since the war, they had taught in various places in the South, now in Georgia, and always with the same intention, that former slaves be taught to read and write, and thus be armed with the only weapons that could make an enduring difference in their lives as free men and women. And every year, the teaching grew more dangerous as white resistance to the education of blacks grew stronger.

"Perhaps it is Aubrey even more than their teaching," Anthea suggested. The family had welcomed Aubrey Edwards because Phoebe loved him, but no one really liked him. He was good at thinking in terms of broad causes, but the little details of daily life escaped him, leaving Phoebe to tend to them and to him as if he were more child than husband.

"You and I are very, very lucky in our husbands," Larissa said, and unconsciously she shielded her belly for an instant with her hand, an ancient gesture of protection for the child within.

"Are you going to tell everyone about the baby soon?" Anthea asked, and Larissa nodded. "I thought it might be a nice Christmas surprise, but I think Gran knows already. She's as hard to fool as you are. And there are Nigel and Max, not to mention Dr. Cameron."

"And not to mention Reid," Anthea said, suddenly aware that her brother-in-law had been hovering more than usual.

Larissa did manage to save her announcement until Phoebe and Aubrey had arrived because she wanted her sister to share in the joy of it. But though Phoebe said all the right things, her sisters saw their worst fears confirmed.

Short, slight, with gilded brown hair, an uptilted nose, dark blue eyes, and a determined chin, Phoebe had always possessed a liveliness and tart humor that had balanced her stubbornness, but now it was as though the light had left her eyes.

"It's worse than we thought," Anthea said to Larissa when they stole a few minutes alone. "She's not even a happy fanatic. She's thirty-one, and she acts as if she's nearer fifty."

Larissa nodded in agreement. "I thought I'd be angry with her, but instead, I feel so sorry for her! She seems so sad, and Aubrey seems more unfocused than ever. It probably doesn't even occur to him that his wife has changed. But whatever their problems, the worst of it is that it clearly affects little Joseph. I've never seen a more solemn child."

Anthea could not blame Larissa's judgment on her heightened maternal state, because she felt the same about Joseph Edwards. He was appealing, with the dark hair and eyes of his father and his mother's nose. And he was clearly physically well treated, sturdily built and rosy-cheeked. But he was far too restrained. He said little, and when he did speak, he was so painfully polite and so obviously anxious about doing the right thing that he seemed older than three. His parents called him "Joseph," as if a nickname would be some breach of behavior.

"Lexy is already calling him Jo-Jo," Anthea said. "And I overheard her asking him why he didn't know how to play and if he'd like to learn."

"Lexy's a love. Maybe she and the rest of the children will be able to teach Joseph a thing or two about being young," Larissa suggested. "The one thing I am sure of is that neither one of us had better say anything. There are some things sisters can't tell each other, and one of those is how to raise one's children."

The rest of the family were no less observant than Anthea and Larissa, and they, too, restrained themselves from intervening. But it was hardest on Philly. She was so happy to have all three of her daughters and the grandchildren together, that she wanted nothing to spoil their reunion. So she spent as much time as she could with little Joseph, and she watched her daughter with worried eyes.

Philly was reluctant to discuss the situation with Blaine because she did not want him to feel obliged to take action, but she doubted he was oblivious; he was also paying an inordinate amount of attention to his grandson, and he was scrupulously polite and not the least bit warm in his attitude toward his son-in-law Aubrey.

Gincie was aware of all the undercurrents, but at first, she was less critical. Phoebe was not her sister, albeit all the cousins had spent much time at Wild Swan when they were growing up and she was fond of them. And though she knew it wasn't true, Gincie felt as if she and Travis were on trial, not only because this was the first time most of the family had been together since her killing of Mark, but also because Alex was going to tell the family of her plan. It was a great relief to find that her cousins treated her no differently from before; and yet quietly, without making a point of it, they let her know that they did not condemn what had happened in California.

As for Alex's plan, rather than causing doubt and resentment, it was greeted with wholehearted approval by both the second and third generations.

Nigel seemed to speak for everyone when he said, "We are all going in so many directions, and none of them lead directly here. I confess, I've had selfish thoughts. I've wanted to know that Wild Swan will always be here, and yet, I've known my work is in medicine. Now I'll feel as if the farm is safe with you helping Gran to run it." He could not bring himself to mention a time when Alex would not be there, but the thought was in his eyes when he kissed his grandmother on the cheek and said, "As usual, you've made a wise decision."

Gincie glanced instinctively at Sam and was very glad to see that she looked as pleased as everyone else, underscoring the fact that she was truly reconciled to the Culhanes' role at Wild Swan.

Travis's fingers curled around her hand, strong and reassuring.

"Your grandmother is a bold player," he said, too low for anyone else to hear. "She risked the peace of Christmas Eve, and she counted on it, too. It would have taken someone a lot stronger than she to protest her plan, and I doubt that person exists on earth. But I honestly don't think there is any rancor, and for that I am very grateful."

The rest of the evening was given to the children, who were, with the exception of Joseph, quite hysterical with the excitement of being allowed not only to have supper with the adults, but also to open presents after the meal.

The house smelled of evergreen and spices, and there was a big fir tree laden with ornaments, most of them made by the children or baked in the kitchen, and candles. The candles were lighted only briefly because of the fire hazard, but it was enough to draw gasps of wonder from adults and children alike.

Even Lexy, usually so responsible, was giddy with joy and whirled around in her red velvet Christmas dress as if she would never run out of energy, and the twins clapped in glee and tried to dance like their sister, ending up in a tangle of chubby legs, still laughing. And for once, Joseph joined in, giggling with his cousins.

"My heavens! They are noisy, aren't they!"

The desperation in Phoebe's voice kept Gincie's temper in check, but her reply was still pointed. "They usually are, when they are healthy and happy and it is a special time like this. Please don't stop Joseph from enjoying it." She was instantly sorry and said so. "I have no right to interfere with how you raise your son and would heartily resent any interference with my children. It's just that . . . well, Joseph is so . . . so . . . ."

"Restrained? Solemn? Sad?" Phoebe's voice was angry, but the anger was self-directed. "I had forgotten how normal children behave. God help me, I had forgotten! Our lives down south . . . our lives are so different from yours here. We have to be so careful about how we behave! So many people, so many white people, hate what we are doing. It's worse than being Caesar's wife; we must all be above suspicion, even Joseph: he must be the perfect child for the perfect family."

Her voice dropped lower, and that made the words even more shocking. "I am married to a fool. Aubrey can never see the reality; he always dreams of what should be according to his imaginary world. Oh, some of that is necessary for the work to go on at all, but

Aubrey will not see that there are creatures loose in the South now who are human only in form; in every other way, they are poisonous slime spreading everywhere. Aubrey thinks they can be reached by reason; reason will never be part of their lives. They roam the night wearing bedsheets or God knows what and calling themselves the knights of this or that or the Ku Klux Klan. At first they said they just wanted to scare the 'nigras' a little, just to show them that white is still the only color worth being, but they grow ever more vicious. And all this talk of laws against them will come to nothing."

Gincie wished Travis were beside her now, listening to the relentless darkness conjured by Phoebe's words, but he was across the room, showing the twins what they could build with a new set of wooden blocks.

Gincie knew about the Klan; nearly everyone knew about them now. Started in Pulaski, Tennessee, in 1866 by ex-Confederate soldiers who chose the name of their secret society to sound like a fraternity, they had started out being fairly satisfied with childish antics in their costumed rides. But the anonymity soon began to cloak more and more members dedicated to restoring the old order of the South, the dominance of whites over blacks. A grand meeting had been held in Nashville, Tennessee, in 1867, with officers fancifully named from the "grand wizard" down to lower ranks. But there was nothing fanciful about their actions. Mischief had turned to malevolence, to burnings, whippings, mutilation, and lynchings, to such extremes that its own officers had disbanded the group. But it was too late. The Klan and other such organizations had caused enough terror in several states, including Georgia, that blacks were losing their access to the political rights so recently granted to them.

Federal regulations did not seem likely to change the course as the whole focus now was on withdrawing federal troops from Southern states as soon as possible, and the new law against the Klan lacked teeth.

"Sometimes the irony is more than I can bear," Phoebe said. "All this fear of Negroes running the states when, in fact, they tend to want to give their support to the same people who ruled them before, to the landowners, the former slave owners. It is a ruling class the freed slaves understand. And it is the poor whites who are their enemies, the whites who have never had much. But they understood the old order and could claim kinship. You know how it is in the South, cousins of every degree are counted kin, and nearly every poor white had a cousin who was in much better circumstances. The new order is unacceptable to them; they will not share anything with a black man, not the government, not the land, not jobs, or anything else. Oh, there are thousands upon thousands of those who would make the best of what has come, but they will not stand against night raiders who think nothing of torturing or murdering those, black or white, who do not do their bidding."

"Mama cross at me?" Joseph was suddenly standing at his mother's knee, peering at her worriedly.

"No, no, sweetheart, I'm not cross at you." Phoebe drew her son into her arms and held him so tightly that he squirmed. She buried her face against his soft little neck, and Gincie saw the glint of tears when she raised her head again. "Have you shown your papa your new ball?" Phoebe asked, controlling the quaver in her voice.

Joseph studied her gravely, considering her idea, and then smiling timidly, he went off with the bright red ball to show his father. Aubrey clearly felt awkward and out of place at the gathering, and he greeted his son with unusual warmth, glad of a familiar diversion.

"Poor foolish Aubrey." Phoebe's voice held wry tenderness now. "He can't help being what he is, and my being impatient with him doesn't solve anything. And poor Joseph; he deserves better parents. We do love him, I swear we do! But . . . we're just not very good parents. The care he should have goes into our teaching. We don't mean to have so little left for him." She wiped quickly at her eyes as the tears threatened to overflow.

Gincie was paralyzed. She wanted to comfort Phoebe, but she didn't know how, the pain was so deep. She felt as if the two of them were under a glass dome, separated from all the others in the room. She wanted to shatter the glass and escape into the merriment swirling around them. But she also wanted to be with Phoebe.

"The time will come when it won't be safe to keep Joseph with us," Phoebe said. "Do you think it will be all right to send him to Anthea or Larissa?"

Gincie finally found her voice. "I think if it is too dangerous for Joseph, it is too dangerous for you."

"That isn't a choice," Phoebe said flatly, suddenly in control again. "There are so few of us to teach so many, and education is the only chance the freed slaves have, the only one."

This was the Phoebe Gincie had known since childhood, unshakably stubborn and committed once she had set her course. And though Gincie could not imagine anything more important than one's own child, she could not dispute the importance of the teaching Phoebe was doing. "I'm sure either of your sisters would be honored to care for Joseph, and so would I. Don't wait too long. If you believe it is too dangerous for him, send him to one of us."

"Thank you," Phoebe said. "I don't want to explain this to my sisters until I must." She paused, staring off into some distance Gincie could not see. "Perhaps you will understand better than anyone. I know you well enough to understand how hard it must be for you to live with the killing of your half brother, even though you had to do it. Maybe you can understand what is hardest, most dangerous for me. It isn't fear of what the night riders might do to me; it is fear of what I would like to do to them. Their violence has become my own. I never knew my heart could hate so thoroughly. I would like to see them all lined up and shot."

The children were playing with their new toys, but tiredly now, ready to go to bed without a fight. The adults were talking to each other and making halfhearted attempts to tidy the room. Travis was talking to Rane, and Rane's right hand rested on Alex's shoulder, stroking gently as he listened. Sam, Morgan, and Adam were laughing at some story Nigel was telling them. Flora was with Blaine and his family. And even Aubrey's tall, cadaverous form looked less tense as he was drawn into the conversation through Reid's kind efforts.

Gincie studied the threads of love and kinship that wove the various small groups into a larger pattern, and she understood the obscenity Phoebe found in her own hate. Phoebe had been raised with love and taught tolerance from the cradle; nothing, not even the war, had prepared her for the violence that was rising in her own soul. Gincie understood that violence too well; she had felt it against Mark. But she did not want to discuss it.

"You have one consolation," Gincie said. "The better you do in your work, the worse it is for the night riders. I can think of no more perfect revenge."

Phoebe considered her words for a long moment, and her smile was genuine. "You are very like Gran, you know, and each year you will be more like her. Though I know the circumstances are difficult, I am glad you and Travis have come back. It is good to know that you will be here keeping Wild Swan safe for Joseph, for all of us, no matter where we are."

Gincie was deeply touched by the compliment, but horrified by the responsibility. "Please, I'm flattered, but only Gran is Gran. If I am like her, then so are you, so are we all; she has had so much to do with raising us."

It steadied her and brought back the joy of the evening when she saw how contented her grandmother was to have the family together. Around her neck, Alex wore the golden circlet of swans that Rane had given her for Christmas so many years ago when she had been living with his family. She had been too young then for such a gift, and Rane had known it, but he had not been able to resist the symbol of the birds Alex loved so much, birds they had watched together. It was a love Alex had brought with her to the United States and given to her descendants, so that they all welcomed the return of the swans to Chesapeake Bay in winter as a special reassurance of continuity.

The matching gold earrings Alex wore had been another gift from Rane years later, sent from England when he had been there during the war. Another symbol, a reminder to Alex that his love continued even when he was far from her.

The party broke up with the younger Falconers, plus Flora, Philly, and Blaine, going back to Brookhaven for the night while the Carrington sisters, their spouses, and their children stayed at Wild Swan. Everyone would gather again for Christmas dinner, this time at Brookhaven.

Travis and Gincie checked on their own children for a final time and found them sleeping soundly, K. C. with a carved wooden horse he had received for Christmas pressed against his cheek.

"That must be very uncomfortable," Gincie whispered.

"Not if it is a magic horse," Travis answered, but he pried the toy out of his son's clutches and placed it carefully beside him on the pillow.

"It was a good Christmas," he said when they were alone. "Even Aubrey came close to enjoyin' himself, and that must surely be a rare circumstance. I saw you talkin' for a long time to Phoebe. Should I have rescued you?"

Gincie drew closer to his warmth, one hand idly playing across the planes of his chest. "No. She needed to talk, and I was safer than her own family." Haltingly she told him what Phoebe had said.

Travis did not dispute Phoebe's perception of the danger in the South, and all he said aloud was, "If Joseph needs a home with us, he'll have it." But he let his hands and mouth speak more eloquently in gentle passion.

He could not fault Phoebe for her fierce dedication to teaching those who were so in need, nor for the violence she felt against those who would stop her, but he could not understand how her son could be secondary, and he was infinitely grateful that he was wed to a woman who would protect her family at any cost.

"Merry Christmas, darlin'," he murmured against her throat, and her little sigh of pleasure as he moved into her was acknowledgment of the final gift exchanged.

Chapter 10

On New Year's Eve, they upheld the old tradition of wassailing the apple trees, a custom Alex had first encountered with Rane's family in Devon. They hung little cakes on the branches, offered cider by pouring it around the bases of the trees, and sang:

> *Here's to thee, old apple tree*
> *Whence thou may'st bud and whence thou may'st blow*
> *And whence thou may'st bear apples enow!*
> *Hats full! Caps full!*
> *Bushel-bushel-sacks full*
> *And my pockets full too! Huzza!*

It was a ceremony that particularly delighted the children, and Lexy and the twins were already familiar with it because Gincie had carried the tradition west. But for the adults, it was also special, a burst of fancy with old, pagan roots, a plea to whatever gods there were to grant abundance from the earth in the coming year.

"We're already assured of an abundant harvest," Reid observed to Larissa, and her laughter rang out as loud as the children's.

Unable to come for Christmas, Alastair Cameron was there for New Year's Eve along with other friends, including Frank Faber and his wife. Frank had been a close friend of Seth's and had fallen in love with Gincie. But though she had never thought of him as more than a friend, he had remained concerned and loyal to the family, going so far as to come to Wild Swan to warn Alex that Union troops were coming to arrest Travis, who was recuperating from his Gettysburg wound. Travis and Gincie had escaped back to Virginia before the soldiers arrived.

A newspaperman like Reid, Frank now worked for the Baltimore *Sun* and was well contented with his wife, a Georgetown girl he had met toward the end of the war.

Frank and Reid were engaged in a lively discussion of the political situation, Frank arguing that the federal government couldn't police the South forever and would simply have to compromise here and there to speed the rebuilding of the Union, while Reid contended that the South deserved to be treated like a delinquent child as long as it behaved so. As he presented his case, Frank's eyes wandered now and then to Gincie. There was no lechery in his gaze, just a shade more tenderness than one would give even a close friend.

"Do you mind?" Alex asked Travis, seeing the awareness in his eyes.

"Does nothin' ever escape you?" he asked ruefully. His gaze moved from Frank to Gincie, who was listening intently to Flora. "No, I don't mind," he said honestly, "because Gincie doesn't look at him in the same way. And I don't doubt that Frank loves his wife; it's just that Gincie was his first love and will always be special for that, but I was lucky enough to marry her." He raised Alex's hand to his lips and kissed it. "Of course, had I met you first, God knows what would have happened."

Alex's laughter caught Rane's attention, and he smiled at her from across the room.

"Then again, it might have been more dangerous than the war," Travis added in mock terror.

At midnight, Rane raised his glass in the toast that had become a tradition since the war. "To those we shall not see again at Wild Swan—we will remember you. And to the living, our family and friends who are safely home again. May this be a good and peaceful year."

Gincie thought of Phoebe facing increasing danger in the South. She thought of Flora facing another year without Caleb, and she thought of how fortunate she and Travis were to have been given a new beginning at Wild Swan.

The work of the farm consumed them immediately. The mares began to foal in January, and outside mares arrived continually to be bred to Wild Swan's stallions, while some of Wild Swan's mares were likewise sent to be bred to prizewinning sires owned by others.

Training schedules for the mares, particularly those bound for racecourses, had to be kept and entries made in stakes races, as the closing dates came well in advance of the events.

And in addition to the horses, there was increasing work to be done in the fields and gardens as the seasons advanced.

The rest of the family went on with their lives, too. In late April, Larissa gave birth to a son, who was named Joshua. Nigel, Max, and Anthea established an office for the practice of medicine in Baltimore. But Anthea was quickly infuriated by the continued prejudice she faced because of her gender, and she sought out her Aunt

Flora because Flora had so long been an advocate of women's rights, even to having attended the now famous Seneca Falls Women's Rights Convention of 1848.

"I'm as highly trained and capable as any man and a great deal more so than many," Anthea fumed, "and yet, only in the most dire emergency will a man even consider accepting my help."

Flora let her rant on for several visits, and then she asked very gently, "Are you allowed to treat the children in addition to the women?"

"Well, yes, because many children, bright little beings that they are, prefer a woman's touch since they are more used to their mother's care than to a man's, even their father's."

"And who needs better medical care than women and children?"

Anthea opened her mouth and then closed it again. A faint blush colored her cheeks. "I won a major battle without even knowing it, didn't I?" she said slowly. "God knows there are too many women who affect ill health to prove how fine and delicate they are or to add interest to boring lives. But there are so many who are worn out by repeated childbearing, by overwork, and by ailments we know far too little about. They deserve the best care I can give them, and so do their children."

"It's very difficult not to want everything to change immediately," Flora said. "Equality in education, in wages, and in political rights seem so basic to me. Sometimes I wake at night thinking I've had a nightmare, that it cannot possibly be true that these essentials are denied to half the population. But it is true. We put aside our demands before the war because slavery was a killing evil that had to end, and somehow, it did not seem acceptable to equate a woman who could not sue for her rights in court, vote in elections, or be educated to the full extent of her intelligence with a slave who was treated like a beast in the fields. But it is slavery all the same. And now that the war is over, there is a tendency to say, 'No more changes; there have been changes enough.' There is so much opposition to granting the vote to black men, I think the possibility that women will be allowed to vote is even further away than it was before the war."

Anthea looked at her in growing horror. "Are you giving up?"

"No, never! But I am growing ever more willing to fight in devious ways. The women your mother and I teach at the school and the children, they will, if we are successful, go away believing more in themselves and their abilities than they did before. And here and there they will be able to earn more than they would otherwise. And women like you will pursue various professions so well that your power will increase. Ignorance makes prisoners of people, men and women alike; education frees them. You cannot keep educated minds imprisoned forever.''

Within a very short time, word got around that Doctor Anthea was to be trusted both as a physician and as a woman, and many of her calls were for those to whom medical care of any kind was a rarity.

She did what she could, usually frustratingly little, for prostitutes who contracted venereal diseases and received various wounds of abuse from their clients or their pimps. She went to the filthy dwellings of factory and piece workers who had nothing and yet produced children year after year. Some of the children flourished despite the conditions, but many died and their mothers, too. Anthea's war on ignorance intensified as she urged the women and the men to do what they could to limit the number of offspring they had. Sometimes there was interest; more often, the reactions ranged from blank stares to shock and outrage that she would even mention such a thing. But even knowing how ruthless it was, she used the skill she offered as blackmail to make those she treated listen to her advice.

For her, it was the one element missing from the usual arguments for women's rights: until women could control when and how many children they had, they would never be free, and many of them would die from the damage caused to their bodies by repeated pregnancies coupled with overwork, squalor, and undernourishment.

Preventing conception was difficult. Anthea did not believe abstinence was a reasonable method, though it was the only one the more radical campaigners for women's rights endorsed, the more moderate being altogether silent on the subject. Nor was the interruption of coitus dependable. The use of sponges offered some protection to the women, but even better were the condoms that had been available since the vulcanization of rubber in 1844. They were more durable and less costly, though still expensive to the poor, than the ones that had been made previously of animal gut, fish membrane, or the like. They were far superior to the douches women concocted of everything from alum, hemlock, or green tea to prussic acid, opium, or alcohol. And though many condemned the use of condoms, there were druggists who stocked them because some men used them to avoid contracting diseases from prostitutes. Where Anthea saw the need would be met in no other way, she gave them to her patients, though she knew that many husbands refused to use them, as if the problem of too many children or an ailing wife was somehow not connected to themselves. Even where there was willingness, the cost deterred many who could not compare that outlay with how much more it would cost to feed another child.

Max was torn between his desire to protect her and his agreement with what she was doing. "You know you can get into trouble, particularly with all the reformers who are beginning openly to condemn control of conception."

"I know, and I know I might acquire a reputation that would put me in the same league as those wretched fakes who sell poisonous potions to women, or worse, butcher them. But I worry more that it might adversely affect you and Nigel."

"That is the last thing for you to worry about," Max said, and then he grinned. "You know how these modern wives are; no one can control them, let alone a mild-mannered fellow such as myself."

He sobered again, and he hesitated before he asked, "What are you going to do when a woman asks you for an abortion? It is only a matter of time before it happens."

"I have thought and thought about it," she admitted. "I don't want to gain a reputation for being a willing killer of the unborn, and yet, I cannot rule it out. Women are willing to risk their lives to prevent giving birth to an unwanted child. I cannot see how I can deny them an alternative to death. I must just take each case as it comes and make my decision then." She studied his kind, homely face that was so beautiful to her. "As you do," she added softly.

Max's practice was general, not specialized in women's problems, but she knew he had performed several abortions in his years of medicine. They had discussed it in the past, and when she had asked him how he felt after the first one, he had answered, "Sad, but convinced it was necessary and relieved that my patient lived."

Anthea wished more regular physicians felt as she, Max, and Nigel did, that the welfare of their patients came before all else, particularly now that the more advanced among them accepted the need for Lister's antiseptic procedures during surgery and could thus make abortion that much safer. But abortion had become a political issue in the past few decades, and the well-being of women seemed to be the last consideration. The Hippocratic Oath forbade it, but it also left all surgery to other than physicians, referring to a system of medical treatment that bore little resemblance to that of the present day. Traditionally the decision to abort had belonged to the woman in the time prior to quickening, the time that might indicate pregnancy by the cessation of monthly courses, but during which no movement of the fetus had yet been felt. It had long been the province of women, of knowledge passed from one to another, of midwives and wise women. For most, there had been no moral blame connected to this practice.

Even when the first laws against abortion in America had been passed in the 1820s, they had been directed against those who might poison women with deadly abortifacients, not against the act of abortion itself.

The view had begun to change in the 1840s. Suddenly it was not poor country women or young women trapped by the consequences of illicit love affairs who were seeking abortions. It had become apparent that women of the upper and middle classes were limiting their families to two or three children, and they were not doing it solely by avoiding conception. Some abortionists, such as Madame Restell, who by the 1840s had offices offering abortions in New York, Boston, and Philadelphia, became infamous for their flamboyant ads promising success and leaving little doubt of what their specialty was. Likewise, newspapers and magazines carried an ever-increasing array of ads for women's remedies such as "French Lunar Pills" and "French Periodical Pills" guaranteed to restore "monthly turns" no matter what had caused the interruption in the first place and without harming those who took the pills.

There were some deaths caused by the inept, but abortion remained far safer than childbirth, and the rising outcry had little to do with protecting women and a great deal to do with the disarray in the medical profession.

The profession, so highly thought of in the days of the revolution, had lost ground and credibility in this century, and a deep division had developed between the regular physicians who went to the biggest medical schools and who took clinical training in hospitals and the vast numbers of outsiders, who ranged from wise practitioners of common-sense treatment to outright quacks. It didn't help the regulars that their results were often no better than those of the outsiders. There was no set course or licensing procedure for all, and the regular physicians, unable to set standards for themselves or other practitioners, began to seek help from the law to do it. They were particularly determined to rid themselves of the outsiders who performed abortions and specialized in various female ailments. Anthea was shamed by the knowledge that it was still not so much that the regular physicians were worried about women as it was the loss of revenue they experienced when women turned away from them for one problem and continued to seek alternative care thereafter.

They were aided in their crusade by the growing realization that white Protestant women of means were the ones who were limiting their families, while the ever-growing population of immigrants with their "foreign" accents, ways of life, and worship were having large families. The nativism that had never been far from the surface since immigration had increased so drastically in the 1840s was clearly evident now. In place of the old midwifery texts and self-help manuals that had matter-of-factly described various means of abortion, there were now pious tracts, many by regular physicians, aimed at scolding white Protestant women of means for shirking their duty to maintain their numbers over the influx of foreigners. And while these same tracts claimed that the only moral action was to accept all the children God sent, there was always at least one passage that stated it was obvious that some people were not fit to breed and should not be allowed to. It was never made clear why God should bless these inferior beings with conception in the first place. Nor was any specific plan put forward to stop them from breeding.

Like many other states in the past ten years, Maryland had passed an antiabortion law, though originally it had been only a rider to a licensing law designed to give a minority of the state's physicians control over who should practice medicine in Maryland. It had been yet another case of various types of medical practitioners fighting for control, and though it passed without provision for the means to enforce it, when an enabling clause was added, the bill was voted down in the state senate, and finally, only the abortion clause became law. Again, it seemed more a case of political expediency than anything else, perhaps as a sop to the Baltimore newspapers that were campaigning against obscenity at the time and had put abortion in that category, as the Comstock laws later labeled the sending of conception-control information through the mails as obscene.

The irony of her situation did not escape Anthea. She was, after all, one of the regular physicians, whether her male colleagues approved or not, and as such, she was fairly well protected under the law which allowed one or more respectable physicians to decide on an abortion. She also had the right to treat women who came for help after a botched job performed by someone else. As long as she was careful, she should be able to avoid conflict with the law. She was probably in more jeopardy from advocating the use of condoms than from performing abortions.

Conflict with herself was another matter and not something that would ever be fully resolved.

But the first time she was actually faced with the decision, it was easy to make. The patient was a pale, blond child of thirteen who had been raped by her uncle. Her mother brought her to Anthea.

"It's bad enough I had t' put up with th' drunken bastard I had for a husband without his damn brother messin' with my little Sally. I don' want her saddled with no brat of his. You don' help her out, I'll find somebody what will."

Anthea didn't know whether true concern lurked beneath Mrs. Birch's belligerent attitude, but it didn't matter. The terrified child deserved her help, and she gave it.

With no demur, Max assisted her, but Anthea performed the procedure, dilating the cervix to cause contractions and washing the uterine cavity with a solution to assist the process, the pregnancy not being far enough advanced to make rupturing the membrane safe. Anthea gave thanks that the sharp-eyed mother had noticed her daughter's condition before the pregnancy was too far along. But then it occurred to her that it was probable that Mrs. Birch had noticed because she had been aware of the rape at the time it had happened and had done nothing to stop it.

She gave the woman no choice about leaving the child with the Kingstons for a week, pointing out that the process might take several days to be complete and that the extra days were necessary for full recuperation. Mrs. Birch seemed relieved to be spared the responsibility of looking after her daughter. Anthea understood why from what little information she gleaned while caring for Sally. Sally was the oldest of eight children. Her father had been killed in a drunken brawl the previous year, and her uncle lived with them along with his own brood of four, orphaned when their mother had died giving birth to the youngest two years before.

Sally didn't speak much unless she was directly questioned, but she was careful to say thank you for every small kindness offered to her, and her blue eyes grew round at the sight of the clean, spacious rooms in the Kingstons' living quarters above their offices, at the plenty and variety of food offered to her, and at the novelty of being treated as a pampered guest. She was wary, but clear intelligence shone in her eyes. Anthea wanted desperately to find a place for Sally where she could be educated and freed from the horrors of her home life, but when she returned after a week, the child's mother would have none of it.

"What am I gonna do if I ain't got Sally helpin' me with all them kids?" she asked, outraged because she did not see that her daughter had any rights not connected to her. She took Sally with her, though not before Anthea had gotten the Birches' address from the girl.

Max was keenly aware of how much of a toll Sally's case had taken on Anthea, and he suggested they go out to Wild Swan for a couple of days. "I've spoken to Nigel, and he assures me he can bear the load for that long."

Anthea didn't even make a halfhearted protest; she longed for the peaceful reassurance of the farm and her grandmother. And as soon as she was with Alex, she realized she also needed a confessor, someone beyond even Max, for all his understanding.

She told her grandmother Sally's story, and then she said, "I don't think I feel bad about performing the abortion. Women of means can find good medical help whenever they need it; poor women almost never obtain it. And Sally is just a child, a child who was raped by her uncle. But I feel as if what I did, which seemed like such an enormous thing to me, is such a small part of what Sally needs. It all seems so hopeless with her having to return to the same home that abused her in the first place."

"I hope you never lose your compassion for your patients," Alex told her. "I believe physicians who are detached from those they serve are worse than useless. There are so many illnesses which cannot be cured, so many times when having another human being's concern is more important than any course of treatment. But you cannot save all your patients from the tragedies in their lives. And until there are strict laws to protect children against the brutality of parents and others who abuse them, there is nothing you can do."

Alex looked as distressed as Anthea felt, and then her expression changed, becoming speculative, almost sly. "Of course, you might offer money for her," she suggested.

"Gran! That's slavery! And while I'd do it, surely not even Sally's mother would dare such a thing."

"She might if you suggest it in the proper way. You see, you would only be paying Sally's wages to her mother instead of to a child too young to have any sense about money. Pay the wages by the quarter, perhaps until she is old enough to have some say in her own life. And in the meantime, turn her over to Flora. Sally can do light housekeeping for Flora, and Flora can educate her. Flora needs a chick to mother. She's terribly lonely without Caleb."

"It might work, it just might!" Anthea felt hopeful for the first time since Sally Birch had come to her. She had seen the worn, angry look on Mrs. Birch's face. It seemed likely that the woman would welcome regular money, even if it meant giving up the services of her oldest child. That the other children faced the same conditions was something Anthea could not consider; it would have to be enough if she could salvage Sally.

"Gran, you're marvelous!"

"No, just experienced," Alex observed dryly. "I blackmailed Gincie's mother into letting her stay here, threatened her with arrest for starting the fire in the stallion barn. If you manage to make an arrangement with Sally's mother, it will be much tidier than that."

A few days after Anthea and Max had gone back to Baltimore, Alex received a brief note from them.

"Mrs. Birch didn't even hesitate; Sally is safe with Flora now. Thank you, Gran. I love you," Anthea had written, and Max had added his own message: "My thanks, too, Mrs. Falconer. Anthea is so much happier now."

Alex was no less grateful than they; that her children and grandchildren valued her advice and allowed her to share so much of their lives was infinitely precious to her. It was part of the same continuity that made her so intent on training Gincie and Travis to have more to do with the business of Wild Swan.

At the yearling sale held in April, she had made sure everyone knew that the Culhanes were not just observers, but nothing would have convinced the horsemen who came to buy Wild Swan stock to trust Travis's judgment had he not possessed such extensive knowledge of the animals and the bloodlines. And with good grace, Gincie accepted the fact that in most cases, the men preferred to speak to another man, rather than to a woman. She reminded herself that if her grandmother had been able to put up with such treatment for so many years and still establish such a legendary stable, then she could do the same.

In June, the Falconers and the Culhanes were at Jerome Park in Westchester County, New York, for the American Jockey Club's spring meeting, and Gincie and Travis found the track as impressive as Saratoga.

Jerome Park had been designed and funded by the financier Leonard T. Jerome, and he had spared no expense. The imposing clubhouse sat on "The Bluff" in a grove of firs with the dome of an old Dutch church rising in the background. The surrounding countryside was verdant with orchards, meadows, woods, and brooks, so that birdsong often seemed as loud as the babble of the legions who attended the races.

Though attendance by women at northern tracks had once been frowned upon, the opening meeting at Jerome Park in 1866 had changed all that; brilliantly dressed society women had, from the outset, placed Jerome Park in general and the clubhouse in particular among their most favored spots.

There was a silly rule forbidding women to cross from the grandstand to the clubhouse unescorted, a rule badly designed to keep out women of loose morals who might solicit for clients, women who were, in any case, turned away before they ever arrived at the space between grandstand and clubhouse. But aside from that, women enjoyed a fair degree of freedom and privilege at the course and were quite uninhibited about wagering considerable sums on cards and the horses.

Gincie enjoyed every minute of their stay there because it was becoming increasingly clear that no matter what anyone knew or thought of what she had done in California, no one was going to challenge her right to be part of the racing set. New scandals had taken the place of old, and no one wanted to challenge Alex or Rane

Falconer, who made it very plain that Gincie and Travis were to be treated with the same respect they themselves received.

Some of the best horses of the county were there, including Chillicothe, Harry Bassett, Hamburg, Preakness, and Helmbold, plus Oysterman, who was so good over the jumps. Wild Swan's entries held their own against the superior field, taking a third in the Fordham Stakes and a third to Harry Bassett in the Belmont Stakes, but winning the Jockey Club Handicap, as well as a one and a quarter mile race for three-year-olds and a steeplechase.

Gincie was particularly excited about the steeplechase because Travis had purchased and was training Toliver, the four-year-old stallion who won it.

The morning gallops were a ceremony in themselves. The parade approached down the elm-shaded walk, the horses shrouded in hoods and body clothes against the morning chill. Then there was a slow trot up to the half-mile ground and a gentle trot for a mile before the body clothes were removed and the horses were taken for a two-mile canter, halted, walked, and let out again, all with trainers and spectators keeping careful count with their watches. The murmured comments on the speed and style of various horses were the chorus to the thudding of hooves. Dust hung in the early morning light, and the smell of warming horseflesh was strong.

Gincie drew a deep breath, and Travis teased, "That is surely the mark of a true turf fanatic."

"I'll plead guilty to that anytime," Gincie said, and she thought how lucky they were to be doing something they both enjoyed so much.

A month later they were at Saratoga for the first summer meeting. Though they had more losers than winners, they all considered the trip worthwhile because Wild Swan's horses won the Saratoga Stakes for two-year-olds and the Sequel Stakes for three-year-olds. Oysterman won both the hurdle race and the steeplechase, defeating Toliver in both, and while Travis was disappointed that his horse was defeated, he admired the power and precision of the winner. In early July, Oysterman had won the Grand National Steeplechase at Monmouth Park in New Jersey. There were few horses in the country who could beat him.

The Falconers and Culhanes were at Monmouth Park for the August meeting, and it was a new experience for all of them. The course had opened only the year before, and they had not attended the inaugural meeting. The track was near the village of Little Silver some three miles from Long Branch, which already had a history of popularity with theatrical people and political bosses, and thus had hotels and dining facilities. Around Monmouth Park itself, the land was green and dotted with buttercups and clover blossoms, and the hot afternoons were cooled by breezes from the sea, which was not far distant.

On race days, the various avenues leading from Long Branch to Monmouth Park were crowded with all kinds of equipages, and the races here were as well patronized by women as those at Jerome Park.

Wild Swan's stables captured the Continental Hotel Stakes for colts and fillies, three years old, and Alex was particularly proud that Lady Lex won it, proving she was still good competition for the colts.

Though two-year-old colts and fillies were often well matched for speed, as the horses got older, colts usually began to gain an advantage in both strength and speed, but there were exceptions, such as the famous racing mares Fashion, Trifle, and Black Maria in the past, and Alex hoped Lady Lex would prove to be in their league.

For Travis, the victories in the hurdle races and in the Steeplechase Handicap were very satisfying, but he was honest enough to admit that the results might well have been different had Oysterman been competing.

After the races had ended for the day, the hotels were lively, with hops held at both the Continental and the West End hotels, the only drawback being that there was a shortage of dancing men so that many of the ladies danced with each other or not at all.

Rane gallantly danced with Alex and Gincie in rotation. Travis did not allow his lameness to interfere with much, but dancing was one thing which made him very uncomfortable because he felt as if he moved like a wooden soldier.

Gincie saw his expression as he watched Alex and Rane gliding gracefully around the dance floor, and she said, "You look better on a horse than Grandfather ever did, and he is a superb rider."

"I was thinkin' how good it would feel to hold you in my arms and move perfectly to the music, as they do. Somehow takin' you up on a horse with me isn't the same as waltzin'," Travis said, and then he laughed when she retorted, "Not the same, but it has possibilities."

Instead, Gincie took Travis dancing on the beach. Feeling like children, they stripped off their shoes and stockings to go for a walk on the wet sand. The moon was glorious, threading the sea with gold and silver and catching in the water that rose in their footprints. Music filtered down to them, mixing with the wash of the waves.

"May I have this dance, sir?" Gincie asked, and here Travis was not self-conscious. They followed their own rhythm, pressed close together as they could never be on a public dance floor, moving slowly on the damp, resilient surface.

"No wonder so many people condemn dancin'," Travis murmured as his manhood hardened in response to her.

Gincie's laugh was low and throaty as she ran her hand down the front of his trousers. "Ah, but it's not the dancing that is so dangerous; it's what happens once you stop."

"Let's stop right now," Travis growled, framing her face with his hands and kissing her deeply.

They gave thanks that they did not run into anyone they knew as they hurried back to their hotel, but even so, Travis had to walk close behind Gincie to disguise his condition.

It was another kind of dancing when they made love, fast and then slowly, Travis's body moving over and inside Gincie's with power and perfect grace.

When they lay contentedly in each other's arms, Travis bestirred himself enough to say, "When Lexy is a little older, I am goin' to tell her that while she might be allowed to dance, she's never, ever to stop."

"I pity the young men who come to call on her," Gincie murmured sleepily. "You are going to be very difficult."

"Lexy is goin' to be the difficult one. She is such a purposeful person already. She will make of her life what she wants it to be."

Of all the things Gincie loved about Travis, his involvement with the children and his knowledge of them were among the most treasured.

The fact of his involvement with his family was brought home to Travis when he went to California at the end of August. He was glad to see everyone at the ranch and to observe that the land was being carefully tended, but everywhere he looked, he wanted to find Gincie and the children. Rancho de Salida del Sol no longer felt like home at all. Gincie's touch, her scent, the sound of her voice, the sight of her bending to one of the children or riding out on the golden land—they were all missing. The ranch still interested him as an investment and as a possible future for one of the children, but the song that had once called him to stay was silent.

It was just as well that this was the case, for according to Boston, Mark Carrington's widow was determined to make vengeance, preferably paid in cash, her life's work. She still lived in Southern California, but she appeared periodically in San Francisco to plead her case before any authority she could collar.

"I don't know anymore," Boston admitted. "While I believe Mark abused her, and while I think money might appease her, I am almost ready to concede that she genuinely mourns the bastard. And that would make her more dangerous to Gincie than anything else."

"It wouldn't be that unusual, would it?" Travis said. "There are all sorts of women, even kind, bright women, who are married to the worst husbands imaginable, and yet when those men die, the women mourn them as if they were saints. Maybe it's a case of not knowin' any better." Then seeing Boston's distressed look, he hastened to explain how he now felt about the return to the East.

"I never expected to feel this resignation, but perhaps it was all meant to be. What your sister has built at Wild Swan is worth hangin' on to, worth fightin' for. And what impresses the hell out of me is that she has managed to make it a payin' business. There are so many who never even cover the basic costs of raisin' and trainin' a racehorse, let alone make a profit at it. But Alex does, year after year. To keep doin' that is challenge enough for anyone."

When Rachel was with them, they exchanged news about the various branches of the family, and Rachel had a special word of thanks she wanted Travis to convey to Reid.

"I wrote to him after Alex sent me the newspaper clipping of his article about the Indian Appropriation Act, but please tell him again how much it meant to have such an articulate man write so eloquently about it."

The act marked a profound change in the legal status of Indians. Prior to its passage, the policy on the books had dated back to the time of George Washington and was supposed to recognize Indian tribes as "distinct, independent, political communities," and as "domestic dependent nations," giving them something like the status of states, with the federal government being the ultimate authority. The new act totally overturned the old policy; now tribes had no treaty-making powers or any others; they had become wards of the state in a country that had never cared well for them.

Reid's article had used lethal sarcasm to point out that it was only sensible for the government to change its policy to reflect what was already true inasmuch as treaties with the Indians had never been respected for longer than was convenient. He had ended the piece with the admonition that if the United States did not learn to respect the differences of its various peoples, particularly its native population, civil war in the country would never end.

"The Cherokee made the fatal error so long ago," Rachel said. "We thought by becoming like the whites we would be accepted by the whites, and so when the government banished us from our lands, it was easier for them than it should have been." It had been more than thirty years, but her face still reflected the pain and loss of the Trail of Tears, which had been marked by thousands of graves as the Cherokee were herded into exile from the Southeast to the desolate Indian territory in the West.

"It will not be so easy with the peoples of the Plains. Already they are fighting, and they will go on fighting for as long as they can." There was no triumph in her voice, and she added, "They will fight, but they, too, will lose. I don't know which is the better way."

"You are too kind to say it," Travis told her, "but surely the best thing for all Indians would have been for the war between the states to go on forever. Everything has gotten so much worse for the Indians since the army has been free to harass them again and since more and more people are moving west."

"I'm not certain what's worse, the army or the missionaries," Boston said, referring to President Grant's plan to insure peace with the Indians by dividing reservations among various religious groups that they might pacify and guide the Indians toward becoming "civilized." The religious groups were squabbling viciously among themselves for control.

"Grant was a fine general," Travis conceded, though he had fought on the other side. "But he is not, in my opinion, a fit president. He chooses venal men to advise him, and whatever his own honor, he seems unable to see that they have none."

Though great fortunes were being made, particularly in the Northeast and by Far West mining and railroad interests, the Thaines and Travis were not alone in feeling that the country's prosperity was an elaborate castle built on quicksand. And they knew that protecting themselves against future losses had as much to do with luck as it did with applying the facts available.

"I think a herd of untried two-year-olds is easier to judge than the futures of our minin' shares," Travis confessed. "And yet, I paid little enough for them, and I think I'll hold the ones I've got left for a while longer."

"You know as well as I do that the shares are being manipulated by the principal owners—fire this week, flood the next, the shares go down, and there is a sudden report of new wealth, and back up they go—after the owners have purchased shares at the lowest prices," Boston reminded him. "But I, too, think there is some value in continuing the gamble."

With his business concluded, there was no reason for Travis to tarry. He was sad to say good-bye to the Thaines, but even that was softened by the prospect of going back to his family. And Gincie and the children greeted his return with such joy, Wild Swan seemed more like home than ever.

Chapter 11

The new year saw the marriage of Adam Falconer to Mercy Starbuck. She was small, slight, and rather plain, with dark hair and eyes, a snub nose, an even mouth, and a rather pointed chin, and she spoke in the clipped accent of New England. But she had a ready laugh and a keen intelligence that illuminated her face. Her family had roots in Nantucket, New Bedford, and Boston and had been connected with the sea in one way or another for most of their history.

Mercy was twenty-two years old, and she had been born and had spent most of her early childhood on board a ship because her mother had no intention of letting her sea captain husband sail without her. Mercy loved the sea, loved Adam, and knew almost as much about ships and sailing as he did.

"For the first time I envy you, brother mine," Nigel told Adam. "It's as if you and Mercy were specifically designed for each other."

"You'll be twenty-seven this year—only a year younger than I am—and you really ought to consider getting married yourself," Adam advised from his newly acquired status of happily married man.

Nigel held his hands up in mock defense. "Don't get any wild ideas; every family needs the old bachelor uncle, and maybe that's what I'll be." He was only partially joking. His medical practice kept him so busy, he couldn't imagine how he could give attention to a wife and possibly children. Anthea and Max managed to spend a good deal of time together, but that was obviously because Anthea was also a doctor. Nigel had met few other female physicians and none he wished to marry.

The family was further enlarged by a visit from Gweneth, Christopher, their eighteen-year-old twins, Hugh and Nicholas, and their fourteen-year-old daughter, Eveline. As a fortieth birthday present from Christopher to Gwenny, they came to spend most of the summer at Wild Swan, and Alex and Rane made no secret of the joy they felt in having them there.

Gweneth looked so much like her parents and her brother that when she, Morgan, Alex, and Rane were together, the dark-haired, green-eyed inheritance they shared was startling. Eveline and Nicholas looked much like them, too, heightening the effect, while Hugh, though dark haired, had his father's silvery gray eyes with the dark ring around the iris.

More than twenty years in England had given Gwenny the accent of her adopted country and an ease with the aristocracy as the wife of the Duke of Almont's son and heir, but she remained as sensible and unassuming as she had been raised to be, and her children had been brought up in the same way, despite the privileges of their birth. They enjoyed the days at Wild Swan as much as Gwenny had in her own youth. And they were patient with their younger cousins, particularly with K. C. and Tay, who trailed after the older twins with all the fervor of four-year-olds who had found perfect heroes.

Gincie gleaned all the information she could about the twins from Gwenny and was reassured.

"It is a bit more difficult, I believe, to have them be of the same sex. Flora and Blaine were bound to develop differences simply from being girl and boy. For a time, I did worry about the boys; they seemed to think with one mind and to be too dependent on each other, but they've become quite different. Nicholas is the one who takes the risks and the lead, but Hugh holds his own in a quieter way," Gwenny explained.

"With mine, it's K. C. who decides what the two of them will do, with Tay trailing along, but both of them will listen to Lexy, thank heavens."

"You should be grateful indeed!" Gwenny told her. "Eveline simply worships her brothers and will put up with almost anything to be allowed to accompany them. But at least they are quite protective of her and kind in a rather rough, older-brother fashion."

Gincie wished she could have spent more time with the Bettingdons, but she and Travis were away for long stretches, taking the horses to various race meetings. This time neither Alex nor Rane went with them.

"I want to spend time with Gwenny and her family," Alex had announced, "and I trust you to do as well as the races as I would."

It was both a test and an act of trust, and Gincie and Travis took it seriously on both counts, seeing to every detail while at the same time trying not to step on Padraic's toes. And they were pleased with the results at the end of the summer, particularly with the performance of Toliver in hurdle races and steeplechases and with the continuing strength of Lady Lex, who was now meeting colts four years old and older and beating them more often than not.

It was especially reassuring to Gincie to see how involved Travis had become in the affairs of Wild Swan. She believed him when he told her that the trips to California, while necessary, were strictly business now. Their lives were growing ever more involved, not only in the affairs of the farm, but also in the wider range of concerns shared by the family.

Due to Reid's career as a journalist, the family had more information and interest in politics than they might have had otherwise, though Alex and Rane, as immigrants, had always been fascinated by the process in their adopted country. This year, with the Democratic Party meeting in Baltimore in July to nominate a candidate for president, it would have been difficult in any case to avoid national politics.

As the Liberal Republicans had done earlier, the Democrats nominated Horace Greeley.

"It is an astonishingly bad choice," Reid declared. "Greeley was one of the founders of the Republican Party, and he's always been antislavery. He has even gone along with Radical Reconstruction because it provides for Negro suffrage. But he is such an odd combination of causes. The Democrats found him acceptable because he has advocated amnesty for the South, because he signed Jefferson Davis's bail bond, and most of all, because he has a national reputation, something to match against Grant's fame as a war hero." Reid felt a kind of personal embarrassment for Greeley because the man had founded the influential New York *Tribune* and had written clear, concise editorials for years. Unfortunately, his passions didn't always seem as clear as his writing.

"I can forgive him any number of his causes, but not his opposition to women's suffrage," Alex said. "I doubt he'll get many votes from this family, even though only the men can vote."

Gwenny shook her head in baffled wonder. "I had almost forgotten how exciting politics are here."

"It makes the elections in England seem quite dull. We will look for the results of your contest in the *Times*," Christopher said, referring to the fact that they would be back in England by the end of August and would thus miss the November elections.

"You won't have to," Reid said. "Mr. Greeley hasn't got a chance against President Grant."

He was proved correct when, after a vitriolic campaign during which Greeley had to spend much time at the bedside of his dying wife, Grant was reelected. And before the year was out, Greeley himself had died.

The election was notable for the attempt made by Susan B. Anthony, president of the National Woman Suffrage Association, to cast her vote. She was not the first woman to attempt to vote in a national election, and two territories—Wyoming in 1869, and Utah in 1870—had already recognized women's voting rights. But Anthony meant to prove legal right. She was convinced that the Constitution already granted it and that the new Fourteenth and Fifteenth Amendments assured it. The Fourteenth, passed in 1868, stated that "all persons born or naturalized in the United States . . . are citizens" and forbade any state to "abridge the privileges or immunities of citizens." Further, the amendment was to insure equal protection of the laws "to any person." The Fifteenth, enacted in 1870, made it illegal for any state to withhold the right to vote from any citizen "on account of race, color, or previous condition of servitude."

The National Woman Suffrage Association's mottoes were to the point: "Men—their rights and nothing more. Women—their rights and nothing less," and "Principle, not Policy. Justice, not Favors."

Miss Anthony had gone to President Grant to request that he make women's votes part of the party platform; his answer was that he had already recognized the "right of women to be postmasters." To him, this so far eclipsed what other presidents had done for women, he felt no compulsion to go further. When Anthony had asked the Republican Party for its support at its June convention, it had been no more forthcoming; its chief aim was to ensure full citizenship and full voting rights for the "colored male citizen" in order that the party might control the South through this new constituency.

"The arguments for a woman's right to vote under the law are so logical," Anthea said to Flora some time before the election, "I don't see how it can be denied any longer."

"I wish I had your confidence," Flora replied, "but I do not. The women who tried to register to vote last year in the District of Columbia were denied on the basis that the granting of citizenship did not necessarily include the right to vote, though God knows what citizenship means if not that. I fear you will find that there is still so much turmoil over granting the vote to black men, women of any color will have to wait a long while or move West to those enlightened parts of the wilderness that count a woman's vote."

Flora was proven correct. A few weeks after the election, not only were Susan B. Anthony and the others who had voted with her arrested, but so were three members of the registry board who had allowed the women to register to vote in the town of Rochester, New York.

Anthony refused to put up bail, wanting to pursue her case to a higher court, but her counsel, unwilling to see her go to jail, paid her bail, thus costing her the right to appeal to the United States Supreme Court because she had not gone to jail. The state decided to prosecute Anthony alone as representative of the sixteen women who had voted.

"I don't mean to sound like an ancient oracle, but you will see, this will all be handled with tight control so that the vote is not granted and neither is Miss Anthony made a martyr," Flora warned Anthea. "It is what I would do if I were on the other side, trying to withhold the vote from women."

Flora was correct about this, too. Before she went to trial in June of the following year, Anthony appeared at all twenty-nine post offices in the county where she voted, lecturing at those popular meeting places about the injustice of denying the vote to women, women who had to pay taxes without representation, who had to stand trial with no hope of having peers on the jury, and who in marriage lost custody of their wages, their children, and even their own persons. She argued that "We, the people," meant "We, the whole people."

It was all for naught. The judge in the case had no intention of allowing a fair trial and directed the jury to find her guilty. And when Miss Anthony refused to pay even "a dollar of your unjust penalty," referring to the hundred dollars plus costs the judge had fined her, the judge countered by not insisting on payment or imprisonment. Far from being conciliatory, he did it to avoid review of his court proceedings and to cut off her opportunity to appeal his verdict.

Reid and many other journalists across the country, even some who did not support women's suffrage, wrote condemnatory articles about the judge's action, but the damage was done.

For Anthea, the outcome of the trial was a personal goad to excellence, and she redoubled her efforts to help the women who came to her. Sally Birch was visible proof that it was worthwhile; she was blossoming by the day into a lovely, intelligent young woman. Once she had learned to read, she devoured books with a desperate passion, overcoming her shyness enough to ask Flora, Philly, or Anthea questions about what she had just read, though she was much more reticent around Nigel, Max, and any other man, which was understandable given her experience with her uncle. And her innate dignity demanded certain barriers that Flora and Anthea, for all their good intentions, could not breach. They would have liked to take Sally with them for Christmas at Wild Swan and Brookhaven, but Sally was quietly insistent on spending the time with her family, and she spent the pocket money Flora gave her on little gifts for her siblings and her mother.

Sally's knowledge of her family was basic and her strategy simple; as long as she could maintain the status of servant, her family would not feel threatened and would not take her back. Beyond that, she was deeply grateful for the changes in her life and did not want to take advantage of her benefactors. On the visits she made to Wild Swan with Flora, she was happy only if permitted to act as lady's maid or to help with the chores in the house, and she never mentioned these trips to the country to her family at all. But to her, Wild Swan was a magical place where even the air was strange and wonderful compared to the noxious fumes of the city, flavored as they were with the sewage dumped into the Back Bay and the assorted odors from the hair-work and curled hair manufactories, leather tanneries, lime kilns, ironmongers, and the like.

Sally's grasp of economics was rudimentary at best, but she knew that things were going very badly toward the end of 1873. She knew it in the most immediate and practical way because her uncle was out of work and growing more surly by the day, so that visits home were even more nightmarish than before, and her mother complained constantly about the uncertainty of her own factory job and the scarcity of money. Sally hated visits home more than ever.

What Sally perceived in the patterns of her own family was happening all over the country. What Travis and Boston and other sensible businessmen had feared had come to pass on September 18 when the brokerage house of Jay Cooke and Company failed due to unanticipated problems in financing the Northern Pacific Railroad, which was to have been a second transcontinental line.

Jay Cooke and Company's failure was the match to tinder that had been accumulating for years in excess trading, production, and speculation in an economy based on too much paper money and artificially high prices. On the same day, thirty-seven banks and brokerage houses closed their doors, and two days later the New York Stock Exchange closed for ten days. Other railroads and thousands of banks and businesses collapsed as the months passed, affecting businessmen, laborers, and farmers everywhere.

The damage was not confined to the United States; European nations were affected, not only because of international speculation, but also because of their own excesses and wars.

The Falconers, Carringtons, and Culhanes had several advantages favoring their financial survival. The most important was that none of them had ever indulged in wild stock speculation, and they all shared a very conservative approach to indebtedness. Through sheer luck, they benefited from the fact that Maryland banks stayed solvent, while many banks in other states closed their doors. Even Gincie and Travis, in their determination to make a new life at Wild Swan, had transferred most of their deposits to Maryland financial houses. Wild Swan's principal offerings, the racehorses, were the least affected because, though many of the wealthy turfmen found themselves short of funds, many others were rich enough and had such diversified investments that they continued as if nothing had happened. The races went on—and people kept buying the best bloodlines available.

But the family was not unscathed. Anthea, Max, and Nigel found many more patients than usual who could not pay their fees, while the numbers needing care rose, particularly among the workers who were hardest hit, having lost their jobs as factories closed or work forces were cut. The doctors treated more wounds inflicted on wives and children by men whose frustrations made tempers flare out of control, aided by liquor consumed too freely even when there was little money for food in the home. The children, more severely undernourished and neglected than before, succumbed even more readily to a host of maladies. Anthea and Max, as close as they were, sometimes found the pain of caring for the children too deep to share verbally, but they held on to each other through the nights when one or the other was not out on a call. And they worried about Nigel, who was taking even less time than usual away from his work and who had no one to comfort him; but there was nothing they could do to make his burdens lighter when their own were so heavy.

For Reid, the financial panic meant delaying the start of his own newspaper even longer. This was no time to start a new venture. And it meant that his articles often dealt with the unfairness of a system that hurt the most helpless first and gave no security to even the best worker. The year before he had written extensively about the Crédit Mobilier scandal first exposed by the New York *Sun*. The affair had involved government officials and the misuse of millions upon millions of dollars earmarked for the building of the Union Pacific Railroad. The extent of the corruption had shaken the nation, but not, Reid had written, enough. He wrote constantly against the tendency to accept corruption as a fact of life or, worse, as some sort of romantic adventure.

Reid believed passionately that newspapers must continue to expose corruption wherever it was uncovered. He was a popular writer with an honorable record as a war correspondent, but even so, he knew his refusal to soften his attacks on influential figures sometimes put him at odds with his editors, the one in Washington and the ones of the newspapers to which he contributed in other cities. Someday he was going to lose his footing entirely on the edge of what the editors considered permissible; he hoped he would be ready to start his own paper by then.

Philly and Flora and their staff went on teaching, but many of their students, young and old, were missing, having no time anymore for anything but the continuous struggle to glean enough to survive.

The teachers helped where they could, giving the children good meals and trying to help the adults with clothing, food, and work when they could arrange it diplomatically, to spare the pride of the recipients.

Phoebe and Aubrey saw the least change; the people they taught were mostly tenant farmers who were so poor, they spent the whole year trying to make their small plots yield enough to pay the rent and to feed themselves with a little over for trade, supplementing this with odd jobs where they could find them. And yet, paradoxically, they were often better off than the jobless in the cities; at least they had the land to feed them, no matter how meagerly.

Phoebe had written more often, but the Edwardses had not been north again since that Christmas visit. Gincie thought of them every time she read another account of the increasing turmoil in the South.

Of all the family's enterprises, the shipyard was hardest hit. The shipping business suffered as cargo orders decreased, and shipbuilding was hurt as investors withdrew. Rane, Morgan, and Adam had all agreed on the necessity for the dredging project intended to insure the continuation of Baltimore as a fit harbor for deep-water shipping, and they had invested heavily in it. They did not doubt the wisdom of that decision or that they would get their investment back in time, but meanwhile, it made finances tighter than they would have been otherwise.

Alex would gladly have lent the shipyard whatever it needed from her own business funds, but from past experience, she knew better than to offer and had to trust that Rane would come to her if his need was dire enough.

The three men did not fear the loss of the company; they were all sure they would survive this crisis. But that was not enough. They did not want to lose any of their skilled shipbuilders or the captains and crews who ran their passenger and cargo services. It was not only the matter of having to train or find qualified men when business increased again in the future, it was also because, as loyal as their workers were to Jennings-Falconer, so were the Falconers loyal to their employees. They did not want to cause them the hardship so many workingmen were experiencing.

The only answer was to do their best to replace defaulting investors on the ships being built and likewise to search out new cargoes to replace those where contracts had been lost. It put them all in a wearying routine of constant negotiation and travel. Adam was best able to cope because he was young and hardy, but he lacked the prestige and connections of his father and grandfather. Rane was a robust man, but he was also seventy-eight, and though he had no intention of letting that interfere with the work he must do, it worried Morgan, who could see his own concern reflected in his mother's eyes. Alex was the strongest woman Morgan knew, but he could not imagine her without his father.

Morgan had never fully accepted the physical limitations brought on by his hellish time in Andersonville prison, and he ignored not only Sam's worry, but also the signals from his own body that he was pushing too hard.

In December, he was in Philadelphia finalizing negotiations with a Mr. Stanhope, who had agreed to take over shares in a new steamer. The deal pleased both sides, as Mr. Stanhope was getting a bargain but paying enough so that Jennings-Falconer could complete the ship without skimping.

Though his speech did not reflect it, Mr. Stanhope was descended from a long line of Quakers who had a knack for astute business dealings. But he was also a kind man, and he eyed Morgan with a worried frown. "You look quite ill," he said bluntly. "Why don't you come home and dine with us? Mrs. Stanhope would like nothing better than to fuss over you. And I would not like to face your father were he to learn we had neglected your health here." Mr. Stanhope was closer to Rane's age than to Morgan's, and he treasured his friendship with Rane as much as he did the business dealings.

Morgan managed a smile as he refused. "I appreciate the offer, but you need not worry; I am just a little tired. I'll be leaving for home in the morning, and I plan to rest for a few days at Brookhaven." He didn't dare to accept the invitation to supper; he was feeling more wretched by the minute and did not want to collapse at the Stanhopes' table.

Short of wrestling Morgan into a carriage and hauling him home, Mr. Stanhope didn't see that there was much he could do, but he left the younger man reluctantly.

By the next morning, Morgan was so ill, everything was blurred, but he managed to catch the train to Baltimore. From there he went directly to Brookhaven. Getting home to Sam was the only thought in his fever-ridden brain.

For an instant, everything was very clear; he saw the welcome on Sam's face turn to terror, heard her cry his name, and he tried to tell her that he was really all right, that he only needed to rest. But the light whirled away and left him in darkness.

Sam wasn't conscious of the other hands trying to help as she sagged to the chilled earth with Morgan in her arms, his name a litany repeated over and over.

"Come on now, Miss Sam, we gets him inside to a warm place. He be too heaby fo' you to carry your ownsef."

The voices of the servants took shape and made sense to Sam, and she let the men lift Morgan, though she kept fierce hold on one of his hands. She had nursed him through these bouts before. Morgan was not going to leave her. She repeated it over and over again to make it true.

Without being so directed, the servants sent word immediately to Wild Swan and to Baltimore.

The fever and chill cycles of malaria, coupled with the blinding headaches and nausea were punishing, particularly in Morgan's exhausted state. Nigel asked Max to come with him because he did not trust himself to treat his father alone, but it was Nigel who talked to Sam.

"You're doing everything possible, keeping him warm when he has the chills, cooling him down when the fever is high, giving him quinine and liquids, but . . . Mother, he . . ."

"He is not going to die! Do you hear me? He is not going to die!"

She looked so fierce, Nigel took an involuntary step back, and then he drew comfort from her ferocity. They had so few medical weapons to fight for his father's life; if his mother's will added even a little more to their side, it might tip the balance.

Sam knew how much love was surrounding them, knew how much everyone wanted to help, but she could not bring herself to leave Morgan. She was terrified he would slip away while she was not at his side.

It was Gincie who persuaded Sam to sleep for a few hours at a time. "When Travis lay close to death after Gettysburg, I trusted you to watch over him so that I could rest and be stronger when I went back to him. Can you not trust me to do the same for you?"

Sam was too hazy with exhaustion to think clearly, but she felt Gincie's strength, and she trusted her to call her instantly if Morgan should take a turn for the worse.

Travis watched Gincie taking charge both at Brookhaven and Wild Swan, and he was very proud of her. For once, Alex and Rane needed strength to draw on rather than the other way around.

"I don't want to live to see another of my children die," Alex sobbed, and Rane knew she was thinking not only of Gincie's father, but also of the little girl, Christiana, who had died in England and of the baby she had miscarried in Annapolis.

Rane wanted to give her the support she needed, but his own heart was breaking. Morgan was proof of their loving over half a century ago, and he was also a magnificent man in his own right. His parents wanted the comfort of knowing he would go on living for years after they were gone.

Though Rane and Alex did everything they could to help in the crisis, both of them suddenly seemed to feel the full weight of their years. To see them appearing old and frail was almost as terrifying to the rest of the family as Morgan's illness.

Sam's world was narrowed to Morgan alone. She hated the pain that made him moan even when he was not conscious, and she hated the delirium more because it took him back to the nightmare of Andersonville and the overwhelming helplessness he had felt in his inability to improve the condition of the younger prisoners who had looked to him for direction and help.

"Hello, Seth. My boy, I have longed to see you again." The change in Morgan's voice from angry despair to gentle welcome was so abrupt, it took Sam a moment to understand what he was saying, and then a chill ran down her spine.

"Seth, I . . ." Morgan started to speak again in the same loving tone, but Sam cut him off, bending over him, holding on to him.

"No, Morgan, no! Seth is dead! And you are not going to die! You can't see Seth. See me, Morgan! Look at *me*! Open your eyes now! I love you! I won't let you go!" She thought she had cried all the tears she had inside, but they poured down her face again and pooled against Morgan's neck.

"Wet," he whispered.

She pulled back and wiped at her eyes until she could see that his own eyes were open and regarding her quite sanely.

Her hands remembered competence while she sponged his face and gave him a drink of water, but the whole while she was laughing, crying, and babbling, "Oh, Morgan, you scared me so! My darling, I love you, love you!"

"Who's delirious?" Morgan murmured, and he smiled.

His eyes started to close again because he was so tired, but he managed to ask, "What day?"

"It's Christmas Day," Sam answered, and as she watched him sleep peacefully, naturally, without crying out to the demons of war, she thought she had never received so valuable a gift.

Though they had all made an effort to keep Christmas for the children, for the adults it had been a dreadful time, and that made Rane's toast on New Year's Eve all the more poignant. Sam had insisted the tradition not be broken, even though Morgan was still confined to his bed and she was keeping watch beside him.

They were all so conscious of what they might have lost, of the name that might have been added to "those we shall not see again at Wild Swan," that the celebration was as torn between laughter and tears as Sam had been when Morgan awakened.

Much to her delight, Lexy was allowed to stay up until midnight for the first time while the twins and younger Tratnor cousins had to go to bed at their regular time. At eight years old, Lexy was already showing signs of being a tall woman, her lank slenderness giving her a deceptively fragile look enhanced by the way her big green eyes dominated her face. But she was agile, strong, and as good in the saddle as many who were twice or more her age.

Tonight she was playing at being a grown-up lady, and Travis felt a lump in his throat every time he looked at her. Not only was he touched by her attempt to live up to the maturity of the occasion, but he also thought that Gincie must have been very like her at the same age. Though Gincie had been only seventeen when he met her, he still wished he had known her even years before that.

Lexy tried to last, but she was curled in a chair sound asleep when the magic hour came. Her parents awakened her. "Just so you can tell your brothers you were up at midnight," Travis told her, and Lexy smiled sleepily and kissed both of them.

As the new year engulfed them, Gincie worried about having less and less time to spend with the children, but she was reassured by the fact that they had so many people at Wild Swan to love them as well as to teach them, and Doris Williams, their teacher, saw that their education had a steady pattern. Public education was still better in design than in application, and tutors had long been a tradition at Wild Swan.

Doris Williams had been at the farm for some time, fitting in quietly and proving herself well able to handle a class of mixed ages which included not only the Culhane children, but children of the workers at Wild Swan and Brookhaven as well. Doris was only in her early thirties, a slender, neatly kept woman with nut brown hair and eyes, but sometimes she seemed much older. She had lost her husband in the war, at Antietam, and six months later, her two-year-old daughter had died of scarlet fever. She was honest in confessing that teaching was her salvation.

Flora and Philly had recommended her to Wild Swan, and everyone was pleased with the arrangement. Doris liked the life on the farm, and she handled the children easily because she believed that teachers and students ought to be partners, not adversaries. Even the twins, who could be more than a handful, behaved for her most of the time because she held their interest. In the summer, she went to visit her two sisters, who were married and lived in the western part of the state, but she considered Wild Swan her home.

"Mrs. Williams says," was an often-heard phrase, to the extent that Gincie sometimes had to remind herself not to feel jealous. Though the twins would be only six this year, both of them read quite well and formed their letters with enthusiasm, albeit their spelling was somewhat creative.

K. C. had, in his experiments with pen and paper, changed the spelling of his name to "Kace."

"It is more like a real name, a real boy's name," he insisted with some strong inner logic, and his mother could hardly dispute him since she had insisted on being called "Gincie" when she was much younger than her son, though her given name had been Virginia, for Alex's grandmother.

"Kace Culhane," Travis said, giving the name its proper dignity and hiding his amusement. "It's a good name. You may have to remind us for a while, but we'll get used to it."

Tay, thinking he ought to assert his own control in imitation of his twin, requested that he be called "Taylor," and everyone complied for a while, but it was Tay himself who called it off. "I keep thinking you're talking to somebody else. I want to go back to the old way."

The children had chores to perform on the farm, everything from collecting eggs from the chickens, ducks, and geese—a sometimes hazardous duty—to helping in the gardens as the seasons advanced, to working around the horse barns. Though there were many tasks connected with the horses that required too much strength or were too dangerous for them, the children were allowed to help with the feeding and with keeping the leather of saddles and bridles clean and supple and the buckles and bits polished. All three of them were so enamored of the racehorses that they even considered mucking out stalls more of a privilege than a duty.

Their parents considered that the time spent learning and observing life on the farm taught lessons every bit as important as those in the classroom, and they were especially grateful that Alex was still here to pass on her own deep harmony with the land.

The enduring rhythm of life at Wild Swan was a major influence on Travis's decision to buy the neighboring farm. With the continuing effects of the financial panic, the family that owned the land had lost so much from speculating in railroads and various stocks, they were selling off assets as quickly as possible. They had not been good or even very interested farmers for several generations, their financial ventures having turned away from the land, the farm relegated to a hobby and country retreat while the family spent most of their time in the capital.

The house and outbuildings were beginning to show signs of neglect, and the fields, once planted with tobacco and grain, were overgrown. But Travis saw the promise. And if he purchased the place, land belonging to the Falconers and Culhanes would stretch from Brookhaven on one side through Wild Swan to these acres that touched Wild Swan on the other side.

It would mean a large initial investment, plus the cost of improvements after purchase, but it would greatly expand Wild Swan's potential facilities both for raising fodder and for increasing the breeding stock.

The irony of the situation didn't escape Travis. While many people had lost or were losing their fortunes, his and Gincie's was improving, most specifically in regard to the mining shares in Nevada. They had cost little because the area had been judged barren of valuable ore, but Travis, Boston, and a few other investors had disagreed with that judgment and had continued to invest in exploration. And now they were sharing in some of the same luck that was making Messrs. Mackay, Fair, Flood, and O'Brien fabulously wealthy from heavy veins of silver.

But neither Boston nor Travis had any illusions about earning the ultimate dollar from their own shares. They had already sold shares that had returned a handsome profit, and Travis trusted Boston to choose the time to sell off more. But they were not the principal owners, and it was impossible to control the mine's output if one wasn't at the site most of the time. Though Boston was making frequent trips to Nevada, he knew he could not oversee the operation the way he did the rest of his enterprises.

Land—it would always be the most important and enduring investment Travis could imagine, something he understood and trusted. Not land that might or might not yield precious ore, but acres that would, with care, produce crops and sustain livestock.

He admitted his lack of vision when he discussed the neighboring farm with Gincie. "It is your money as much as mine that will be invested, and with the stock exchange still in such disarray, there are undoubtedly stocks that are undervalued now, that might prove highly profitable before too long. It's slow, but the country will recover; I'm sure of that. There's too much wealth for it not to. The farm is no sure thing, not for an investment we could resell any time soon. It's good for us just because more land means more room for more horses. And it would take a lot of fixin' in the next few years, a lot of money."

"Are you trying to talk me out of it?" Gincie asked with a smile. She was ecstatic about the idea of buying the farm. To her, it meant that Travis's commitment to their life away from California was growing deeper and deeper.

"Do you mean for us to live there?" she asked. She didn't want to leave Wild Swan, but she saw how he might.

He quickly put her fears to rest. "No, I think the big house ought to be repaired and kept up, just so we don't lose it, but I don't want us to leave Wild Swan. It will still be the center of our work, and more important, I don't want the children to lose what they have here. They wouldn't see their great-grandparents as much, nor Della, Padraic, and the rest if we lived over there."

A shiver ran through Gincie, and Travis looked at her inquiringly.

She took his hand and pressed it to her cheek for a moment. "Hard to explain," she murmured, her throat suddenly tight. "Just that it's one of those times when I'm so happy, it's hard to contain it all at once."

Travis put his arm around her, hugging her to his side. "What do you say to namin' it 'Sunrise Farm'? Somehow that sounds better than 'the old Sprague place.' "

La Salida del Sol, the golden acres in California; Sunrise Farm, the green land in Maryland: By the choosing of the name, Travis was acknowledging his belief in the continuation of their dreams, first in California and now in Maryland. It was, to Gincie, a gift beyond price.

Chapter 12

By late spring, Sunrise Farm belonged to the Culhanes. Alex was as pleased as Gincie by this development, for while she had once resigned herself to the possibility that Wild Swan would end with her own death, now it seemed ever more certain that Gincie and Travis would carry it on. Her only worry was that the couple would over-work in trying to improve the property without neglecting Wild Swan; after nearly losing Morgan, Alex did not want to see any of the rest of the family so endangered. But Gincie assured her that they had every intention of taking it slowly and of delegating authority to a good overseer.

They hired Lemuel Washington. Though his parents had been slaves on the Eastern Shore of Maryland, Lem had been freed while he was still quite young. He was in his early thirties, could read and cipher on a basic level, and could do anything with horses.

They hired others, black and white, not a huge number, but enough to work the land efficiently, and they were so pleased to have solved the problem of staffing Sunrise that it came as a shock when Della and Padraic approached them to tell them that all was not as settled as it seemed at the new farm.

"I know that Lem looks like Samson did in his young days," Della told them bluntly, "and with horses, he may be nearly as skilled as my husband was. But he's not the same man. He's not dishonest or anything of that sort that I know of, but he's no good with the other workers. He demands too much with too little explanation and no patience at all."

"It's true. He's got a foine idea a' how Sunrise should be, an' he expects everyone there to be seein' it his way. You'll be losin' good men if Lem doesn't cease to be so unraiseenable." The Irish in Padraic's voice was very evident in his intensity.

Neither Travis nor Gincie wanted to believe it, but it was difficult to ignore the words of these two they trusted so well, and after hearing the report, the situation at Sunrise looked different to them from the way it had previously. None of the workers came forward to complain, but they were too quiet, casting furtive glances at each other while Lem was pointing out this or that improvement. It was not difficult to understand the reticence; good jobs were difficult to find, given the number of freed blacks who were still drifting northward looking for a better life.

"Della's right," Gincie confessed to Travis. "In some ways, Lem does remind me of Samson, and Samson was such a wonderful part of my life at Wild Swan while I was growing up, it's made me blind."

"Damn! I hate the idea of havin' to tell him it's not workin' out, but it's got to be done," Travis said, and in the end they went together to face the disagreeable task.

It was an agonizing interview. Lem obviously thought Travis intended to speak to him about a new project or to praise him for work already done, and as it began to dawn on the man that this was not the case at all, Gincie watched his expression change from confidence to bewilderment to hopelessness.

"I want you to know that no one at Sunrise has said anything against you, not a word, but it is evident that things are not goin' smoothly. No one could doubt your skill with the horses, but you don't seem to handle people as well. Mrs. Culhane and I have enough to worry about without frettin' that the workers will grow discontented enough to leave. I regret very much havin' to tell you this, but it just won't work out with you being' the overseer at Sunrise."

It would have been much easier if the big man had raged at them, but he didn't. His hands pleated the brim of his battered hat, and his throat rippled convulsively. Gincie's own throat tightened as she saw how close Lem was to tears at the wreck of his great opportunity.

"It may not be something you wish to do," she said. "After being in charge, you may not feel like working at someone else's command, but you are so good with the horses, would you consider staying on to work with them? It would mean doing so at the direction of another man, but if he is good at his job, then you should be allowed to do yours well, too."

It was not an offer they had intended to make, but Travis was willing to try it; he felt as badly as Gincie did at Lem's distress.

The meeting was taking place in the main house, but the sounds of the farm drifted in, loud in contrast to the silence of the three in the room.

For a long time, Lem studied the floor, and when he spoke, his voice was so low, Gincie and Travis had to strain to hear. "I neva been th' boss befo'. I want to do it right, but I know it's goin' wrong from th' start. I jes' doan know how t' tell a man t'do somethin' without tellin' him jes' how t'do every bit of it. Hosses you kin tell that way, but no man with any brains gonna put up with that. I be betta workin' jes' with th' hosses, an' I thanks you fo' th' chance." He paused, his hands once more working his hat. "Mebbe you make that Mr. McCoy th' boss. He do a good job."

"We'll certainly consider it," Travis managed to say, though he was surprised at the suggestion. He extended his hand. "I'm pleased you have decided to stay. The horses are very important to us, and we will know they are in good hands."

As soon as Lem had gone, Travis asked Gincie, "Why in the world would he suggest Michael McCoy? Among other things, the man has only been here for a short time, and he's white."

Gincie considered the matter carefully before she ventured a guess. "I think it might be just because of those things that Lem could bear to work under him, a matter of saving dignity. It's the usual thing after all, for a white man to be boss to black men, and the very fact that McCoy has only been here for a short time will make it seem plausible that we intended to replace Lem all along with a white man as soon as we found someone suitable."

"It makes sense," Travis conceded. "But it has little to do with how we really feel about the situation. It reinforces old ways we fought so hard against."

"So we have a choice," Gincie said. "If McCoy is qualified, we go along with Lem's plan and seem just as prejudiced as the people we despise, even though black and white workers, aside from the overseer, have equal rights here. Or we take the chance of losing Lem altogether if we choose some other man, black or white, from here or someplace else to superintend Sunrise."

"Carin' about what other people think is a waste of time,"

Travis said, and Gincie knew he was talking about more than their current situation.

"So we'll see if Mr. McCoy wants the job and if he can do it," she finished for him.

They made a point of explaining to Michael McCoy that Lem was relinquishing his position as headman because he thought he could be more useful with more time to spend on the horses. McCoy betrayed no sign that he was aware there were other reasons, and he was openly grateful that Lem had recommended him.

Michael was a simple man in the best and rarest sense of the word. Differences in skin color did not concern him. He judged a man by how well he could do a job, how well he could provide for himself and his family, and how fairly he treated other people. He was thirty-five, had been raised on a Pennsylvania farm, and had married his childhood sweetheart when they were both eighteen. He had gone to war with the Union Army when he was twenty-two, and after the war, he had taken his family west to Ohio. He and his wife, Mildred, had had three sons: Willy, born a year before the war ended, and Timmy and Johnny, born right afterward, in 1866 and 1867. But in 1872, Mildred had died in childbirth and the infant with her, and Michael had given up life in Ohio to return to the Eastern Seaboard. For the past two years, he had been living and working on the family farm, but it was crowded with two of his brothers and their families there as well, and besides, he had always had an interest in blooded horses. The opportunity to work at Sunrise, with its connection to Wild Swan, appealed mightily to him.

He was redheaded, freckle-faced, and rawboned, and his sons looked so much like him it was difficult to discern what impact Mildred had had on her offspring, unless she had looked exactly like her husband. The three boys had already formed tentative ties with the children at Sunrise, Wild Swan, and Brookhaven, and that pleased their father greatly. He knew how disrupted their lives had been by the loss of their mother.

Michael was more than willing to accept the position at Sunrise and confident that he and Lem and the other workers would get along fine.

The Culhanes were relieved that the arrangement seemed to be working, for it was a busy, confusing season. Though the yearling sale went well, Wild Swan's entries for the racing seasons were plagued by injuries and illnesses, despite the good care the horses received. One of the best two-year-olds ran himself into a fence and was out for the season. Two of the three-year-olds contracted a respiratory ailment that would keep them out of racing at least until the fall season and possibly beyond that. And one of Travis's best jumpers suddenly began, for no explicable reason, to refuse hurdles he had sailed over before.

They tried to console themselves with the knowledge that they had a fine crop of new foals for the future and some steady, healthy older horses who were entered in the races. No stable escaped off years; such were part of the game. And good care of their livestock kept them in the running more often than not. Still, it was difficult to know they would have to forfeit some races and would give a doubtful showing in others. Alex and Rane decided to accompany the Culhanes to most of the meetings, to provide moral support, as Alex put it.

But before they left for the first of the race meetings in New York State, they had a visit from Phoebe. She arrived with no warning, and she had Joseph with her but not Aubrey. Gincie was not the only member of the family who wondered if Phoebe had left her husband for good, but Phoebe quickly disabused everyone of that notion.

"I just needed to get away from our work for a while, and Joseph needs to see his cousins. It's been four years."

Gincie was saddened to see how worn and tired Phoebe looked, so much older than she had four years before. But at least there had been visible improvement in Joseph. At seven years old, he was far more outgoing than he had been as a small child, and he played happily with his cousins.

"We've really tried," Phoebe told Gincie. "Our visit that Christmas made us both see how burdened Joseph was with our work, our attitudes. We were making him into a little old man."

"I think you've done very well," Gincie told her.

"It grows harder every day to think of being without him, but the time will come," Phoebe said, and there was a world of sorrow in her eyes. "I have discovered I have more maternal feelings than I knew."

"But surely he is doing so well and is so much a part of your life now . . ." Gincie's voice trailed off.

"Aubrey and I have changed in our behavior toward our son, and as a result, Joseph has changed. But the work we are doing and the way it is received by too many whites has not changed. And we can't stop teaching." She stared at her hands as she interlaced her fingers first one way and then another. "There are good and bad men, black and white, who are, in their various ways, using or abusing power to reshape the South. But the overwhelming truth is that the bigots will win. They are willing to use violent means, and they increasingly have the sympathy of those who, while they would not commit acts of violence themselves, are determined that blacks will have no share financially, politically, or otherwise in the South, not as long as the share means power. And even the mildest of Southerners hates having federal troops policing the large cities. Yet when the last of those troops are withdrawn, the South will be free to do as it wills. Consider Louisiana. There is open rebellion there now against federal authority."

While Gincie sympathized as much as ever with her cousin, she found it difficult to do more than listen; there was little she could think of to say. She herself had taken great risks in helping to guide slaves out of bondage before the war, but she had had no children then, no division of loyalty and responsibility.

Phoebe was accustomed to being loved by her family and to being supported in whatever she endeavored to do, but she was not accustomed to full understanding of her single-minded devotion to teaching the freed slaves in the South. It wasn't that the members of her family did not take their own various pursuits very seriously, it was that they had other interests and a more tempered view of what life ought to be. She knew they worried about her, and she appreciated their concern, but they pitied her as well, and that made her uncomfortable and resentful, even though she knew she ought to be hardened to it by now. It created a subtle barrier that was always there between herself and them, and she regretted it most of all between herself and her sisters. She was as careful in what she said to them as they were with her. On her last visit, she had found it easier to talk to Gincie than to her sisters, and she dreaded seeing them this time, as necessary as it was.

Leaving Joseph securely ensconced at Wild Swan, she went first to Georgetown to visit Larissa. She admired her niece and her nephews, toured the nation's capital, understood Larissa's pride in her children and her husband, and felt all along that they were even further apart than they had been before. Larissa's life seemed to bear no resemblance to her own.

She expected to have the same experience of alienation when she went to Baltimore to be with Anthea and their parents, and at first it was. Then, quite suddenly, it changed.

Since Anthea's normal working day began early and finished late, Phoebe spent the days visiting with her mother at the school and her father at his office, as well as seeing Rane, Morgan, and Adam at the shipyard. She also had supper one evening with Adam and Mercy, who was happily pregnant with their first child. Anthea, Max, and Nigel she saw only briefly, when their medical practice allowed.

But one afternoon, Anthea sought Phoebe out at their parents' house, where Phoebe was staying, and found her alone.

"You look as if you could use a cup of tea," Phoebe said. It was difficult not to stare because Anthea was behaving so unlike her usual calm self. Her eyes were wild, her movements sharp and graceless.

"I could use a quart of brandy, but I'll settle for a cup of tea," Anthea said after gazing blankly at her sister for a moment, her mind far away. She stopped pacing and sank into a chair, pressing her fingers hard against her forehead as if to stop the thoughts rolling around in her brain.

"How do you stand the hate? Your own hate, how do you stand it? How do you keep from doing violence with it?" Anthea's voice hissed and then dropped to an elaborately even tone that was somehow all the more furious. "I lost a patient today. She died giving birth to her sixth child. The baby lived, but the mother died. She was all of twenty-five years old. She looked closer to fifty. I told her and her husband two babies ago that she was not strong enough to bear more children, that there were ways to prevent conception without giving up their physical love for each other. But they had been taught that intercourse is for creating children and that a woman's duty is to bear as many as God chooses to give her. God chooses! Ignorance chooses, not God! So now the man has four small children to raise—two of them have already died of the squalor and disease they live in—and no wife to help care for them. He hardly earns enough to feed himself. Before long, I'll be called to treat one or another of the remaining children, and if one or two of them survive into adulthood, it will be a miracle." She was shaking, and tears of rage filled her eyes.

"There is a movement afoot in this country to make it more and more difficult to obtain even the most basic information about preventing conception; Mr. Comstock's law makes it a criminal offense to send such information through the mail. And if he has his way, he will further reshape this country in his own mad image. He does not act alone; Congress passed his law last year. And even when I tell couples what they can do, I run up against the kind of attitude that killed my patient today."

She got up and began pacing the room again because she couldn't bear to be still. "Sanctimonious ignorance is being enshrined as never before. Matters pertaining to sexual congress and reproduction were more openly discussed when Gran was young than they are now. We are going backward!"

Her impassioned voice sank to a whisper. "My fury never leaves me these days. It is always here, inside of me."

When Anthea had started her tirade, Phoebe had thought she was being reprimanded, but she had swiftly realized that this was not the case, and she had sat in stunned silence, feeling so many things at once, it was difficult to sort them out. Empathy, compassion, wonder, admiration, and love, she felt all of these and more, that she had found a companion after years of being alone in her own family.

"I do what you do," she said as she recognized the truth. "I teach day by day in the hope that somewhere, sometime, I will make a difference. But you make a measurable difference. You save lives. Not always, I know. Today you lost someone. But remember all the others who are alive because of you."

Phoebe thought of how strange it was to have come from such openly affectionate parents and to be so awkward about expressing her own love. She swallowed nervously, and then she said very firmly, "I love you, Anthea. I love you and admire you enough to ask you if you and Max will take Joseph when it is time." Saying the words aloud gave her strength.

Now it was Anthea's turn to be stunned into silence as she listened to Phoebe explain, as she once had to Gincie, why Joseph could not remain with his parents indefinitely.

"Even if the political situation improved," Phoebe said in closing, "the world we have down there is too small. Joseph needs a wider horizon than we can offer him there. Next year or the year after that at the latest, I would like to send Joseph to you."

Though Anthea had not yet seen the change in Joseph, she could not doubt the sorrow in her sister's eyes as she spoke of sending Joseph away from her. She had never seen Phoebe so soft and yet so strong, and she could not mistake the depth of the trust and love her sister was offering. She knew that Phoebe had already visited Larissa, Larissa who had three children and a much more settled home life than the Kingstons, but she did not ask why Phoebe had not chosen the other household. She accepted the fact that her own fire, which made her so uncomfortable much of the time, was what made Phoebe comfortable with her now. And she knew that while it would affect Max as much as herself to take responsibility for Joseph, Max had so much love to give, he would have no reluctance.

She finally found her voice. "Max and I will do our best to make a good home for Joseph." She paused and then added with a shaky smile, "Do you ever wonder what it would be like to lead a normal life?"

Phoebe's peal of laughter was startling and welcome. "Normal? Growing up in our family? I don't mean it unkindly, but I suppose Larissa is the most 'normal' person I know, and frankly, her life doesn't seem real to me."

Anthea understood exactly what she meant.

Anthea and Max had felt both pity and affection for Joseph the last time they had seen him, but this time they fell in love with him. They visited with him as much as they could at Wild Swan before Phoebe took him south again, and though they did not frighten him with the possibility of being separated from his parents, they discussed the idea of his coming to them so that he could go to school in Baltimore some day.

"All the children in our family do that," Phoebe told her son. "And you'd have not only your Aunt Anthea and Uncle Max, but also your Grandma Philly and Grandpa Blaine and all the rest of the family to be with."

Joseph pondered this gravely before he said, "I guess it would be okay when I'm bigger."

He was considering it a plan for far in the future, and they did not enlighten him further, but Anthea's heart ached for the period of adjustment that would come sooner than the little boy knew.

Gincie was grateful that Phoebe had made the decision about which of her sisters would take Joseph, and it made her even more appreciative of her own three children.

"Please behave and try to stay out of trouble while we're gone," she cautioned them before the racing party went north. And then she added special words for Lexy. "I trust you to keep an eye on your brothers." And to the twins, "Please listen to your sister and don't make things difficult for her or for Della."

Gincie's last sight of them as she and Travis and the others left Wild Swan was of the three small straight figures standing side by side, waving furiously.

"We're very lucky," Travis said. "They're good children. They'll be fine while we're gone. Summer is splendid for them at Wild Swan."

Picturing them fishing, swimming, riding, and engaging in countless games as they did every summer made Gincie feel better about leaving them, just as Travis had intended.

Chapter 13

There were so many adventures to be enjoyed at Wild Swan, and they were given so much freedom, the children saw little reason to step outside of the few rules imposed for their safety.

They rose early in the morning, did their chores, and played so hard that nightfall found them happily exhausted. And they had every intention of behaving and managed to do so until the day before their parents were due home. But by then the Tinker had arrived.

The children had feared the Tinker from the first time they saw him, but he fascinated them nonetheless. His caravan made tinny music as it moved, with a seemingly endless array of tin pots, pans, and other domestic items clinking together. He sold all sorts of other oddments, ranging from ribbons to pins to secondhand clothes to nails and tools. And he would sharpen scissors and knives for a fee.

The children speculated about how many things the man was able to cram into his wagon. Tay guessed an even four thousand, but Kace thought the figure was somewhat less than that. Lexy wondered if the Tinker himself knew how many things he had.

The man was as strange as his conveyance. No matter what the weather, even now at the height of summer, he dressed in layers of old, flapping clothes, a dirty hat pulled down over his forehead, creating a shadow from which his dark eyes gleamed. He was probably of medium height, but it was hard to tell because he was stoop-shouldered, his head lowered as he peered out from under his hat. He never offered his name, and no one ever asked.

"He talks to himself more than to other people," Kace said. "Do you think he's really a crazy man?"

"Maybe he just likes talking to himself better than to other people," Lexy suggested, wanting to give the man the benefit of the doubt, but a shiver ran down her spine when she thought of him.

No one at Wild Swan liked having him about, and Della objected to his presence too near the buildings because she believed he'd steal anything that wasn't nailed down. Della always had the children count the poultry when the Tinker was near. But Alex and

Rane maintained that as long as he caused no harm, the man was welcome to camp on their land on his way through the area.

Lexy and the twins had spent the hot summer afternoon getting as close to the Tinker's camp as they dared, feeling excited and guilty as they spied on him, and now they were resting safely in the woods.

"I want to get closer to look at that old horse. I don't think the Tinker treats him right," Tay said.

Of the three of them, he had the tenderest heart when it came to the animal kingdom. He could not bear to see any creature suffer and spent hours watching his great-grandmother, his mother, Padraic, and anyone else who doctored the livestock.

Conscious of her role as the oldest and wisest of the three, Lexy felt compelled to tell the truth. "That horse belongs to the Tinker. Even if it doesn't seem right, I think that means he can do what he wants with it. Willy McCoy told me that some people even eat horses." Her own horror at that idea was reflected on the twins' faces.

"Too bad horses aren't like lions, then they could eat them back," Tay suggested after some thought.

This brought a snort of disgust from Kace. "Then if you fell off your horse, he might eat you before you could get back on."

"And instead of hay and grain, Mama and Papa and Gran would have to raise chickens and pigs and cows to feed the horses." Lexy joined in the nonsense, hoping to divert Tay from his plan of further spying, but he was single-minded when it came to the welfare of an animal.

"I still want to get closer to look at that horse," he insisted.

"We've been told to stay away from the Tinker," Lexy reminded him, but it made no impression.

"I'll go by myself if you won't go with me," he said, looking first at his twin and then at his sister.

"Well, I guess we could," Kace agreed, and Lexy surrendered, knowing that he was already plotting the best way to accomplish what Tay wanted. Short of tattling on them, there was no way to stop them.

"He goes fishing and after rabbits all the time. We could get closer then. He just leaves his things there." Just for a moment, guilt was clear on Tay's face as he considered the fact that the Tinker felt so safe on Wild Swan land that he trusted nothing would happen to his possessions. But then his concern for the animals reasserted itself. "Nobody should be mean to animals!"

They briefly considered enlisting other children from Wild Swan or the McCoys from Sunrise to serve as added troops, but they all decided that that would just add to the difficulty.

" 'Specially that Willy McCoy," Tay said. "He shows off so much, he'd do something dumb."

Lexy thought the three of them were doing something dumb, but nonetheless, she went sneaking belly down with her brothers through the lush growth of summer. Her last hope for a reprieve faded when, after long moments, they saw the Tinker leave with a fishing pole and a gunnysack. There was still bright light in the summer afternoon, and they were sure the Tinker knew as well as they that the fish would not be biting for a long while yet, so he planned to be away for some time. Still, they waited some more to be sure he wasn't coming back immediately. Lexy felt the beat of her heart as if it were a separate wild thing trying to jump from her chest.

Finally Kace whispered, "Come on. It should be all right now."

Curious as they were about the Tinker's caravan, they were careful not to touch anything. The horse was their only goal, and they lessened their guilt by reminding themselves that the Tinker had two horses—the young, fairly healthy looking bay that pulled his wagon and the older horse, who didn't look strong enough to pull anything, though he had gall marks that showed where he had carried bundles on his back.

The minute Lexy and Kace got a closer look at the animal, their doubts about what they were doing vanished.

The gelding's brown coat was dull and mangy; his bones tented the hide in prominent ridges. Flies buzzed around the sores where the packs had rubbed him raw. Deep hollows etched his temples, and he stood with his eyelids drooping, his head down as if it were too heavy to support.

"Poor fellow," Tay crooned, offering a hand for the animal to sniff by way of introduction. "Padraic could fix you. I bet it's your teeth that're causing you to look so sorry."

"You know, if he wasn't so skinny, he wouldn't be a bad-looking horse," Kace observed. Young as they were, judging horse-flesh was something they'd been learning from the cradle.

"If we're really going to take him, we'd better do it," Lexy said, glancing around to make sure the Tinker wasn't coming back. She was resigned to her brothers' intention to rescue the horse.

Aside from a soft nicker to the younger horse, the brown went with them without protest, nuzzling Tay's shoulder as he led him.

Kace carefully wiped the ground with a branch wherever their prints showed, but he knew that wasn't going to be enough to hide what they'd done. "Lampblack and boot polish!" he exclaimed.

"What are you talking about?" Lexy asked, wishing they were miles away.

"Della keeps lampblack, boot polish, and stuff in her cupboards. We can use them to make the horse look different," Kace explained. "At least until we're sure the Tinker won't find him."

"I think we ought to call him 'Tinker,' " Tay said, wholly involved in leading the horse and talking to him on the way.

"I think we'd bettter only call him Tinker to ourselves for a while, and we've got to find a place to hide him, and we've got to feed him," Lexy pointed out. She wished she weren't so good at thinking of the consequences of everything, and she didn't want to think at all about the fact that her parents and great-grandparents would be returning to Wild Swan on the morrow. She took courage from the poor condition of the horse; he needed their help, and that was that.

It was Lexy who slipped into the house to pilfer the necessary items, flattening herself against the wall and shaking with the pounding of her heart when she heard Della speaking to one of the housemaids close by. Even when she was outside again with her bundle, she felt as if guilt were written all over her, and it was all she could do not to break and run for the woods. Instead, she skipped along as if she hadn't a care in the world and nodded a return to the greetings of various workers.

Kace had been on his own mission, invading the stables to procure some grain and a pot of salve for the horse's sores. "Jotham almost saw me, but I hid behind some feed bins," he said proudly, but his face was as pale as Lexy's.

"Try not to get too much on your hands," she cautioned her brothers as they began to transform the horse from brown to black, "or Della will notice."

They used the rags Lexy had brought, and they darkened the coat with lampblack and a little water and used the thicker boot polish to cover the white markings on the horse's forehead and his two white stockings. Tay carefully applied salve to the sores. Throughout the entire procedure, the horse stood patiently, seeming to enjoy all the attention. However, he didn't do as well with the grain they offered him. He tried to eat it, but Tay's diagnosis of bad teeth was obviously correct, and more grain fell out of his mouth than went down.

"We're going to have to get Padraic to fix his teeth," he repeated.

"Well, we can't do that now. Padraic won't be back until tomorrow," Kace pointed out reasonably. "And anyway, we're trying to hide him, not show everybody we've got him."

There was no way the ailing beast would blend in with the blood horses, so they decided to put him out to pasture with the workhorses and the hacks that some of the workers kept and traded.

As long as the hands got their work done, and as long as there was sufficient room on the farm, they were allowed to carry on horse trading of their own.

The children were conscious of the hour growing later. Soon Della would be looking for them for supper, and the last round of chores for the day would have the men wandering about. But still they stayed long enough to be sure the other horses would not turn on the newcomer. They knew enough about herd habits to know it was less likely to happen here where there were no stallions, only geldings and mares, and where the members of the herd changed as horses were frequently bought, sold, and traded, thus preventing clear dominance.

Aside from a few sniffs, snorts, and sharp little squeals, the newcomer was accepted quite readily, and for his part, seemed quite willing to make new friends where allowed.

"It's still so hot, they probably don't have the energy to fight," Lexy suggested.

"I think it's because he smells more like a lamp or a pair of boots than a horse," Kace said, and that set them off in nervous giggles.

Following Lexy's dictates, they had managed to keep most of the black off of their persons, but they were still a dirty, disheveled group even after washing as best they could in one of the horse troughs.

Della took one look at them and said, "Soap and water, lots of soap!" But she wasn't angry, and she suspected nothing out of the ordinary. The children at Wild Swan were expected to play hard and to get dirty in the course of it. However, when the three of them appeared scrubbed and brushed for supper, she eyed them more closely. They seemed subdued and excited at the same time, all three of them, and they were paying extraordinary attention to their plates.

"Is there anything you would like to tell me?" she asked and waited.

Lexy thought the silence was going to strangle her, and she could have kissed Kace when he said, "I guess we're just excited about Mama and Papa and everybody coming home tomorrow."

Though it sounded like a reasonable explanation, Della wasn't convinced, but as long as none of the children seemed to be injured, nothing at the farm had burned down, and none of the men was reporting damage anywhere, she decided not to press them further.

For Lexy and the twins, the next couple of days and nights seemed to be the longest in their lives. None of them slept much, and they spent the next day waiting for their plot to be discovered by someone on the farm or by the Tinker himself. In addition, they tried to avoid their usual playmates, fearing they would give something away.

After suggesting a variety of activities and receiving refusals for his pains, Willy McCoy took his brothers and stalked off, declaring that there were other children at the farm who were more fun to play with than the Culhanes.

Hardest of all was staying away from the horse, but the three of them agreed that was the most important thing they could do, so as not to draw attention to him.

The Tinker arrived before their parents did, and the minute they saw him, Lexy and the twins headed for the hay barn, hiding in the dusty darkness, their shaky whispers blending with the eternal rustle of cats, mice, and birds.

"He didn't ride the other horse; he just walked in, so the other horse isn't here to call to ours," Tay said. He at least had no doubt about who the brown-black gelding belonged to now.

"Unless he looks real close, I don't see how he'd know that black horse is his. And there're a lot of horses here," Kace offered.

Lexy's thoughts were more complicated. "He didn't *march* in, he just walked in, so I don't think he really expects to find the horse here. And there's something else—he isn't kind to his animals, so why would he ever think anyone would steal a horse to help it? He probably thinks if anyone was going to steal one of his horses, they'd take the younger, stronger one. So maybe he believes the old one just wandered off, just like we want him to believe."

"I wish he didn't look so poor," Tay whispered, and his siblings stared at him in dismay. But neither of them was surprised. It had been his plan in the first place, but his exceedingly kind heart was sometimes as difficult for them to live with as it was for him.

"Being poor doesn't make being mean all right," Kace insisted, and Tay had to concede the point.

By the time they crept out of the barn, the Tinker was long gone, and though they dared not ask anyone directly what had happened, the muttered comments they overheard told them enough.

"Lookin' fo' his hoss, jes' bet. Mo' like Della say, here fo' chicken stealin'."

"But Della gave him somethin' to eat."

"Della feed de Debil she think he hungry."

"I hope he wasn't really hungry," Tay muttered.

By the time their parents, great-grandparents, and the rest of the racing party arrived home, the children were dazed with the tension of their secret, and even in the confusion of greetings, Gincie noticed. She touched Lexy's forehead. "Are you feverish?"

"No, Mama, truly, just glad to have you home."

Gincie had to accept the explanation, for none of the children seemed to be ailing physically, but Travis agreed they were up to something or had been.

"It's probably not serious except to them," he said with a smile. "Maybe Tay's savin' mice from the barns again. The other two never have the heart to stop him."

"I don't mind if he saves them from the cats as long as he doesn't keep them in the house," Gincie retorted. "I wonder if Tay appreciates how patient his brother is about the creatures that have shared their room from time to time."

But when she asked Tay, he looked completely blank before he answered, "No, Mama. There's no mice in our room, honest! Unless they're living there on their own."

Mice were the furthest thing from Tay's mind. Now that Padraic was back, he wanted to ask him to look at the horse's teeth, and he kept suggesting ways to enlist the Irishman's aid without giving away the secret.

"We can't do it yet!" Lexy told him in exasperation. "We have to make sure the Tinker's gone, and then we're still going to have trouble explaining where we got the horse."

They suffered through the evening meal of their parents' first night home waiting for the subject of the Tinker's missing horse to be raised by Della or someone else. When it didn't happen, they breathed a collective sigh of relief. But when the next day dawned, they had to face the fact that their parents and their great-grandmother would be walking and riding about the place all day long, checking on how things had gone in their absence.

"I wish they were all going back to Baltimore with Grandpa Rane," Tay grumbled.

"I care about the horse, but I don't want to be an orphan for it," Lexy said, though it had occurred to her that if their parents found out what they'd done, it might be better to be an orphan.

Kace managed to sneak off to the Tinker's camp and returned to report that the man was still there. "Maybe he thinks his horse will just come back. Maybe he's going to stay there until it does."

"That's the worst idea yet," Lexy said.

By nightfall, no mention had yet been made about the horse, and the children began to think that perhaps he would just become part of the farm without anyone noticing.

The next morning was the beginning of the end, though none of them realized it. The day was hot and more humid than usual because the sky was heavy with building clouds, and by afternoon, the rainstorm had begun. As the first drops began to spatter on the ground, Lexy's eyes widened, and she clapped a hand to her mouth. "Uh-oh!"

Kace shared the thought, followed swiftly by Tay. Without another word, the three of them scurried to the barn for shelter from more than the rain.

Their hope that the rain would be light and pass over quickly was dashed by the thunder of sound on the barn roof.

Finally Lexy said, "We can't stay here forever." They stayed only until the rain let up, and when they emerged, it was to discover that their dread had come true.

The horse had been led up to the main paddock area. Water dripped in black rivulets from his coat, but now he looked more brown than black, though the boot polish still covered the white markings fairly well.

Jotham was leading the horse; Padraic looked curious, and the children had never heard their great-grandmother sound so angry before.

"You all know I do not object to your horse trading," Alex said, "but I will not tolerate any sort of chicanery, and I cannot think of any honest reason to disguise a horse's true identity." She looked from one face to another as the workers continued to gather. "Unless, of course, one of you had been deceived and purchased this beast thinking it was another."

She waited for someone to volunteer information, but no one did.

Lexy could hardly bear the expressions on her parents' faces as they stood flanking Alex, and worse, she saw the dawning comprehension on the workers' faces. They were obviously connecting the disappearance of the Tinker's horse with the animal before them and with the children, yet not one of them suggested that Lexy or the twins might be involved.

"We did it," Lexy said softly, and then she repeated it more loudly as the three of them stepped forward.

Suddenly the children were the focus of all eyes, and then Tay squared his shoulders and announced, "It was my idea." He stepped up to the horse and rubbed its head gently, smearing wet lamp black and waxy boot polish on his hands and earning a rumble of welcome. "The Tinker wasn't taking care of him. He has sores, and he needs his teeth fixed so he can eat better."

"It might've been Tay's idea, but we helped," Kace confessed, and he and Lexy went to stand beside their brother.

Travis had a strong and totally unacceptable urge to laugh as he contemplated the fact that his children were surely the youngest horse thieves in the country, but he suppressed his smile.

Alex and Gincie were having the same problem, but Alex's first concern was to set matters straight with her employees. "I apologize for suspecting you of this deed," she said. "I should have known none of you would indulge in such a scheme." To her relief, the hands looked as amused as she felt, but Alex and the Culhanes knew that they had to impress the children with the seriousness of the crime.

"The first thing the three of you will do is to give that animal a thorough bath," Travis told them gruffly. "Then you will come inside, and we will discuss this matter."

"Papa," Tay called softly as Travis turned away, "as long as the horse is here, can Padraic look at his teeth?"

"All right," Travis agreed. As they went into the house, he said to Gincie and Alex, "We think of Lexy and Kace as being the leaders, but no one is more stubborn than Tay when he's out to right a wrong."

The first audible laughter escaped from Alex once she was safely inside, and then Travis and Gincie were laughing with her. "I know it is perfectly reprehensible to be so amused, but I can't help sympathizing with them, and it's only too easy to imagine what an extraordinary amount of effort they put into this project. It's no easy task to disguise a horse head to tail. I'll leave you to explain the morality of the situation to them. There are some privileges to being a great-grandmother." It was Alex's graceful way of saying she would not interfere with parental authority.

Gincie and Travis had managed to control their mirth by the time the children appeared before them. While the horse might have improved in appearance with the bath, the children seemed to have transferred most of the blacking to their persons.

"It was harder to get it off the horse than to put it on," Lexy explained.

"We think we'll call him 'Tinker,' " Tay said, his chin set just so, indicating that while he knew he had to face the consequences of his action, he was not willing to give the horse back.

"The horse belongs to the Tinker," Travis reminded him. "You stole it from him, and you must return it."

Tay shook his head vigorously. "No, Papa, that just isn't fair! The Tinker doesn't deserve to own that horse if he can't take care of him."

"Taylor Culhane, that is not the way it works, and you know it," Gincie said. "The law says he owns that horse, and no matter what your reasons for taking it, it's stealing."

"Maybe he doesn't own it; maybe he stole it," Kace offered, coming to his brother's rescue.

"You have no reason to suspect that," Travis said, "and even if it were true, I believe you've heard the sayin' that 'two wrongs don't make a right'?"

Kace nodded reluctantly.

"The fact is that you've done the wrong thing for the right reasons," Travis explained, giving the children time to absorb what he was saying. "You would not like it at all if someone thought we didn't take good care of the horses at Wild Swan and decided to steal them from us."

"But the horses are taken care of here!" Lexy exclaimed, unable to keep silent at the suggestion of anything less than perfection at her beloved farm.

"You know that, and I know that," Travis agreed, "but there are more than a few people who think it is wrong to breed horses for sport."

Lexy's amazement at this heresy showed plainly on her face, but because her father had said it, it had to be true.

"Could we buy the horse?" Kace asked, and Travis groaned inwardly. He was no less vulnerable to the deplorable state of the stolen horse, and he found it no less difficult than the children did to imagine the horse going back to the neglectful owner. He didn't know quite how they were accomplishing it, but as the minutes ticked by, he was becoming more and more an ally of the children, rather than a disciplinarian, and Gincie wasn't helping.

"Do you think you have enough money?"

"I don't know," Kace admitted. "How much does a horse like that cost?"

"Too much, I fear, because the Tinker is goin' to be angry when he finds out that his horse was stolen instead of just wanderin' off."

To their credit, none of the children suggested the Tinker not be told of the theft, though Travis knew they were thinking how much easier it would be if they could just pretend to the man that they had "found" the horse and then ask him to sell it to them.

Money was a rarity in the children's lives. They earned pennies and nickels and sometimes a dime here and there for doing extra chores and from visitors who sometimes tossed a coin to them for carrying bags or doing some errand. But despite these contributions, the entire fortune of the three was three dollars and twenty-seven cents.

"Even I know that isn't enough to buy a horse," Tay said sadly.

At that moment, Travis lost the battle, and glancing at Gincie, he saw that she had too; she looked as downcast as the children.

"I tell you what," he said, "I'll take your three dollars and twenty-seven cents, and I'll add to it to buy the horse if the man will sell. But you're goin' to have to come with me to the Tinker's camp to tell him what you did and to apologize. Fair?"

The three faces brightened; they didn't fancy the prospect of apologizing to the Tinker, but they were heartened by the prospect of saving the gelding after all.

All five Culhanes trooped out to the Tinker's camp, but they left the horse behind. Travis didn't want the man to see the care that had already been lavished on the beast, though he didn't explain this bit of reasoning to the children, who had already faced their share of moral dilemmas this day.

The Tinker watched them approach his wagon. He gave no greeting, and his stance was less than welcoming.

"Our children have something to tell you," Travis said, and then he looked to the three.

Holding hands, they approached the man nervously, stopping just out of his reach. Lexy was afraid of what Tay might say, so she spoke first.

"Sir, we took . . . um, stole your horse, and we're sorry, really we are. We were worried about him." That was as diplomatic as she could manage to be. "But we shouldn't have done it anyway."

"We're sorry," the twins added in chorus.

The Tinker looked from one face to another without saying anything, and then he looked beyond the group, expecting the horse to be somewhere in the vicinity. His gaze swung slowly back to the Culhanes.

"So where's my horse? If th' brats harmed 'im, I'll have th' sheriff on 'em." His voice was as harsh as crows.

Not even the fact that his life was undoubtedly hard and lonely softened Gincie's flare of anger at his lack of direct response to the children and his reference to them as "brats," but she stopped herself from snapping back at the man because she now wanted the horse as much as the children did.

"Gincie, why don't you and the children go on back," Travis said, and playing the obedient wife, Gincie went, the children trailing behind her, though they would rather have stayed to see if their father succeeded in buying the horse.

When they got back to the house, Alex met them, her curiosity evident in her expression even before she spoke. "Has Wild Swan acquired the beast?"

"Not yet," Gincie replied, "and the advantage is surely the Tinker's. I fear this will not be Travis's best bargain in horse trading."

When Travis came in, his expression was such a mixture of triumph and outrage, Gincie laughed aloud. "How much did we pay for the horse?"

"Seventy-one dollars and seventy-three cents more than the children had," he admitted with a grimace.

"Seventy-five dollars for that animal!" Gincie exclaimed. "The Tinker ought to be charged with extortion."

"At least I got a promise that he won't come here again." Travis could too easily imagine Tay rescuing every ailing horse the Tinker chose to bring through.

But the fact that he had had to pay seventy-five dollars impressed the children immensely.

"That's so much money!" Lexy gasped, and the twins were as stunned as she. It was a sum so far out of their ken, they could scarcely picture the pile of coins it would take to equal it.

Travis used their awe to his advantage. "It is indeed. And I want all of you to promise you won't ever take it upon yourselves to steal another horse or any other animal to rescue it. Come to us if you see a creature being abused, and we'll do what we can. But the fact is that until there are better laws to protect animals, there isn't much we can do, and we certainly can't afford to buy every beast that has a bad owner." They looked so distressed, he couldn't resist adding, "But now, you own a horse that needs special care. 'Tinker's Ransom' might be a better name, but I guess 'Tinker' will do."

They brightened immediately at the prospect of going to see how their new acquisition was doing, and they were on their way, except for Lexy.

Gincie stopped her momentarily. "I know Tay is difficult to resist, but you are nine years old, three years older than the twins. Please do try to keep them out of further mischief, at least for a few days."

Lexy nodded dutifully, but Alex saw that her green eyes were suddenly tear bright as she followed her brothers.

It was too much for Alex. "My dears, I cannot think of better parents; you are raising marvelous children. And I can't think of anything worse than a great-grandmother who interferes. But I must plead Lexy's case. She does the best she can with two very lively brothers. They look up to her, and she adores them. But she is not a parent. She's just their sister. They know when they're doing something wrong, and she is not responsible for what they decide to do, only for what she does. In the case of this horse, they all did wrong, but they all acted out of good heart. Lexy is already the voice of conscience for the trio; it would be sad if she felt she had to be the jailer, too."

Gincie wanted to protest that she was not guilty of overburdening Lexy, but she could hear her own voice saying, "You're older, you must be more responsible than your brothers," too many times. She looked at Travis, and he shared the thought, admitting, "Lexy's always seemed so grown-up, we do expect a great deal of her. And when I think of how much trouble we have outthinkin' the twins, it seems pretty unjust to expect Lexy to do it even better."

Gincie gave her grandmother a quick hug. "We'll speak to her, I promise."

Gincie and Travis were even more grateful to Alex's advice once they talked to Lexy because she was so relieved. "I do try," she said, "but they think of new things to do so fast! And sometimes they make me see it their way even when I know it's wrong." Given the persuasive powers of the twins, this was not a startling revelation.

"They do the same thing to us," Travis told his daughter.

He couldn't help but think that the twins had some special spirit guarding their mischief, a spirit particularly evident in the horse Tinker. Once Padraic had floated the gelding's teeth, filing them to give a more even eating surface, the horse began to put on weight and to acquire a glossy coat in the process. He had looked ancient in his neglected state, but with care, his true age of nine or ten became evident. He had been trained to saddle and also to working in harness. When they tried hitching him to a light gig, he took to it immediately. And he carried himself as if he took great pride in being back at work. But this picture of dignity was somewhat spoiled by the friendship that developed between Tinker and a hound kept by one of the hands for coon hunting. The two animals seemed utterly content in each other's company. When Tinker was ridden by the children or hitched to the gig, the hound, Blue, went along with them. And when let out of the paddock, Tinker could be trusted to follow the children as readily as the dog followed him.

Watching the procession heading for the woods one day, Travis said, "I'm beginning to think that seventy-five dollars was a bargain for that horse."

Chapter 14

When Phoebe left Maryland, she felt more at peace than she had in years, not only because she had found an ally in Anthea, but also because she finally felt that Joseph's future was assured. She had no doubt that Anthea and Max would take good, loving care of him, and she began to make firm plans to send him north the following year when he was eight. She envisioned him spending a few carefree weeks at Wild Swan next summer and then starting school and a new life in Baltimore in the fall.

She mentioned her plan to Aubrey casually, as if it were only a vague possibility to be considered in the future. She did it as a means of laying the ground, so that when the time came, she could claim, "Remember, I spoke to you about this."

She had long since realized that Aubrey's defense against the worsening situation around them was to retreat more and more into his vision of a perfect world. Often she thought he would be better off living in a utopian community somewhere rather than coping with the daily reality of trying to teach frightened, impoverished blacks to read and write in a place where some whites were willing to kill to keep that from happening.

The number of their pupils, children and adults, increased as the seasonal work slackened with the onset of cooler weather. Sometimes Phoebe found herself moved to tears by the simplest things, by the painstaking care her pupils took to appear neat and clean when they came to school, even if their clothing was in tatters, and by the pleasure so many of them took in each small advancement in their education. She thought of how much she and others who were raised in a tradition of learning took schooling for granted, while for these people, each step was a treasured gift.

But in spite of the satisfaction she still got from teaching, Phoebe discovered that her new bond with Anthea underscored a definite lack in her life. She had not realized before how isolated she was from normal friendships, particularly with other women. All of her contacts in the rural area where she and Aubrey taught were connected, for good or ill, with the work they did, and they had a special status as teachers, which made close, equal friendships difficult.

Phoebe had tried to cross what she considered artificial barriers, but her students were insistent on maintaining the separation. And one specific rebuff still brought sorrow when she thought of it.

Rufus, one of the young pupils, was a special friend of Joseph's, and Rufus's widowed mother, Beulah, often stayed late at the school to tidy up, taking special pride in making sure everything was as clean as it could be with the red dust constantly trying to move in and settle.

Once, as evening drew on while the boys still played outside, Phoebe asked Beulah if she and her son would stay for supper.

"Oh, no, Miz Phoebe, we's got to go on home now." Beulah's answer was swift and absolute, but her eyes said more than her words. They held Phoebe's for a moment and then slipped away, but the black woman's distress was plain. The idea of sitting down as an equal at the Edwards's table horrified her, and there was a feeling of betrayal as well as hurt that Phoebe had put her in such an uncomfortable position by asking her to supper.

"Of course," Phoebe managed to say, but she wanted to plead, "Please, if our sons can be friends, why can't we? I need a friend in this lonesome place." But she reminded herself that while Beulah might want to learn skills the whites could teach and could revere the role of teacher, she had little reason to trust whites on a personal level. She had been raised as a slave, and her husband had died a few years before as a result of the long years of abuse he had suffered under the "peculiar institution." Slavery had made him an old man long before his time, and emancipation had not come soon enough to save him.

It had taken some time for Beulah to feel comfortable at the school once more, and Phoebe had been careful not to violate the boundaries with her students again.

Friendships with the local white population were no easier to achieve. Though there were scores of poor whites who would have benefited from schooling and who would have been welcomed to the classes, not one white face appeared among the black. To do so would be to side openly with the Edwardses and thus to risk the wrath of the night riders. Even those whites who did sympathize with the work were very circumspect in the kindness they extended to the family. Sometimes offerings of food or even books appeared at the schoolhouse door, and sometimes a quick nod or a smile at the crossroads store would tell Phoebe that not every white considered her an enemy. But those who hated were more open and vocal, so that sometimes she felt as if she were running a gauntlet when she went to buy basic necessities such as flour and salt.

"Nevah seen sech a pursy-lipped whoah afaoh this 'un, but heared she likes them bucks."

"Reckon that boney man a' hers ain't got bones in th' right places."

They lazed on the porch of the store, talking just loud enough to be sure she'd hear what they were saying as she went inside. Head high, she went past them as if they didn't exist, but inside, her rage boiled so that she could taste it at the back of her throat.

She had Joseph by the hand, and she had told him over and over not to pay any attention to such ignorant louts, but it was difficult to answer him when he asked very softly, "What's a 'pursy-lipped whoah'?"

"It's a very bad name to call a woman, but those men haven't any sense or manners, so there's no use in letting it bother us," she told him.

"When I get bigger, I'm going to kill them all," Joseph said very calmly.

Phoebe's heart jumped painfully at hearing her own hate coming from him, but she kept her voice even. "It wouldn't be worth it. You'd probably be hanged for doing it, and then what use would it be? What happens when you kick horse manure?"

"It goes all over, but it gets on your foot, too," Joseph answered with the giggle Phoebe had hoped for when she'd offered the crude parable.

There was another laugh, this from Mr. Crowper who owned the store. "Yoah mama's right, little 'un, th' likes of them out theah ain't woath gettin' yoah boots dirty."

Phoebe smiled at him gratefully. Mr. Crowper was an ally, though he had to be as careful about it as anyone. But he always offered Joseph a stick of candy when they came to the store, and quite often Phoebe found little extras tucked into her grocery order. Mr. Crowper had fought for the Confederacy even though he had already been middle-aged at the time, but he had also accepted the defeat and the fact that life in the South must change.

Sometimes Phoebe was tempted to keep Joseph away from everyone except the pupils at the school, but she knew that that was too unhealthy for the child, and the outings to the store were made worthwhile by Mr. Crowper's attitude.

Today he was as patient as always as Joseph chose the flavor of candy he wanted, but his eyes watched the door warily as he kept careful track of the men on the porch, and when Joseph wandered over to study the fascinating things on the shelves, Mr. Crowper spoke very low to Phoebe. "Some a' them out theah don't keep theah bedsheets wheah they belong, an' some a' them have been gettin' pretty ugly 'bout yoah school, sayin' the niggras are bein' moah uppity 'cuz a' th' ideas you an' yoah husband teach 'em. Jes' wanted you t' know, so's you kin keep a watch."

"Thank you, Mr. Crowper," Phoebe said, meaning it because she knew the risk he took in warning her, but inwardly she wondered what he expected her and Aubrey to do against the night riders. Without an arsenal and an army, no one was proof against their attacks.

Because they were out in the country, there was little sign of a federal presence here, but the fact that their school was supported by Northern agencies gave them some protection, or was supposed to. It was thin armor at best.

Walking back to the school, she grew more and more convinced that Joseph ought to be sent away earlier than planned, but when she proposed the idea to Aubrey and told him about the unpleasantness at the store, he failed to share her urgency.

"It's been like this all along," he pointed out. "I doubt it's gotten any worse just because Mr. Crowper has overheard more than usual. We have so little here; a one-room schoolhouse and a poor excuse for a house. We're not worth their trouble."

"You of all people should know it is the ideas taught here that they object to, not the damn buildings!" she said in a flash of temper. "And they find the shacks of poor black farmers targets worth their trouble, so why not us? Do you think the broken windows and the other 'accidents' we've had around here happened by themselves?"

Two days later, she went back to the store, without Joseph, and she waited until the store was empty before she spoke to the proprietor. "Mr. Crowper, I don't want to endanger you in return for your kindness, but I need a great favor. I need a safe place for Joseph to come to in case something happens to his father and me."

Mr. Crowper thought about it for a long time, his reluctance to become further involved clear, but finally he said, "I ain't turnin' away no child 'cuz a bunch a' cowards cain't face th' world th' way it's gonna be now. You jes' send him t' me if theah's trouble out yoah way."

Phoebe could have embraced him, but she contented herself with thanking him, and then she gave him a letter to be sent to Anthea, since the store served as the post office for the area. But she also gave him a slip of paper which listed her parents' address, Anthea and Max's, and Wild Swan. "If something happens to us, please make sure Joseph gets safely to Wild Swan. I promise you that my family will reward you well."

Even with her most immediate family living in Baltimore, Wild Swan remained the place of refuge. And though she didn't want to explore it fully in her own mind, she wanted to know that the family would be together at Wild Swan if they had to face whatever the awful circumstance that would see Joseph escorted by Mr. Crowper.

Mr. Crowper watched Phoebe leave, and then he tucked the paper away, hoping he would never have to refer to it.

Still resolute, Phoebe told Aubrey what she had done and what she planned to do. "I'm going to take Joseph with me, and I'm going to leave him with Anthea and Max. I would, of course, like you to accompany us, but one way or the other, Joseph is going to be living safely in Maryland by Christmas Day."

They could hear the sound of Joseph's voice as he played outside with some of the younger pupils.

"I have nothing to say about this?" Aubrey's voice was mild, but for the first time in a long while, Phoebe saw that he was fully focused on her, not drifting as usual in his own view of the world.

"Nothing at all." She was revealing the truth of their marriage—that she had always been the dominant one.

"I do love our son," Aubrey said.

"I know you do," Phoebe answered. "But I will not allow your refusal to see the truth to put him in jeopardy. You are wrong about how things are going here. They are getting worse. Do you object to the Kingstons as guardians for Joseph?"

"No," he said. He closed his eyes and then opened them to stare at her intently. "I object to my own ineptitude. Are you sorry you married me?"

Of all the responses she had expected, this question was not one of them, and it shocked her so, she made no effort to dissemble. She studied him as openly as he was studying her, and her resentment melted away.

For all her impatience with him, she realized anew that his reserve was the perfect balance for her fire. If she had had a husband more like herself, they would surely have destroyed each other and their work long before this. Though she had wished countless times that he were more forceful and realistic, he was something more; he not only dreamed of a better world, he lived the dream day by day, never faltering as she did. And without him, there would have been no Joseph.

"I am not the least sorry I married you," she told him. "I loved you then; I love you now. I'm only sorry I haven't made that clear more often." She went to him and drew his head down so she could kiss him. He put his arms around her.

"Without you, I would surely have been no more than an odd old bachelor," he murmured. "I dread to see Joseph go, but I want him to have the kind of life your family can give him. It is a good decision."

Only now did she understand how much she had dreaded fighting him about this, and she was infinitely grateful for his capitulation.

They decided not to tell Joseph of their plan until it was time to take him to Maryland, but Phoebe did tell him about the arrangement she had made with Mr. Crowper in case of trouble, couching it in the least threatening terms she could manage. But Joseph was a bright child.

"You're talking about those men on the porch and their friends, aren't you?" he asked. "Rufus told me some of them dress up like ghosts at night and go around doing bad things."

"We don't know if those men on the porch are part of the night riders," Phoebe told him. "They may only say bad things, not do them; some people are like that. But we have to be ready for trouble, and that means that you promise to go to Mr. Crowper if I or your father tells you to. Promise?"

Promises were not lightly given in the Edwards family, and Joseph's chin set stubbornly against giving this one. He was unhappy with the idea of abandoning his parents in time of trouble. But Phoebe's will was greater than his. Finally, he nodded and mumbled, "I promise."

Having faced the danger squarely, having Aubrey face it with her, and having made definite provision for Joseph's protection made Phoebe feel safer than she had for a very long time.

A week later, she knew how foolish the sense of security had been.

They came in the darkness, banshees wailing their hate. "Come out, nigra lovahs! You, school masta, an' yoah whoah!"

The nervous stamping of the horses' hooves was as loud as the voices in the still night.

Phoebe had wondered how she would react if the raiders came, and now she was hardly reacting at all. She supposed she must be terrified, but she felt removed, as if she were watching it happen to someone else.

Her detachment allowed her to go to Joseph as Aubrey was rising from their bed.

Joseph was awake, cowering in his bed, and when she came to him, he threw his arms around her. "Make them go away!" he cried.

"We will certainly try. But you must go to Mr. Crowper now. You promised."

She picked him up as if he weighed nothing and carried him to a window at the back of the little house. "You have to go right now before they surround the house."

The men outside sounded so drunk, she wondered if they would even think of coming around to the back. The alcohol had surely dulled their fear of repercussions as well.

She boosted Joseph over the sill. "Go now! And don't look back! We love you very, very much, and we need you to do this for us. Run as fast as you can, but hide from the horsemen if you must; don't let them see you. We'll come to you as soon as we can."

She kissed him and then shoved him outside. He hesitated for a moment, and then he fled into the darkness. She waited only until she saw the woods swallow him.

She went back to Aubrey. "We may have time to get out the back. Joseph is already on his way." The calm detachment remained with her; she might have been talking about the weather.

"You go," Aubrey said. "If I can keep them busy here for a while, you and Joseph can get safely away. I won't be driven from this place. I recognize those men. I want to talk to them."

A stone crashed through one of the front windows, and a bright glow lit the house, light from the fire burning the schoolhouse. The voices outside kept yelling obscenities and challenges made more menacing by the drawl that should have softened the words but did not.

Aubrey had pulled on his clothes, but Phoebe had to content herself with a robe over her bedgown. "Where you go, I go," she said. "It's always been that way for us. And if we both confront them, Joseph has a better chance."

"My blessedly practical Phoebe," Aubrey murmured. He kissed her, and then he took her hand. His was warm, dry, and absolutely steady, and she had the fleeting, mad thought that perhaps this was what he had been born for, this unswerving last-hour courage, and perhaps she no less than he.

They went out together. Their appearance caused a sudden silence, and then the babble broke over them again: "Nigra lovah," "Whoah," "Yo'ah makin' it bad foah yoah own people," "Teach you a lesson . . ." Much of it was unintelligible and better so.

"We are not hurting you. We are helping you as much as our students. All of us must live together, and education makes life better for everyone." Aubrey's voice rose strong and clear, and his calm reason had, for the moment, the effect of dashing them with cold water. Silent in their shrouds, they were at once menacing and ridiculous. Phoebe wondered if their wives kept their costumes clean, and she wondered if the men really thought they were anonymous when their voices and horses were known.

"I surely know horses." She didn't know whether she'd said it aloud or not. She felt the edges of terror and hysteria now, but like everything else, they seemed to be moving very slowly in a place far away.

"Hank Willet, Beau Corey, I know you; you are better men than this," Aubrey said, and he continued to name names, nearly all of them, wanting to appeal to them as individuals.

"Shee-it! Th' bastard knows who we are!" Beau Corey howled, and whatever restraint they might have shown was gone. The few weak voices mumbling their doubts, "Ah, hell, let's jes' get out a' heah," were drowned out by the others.

"Wheah's th' whelp?" Hank Willet asked, and Aubrey moved toward him. "You leave our son out of this," he commanded, glancing back as if Joseph were hiding in the house.

Hank's horse bucked with his rider's nervousness, and as the horse came down, Phoebe saw Hank's pistol. "No!" she screamed as he fired.

Aubrey fell, part of his face blown away.

"Now we gotta find thet kid!" she heard someone shout, and she did not know who it was.

"If he's in theah, he's dead already."

The house was crackling into flame behind her. They were going to kill her anyway; they had to now. Saving Joseph was the only thing. She ran straight into the fire, screaming his name, the perfect image of a mother trying to save her child. Her last thought was clear. "Dear God, keep Joseph safe."

Joseph watched it all from his hiding place. He saw his father fall, and he heard his mother scream his name as she ran into the flames. And then he began to race through the night, going to Mr. Crowper as he had promised, avoiding all the houses, black and white, between his burning home and the store because somehow he knew that some of the people in them were part of this nightmare, even those who were not riding with the white-robed monsters; some knew about this night and had done nothing to stop it.

Mr. Crowper kept his word. By the next morning, Joseph's words, "I promised to come to you. My mother and father are dead," were confirmed. Everyone knew what had happened at the Edwardses' school.

Mr. Crowper closed his store with a "Gone Fishing" sign and spirited Joseph away that evening. He was sick at heart and determined that the least he could do was to save the child, but he would have felt easier if Joseph had raged or wept. Instead it was as if he were accompanying a little old man disguised as a child. Joseph did exactly as he was told, sitting quietly on the train, eating when food was given to him, but offering no reaction.

Joseph's arrival at Wild Swan made the horror of what had happened immediate and undeniable.

Alex sent for the family. Mr. Crowper told her how specific Phoebe had been about bringing the child to the farm, and Alex understood what Phoebe had wanted.

All the family came, even the three doctors, who had to find others in their profession to oversee their patients; they all understood this was a summons that was not to be ignored.

Rane arrived first. Before Alex even spoke, he knew that death had come to the family again. When he heard that Joseph was at Wild Swan because Aubrey had been shot and Phoebe burned to death, his whole body convulsed as he put his arms around Alex. "Oh, God," he moaned over and over, and he wept fierce, bitter tears. And then he gathered his strength, as Alex did, to support the rest of the family.

Philly, Blaine, and Phoebe's sisters were sustained by Joseph's survival. That alone kept their hatred for what had been done and their grief at a manageable level. According to Mr. Crowper, there was little doubt that Joseph had seen what had happened; he had known that his parents were dead when he arrived at the store, but he continued to keep his silence, and no one wanted to question him directly.

"I want Phoebe and Aubrey to be buried here," Philly said, and all agreed. But they gave Mr. Crowper time to return to his store and promised that they would give no indication that he had carried the news and the child to them.

"Do you know who killed my daughter and my son-in-law?" Blaine felt compelled to ask as the man was preparing to depart, though Mr. Crowper's avoidance of the subject was sure indication that he did not want to talk about it.

Mr. Crowper had been braced for the question since his arrival at Wild Swan, but it was no easier to answer for having anticipated it. "Suh, I wasn't theah. I kin tell you thet theah are men who are capable of it, men I'd guess weah theah, but I cain't tell you they did it."

He glanced around with a look of bafflement. "I doan undastand. Yoah daughta, she came from all a' this. Why evah did she give it up foah teachin' down theah?"

Blaine straightened his shoulders. "Because she was a soldier. The war didn't end for her or for her husband at Appomattox."

"I reckon it didn't end foah a lot of us," Mr. Crowper said, and hesitantly he held out his hand.

Blaine shook it firmly. "We are forever in your debt for bringing Joseph home."

Mr. Crowper had been handsomely recompensed for the deed despite his protests that payment of the travel expenses was more than sufficient. But he found that Mr. Carrington's's gratitude meant more to him than the money.

He cleared his throat nervously. "Someday I'd 'preciate gettin' word 'bout th' boy. I hope he's gonna be all right."

"We'll send word," Blaine promised.

When Blaine went south to retrieve the bodies, he did not go alone. Travis, Reid, and Morgan accompanied him, and they made no secret of who they were or of why they had come. Mr. Crowper, betraying nothing of what he knew, noted with satisfaction that the men from Maryland had a sobering effect on a good number of the community's inhabitants, and his porch was noticeably bare of braggarts. But it was a small victory. No names were revealed; no one was charged with the murders.

The black pupils had buried their teachers with sorrow and

honor, but they thought it fitting that the family had come to take the pine caskets home, and they willingly opened the graves. The two wooden markers listed not only Phoebe and Aubrey, but also Joseph.

Julius, a slight, elderly man who seemed to be the accepted spokesman for the group, hastened to explain. "Suh, we never finds liddle Joseph. We puts his name heah wid his mama so dey thinks he dead too an' doan look foah him no mo'. Mebbe he be alive somewheahs."

The old man's face looked so hopeful, Blaine wanted to tell him, but nothing could be allowed to threaten his grandson's safety or Mr. Crowper's, and even innocent rejoicing might do both.

He met Julius's eyes squarely. "We are mourning the murder of my daughter and her husband. Since he does not lie here with them, we will not mourn my grandson."

Julius studied his face, and then he bowed his head and whispered, "I pray to de Lord it be true."

Nothing demonstrated the division in the South more clearly than the fact that while the men felt perfectly comfortable and comforted by the blacks of the Edwardses's school, there was no such ease with the whites of the community. They wondered at each white face they saw whether this person had been connected with the killings. Not even the women were exempt, for surely the wives of the night riders knew what their men did. Some whites watched them warily, a few stared belligerently, most seemed to want to pretend they were not there at all. But a few had the courage to come forth as the coffins were being loaded on a wagon to take to the nearest railhead.

"We'ah sorry foah what happened heah," one of the onlookers offered.

Blaine nodded in acknowledgment, not trusting himself to speak. A terrible rage burned inside of him. These people might be sorry, but they weren't sorry enough to stop the men who were responsible for the charred death he was taking home.

Travis's grief and rage were nearly equal to Blaine's. He had fought hard for the Confederacy because Virginia had been part of the rebellion and because he had understood that the economic policies of the federal government had been leaning more and more to the advantage of the North with its factories and merchants. But he had never fought so that domination of one race by another could continue. It was agony to be here in this place where it seemed the war would never end but would be carried on by creatures who thrived on violence in the darkness.

By the time they arrived back at Wild Swan, he looked as worn and bleak as Blaine. And when the words Mrs. Howe had written for the Union troops were sung at the graveside, Travis's voice was strong with the rest.

Mine eyes have seen the glory of the coming of the Lord.
He is trampling out the vintage where the grapes of wrath are stored;
He hath loosed the fateful lightning of His terrible swift sword:
His truth is marching on. . . .

Chapter 15

Though Anthea had every intention of carrying out Phoebe's wishes, she dreaded confronting her parents and most of all, Larissa, with Phoebe's choice for Joseph. But once it was done, she found, to her chagrin, she had underestimated her family.

"We are too old to raise a child now," Philly told her sadly. "But since Joseph will be with you, we will get to see much of him."

And Larissa said, "Our sister made a good choice. Reid and I have three children already, and Joseph will need more attention than we can give him, at least in the beginning. But when he's settled, I hope he'll be able to spend time with his cousins." She did not have to express her doubts about when Joseph would be "settled" because everyone shared them. They all wondered how the child could ever adjust to the nightmare he had witnessed.

He continued to do everything that was asked of him and to express no emotion at all. They had allowed him to be at the graveside when his parents were buried not only because they felt it was his right, but also because they hoped that seeing the burial would help him to understand that as horrible as the murder of his parents was, it was over.

"I swear that he is seeing it continuously behind those quiet eyes of his," Max told Anthea. "And surely in his sleep. He is never free of it."

Joseph did not cry out loudly in the night, but he breathed with little whimpers, and his body often shivered with distress. New as they were to parenting, Anthea and Max were stunned by the overwhelming love they felt for the boy.

"If we don't go carefully, we'll smother him, but it is so hard! I just want to wrap my arms around him and promise him that nothing will ever hurt him again," Anthea said.

Without hesitation, they rearranged their lives for Joseph. Nigel moved into the quarters over their offices, and the Kingstons moved into a house two doors down, a house with its own yard where a child could play. Philly and Blaine insisted on helping the Kingstons purchase the house.

"Please don't let pride interfere with this," Blaine said. "Joseph is our grandson, and you are changing your lives out of love for him. Let us help, too."

Although it meant neglecting her own medical practice, Anthea spent many days at Wild Swan because she and Max agreed that the best thing for Joseph now was to gain a sense of the family. They could only imagine how alone he had felt when he had seen his parents die.

Lexy and the twins did their best to welcome their cousin, but their efforts were hampered by their own insecurities, and they treated Joesph far too carefully.

"He is a child just like you," Travis pointed out. "I don't mean for you to be rough with him, but it would be good if he could join in some of your games."

"We've asked him if he wanted to ride on Tinker," Kace offered, but he didn't quite meet his father's eyes.

Tay looked at him directly. "Are you going to California again?"

"Yes, but not right away. I've already been this year, as you know. But next year, I'll have to go again because we still have business there."

"Don't go! Don't ever go again, and not to the races either!" Tay's voice was a wail of pleading, and Kace and Lexy looked as if they were the silent chorus of the plea.

Suddenly Travis wished Gincie were in his place, but since she wasn't, he drew a deep breath and tackled the subject of the mortality of parents.

"Your mother and I can't promise never to be out of your sight. And we can't promise we will live forever. But we do take care of ourselves." He wasn't sure what he'd say if one of them mentioned the risks he took in jumping horses, but none of them did, probably because to them, work with horses was so natural, it did not seem unusually dangerous.

"We want to be with you for as long as we can be. We want to see what you make of your lives. We want to be at your weddings if you marry and to meet our grandchildren if you have families of your own."

Speaking of events so far in the future the children could hardly imagine them had the desired effect. The fear faded from their eyes, and they were a bit more natural around Joseph, but there was no denying that he still carried the worst of all childhood stigmas—he was an orphan, and if his parents could die, then so could anyone else's. It would take time for the children to think of Joseph as belonging to Anthea and Max.

Even during the holidays, Joseph remained impassive, thanking everyone politely for his gifts, but evincing no pleasure in the new toys.

"He is a survivor," Max observed quietly to Anthea. "He eats and sleeps enough to stay alive; he is always on his best behavior, and he watches, he watches as if he is in a foreign land among people who speak a foreign tongue. It must seem exactly like that to him. And somewhere inside there must be more fear and more hate than we can imagine. I think the time has come to have a talk with Joseph. He's been taught to be so well behaved, I am not sure he understands he has a right to express what he feels instead of what makes others comfortable."

"You are a good father, my love," Anthea said. And inside she added silently, "Phoebe, we are trying to do our very best."

"I'm not a good father yet, but I'm willing to learn if Joseph will help teach me."

With the new year, Joseph had started attending Flora and Philly's school, but even this exposure to other children of various ages had not changed his withdrawn demeanor, though he obligingly did his schoolwork.

Max often used Joseph's studies as a point of reference, trying to coax him to talk. So far it hadn't been an overly successful tactic, but at least it was a familiar one to the little boy, and now and then he ventured a brief flash of enthusiasm about something that had sparked his interest in school or betrayed his distaste for something that bored him.

This time Max began by asking Joseph about arithmetic. He got the expected response when Joseph gave a little shrug and said, "It's all right. I can do the problems, but I don't care much when they're done."

"I know what you mean. I didn't like mathematics when I was your age either, though I know one has to study the subject because there are so many occasions when it is useful."

"When?" asked Joseph suspiciously, and Max hid his elation at Joseph's participation.

"Well, when you go to the store, if you can't do your sums, you won't be able to tell if you have enough money to buy what you want or if the prices are fair. And if you need to measure something, to build something, for instance, you have to know how to do it. Of course, I still like reading better, as I did when I was in school."

"I like it, too," Joseph said softly, and Max wondered if he were remembering his mother or father reading to him or, more likely, teaching him to read, something they had begun when Joseph was very small.

Max smoothed out the newspaper clipping. "You know your Uncle Reid writes for several newspapers, and lots of people read what he writes. This was a special piece of writing he did after your parents were killed. I think you ought to hear what he had to say about it."

Joseph's hand darted out and then pulled back as if the paper were something venomous.

"I think you could probably read it yourself, but maybe it would be better if I read it to you, and maybe you could follow along if you sat on my lap." He held his breath as Joseph hesitated and then tried to act nonchalant when Joseph climbed into his lap. But he wanted to hold the little boy against his heart and heal the hurt inside of him more than he had ever wanted to bring surcease to anyone.

He cleared his throat and made himself read the article in a steady voice:

When incidents of violence are reported from the South these days, more often than not they are discounted as evidence of "waving the bloody shirt," lies told to enable the Radical Republicans to maintain their power in the South. Sometimes, lies have been told for that purpose. But, tragically, such tales are too often true.

Yesterday, I attended the burial of my sister-in-law and my brother-in-law. They were cruelly murdered by cowards who roam the night, hiding themselves in their bed sheets. My relatives' only "crime" was to teach those who were once slaves how to read and write that they might enjoy and employ their freedom with the skills provided by education. It is to all our good that all citizens of this Republic be as well informed as possible.

I do not endorse any political party, nor do I deny that there have been violent excesses on all sides, but I do avow that the murderers did not ride alone that night. Every citizen who approves their crimes, every person who knows who they are and yet continues to treat them as members of the community, rode with them, killed with them. Until everyone of whatever race or creed in this nation is safe from such savagery, none of us will be free, and the war will never end.

When Max finished reading, Joseph was absolutely still on his lap.

"We've all talked about how your mother and father were murdered, and your Uncle Reid wrote about it so that many, many people could read about it, but you have never said a word about what you saw." Joseph's body jerked, and Max wrapped his arms around him. "We do know you saw it."

Max didn't know how long he had held Joseph before the tremors started, small ripples that grew stronger and stronger, as if the child were having a fit.

"They shot Papa, and then Mama ran into the fire to make them think I was there, so I could get away."

Though Max had suspected it might have been that way, to hear the thin, high voice bearing witness was unbearably painful. But then the voice changed, growing stronger, boiling out in a raging fury that was far larger than the small body.

"I will kill them, kill them, kill them all! When I'm big, I will kill them all! I will shoot them and burn them, shoot them and burn them, kill them, kill them, kill them all!"

Despite Joseph's small size and tender years, Max could not deny the power of the atavistic chant, and at that moment, he knew that unless the course was changed, someday Death would wear Joseph's face. For now, it was enough that the festering sore was open to the light.

Max held Joseph, rocking him in slow counterpoint to the frenzy. "Who were they? If you know their names, we can report them to the authorities and have them arrested." He hoped that was true, but it made no difference anyway. Joseph had revealed more than he wanted to already and had no intention of saying the names he thought he'd heard.

It haunted him that he was not sure. He thought his father had spoken directly to Hank Willet, Beau Corey, and several others, but he had been too far away to hear clearly, except for his mother screaming his name. That he would hear forever. But the images of that night were so horrific and jumbled, sometimes he saw the mean men from the porch of Mr. Crowper's store riding in that night without sheets covering them, and he knew that couldn't be true. He remembered their horses more clearly than anything else. His mother had never lost the early influence of her life, and together they had made a game of judging the horses they saw, even aging cart horses.

Somehow he would sort it all out when it was time. He tried to hold on to the strength of that idea, but it wasn't enough. As he had kept the anger inside, so had he kept the sorrow, but now it sprang upward like a live thing, tearing at his insides, so that he clung to Max and moaned in pain.

"Mama, Papa! They're never coming back, never, never."

Max held him and wept with him, and murmured, "Your aunt and I aren't the same as your parents, I know, but we love you dearly. You aren't alone, little one. We're here for you, and so is the rest of the family, all of the other people who love you."

It was harsh, but it was a beginning, and Anthea and Max even considered it a good sign when Joseph began to show flashes of temper as well as interest and merriment, all normal reactions of children his age.

But though they were making progress, Anthea worried about companionship for Joesph when she and Max were busy with their patients. Joseph was improving, but he still tended to be a loner, preferring his own company to that of neighborhood children. He had always been an adult child. They had a cook and a cleaning woman, both kind enough, but not exactly what Joseph needed.

It was Flora who offered the solution. "Sally would be a perfect companion for him. She's very mature for her age; she's had experience with children; and she knows what it is to live through a tragedy. She could be at the school during the day, as she is now, but the rest of her time she would be part of your household. That way she could take Joseph to school and bring him home in the afternoon."

"It's a very generous offer," Anthea said. "But what about you? Sally has proved herself a willing and useful part of your household."

"To be honest, I am more in need of privacy now than of a lady's maid."

To her amazement, Anthea saw that her sixty-year-old aunt was blushing, and it occurred to her that Flora had been looking much happier and healthier lately, losing the fragile appearance that had come with Caleb's death. She thought of the man who had been escorting Flora to various social functions and entertainments lately. "Marsh Whitcomb?" she asked, and Flora's blush deepened.

"I must seem like a very foolish old woman to you," she said, "but Marsh is a wonderful man. We are being discreet. I don't want the school to suffer. But I have discovered that my life as a woman is not over yet." There was a trace of defiance in her voice, but she appeared more apprehensive than anything else, and it touched Anthea that Flora feared her judgment.

She was seeing Flora in a new light, as a still beautiful woman instead of a widowed aunt, and it was a startling change. She thought of Marsh Whitcomb and found nothing lacking. He was a gray-haired, blue-eyed, tall, spare man in his midfiftes. He had made his fortune in the shipping business, particularly in transporting huge cargoes of grain to Europe. He had lost his wife some years before, and his children were grown. Anthea knew a good deal about him because of his business, which made him familiar through the Jennings-Falconer company.

"I think it's quite wonderful," she said. "Mr. Whitcomb is, from all I know, a very respectable man." She grinned. "He's also very handsome. Uncle Marsh—it sounds rather nice."

"He has already asked me to marry him, but I'm not going to," Flora said without sorrow or regret. "It's not that Marsh is younger or that I think Caleb would object; he was such a generous, loving man, he always wanted my happiness more than his own. But Marsh has one fatal flaw. He is willing to indulge my enthusiasm for the legal rights of women because he knows it is vital to me. But indulgence is not the same as belief. Caleb shared the belief, and I would never marry a man who did not. Marriage is a legal, binding contract, and surely shared beliefs are a necessary part of making that contract work. I enjoy Marsh's company and his love, but that is enough for me. It may not be for him. Contrary to the myth, men are often far more proper and desirous of a legal domestic arrangement than are women, even when the women are, as I am, past the age of childbearing."

She hesitated, and suddenly she looked very young. "Your father's reaction is the one I dread the most. Isn't that foolish? But even after all these years, he is still my twin brother, and behavior he would accept in others, he finds shocking in me. I do dread a scene with him once he realizes what is going on."

"Mama's good at calming him down." Anthea smiled as she pictured her diminutive mother's feisty approach to her tall, reserved father when Philly thought Blaine was being too stuffy and judgmental.

"I think she already knows what's going on," Flora said. "And she seems to approve of Marsh, so I trust you're right and that I'll have an ally there." She looked thoughtful for a moment and then added, "It's odd, but I never worry about what Mother will think. She has lived through so much, she seems to understand what people need before they themselves know."

Anthea nodded in agreement. "I feel as if I could tell Gran anything in the world, and no matter what I had done, she would have some sensible, comforting plan to make things better."

Flora's talent for judging how people could help each other was as keen as usual. Sally Birch was a perfect addition to the Kingston household, old enough at seventeen to exert some authority over Joseph and yet young enough to encourage the child in him to play. And her loyalty to the Kingstons was unquestionable; as far as she was concerned, she owed not only her physical life, but also all the good things she had experienced in the past few years, to Anthea and Max.

Flora was also right about Blaine's reaction to her relationship with Marsh Whitcomb. Flora began to include Marsh in more family occasions, and Blaine's cordial attitude began to cool until finally he said to Philly, "I hate to believe it, but I think my sister is having an affair."

Philly went on with her preparations for the night, taking off her earrings and beginning to unpin her hair. "Will you please unfasten my dress?" she asked, presenting her back to him. Then she added casually, "You're right; anyone who knows Flora could tell that she is much happier lately and that Marsh Whitcomb is the reason. I like him."

A button flew off of her dress.

"Blaine! Do be careful! It's no use taking your brotherly rage out on my innocent dress."

"Your dress might be innocent, but you're not!" he snapped, turning her around so he could see her face. "You've known about this since it started, haven't you?"

"Almost," she agreed placidly.

"And you didn't tell me!"

"Of course I didn't, because I knew you would behave just as you are now. What did you expect Flora to do, wear widow's weeds for the rest of her life?"

Blaine had managed enough of her buttons so that she could pull the fabric off of her shoulders and let the dress slip to the floor. She leaned against him clad in her lacy undergarments, and she ran her hand down the front of his clothes until she encountered the evidence of his sex. Her blue eyes held his as she teased him in the patterns learned from years of loving.

"Did you expect her to never feel the delight of her body again?"

Though her body continued to entice his, suddenly her eyes were somber. "There is so little time for loving, for any of us. Flora and Marsh aren't hurting anyone. Don't begrudge them their pleasure in each other."

They still had trouble talking about Phoebe; her death had been so horrible. But they thought about her constantly, and Blaine could hear her name between them as if Philly had spoken it aloud. He could not stand against Philly's plea for compassion and tolerance, particularly when she made him realize how childish his own reaction was.

He held her against him, and he tried to imagine what his life would be like if he did not have her to love and to love him. The awful chill of it swept through him, and he understood better than he ever had how Flora must have felt in these years since Caleb's death.

"The family considers me the rational one, but you are the voice of reason in my life. I have always had difficulty thinking of my sister as a woman," he admitted, "but you make me see. I promise, Flora and Marsh will have nothing to complain of from me."

He was as good as his word and was amply repaid for the adjustment by observing how happy his twin was and by having her treat him with her old warmth, the apprehension gone. He even managed a measure of grace in accepting her decision not to marry Marsh, an offer she told Blaine about in order that he would know Marsh was an honorable man.

"As opposed to my sister, the adventuress," he told Philly, but the words were said with rueful humor and the knowledge that the term did not fit Flora at all.

Chapter 16

For the Culhanes, the Falconers, and the rest of the racing world, 1875 saw the inauguration of a new racetrack and of a race that excited interest throughout the country. The track was the Louisville Jockey Club, located outside of Louisville, Kentucky, on one hundred and eighty acres. Colonel M. Lewis Clark was responsible for establishing the track and for inaugurating races patterned on the classic events in England and France. He had traveled to those countries to visit their racecourses, and the first running of the Kentucky Derby, named for the famous Derby that had been run in England every year since 1780, was attracting a magnificent field of three-year-olds.

Though Wild Swan's horses were not usually sent to races as far west as Kentucky, Alex and the Culhanes had decided this was an event worth attending, and they had entered Moonraker.

Alex had chosen the name, and the children loved the legend of it. It was said to have come from a small village in England where the populace had hidden smuggled goods in a pond and were using rakes to retrieve the goods when revenue officers came upon them. The moon was shimmering on the water, and the villagers pretended to be raking the light, as if they were mad, thus evading arrest. The children begged to hear not only the legends, but also the real accounts of Rane's free-trading days over and over again, and Alex told them those, too.

Moonraker was the result of breeding a black mare who carried the Swan and Fortune lines, as well as the strong blood that had been added to those lines, with Leamington, the famous brown stallion imported from England in 1865, sire of such famous racers as Enquirer and Longfellow. Leamington had served the 1866 season in Kentucky but had been on the East Coast since 1867 and was now at the Erdenheim Stud near Philadelphia.

Moonraker was a true black with a white crescent moon on his forehead, fitting for his name. He was the colt who had run himself into a fence the previous year and had thus missed the spring and summer racing seasons, but he had come back in the fall to do very well.

Since they were making the trip anyway, they shipped a few other horses west for entries in other events. As usual, Padraic and some of his men went ahead with the animals to get them settled.

Kentucky had a long and admirable tradition of flat racing, and it was hoped that the establishing of the new Louisville Jockey Club would promote racing in the South and the West, both areas that lagged far behind New York State now. More and more stud farms were being located in Kentucky because the lush bluegrass and the limestone-rich earth contributed much to healthy, strong-boned race-horses. It was doubtful that the amount of alcohol, particularly in deceptively smooth mint juleps, consumed by the racing set was as healthy, but the hospitality in Kentucky was gracious and difficult to turn down.

"It's a good thing the horses are runnin' and not us," Travis confided to Gincie after a late night.

"Speak for yourself," she retorted with a laugh, only to discover he was already asleep.

But whatever the revelry that surrounded them, the races were the focus of attention and the Derby most of all. It was the second race of the day on May 17, and of the forty-two horses originally entered, fifteen came to the post. In the betting, Mr. McGrath's entries, Aristides and Chesapeake, were the public's favorites, and Padraic and Alex had their eyes on Aristides, a chestnut sired by Leamington.

"He was cut up at Lexington in the Phoenix Hotel Stakes, and he's one of the smallest horses in the field," Travis pointed out. "And Moonraker has the same sire and a longer stride."

"But Price McGrath has a good record for breeding winners," Alex said, "and Aristides got far more experience last year than Moonraker did. He won three of nine starts and was second three times. And he seems quite recovered from his injuries."

Alex had known Mr. McGrath for years, and they admired each other's knowledge of Thoroughbreds. Price McGrath had been born to poor parents in Woodford County, Kentucky. He had gone west in 1849, and had earned a living gambling there and in the south. In 1864 he had gone to New York, and had become part of a syndicate which established a highly profitable gaming house. When he withdrew from the syndicate in 1867 to return to Kentucky, his fortune was estimated to be nearly half a million dollars, and he had used his money lavishly to create McGrathiana Stud outside of Lexington.

Like Alex, McGrath was of the old style of horse owners, involved in every step of the operation rather than viewing racehorses as nothing more than another investment.

Ten thousand spectators were on hand to see the Derby run, and Moonraker was so nervous, Alex, in addition to being apprehensive about the large field, feared that he would run his race before the official start. But the horses got off at the first attempt, and Moonraker took the lead, with Verdigris, Aristides, and McCreery close on his heels, the rest a length or two behind. Chesapeake was one of the last to get away. They ran in this order for the first half mile, but then the pace began to tell on some of the rear division, and Enlister, Vagabond, and Chesapeake fell back.

"Keep it up, you can do it," Alex murmured, and Rane put a comforting arm around her shoulders.

But Travis now had his doubts, and he could see them reflected in Gincie's eyes before she said, "The pace is very fast!"

Aristides took second place as they ran along the backstretch, and then he lapped Moonraker as they reached the half-mile pole, the starting point, and was in front, steadily increasing his lead as the fast pace spread the field further and further behind him.

Alex took her eyes off the horses long enough to see Mr. McGrath standing at the head of the stretch where his jockey could see him. Mr. McGrath waved at the jockey to go on, and the jockey obeyed by loosing his pull on the bridle.

Seeing the power unleashed in Aristides, Alex sighed, "I fear we've lost," and her heart went out to Moonraker as she watched him coming on with a determined rush that was still not enough to overtake Aristides, who won by a length and a measureless gallantry for his small size.

"He deserved to win," she told Mr. McGrath when she sought him out. "You have my congratulations."

"Your horse gave him a good run," McGrath returned. "And who knows what he might have done had he not missed so much of the racing last year."

In addition to the prize money, Aristides won the Derby trophy, a massive thousand-dollar punch bowl made of three hundred ounces of sterling silver. Moonraker won two hundred dollars for Wild Swan.

"As impressive as the punch bowl is, I think we can survive without it," Rane said to Alex.

" 'Impressive,' but a bit much, isn't it?" she said, and for an instant, Rane saw the young girl he had escorted to the Barnstaple Fair in Devon, the young girl who had viewed everything with bright interest, but had coveted none of it.

"It's extraordinary," Rane murmured.

"The punch bowl?" Alex asked, puzzled at his continued interest in the prize.

"No, not that. It's extraordinary that even after so many years, you still fascinate and delight me as much as you did when I first met you."

"It is you who are extraordinary," she said, smiling mistily. His ability to articulate his love was a rare and wonderful gift for which she never ceased to be grateful.

"I hope you know, but I doubt I tell you often enough how much it means to me that you have always been so willing to take time from the shipyard for my business."

"I shall never have the passion for horses that you do, but I must confess, the excitement of the racecourses has drawn me in over the years. And it has not hurt Jennings-Falconer either, particularly recently."

He was referring to the fact that many of the wealthy patrons of the races were also interested in other sporting pursuits, and the shipyard was finding a lucrative new life in building luxurious yachts for them. Without the racing connection, many of the buyers would undoubtedly have chosen shipbuilders further north, even though the Jennings-Falconer yard had a fine reputation.

"Now that the business is steady again, Morgan and Adam are quite capable of carrying on without me, though they would never be so unkind as to say so. And the younger generation is coming on. Adam and Mercy are determined that their son will know ships and the sea even before he walks. Mercy insists little Nathan begins to smile as soon as he hears the noise of the docks," he said, referring to the child Mercy had borne the previous year. He tucked her arm more closely against his side as the color and noise of the track swirled around them. "It is a wonderful thing to live long enough to see one's work being carried forward in competent hands."

They shared the sight of Gincie and Travis standing a short distance away, talking to Padraic.

While they hadn't won the Derby, the second-place finish and the good showing in other events made the trip to Kentucky more than worthwhile, generating additional interest in Wild Swan's blood-lines and particularly in the combination that had produced Moon-raker, for the future when he would stand at stud.

Since the Louisville Jockey Club racing dates were so close to those at Baltimore, they missed the Pimlico spring meeting, but none of them minded as it gave them a respite at Wild Swan before they were due to go north to Jerome Park and Saratoga Springs.

The children were reassured that Gincie and Travis had gone away and returned. Though they had not protested their parents' departure for Kentucky, they had been more anxious than before Joseph had lost his parents. It was important to Gincie and Travis that the children readjust to the demands of the business, but it was equally vital that they know that nothing ranked above their basic need for love and reassurance.

With classes ending and Doris Williams leaving for the summer, it was a good time to be with the children as they exploded into their season of freedom. Even with chores to do and with rides with their parents, the children had long hours to pursue their own interests, and it was fascinating to observe the way they bustled through their days, the three frequently joining forces for an adventure and further enlarging their ranks with children from the farms, often the McCoy brothers from Sunrise.

Anthea and Max brought Joseph to Wild Swan so that he could enjoy summer in the country, away from the reek and infections of the hot season in Baltimore, and they were pleased that he seemed to feel at home there and that his cousins were more at ease with him now. Sally Birch accompanied him and stayed when the Kingstons returned to the city. Their real intention was that the young woman would also have a gentle summer, but Sally was so conscientious and so careful about not taking advantage, the only way to make her accept the interim was to cloak it in terms of work.

Joseph was still more aloof than the other children, but he made a patient effort to share their interests, letting Kace instruct him in the finer points of riding and of swinging from the rope in the barn, patiently assisting Tay in his wildlife rescue efforts, and serving in any capacity Lexy assigned him while she produced copies of the *Wild Swan Journal*, the newspaper she had founded after receiving a child's-size printing press for Christmas.

Since its inception, the journal had created hilarity among the adult population of the farm, though everyone was careful to read it with a straight face when the children were present. The paper presented a strange mix that made no distinction between such things as snippets of national news gleaned from Cousin Reid's columns and barnyard reports about which chickens were laying, which horses were foaling or racing, and which cows had produced the best calves. Lexy also included academic reports that, typically, noted Tay's arithmetic was better this week or "Willy McCoy read aloud last Thursday."

Lexy had already learned that bad school reports were received with less than good grace by her siblings and playmates.

To Joseph, all three of his Culhane cousins seemed special, children as he thought children ought to be—happy, strong, and loved by their real parents. He could not have articulated the difference, but inside he knew he could never be quite like them, though he was now convinced of how much his Aunt Anthea and Uncle Max loved him. And while he was careful to show no preference for one cousin over another, he especially liked the time he spent with Lexy. She was more serious and responsible than her brothers, and he was as captivated as she by the process of setting up the type and having a backward line come out the right way 'round. They both enjoyed the game of rewriting lines to accommodate a shortage of this or that letter.

Joseph was not so at ease when the Culhanes and McCoys joined forces. He found the McCoys a little rough and tumble, but he went along gamely. He sensed that Willy McCoy would rather he didn't join their games, and that it had something to do with Lexy, but he wasn't sure what. Willy was eleven this year to Lexy's ten, and since Joseph was only eight, he couldn't see how he could be any threat to the older boy.

This June day started out particularly well to Joseph's mind. It was hot and still, and the cousins decided to play in the wood where it was cooler. Best of all, it began with just the four of them, with no McCoys in sight. Joseph knew it was unkind of him, but he hoped the McCoys had chores that would keep them away all day.

They'd only had a few games of hide-and-go-seek before a babble of voices and calls heralded the arrival of the McCoys.

Willy was in hectically high spirits from the beginning, talking and shrieking so loudly that Joseph felt the inner part of his ears trying to shut out the sound. He glanced at Lexy and saw that she didn't look much more pleased than he felt.

Lexy thought Willy was acting very silly, but she didn't want to embarrass him by saying so. She knew he was showing off for her, and it made her sad for him. He was such a stringy, freckled gawk of a boy, with his ears sticking out on the sides of his head. He seemed to need to attract attention to his antics, as if he were saying, "See, it doesn't matter how I look, I can make you laugh." Lexy wished she could tell him it truly didn't matter how he looked, that he didn't have to dance about like a crazy person. She had caught glimpses of a quieter side of him, and she much preferred it.

The cold water of the stream felt good on her bare feet, and she wished they'd brought fishing poles with them. She was tired of playing hide-and-go-seek and would have liked to do something quiet for a while.

But Willy was still hopping about as if the day weren't so hot and muggy.

"Let's play stagecoach robbers," he said, and then with a wide grin of triumph, he produced the surprise he had hidden in his baggy clothes, the big horse pistol that belonged to his father.

The whole mood of the day changed.

"Put that down right now, Willy McCoy, before you hurt someone!" Lexy snapped, and out of the corner of her eye, she saw Joseph frozen in place, eyes fixed on the gun.

"Aw, it ain't loaded," Willy protested. "You're just a girl. I was gonna let you be a stage robber, but now you can't play."

"I don't want to play. Joseph, Kace, Tay, come on, we're going home now."

Joseph started to edge away toward the deeper shadows of the trees, but the twins eyed Willy and his two brothers longingly. They were younger and felt honored to be able to play with the group, and it was hard to have to side with their sister, the only girl.

"Let's stay, please, Lexy," Kace pled.

Lexy was implacable. The more she considered Willy fidgeting with the weapon in his hand, the more frightened she became. "No, you know what Papa says about guns. We aren't ever, ever to play with them. And if Willy won't put that down, then we have to go home."

The mention of their father did it for the twins; they had no trouble remembering the numerous lectures he had given them regarding firearms. He seldom interfered in their play, but he had left no doubt about the terrible things that could happen if guns were in the wrong hands. And it occurred to Kace that he knew a lot more about how to handle that pistol than Willy McCoy did. Travis had taken care to show all three children how to shoot and how to care for the weapons so they would not blow up in one's face.

"Come on, Tay," he said, taking his brother's hand. "I think we'd better do what Lexy says. That old Willy doesn't know what he's doing."

Willy felt more foolish than usual in front of Lexy, and he brandished the pistol in both hands, trying to look as he imagined a Wells Fargo agent would. "You can be the bandits if you stay," he offered.

"Put that pistol down!" Lexy ordered, reaching for Kace's hand.

They both felt as much as heard the sharp crack because Kace was holding Tay's hand, and when the bullet hit Tay, the shock of it traveled through Kace to Lexy. But at first, they were too shocked to understand what had happened.

Willy understood immediately. He dropped the pistol as if it were a rattlesnake, and his mouth pulled wide in a rictus of horror. "It wasn't loaded, wasn't!" he screamed.

The sound of Willy's voice was drowned out by the inhuman screech of fury from Joseph, springing from the shadows after Willy and his brothers as they turned and ran.

Tay crumpled to the ground, blood rapidly staining the back of his shirt and his breeches. Kace fell to his knees beside him, tugging at his arm. "No, Tay, you're all right, you're all right! Get up now!"

Lexy wanted to deny the truth, wanted to run home, but her mother and grandmother had already taught her too much about the healing arts. She grabbed Kace by his shoulders, and when he didn't respond, she shook him hard. "Run home as fast as you can, do you understand? As fast as you can! We need help *now*!"

When Kace only blinked hazily and murmured, "I can't leave Tay," Lexy slapped him and then shook him again. "Run! Tay is going to die if we don't get help!" She made herself say the word "die," and it got through to Kace.

Lexy heard Kace's footsteps sprinting away as she crouched over Tay, and then there was nothing except her little brother. She searched her mind frantically for all the things she had learned that might be of use. It steadied her when she conjured the voice of her mother saying, "Bleeding is one of the most dangerous things of all. If someone is bleeding badly, if they're still breathing without choking, nothing is more important than stopping the bleeding."

The bullet had entered his back to the side and just above his waist. She managed to turn him on his side enough to discover there was no exit wound in the front, so she only had the one hole to worry about. He murmured but didn't cry out when she moved him, and that seemed more frightening than if he'd screamed, so she started talking to him as she worked.

"Tay, listen to me! Kace has gone for help. Mama and Papa will be here soon, but I'll take care of you until they come. I know what to do." She hoped he didn't hear how much her voice was shaking.

"Willy shot me, didn't he? Dumb ol' Willy. Boy, is he gonna be in trouble. Don' worry, Lexy, doesn't hurt." His voice wandered and wavered as if he were speaking from underwater.

Lexy was glad and at the same time scared that he didn't feel anything, but she kept working, wadding up her shirt and pressing it against the wound, stripping off her breeches to add a little more warmth for Tay because she could feel the chill on his skin, despite the heat of the day.

When Travis and Gincie, led by Kace, rode in, Lexy, wearing only a pair of cotton drawers, was huddled over Tay, keeping pressure on the wound and trying to share her body's warmth with him.

As Gincie knelt down beside Tay, Travis lifted Lexy up and wrapped her in his own shirt, feeling her tremble against him like a trapped bird. "It's goin' to be fine, little darlin'; we'll take care of him now. You and Kace have done well." His own heart was pounding so hard, it sounded louder to him than his words, and he was nearly as worried about Lexy and Kace as he was about Tay. That Tay might be dying here on the warm summer earth was something he could not allow himself to consider.

A cart was following them from the farm, but Gincie said, "We can't wait. We have to get him home as fast as we can." Her face was as white as the children's.

"Lexy, wasn't Joseph with you?" she asked, afraid if she looked further, she'd find another fallen child.

Lexy nodded, trying to put the jumbled terror into order. "He ran after Willy," she finally managed.

"We can't worry about him now," Travis said grimly. "The pistol's here, so at least there won't be any more shootin'."

Travis cradled Tay before him on the saddle, and Gincie took the other two children up with her, Lexy holding on behind, Kace in front, and when her mount started to buck a little in protest, Gincie's sharp command and a flick of the reins warned the horse that no nonsense would be tolerated.

"You're goin' to be all right, son; just hang on, and we'll have you home in no time." Travis kept talking to Tay, hoping his voice would somehow get through to his son. Tay felt so fine-boned and small in his arms, not at all like the sturdy little boy who had gone off to play this morning.

Alex had immediately sent word to Nigel to bring the best surgeon he knew to Wild Swan; she had hoped the call would be unnecessary, but the minute she saw Tay, she knew it would be a miracle if the doctor got there in time. And there was no question of taking Tay to Baltimore; he was already too weakened from blood loss to sustain such a rough trip.

Sally was sent to Sunrise to look for Joseph, and she found him dirty and disheveled, but on his way back to Wild Swan.

"Do you want to tell me what happened?" she asked gently.

He stared at her for a long moment before he said, "I beat Willy McCoy with my fists. I made his nose bleed, but I don't think I broke anything, except maybe that nose. I thought he was those men. I stopped when I knew it was only Willy." His throat worked convulsively, and his eyes pled with her to understand.

She left him no doubt that she did. "Of course you thought that. It must have reminded you of terrible things when Tay was shot." She was careful to speak as if the transformation of an eight-year-old boy into an angel of vengeance was nothing out of the ordinary; Joseph did not need to feel any more the outsider than he did already.

"Is Tay d . . . dead?" Joseph asked.

"No, and everyone is doing everything possible to make sure he gets well," she told him firmly. When she got him back to Wild Swan, she helped him to clean up, and then she tucked him into bed and gave him a glass of milk with nutmeg, sugar, and just a drop of brandy in it. Della had fixed it, understanding exactly how shocked Joseph was by his own behavior.

The unfamiliar taste of brandy made Joseph feel as if he were an adult and paradoxically made it all right when Sally held his hand as if he were a baby while he fell asleep.

Sally knew what it was to feel young and terrified, and she remembered how safe she had felt with the Kingstons. She wanted to make Joseph feel as much of that security as she could.

It was as if the heartbeat of Wild Swan hung suspended. Only work essential to keeping the animals fed and comfortable was done; everyone's attention was focused on Tay's condition.

Travis had to wrench himself away from Tay's bedside, but with Gincie and Alex hovering over the boy, there was nothing much he could do there, and he was still worried about the other children. He checked with Sally first and then found Kace and Lexy with Della.

She was trying to tempt them with cool drinks and cookies, but they both just sat there, their eyes huge in bleached faces. When they saw their father, they both began talking at once.

"Willy McCoy was showing off for me. I should've made him stop it," Lexy said. "It's my fault."

"I wanted to stay and play. If I hadn't made us wait, we wouldn't've been there when the gun went off," Kace said. "So it's really my fault."

Although he had only Kace's first babbled account of what had happened, Travis spoke firmly. "Neither of you is to blame, and neither is Willy McCoy. I'm sure he didn't mean to shoot Tay." It was difficult for him to add this absolution. If Willy were before him, he wasn't sure what he would do.

He stretched out an arm to each of the children, and they came to him, nestling against him. Kace began to sob, a quiet, helpless little river of sound, but Lexy was still too shocked for tears.

"The bullet didn't come out, Papa. It's still inside him. He needs an operation, and people die from that." The words were a monotone, as if she were reciting a lesson she didn't understand.

"People also live because of surgery," Travis reminded her. "And your Uncle Nigel is going to bring the best surgeon he knows."

"If Tay dies, then I die too," Kace said. It was not a question.

"No, you won't! You and Tay are twins, but you aren't the same person! You hear me, Kace, you are separate!" He felt as if he were choking on Kace's despair because, though Kace nodded obediently, he obviously did not believe a word his father was saying. "Tay is still alive, and we're goin' to do everythin' we can to make sure he gets better." He wondered whether he was saying the words aloud for the children or for himself.

"Is Joseph all right?" Lexy asked, suddenly seeing his face as it had looked when he lunged for Willy. "He was so angry!"

"Sally has put him to bed," Travis told her. "He'll be all right. I'm sure the gun made him think about what happened to his parents."

Lexy's hand stole into his as she thought about that.

It seemed as if days had passed rather than hours by the time Nigel arrived with Dr. Samuels in tow, but the two physicians had ridden as hard as they could. And Dr. Samuels had been prepared by Nigel to deal honestly with Tay's parents and with Alex, and he was impressed by the clear account he received.

"He's been conscious only once since we brought him in," Gincie told him. "He was in great pain, but the period of consciousness lasted only a few minutes. The exterior bleeding has stopped, but God knows what's happening inside." Her face was gray, her green eyes muddy, but her voice was steady.

Dr. Samuel's examination was thorough but quickly done, every motion bespeaking his knowledge of time running out.

Alex slipped away to summon Travis, and the surgeon spoke to both parents. "It is a difficult decision. Surgery is always a risk. He was clearly a strong, healthy little boy until the moment he was shot, and that's all to the good. But his body has already sustained massive trauma. There is a possibility that he could live with the bullet inside him; it has happened before. But in my opinion, that's a very slim chance. Bullets travel in strange and awful ways, wounding various organs as they go and causing infection."

Dr. Samuels was tall and lanky with a rather severe face, but his eyes were kind, his hands well kept and steady, his forty or more years indicating experience, and Nigel had chosen him, Nigel who adored all the children. It was precisely because Nigel and the Kingstons so loved the children that Alex had requested an outside physician.

Unmindful of the others in the room, Travis touched the place where Gincie's scar lay beneath the material of her dress. "You survived my rough surgery. Tay is made of the same blood and bone as yours, as ours. He'll have better care than I could give you, and he'll survive, too."

Their hands locked together, and Travis nodded to the doctor. "We trust you and Nigel to do the best you can for our son."

"Do you need Gincie or me to assist you?" Alex asked, her voice leaving no doubt that either or both of them would, but Nigel shook his head. "I promise, Gran, I'll call you if we need you."

They did not try to hide anything from Kace and Lexy as they waited for the outcome of the operation, but it was heartbreaking to see the too-adult reserve on both of their faces, the blank hopelessness in their eyes. And it was especially painful to look at Kace. He and Tay were not identical twins, but they were so alike and so attuned to each other, it was like having him near death in the room above and, at the same time, here with them. It added chilling weight to what Kace had said about dying if his twin died.

Della quietly offered food and drink and kept the others at Wild Swan informed by reporting periodically to Padraic, but even as Rane and other members of the family began to arrive, her main concern was Alex. They had been bound together through so many years, through so much triumph and tragedy, she could scarcely bear the thought that Alex might now lose her great-grandson as she had lost children of her own and her grandson Seth. It was too much. And yet, it was Alex who, with Rane's arm around her, explained the situation as the family arrived, excluding the Kingstons, who had patients they could not leave, in addition to caring for those of Nigel's who needed immediate attention. Anthea and Max had to trust that Sally and the others would care for Joseph, and at this point, having heard only that Tay had been accidentally shot by Willy McCoy, they had no knowledge of Joseph's involvement.

Finally Nigel appeared. "He's holding his own, and we found the bullet. There was some internal damage, but we think the bleeding is under control. In one way he was lucky; a rib deflected the bullet and slowed it down. The damage could have been much worse. Now it's just a matter of time, and of the kind of healing you," he looked at his grandmother, "and Gincie do better than we."

"Can I see him?" Kace asked.

"It would be better if you waited," Nigel told him gently. "He wouldn't know you were there right now."

But Kace stood his ground. "Twins know things about each other. He will so know I'm there, even if he can't talk to me."

Nigel shot a questioning glance at Travis and Gincie and then turned his attention back to Kace, holding out his hand. "All right, you can see him just for a minute. I'll take you up." He offered his other hand to Lexy. "And you, too."

Inwardly Travis blessed Nigel's sensitivity in understanding that Lexy's need was as great as Tay's, though she would not ask because she wasn't a twin. Travis and Gincie followed the procession, but allowed their children to go in first with Nigel. Their three offspring were so close, not even parental rights superseded theirs to be together.

Dr. Samuels raised his eyebrows at the intrusion, but it took only seconds for him to understand the situation. He found he had to swallow hard against the lump in his throat.

Kace and Lexy approached the bed timidly, their eyes wide and frightened as they stared at their brother. One of the rooms usually reserved for guests had been turned into a sickroom, and Tay looked very small in the big bed. He had been propped up against the pillows to aid his breathing, and his face looked nearly as pale as the linens, as if all the tan of summer had drained away with his blood. Dark shadows already circled his eyes.

Lexy was afraid to open her mouth for fear she would cry, but very carefully she patted one of his hands that lay on the coverlet, and the words she couldn't say tumbled around in her head, endless pleas that he get well.

Kace's breathing was suddenly loud in the room, as if he had been running hard, but he finally managed to control it. He leaned very close to his twin and whispered, "Tay, it's me. I'm here, and the whole house is full of people who want you to get better. Tay, you can't . . ." his voice broke, and he steadied it, "you can't die. You an' me, we're twins, that's what we're always supposed to be, but there's gotta be two to be twins." His whisper faded away, and then he said very softly, "Tay, I love you, don't leave me." He backed away from the bed.

Nigel, his vision blurred by tears, escorted the children from the room.

For the first twenty-four hours, Gincie and Travis stayed beside Tay with only brief absences. Travis couldn't stop breathing in Tay's rhythm even when he tried. It was as if the action of his own heart and lungs could help sustain his son's.

Gincie didn't want to think about it but could not stop considering what life would be like without Tay. She remembered how it had felt when her body had carried the twins, swelling with their presence until they possessed all her days and nights. And she remembered how hard she had labored to bring them forth, not sure, though she had suspected, that there were two babies, not sure until they were born and she held them in her arms. That all the loving and pain that had created Tay would end because of an idiotic accident during a child's game was inconceivable.

When Michael McCoy came to the house with Willy, Rane conducted the interview, making the decision that Gincie and Travis were going through enough without this.

He was a straightforward, hardworking man, not given to subtleties. That his son had shot his employer's child was a complexity that was beyond his imagination. He seemed to have aged years overnight, and the change in Willy was even more severe. His freckles stood out as ugly splotches against his fear-bleached skin. He looked more awkward and ill-made than ever before, and though he was a year older than Lexy, his thumb kept stealing into his mouth as if he wished to be a suckling babe again. His nose was swollen, and he had a black eye, marks of Joseph's fury that not even Willy's brothers had been able to quell. All the spirit and mischief had been eclipsed. He cringed at his father's side, and Rane had no doubt that he had been soundly thrashed by his father as well as by Joseph.

It was clear to Rane that if Tay died, Willy McCoy would never recover.

"Mr. Falconer, I'm sorry we been so long comin' to you, but the boys, they kept it all a secret until Willy broke down an' 'fessed up to what he done." Mr. McCoy's mouth worked with the effort to get the next words out. "The little 'un, Tay, is he . . . is he . . ."

"The bullet's out, and he's holding his own," Rane said. "We have every hope for his recovery."

Willy slumped against his father's side and would have crumpled to the floor had his father not held him in an iron grip. "I never meant . . . I never . . . I'd never hurt nobody, not Tay or Kace or Lexy . . . I'm so s-s-sorry." Sobs engulfed him.

Rane couldn't bear any more. "Willy, everyone knows it was not intentional. The best you can do is to cease blaming yourself and help to teach your brothers that weapons are not playthings." Rane wondered if Mr. McCoy had ever instructed his children about such things, but he didn't ask.

"Mr. Falconer," Michael McCoy said, "I would thank you if you'd tell the Culhanes we'll be gone from the farm in a few days, if that suits them. It'll take me that long to pack up everything."

There was no question in the man's mind that the Culhanes

would demand the McCoys leave, but it was a possibility that Rane had not even considered, so it took him a moment to reply.

"I can't speak for them," he admitted, "but I doubt that they will want you to leave Sunrise. You have done a good job for them there. The accident doesn't change that. Please continue with your work until you hear from them." He didn't know what the situation would be if Tay died; he wasn't sure the two families would be able to stand the sight of each other then.

Mr. McCoy thanked him sincerely, but the sorrow in his eyes was indication that he was considering the same thing.

"We'll keep you informed of Tay's condition," Rane assured him, and then quietly he asked a favor of the man, "Please, don't belabor the boy any more. He has surely suffered nearly as much as Tay in this tragedy."

When Rane discussed the interview with Alex, she agreed there was no reason to trouble Travis and Gincie with it now.

Rane wrapped his arms around Alex and held her while she rested her head wearily against his shoulder.

"This awful time is a reminder of how fortunate we have been with the great-grandchildren. Aside from minor complaints, they have been so healthy. And now this."

The household quickly settled into a routine, with Travis and Gincie taking turns keeping the longest vigils beside Tay's bed, and the others filling in when they could persuade the parents to rest. Reid went back to Georgetown, but Larissa remained at Wild Swan to help where she could, and the rest of the family came and went, doing what they could, too.

Sally tried to keep Joseph amused and out of the way, but early on, she begged a favor from Nigel. "I know the Kingstons will be here as soon as they can, and then everything will be easier for Joseph, but I think he would feel so much better if you talked to him about Tay. Joseph trusts you." She did not have to add that she did also; it showed in her eyes. Nigel was part of the family that had saved her; therefore, he was one of the small number of men she trusted.

Nigel didn't lie to Joseph. He told him what Tay's injuries were and what had been done to help him.

"I should have taken the gun away from Willy the minute I saw it," Joseph whispered. "I know what guns can do."

"It was an accident, and it happened very quickly," Nigel reminded him. "If you had tried to take the pistol from Willy, it might have been far worse." He searched Joseph's dark eyes. "It would not have been better if you had been shot instead of Tay. The only thing that would have been better would have been if no one at all were hurt. I know it is going to take you a long time to believe it, but Anthea and Max love you very, very much, so much that if anything happened to you, they would be just as sad as Gincie and Travis are about what happened to Tay. And the rest of us would be just as sad, too. You're a very important part of this family. I swear to you, I wouldn't say any of this if it were not true."

Joseph's trust of his cousin Nigel ran deep, and his worry and guilt lessened.

Out of Joseph's hearing, Sally thanked Nigel and added, "He's such a sensitive little fellow, and so much has happened to him already. I wish it were possible to make sure he is never hurt again, but I know it's not."

Nigel listened to her soft, cultured voice, all the rough edges smoothed by the time with Flora. He saw her clearly for the first time in years, saw that at seventeen, she was quite lovely with her deep blue eyes, blond hair, symmetrical features, and the soft curves of womanhood. He saw the love and compassion she had for his young cousin, and he thought that Sally ought to have children of her own someday. And then he thought that it was a shock to be thinking of Sally Birch this way and that it must surely be because he was so tired.

"Dr. Falconer, are you all right?" Sally asked anxiously, not understanding the strange expression on his face.

"Please, call me Nigel," he said, and then seeing her doubtful look, he continued, "It's just because Dr. Falconer sounds so formal, as if I'm decades older than you." He would be thirty this year, thirteen years older than Sally. Was that too old? Too old for what? He rubbed his face wearily, thinking he was getting in deeper every minute.

"Pay no attention to me," he said. "I seem to be tired enough to talk nonsense."

Sally smiled at him, showing a sudden flash of mischief and humor. "The elderly Dr. Falconer speaking nonsense? Why, it could never happen!"

She left in a flurry of skirts to return to Joseph, and Nigel stared after her, still seeing how beautiful she had looked when she smiled and wishing he could protect her from pain and worry as she was trying to protect Joseph. He focused his attention on Tay again, but in the back of his mind, Sally's image lingered, and it continued to haunt his dreams when he turned his vigil over to the Culhanes and sought his own rest.

In the early hours of one morning, Travis heard a noise outside the door of Tay's room, and when Gincie did not come in, he got up to investigate. He found Kace sitting on the floor by the door, his head resting on his knees.

Kace realized his father was standing over him, but he was so tired, he could hardly lift his head. Travis didn't question why he was there; he picked him up and carried him to Tay's bedside, settling down in the chair again with Kace on his lap.

After a long silence, Kace asked softly, "Does he ever wake up?"

"He has a couple of times," Travis told him. "It was just for a little while, but it's a good sign."

"What if he doesn't wake up again? What if he dies after all? Will I find him again when I die, too?"

Kace did not raise his voice, but the questions were as loud as thunder to Travis. In despair, he thought that these were the sorts of questions dreaded by every parent because there were no perfect answers, even if one were an orthodox believer, which he was not.

"The truth is, I don't know," he said. "No one has come back from the other side to tell us what happens after we die. But I can tell you what I think. I think the human spirit, that part of you that's inside, that's especially you and makes you different from everyone else, even from Tay, I think that part probably goes on forever, somewhere, somehow."

His arms tightened around Kace. "The one thing I'm sure of is that you don't have to worry about it because you can't change it, whatever it is. But you can do your best while you're livin' here on this earth. That's all anyone can do. And you can believe your brother is gettin' well. I can't make any promises, but I think the two of you will be plottin' all sorts of mischief before too long."

He felt Kace settle against him and relax in sleep. If there was anything more satisfying and, at the same time, more terrifying than the trust of a child, Travis did not want to know about it.

By the end of a week, they were all breathing easier. Tay still looked very frail, tired easily, and was very sore, but he was definitely on the mend. Though he slept a great deal, he was alert when awake, his appetite was improving, and most encouraging of all, he was anxious to get out of bed.

"I sure hate missing all this vacation," he complained, and Gincie had to turn away until she got control of her tears. She could not imagine how she would explain to Tay that now that he was getting well, she seemed to be falling apart.

On the first night they had back in their own bed, together, with no vigil beside Tay to break the night, Travis was just sinking into exhausted sleep when he felt Gincie begin to tremble. Her skin was chilled, and when he touched her face, he felt the tears streaming down her cheeks before he heard the first muffled sob.

He turned her over so she faced him and put his arms around her, rubbing her back.

"I'm be . . . being ridiculous!" she choked. "It's all over, and I'm . . ."

"Go ahead and cry, darlin'. Scream your head off if you want. You stayed strong while it mattered."

"Oh, God! We came so close to losing him!" she wailed. "I thought I knew how Gran felt when my father died, how it was for Sam and Morgan when Seth died, but I didn't, I didn't know!"

The tears overwhelmed her, and Travis kept on holding her, his own cheeks wet, until the storm passed, and Gincie whispered, "Love me."

Fragile, weary, and infinitely vulnerable, they came together, taking great care to love each other well. There were no great explosions of passion, but the beat of one heart echoed the beat of the other, and Gincie found refuge by sheltering Travis's flesh in her own. They fell asleep still intertwined, unwilling to lose the mutual comfort.

Chapter 17

By the time Anthea and Max were able to come to Wild Swan, Nigel had had his talk with Joseph, and Tay was in the first stages of recovery. When the Kingstons heard the details of the shooting, including Joseph's reaction to it, their guilt was instantaneous.

"We should have come immediately," Anthea said. "I should have thought of what it would do to Joseph even if he hadn't been right there to witness it. But we've had so many emergencies, one after the other."

"I told him I would always be there to listen, and I wasn't," Max said.

"Sally has been very attentive, and Nigel spoke to him," Gincie told them, "and while I'm not saying he is a substitute for either of you, you know how wise and kind he is. Joseph seems to be doing quite well. I realize the case is different with him, but all the same, you ought to be able to depend on the rest of the family, just as we all do. You had patients who needed you, and it wasn't as if Joseph were left alone on a doorstep."

Their anxious expressions eased, and Anthea smiled at Gincie. "You sound more like Gran every day."

They soon learned the truth of Gincie's words, because it was some time before they saw Joseph, since he was out playing.

After a hurried greeting, he informed them, "We think Tinker and Blue miss Tay 'specially, but we've told them that Tay's getting better."

The "we" indicating he identified himself with his cousins was particularly good to hear. And in a more serious vein, he spoke to Max without prompting.

"I 'pologized to Willy for hitting him, and he said it was okay because he deserved it. But he didn't, not really. He didn't mean to shoot Tay. And I didn't really mean to hit Willy. I got awful mad, like . . . like." Only then did he hesitate, and Max suggested gently, "Like when your father was shot?"

Joseph nodded, looking puzzled. "It seemed like the same thing, but it wasn't."

"That happens to everyone," Max assured him. "When something very good or very bad has happened to us, we remember it, and sometimes another good or bad thing can make us confuse the past with the present." He wasn't sure Joseph understood what he was saying, but the little boy was comforted by the fact that his had not been a unique experience.

"I didn't like hitting Willy," Joseph confided. "Even when I couldn't stop, I didn't like it."

"That's good," Max said. "Hitting other people hardly ever solves anything, though sometimes there doesn't seem to be any way to avoid it." He was infinitely heartened to know that Joseph had not enjoyed his excursion into violence. He knew that he had a great well of violence and anger trapped inside, but day by day, it was becoming clear that the child's basically kind and thoughtful nature was still intact. Max hoped it would always be dominant.

When Gincie asked that Joseph be allowed to stay at Wild Swan for more of the summer, Anthea and Max agreed. They missed him dreadfully, but the city was disease ridden in the heat, and he was at risk by the very nature of their medical practice, which brought the sick into close proximity to them and thus to him.

Though Gincie was torn by conflicting demands, in the end she had little doubt where her major duty lay. She decided to stay at Wild Swan with the children while Travis, Alex, and Rane went to the races.

"I wish I could tell you that I think you ought to go with me, but I can't," Travis said. "One of us ought to be here until Tay is fully recovered. But I will offer to stay in your place. I might not have your maternal instincts, but Della could assist me over the difficult parts."

Gincie loved him for the offer, but she shook her head. "If I can't be with you, I'd rather be here. I know that the subject of Mark is not raised, at least not in my presence, but I'd rather you faced everyone without me beside you than the other way around."

With the McCoys' and the Kingstons' permission, Travis did accomplish an important task before he left. He took the three McCoy children and Joseph out for shooting lessons.

The children were flattered by Travis's attention and, at the same time, unenthusiastic about the lesson. Since they had witnessed the accident that had nearly taken Tay's life, guns had ceased to hold any attraction for them. But Travis was calm and patient, instructing them over and over again in the principles of safety, caring for weapons, and shooting accurately.

Willy was shaking so much that, even with two hands, he could not hold the pistol Travis was using for the demonstration; but Travis wrapped his own hands around Willy's to steady them.

"This is too heavy for any of you to handle alone," Travis told them. "You're as likely to shoot off your own foot as you are to hit a target. But someday, when you're older, you might need to use a gun or you might wish to learn to hunt. For now, you're old enough to understand that guns are never, ever to be used as playthings."

Willy's eyes filled with tears, and he hung his head. Travis reached out and ruffled his hair. "That's a lesson for everyone, and you've surely learned it already."

It was difficult for Gincie to see her grandparents and her husband leave without her, particularly because Travis would be going on to California after the summer racing season closed. But there were compensations. The days of summer, unbroken by the racing schedule, were patterned instead by the activities of the children and the rhythms of life on the farm. She got to visit with the rest of the family as they sought brief respites from Baltimore, Washington, and Georgetown. And though Morgan, Adam and Mercy and their son, and Nigel naturally stayed at Brookhaven, they, with Sam, were often at Wild Swan.

It made Gincie very aware of how central to the lives of the family Wild Swan was, how much of a refuge and home Alex had made it.

Reid made sure that Gincie received the sporting news as soon as possible, and so she was able vicariously to enjoy the performances of Wild Swan's horses, especially Moonraker, who was running with such speed and grace that the turf writers were lavishing him with praise, and in so doing, were also writing extensively about the Falconers and the Culhanes. One piece noted that "the lovely Mrs. Culhane was missed by all, but her absence was forgiven as she remained at Wild Swan to care for one of the Culhane children who is recovering from an accident." Considering what she had once dreaded to read in the papers about herself, Gincie found the piece very flattering.

Lexy was fascinated by the mentions in the newspapers, and she questioned Reid about how such information got into print when he hadn't written it.

"Wild Swan's horses, your great-grandmother, and now your parents are well known in the racing world," he explained. "So newspaper reporters, even the ones in New York State, are interested in them."

Reid had a special fondness for Lexy. "I think she'll become a good reporter someday," he told Gincie. "She's been interested since the first day she smelled printer's ink, and she grows more, not less, involved as she grows older."

Reid enjoyed the visits the Culhane children and Joseph made to the capital, where in company with the Tratnor three, they were taken to see various sights and exhibits. All the children were bright and inquisitive, but Lexy was the one who asked the most penetrating questions about why things were the way they were, and she never accepted easy or complacent answers.

The Culhane and Tratnor children had been spellbound by the sight of the visiting Sioux chiefs in Washington in early May, but it was Lexy who had wanted to know all the details of why they were there. She had not forgotten the poor Indians she had seen in the train trip across the country, and the Sioux chiefs, cloaked in somber dignity despite the motley of white man's and Indian garments they wore, seemed much more as she thought Indians should be. Even their names—Red Cloud, Spotted Tail, White Swan—enchanted her.

Reid did not try to soften the truth. "They are here because our government keeps making promises and giving them land and then taking it away when white men want it."

He showed her the account of Red Cloud that his paper had printed:

"When I speak, I always call on the Great Spirit to hear me, because I tell the truth. The white men tell me many lies, and I became so troubled, I wanted to come to Washington and see the Great Father himself, and talk to him. That is why I have come to see you."

After a moment, Red Cloud arose and added, "When I spoke of white men telling me lies, I did not mean the white men present." His sly humor provoked laughter from both sides.

"It's wrong to take away the Indians' land," Lexy said flatly. "How can they do that?"

"Unfortunately, 'they' are our government, which means all of us, even if all of us do not agree. There are many, many people in this country who do not want Indians to live anywhere. There has been a lot of killing on both sides, and that's hard to forgive or to forget, though too many white people find it convenient to forget that the Indians have killed because their lands are being taken, the buffalo they depend on for food slaughtered, their homes destroyed, their people attacked."

"I think that must be why Aunt Rachel looked sad sometimes," Lexy said. "I don't remember everything about California—I was so little then—but I think I remember that. Someday I'm going to write about why we ought to treat people better, Indians and everybody."

"I expect you will," Reid said, but the pride he felt in his niece was mixed with sorrow; she was always going to choose the more difficult path when her sense of justice demanded it, which would, no doubt, be frequently.

Lexy had always been an observant child, and the family was accustomed to it, but Gincie was shocked when her daughter said, "Do you think Cousin Nigel will marry Sally Birch?"

Gincie stared at her. "Marry Sally! Why ever would you think that?"

It was Lexy's turn to be surprised because it seldom occurred to her that everyone did not see things as plainly as she did. "Well, he comes to Wild Swan more than ever before, and he always wants to see Sally first, even when he tries not to be anxious. Sally could keep Cousin Nigel from being lonely by being his wife."

"Have you said anything to them?" Gincie managed to ask.

Lexy shook her head in vigorous negation. "No, because they're sort of bashful about it."

"How wise of you. I think perhaps we ought to keep it a secret until they decide to tell us," Gincie suggested. Inwardly, she was already beginning to accept the idea of a romance between Nigel and Sally. Not only was Lexy seldom wrong, but now Gincie was seeing Nigel's visits in a new light. She had no doubt of the validity of Nigel's concern and love for Joseph, a bond that had been strengthened in the aftermath of Tay's accident, but his attention went beyond that. Sally's actions were more difficult to judge; she did not seem any different when Nigel was there.

Gincie had been very fond of Nigel since their childhood, and she thought of what a good husband and father he would make. She thought of what a fine young woman Sally was. And then she thought of Sally's awful family, and her heart sank. She knew how careful Sally was to keep them separate from her job with the Kingstons, how careful she had been since the beginning, when she had been with Flora. But if she married Nigel, there would no longer be any way for her to pretend that she was nothing more than an employee.

Sam had also begun to notice, and her thoughts were parallel to Gincie's. She was relieved when Morgan came to Brookhaven.

"Have you noticed anything different about Nigel?" she asked him.

Morgan cocked his head, studying her. "You wouldn't ask me that unless there was something different, so let me think. He seems as happy and dedicated as ever in his work, except that he has managed to spend more time out in the country this summer. . . ." His voice trailed off as he considered that more closely. "And Nigel, being as normal as any young man, would probably not have changed his pattern unless there was a young woman involved."

"A very young woman," Sam supplied, and had the satisfaction of seeing the shock she'd felt register on her husband's face as he exclaimed, "My God! Sally Birch! Well, it is not so odd. She is quite beautiful, well spoken, intelligent, and gentle-natured." He followed his train of thought further. "And she has a horrible family. Even that would appeal to Nigel. He's always been a champion of the helpless. The chance to protect Sally from her relatives would please him mightily."

"As it pleased you to protect me," Sam said quietly. "I didn't want to see the similarity, but it's there. My family wasn't horrid in the same way, but it was bad enough." She touched his lean face. "And nothing could be worse than my father's refusal to get you out of Andersonville until I blackmailed him into it."

Morgan turned his head as he captured her hand in his own and lightly kissed her palm. "In any case, there is nothing for us to do until Nigel and Sally decide what they wish. Sally may be only seventeen, but Nigel is thirty."

"That makes me feel ancient when I consider it," Sam admitted. "Sometimes I find it nearly impossible to believe that my youngest son is that old."

"I have ways of making you feel young again," Morgan offered with an exaggerated leer as he pulled her into his arms.

Sam's last coherent thought was that no matter what the difficulties, she would not want to deny to Nigel the chance of having the same warm loving she and Morgan shared.

Nigel was aware that his family was beginning to suspect his visits to Sally, though no one said anything. It was impossible that it would be otherwise in such a closely knit clan. It did not concern him as long as it didn't make Sally any shyer than she was.

Nigel was sure there had never been a more careful courting than his of Sally. When he wanted to tell her that her hair was glorious, or her eyes entrancing, he spoke of the latest news from Baltimore. When he wanted to take her in his arms, he asked her about the books she'd read recently. When he wanted to tell her that she was the first woman he had imagined as a companion, not only for the bright passion he felt now, but for the years of old age, he talked to her about the harvest and horses of the farms.

In some ways, Sally was very open, in her devotion to Joseph's well-being, in her endless gratitude for what the Carringtons, Falconers, and Culhanes had done for her, in her enthusiasm for the world of learning that Flora had opened for her, and in her love for the beauties of nature, whether they be as small as a butterfly or as large as the racehorses.

But in other vital ways, she was a hidden soul. She took each day as it came and betrayed no hopes or dreams about what she might be doing in the future. She never expressed any personal desires, not for possessions, not for anything, not even for one kind of food over another. When a meal was served, she obligingly took a small serving of whatever was offered, but she never asked for more of this or that, though she must surely like some things better than others; and though there was never any shortage of food, and dishes were refilled if they were emptied too soon, she would automatically refuse a dish if it were too depleted.

Nigel watched and noticed everything about her, and he was alternately fascinated and appalled. He understood that she had come from a family where there was seldom enough to eat, and because she had been like a mother to the younger children, she had long ago learned to consider her own needs last. It was a pattern so well established, not even her years with Flora and the Kingstons had changed it. It was the same with everything in her life; deprivation had been the rule for so long, she did not trust plenty to continue in any form, least of all in love; her uncle had taught her a brutal lesson on that count. She had learned to accept praise for work well done because it was a direct exchange, but Nigel could imagine only too well what her reaction would be if he offered her his love. Sally did not consider herself worthy of love; therefore, she would undoubtedly flee in fear and confusion from the offer of it—unless he could change her perception of herself.

His strategy was simple. He planned to love her subtley, relentlessly, until she had grown so used to his presence and attentions, it would be impossible for her to imagine being without him.

He felt he was making progress during the summer. When he brought her his first gift, copies of two new books, *A Winter in Mexico* and *Dolores*, she flushed in embarrassment and stared at him in confusion.

"For taking such good care of my nephew," Nigel explained smoothly. "And please don't tell me it is your job; you give him much more tender care than that."

Her blush deepened at that, but she accepted the books. The next time it was an elegant box of chocolates, and Nigel's excuse was that she could share them with Joseph and the other children. "And if you refuse them, they will simply melt away in the summer heat," he added. He felt no guilt for maneuvering her into acceptance. He did not mean to lose this campaign.

He was collecting other gifts—ribbons that matched the blue of her eyes, a bottle of delicate scent from France, a pair of combs for her hair, gloves, and handkerchiefs—an array of feminine articles he knew he could not give her yet, but which he was determined would eventually be hers.

Nigel was not so besotted that he was blind to his condition. He viewed himself with wry humor. He had enjoyed the company of a number of beautiful, intelligent women since he had reached his majority, but none of them had ever been of overwhelming importance to him, and as he had told Adam, he had begun to think of himself as apt to remain a bachelor. The image had not distressed him. His work demanded a great deal of him, and he had been comfortable in his life.

Now that was a thing of the past. He dreamt of Sally. He imagined sharing a home with her. He thought of how wonderful it would be to find comfort in her arms when a case had gone badly and his inability to heal everyone who came to him became a burden too heavy to bear alone. He thought of sharing the triumphs. And he considered the joy he would find in watching Sally grow into confidence in herself. He did not dwell on the fact that she had not yet even called him by his given name.

Sally was indeed oblivious to Nigel's intentions. She thought he was being extraordinarily kind to include her in his attentions to Joseph and to his other cousins at Wild Swan. It did not surprise her. She had come to consider Dr. Falconer one of the kindest men in creation. She admired everything about him, from his professional skill to his compassion to his gentle humor. But the idea that he might desire her as a woman never occurred to her. When her uncle had taken her for his brutal pleasure, Sally had been on the edge of womanhood. When she lost her virginity, she also lost her perception of her own allure and value.

It was Joseph who turned her world upside down. They were packing to return to Baltimore when he said, "Cousin Nigel won't have to go so far to see you once we're home. When you marry him, can I come visit you at your own house?"

Sally's hands stilled on the clothes she was folding. "Oh, Joseph, you've got the wrong idea entirely! Your cousin has been coming to see you and his other cousins; he hasn't any special interest in me."

If Sally had known Phoebe when Phoebe was Joseph's age, she would have seen the image of the mother in the son. Joseph was polite but implacably stubborn; he knew what he'd watched all summer was true. "I know Cousin Nigel liked seeing me, but he really came to see you. He doesn't look like that for anybody else." He paused, regarding her worriedly. "Don't you want Cousin Nigel to love you? He's a nice man."

Only the fact that Joseph was so obviously in need of reassurance enabled Sally to answer at all, and her voice sounded thin and scratchy to her own ears. "Your cousin *is* a very nice man, but I am not the sort of person he would consider for a wife."

This made no sense to Joseph, and Sally struggled with the difficulty of explaining. "You see, I come from a family that is very different from yours. It just wouldn't be right to try to mix them."

Joseph was only eight years old, but he was no child when it came to recognizing prejudice; it was what his parents had continuously fought against. "That doesn't make any sense!" he declared. "And anyway, Cousin Nigel wouldn't be marrying your family, just you."

Sally closed her eyes for an instant, and she saw her uncle so clearly, her heart quickened in fear. She wished she could kill him. It was the ultimate bond she shared with Joseph. She understood the violence that remained in the shadows of the boy.

She held to her patience. "I think this is a foolish conversation, don't you? There really isn't anything to be done right now, anyway. I am quite content as I am, and I don't have time for gentlemen callers, not even your cousin."

Though Joseph obligingly let the subject drop at this announcement of female privilege, Sally knew he had not changed his mind.

But he had changed hers. She tried to hold back her thoughts, but once they started, they would not cease. Sally remembered how Dr. Falconer had looked when she had asked him to speak to Joseph; the change had happened exactly then. What she had taken for the exhausting emotional climate of that time had been something quite different. She recalled every one of his visits since then, seeing them through newly opened eyes, admitting to herself that what Joseph had seen was the truth.

The realization did not change her opinion of her own unworthiness; it made her think Dr. Falconer was suffering from some sort of madness which she hoped was temporary. She was miserably embarrassed in anticipation of seeing him again and began to devise elaborate plans for avoiding him, knowing all the while it was going to be impossible. She was an integral part of the Kingston household, and Nigel, even before he had displayed this alarming interest in her, was a frequent visitor.

Nigel thought he was doing well to resist visiting the Kingston house for two days after he knew Sally and Joseph were home, but for Sally, it was much too soon to face him.

She was downstairs when he entered the house, and her panic at the sight of him was obvious as she turned to flee up the stairs.

"Sally! Wait! Please wait."

Sally turned back to him, frozen in place by the few words that were command and plea.

"Who told you, or did you figure it out for yourself?" he asked bluntly.

"Joseph," she said, bowing her head because she could not bear the directness of his bright green eyes.

"Joseph and Lexy, they were surely the first ones to know. Lexy because she sees everything, and Joseph because he sees you so clearly." He didn't sound distressed about it.

"Dr. Falconer, this is very unsuitable," Sally mumbled.

"My name is Nigel, and certainly after all of this time, you can say it. I asked you months ago. Why is it unsuitable? Are you already married? And why are you trying to sound as if you are seventy years old and bound for mission work?" He was trying to make her smile, but her distress was too great for that, and to his horror, he saw all the color drain from her face and her eyes fill with tears.

"Oh, my dear," he said softly. "How arrogant I've been! I've been so carried away with my own vision of how it could be between us, I have not even considered that you might feel no attraction to me."

It was hard to believe that he could feel so strongly about her while she felt nothing except embarrassment, but he realized he had truly been arrogant in his perception of all that he had to offer her in comparison to her background. Many people married for less reason, but it was not the kind of marriage he wanted, and Sally's sense of honor would never allow her to marry for material gain. While he had never considered himself a great romantic hero, he had always been romantically successful. The possibility that the one woman he had ever truly cared about felt no physical attraction to him was not only ironic, it was a severe blow to his hopes for the future and to his masculine pride.

Sally had never seen in Nigel any of the strutting arrogance she detested in other men, but he had always had an aura of easygoing self-confidence. Now she saw the uncertainty in him and the beginning of the humble acceptance that he was somehow not good enough for her, somehow lacking in what she wanted from a man. She could not bear it, and she stumbled over her words and the truth as she sought to reassure him.

"No, it's not you! You're . . . you're exactly what most young women would want in a man. But I don't want a man! Not you or anyone else! And you can't want me! You've got to be mis . . . mistaken! You know what kind of people I come from. You know!"

Her passionate defense of him was all he needed to hear. He moved toward her slowly, willing her not to run. Very carefully he took one of her hands in both of his, cradling it as he would have liked to cradle her.

"I am not mistaken. I love you, and I fear that is not going to change. I do know about your family; I know what your uncle did to you." Her hand tensed in his, and he held on just hard enough so that she couldn't pull away. "Your uncle was to blame, not you. What he did has nothing to do with what you are. A mirror can tell you that you are beautiful, but it will not tell you that you are intelligent, kind, loving. I can tell you that as truth." His hands stroked hers gently, as if soothing a wounded bird. "You are very young, and perhaps I am too old for you. But I won't give up, at least not until you know your own worth and can make a clear choice. Your uncle had no right to touch you, to rape you," he made himself say the word, "and he has less right to determine how the rest of your life will be. More than I've ever wanted anything in my life, I want you to marry me. Not today or tomorrow, but when and if you have learned to trust me, to love me. You needn't love me as much as I love you; I don't think that's possible; a fraction of it will do."

He was offering her so much, she suddenly found she could give no less than the truth in return. "I cannot bear the idea of a man touching me . . . that way again. I cannot! Not even you. What if I always feel that way? What if it never changes?"

The anguished whisper clawed at Nigel's soul. " 'That way' has nothing to do with what happens between a man and a woman who love each other. I will not lie to you. I desire you physically. But that is only part of the way I love you. And if physical love is not enjoyed by both, it is not loving at all. There are many couples who, for one cause or another, do not have sexual congress in their marriages and yet are happy. If that is your choice, then it will be mine, too."

She believed him, and she was awed. That a man as virile as Nigel Falconer could love enough willingly to accept a celibate marriage bed was beyond her experience. Where she had come from, women escaped the sexual attentions of their men only in the final months of pregnancy, when they were severely ill, or when the men had consumed so much alcohol that they were rendered incapable or unconscious before they could satisfy themselves. And she had seen enough of Nigel's family to know that these were men and women who loved each other physically and in every other way. And children, children were beloved in the Falconer, Carrington, and Culhane families. Nigel was offering never to look on a son or daughter of his own. If he ever made a marriage vow he would keep it; Nigel was not the sort of man who would sire bastards.

She did not realize that she could see how Nigel's children would look; that she was thinking of him as "Nigel," not "Dr. Falconer," and that standing with her hand held in his, she felt safer than she ever had before. All she knew consciously was that everything was even more complicated than before, but that she did not want Nigel to disappear from her life. The tears she had been trying to keep in check overflowed, and she gave an undignified sniff.

Nigel took out his handkerchief, tipped her head up, and carefully wiped the tears away. "I really can't bear it when you cry. And think of what people will say if you weep at the sight of me. 'Such a cruel man he is, making the lovely Sally weep. There must be terrible things only she knows about him.' "

Her smile was tremulous, but it was enough for Nigel. He had felt her hand tighten before he let it go, had seen the myriad emotions sweeping across her face. For now, it was enough.

"Nothing is changed. It will be just as it was this summer, just two friends visiting," he assured her, though he knew that, in fact, everything had been altered by the truth that now lay between them.

Chapter 18

Though Travis left for California shortly after his return from the races in New York State, he was back in time for the meeting at Pimlico in Baltimore.

Moonraker again placed second to Aristides when they ran for the Breckenridge Stakes, but overall, he had done exceedingly well, earning nearly eight thousand dollars in prize money and various pieces of silver plate. If he remained sound and fast, he would be entered in races for two or three more years and then retired to stud. There was already a list of horse owners who wished to be informed when the stallion made his first season.

Alex was particularly pleased by the letter of congratulations from Hugh Bettingdon. He subscribed to racing calendars and sporting journals from the United States, and since he had had so much to do with the bloodlines at Wild Swan from the beginning, it was a special delight for him to read of the farm's successes:

It is just as well such a broad expanse of ocean separates our countries, for otherwise, a champion like Moonraker would surely challenge the complacency of English horse owners.

Alex could see him smiling as he wrote it, and she rejoiced that his wry humor was still intact. Angelica had been in ill health for much of the year, unable to recover from a respiratory complaint she had contracted the previous winter, and the family had been so worried about her that Gweneth and Christopher and their children had canceled a visit to the United States. It was a mark of how much everyone loved Angelica that none of the family would consider being too far from her side. But she was doing well now, and Hugh planned to take her to the warmth of the Cornish coast if he saw the slightest sign of the cold weather bothering her again. Christopher and Gweneth had rescheduled their trip for the following year.

In addition to notes and best wishes from everyone, Hugh had sent new photographs of the family. Alex could not look at them without getting misty-eyed and wearing what Rane called her "grandmotherly smile," which was, according to him, "composed of equal amounts of love, indulgence, and idiocy, as if no other children and grandchildren in the world were as perfect."

Alex didn't mind his teasing because he was no less smitten than she. "I can look at you as my mirror," she told him.

Indeed, Rane thought it as wondrous as she that their daughter, Gweneth, was the mother of the tall, handsome twins, Hugh and Nicholas, who were twenty-one years old now, and of Eveline, who at seventeen was rapidly shedding the last awkwardness of adolescence.

The good news of Angelica's recovery added to the joy the family shared during the Christmas season, and Adam and Mercy's announcement that they were expecting another child in the late spring or early summer was another gift.

Marsh Whitcomb and Flora spent part of the holiday with his grown children and part at Wild Swan, and they were so accepted as a couple now, there was no unease. Because Marsh was a well-read man with diverse interests, he fit in easily at Wild Swan, where everyone had opinions about everything. With exposure to Alex, Sam, Philly, and Gincie, in addition to Flora, Marsh had come to expect women to have intelligent comments to make about current affairs, rather than being surprised by the process as he had first been when he and Flora were in the early stages of their affair. Flora wisely kept her satisfaction to herself until Alex said, "You're training him quite nicely, I think. A little more time, and you will have him petitioning for woman's suffrage."

"Mother, you never miss anything!" Flora exclaimed. "And I can't take all the credit; you and the rest are doing your part."

In the wide-ranging discussion of various topics, Marsh made the mistake of defending President Grant. It was a measure of how accepted Marsh was by the family that no one refrained from disputing him.

"I truly feel sorry for the man. I think he has been ill used by those he trusts," he said when someone mentioned the newest revelations of the Whiskey Ring Scandal, a story Reid had been writing about since the first exposures of last year, 1874. Revenue officers from the Treasury Department had been defrauding the government of the whiskey tax revenue in the amount of one hundred thousand dollars a year and had involved, among other notables, President Grant's private secretary.

"Mr. Whitcomb, are you sure you wish to defend the president?" Alex asked. "Though he may be acting like a simple storekeeper who extends credit unwisely, he is the leader of this country, and his questionable judgment affects all of us."

"It's not as if this is the first time," Sam pointed out. "We have already suffered through the Crédit Mobilier scandal and Black Friday. If the president had stopped Gould and Fisk as soon as they began to try to corner the gold market, many ruined banks and businesses might still be functioning today. Instead, he let it go on so long that the whole country was hurt."

"I come and listen to them before I write my columns," Reid told Marsh with a grin, but then he sobered. "I think most people wish Grant well as a man, but shudder at the bad advice and shallow friends with whom he surrounds himself. I confess, though I am a newspaper man, it is difficult not to dread the next revelation. The country needs to heal, not to be plagued by questions about its government's morality. Even Grant's 'Peace Policy' is proving a disaster. At the time of its promulgation, few noticed the caveat that Indians who would not make peace on the government's terms would be met with 'a sharp and severe war policy.' Our army is now at war with every Indian who will not live as if in prison on a reservation and with many others who *have* agreed to our terms. If we don't get control of people like George Custer, the battles aren't going to end until the dead are piled high enough for everyone to notice. Even those who admired Custer during the war called him a 'reckless boy,' among other things. In my opinion, it is too bad his conviction at his courtmartial didn't have more lasting results.''

Everyone was familiar with the events to which Reid referred. The previous year, in the area of the Southern Plains, the Peace Policy had been superseded by the authority given to General Sheridan to make war on hostile Indians wherever he found them. Though they had a long list of grievances, the Indians were particularly enraged by the depredations of the buffalo hunters, who slaughtered the animals by the millions for tongues and hides alone, leaving to rot the meat that had fed the Indians since their memories began. The Kiowas, Comanches, and Cheyennes had banded together to attack white settlements, buffalo hunters, and wagon trains, and to raid across the borders into Texas and Mexico. But there the Indians had lost their bid to retain their old way of life. The end of the Red River War had been the end of hostilities in the region. General Sheridan had consolidated his victories by sending the war leaders of the tribes off to various prisons, some as far away as Florida, to make sure those leaders could not foment further trouble with their followers.

But no such enforced peace existed in the Black Hills of South Dakota. In the Fort Laramie Treaty of 1868, made following Chief Red Cloud's war, the government had agreed to abandon the Bozeman Trail and its forts, and to regard the Powder River country as "unceded Indian territory" on which the Sioux could still roam freely. But as usual, there was a snake in the Eden offered to the Indians. A reservation was established next to the unceded land, and the right to hunt on that land was to exist only "so long as the buffalo may range thereon in such numbers to justify the chase," obviously a condition to be judged by white men and a condition that was being changed by white men whenever they sighted their rifles on the animals. And then there was the matter of gold.

It was Custer who had followed the rumors of the precious metal and had trespassed during the previous year into the holy lands of the Sioux in the Black Hills. It was Custer who, when the gold was found, had made sure that the news was widely broadcast so that prospectors would flood the land, thus making it impossible for the Indians to retain it. When the gold seekers started rushing in, the government tried to buy the land, but the Indians refused to leave.

Chief Red Cloud was one of the Indians the children had seen in Washington in May, and Reid remembered Lexy's outrage when he had told her why the Indians were there. He described the outing, and then he said, "If a child can so accurately judge the injustice and see the remedy, while our governmental policy continues to be the implementation of injustice, there is something tragically awry. Custer was courtmartialed and suspended from his duties for a year in 1867 because his rabid pursuit of Indians put his own men in needless jeopardy and because he jumped a train to go visit his wife while his regiment still needed his guidance. When I compare him to Chief Red Cloud, I am embarrassed that Custer is our representative."

Marsh knew that these people had a special, personal interest in the fate of the Indians, but it did not trouble him. He, too, believed that Indian affairs had been shamefully mishandled, but he asked Reid, "What end do you see?"

"I wish I knew. The simple, obvious solution is for us to abide by our treaties, even at the cost of ceding wealth and territories to the natives. But we have proved ourselves unwilling to do this, unwilling to the point of tacitly sanctioning the massacre of women and children in undefended villages. So that must mean we intend to continue as aggressors against people who are known for their prowess in battle. The Cheyenne and Sioux are ever more willing to act in concert against a common enemy. I confess, every time I learn of a new skirmish between our troops and the Indians, I recall how difficult it was to contain violence during the war, how the first engagements, terrible as they were, only foreshadowed the unimaginable carnage of Antietam and Gettysburg."

"The Indians are doing no more than we did to form a nation from disparate colonies," Flora offered. "White men do not take kindly to being told where to live, how to live, what to eat, what to wear, and what god to worship; it is insane to expect the Indians to accept the yoke white men will not wear."

Marsh regarded her with admiration for her eloquence and for the parallel she had drawn. It was a paradox that while most whites thought of Indians as being all the same, it was also common knowledge and a comfort that various tribes were traditional enemies of each other, to the point that some, such as the Crow, were employed as scouts by the Army. This rivalry was often used to illuminate the savagery of red men without any reference to the fact that the same sort of strife had existed for centuries among the peoples of Europe.

"But even if the Cheyenne and Sioux band together in their greatest numbers, and even if they had others to join them, they would lose," Marsh pointed out. "There would still be too few of them with too little opportunity for resupply of weapons and food.

And unlike the colonies, they have no France to come in on their side."

"That's true," Flora agreed. "But that will not stop the bloodshed that may well occur before the Indians surrender."

They all shared the nightmare vision of western settlements attacked and burned to the ground. Despite sympathy for the Indians, no one was unaffected by the knowledge of how gruesome their vengeance could be; slow death by torture was a common fear in the West.

"Mrs. Falconer, I concede the original point," Marsh said to Alex. "If President Grant were a better leader surrounded by men of higher caliber, perhaps even the Indian situation would be more wisely handled. Listening tonight I have realized I could not run my business as Grant runs the country without risking ruin."

"Now I shall play the devil's advocate and offer the only sympathy I can," Alex returned. "Grant was a good general when we desperately needed him. It seems that we ask too much of him and he of himself that he also be a good president. It is ironic—is it not?—that there are Indians, so-called savages, who have separate chiefs for peace and war because they do not believe the two impulses compatible in the same man."

The conversation moved on to other topics—to newly published books; to the slow but sure recovery in shipping and other businesses from the financial panic of two years before; to the worsening relations between employers and workers in major industries such as coal mining and railroads; to last March's congressional ruling that the Fourteenth Amendment to the Constitution did not grant the vote to women; to past horse races and races to come; to the merits of this bloodline over that—the conversation swirled and settled and rose again.

Suddenly Flora noticed that Marsh had shifted from participant to a sad distance. "Are we too aggressive for you?" she asked softly.

He started and then smiled at her, but he still looked sad. "No, quite the contrary. I was thinking how much my children missed, especially my two daughters. In our home, we discussed only 'polite' subjects, bland and safe as bread pudding. No one was ever offended; nor, I think, was anyone ever interested. Being with you and your family has made me see what an act of trust it is for people to speak honestly with each other and to face difficult issues together."

It was hard for Flora to argue against his own judgment of his family, for she found his children, particularly his daughters, drearily conventional. But at least they all treated her civilly for their father's sake, though she was sure they were scandalized by the affair. She felt she owed them something for that. "Your children are all doing well and leading productive lives; perhaps it is wrong to ask more than that," she offered.

"Once I would have believed that; now I think it is essential to demand far more than that," Marsh said. "But it is too late for me to do that with my children. Maybe I ought to introduce my grandchildren to the delights of dangerous discussions." He and Flora shared a wry smile at the image of how his children and their spouses would react to that; undoubtedly they would judge that Flora had corrupted him utterly.

"Maybe you had better leave well enough alone," Flora countered.

Watching the interplay between Flora and Marsh, Alex said to Rane, "Flora was always the one I worried most about, and yet, after her first disastrous marriage, she has made wise, strong choices for her life and for her loves—Caleb, and now Marsh. Sometimes I wonder if she would have found so much strength had she not married that awful Carlton Fitzhubert."

"Perhaps not," Rane conceded. "Perhaps she would never have known the need for strength. But certainly the way you raised the children has given them weapons to fight back when faced with adversity."

"And you," Alex said, "you have had so much to do with raising them."

She studied his face and thought how incredible it was that he was eighty this year and she seventy-five. In some ways it seemed as if life had been long, but in others, the fact of so many years having passed startled her. So many things seemed to have happened just a short time ago when, in truth, it had been decades.

"I wish I really believed in Heaven, in another place where life goes on as it does here, but without the pain. I would like to be with you for eternity. But even the best descriptions of Paradise make it seem a bloodless place, no passion, no earthly delight. I think I am too rooted here to imagine that as a better existence."

"So am I," Rane agreed, stroking her hand with a slow intimacy that even after all these years had the power to make her pulse quicken. "Perhaps we shall be allowed to go somewhere where there are swift horses and swift ships and loving is not lost."

Only Nigel found the holidays difficult to witness, and for that reason he had volunteered to spend far more time at the medical office than the Kingstons, freeing them to be out in the country. But tonight was his turn, and he wished it weren't. The obvious love between his grandparents, between Flora and Marsh, between all the couples present, made him feel achingly empty inside. He knew that Philly and Blaine mourned Phoebe's death and that his own parents never forgot that Seth would have been with them, save for the slaughter at Gettysburg, but even these tragedies seemed to bind the couples closer to each other.

Nigel had tried to persuade Sally to come with him to Brookhaven and Wild Swan, but she remained adamant about spending her time off with her family, about maintaining the fiction that she was nothing more than an employee to the Kingstons and to himself. He had promised he would not rush her, but his patience was running out. All through the autumn he had spent as much time as he could with her, coaxing her in every way he knew to trust him, to trust his love. But her refusal to spend any of this special time with him made it seem as if he had made no progress at all.

"Father Christmas doesn't seem to have offered you any cheer," a gruff voice observed, and Nigel found Dr. Cameron at his side. "It is unfortunate that the lovely Sally is not here."

"Christ! Does everyone know?" Nigel snapped and then felt guilty, but Alastair took no offense. "Everyone who cares about you," he answered calmly.

"Everyone except her family," Nigel said. "And they don't care about her or about me, only about the money she brings to them."

"I am not sure what you should do about that, but I can tell you that you can't afford to let it distract you too much. You're a fine physician, and your patients deserve the best from you every single day." He paused, his eyes roving about the room, studying the occupants as Nigel had done. "Marriage didn't work for me. My wife was perfectly justified in fleeing from my less-than-tender care. I was so obsessed with medicine, I hardly noticed she was gone. But I don't think your case is the same. There is a tradition of loving long and well in this family, and I think you will feel the lack if you do not win your Sally. But she must make a choice, and I gather that is something she will not do, or else she would be here with you."

Despite the genuine concern Alastair was expressing, Nigel had no intention of telling the old doctor just how complicated Sally's problems were, but he did ask, "Do you think she is too young for me?"

Alastair shook his head. "I don't think Sally Birch has been young for a very long time."

It was no more than a wry observation, but it made Nigel see things very clearly, made him realize that the gap between his age and Sally's had made too much difference to him. And it made him believe that left to her own devices, Sally would never make a choice, would remain forever in the purgatory of her fear, preferring the devils she knew to the unfamiliar—to life with him.

It was two days after Christmas before he could go to her, but he arrived at her home laden with packages for her mother, for those of her siblings and cousins who still lived there, and most of all, for her. This time he had not brought her books or chocolates to share with the children. Instead, he had wrapped all of the frivolous, personal items he had collected for her over the months.

The children were excited by Dr. Falconer's arrival with his great bundle of packages; Mrs. Birch was at once intrigued and suspicious; the uncle was too drunk to express anything clearly; and Sally was horrified.

"What are you doing here?" she gasped, knowing it was a stupid question even as she asked it.

"I've come courting," he said. "I've missed you too much this Christmas; I don't intend to do without your company again." He directed his attention to her mother. "I wish to marry your daughter. She hasn't made up her mind yet, but I want to court her openly, with your permission, of course."

His words were polite enough, but his eyes dared Mrs. Birch to refuse, and she bowed to his will, as she had always done with the men in her life, from father to husband to brother-in-law.

If it hadn't so much to do with his hope of happiness, Nigel would have been cynically amused by the chase of expressions on Mrs. Birch's face. She was stunned that Dr. Falconer wanted to marry her daughter; she was angry that she had not known until now; and she was already beginning to calculate what further benefit this could be to herself. She managed a mumbled greeting which, though it lacked warmth, was better in Nigel's view than being told to leave.

The children's excitement over the sweets, fruit, games, and toys that Nigel had brought was a good diversion, and under cover of the noise, he focused his attention on Sally.

"You're not opening your gifts. I've collected them for a long time, and I'd like to see if they suit you."

Obediently she began to pick at the wrappings, the uncharacteristic clumsiness of her hands evidence of her reluctance and of her knowledge that these were not going to be impersonal tokens, easy to ignore. The pile of bright, feminine articles grew until Nigel placed the last box in her hands.

The gold necklace was delicately set with pearls and turquoise in a pattern of little flowers. It was of French origin, from the early years of the century. It was exquisite, and it reminded Sally that Rane had given Alex the swan necklace so long ago. She had seen Alex wear it, and Anthea had told her the story, part of Anthea's continuing efforts to make Sally feel she was a member of the family.

But Sally knew such a gift had everything to do with Nigel's world, Nigel's family, nothing to do with hers.

"Thank you," she murmured, still obedient, but when she raised her eyes to his, he saw a world of hurt and the accusation of betrayal in hers. The necklace slipped out of her fingers to lie with the rest of the gifts.

The odor Nigel had managed to ignore until now assailed his nostrils. It was a blend of old cooking, of bodies not washed often enough, of the lack of sanitary facilities, of poverty, ignorance, and weariness. That the children were adequately fed and clothed and the few bright touches in the room were due to the money Flora still paid to Mrs. Birch and to the wages Sally spent on little else except the family. Though the older children, aided by Flora and Anthea in finding employment, were leaving as soon as they could, the family's needs were still great.

The sounds of neighbors who lived too close and too many to a room was audible even over the squeals of the Birch youngsters.

Nigel had thought he understood, but now, faced with the reality of Sally's home, he could not imagine what bound her to it. For the first time, he knew it was more than fear.

"Come with me, outside for a while." He meant it to be a request, but it sounded like a command.

Sally stood up primly, like a little girl waiting to be taken on an expedition she didn't fancy, but Nigel hesitated only long enough to wrap her in her cloak before he led her outside by the hand.

He took a deep breath of the chill air, though the smell, detectable in spite of the cold, of the refuse-littered street wasn't much better than the odor inside the house. He started to walk, still pulling her along, until her voice came to him, protesting, "You walk too fast!"

"Sorry," he apologized, slowing his pace, but he couldn't slow his thoughts. They tumbled around in his brain with images of the bleak life this district represented. His nose wrinkled from the assault of fumes from paint factories, tanneries, and establishments that made hairpieces. Savagely he kicked aside a spill of greasy rags in his path. He felt as if his senses were being attacked on all sides.

"My God! How can you stand to come here when you don't have to?" he demanded harshly. "You don't belong here anymore; you never did. Your uncle, the drunken sot, just sitting there, and your mother allowing it. How can she? How can she allow him anywhere near you and the other children knowing what he did to you?" Only now did he realize how enraged he was to find the man still with Mrs. Birch and her brood.

Sally planted her feet and refused to go another step. Her face was pasty white except for the red spots of cold and anger on her cheeks. "That is my family. That is where I come from, where I belong!" she screeched, unmindful of passersby. "Everything else is just an illusion. How dare you do what you did today, how dare you! You promised you'd be patient, and instead, you march in as if you own me, making it clear to all of them that I haven't told them the truth about my life at the Kingstons'. You're just like the rest of them."

It was the cruelest thing she could say, and she knew it wasn't true. Nigel's only crime was that he loved her too much. She thought of the pile of gifts and the necklace, and she felt small, dark, and shriveled inside.

"I shouldn't have done it," Nigel admitted dully. "But seeing everyone together at Christmas was too much. I wanted you to be with me. You're right; I didn't think of what was best for you; just what was best for me. I am like them." The bleakness in her settled in his own heart. "Not only do I not have the right to make you see yourself differently; I don't have the power to do it.

"This mustn't endanger your job with Anthea and Max. Joseph would miss you terribly if you left, and so would everyone else. I can't avoid seeing you; my medical practice is with Anthea and Max, but I swear that I will treat you as no more or less than a casual acquaintance."

She was hardly conscious that he had been leading her back to the house that sheltered too many people—her family and other tenants. By tonight, they would all be talking about Sally Birch walking out with the gentleman, and most would know it was Dr. Nigel Falconer, many because he had treated them for this ailment or that. Some would think she was putting on airs to be seen with such a man; others, those who still had dreams in spite of the grinding circumstances of their lives, would wish her well. And none of it would make any difference, because she was sending him away.

The words to give herself and him another chance rose in her and died. This was the better way. Nothing had changed. She had not changed. That Nigel believed her worthy of his love did not make it so.

"You needn't come in," she said when they reached the front of the house. "And don't worry, I will continue to work for the Kingstons." Her gaze was fixed somewhere over his left shoulder; she refused to meet his eyes.

"Please make my excuses to your family," he said, as stiffly polite as she, and then he turned and walked away.

When Sally went inside, her mother immediately asked where Dr. Falconer was.

"He's gone. I sent him away," Sally told her, watching her and wondering what her reaction would be. She didn't have long to wait. Her mother's hand lashed out so quickly, Sally didn't have time to step back before the blow landed hard on the side of her face.

"You fool! You . . ."

When her mother came at her again, Sally grabbed her flailing hand with a strength that shocked them both.

"Don't you ever hit me or the others again, not ever! If you do, I'll leave. I'm old enough to do that now. I'll leave, and you'll never see another penny of my wages or of Mrs. Jennings's money." She knew Flora could have stopped the payments by now, but Flora was too tenderhearted and would probably keep paying until all the children were old enough to survive on their own, but Mrs. Birch didn't understand that.

Sally swung around to confront her uncle as she felt his stare. He had paid her little mind when she had visited during these past years, and she suspected it was because her association with Flora, with the Kingstons, and thus with the Carringtons and Falconers, had given her protection, even in his alcohol-hazed mind. But now he was eyeing her with a renewed spark of interest, as if her refusal of Nigel's suit had somehow made her fair game once again.

She wheeled on him, her fury unabated. "And you, you will keep your filthy hands off me and the others if you want to keep yourself in drink." She knew what a threat it was to him; he had seldom held a job for more than a day in the past couple of years. She was sure his drinking was now far more important to him than molesting her or one of the other children.

Once her uncle would have come at her for her defiance, and her mother would have cowered and allowed whatever violence the man wanted, but the power had shifted dramatically to her. Confirmation was in the awed eyes of her siblings and cousins. But Sally did not see the change in her that Nigel had already wrought; she saw only his strong silhouette as he walked down the street, away from her. The desolation she felt made everything else pale by comparison, and defiance was easy; she had nothing else to lose.

She gazed around the room, seeing what Nigel had seen, and she was more sure than ever that he and his family did not deserve to be connected to this as they would be if she and Nigel married. She looked at her uncle, and for the first time in a long while, she allowed herself to see his abuse exactly as it had happened, rather than as a blurred nightmare. Her loathing was so obvious, her uncle looked away, but she did not notice his reaction; she thought that Nigel did not deserve to have her uncle's leavings.

*　　*　　*

Though the carefully wrapped package containing the necklace had already been delivered to his quarters, it was after New Year's Day before Nigel saw Sally again. The bruise from her mother's blow had faded, but it was still visible.

For an instant, his face contorted as if he had taken the blow, but his voice was devoid of emotion when he asked, "Your uncle?"

"No, my mother," Sally answered honestly, knowing Nigel would take no revenge on a woman. "It doesn't matter; it won't happen again."

He tipped her head up, angling the bruise to the light so he could see it more clearly. "There doesn't seem to be any damage to your eye. Have you had any problem with your vision?" He seemed coolly professional, but his stomach roiled at the image of Mrs. Birch striking Sally so hard that the damage still showed. He had no doubt that it had happened right after he had left her at the house.

"I bruise easily," Sally told him. "It wasn't as bad as it looks."

Though he made no comment, she knew how disgusted he was by the whole business; the members of his family did not strike each other. It was another measure of the differences between them.

They turned away from each other at the same time, both of them thinking that it must get easier; day by day, the caring between them would surely diminish because they were making such an effort to kill it.

As Nigel had told Sally, it was impossible for them to avoid meeting as long as he practiced medicine with the Kingstons. He forced himself to spend every bit as much time with them as he had before, and he watched Sally striving to maintain the same fiction that nothing untoward had happened. But he soon knew how useless it was, at least as far as fooling his relatives. They all kept politely silent on the subject, but they regarded him with such visible concern, it made him grit his teeth.

Before he had fallen in love with Sally, his work had consumed most of his time. It had been sufficient before, and he was determined it would be again. Alastair had reminded him of his duty to his patients. He had always been conscientious, but now he began to expand his practice until he was seeing patients from early in the morning until late in the evening and answering pleas for emergency aid so often during the night that what little sleep he had was, to his relief, deep and dreamless.

Anthea and Max watched him with growing worry as the days became weeks of overwork. Finally, Max felt he had to say something.

"Are you trying to win a prize for having more patients than any other physician in Baltimore? You haven't had a full day off since . . . well, for too long."

"Do you think I am giving less than good care?" Nigel asked, trying to keep his voice even, though he felt a flare of temper for Max's interference.

"No, I think you are offering superb care to each and every person you see. I would have spoken sooner if I did not believe that. But no one can maintain the schedule you've set yourself. I'm speaking not only as your friend, but also as a physician. It won't do any of your patients any good if you collapse. And frankly, you've increased your practice so much, Anthea and I might not be able to take over for you if it becomes necessary."

Nigel's shoulders slumped wearily. He couldn't hold on to his anger in face of Max's genuine concern and reasonableness.

"I'll ease my pace, take more time for myself," he assured Max, and he truly meant to do so, but he found it easier said than done. The only contentment he could find came from his work, and since Sally would not accept the care and tenderness he wanted to offer her, he needed to offer it in another form to his patients, who were, with few exceptions, in dire need of his ministrations.

Though Adam's days with the shipyard and his family were busy, he repeatedly made efforts to draw his brother out and ease the burden, but he ended up by feeling that the time Nigel spent with him was just added work for his brother. And Morgan fared little better. He was constrained from overt interference in his son's life by the mutual respect that had characterized their relationship since Nigel had been a very young man, and though he hated to see Nigel looking so worn, he had no easy answers for him, particularly when his son confronted him directly.

They were having dinner together, carefully skirting anything personal, when Nigel took Morgan by surprise, asking, "What would you have done if Mother had married Justin Sinclair after all?"

"You mean in spite of my making a complete ass of myself at her engagement party?" Morgan asked, and was rewarded by a faint smile from his son.

"Yes, in spite of that."

Morgan sobered, remembering vividly the terror that had filled him at the idea of Sam marrying Justin Sinclair, the wealthy Virginian who had courted her so honorably. The terror had been great enough to drive Morgan to behave like a madman in front of his family and all of the guests who had been at Brookhaven that night.

"I cannot imagine what my life would have been like without your mother," he admitted. "I have never ceased to be grateful that when I challenged Justin with my fists, he won. If your mother hadn't seen me laid out on the floor, she might well have married Justin instead. He loved Sam enough to relinquish his claim when he witnessed how much she cared for me. I had treated her so shabbily, I am not certain what she would have decided had he continued to press his claim. He was a kind, civilized man. He, no more than Seth or any other, deserved to die in the war." He paused, wondering how far he could trespass, and then he asked gently, "But it isn't another man in Sally's case, is it?"

"I wish it were," Nigel said. "That's something I might be able to fight. But Sally doesn't want any man, including me." He gave a self-deprecating shrug of his shoulders. "Her home is dreadful, and yet, she will not use me to escape it."

"Bless her for that," Morgan said. "No matter how much you love someone, you cannot solve all her problems, and you cannot heal all her wounds. Your mother will always carry the hurt of her father's indifference. I can't change that; I can only make her feel secure with me. Maybe Sally will come to see that she has room in her life for you to love her, perhaps not. You asked me what I would have done had Sam married Justin. The fact is, I don't know because that's not the way it happened. But I would hate to think that if Sally remains firm in her refusal, you will condemn yourself to a life without love. You have a great deal to offer a woman, and it would be an odd world if there were only one woman who could content you." He wished his words carried more conviction, but he was hampered by his mental images of Sam, Sam for all the years he had known her and loved her.

Nigel saw his father's dilemma clearly, and he couldn't help but smile again. "It was a fine effort, Papa, and I appreciate it."

Morgan had done his best, but he felt there was someone who could counsel Nigel more effectively, and he was not above manipulating the situation for his son's benefit. Nor did Nigel even consider refusing the invitation to dine with his grandparents at their Baltimore house, though he kept hoping that an emergency, if it were going to happen anyway, might happen in time to save him from his grandmother's knowing eyes. With others in the family, even with his parents, it was possible to keep a last protective distance from the heart of things, but not with her.

Alex had intended to be subtle, but once she saw how unhealthy Nigel looked, how much weight he'd lost since she'd seen him last, she found it difficult. She watched him struggling to eat the carefully prepared supper, and she listened to the husky weariness of his voice as they discussed safe topics that ranged from new foals at Wild Swan to the latest scandal of the Grant administration wherein Secretary of War William W. Belknap had been discovered to be taking bribes as payment for lucrative sutlerships in the Indian Territory. Washington was buzzing with the gossip attached to the case because Mrs. Secretary Belknap claimed that the bribes had been paid to her, and thus she was responsible, a questionable assertion since the checks were made payable by her to her husband, indicating the secretary's complicity in the affair.

"The secretary and his wife make such fascinating reading, no one seems the least concerned about what effect the fraud might have had on the treatment of Indians in the regions where the trading posts are located," Rane said. "And while column after column is being devoted to the Belknaps, few people in the East seem concerned by the fact that the Cheyenne and the Oglala Sioux have shown enough united strength to drive the cavalry back recently."

"People are growing accustomed to the constancy of the Indian wars," Alex observed. "And they are so far away for most people, it is far easier and surely more entertaining to concentrate on Mrs. Secretary Belknap's activities."

Nigel was so lulled by the discussion of events far removed from his own problems and so much more important in the scheme of things, he had begun to think he was going to escape any close scrutiny by his grandmother. But that illusion vanished when Rane abruptly made an excuse about papers to attend to and abandoned Nigel to Alex.

It did not help Nigel to remind himself that he was a grown man; his grandmother was more than twice his age and eons older in experience.

"We cannot solve the nation's problems tonight, and I doubt yours can be easily solved either. But there must be a better course than your present one," Alex said. " 'Men have died and worms have eaten them, but not for love.' Shakespeare had a great many wise things to say; I hope he was correct about this, but I am not altogether convinced." Her green eyes held him so that he could not look away.

"I was going to go gently with you, Nigel, until I saw you. Now I have decided to cast aside all delicacy. You look like my son Nigel looked the last time I saw him alive. He worked himself to death because he could not find a way to rid himself of his horrid wife and because he felt he had failed to be a good father to Gincie. Your profession is hazardous; you are exposed to every contagion, and if you drive yourself to exhaustion, you invite the worst consequences, just as your uncle Nigel did. You have no right to do that. Death comes anyway, without a special invitation. You have no right to make an early appointment. Your parents and Rane and I, all of us, have had to adjust to life without Seth; you must not ask us to face it without you."

Her fierceness he could bear better than the tears that suddenly filled her eyes, though she ignored them by refusing to wipe them away.

"Sally Birch is not worth this; no woman is," she said flatly. "If she cannot see what a marvelous man you are, it is her blindness and should be her loss."

"Oh, Gran, it isn't like that!" he protested, and for the first time, he found it possible to relate everything that had happened between himself and Sally, everything he had seen at her house, everything he guessed and everything he wondered about.

Alex regarded him for a long moment, and the sorrow was still in her eyes, but when she began to speak, he realized it was from another source now. "When I learned my mother had died in England, long after I had come to this country, long after I thought I was resigned to the fact that she would never love me, I realized there had always been part of me that dreamt she would tell me she had loved me after all, all along. My father loved me, though he could not protect me from my mother. My grandmother and Rane's family loved me enough to give me a joyful new life. And for more than sixty years, Rane has loved me more than anyone deserves to be loved. And yet, there is still that part of me that is a little child wondering what dreadful sin I've committed that my mother cannot love me. My mind knows she was a cold, angry woman, but my heart will not learn the lesson.

"And Gincie, who has been brave and loving and loved since she was very small, still quails before the knowledge that her mother did not love her and may still be somewhere, despising the thought of her. Your mother likewise, though it was her father who did the damage by neglect.

"I don't know your Sally well enough to be sure of anything, but from what you've told me, I suspect it is her mother, not her uncle, in spite of his crime against her, who has damaged her by not loving her, not protecting her, not giving her the confidence to go out in the world."

She studied her grandson's face, understanding his confusion and despair. "It is difficult to accept that it has so little to do with you at this point. But you must remember the end to all the stories I've just told you. I married Sinje and then Rane, and I have loved both of them. Gincie adores Travis, and your mother would not relinquish her marriage to your father for anything on earth. We all found a way to love despite feeling unlovable. There is every bit as much chance that Sally will do the same. I know it would be complicated to leave your practice, but perhaps it would be best if you could arrange to do so for a while. It is all very civilized to go on seeing Sally nearly every day as if nothing has transpired, but it allows her to see you, even in so unsatisfactory a manner. It teaches her nothing about how her world would be were you gone."

Nigel contemplated the idea with hope and dread. "And what if she finds she can manage very well without me?" he asked.

"Then you will have your answer, bitter as it may be," Alex said. "And you will have the best reason of all to stop this self-destruction. It is not knowing that wears down the best of us." She knew she was a far from impartial judge regarding her grandson, but she could not believe that Sally Birch would really allow Nigel to disappear from her life.

The wisdom of the plan began to take hold in Nigel's mind. Anything was better than the weeks that had just passed. He thought he might go as far as California to visit Boston and Rachel and to see the Culhanes' ranch. With his grandmother's recommendation, going away seemed like a positive thing to do rather than a retreat.

Alex saw the tension lessen in his face, and her own anxiety about him eased. He was, after all, a Falconer male, and all of those she had known, clear back to Rane's father, were men of action who could face anything except doing nothing.

"Gran, I think you've spoiled all of us. If I could just find someone like you, I wouldn't be in such a quandary," Nigel told her.

Alex put up her hands in protest, laughing. "If your grandfather wasn't such a courtly man, he could tell you tales that would make you grateful you haven't fallen in love with my double. Believe me, it hasn't always been easy or even sane; it's just that at this point, we've had a very long time to adjust."

Nigel left his grandparents' house with a light step. He was still wide awake and making plans in the small hours of the morning when the bell clanged to indicate someone needed a doctor.

He found one of the Colley children on the doorstep. "Petey, isn't it?" he asked, and the little towheaded boy nodded vigorously, pleased to be remembered, but then new tears started down the dirty tracks left from a previous bout.

"It's Mama again. Papa . . . She fell down again," Petey sniffed.

"Then we'd better go see what we can do for her," Nigel said, letting his own calm wash over the child.

Nigel hadn't met the man because he was never called until the culprit had left the scene, but he had no doubt that Mrs. Colley's "falls" were the result of Mr. Colley's fists and boots. He had tried to speak to her about it, but that had evoked more terror than her injuries, and he had desisted lest she cease to seek his aid. He had treated her for various cuts, bruises, a couple of fractured ribs, and a broken arm, and he feared someday she would be beaten beyond help. The only thing he found to be thankful for was that the long stepping-stone line of children did not seem to receive the same degree of brutality from their father, though they had not escaped a bruise or two.

"Mama's talkin' funny," Petey said, his voice quavering. "She never done that before."

Because she has somehow managed to avoid having her skull cracked before, Nigel thought, but he murmured soothing words.

If anyone else came needing assistance, he would have to go to the Kingston house down the way, but that was standard procedure, known by all their patients and by everyone on the street, should a stranger come looking for one of the doctors. Nigel left a scrawled note for Anthea and Max, telling them where he'd gone.

The Colleys lived in what had once been the luxurious home of one family but was now the shabby shelter for many, the fashionable having long since abandoned this district for better surroundings in less congested areas. It was depressingly like the house where Sally's family lived and not far from there.

The children were clustered in a small army around their mother's bed. The oldest child, a girl, was only ten, but she was trying without much success to bring some order to the chaos of weeping children. She greeted his arrival with such relief, Nigel had to swallow the lump in his throat.

He shooed the children away so he could examine their mother, and they obeyed him instantly. Dr. Falconer had made their mother all right before; he could do it again.

At first, he feared their confidence was misplaced. Mrs. Colley, in addition to various other contusions and abrasions, had a dark stain of purpling flesh over her left eye and temple and was alternately silent or muttering incoherently. He spoke to her coaxingly and then sharply, demanding she waken. "Mrs. Colley, it's Dr. Falconer. You're going to be all right, but you must wake up now. Your children are very worried. Come on, Mrs. Colley, open your eyes and look at me!"

At last she did as he commanded, making an obvious effort to resolve his multiple image into one.

"Who am I?" he asked.

"Dr. Falconer," she answered, puzzled that he would ask, and she was rewarded by his smile.

"Mrs. Colley, your . . . er . . . fall gave you a bad crack on the head, but you're going to be fine." He held up two fingers, then five, and she was able to answer correctly when he asked her for the count. There was little he could do for her, but he had no intention of leaving her until he was sure she was not going to lapse into a coma. He treated her split lip and various other wounds with great tenderness, as much to assure her that someone cared as for any medical good it would do.

He was so intent on her, he thought the commotion behind him came from the children until he saw his patient's eyes widen in horror.

Mr. Colley was huge; that was the first thing Nigel noticed, and the next was that the man was very drunk. The fumes of high-proof rum reached him across the room.

Nigel got to his feet. "I'm Dr. Falconer, your wife's physician. She seems to have had an accident." He tried to keep the accusation out of his voice. "With rest and care, she ought to recover fully."

He put his hand out in the vain hope that by treating Mr. Colley with politeness, he would receive it in return, but instead of a handshake, he got a roar of rage as Colley charged at him, screaming that his wife was a whore, among other things.

Though his life was dedicated to healing, Nigel had been raised with two active brothers by a father who believed every man ought to know how to defend himself. He sidestepped the first charge and put out his foot, sending the giant crashing to the floor. And still unwilling to give up reason in the midst of this insanity, he kept talking. "Mr. Colley, I assure you, I am your wife's doctor, nothing more. Please consider her well-being if nothing else; she has had quite enough violence tonight."

The words sounded weak to his own ears when matched against the furious bulk of the man, and the part of Nigel that always observed his own actions as closely as it did the actions of others conceded that he was going to have to disable Colley very swiftly if he wanted to survive.

When the man got to his feet and lunged again, Nigel was ready for him, but he wasn't ready for Petey's misguided efforts to aid him. Petey ran between the two men, screeching, "Stop, Papa, stop it! He came to help Mama!"

There wasn't any choice. Nigel lost his advantage when he reached for Petey and swung him out of the path of the oncoming monster, and only at the last second did he see that Colley had a knife, a very large knife. He tried to twist away, but the blade slashed across the top of his right arm, slicing through cloth and flesh and then with a turn sank into his back below his shoulder. As he fell, he saw the room in a kaleidoscope of humanity, Mrs. Colley trying to get up, the children dancing in a mad frenzy and screaming at the top of their lungs.

It seemed to him that it took a very long time to make contact with the floor. He curled on his left side, trying to lever himself up with his left arm; his right arm had gone instantly numb, though he could feel the hot edges of the pain that would be. He expected Colley to finish him, but instead, the pack of screaming children had turned on their father, beating him with their small fists. The man stood shaking his head like a bull unsure of where to charge next. Then the first small light of understanding flickered in his eyes, and he turned and fled, leaving sudden shocked silence in his wake.

Nigel knew he didn't have much time to give instructions. He could feel the blood pouring from the first cut and welling around the knife blade. When the ten-year-old, glassy-eyed but resolute, reached for the knife hilt, he stopped her. "No, don't touch it! There will be too much bleeding if you pull it out. I need to get back to the other doctors, to the Kingstons. Can you get help to take me there?"

Dispassionately he noted that his voice already sounded breathy. He heard Mrs. Colley saying, "Oh, my God!" over and over, prayer or curse, he couldn't be sure, and he was very thankful when she stopped it and rattled off names, some of which he recognized, telling the children to fetch the neighbors.

Petey guided the men who carried Nigel back to his own street and dumped him in front of the Kingstons' house. When the bearers fled for fear of being accused of the crime, Petey stayed to ring the bell, not running away until he saw the door beginning to open and knew that someone would help Dr. Falconer.

Nigel tried to thank him, but he wasn't sure he'd said the words aloud. The first light of the sun was beginning to creep across the sky, but for him, night was falling again, and when he heard renewed screams, he thought he was dying on the Colley's floor after all.

Chapter 19

Sally stopped her screams with her fist, cutting through the skin of her knuckles with her teeth, but even as she turned to summon help, Anthea and Max were coming to the door, belting their robes.

"It's Nigel," Sally said, not noticing that she had called him by his given name as he had repeatedly asked her to do.

"What the hell . . . ?" Max's voice trailed off as he saw the knife hilt and the blood soaking Nigel's coat. And then he swore, "Good Christ Almighty! What have you done to yourself?"

"Looks as if he had some help," Anthea noted grimly. As the

two of them spoke, they were checking him for pulse and other vital signs.

"Come on, Sally, help us get him inside," she ordered, and was glad to find that the girl wasn't too shocked to help.

Nigel was heavy in his unconscious state, but the three of them got him inside and laid out on the dining room table.

Joseph was still sleeping, despite the commotion, and so Anthea asked Sally, "Can you help here?"

Sally had proved herself a good nurse when they needed one, but Anthea knew how different this situation was.

Though her face was nearly as pale as Nigel's, Sally said, "I'll do anything, anything at all to help him."

Anthea left her with Max to cut away Nigel's clothing, and she ran to the office to gather everything they needed, knowing Nigel must not be moved any more than necessary, knowing precious seconds were ticking away.

Nigel moaned but did not rouse fully as Max and Sally worked on his clothing. Max glanced at Sally. "If it's necessary, we'll give him chloroform before we take the knife out." He needed the reassurance as much as Sally did; he had grown to love Nigel as a brother.

However, when Anthea and Max removed the knife, cleansed the wounds, staunched the bleeding, and sutured the cuts, Nigel remained unconscious, not even moaning anymore. Sally's hands were steady as she assisted the doctors, but she knew as well as they that not only had Nigel lost a great deal of blood, but also dirt had undoubtedly gotten into the wounds from the broad, two-edged knife.

"Let's get him upstairs while he's still out," Max said, and they carried him up to the bedroom kept for guests.

Joseph found them there, and Anthea explained swiftly, before he could panic. "Nigel has been injured, but he's going to be all right. He just needs rest and care, and we're going to give that to him here." She hoped the prognosis would prove accurate.

"Come on, we'll have to hurry to get you ready for school on time," Sally said, though all she wanted to do was to stay by Nigel's side. But her reminder of the commonplace routine comforted Joseph.

At the school, Sally told Flora and Philly what had happened, and they promised to get word to Morgan immediately, as well as to bring Joseph home when school was out for the day. She knew that by the end of the day, the whole family would know about Nigel and would begin to gather to share the burdens of his care and their concern. She knew she had forfeited her claim to be with him by refusing his suit, and she wasn't sure how she was going to bear it, but the Kingstons had other ideas.

"Do you love him after all?" Anthea demanded.

"Yes, I do." Even under such dire circumstances, it was a relief to say it, a relief to know it was true, and a terror to know that Nigel might not live long enough for her to tell him, or might not care if she did.

"Then you will surely be the best medicine we can offer," Anthea told her.

Sally's fear that the rest of the family might not prove so generous was groundless. Even Nigel's parents accepted her presence as if she had a long-established right to be there.

It hurt to look at Nigel, but it was worse to be away from him. No one had to tell her that his recovery was going to be more difficult because he had overworked and lost weight and sleep because of her refusal of his proposal in the weeks before the stabbing. She would have liked to stay beside him without pause, but she obediently took her turn with members of the family. When she was with him, she listened to each breath he drew and waited for the next one. She monitored his fever, sponging him down when it rose too high. She coaxed him to swallow the liquids to replace the fluids he burned away in his fever. And she talked to him, telling him she loved him, telling him he was not alone. She didn't care that others heard her litany. Her world had narrowed to two people—the pale figure on the bed and Joseph.

Even in her concentration on Nigel, there was room for the child. She knew how unsure and afraid he often was despite his brave show, and she did not want him to feel lost and neglected in this crisis. However, she found that in his old man–little boy way, he was equal to the challenge.

"I don't understand everything," he told her earnestly. "First I thought you loved Cousin Nigel, and then I thought you didn't. Now I think you do again, and he's real sick, so you'd better make sure he gets well."

Sally hugged him and ruffled his hair. "I do love him, so much. I did even when it seemed like I didn't. You're a wise young man, and I am very, very glad you are my friend."

The first day, Nigel never roused fully, only enough to plead over and over, "No, Petey, stay out of the way!"

It was harder on the second day, when his fever rose and he babbled about Sally, apologizing over and over for breaking his promise, for not understanding.

"It's all right, my darling, it's all right," Sally crooned, but by the afternoon his fever was so high and he thrashed about in the bed with such violence, Morgan and Adam had to restrain him until Anthea and Max could get him packed in ice.

Sally stood unnoticed, her back pressed hard against the wall and tears rolling unchecked down her cheeks as she listened to Nigel's father.

"That's it, old son, quiet now, quiet," Morgan murmured, while Sam clung tightly to her son's hand.

When Nigel's teeth began to chatter, they warmed him up again, just enough to counter the chill, and then he lay in a stupor that was as frightening as the violence.

The third day was a repeat of the second, and Nigel was beginning to look so frail, Sally knew she was not the only one who despaired of his recovery. But this time, once they'd gotten his temperature down, he fell into a natural sleep, and by morning of the fourth day, everyone was breathing easier.

The first faces Nigel saw when he opened his eyes were his mother's and his grandmother's. He blinked at them, not understanding why they were there until he tried to move and pain shot through his shoulder, reminding him of what had happened. He clenched his jaw, closed his eyes, and waited for the pain to ease before he looked at the faces again.

Sam and Alex were both smiling, both weeping, and their glad voices broke over him as he was offered cool water for his parched throat. His pillows were fluffed, his linen straightened, and the hair brushed back from his forehead, little touches telling him how much they loved him.

"Please, don't fuss," he croaked, but they paid no attention, and he was determined to recover as quickly as possible.

"California, I meant to go," he said to Alex as he felt sleep drift over him again.

"It would have been an easier journey for you and all of us, but I believe you've accomplished your goal nonetheless."

He could hear the smile in his grandmother's voice, and the words swirled around in his head as he fell asleep.

He understood them when he surfaced again to find Sally beside his bed. She looked as ragged as he felt, her face pale except for the dark circles around her eyes, but the eyes were shining with love, and her first words confirmed it. "I love you," she said, and then she buried her face in her hands, sobbing, "and I thought you were going to die before I could tell you."

"Well, I didn't," he said slowly, trying to absorb this drastic change, thinking perhaps he'd heard her say the same thing in his fever. He also tried to reach out to her with his right hand, but he discovered that not only was his arm bound against his side, his hand didn't seem to be responding to his command anyway. And when he managed to move his left hand, he was too weak to move it far enough to touch Sally.

She looked up and saw his struggle.

"This time you'll have to come to me," he said, and his efforts to move and talk were well rewarded when she took his left hand and cradled it against her cheek and then bent down to hide her face against his for a moment.

She answered all his questions before he asked them. "If you still want me, I will be your wife. I still think you could do better. I still doubt I can be what you need. But I love you, and nothing matters more to me now than that, not my family, not yours. When I saw you lying there on the street, it made everything change, or maybe changes had already come, and I just didn't recognize them. I only know that I don't want to be in a world that you have left."

It was worth the searing pain in his shoulder, it was worth anything to have Sally beside him, but it made him anxious to get on with his life.

He was a terrible patient. While he was still too weak to sit up without assistance, he demanded to know what the doctors thought about the damage to his right arm.

"You know the answer," Anthea said gently. "We don't know. It's possible the damage is permanent, but it may also be a temporary condition. We could not tell when we patched you up; you wouldn't have been able to tell if you'd done the surgery on yourself." She studied him for a moment before she shook her head in teasing disgust. "Men! Honestly, Nigel Falconer, you are asking things of yourself you would never ask of a patient. It's your foolish male pride. You think you ought to be able to get right up as if nothing happened. Well, it's true you might not be so weak now if you hadn't been neglecting yourself before. But for heaven's sake, you weren't pricked with a penknife! You were slashed and stabbed with a blade big enough to kill a bear. And Mr. Colley might not have kept the weapon clean, but he kept it sharp."

"Just my luck to be attacked by a meticulous dipsomaniac," Nigel muttered with a flash of his old humor, and then his attention shifted. "Petey Colley! He saved my life. It's all blurred, but I'm sure he stayed until Sally came to the door, and he's the one who led the men who carried me here. I've got to thank him and to check on his mother."

"We already tried," Anthea said. "I found the note you left, but by the time we could gather our wits enough to check on the Colleys, they were gone. Undoubtedly they feared Mr. Colley would be jailed for what he did, which might have been the best thing. But who knows? The neighbors reported that, though he consumed too much of his wage in drink, his family did manage to get enough of it to stay alive."

"Damn! Poor Petey, poor Mrs. Colley and the rest of them." He sank back against his pillow and closed his eyes, exhausted as much by the contemplation of the Colleys' bleak lives, now beyond the reach of his help, as by the energy he had expended in talking to Anthea.

But as soon as he had collected a small store of strength again, he concentrated on moving his arm and on flexing the rest of his body so that he would not grow too stiff in bed. Though he tried to be gracious about being fed, washed, and tended like an infant, he was determined to end the solicitousness by getting up as soon as possible. The logical, scientific part of him knew he was wearing himself out needlessly, but he was sure he could win by sheer willpower.

He questioned Gincie closely about how soon mobility had returned to her arm after she had been shot in the shoulder, and she answered willingly enough, but she thought it early for him to be pushing so hard.

"If only he would treat himself as kindly as he does his patients," she fretted, joining the family chorus Nigel was ignoring.

"He will," Sally announced, too worried about Nigel to be shy any longer, and the family watched in wonder and appreciation as a new Sally emerged.

Using wiles she would never employ for her own gain, Sally became the dictator of Nigel's sickroom. When he didn't eat enough or wanted to get up for too long once he could sit and then stand without passing out, Sally let her big blue eyes well with tears as she pled with him to eat just a bit more or rest for her sake. He did not want to take landanum or anything else for the pain because he hated the artificial sleep it induced, but when Sally saw his color fading and the taut lines framing his mouth, she let her own face mirror his suffering so accurately that when she offered the potion again, he took it as obediently as a child.

When he fretted that he would hardly be fit to practice medicine without the use of his right arm, she stared at him blankly and then asked, "Do you think that would bother me after nearly losing you altogether? You must think me very shallow if you judge that such a small thing would make any difference in my love for you. And I know you better than to think you will not find a way to cope if the condition is permanent."

Nigel hadn't meant to imply any lack on Sally's part and assured her that indeed they would be fine, no matter what happened.

It was Sally who first saw his right hand move, and she waited for it to happen again, so she could be sure, before she covered his fingers with hers and said very calmly, "Now you can find something else to worry about since your hand just moved."

He looked at his hand as if it belonged to someone else, and then he watched the fingers move when he commanded them to do so. The smile he gave Sally made her tears overflow, and she wiped at them like a child.

"I weep too readily these days," she sniffed, "though all the cause for weeping is past."

It made Nigel see how gaunt, pale, and bruised-eyed she was, and it was he who proposed that they go to Brookhaven as soon as Anthea and Max said he could travel.

"It's exactly what we would have prescribed, but we expected he'd claim that if he were well enough to go out to the country, he was well enough to work again. I don't know how you persuaded him, but I'm glad you did," Anthea told Sally.

"In this case, it was his idea," Sally reported happily, and though Anthea guessed accurately at Nigel's motive, she did not mention it. Let the two of them heal together out in the fresh air.

The land was growing greener by the day as April advanced, and for the first time Sally allowed herself to imagine what it was going to be like to be part of Nigel's family without the distance she had always maintained. It was at once a comforting and a daunting prospect, and despite all evidence of welcome, she still wondered if Nigel's parents were really resigned to his choice of a wife.

"I will try to take very good care of him," she said to Sam one afternoon as they shared the pleasant task of working in the flower garden.

"Oh, my dear girl, you mustn't have any doubts! His father and I certainly don't. We have already seen you take very good care of him!" She peered at Sally's face, shaded under the brim of a sunbonnet. "Don't worry. You and my son have enough love between you to help you over the rough spots and to enjoy the smooth."

Sally was suddenly enfolded in Sam's arms, and for a moment, she thought she was going to burst into tears; she could not remember her mother ever hugging her or showing any affection.

"I love my sons, but I always wanted a daughter. And now I have Mercy and you. I could not wish for better," Sam murmured.

Sally found warmth and welcome also awaiting her at Wild Swan and, to her relief, she made a practical discovery, too. She had her first riding lessons and enjoyed them immensely. She had always begged off when Joseph had gone with his cousins, but now she felt she ought to know how to do it since horses mattered so much to Nigel's people.

Gincie started Sally's lessons, and then Nigel took over when his arm and hand were strong enough.

"Isn't it wonderful that I can do this!" Sally exclaimed, bouncing a little with excitement and then remembering what she'd learned about keeping her seat in the saddle.

Nigel laughed aloud at her pleasure and then sobered, understanding the anxiety that had preceded the exuberance. "I'm pleased that you enjoy this," he said, "but being a good horsewoman is not a prerequisite for marrying me. I love you just the way you are. I don't want you spending your life trying to live up to some foolish ideal you've conjured in your own mind."

She nodded her agreement, looking at him with her heart in her eyes, but Nigel thought he'd have to watch very carefully to make sure her budding self-confidence continued to grow.

If he had his wish, they would be married immediately, but for her sake and their future happiness, he was willing to take everything very slowly. He spoke to his mother and his grandmother about his plans.

Alex offered to give an engagement party at Wild Swan in late May and would have been willing to have the wedding there, but she understood why he decided it would be at Brookhaven, and he made sure his mother understood, too.

"Whatever Brookhaven was when your father owned it, it's changed since Papa bought it for you, since you've made it into a home."

Sam recognized the words for the gift they were.

Though he was prepared to give Sally her way in most things, Nigel would not allow her apprehension to spoil the plans for the engagement party or the wedding.

"We are not going to hide our love; we are going to celebrate it."

She recognized his implacability, but she made a last attempt to change his mind. "What about my family?' she asked, her voice shaking.

She looked away from his steady gaze, and then the thing she had never been able to tell him before rose up and spilled out. "My mother knew that my uncle was . . . bothering me. That's why she was watching me so closely for pregnancy. He didn't want her; he wanted me. And she was afraid to be without a man. She was more afraid of that than she was afraid for me." Sally's eyes, wild with hurt, met his again. "How could that be?" she whispered. "How could that be?"

Nigel remembered everything his grandmother had told him about herself, about Gincie and his mother, about the pain that remained with them all, and he made himself be more cautious than he had ever been before. "I don't know how that could be," he admitted grimly. "I do know that you deserved much, much better than that. But it has nothing to do with you. It has to do with your mother's troubles. And I can't tell you what to do about your mother. I am unfit to judge for you because I was raised by two people who still love each other and who would die before they would allow harm to their children. I don't know how much you need her in your life. And I cannot forgive her as you might because I love you more than you love yourself. But I will promise to be civil to her if that is what you wish. And I will not forget that had she not brought you to Anthea, I would never have met you." And you might have died in other hands, he added silently, his heart clenching at the thought.

The horses fretted with the inactivity, and Nigel and Sally rode on in silence.

By the next day, Sally was ready to talk about it again. "I have decided to decide nothing. If my mother wishes to celebrate with us, she may. If she does not, that is all right, too."

"Agreed," Nigel said calmly, but inwardly he was lauding the quiet strength he heard in her voice.

Part of him would have liked to stay in the country doing nothing but sharing the days with Sally, but he knew how much heavier the Kingstons' burden of cases was without him, and part of him was anxious to return to his practice.

To Sally, the city was a shock after the days of spindly-legged foals and green meadows, but she had already learned that home was anywhere Nigel was, and she continued to adjust to the changes in her life. She found it impossible to refuse the dramatic expansion of her wardrobe, a project the women of the family took on with great delight and with a concerted and successful effort to overcome her objections by pointing out how much this or that dress would please Nigel. But she remained firm about her job with the Kingstons.

"It's a perfect position for me," she insisted. "Nigel will be busy all day, and I have no wish to be idle. Joseph and I get along very well. He won't need me forever, but for now, I think things ought to go on as they are."

"I hate to admit it, but for selfish reasons, I won't try to dissuade you anymore," Anthea said. "I was already wondering how we were going to manage without you."

When Adam's wife, Mercy, was delivered of another boy, Zachary Falconer, Sally felt her own private joy in knowing she would be the baby's aunt before too long. And she cheered with the family at Pimlico when Moonraker showed that his promise as a three-year-old had only grown during the off-season. Due to his winning record, he was going to have to carry more weight than many of the other entrants of his age in handicapped races, but he was big and strong in his fourth year and should be able to handle weight within reason, though every horse had its own limit to the burden it could carry and still run with speed.

Nigel was openly proud of Sally, not only of how beautiful she looked in her new finery, but also of how quickly she was learning the intricacies of Thoroughbred racing.

"It would be difficult not to be charmed and fascinated by them," Sally said in answer to his praise. "They are such exquisite creatures!"

"So are you," Nigel murmured. He wanted to kiss her right there in the middle of the crowd, but he contented himself with nothing more than a gentle squeeze of her hand. Even when they were alone, he was careful about any physical display of his love. Though Sally tried to hide it, he could feel the tension in her when he pressed, no matter how inadvertently, too close physically. It was frustrating, but the wounds of her past were part of Sally, and he had every intention of winning by patient wooing and patient waiting.

The engagement party at Brookhaven was held at the end of May, after the Pimlico races and before the Culhanes and Alex and Rane were due at Jerome Park, though Padraic and some of the hands went ahead with the horses as usual. Alex had asked Padraic if he would like to stay for the party, but he would not allow his precious charges to go north without him.

Mercy was recovered enough from the birth of Zachary to attend the party, and she went out of her way to reassure Sally about how pleased she was to be gaining a sister-in-law.

"I'd be glad to watch Nathan and Zachary for you should you and Adam want some time to yourselves," Sally offered in turn.

"We might well take you up on that," Mercy said, "though you may want to reconsider, for you will surely be running after your own brood soon enough."

Mercy's beaming face was eloquent proof of how joyful she found the task, but Sally had all she could do to repress a shiver of dread. Having children meant having a man in her bed, in her body.

Nigel came up beside her at that moment, "Forgive me for neglecting you, my dear. But hard as it may be to believe, there are requests for medical advice even at a function such as this one."

It will be Nigel; not anyone else, just this very kind and loving man, Sally reminded herself. Her frantic pulse slowed to normal, and she touched the necklace Nigel had given to her a second time. "And what advice did you give?" she managed to ask.

"I told him the truth. I told him I wasn't competent to practice medicine tonight because I am too enchanted with my intended bride. I suggested he take his problem to Anthea or Max."

Sally and Mercy spotted Max, trapped in a corner by a large man who was talking very fast and pointing to various parts of his own anatomy.

The two women giggled, and Nigel made a great show of being insulted. "Such a lack of sympathy for the hard-pressed Dr. Kingston," he chided, but inwardly he was relieved to feel the tension ease from Sally, while he wondered what had caused it in the first place.

Alex wondered the same thing about Rane, but his tension never eased. He was saying and doing all of the right things and had been since his arrival the day before, but she was not deceived by the facade. She was waiting for him to tell her what was wrong, but her patience was wearing thin and wasn't improved when Gincie came up to her to inquire softly, "Gran, is something troubling Grandfather? He seems so . . . I'm not sure . . . distant, I think. And sad. Doesn't he approve of Nigel's choice?"

"As far as I know, he does approve," Alex said slowly, studying Rane where he stood some distance from her, speaking with a group of their guests. "But you're right, something is wrong, and I intend to find out what it is."

Gincie didn't mind that she'd been forgotten as she watched Alex move toward Rane; her grandparents were so much the center of all of their lives, discord between them was a risk for everyone.

Rane felt Alex approaching before he saw her. He was so attuned to her, he had never lost track of where she was in the room. And he knew the other side of the coin was equally true. It was usually comforting to know that she shared his moods as he shared hers. But this time, he wished it were not so. He was determined to keep the news he had received yesterday to himself until tomorrow. He wanted her to savor the joy of Nigel's engagement without any shadows. He wished he himself did not know what had happened; it made him want to weep in the middle of the rejoicing.

Alex spoke to the group, apologizing for her intrusion, and then at her most gracious, she asked, "Will you forgive me if I steal my husband for a few moments? There is a matter I would discuss with him."

The guests' smiles were benevolent with the assumption that the Falconers had no problem more pressing than a consultation on the wine and food being served.

"Is it Nigel and Sally?" Alex demanded without preamble when they were alone. "Do you disapprove after all?"

Her question was so far off the mark, Rane was dazed, and then he realized just how deeply his dark mood had affected her.

"No, it has nothing to do with them, nothing! I think Sally will be a good and loving wife to Nigel, and Nigel no less a husband."

"Will you tell me then what burdens you so?" she asked, so much love in her voice and her eyes that he had to turn away for a moment.

"I will tell you tomorrow; it is soon enough. It is not important to this night, just a problem at the shipyard, and soon solved. I am sorry I have let it intrude on this celebration."

Rane felt the seconds of her silence passing very slowly, and then she said, "Is this lie very important to you?" and the hurt and the kindnesss were equal in her voice.

Rane swallowed the lump in his throat. "It is important that you allow me to explain tomorrow, not tonight."

"I will let it go if you will assure me of one thing." She planted herself in front of him so that she could see his face. "Promise me this has nothing to do with your well-being. Nothing on earth, no one, including Nigel and Sally, is more important than you are to me."

He put his arms around her and pressed her close, inhaling her fragrance and the separate scent of delicate silk. "I promise I am very well. I swear it."

She tipped her head up for his kiss, believing him, loving him. And she let the matter of his secret drop because it was important to him that she do so, and because she could face whatever he had to tell her whenever he chose to tell her, as long as she had him with her.

The party continued to go smoothly, and no one was less than courteous to Sally. The Falconers, Carringtons, and Culhanes had given their stamp of approval to the young woman, and that was enough.

"It's a nasty little thought, but I'm glad Sally's family isn't here," Gincie admitted to Travis. "I think they would have made this evening very difficult for her."

"Perhaps Mrs. Birch has some love for her daughter after all," Travis suggested. "The choice was hers, and she declined to come."

Gincie thought it more likely that the woman didn't want to face a gathering like this one for reasons of her own comfort, but whatever the cause, it was better for Sally this way.

She saw her grandparents return to the party together, and because they both looked more at ease than before, she stopped worrying about her grandfather and concentrated on making sure the festivities continued to run smoothly with no lack of food or drink.

*   *   *

As always, Alex awakened early, and she found Rane propped on an elbow, watching her. He sat up and pulled her into his arms, cradling her head against his chest. "Hugh Bettingdon is dead. He was trying out a new hunter. He died instantly of a broken neck when the horse fell." Rane felt the current of shock run through Alex's body, and he held her tighter. "It will be in all the papers soon. Christopher and Gwenny sent a transatlantic telegram so that we would know as soon as possible."

Alex listened to the beat of Rane's heart, to the steady drumming assurance that he was alive and with her, and she made herself believe that what he had told her was true.

Hugh, who had protected her when St. John would not; Hugh, who had made St. John see how much he loved her; Hugh, who had been godfather to her children in England, who had supported her spirit in so many ways through all the years, who had even had much to do with the excellence of the Thoroughbreds at Wild Swan. Hugh, who had thought enough of her, of Sinje, and later of Rane, that he had rejoiced when his son and heir had chosen Gweneth Falconer for his bride.

"Poor Angelica, she will have to go on without him now," Alex whispered. She held on to Rane as if she feared he would slip away from her. She could see Hugh for all the years she had known him from young man to old, but she could not see him dead. Her tears fell warm and wet on Rane's chest.

"You meant a great deal to the duke," Rane said, his voice infinitely gentle. The jealousy he had felt years ago had long since vanished in the understanding of the special bond between Alex and Hugh, a bond that had not threatened either of their spouses.

Suddenly, Alex stiffened and pulled away from Rane, wiping at her eyes. "My God, Christopher will be the Duke of Almont now and Gwenny his duchess! Though they have known it would be so someday, what a shock it must be."

The rest of the family had to be informed, letters of condolence had to be written, and the inevitable interest from newspapermen had to be handled, though Reid made this last task much easier. Not only had Hugh Bettingdon, Duke of Almont, been well known in sporting circles in England and America, but the fact that the new duchess was an American, though born of English parents, was deemed a noteworthy story everywhere.

For all their professed contempt for titles, Americans were fascinated by them and never more so than when an American attained one. It was inevitable that parallels were drawn between the case of Jennie Jerome, who had married Lord Randolph Churchill two years previously, and Gweneth Falconer Bettingdon, particularly because Mr. Jerome was a highly respected figure in the racing world, as were Gweneth's parents. A few papers were crass enough to call the two women "America's Thoroughbred Fillies." And a few had the bad taste to point out the financial differences; Lord Churchill was known to be chronically short of funds, while the estates and commercial holdings of the Duke of Almont, past and present, were vast, solvent, and growing by the year.

"Thank God Gwenny is so sensible! I am sure she has been married to Christopher for too long to allow this sort of nonsense to bother her," Alex said, and she tried to ignore the newspaper articles, too.

The plans for the summer changed. Originally the Culhanes and Alex and Rane were to begin the racing season in New York State in June, and the Falconers were to return to Wild Swan in time for the arrival of Gwenny and her family in July. Gincie and Travis were to have had time with Gwenny and the others after the race meeting at Saratoga.

Now there would be no visit from England this summer. But Flora and Marsh were going to make the crossing the other way, and Alex was grateful. Flora had always been fond of Gwenny, and she and Marsh would be able to offer support without causing extra work.

Alex and Rane discussed whether or not they ought to go to England and had decided against it. The last thing Gwenny needed in this time of transition was to worry about seeing to the comfort of her aged parents.

Rane winced at the word "aged" when Alex used it, though he conceded it had a certain public truth. "As long as we don't believe it in private," he amended, and was rewarded by a smile from her, something he sorely missed in these somber days.

Alex had admitted that she did not feel up to attending the races this summer, and Travis and Gincie did not press the Falconers to accompany them.

"The children will love having you with them for the summer," Gincie told her grandmother, and to Travis she said, "I'm glad they're not going with us. I would hate to watch Gran having to answer endless questions about the duke and Gwenny while the loss is so fresh."

All of the decisions Alex was making were sensible ones, and yet, as Rane applauded them, he also worried about her. After the first tears, there had been no others, and he wondered at her continued control in face of so grievous a loss. And finally, reminding himself that the best of their lives together had been the truth between them, he asked her point-blank whether she was really all right.

She considered the question for a long time before she answered. "As well as you know me, you might still think me mad for this. I know that Hugh is dead and I will not see him again. At least, the practical part of me knows this. But there is another part that never quite believes in death at a distance. That part of me is quite able to believe that the people I loved who died so far away in England are there yet. I can see my grandmother still working in her garden, welcoming me when I come to help. And my father is busy in his chandlery with all the stores that will outfit a ship to sail anywhere in the world. Your parents, too, they're waiting in the house at Clovelly—your father Magnus, so big and hearty that he frightened me until I knew how kind he was—and your mother, glad that Magnus has escaped the sea and the revenue cutters once again. And Hugh is there no less than the others. Hugh in his forbidding dignity that disguises such a quick mind and kind heart . . ."

She paused, gazing off at her own vision. "My practical side is thankful that he did not linger, trapped in a crippled body as Sinje was. But the other side sees him still riding his blooded horses, still loving Angelica and his children and grandchildren, still protecting everyone who depends on him . . . still, just Hugh, just Hugh as he has always been."

"Sweetling, I think you might defeat even Death," Rane said, and his use of the old endearment told her of the depth of his understanding.

Rane found himself spending a great deal of time at Wild Swan, and when he could not leave Baltimore for a few days at a stretch, Alex was there, in spite of her distaste for the noise and filth of the city in summer. The city visits also made it possible for her to see more of the rest of the family who dwelt in Baltimore. And in order to make the heat more bearable, Rane and Alex stole time here and there to sail out on the bay or to take advantage of the cool green shadows of Druid Hill Park and of the pleasant, stream-laced countryside that beckoned not far from the city limits.

One afternoon while they were strolling arm and arm in the park, Rane was startled when Alex suddenly laughed. He looked at her inquiringly.

Her expression grew serious as she searched for the words to explain. "I was thinking how we must appear to the children and the young couples here. We must seem so ancient, and they must wonder, at least now and again, what it is like to be so old." She paused and then added softly. "And they would never accept the answer, that experience and memories grow, but that the physical changes they can see have nothing to do with what is inside. That stays the same. I love you as I always have, and the Alex I am now is little different from the one who existed long ago. Sometimes I am quite shocked to see how I look in a mirror, to see how I look to other people. The white in my hair and the lines on my face seem like a disguise of some sort, though I know I've earned them."

"Then I have certainly been better paid," Rane said with a grin, indicating his own hair, which was all silver now in contrast to the dark and light of hers, and his skin, which showed the years of exposure to sun and sea. But then he grew serious, too. "It is one of the best things of all about growing old together, growing apace, and thus staying the same."

Having her trim and tall beside him, her fragrance drifting to him with the scent of summer flowers, he felt the stir of passion, not swift and piercing as it had been in his youth, but so deep and strong, he wished they were back in the privacy of their bedroom or in the cabin of his ship, the *Falcon*.

"I know that look," Alex murmured. "Let's go back to the house."

Neither of them was considering any longer how younger people might be viewing them.

Most of the country was a bit giddy this summer, excited by the prospect of the centennial of independence. Special celebrations were planned in a multitude of cities and towns, with the greatest to be in Philadelphia, where a grand exposition of mechanical marvels paid tribute to the inventiveness of the human mind and to the industrial progress being made.

Alex and Rane felt that the holiday had a special significance for them because they had left their birthplace to build new lives here, and to honor the day, they planned a gathering of family and friends at Wild Swan. The children were already delirious in anticipation of the games, food, and fireworks, though they knew their great-grandmother meant it when she said the fireworks were to be set off far from the horses and with adults in charge.

The family began arriving at Brookhaven and Wild Swan a few days before the Fourth. Alastair Cameron came too, glad to celebrate with the people who had become like his own over the years.

When Reid, Larissa, and their children arrived on the third, it seemed like part of the general migration until Alex got a closer look at the adults' faces.

Larissa kissed her grandmother on the cheek and asked urgently, "Gran, may Reid and I see you and Grandfather alone, please? We're all right, but we have some news to tell you."

The Tratnor children scampered off to play with their cousins, and Rane was summoned from yet another consultation with the other men about how to get the best display from the fireworks without causing a disaster.

"It's a good thing Morgan, Adam, and I agree more easily on shipbuilding than on pyrotechnics," he said as he greeted the Tratnors, but his smile faded as he picked up their tension.

"There is no easy way to tell this," Reid said. "We've known all along it was possible, even inevitable, but the reality is stunning. General Custer and all of the men who rode with him were annihilated by the Sioux and the Cheyenne at the Little Big Horn River in Montana Territory. It happened about a week ago. The accounts are still coming in; there's considerable confusion; and some people still won't believe it happened at all, but I'm convinced it's true. The military details are too believable for it to be otherwise. Some of the men with Major Reno and Captain Benteen survived, but all of Custer's detachment died, including his two brothers, his nephew, and his brother-in-law. The total army dead, from Custer's troops and the others, are said to number over three hundred. There are few wounded. And there are reports that many of the bodies were mutilated, though Custer's remains were not."

"Tribute from the Indians to a brave enemy," Alex whispered. "A brave fool . . . those poor young men who followed him." She looked at Reid with the question in her eyes.

"Again, the reports are confused, but it is possible that there were so many Indians that not even reinforcements would have saved Custer. But in any case, he did not wait for the columns that were to join him. And in the beginning, he had been offered some of Gibbon's cavalry but said he didn't need them, preferring his own regiment. He also refused a battery of Gatling guns, claiming he was strong enough without them. General Terry says if Custer had waited for the troops that were to meet him, the expedition would have been successful. General Sheridan claims likewise that if the junction had been made, the column would have been sufficiently strong to handle the Indians, and Sheridan is a supporter of Custer." He paused, rubbing his face wearily.

"For the first time since I met all of you, I wish I were not connected to this family because I would spare you any blame for what I've done and will do. I've written a piece about the battle, about the fact that the Indians only did what our cavalry intended to do to them. I've written about the danger of sending officers who have too keen a taste for glory, too little sense, and little care for their men. And I've written that we have no right to harry the Indians from this land.

"There is so little time for truth. Already it is being altered; in a week or a little more, Custer will be a hero again. It is inevitable. Men are starting to volunteer; men who want to ride out and kill every Indian they find.

"I have calculated this very closely. In the first confusion, I believe, my columns will be printed. The first one will appear two days from now. I've never shrunk from controversy, and my reputation is good enough to carry me for a while," he said matter-of-factly, without arrogance, "but when the tide turns, the owner of my paper here and of the other papers that carry my articles are going to turn with it. I expect to be out of work fairly soon."

Alex was watching Larissa's reaction as carefully as she was listening to Reid, and she saw that her granddaughter was in complete agreement. Larissa's hand was tucked firmly in Reid's.

"I've always wanted to own my own newspaper, but I've grown complacent," Reid admitted. "There is a lot of security in working for others, in letting them take the financial risks, particularly in a city like Washington, which is known as a graveyard for newspapers. But current circumstances are going to force me from the nest."

"We know it won't be easy," Larissa said, "but we'll make a success of it because not only is Reid a very good writer, he knows how a newspaper should be run. And I think I could persuade merchants to have advertising accounts with us; I'm already practicing how to approach them. You do see why Reid must write the truth as he sees it, don't you?"

"Of course we do," Rane answered. And Alex added, "My dears, this family has never shied away from controversy. How we will be affected is not something to consider. Our views on the shameful treatment of Indians have been well known since Boston married Rachel."

Larissa's serenity did not falter when Reid told them the rest of his plan. "I realize it's already late for this, but I'm going to the Sioux territory to see if there's anything more to be learned there."

This was more difficult for Alex to accept, but she held back the words against his journey. His firsthand accounts of battles during the war had established his reputation for vivid, honest writing while so many other newspapermen had done their reporting from the hotels and bars of Washington. If Larissa could let him go this time, to another battlefield, then no one else had the right to argue against it.

"Travel safely," she said, and Rane offered Reid his hand. "Good luck. If there is anything we can do from this end, send us word."

Reid was gone by the time Philly and Blaine arrived from

Baltimore, but Larissa explained everything to them and was gratified that their support was instantly given.

Reid had left a copy of the article so that the family would know the text before the newspaper's readers did. Slowly Blaine read it aloud, giving every word its own weight.

We are celebrating a hundred years of existing as a free country with "justice for all." We have much to be proud of, but we also have far to go to fulfill the promise of this nation. Slavery was not honorable, and we ended it by a long and bloody struggle. Our treatment of the Indians has not been honorable, and we are trying to extinguish them in ways more bloody than we saw in the war. We have ridden them down in their villages, killing their women, their children, their elders. We have proven ourselves incapable of keeping the treaties we ourselves have written.

We are celebrating the time when we declared England's domination of our national life to be intolerable. And yet, we were brothers in tradition. How much more difficult it must be for the Indians, who are not part of our tradition and who must see us as the most foreign of tyrants when we tell them where they must live and how. In resisting this, they have done no more than we did one hundred years ago.

It is a tragedy that General Custer and his men were killed. But it is not the first tragedy. The first tragedy was that they were there at all and for the purpose of attacking the Indians, because the Indians do not understand why they should be forced from their homeland because white men crave gold.

There is no easy answer to this, but honor is seldom easy. And unless we wish to live with a legacy of dishonor that will haunt us for generations to come, we must, all of us, men and women, choose the honorable course, even at cost to ourselves.

It is late in the day, perhaps too late. We have killed so many of them and lost so many of our own; we have broken so many promises. But still, my fellow citizens, I beg you to call for a more reasonable way of meeting with the Indian nations, not for more blood.

"Your husband is a brave and eloquent man," Blaine said.

"He is, indeed. But his words will be on the same page as the report of the battle, and he knows better than anyone that too few people are going to consider anything except the fact that Custer and his men are dead. Even many of the people who have pled for years for just treatment of the Indians will be silent now. And the support for Sherman and Sheridan's strategies against the Indians will grow." Larissa hesitated and then added softly, "I thought I knew how much I love Reid, but I have never loved him as much as I do now."

For the adults of the family, it was a strange Fourth of July as they tried to enjoy the festivities for the children's sake even though their minds were filled with speculation about the repercussions that were sure to follow the massacre.

Alex thought of Gincie and Travis, north at the races, and knew it would be hard for them to be away from the family when they heard the news. And she thought of Rachel and Boston far away in California. Rachel, more than anyone, would understand how the government was likely to treat the Sioux and Cheyenne for winning the battle of the Little Big Horn—Rachel, who had traveled the Trail of Tears with her people when the Cherokee had been removed from Georgia and other southern states because of the gold and the land white men wanted.

When Michael McCoy and Lemuel Washington came to report that workhorses and a few head of prize cattle had been stolen from Sunrise during the night, Alex regarded them blankly.

"The Culhanes are going to be right angry, an' I don't blame 'em, but whoever it was just sneaked right in an' took the beasts," Michael said, with Lem nodding vigorous agreement. They were outraged and clearly expected Alex to share their feelings.

She felt like telling them that the loss of the livestock hardly mattered in comparison to Reid's news, but since they didn't know about that yet, she made herself concentrate on the problem at hand.

"Though it is regrettable that the animals were stolen, I am sure Gincie and Travis will understand that it was not through any negligence on your part; no one could protect their interests at Sunrise more fiercely than the two of you do." That was no exaggeration. Particularly since the shooting incident between Willy and Tay, Michael McCoy had offered such devotion to his duties that Travis had confided that Michael made him feel like a feudal lord. And Lem, unable or unwilling to manage men, was completely competent with the horses and other livestock.

"I suggest you ask around and circulate descriptions of the

beasts just in case the thieves try to sell them nearby, but it's more probable that the men and the animals are headed far away by now."

Even so many years after the war, there were still ruffians left who drifted from one nefarious deed to the next, apparently having enjoyed the pillage of the war so much that they could not adjust to honest work.

Alex made herself concentrate on the children to share their joy. They, at least, saw no shadows on the horizon. They shrieked and giggled as they hobbled through three-legged races and other contests, and Willy McCoy let Lexy's team win in the tug-of-war. If Michael gave feudal obeisance to the Culhanes, Willy was Lexy's devoted slave, following her around whenever he could to the point that Alex thought Lexy showed great restraint in her patience with the boy.

"He's like a big, clumsy puppy," Lexy had told her great-grandmother earnestly. "I can't be mean to him, even when I wish he'd go away sometimes."

But in the matter of the tug-of-war, Kace, who was on Willy's team, was not so understanding. "You let her side win! You slacked up on the rope!" he proclaimed in outrage, causing Willy's freckles to disappear in a blush of embarrassment.

"He slipped," Lexy lied stoutly. "But just so you won't feel cheated, let's do it again; only this time, Willy and I'll stay out of it."

Kace was mollified enough to comply, though not overly pleased when Lexy's team won anyway. Willy was starry-eyed at being defended by his heroine.

"Very diplomatic," Rane murmured to Alex, having observed the scene with her, "but not a very good way to discourage her knight-errant."

"I believe that would require a degree of rudeness from Lexy that is beyond her," Alex said.

Though he had helped to set up the fireworks, Rane allowed the younger man to set them off while he watched. The "oohs" and "aahs" were ample payment for the time spent in preparation.

But then Alex said, "They look so small against the darkness, but so bright and so fierce."

It applied to both the fireworks and the children, Rane thought. And whatever was done to or for the Indians in the aftermath of Custer's disaster would be the legacy for these children dancing with joy in the brilliant fractures of light shooting from amusements made of gunpowder.

Chapter 20

Reid traveled by rail, by riverboat, by stagecoach, and on horseback and was in Bismarck in the Dakota Territory in a week, before the army reinforcements had arrived from various forts via Chicago and other embarkation points. He used every political, military, and journalistic connection he had. And as he traveled in the Dakota and Montana territories, he listened to every rumor and interviewed everyone who would talk to him. He spoke to seasoned veterans of the Indian wars, to soldiers newly arrived, to ranchers, sutlers, scouts, some of them Crow Indians, and to Sioux on the reservation lands.

He was there in time to hear the truth, that Custer had been warned by scouts that the Indians had gathered in huge numbers, and he was there long enough to hear the truth being changed just as he had predicted, to hear a string of excuses being made for the general. And everywhere there were gruesome tales of hearts cut out and laid across the soldiers' faces, eyeballs dug from their sockets, entrails, genitals, and limbs hacked off, even beards dug from the faces and taken like scalps. But Custer, "Long Hair" to the Indians, had indeed been spared this treatment.

Reid learned that Chief Sitting Bull had not been killed, as some of the first reports had claimed, but had fled toward Canada. And he learned other things from a source he considered impeccable.

Paul Atkins was slightly built with graying hair and brown eyes mild behind spectacles. He was a Quaker who had come to the region as part of the president's Peace Policy, but had found himself changing rather than changing his charges.

Everything was made easier by the fact that Mr. Atkins was well read and familiar with Reid's work, though the eastern newspapers came to him only as gifts from friends and after long delays. Further, he was aware of Wild Swan's contribution to the Underground Railroad before the war.

"I can't claim any credit for that," Reid said. "I didn't meet the family until the war was well advanced."

Mr. Atkins brushed his protest aside. "Thee is kin to them, and thy writing shows thee agree in spirit."

It was through Atkins that Reid approached some of the Indians, but he soon found they were not willing to speak of anything more personal than the need for a fair government policy toward themselves.

"They have been told before that this white man or that one is their friend, and it has most often proved untrue," Mr. Atkins said sadly. "But I can tell thee that some of the people thee saw today were with the Sioux and the Cheyenne in the camp by the stream they call the 'Greasy Grass' and the Army calls 'Little Big Horn.' They need food and shelter because the Army is set to go after Indians everywhere outside of reservation boundaries. And there is already talk of a new treaty ceding the Black Hills to the United States, a treaty that will be made by reservation Indians because they have been warned that the old terms are running out and no more food will be provided unless they do what the government wants. I call that blackmail of the worst sort."

His eyes were suddenly blind-looking behind the spectacles, as if he were gazing inward. "I came here convinced that I could 'save' the Indians, that I could teach them our ways. And now I have come to a crisis in my own faith. Oh, it is not that I doubt the truth of my beliefs, but I doubt the truth for the Indians. I know it is being said that Sitting Bull was one of the war chiefs leading the battle against Custer, but it isn't true. On that day, he was the medicine man, apart from the warriors, reading his visions which foretold the coming of the soldiers. I believe in those visions—not for me, but for him, for his people. And Crazy Horse, that translation of his name suits whites just fine, but it's wrong. It would be more correct to call him 'Enchanted' or 'Magic' Horse in English. His name doesn't mean deranged; it indicates strong spiritual powers. And I believe he has them."

He looked away for a moment, as if shamed by these admissions, but he did not cease his confession. "They are a wild, fierce people, as their gods are. There are wise Indians and fools, greedy ones and the generous, the cruel and the kind, but even in these traits that ought to make us brothers, there are vast differences. What is wisdom to a white man is foolish to an Indian and vice versa. How can I tell the Indians that white men are civilized when they see them killing each other and anyone else for gold, for something without practical value? And how can I tell the whites that Indians can live in peace with them when an insult the whites don't even recognize as such can mean the bloodiest revenge? In my experience, Indians are the most loyal of friends and the most implacable of enemies."

"Then you see no way for the two races to live in peace?" Reid asked.

"I do see a way," Mr. Atkins said slowly, "but I doubt the majority of our citizens will ever approve it. We must treat them as sovereign, foreign nations, respecting their borders and their traditions as they must respect ours. It would mean settling boundaries and abiding by them for all time no matter what wealth was there enclosed."

He regarded Reid speculatively. "There is a man I think thee ought to meet. He is not an Indian by birth, but he is as close to them as any white man could ever be. Jericho Baines is one of the last of the mountain men. He has a small place some miles from here. I will give thee his direction. Take some whiskey; he still regards it as worthy barter. And I caution thee not to judge him by his appearance; thee will find his heart better kept. Do not fear for thy passage; I will pass the word that thee are going to see Jericho on my advice. I have the influence to gain honorable behavior from the Indians but not from my own kind." Bitterness and regret colored his words.

At his first sight of Jericho Baines, Reid understood why Atkins had warned him against quick judgment. The man was wearing buckskins that were so ancient, they seemed preserved by their layers of grease, sweat, and dirt. And the worn stock of his rifle seemed as well tailored by use.

"Yur name," the man demanded.

Reid gave it and was relieved to see the rifle was no longer pointing at him. Clearly word had already come to the man that Paul Atkins was sending Reid out to see him. Reid wondered if Indians had followed his progress and then gave an inward shrug; if they had, they had let him pass without harm.

Jericho Baines was big and hard muscled, though he was in his seventies. His hair was white, his skin seamed with a network of wrinkles and weathered Indian dark, but his blue eyes were still sharp and farseeing. He had spent nearly all his life hunting and trapping in the West, and he knew the land and the peoples on it intimately.

He studied Reid for a long time before he asked, "Why should I talk to you, boy? You want lies fer them eastern newspapers?"

Reid bore his scrutiny without flinching and did not take exception to being called "boy"—to this old man, he probably seemed no more than that.

"Mr. Baines, I have some good whiskey to offer, so that might be reason enough. But it's not lies I want. Those are coming from every direction and growing by the day. You must know as well as I do that the Indians don't have a chance now. The United States government is not going to allow Custer's death to go unavenged.

And I can't promise that I'll be able to be a voice for the Indians for much longer, but I want to try." Briefly he told the man about what he'd already written, about what he thought of Custer's incursions into the Black Hills and of the treatment of Indians in general.

The blue eyes studied him again, and Reid could almost feel them probing beneath the surface. Then the old man nodded as he reached his conclusion. " 'Jericho,' not 'Mr. Baines,' and you're 'Reid.' " He made the exchange of their names seem like a ceremony.

"I ain't got this old by bein' easy t' fool. I know an honest man when I sees him, white or red. Reckon you come t' me 'cuz I was a squaw man. An' thet's true far as it goes. But I didn't jus' take me an Injun woman t' keep me warm a' nights like some men do. I loved thet woman, an' no man ever had a better wife. I paid fine horses fer Singin' Bird, but she chose me an' I chose her. We made a good life together an' had us two sons."

Reid listened as Jericho's gruff voice softened and flowed into the years he had spent loving Singing Bird. He had admired her kin as much as he had loved her, and he spoke of the way their lives had moved with the seasons, sometimes with her people, following the herds of buffalo or deer or other game animals, going to higher elevations as summer advanced, retreating to lower lands as winter returned. And Singing Bird went with him away from her people when he needed more isolation to hunt and trap for furs to sell.

"I didn't know it, but I was part a' th' trouble comin' t' th' Injuns," the old man admitted. "Th' best of us lived with 'em, lived like 'em, but we was still white, an' we opened th' way fer other whites. Whites kilt Singing Bird by bringin' th' smallpox t' her all them years ago."

"Your sons?" Reid asked, thinking of Larissa and his own children.

"Whites kilt them outright," the soft note was gone, and the old face was set in such harsh lines, Reid caught a glimpse of what a formidable man Jericho must have been in his younger days. "Our sons was part a' both worlds, red an' white, but th' Injuns accepted 'em where th' whites wouldn't. Came t' pass they gave up on th' whites 'cuz th' whites gave up on them. We knew other tribes 'sides th' Sioux, an' my boys married sisters who was of th' Southern Cheyenne. They was Black Kettle's people."

Reid closed his eyes, feeling Jericho's pain as if it were his own. He knew the story. Black Kettle had believed that the only way to survive was to make peace with the white men, and he tried to do so for years. Treaties made with the Southern Cheyenne and the Arapaho had been deteriorating as whites found more and more reasons to want more and more Indian land, particularly for building railroads that would in turn bring settlements.

And then in the spring of 1864, the once Reverend, then Colonel, J. M. Chivington, a power in the Colorado Volunteers, claimed that Indians had stolen cattle from a government contractor's herd.

"Hell, it were an excuse for killin', nothin' more," Jericho swore. "Every time some idiot had a cow stray, the' Injuns was blamed. Colonel Chivington had hisself a grand ol' time attackin' th' Cheyenne who didn't have no idea why. But they got themselves up on their own ponies an' attacked white settlers jus' like they'd been attacked, an' war started all over agin."

By autumn, Colorado's governor had managed to persuade some of the Cheyenne to come to Denver for peace talks. The Indians were lead by Black Kettle and the renowned war chief White Antelope. They talked to the governor and took the advice of the military commandant of Fort Lyon, establishing their village on Sand Creek, thirty miles from the fort.

"Chivington had hundreds a' men with 'im, mostly them volunteers"—Jericho made the word sound like an obscenity—"when they rode down on thet village, an' he tol' his men, 'Kill an' scalp all big an' little Injuns; nits make lice.' An' they done it. I had four little grandbabies, three boys an' a little girl who looked like her grandma. They bashed her brains out, caved in her little skull like a pun'kin. An' th' little boys, they was all stabbed an' bashed an' pulled apart. Their mamas was scalped an' cut up.

"Black Kettle was a good man, an' he couldn't believe what was happenin'. He ran up an American flag an' a white flag, an' he kept callin' to his people thet it was all a mistake. A mistake thet put nine bullets in his wife, though she lived. Black Kettle finally managed to escape, but White Antelope, near as old then as I am now, jus' stood there in front of his lodge an' sang his death song: 'Nothin' lives long, except th' earth an' th' mountains.' "

Jericho's voice rose, singing the words in a minor key, first in English, then in what Reid took to be Cheyenne, and the hackles on Reid's neck rose in response.

Jericho's sons survived that day, only to be killed within the year when they joined other survivors raiding in revenge for Sand Creek. Thus, the war went on, though Black Kettle kept trying to find peace. Then, in the winter of 1868, he and his followers were camped on the Washita River when the troopers attacked with orders to hang all the men and capture all the women and children. "Only they wasn't too fussy," Jericho said, bitterness edging his voice. "So they kilt themselves some women an' children, too, before some Commanche, Kiowa, an' Arapaho come t' help. But it was too late for Black Kettle. Him an' his wife tried t' escape, ridin' double on a horse, but th' troopers shot 'em. Black Kettle still had his flags an' was still tryin' to' keep th' peace.''

For the first time, Jericho broached one of the bottles of whiskey Reid had brought and took a big swallow to wet his dry throat. His eyelids drooped, and a sly smile tilted his mouth. "Th' commander a' them troopers hightailed it out a' there, leavin' nineteen men behind. Them men had thought t' catch themselves some prisoners; instead, they got caught an' kilt, every one of 'em. Thet commander was George A. Custer. I reckon th' devil jus' took a while catchin' up with 'im, an' along the Greasy Grass was as good a place as any.''

He took another long pull on the whiskey and offered the bottle to Reid. "Drink t' Black Kettle an' th' Battle of the Greasy Grass?"

Reid took the bottle and raised it. "To Black Kettle, to the Battle of the Greasy Grass, and to your family."

"Afore you leave th' territory, look 'round you an' let yourself see. This land ain't no use t' most white men. Th' gold'll only go t' a few, an' cattle need kinder country than this. They'll eat what they can an' take thousands a' acres t' do it, an' still they'll die when th' summer's too hot an' dry or th' blizzards come in winter. They ain't like th' buffalo an' deer who know how t' move with th' grass. An' white men ain't like Injuns. Th' Injuns know this is land t' travel on without takin' root fer too long. White men will take this land, but it'll never love their bones like it does th' Injuns'.''

Reid did not have to ask why Jericho had settled here in one spot, because he hadn't settled at all. He had just found a place for his old body to wait for death. His heart and his spirit still roamed the grasslands and the desolate spaces and the mountains with the ghosts of the Indians who had become his family.

Reid spent the night at Jericho's place, sharing a meal, a tasty stew whose main ingredients he thought it better not to question. They shared the whiskey, too, and Reid told Jericho about how he had met Larissa and fallen in love with her instantly; he told him about Wild Swan and the family, about Boston and Rachel going on the Trail of Tears together, and most of all about Alex, about how central she was to the family.

"Now thet's a woman I'd like t' meet," Jericho said, and Reid thought Alex would probably like the old man very much.

"Write th' truth. Bear witness." The words followed Reid as he rode away the next morning. There were alarms everywhere about the danger from Indians who were slipping on and off the reservations, but he felt no physical danger. It was his white man's soul that was in jeopardy. He understood Paul Atkins very well now. He felt small and inadequate inside, as if the air around him were full of spirits as vast and alien as the land. He would never be able to tell that part of the story as it should be told. Not only would it sound mad, it would claim a spirituality for the Indians that was at least equal to, if not, in many cases, superior to, that of white men, and that would be intolerable.

It was time for him to go home. He had been sending dispatches to his papers, using any method that seemed to promise swift delivery, but he had no idea how much had reached the papers or how much they had printed. And he hoped Larissa had not had to face too much trouble without him.

He arrived home to discover that the papers had been so desperate for firsthand information, besides being aware of Reid's popularity with readers plus the lure of a controversial stand, they had been printing what he sent as it was. But the tolerance was wearing thin. The piece entitled "I Met a Man Named Jericho" finished it.

The country was growing increasingly anxious to punish the Indians for killing Custer, and Oscar Bryant, the paper's owner, was having to face the prospect of canceled advertisements and adverse reader reaction to Reid's opinions.

"Some people are beginning to call your view treasonous," he said.

" 'Some' are considerably more than a 'few,' " Reid acknowledged peaceably, "but that doesn't make them right."

He liked Mr. Bryant. Though the man showed paunchy evidence of overindulgence and was hardly prepossessing, with his short stature and balding dome, he had once been an eager reporter for the Baltimore *Sun*, and when he had married a woman who had a small inheritance, his astute investment sense had greatly improved their means. Reid didn't want their parting to be acrimonious, particularly because Mr. Bryant had long given him editorial control of the paper.

"Would you consider softening your stance, at least for a while?"

Reid thought of all he had just seen; he thought of all that Jericho had made him see, and he shook his head. "No, I couldn't. I know it must seem impossible for you to believe, but what I have been writing is already less forceful than I would like, deliberately so that I might change at least a few minds. Not 'some,' but at least a 'few.' Sir, a whole people is being put to death, some by hunger, deprivation, and disease, some swiftly by the gun or sword, because they are different, because they refuse to relinquish the land that is theirs by every right of tradition and use. What the government is doing in our name is wrong by every decent code. To write gently about it is to deny the truth. You hired me in the beginning because you wanted me to write the truth as I saw it. To stop doing that now would be a betrayal of both of us. But I understand your position, and because I do, I offer you my resignation."

He handed Mr. Bryant the letter containing the formal wording, and he did not blame the man for looking relieved; Mr. Bryant did not want bad feelings between them either.

"What will you do now?" Mr. Bryant asked.

Reid answered honestly, "I'm going to start my own newspaper."

His former employer groaned aloud. "I feared that might be the case. Mind you, I think you'll have a difficult time of it for the present, things being as they are, but you're a good writer and a good managing editor, and that'll surely count for more in the end. It's against my own interests, but I wish you luck." He offered his hand, and Reid again thought of Jericho and the inevitability of his own decision.

While Reid understood his commitment, he was worried that the changes in Larissa's life would not be acceptable to her, despite her assurances to the contrary. But as the days passed, he found that acceptance was too pale a word for her reaction: she was exuberant. Even the social slights that came from espousing an unpopular cause did not seem to trouble her.

When they attended a party that included many of the socially prominent citizens of Washington and Georgetown, a woman whom the Tratnors had entertained in their own home cut Larissa dead, muttering about "consorting with savages and condoning murder."

Reid, a short distance away, saw and heard the whole thing, but before he could go to Larissa's defense, she said, "Who is civilized and who is not is often difficult to judge, but not in this case." There was a ripple of laughter, and Larissa had no lack of smiling attention from other guests while her attacker withdrew to a small cadre of supporters.

"How much of that kind of treatment did you receive while I was gone?" Reid asked her once they were home again.

"Not enough to make any difference, just enough to tell me who our real friends are. And we're still being invited out," Larissa replied. "Don't look so grim. Surely you expected it to happen?"

"Yes, I did," Reid conceded reluctantly, "but I didn't really consider what it would mean to you."

"Now that is more insulting than what Mrs. Canby said to-night," Larissa snapped. "You imply that it must mean more to me because my concerns are smaller, less significant than yours. It must matter more to me that I will not be welcome in some social circles because parties are the center of my life." Seeing the shock on Reid's face, she drew a deep steadying breath to control her anger.

"It isn't fair to blame it all on you. I've enjoyed raising our children and entertaining our friends, but it's time for me to be doing something else. The children are well cared for, and I will not neglect them. I confess, I like things to be peaceful and orderly. I always have and more so since the chaos of the war." She smiled at him with the warmth of her love back in her silvery eyes. "You know that better than most. You upset the order of my days from the first time we met, and I wasn't very nice about it, you'll remember. But I married you anyway, or maybe even partly because I knew things would never be too peaceful for too long with you. In turn, I hope you can trust me to make adjustments when they're necessary in our lives and to be able to think of more important issues than how some old cats might behave at a party."

Reid's heart lifted, freed of a burden he had not known he'd carried, the last doubt that his choice was right for Larissa and the children. He kissed her fiercely, lifting her off her feet, and swinging her around in his arms.

"I love you, Lissa mine," he declared, letting her slide down his body until she was on her own feet again. "And to prove how much I respect you, I'm going to work you very hard."

He was as good as his word, and together they tackled the myriad aspects of launching a new paper. They found a journal that was going out of business and willing to sell the building and the presses, which were not of the newest design but were at least in working order, though much of the type was worn and needed replacing. Reid had known that the journal was floundering for a long time, and he was not surprised that the owners accepted his offer.

"This part is frighteningly simple," he observed to Larissa, "clear proof that newspapers disappear easily in the capital."

"Well, ours is not going to disappear," Larissa said serenely.

Some of the people who had worked for the journal were grateful to be kept on to run the presses and to do many of the other mechanical chores, but Reid had a very precise idea of what kind of reporters and writers he wanted on his staff. He had no objection to taking on some young and inexperienced writers, but he needed experienced ones as well, and they were difficult to find and employ.

Both the Tratnors were not only pleased, but also taken aback, when Frank Faber, Gincie's old suitor, came to them to ask if he could join the new enterprise.

"My immediate answer is 'yes,' but it's followed by 'why?'" Reid admitted. "You have a very secure position on the *Sun*, and it's one of the best papers in the country."

"It is," Frank agreed. "But I'd like the chance to be in at the beginning of a good paper. My wife says she has no objection; a new

paper is better than a new woman." He could say that because he
was happily married and not the philandering sort.

It was agreed that Frank would remain in Baltimore to gather
news there and would direct sources in Philadelphia as well. Reid
planned to have staff covering the major cities in the North and the
South as soon as possible, because he believed that only with a wide
appeal would the paper survive.

With each person they added to the staff, with the contracts
they signed for paper and ink in addition to the purchase of the
property, they watched their capital diminishing. They had known it
would be so, but the reality of it was sobering. One of the major
New York papers was still carrying Reid's columns, but it was difficult for him to keep up with his writing with so much business to
conduct. Larissa did what she could to give him time to keep his hand
in and to be paid for his work, and some tradesmen were disconcerted
to find themselves dealing with Mrs. Tratnor instead of her husband.
She kept her temper, tried to be as charming as possible, and made
the best bargains she could.

But it was far more difficult to sell advertising space and sub-
scriptions than to purchase supplies. Curiosity would sell some copies, but advertisers wanted a good return on their investment, and
they didn't want to be associated with a doubtful publication. The
space they managed to sell for the first issues was sold in the main to
businesses with which they were personally connected, many through
the family, such as horse farms, ship chandlers, and clothing stores,
bookshops, and the like which the family patronized.

Even knowing it was impractical to consider not accepting such
accounts, Reid felt some guilt for using the connections, but Larissa
did not share his reluctance.

"It's going to be a splendid newspaper, so it is to their advantage to advertise in it," she insisted. But both she and Reid knew
they were going to have to give very favorable rates, perhaps for a
long time, and might even have to give free space to entice certain
accounts.

When his father-in-law approached him with another plan entirely, Reid was stunned. Quite simply, Blaine suggested that Reid
sell shares in the paper in order to expand its financial base beyond
his own funds, and he proposed that the shares be offered exclu-
sively to the family.

"It would, of course, allow Philly and me an opportunity to give
Larissa and our grandchildren that additional edge of security. But I
would not consider it at all if I did not think the enterprise worthy
and that in time the shares will show a profit. If I did not believe
that, I could as easily set the money aside for Larissa without any

link to the paper. None of us has any idea of how to run a newspaper, nor any wish to do so, save perhaps for Lexy, who is already your competitor."

Reid made himself answer Blaine's smile, and he thanked him graciously for the offer, promising to consider it, but inside he felt a little sick. It was not that he feared the Carringtons' interference in the business; he knew how blessed he was in the good relationship he had with Larissa's family. They had offered him a sense of belonging he had lacked in his own upbringing. But he was discovering that an abundance of faith in his ability to make the paper prosper was in some ways more terrifying than doubt would have been. It was one thing to fail one's self, quite another to fail a league of believers.

And it did not end with the Carringtons. Alex and Rane, and then Gincie and Travis when they returned from the races, approached him with basically the same idea that Blaine had broached. Even Sam and Morgan, who were so involved financially in the shipyard and Brookhaven, offered.

Larissa understood his reservations in this case, but she pointed out the one undeniable fact—with the added capital, they could insure wide distribution from the beginning. "You don't intend that the paper appeal only to the inhabitants of Washington, do you?"

Reid had to admit that he had a wider audience in mind, and it came to him that if the family could believe so devoutly, then he could do no less. He faced the truth that his pride more than anything else had been getting in the way, a determination to do it on his own, when Larissa and the children were already involved in the risks and when the paper had to mean more than personal considerations if it was to be of the quality he envisioned.

He went to Blaine, and the papers were drawn up to make the transaction legal.

Larissa believed that all the decisions they had made, including the selling of shares, were good ones, but she had her doubts when she awakened one night to Reid's restless tossing. And then she identified the choking, whimpering sounds. When she reached out and touched his face, she felt the wetness of his tears. For a moment, she was frozen, not sure whether he was awake or asleep, not sure of what she ought to do. But his weeping tore at her heart, and she called his name softly, putting her arms around him.

When he tensed into sudden stillness, she knew he had been dreaming, and she could sense his disorientation.

"Darling, it's all right, whatever it is, it's all right. You were having a nightmare. You're here with me." She continued to speak to him, kneading his sweat-dampened shoulders, waiting for him to come fully awake. "You've been working so hard on the paper, maybe too hard. It is the shares? Do you regret selling them? Please, talk to me."

Reid heard her voice, felt the tenderness in her touch, and gradually realized that the few sounds filtering into the room were those of carriages and horses going home late, of occasionally raucous city voices, not the vast human silence of the territories with only the wild beasts singing. But the nightmare was no less vivid for waking.

"It isn't all right; it never will be. It was Jericho's story become my own," he murmured. "It was you who died of disease, our children who were beaten and stabbed to death. I saw their faces bashed in, their arms and legs torn off. Ben, Jilly, and Josh, all of them dead. And Black Kettle, I saw him die with his wife, and it was as if I knew them, had known them for a long, long time."

He shuddered violently and was not aware that he was weeping anew. Larissa held him in her arms, her own heart twisting with his grief.

"Jericho bade me to bear witness. It is so little to do in face of this tragedy, but the paper will do it."

They lay together, holding each other against the darkness, and the name of the paper was irrevocably set as the *National Witness*, pledged to "bear witness today that we may fulfill yesterday's promises and tomorrow's dreams."

The words of the masthead would be as fittingly florid as any of the other papers of the day, but Reid and Larissa would always know how personal were the name and the pledge.

Chapter 21

Gincie and Travis were especially glad to be back at Wild Swan, having completed their summer racing dates by attending part of the meeting at Saratoga. They were pleased with the showing their horses had made, particularly Moonraker, who had continued to race brilliantly, not only against other four-year-olds, but also against older horses.

Socially, it had been a trying time at the racecourses. There had been endless questions about the Bettingdons, specifically about

Gweneth and what might be expected of her in her new position. And after Custer's death and Reid's articles, there had been less cordial inquiries. They were not alone, but they were certainly in a minority, allied with those who thought the Indians had grievances that deserved just redress. And because of the scandal that had previously sparked interest in Gincie, there was an added sense of the Culhanes' involvement. "As if," Travis observed, "we might have told the Indians where Custer was goin' to be."

It would have been easier for them had Rane and Alex been with them, because so few dared to challenge the Falconers on any level, but in a way, it had been a good test of the Culhanes' own standing and strength. All in all, they had managed well enough, and coming home to Wild Swan with trophies and prize money was the reward.

The children were full of summer adventures, and their parents listened avidly to the tumble of words, eager to absorb all the growing their offspring had done over the past weeks.

"I'm teaching Tinker to count," Tay claimed.

Kace rolled his eyes and said, "He's teaching him to thump the dirt."

"Why would a horse need to count anyway?" Lexy questioned reasonably.

"Just 'cuz he wants to," Tay insisted with his own logic, and Gincie felt all the tensions of the time away easing, replaced by a honeyed warmth stealing through her veins. In that moment, she loved the children and Travis so much, it brought tears to her eyes.

Her emotions were varying widely lately anyway, and she judged it time to tell Travis her news.

"I wanted to wait until we were home in our own bed," she said as they lay listening to the August night singing outside. She took his hand in hers and placed it over her abdomen. "Not until March, I think, but then we will have another child."

She felt him tense and heard him murmur, "I've wondered. Are you . . ."

"Don't be afraid! I've wanted another child. Lexy and the twins are growing so swiftly! And I'm only thirty-four, not too old yet."

The absurdity of it struck him: she was trying to reassure him when the risk was hers. And he could not doubt the sincerity of her wish for the child. He thought of how intelligent and appealing their three children were, and he thought of another such special being growing inside of Gincie. Please God, one child, not another set of twins to tax Gincie's strength.

"I might not be able to go to the races next year, but after that we'll manage . . ." her voice trailed off as his mouth claimed hers.

He kissed her, and his hand moved over her belly with infinite tenderness.

"Here you are talkin' about next year while I'm still adjustin' to right now," he chided gently. His lips traced the contours of her face and trailed down along the hollow of her throat. When he suckled at her breasts, she felt her whole body responding, not only to Travis, but to the tiny mouth that would draw its sustenance from her in seven months' time. The mixture of erotic and maternal love was so heady, she shivered beneath the onslaught of Travis's loving, voicing her need with little cries.

His mouth traced the contours of her belly, his hands touched her everywhere, fingertips teasing with the lightest of pressure, leaving ripples of warmth along her arms and ribs and the soft skin of her thighs. When his mouth sought the secret petals of her sex, her body arched, and his name was a wail of demand and surrender, but he would not be hurried. Even when he possessed her fully, he controlled every movement, thrusting in the patterns and rhythms he knew her body craved, bringing her to pleasure again and again before he allowed himself release.

As she slipped into sleep, Gincie was aware of his hand once more resting over her womb, his body curved protectively along her back, and she thought that the safe harbor he offered her was equal to the passion. She was too satiated and sleepy to do more than murmur his name, but it was enough; he understood.

They quickly readjusted to the pace of life at Wild Swan, so different from days spent on the racing circuit, and they reinvolved themselves in the lives of the family, too, in a way that was not possible when communication was limited to letters.

Gincie shared the Tratnors' excitement about the new paper, and she heartily agreed with Travis's wish to invest in it. She knew he was still vaguely troubled to have done so well on the mining shares, not just because so many had lost so much in similar investments, but more because he didn't feel he'd worked for the wealth.

"You are surely a farmer at heart," she teased. "If you didn't plant it or breed it, there must be something wrong with it. The fact that you took the risk doesn't seem to count at all. But Sunrise and being able to invest in the paper are results of taking that risk."

He didn't dispute her logic; not only was what she said true, but he was also hampered by the rosy glow that seemed to color everything now he knew he was going to be a father again.

They had thought to keep the news of Gincie's pregnancy secret for a while longer, but that was a hopeless prospect in this family. Alex knew almost as soon as Travis did, and Anthea and the other women would surely have guessed soon if they hadn't been told.

"If I had not seen the changes in Gincie, I would surely have noticed them in you," Alex said to Travis with a fond smile, but then she glimpsed his lingering fear beneath the joy. "You mustn't worry. Gincie is a healthy woman who wants this child. There is no reason to fear that this pregnancy will be anything like the one that produced the twins. Each one is different." She said it with the authority of her own experience, and Travis was comforted because he knew that Alex loved Gincie nearly as much as he did.

The Culhanes' reaction to the livestock losses at Sunrise were as Alex had predicted: they trusted Michael and Lem too thoroughly to suspect any neglect on their part, though for their sake, they tried to take the incident as seriously as the men did. But the men had to admit, albeit grudgingly, that there had been no further trouble, and some other farms in the region which had suffered theft at the same time hadn't reported further losses either.

Though it was going to be a relatively small affair, most of the family's collective attention was centered on plans for Nigel and Sally's wedding.

Normally Travis would have been on his way to California by then, but he was postponing this year's trip in order to be at the wedding. He, no more than any of the rest of the family, wanted to miss the celebration.

Flora and Marsh arrived home from England, and Flora's special gift to Sally was a wedding gown designed by Charles Frederick Worth, the Englishman who had founded the House of Worth in Paris nearly twenty years before and whose creations were worn by the most elegant women, including royalty, in Europe. The gown for Sally was a subtle blend of innocence and sophistication in ivory satin trimmed with the finest lace. The neckline was square cut, and the cuirasse bodice fitted to a vee below the waist where the soft drape of the narrow skirt began. A square court train covered the skirt in the back, and the fine details of the gown showed in every stitch.

It hadn't been difficult to keep the secret from Sally; she was so unaccustomed to the new plenty in her life, she had planned to wear one of the dresses she had already been given. She was overwhelmed by the extravagance of the gift, but Flora made it impossible for her to refuse it.

"It was made especially for you, won't fit anyone else, and Mr. Worth would surely go into a decline if I were to send it back to him," Flora said. Despite her advocacy of financial and political rights for women, she saw no loss of dignity in enjoying the most feminine of fashion when the occasion called for it. As she had once explained to Anthea, "I would like to be able to wear a frock coat and trousers if I cared to, but I wouldn't want to wear them all the time; men's fashions are so dull! And I am too vain to disguise myself as a drab sparrow to further the cause."

Flora was relieved to be home.

With mock seriousness, Marsh told Alex, "I'm not sure she would have been able to avoid arrest for treason, or at the very least, for disturbing the peace, had we stayed much longer."

"Well, truly, it was frustrating to see how little the queen thinks of women," Flora said. "There she is, a woman herself, and one of the most powerful leaders in the world, and she makes not the slightest effort to help her own sex gain equality. Instead, she expects women to be docile keepers of the hearth without a thought in their heads beyond maintaining peace amongst the kitchen staff. She doesn't seem to understand that there are all sorts of women in her country who haven't got any servants or ease of any kind, who must work in factories and shops to survive, and that there are others who want more for their minds than that, even if they do exist in good circumstances.

"But, Mother, you would be so proud of Gwenny! She manages to fulfill all the duties of the stilted life her position demands of her, and yet, she is still the same independent woman she has always been. And she is treating Angelica very cleverly indeed. It would be so easy for Angelica to just slip away now. She misses Hugh desperately, and with Christopher and Gwenny taking over the duties of the title, there could be even more time for her to brood. But not only does Gwenny make sure she is included in everything, she consults with her constantly, claiming a great need for counsel. Angelica would have to be rude to refuse, and she is, as you know, one of the most gracious people on earth, so she finds her days very busy. Her grandchildren are part of the conspiracy, and I expect before long there will be great-grandchildren for her to fuss over. Nicholas and Hugh are both committed, though the marriages will have to wait until the period of mourning is over—another silly convention embraced by the queen. Since the Prince Consort died, Victoria has elevated formal mourning to the status of art. So Nicholas and Hugh must wait, though their father would have been the first to tell them not to delay. At least they are all spared having to spend their days at court."

Though they had been most concerned with family affairs, even so far away, they had not escaped the repercussions of Custer's death.

"With their empire expanding, the British have their own worries about 'native uprisings,'" Marsh said, "and for the most part, they haven't any sympathy for the Indians, for all they're fascinated with tales of the red man. I believe they see it as a matter of expediency, which is the way most citizens of this country view it, too."

Marsh and Flora questioned Reid closely on further developments of the Custer affair and saw no more alleviation of the trouble then he did.

"Sitting Bull has sent word from Canada that he will not harry the whites south of the Black Hills, but will fight incursions in the sacred grounds. How well he could carry out his threats isn't known. The reservation Indians still seem ready to give in. And meanwhile, our Army generals are squabbling over their commands. But the war will grind along in any case."

They were all glad to have Nigel's marriage as a cause for rejoicing after the tensions of the past months.

The engaged couple's tensions were internal. Nigel could see Sally's panic growing as their wedding day approached. After having gone through so much to win her, he was not complacent now, and despite the pressures of his medical practice, he wrenched extra time from his days to spend with her.

One afternoon, he took her to Druid Hill Park, and when they had found a shadowy bench on a high spot with a view of the city, he asked softly, "Are you thinking of leaving me at the altar?"

Her hand jumped in his, and he stroked it, seeking to calm her with his touch. "Gran and Grandfather come here quite often when she's in the city. I know because Gran always notes the flowers that are blooming here. They've been together for so long, and my parents, too, for that matter. It's not just habit, nor is it the desperate fear of being alone that keeps them together; it's because they still love each other."

He raised her hand to his mouth and kissed it. "I promise you, that is how it will be for us, years and years together just because we love each other. There is time for us to learn each other, physically and otherwise. I do not expect you to speak the vows and suddenly lose all your fear. We'll get accustomed to each other first, and when you're ready to be my lover, that will be soon enough."

Sally had known all along that Nigel would not force her, but she needed to hear him say it again so close to their wedding day, and she offered him the truth in return. "I am not afraid of you. I am afraid of myself, of how I will be as your lover. I am afraid that that young girl who was so terrified and hurt is still somewhere inside me. I'm afraid she'll keep me from pleasing you."

"You already please me," he said, and kissed her. He laughed when she blushed. "It doesn't matter if someone sees us. Soon you'll be an old married woman just like Gran and my mother."

The panic that had been growing in Sally for weeks lessened.

Above all people, she trusted Nigel, and he had chosen the perfect images when he compared their situation to his grandparents and parents. She also realized that all the plans being made for the wedding and the honeymoon had been tailored to be the easiest way for her. The guest list could have been immense, given the numbers of people the family knew, but it had been limited to immediate family and very close friends in order to make it possible for her to enjoy the intimacy of the ceremony rather than feeling she was performing for a vast audience. And she and Nigel would spend the first night at Brookhaven, a place now warmly familiar to her, before going on to Annapolis for a quiet week at the Wild Swan Tavern and Inn. The Wild Swan was no longer as closely connected to the family as it had been when Timothy and Mavis Bates had run it, but it was still a symbol of the family's beginning in America, and it was where Morgan and Sam had gone for their honeymoon.

Sally went to Brookhaven several days before the wedding. Though she accepted the fact that Nigel would not be able to join her until the night before the ceremony, she missed him, further proof to herself that she was doing the right thing in marrying him.

Sam and the rest of the women had matters well in hand, but they made sure Sally was kept occupied, and the comings and goings between Brookhaven and Wild Swan hurried the days in their passage.

Seeing the last of her grandchildren married had a special significance for Alex. She was donating the best provisions, late flowers, and the choicest bottles of French wine from Wild Swan, as well as riding over daily to turn her hand to anything that needed doing.

On the day before the wedding, she enlisted Padraic's aid, having him drive the loaded wagon while she rode along beside on one of the young half-bred horses they were training as field horses. Padraic made feeble protests about being consigned to the rumbling wagon, but in truth, he always enjoyed watching Alex's grace and skill in the saddle, and from the wagon, he could observe Alex and the action of the horse.

"He's a foine one," he declared with satisfaction.

"He is," Alex agreed. "He's got a good floating gait. One could ride him all day and not tire, nor will he. And Travis says his jumping capabilities are worthy and should be very fine by the time he's a bit older."

On the way back to Wild Swan, the empty wagon rattled more than it had when loaded, and Alex's mount objected to the sound, trying to shy away from the contraption that caused it.

Alex kept him reined under a firm hand and soothed him with her voice. "No, young one, you've got to get used to such things. No one wants to ride a horse who needs the road all to himself. There, now, that's a good boy."

The horse was quieting down when a rabbit skittered across the road right at his feet. That was too much for him. He gave a snort of fright and jumped into the air. Alex was still in control, keeping her seat, but when the horse landed, he stumbled, going nearly all the way down and tossing his rider over his head.

Even thrown, Alex kept hold of the reins. For a horrified instant, Padraic feared the horse was going to step on her. But the animal had been trained to ground tie, and he stood where he was, looking as if he were faintly puzzled by his own behavior, and then he nuzzled his fallen rider.

Without knowing he had left the wagon, Padraic knelt beside Alex. "Oh, Sweet Jaisus!" he kept repeating, his normal competence wholly gone.

Alex opened one eye and then the other. "Is he all right? He didn't break anything, did he?"

Padraic stared at her, and then he started to laugh and cry at the same time. "Damn th' beast! He's standin' quiet as a stump now. What about you, Alex, what about you?" It was a measure of his distress that he called her by her given name.

Alex took careful stock of herself. She had a bump on her head, and her ribs were bruised from striking an uneven, stony patch in the road, but she was sure nothing was broken, and at her age, that was fortunate. "I seem to be all of a piece," she said. "A little battered, but that's all."

With Padraic's anxious assistance, she got to her feet, brushed herself off, and turned her attention to the horse, checking him closely before she was satisfied that he had come to no harm.

"You're not gettin' back up!" Padraic roared when she asked for assistance in mounting.

"I certainly am," Alex retorted, "with or without your help." Her voice wasn't raised, but this was Alexandria Carrington Falconer at her most authoritative, and not even for her own good could Padraic refuse to do as she asked, though he mumbled under his breath the whole while.

"Poor Irish," she said, looking down at him from the saddle. "I did give you a fright, and I apologize. But truly, there is no cause for a fuss. You know as well as I that no one who rides stays in the saddle all the time. And I'll thank you not to go worrying anyone about this, most particularly Rane."

Padraic was glad she had not required a solemn oath on that because he would have broken it. First he told Della so she might keep a discreet eye on Alex, and then as soon as Rane arrived that evening, he told him, too, with Della a willing member of the betrayal.

"As if he wouldn't notice anyway," Della had sniffed, "knowing her the way he does. But you tell him just to make sure."

When Alex saw Rane's face, she sighed. "Padraic told you and Della, too, I believe, since she's found some excuse or other to check on me at least a hundred times since I returned from Brookhaven. Do you wish me to dance a jig to prove I'm all right?"

But Rane was not to be cajoled, not while his heart was still pounding with terror. He cupped her face in his hands and inspected the bruise and swelling near her temple, most of it covered by her thick hair. And then he kissed her very softly, not daring to put his arms around her because he was so afraid of hurting her.

She could feel the frenzy of his pulse, and she put her hand inside his jacket where his shirt covered his heart. "I swear to you, I'm just a bit bruised. Nothing is broken. I wasn't racing or doing anything extravagant. The horse and I simply lost our balance together."

For Rane, the image of Winter Swan tumbling over with a broken leg and landing on Alex had never faded, though it had happened so many years before. And added to that was the fact that St. John had been crippled by a horse. And this year Hugh Bettingdon had been killed.

After her accident on Winter Swan, Alex had promised Rane she would never race or test a horse at racing speed again, and she had kept her promise. Though he would have liked her never to get on a horse again, he knew he would not ask that of her any more than she would ask him to give up his time aboard ship on the sea he loved and she feared. And suddenly he realized that it would be a far more frightening day than this one if the time ever came when Alex admitted she was too old or frail to ride anymore.

Rane's tense muscles relaxed as he accepted the truth that she really had come to no great hurt. "I hope you won't be too cross with Padraic; he has only your good at heart."

"Cross with him? What possible use would that be?" Alex asked with a rueful grimace. "I expect I would have done the same in his place, but I hope we don't have to tell anyone else. This is Nigel and Sally's time, and I don't want everyone fussing over me as if I were an old woman."

"They wouldn't dare!" Rane said, his eyes beginning to dance with barely suppressed mirth, and this time he kissed her soundly.

If Alex moved less gracefully and Rane was more solicitous than usual that night at supper, Gincie and Travis made no note of it in the general air of excitement that enveloped all in anticipation of the wedding.

"Sally is going to be a gorgeous bride," Gincie said. "And I'm glad for her sake that her family isn't going to be there."

Travis knew she spoke from her own harsh knowledge that blood bonds were often not enough to insure kindness, but he still felt obliged to say, "Perhaps it is the one gift Mrs. Birch can give to her daughter, lettin' her have her weddin' day without the shadows of the past." As I wish you could have your life, he added silently, and then turned his attention to the children, who, having assuaged their hunger, were full of questions.

In spite of having heard all of it already, Lexy wanted to know the details of what would happen at the wedding, while the twins wanted to know if they were going to be subjected to "kissing and other silly stuff."

"Oh, I guess everyone there will probably kiss you and tell you what darlin' boys you are," Travis drawled, rolling his eyes and doing his best to simper. "I reckon you'll just have to be as brave as you can."

The twins surrendered to the general laughter at their father's antics.

By the next morning, Alex's headache had eased, but a deep purple bruise ran across her ribs, and she was stiffer than she'd been the day before. However, she was still thankful to have gotten off so lightly.

Rane winced just looking at the bruise, and he was determined that they would make an early night of it, despite the wedding.

They went to Brookhaven in the late afternoon, he and Alex in a carriage, the Culhanes following by wagon, and other people from Wild Swan and Sunrise coming along in various conveyances. The employees had drawn lots to see which few would remain behind so that the livestock would not be totally deserted.

With Max and Anthea as their attendants, Nigel and Sally were married in the garden at Brookhaven as the sun was going down. The air was scented with the last roses, and in spite of great clouds in the sky, not a drop of rain fell. The half dark, half light provided a magnificent canopy shot through with lavender and gold and silver. And when Nigel said his vows in a clear, sure voice, distant thunder echoed him, causing a ripple of appreciative laughter to run through the guests.

"Nigel seems to have invited some powerful witnesses to his wedding," Rane whispered to Alex, who quickly disguised her laughter with a little cough.

Gincie watched the ceremony and remembered her own wedding at Wild Swan with the war looming over everyone. She remembered how earnestly Travis had tried to protect her by setting her free until the war ended, until they would know who survived. She was very, very thankful that she had been too stubborn to listen to his logic.

"I know Sally's dress is magnificent," Travis murmured, "but I still have a taste for brides in green velvet and marriages consummated in the heart of winter."

Sam and Morgan watched the marriage of their youngest with glad hearts because Sally's voice, as sure as Nigel's, and her expression as she gazed at Nigel left no doubt that she loved their son.

Sally herself, who had thought she would be terrified at being so exposed to all the guests, found instead that it all had a dreamlike quality with the only sharp focus being Nigel. All her doubts had vanished. He was dear, familiar, and he looked happier than she had ever seen him before. That alone was enough to banish the last of her reluctance. There were still traces of guilt because she had not insisted that at least her siblings, if not her mother, be here. But she also understood the harsh fact that if she were to embrace this new life, she had to leave the old one behind, not only for her own sake, but for Nigel's. No one had given her into his keeping; she alone had made the gift.

With the formalities over, the guests waited patiently to congratulate the couple, and then the employees dispersed to their own party in one of the barns, while the rest of the company went into the house to eat, drink, and dance to tunes provided by musicians from Baltimore.

Kace asked if he might go to the barn party instead. "I know it's going to be more fun," he announced, and rather than disputing that, Travis suggested that the twins divide their valuable time between the two gatherings. He hid a smile at Lexy's dilemma; she was torn between her desire to be at her most sophisticated at the more formal celebration, and her common sense, which told her that Kace was probably right that there would be more fun to be had in the barn. The lively notes from a fiddle were already drifting up from there.

Nigel and Sally danced at both parties, and Nigel could scarcely take his eyes off his bride. "You are simply the most beautiful woman I've ever seen, Mrs. Falconer," he told her, and his eyes lit up at the use of her new name.

Courtesy of Reid, the first edition of the *National Witness* had carried, along with national and local news, sporting news and social notes, an announcement of the forthcoming marriage of Sally Birch and Dr. Nigel Falconer, which concluded, "After their honeymoon,

Dr. and Mrs. Falconer will be residing in Baltimore where Dr. Falconer has practiced medicine for five years."

Sally had cut out the announcement. She intended to keep it forever. "It makes it seem wonderfully official," she had told Reid.

And she felt particularly blessed when Alex said, "I am pleased that my grandson has chosen his bride so wisely. And I can assure you from experience, Falconer men love fiercely and faithfully. I hope your years with Nigel will be as many, as full, and as happy as mine have been with his grandfather."

Whether Alex wished it or not, she was the central power in the family, and her approval meant a great deal to everyone in it. Sally expected she would always be somewhat in awe of her, but she could not deny the warmth of the welcome Alex was offering.

Alex chatted with the guests and even, at her insistence, danced a waltz with Rane, claiming, "It would appear very odd if we did not, and in any case, I cannot forgo an opportunity to dance with the most handsome man here."

Rane led her gently through the steps, but he could see she was tiring, and she did not protest when he suggested they go home after the dance. Their excuse was that some of the guests would be spending the night at Wild Swan and they wanted to make sure everything was in order, but Rane told the truth to Nigel and Sally so that the couple wouldn't feel any censure in the early departure.

"I could tell you that we are simply too old for late nights," Rane said, "but the truth is that your grandmother came a cropper yesterday and is still feeling the effects of it."

Nigel instantly became the physician, examining his grandmother with critical eyes, seeing the bruise she had carefully concealed with her hair, but before he could go any further, she forestalled him. "My dear, that is exactly the sort of reaction I wish to avoid. Ever since I hit the ground, I have been saying, with absolute honesty, that I am all right."

Nigel kissed her cheek, conceding, "Gran, you've been practicing good medicine for a lot longer than I have, so I'll have to take your word for it. But pray remember, should you need another opinion, we are well stocked with physicians here tonight."

He watched his grandparents walk away, both so tall and straight, though now that he knew, he could see that Alex was moving a bit gingerly. And then he gave a rueful laugh. "You must fear you have married into a mad family. Where else would you find a seventy-six-year-old grandmother who is still active enough to have fallen off a horse?"

"Nowhere else," Sally agreed happily. "You and your family are utterly unique!"

Clouds still rolled across the sky, obscuring the moon and then setting it free only to hide it again, but still no rain fell as Rane guided the carriage toward Wild Swan.

"They were all there tonight, weren't they, at least for you and for me?" Rane asked, and Alex nodded, her face silvered as the moon broke free again.

"Yes, each one. I thought of my son Nigel and how proud he would be of Gincie and of his grandchildren. And of how much he would have liked his namesake. And I know Seth would have approved his brother's choice of a bride. And Phoebe would be so happy to see what a fine young man Joseph is."

Rane knew that St. John Carrington had been there also, in both of their minds, but that too was fitting.

By the time they were ready for bed, Alex could hardly keep her eyes open.

"I hope we'll hear them when they come in. We really ought to be awake to make sure everyone is comfortable for the night," she said, yawning widely.

"Gincie and Travis will come back with them, not to mention Della, Padraic, and the rest of the staff. No one will lack a place to sleep. But just to put your mind at ease, we'll leave the door cracked; that way anyone who really needs us can give a yell for aid."

Rane had no qualms about the younger generation's ability to manage, but he understood that thinking of her duties at Wild Swan was as natural to Alex as breathing. If she wanted to believe that she would be up and about in a short while to assist their guests, that was fine with him, but he knew she was so exhausted from the festivities coupled with her fall from the horse, she would sleep the clock around. For that matter, he was weary as well. He wasn't quite ready to admit that he felt all his years, but sleep would be as welcome to him as to Alex.

Her conscience satisfied by Rane's assurances, Alex climbed into bed and settled against him with a sigh of contentment when he joined her. "They're all married now. Next it will be the turn of the great-grandchildren," she murmured.

"Not yet, I trust," Rane laughed. "I'm not quite ready to see Lexy pledge her life to some bold eleven-year-old."

Alex fell asleep with a smile still curving her mouth, and Rane followed her, his mind filled with images of how she had looked when he first saw her, when she was thirteen, not much older than Lexy. And then the images turned to dreams of how she had looked on their wedding day, and in the dreams, it seemed perfectly logical to see her as she had been in all the years before their marriage and all the years since, the days turning, dancing to the graceful, erotic music of a waltz.

Later, Alex stirred restlessly, dreaming that the stud barn was burning, dreaming that the nightmare Gincie's mother, Piety, had caused was happening again, the stallion Wild Swan screaming in terror and agony.

She whimpered in her sleep, and instinctively, Rane drew her closer, giving her comfort, neither of them waking. Rane's touch eased the old terror from Alex's mind, and she slipped into the best of the days she had spent with him, so many shining, joyful days shared over so many years.

The hot, muggy night was ruffled by a little breeze, legacy of the storm clouds that would not yet spill their rain.

The fire generated its own motion, smoke stealing up the stairwell, up the side of the house, through the small opening left between the bedroom door and the hall, through the windows open to the night air.

Alex and Rane slept on, dreaming each other's dreams, wrapped in each other's arms.

Chapter 22

Jimmy Bethune had no pangs of conscience about the plan. His goal was not to kill people at Wild Swan; it was to take the horses, as many as he and his four companions could drive off. He had been planning it ever since he and Harv had run off the livestock from Sunrise Farm months earlier. Even then, he had known that far more valuable animals were kept at Wild Swan. But he had also known how fortunate they had been in the first theft because both farms were well staffed. He had bided his time, waiting for the opportunity for bigger game.

The wedding at Brookhaven was the perfect answer. It had not been difficult to glean the information that nearly everyone from Wild Swan and Sunrise would be there. Not only was news of the wedding no secret, for weeks it had been a source of gossip and anticipation for miles around. And the habitual hospitality offered at the farms had made it easy for him and his companions to drift in singly, begging a drink of water or a bite to eat and looking the places over all the while.

Jimmy did not see anything wrong in twisting this hospitality to his own purposes. The Falconers, the Culhanes, and the rest meant nothing to him beyond the fact that they possessed power and wealth that he would like to have. His reluctance to kill any of them came not from any moral reservations, but from the fear of facing return fire. Still, he thought they ought to be grateful that he hadn't more murderous intentions in mind.

"I don' see why we gonna burn th' house down if it's only them horses we want," Harv whined, and Jimmy controlled his temper with an effort. Harv was slow, took some convincing, but would do almost anything if it were explained the right way.

"We're gonna burn down th' house so's anybody left guardin' th' place will come runnin' to put out th' fire. Else they'd be watchin' th' horses."

Harv's mutterings subsided.

Softly lighted by lamps left burning to welcome those who would return late from the wedding, the house at Wild Swan lay open to the predators. Jimmy had considered the problem carefully. The house was brick, which would not burn, but the floors, decorations, and furnishings would surely ignite with a little help from the kerosene he and his men had brought with them.

Though he expected to meet no one inside the house, he cautioned the others to be quiet. "We don' need no one comin' t' see what's goin' on."

It was more difficult to restrain his men once they saw the silver racing trophies. "Leave 'em!" he hissed. "We come fer th' horses, an' they's wuth their weight in gold. You take that stuff, it'll slow you down an' clank like chains. It ain't no use t' us 'cept melted down, an' then what'd we have?"

The men obeyed him as much from fear as from the reasonableness of what he said. They were not afraid of Jimmy, though they knew he could be violent if he were displeased; they were afraid of the house. Being inside it was different, vastly different from talking about it. The quiet elegance, the long history, was settling around them like a shroud, alien and imposing.

Jimmy could feel their courage ebbing. "Jus' pour th' damn kerosene an' get out!"

They sloshed it everywhere, until the smell of it overpowered decades of the sweet oil, linseed oil, and turpentine used on wood, the rich scent of leather, the spicy perfume from bowls of potpourri Alex kept in every room. And when they lighted it from the front of the house, the flames leapt and danced from room to room, rolling oily smoke in their wake. Even if the fire did not manage to level the house, it would certainly create the necessary diversion.

They were away from the house, sheltered by trees, when the dogs began to bark and the few stablemen left at the farm discovered the fire. Jimmy didn't have to hear the men's words to know their confusion; there were far too few of them to fight the fire, and they had to make do with one less so that they could send for help from Brookhaven. One of them rode off, bareback on a skittish horse. No one was left at the stables.

Jimmy had counted on everything except the temperament of the Thoroughbreds. He was used to hacks that more or less did what the rider wanted, more when the rider insisted. But Wild Swan's racehorses were accustomed to being handled carefully by familiar attendants. They reacted badly to having strangers trying to drive them out of comfortable quarters in the middle of the night, particularly with the smell of smoke filling the air.

Jimmy's plan of calmly herding the horses away from the farm quickly degenerated into chaos. Stallions screamed in rage and fear; brood mares kicked out; and the youngsters still out in summer pasture squealed and ran away in the darkness when the gates were opened.

These were not horses as any of the raiders knew them; these were fiery beasts that loomed huge in the night, challenging the mounts the thieves rode. The men began to shy like their horses, their voices rising in hysteria: "Let's get out a' here!" "It's takin' too long." "I want t' get rich, not kilt!"

"Shut up!" Jimmy roared. "We'll take what we can get! Circle that bunch an' drive 'em out!"

Tinker, caught in the maelstrom, whinnied frantically for Blue, and the hound, shaken out of his normal docility, bayed and barked in protest, darting at the mount of one of the men. The horse kicked out, sending Blue flying through the air, and Tinker plunged after him, tangling with another horse, falling to his knees, but getting up, determined to get to his companion. When he broke away from the other animals, Harv tried to drive him back, but even in the flickering light of the moon and the fire, Jimmy could see the horse was not one of the Thoroughbreds. "Leave 'im!" he commanded.

Everything was happening very quickly, but he was conscious of time running out. Reinforcements would surely arrive soon. Suddenly he saw one of the fire fighters running toward the horses, having seen what was going on.

They rode the man down, the horses doing their best not to step on him but unable to avoid it completely because they were being herded so closely.

The raiders and the horses were barely out of sight when the first riders arrived from Brookhaven, but no one had any thought of anything except the burning house. On horseback and in carriages they streamed into Wild Swan, the adults of the family, workers, and male guests, as well as some of the women who were determined to help. Sally and Flora, though they wanted to go to Wild Swan, remained at Brookhaven to watch over the children.

With the fire raging and so many people dressed in evening finery, the scene was like a macabre etching of an affluent corner of hell.

The family knew that Alex and Rane had returned to Wild Swan hours before. One by one they had noticed their absence and had inquired, and since his grandparents had effectively made their escape from the party, Nigel had felt no guilt in telling his other relatives the true reason for the elder Falconers' departure, while insisting that he was confident that Alex's self-diagnosis was accurate. Thus reassured, they had all shared his rueful amusement at Alex's indomitable will to lead life as she wished.

And even riding to Wild Swan with their hearts pounding in terror, they had not faced the fact that Alex and Rane might be dead. It was so unthinkable; they expected to see them outside, fighting the fire.

Gincie searched frantically, grabbing one of the weary men who had been fighting the fire since the beginning. "Where are they? Where are my grandparents?" she screamed.

He looked at her uncomprehendingly. "Dey at de weddin' wid you."

"No! No, they're not! They came home hours ago! Didn't you see the carriage?"

"Doan know, we doan know," the man moaned.

"Gran!" Gincie wailed the word in a long cry of despair and lurched toward the fire. The heat slammed into her like a living creature, searing her skin, her eyes, and her lungs. She could feel it trying to burn away all the moisture in her body in the instant, could hear it howling at her to come closer, to come in where her grandparents were.

As she took another faltering step forward, Travis grabbed her and pulled her back, shaking her hard. "Stay clear!" he shouted at her. "If not for yourself, think of the child you carry, the children we already have! No one can get inside the house yet, no one! Do you understand me?" He gave her another shake, terrified by her blank stare. She blinked, and he was relieved to see sanity reflected in her eyes with the fire. "Oh, my love, we'll do the best we can. We cannot lose you, too." He hugged her and then let her go.

"I'll stay safely away," she mumbled, knowing he needed to help the other men.

She understood that throwing herself on the flames would accomplish nothing, but she had no intention of standing idly by. She found a position in the bucket brigade that was out of Travis's line of vision, and she willed herself to think of nothing except handing the heavy pails of water along. She tried not to look at her relatives' faces. Blaine, Philly, Morgan, Sam, Larissa, Reid, Anthea, Max, Nigel, Adam, Mercy—every face looked alike in the grim horror they shared. Most of all she tried not to think of Travis's words, "We cannot lose you, too," but they sounded in her head over and over, a death knell for her grandparents. She knew they were dead. It was not just the rational knowledge that they would have tried to get out if they were still alive, it was something more, a horrible stillness in the center of her, as if their hearts had beaten there once along with her own and were now silent.

The house, built of such durable brick, was burning erratically as if reluctant to surrender. Flames jetted one way and then retreated, only to attack again; smoke rolled from upstairs windows, and part of the roof began to sag, but the flames had not engulfed the upper levels when the sky opened and hard rain pelted down.

The people fighting the fire were so mesmerized by their tasks, it took them a moment to realize what was happening. There was no cheer of jubilation. Shoulders slumping, they just stood there as the rain drenched their soot-stained, water-splashed silks and satins. And then they started passing the buckets once more, able to get further into the house as the atmosphere around it was saturated and cooled down by the rain.

It was Michael McCoy who first caught sight of a few of the racehorses wandering amongst the saddled horses and carriages that had carried everyone from Brookhaven.

Michael peered through the confusion of rain, horses, and vehicles, and bellowed, "What th' hell!" but there was nothing anyone could do until men could be spared from the fire line to find out what had happened.

It was murky dawn with the rain tapering off before they knew the full extent of the devastation—the badly injured stablehand, the scattered horses and the missing, including Lady Lex, Moonraker, and horses in training, ten prize animals in all. In the pasture, a yearling was down and had to be shot because both forelegs had been broken by the fall he had taken in the dark panic of the night. Tinker, bruised and patient, stood over Blue, who had not moved since being kicked.

And over it all stood the ruined heart of Wild Swan. No one

doubted that Alex and Rane were inside the house. Travis had never felt more dread than now when he, Morgan, and Nigel, quickly chosen by lots, went inside, the other men remaining outside to share the tension with the women. Despite his game leg, no one questioned Travis's right to go to the second-story rooms. And Gincie knew she could have insisted on going with him, but she did not; whatever the men would find, Alex and Rane as she had loved them were no longer there.

The house was rank with the smell of burned cloth and wood soaked with water. They had to tread carefully because some of the floorboards had burned through, and others creaked ominously. And so much of the staircase had burned away, they had to be as cautious as if they were scaling a cliff face, testing each foothold.

Above the first floor, the damage was much more uneven than below, some rooms scorched and burned, others nearly untouched, though smoke had tainted every space.

Flames had not touched Alex and Rane's room, and for an instant, the men shared the thought that by some miracle, the couple were only sleeping.

It was Nigel who broke the spell. "The smoke killed them. They never awakened." His voice broke: "And they never will again."

"Mother. Father." Morgan's whispered words were loud in the quiet.

It was harder now to face the others outside than to face death in the house.

Travis's eyes sought Gincie's and saw that hope had already fled from hers. He opened his arms, and she came into them. "They're gone, darlin'. I know it doesn't make them live again, but they didn't suffer. They aren't burned. The smoke suffocated them."

He felt her shudder against him, and his throat closed as the tears came. "God, oh, God, I'm sorry."

"Why?"

Though Travis thought it was a wider question, he answered, his voice still choked, "Because they wanted the horses, and they fired the house as a diversion. It is the only thing that makes sense."

"No, it isn't," Gincie said so softly that Travis did not hear, his attention taken by the rising sound of mourning around them.

Della and Padraic were weeping with their arms around each other, an incongruous pair bound together by the depth of their loss. They had worked for Alex for decades, but beyond that, they were tied to her and to Wild Swan by shared tragedy and triumph, by respect, by love.

But none of them could afford the luxury of remaining immobilized by their grief. The injured colt had already been destroyed. Alastair Cameron and Anthea were tending the man who had been trampled, while Nigel and Max treated the fire fighters for various burns and bruises. Reid left to take the news to Brookhaven, and the Culhanes knew they had to go there soon, too, to be with the children. But first they had to oversee the rounding up of the remaining horses that were loose and check them for injuries.

Michael McCoy approached them tentatively. "Tinker's sound enough, just a little stiff an' scuffed; 'spect he took a fall last night. But Blue's hurt bad. You want me t' put him out of his misery?" His face reflected his dread of what effect this would have on the Culhane children.

"No!" Gincie said. "He's got to be all right! I won't let the children lose him, too!"

It was something to do, something to focus on. She went to the hound and checked him over carefully while Tinker, held by McCoy, snuffled and whickered his distress.

Alastair knelt beside Gincie. "Your man will recover, though it will take some time. He's got a broken leg, but it's a clean break, and he's got multiple cuts and bruises. And how is this fellow?" he asked, as if Blue were another human patient.

"Not very well, I'm afraid. He's got some broken ribs and, worse, a head wound. He must have been kicked very hard."

Her hand stroked the rough coat gently. She glanced at Alastair and then away. Like Della and Padraic, he had known the Falconers forever, and his loss was as profound as anyone's in the family. He had always seemed invincible to Gincie, but now he seemed very old and frail. His gnarled hands were steady though, as he reached out and touched the dog.

"His heartbeat is strong. And his friend surely cares for his recovery. I'd say it's worth a try."

They both knew it was more important than saving the children's companion; they simply could not bear any more death.

"I'll take charge of him," Alastair offered, and Gincie nodded, beyond words.

Facing the children was a terrifying ordeal. They had been told about the fire and about the deaths of their great-grandparents, but none of it was real to them yet.

At first the twins asked practical questions.

"Bricks don't burn," Kace said, "so how could the house be gone?"

"Much of the house is still standin'," Travis answered patiently, "but the fire burned wood and furniture, things that aren't made of brick, and the smoke ruined a lot, too."

"Is all our stuff burned up?" Tay asked.

"No," Travis said. "The fire didn't burn so much upstairs." He forced himself not to think about Alex and Rane. "But your things will have to be aired out for a while to get rid of the smoky smell."

Gincie saw Lexy's question before she asked, "Are Gran and Grandpa really dead?"

Lexy's eyes were enormous, and Gincie would have given anything to be able to tell her daughter that it was all a mistake, that no one had died. Instead, she had to confirm the nightmare, and her words sounded hollow to her own ears when she added, "They did not suffer. They breathed the smoke and died while they slept."

Suddenly Lexy's face was contorted with sorrow and hate. "I hope they catch the men that did it, and I hope they kill them!"

And then Tay asked about Tinker. The children had already been told that some of the horses had been stolen, but no one had said anything about Tinker and Blue.

Gincie found she couldn't open her mouth, couldn't tell the rest of it, but Travis filled the breach.

"Tinker is a little stiff, probably from a fall, but you'll be able to ride him again in a few days. But Blue was badly hurt. Tinker was keepin' watch over him when we found him, and now Dr. Cameron is doin' his best to take care of him."

For Tay, believing that he would not see Alex and Rane again was, for the moment, impossible, but the fact that Blue had been hurt was very real. Tears poured down his cheeks as he threw himself into his father's arms, and that set off the other two children. Their parents weren't any better off than their children, and the rain beginning again outside made it seem as if the earth were weeping with them.

Travis tried to watch over Gincie without crowding her too much, but it was difficult. He knew it was dangerous for her to have gone through so much in her pregnant state, but it was futile to demand that she take to her bed and leave all the tasks that needed to be done to the rest of the family. The best he could do was to turn his hand to whatever needed doing, and he was grateful that the others were obviously doing everything they could to share the burden.

The Culhanes were going to stay at Brookhaven until after the funeral, but then they would move into the house at Sunrise, and Travis had the men begin airing and moving clothing and various possessions from Wild Swan to Sunrise, after the damaged staircase had been shored up and made stable enough for safe passage.

Reid was particularly helpful in handling the inquiries about the tragedy from various newspapers, and Flora sent word to the family in California and England.

Travis spent long hours talking to authorities and composing advertisements for newspapers and fliers which would be widely distributed with descriptions of the stolen animals. But he wondered what success they would have. The rain had washed away the tracks, giving the raiders the advantage, and it was difficult to know where to look for them, though the best guesses were that they had headed either south or west past Washington City because the North seemed dangerously populated. If the thieves stayed together with the ten missing horses, they would certainly be conspicuous, but Travis suspected they would soon realize that that was a precarious plan. He tried not to think what kind of treatment the horses might be receiving. The animals were the result not only of years of careful breeding and training, but also of affection lavished on them from every quarter. He doubted their new masters would offer the same care.

As he was trying to ease Gincie's burden, so Travis saw the people at Wild Swan trying to do the same for Della and Padraic. Even Cassie and Polly, sisters who, with their husbands and children, had long histories at Wild Swan, deferred to the grief of the two who had been so intimately connected with Alex. But like Gincie, Della and Padraic needed to keep busy.

For Lexy, Kace, and Tay, the fire became a reality when they visited Wild Swan to see Blue and Tinker. Gincie and Travis knew how hard it was going to be for them to view the devastation, but they had to see it sooner or later, and it was important for them to be reassured that Tinker was all right and that Blue was at least holding his own, cared for now by Padraic.

The children's reaction to the ruin of the house was wide-eyed silence, but they released their feelings with Tinker, hugging, patting, and crooning to him, and with Blue. They were careful not to touch the hound, but when they spoke to him, Blue's tail wagged feebly, the first response he'd shown since he was hurt.

"See, he knows we're here!" Tay exclaimed. "So now he can get better for sure."

Gincie swallowed convulsively to prevent tears from overwhelming her again, though she had thought she had already cried more of them than any body could hold.

For Nigel and Sally, it was as if the happy hours of their wedding celebration had never happened. Of special concern to Sally, and to Nigel as well, was Joseph's reaction to the fire. As his mother had died, so had his great-grandparents, threatening all the hard-earned gains in his feeling of security. He hadn't wept or talked about the tragedy at Wild Swan since he'd learned of it; he'd retreated to watch warily from the silent, distant place he'd occupied after the murder of his parents.

Anthea and Max were grateful for Sally's willingness to spend so much time with Joseph, because it added a certain normalcy to his days, shaping them in the usual pattern.

Joseph's nights were not silent; they were filled with nightmares. Anthea and Max hardly slept, listening for his cries, and they took turns going to him to wake him up gently and to reassure him that he was only dreaming.

But finally Joseph twisted in Max's arms and sobbed, "I'm not going to love anyone ever again! Not ever!"

Max held the nine-year-old, not letting him get away, wondering how on earth to make things seem right when they were so obviously wrong. He rocked Joseph in his arms, as much for his own comfort as for the boy's.

"You're right. Loving people is always a risk. Because part of loving them is knowing you're going to lose them someday, or they are going to lose you. But it is so much worse if you don't love; you're not even alive, not really alive. The people who burned Wild Swan, I doubt they ever loved anyone."

He could feel Joseph listening, but he couldn't judge how much he was understanding or accepting. A terrible rage rose up in Max as he thought of the damage the killers had done to Joseph after all these careful years of healing he, Anthea, and the rest of the family had tried to give him. And then the rage died in the wave of love he felt for the child.

"I love you very much," he said. "And nothing could ever change that. I will always be sorry for the tragedy that sent you to us, but I will always be grateful to your parents for choosing us to care for you when they no longer could."

Joseph said nothing, but rather than try to pull away again, he cuddled closer and fell asleep in Max's arms. Anthea found them together like that, and she settled down beside them, putting her arms around both of them. For all her strength, Max knew she felt nearly as lost as Joseph.

Alex and Rane were buried at Wild Swan three days after the fire, and until the morning of the funeral, the family had no idea of how many people shared their grief.

They came in legions on horseback, in carriages and wagons, and on foot. There were people from the shipping industry, from the lowliest workmen to the men who owned their own shipping concerns—men and their families who honored Rane Falconer for the swift ships he and Caleb Jennings had built with such care.

There were statesmen and politicians from Maryland's statehouse and from the Congress of the United States. Ex-governor Oden Bowie was there. There were Quakers and others who had known of Wild Swan's involvement in the Underground Railroad. There were blacks and whites who had, in one way or another, by Alex or some other member of the family, been helped by being given jobs or education or medical aid. And there were people from every corner of the horse racing world, from owners to trainers to stable hands and jockeys. Alexandria Carrington Falconer had known as much about Thoroughbred racehorses as anyone in the country, and the horsemen came to mourn her as one of their own. Even President Grant was represented in the person of his special emissary from the Department of the Navy, officially in recognition of the work for the Union Navy that Rane Falconer had done before and during the war, but also, everyone knew, because the president had a good eye and a liking for fine horseflesh. Political differences with Reid and the rest of the family over Indian policy were forgotten for the day.

The sea of mourners was dressed in everything from the finest silk, muslin, and broadcloth to rougher and often patched clothing, but they stood elbow to elbow, and some who had not spoken to one another since the war had so divided them, spoke civilly to each other this day.

Alastair, who had read the words for the dead of Wild Swan before, did not flinch from the duty because of the crowd. In the sorrow of the occasion, he found consolation in seeing such a mixture of class and race, a vision of people cooperating as Alex and Rane had always believed they should and could. And beyond the press of the day was his own wish to honor the two people who had been his family for so long, and, when he was honest with himself, most of all to honor Alex, whom he had loved in his own way and quite steadfastly nearly from the day he had gone to meet the woman who had such a reputation for healing.

"You healed me well, Alex," he thought to himself. "You gave me a family, generations to cherish. And you, Rane, you loved her so well for so many years, and you understood how so many men who met her fell just a little and sometimes more in love with her. Oh, my friends, I will miss your good company for all the rest of my days."

He knew it was an inconsequential thing compared to all the rest, but still, he hoped that somehow Alex knew that he and Padraic had tapped the hives and turned them, telling the bees of the deaths, as the creatures must, by the lore Alex had learned from her grandmother, always be told important family news, so that they might feel a part of it all and not desert their hives. It did not seem outlandish to him to believe that even the smallest creatures at Wild Swan were mourning the loss of Alex.

His voice was strong and clear with the soft burr of his Scottish heritage giving an added majesty to the words:

> To every thing there is a season, and a time to every purpose under heaven.
> A time to be born, and a time to die; a time to plant, and a time to pluck up that which is planted;
> A time to kill, and a time to heal; a time to break down, and a time to build up;
> A time to weep, and a time to laugh; a time to mourn, and a time to dance . . .

The sonorous words from Ecclesiastes rolled over the crowd.

He spoke briefly of the couple's embrace of their adopted country, of how they believed so deeply in the principles of equality, liberty, and justice, so deeply that they had lived by those principles, giving far more than lip service to them. "And kindness," he added, "kindness extended to all of us, day by day. They lived with rare grace and humanity."

When he began the Twenty-third Psalm, "The Lord is my shepherd; I shall not want," a great swell of voices joined him, rumbling through the still, warm air.

"They will not be alone," Morgan whispered to Sam, holding her hand tightly and thinking of their son Seth; of St. John; of Virgil Winslow, the scholarly uncle who had raised Philly; of Horace Whittleby, for years the tutor for the children of Wild Swan; of Katy, Padraic's wife; of Samson; of Mavis and Timothy Bates; of Phoebe; of Aubrey; and of others, all buried here.

"I'm not sure I believe in heaven," Gincie heard Tay murmur to Kace, "but I hope Gran gets to see all her horses again, the ones that died, I mean."

Gincie felt a prickle of tears, but she was distanced from the proceedings around her, concentrated inwardly instead. She'd had a vague crampy feeling ever since the night of the fire, when she'd lifted and passed the heavy buckets of water for so many hours, but she had denied to herself that anything was amiss. Now the denial was growing more difficult by the moment as the cramps intensified.

Travis looked at her inquiringly, and only then did she realize that she had been tightening her hold on his arm in rhythm to the pain, in rhythm to the contractions. The word came into her mind unbidden and would not go away. She made an effort to ease her grip on Travis and was glad she was wearing a veil that kept her face obscured. But Travis was not so easily put off.

"Are you all right?" he asked urgently, although he acknowledged to himself that it was a ridiculous question on this day.

Even as she murmured, "I'm fine," her eyes sought Anthea, and she was reassured to see her cousin close by. She concentrated all her energy on getting through the rest of the service without disgracing herself or causing a panic.

When Alastair's voice had died away and the service was finished, the day was still not over. People had brought an endless array of food from cold meats and fowl to cheeses, fruit, breads, and cakes, and at Brookhaven, any object that could serve as a table or bench was pressed into service as many of the mourners stayed to share a meal and their memories of the Falconers, and to extend their sympathies to each member of the family.

It didn't take Gincie very long at Brookhaven to know she was not going to last through all the civilities. She felt a small trickle of warmth between her legs. She slipped away from Travis while he was talking to some of the guests, and she found Anthea.

"I need your help. I'm losing the baby," she said bluntly. "Please don't tell anyone else yet."

Anthea reacted calmly, steering Gincie through the crowd into the house swiftly and with a minimum of fuss. She hoped Gincie was wrong, but as soon as she saw the ever-increasing amount of blood, she knew there was no doubt about the miscarriage. The terrible irony of it struck her; she so often saw women who were desperate to end their pregnancies, but here was Gincie, who desperately wanted to continue hers, and Nature did not cooperate in either case.

By the time Travis found them a short time later, Anthea had Gincie tucked into bed and had given her a draught to help her relax and sleep.

Travis had noticed Gincie's absence. Finding her like this with Anthea in attendance sparked instant terror in him. Anthea took one look at his pale face and explained, "I'm sorry, she's losing the child, but she'll be all right with a few days' rest. She isn't bleeding violently."

Her heart aching for both of them, Anthea left them alone.

Gincie opened her eyes and focused on Travis. "I didn't mean to harm the baby," she said, tears filling her eyes.

He bent down and kissed her gently. "Hush now, darlin'. I know you didn't mean to, I know." The sorrow of the day and this was lodged in a solid lump of pain in his chest, but her next words caused a chill to chase down his spine.

"It had to be them, one of them. It will never end. I thought it would end with Mark, but it didn't." The medicine Anthea had given her was making it hard for Gincie to focus on what she was saying, and the words were slurred, but Travis understood.

"Them? Gincie, you can't mean your mother or Matthew; you haven't seen either one of them for years! They can't have had anything to do with the fire!"

Her eyes closed again, but her voice drifted up to him. "They can. Like my mother burning down the stallion barn, killing Wild Swan, all those years ago. This time all of Wild Swan died."

Travis took one of her hands and pressed it hard between his own, trying to anchor her to reality. "The most plausible explanation is that horse thieves were responsible for all of it, just thieves, men who knew how valuable the race horses are without knowin' how hard it's goin' to be to get their full price without papers. The fact that everyone was goin' to be at Brookhaven for the weddin' was no secret. I don't think the thieves even meant to kill anyone. But if you're lookin' to take the blame, I think you'll have to wait in line. If it were some personal vendetta, the whole family has espoused unpopular causes for years. Hell, I'm a Southerner who didn't believe in slavery but fought for the Confederacy; that's surely enough to make more than a few people angry. For God's sake, even Michael McCoy and Lem Washington are takin' the blame because they're sure it was the same men who raided Sunrise months ago, and they believe that if they'd stopped them then, this wouldn't have happened."

Gincie had retreated into sleep, but Travis doubted his arguments would have made an impression even if she were perfectly alert. They had lost a child, and it ought to be the only thing they were thinking of, but instead, Gincie was trapped again in her old nightmare of her "bad blood" harming those she loved. The idea that her mother or her half brother might have engineered the raid on Wild Swan seemed mad until he reminded himself that Mark's threats had been very real.

As he watched over Gincie, he determined that he would track her relatives down, one way or the other, to determine for all time whether or not they posed any threat. He wasn't sure what he would do if it proved to be Piety who was guilty, but if it were Matthew who was carrying on Mark's vengeance, Travis had every intention of killing him himself.

Chapter 23

It was Sam who sent Nigel and Sally on their way to Annapolis. "There are few enough days of your honeymoon left," she allowed, "but the two of you have suffered enough in this time that should have been the happy beginning of your marriage. There is nothing you can do for Gincie or for any of us that is more important than your spending time alone with each other."

She shook her head sadly as she looked at Sally. "My dear, I am so sorry that the family's tragedies should fall on your shoulders so soon."

"Oh, please, you mustn't feel that way!" Sally protested. "I meant my marriage vows. What happens to Nigel happens to me, for good or for ill."

Sam noted with satisfaction that much of Sally's former shyness was absent now when she looked at Nigel.

In fact, Sally was well aware of the changes in herself. The past few days had been trial by fire, not only physically, but also in her mind and heart. And she had been tempered by the experience. Nigel had needed her for company and comfort while he was recovering from the knife attack, but she recognized a far greater need in him now. His grandparents and Wild Swan had meant an enormous amount to him, particularly Alex, who had been the one to inspire his love of healing, giving him an early focus to his life. To have it all swept away so brutally had left a deep wound that Nigel, in his customary fashion, was doing his best to ignore by turning his attention to everyone else's needs except his own. She knew better than most how selfish men could be, and it struck her as wryly amusing that one of her tasks was surely to teach Nigel to give more weight to his own wants.

They had slept together at Brookhaven after their wedding, but sleep was all it had been, sleep grasped in short stretches as refuge from the turmoil caused by the fire, both of them too exhausted to feel any sexual tension. Already Sally had learned that she felt more secure with Nigel sleeping beside her than when she slept alone. But most remarkable, she no longer feared consummating the marriage.

She doubted she would be a very adequate lover, not at first, but she finally recognized that the gift of herself, of her body, was the one thing she could give Nigel. It was as if it were her dowry, the only one she had and slightly tarnished at that, but still hers to give.

When they first settled in at the Wild Swan in Annapolis, Nigel was not so convinced his mother's idea had been a good one. So much about the place reminded him of his grandmother because this was the first business venture she and St. John had had in the United States. He told Sally the story of how angry the aristocratic St. John had been at the idea of being a publican and how in apology for his temper, he had presented Alex with the carved sign that still hung over the entrance to the tavern and inn.

In telling the old story, he felt the tightness in his chest begin to loosen. "Gran is here," he said, "and Grandfather, too, though he wasn't married to Gran then. I won't ever stop missing them, but I'm beginning to realize that everything they taught us and gave us continues, though they are gone."

They had had supper and had walked about the town which, despite being the state capital, the county seat of Anne Arundel County, and the site of the Naval Academy, had the elegant, slightly faded air of a place that had had its flowering in the last century and had decided to stay there in time. Annapolis was still very English in atmosphere with its Georgian houses and with street names such as Duke of Gloucester and King George. No wonder Alex and St. John had found it a good place to begin their lives in America, and Rane had formed ties here also, with Caleb Jennings's family, though the shipyard had by then been moved to Baltimore.

Night was stealing over the town, making the room Nigel and Sally shared cozy with the flickering light of lamps. Nigel let the peace slip into his bones. But Sally felt far from peaceful. She knew that the first move was up to her; Nigel was prepared to be patient forever.

She cleared her throat nervously and then blurted out, "I don't know how to do this gracefully, how to seduce you, but I want to be your wife physically as well as every other way."

She looked so vulnerable, standing there in her nightgown with soft color flushing her cheeks. Nigel knew how much courage this took. For a moment, he was frozen in place, disoriented by her sudden boldness. And though he thought he had subdued all passion for her, he found it surging back with such force, he feared his response would terrify her anew.

"Do you not want me anymore?" she asked softly, mistaking his hesitation.

"More than you can possibly know," he answered, taking her in his arms, though he knew she would feel the swelling proof of his desire. He needed to hold her and to reassure her. But still, he offered her a way out. "You know you don't have to do this, don't you?"

Sally's laughter was low and husky, and she squirmed impatiently in his arms. "I do know! But I never thought you would steal my role of shy bride." She had meant this to be her gift to him, but she was feeling a singing in her own blood, an unfamiliar warmth that made her want to curl into his bone and sinew and become part of him.

Mischief began to dance in his green eyes. "Shy bride, indeed!" He nuzzled her throat and licked lightly at first one earlobe and then the other. His hands tangled in the blond silk of her hair, and he cradled her head as his mouth took hers, softly at first, then more forcefully.

"Open to me, sweetheart," he murmured, and she obliged, shivering at the delicious invasion of his tongue as it flickered in her mouth. A heavy, waiting pressure began to build deep and low in her belly, and she felt the swell of warmth between her legs. Her knees gave way, and Nigel swept her up and placed her on the bed.

The awkwardness that Sally had dreaded never intruded, because Nigel was too skillful to allow it. When he stripped her of her nightgown, he made a slow erotic ritual of it, his hands and mouth stroking her pale skin as he uncovered it, his low words of appreciation vibrating against her.

"You are so lovely, more than I knew, more than I knew." Nigel was drowning in the sweetness of her, but he was determined not to lose sight of her pleasure. It was even more delicate than making love to a virgin, for Sally had experience enough to hate everything about sex, or at least sex as she knew it. His heart pounded harder at his joy in the trust she was showing. "Tell me if you don't like something I'm doing. Tell me if there's something you want me to do," he murmured.

Beyond words, Sally let her body tell him that everything he was doing was delighting her. Her uncle had made her feel dirty and violated with as little as a look, but for Nigel, she lay open and unashamed, so captivated by his touch that she did not even tense when his fingers stroked the center of her passion and slipped inside her body. And her last coherent thought was of wonder, not fear, as her body shimmered with the waves of sensation Nigel created.

He covered her body with his and entered her, finding the way open and slick in welcome, the hot flesh fitting around him and pulsing with the pleasure he had given her, the pleasure he kept giving her until he could bear no more and surrendered to his own need.

When he started to move off her, Sally held him close. "Not yet," she pled, loving the weight of him, loving everything about him. She thought of the seed he had spilled inside her, and she hoped they would conceive a child this night, a child that would be created from mutual love, so different from the vile predation of her uncle.

She ran her hands through his hair and traced the clean contours of his face. "I should have known, but I didn't," she murmured.

"Should have known what?" he roused himself to ask.

"That you would be as good at this as you are at everything else. You are so skilled, kind, and thoughtful in your practice of medicine, in your life; I should have known you would be no less in lovemaking."

Her face looked so dreamy and satisfied, Nigel smiled. "I'm flattered, my darling, but the credit must be shared. Where so much love exists on both sides, making love is easy, not to mention immensely enjoyable." He raised himself off her enough to nip playfully at the slender cords of her throat, and to his surprise, he felt himself growing hard inside her.

"Can we do it again?" Sally asked, arching her hips up against him, her expression an intriguing blend of the wide-eyed innocent and the happy wanton.

"Indeed we can," he said, but when he would have concentrated once more on arousing her, she protested, "Please, I can't think when you do that! This time I want to give to you. Teach me what to do to pleasure you as you pleasure me."

It was a new experience for Nigel to have a woman who loved him lavishing such care on his body, and her willingness more than compensated for lack of expertise. Because it was Sally touching him with her hands and mouth, with the silk of her hair and skin, his body responded as if every inch were erotically sensitive. His small male nipples became hard pebbles when she licked them, his skin shivered and moved with the ripple of the muscles beneath when she ran her hands over him. She explored his rib cage, his flat belly, the muscled strength of his hair-roughened legs, and even his feet, high-arched, long and lean like his hands. She teased the vulnerable spaces behind his knees and discovered that they were as sensitive as the like spaces on her own body. She dug her hands underneath him and massaged the taut tuck of his buttocks. She felt female power as she never had before as she reduced him to a groaning, shuddering state of bliss.

Finally when she circled his hard shaft with her fingers, Nigel gasped, "Enough!" and joined his body to hers again.

It would be a very long time before the pain of his grandparents' deaths would truly fade, but for now, she had given him the surcease of mutual passion. And he had returned to her the sovereignty of her own body, stolen those years ago by her uncle.

They returned to Brookhaven before settling back in Baltimore, and no one had to ask about their brief honeymoon; they shone with the joy they had found in each other.

Travis did not begrudge them their happiness, but he wished desperately that his own life with Gincie were so simple. Physically, she had recovered quickly from the miscarriage, and outwardly she maintained a facade of calm control. But he knew her too well to be fooled. She was wound as tightly as a spring; she was as terrified as she had been when Mark was stalking her. She was trying not to be obvious about it, but she was watching the children so closely they could not help but notice it.

"What do you think will happen to us if we go into the woods?" Lexy asked. "We've always played there, here at Brookhaven and at Wild Swan, too."

Gincie saw her own fear beginning to be reflected in her daughter's eyes, and she tried to control it. "You're right, of course; just keep track of each other."

But Lexy, once alerted, was not to be put off. "It's the people who burned down Wild Swan and killed Gran and Grandpa, isn't it? You're afraid they're still out there."

Gincie was afraid of exactly that, but to hear Lexy say it made it sound crazy. "No," she lied, "I'm sure they're not out there. Your father is certain they have gone as far away as they can in order to sell the horses, and I am sure he must be right."

She put all the conviction she could muster into her voice and met Lexy's eyes squarely. She didn't know whether Lexy was completely convinced, but she and her brothers did go off to play. Gincie asked the hands to help her keep track of the children without making it obvious at Brookhaven and at Sunrise.

Travis quickly gave up trying to talk her out of her obsession. The one hope he saw was to find her family, and he spared no expense, hiring private detectives to pick up whatever trails Piety and Matthew had left. There was little hope of tracking Piety and the preacher with whom she had last been seen, but Matthew had been of military age during the war, and perhaps he would show up on the rolls somewhere, either as Thurgood, his natural father's name, or Carrington, if he had kept his stepfather's name. And

Travis waited to hear from someone, anyone, in the racing fraternity that the stolen horses were being offered for sale.

One unavoidable result of the disaster was that there was so much to take care of in the aftermath, there was little time for brooding. Though Sam was sincere in her insistence that the Culhanes must stay at Brookhaven for as long as they wished, they knew that the sooner they were settled at Sunrise, the better. They were glad they'd had the house refurbished when the farm was purchased, and it was more than adequate for their needs, but they were all conscious that it would never be Wild Swan.

Alex and Rane had left their estate in perfect order, with bequests to the family and to faithful workers. The shares in Wild Swan were exactly as Alex had discussed with the Culhanes. But the living heart of Wild Swan was gone. And rebuilding the house would require a small fortune.

To complicate matters further, Travis had news from Boston Thaine that he could not bring himself to share with Gincie, not yet. Boston had sent the letter just before the fire at Wild Swan, and it had arrived just after. Mark's widow was dead. Boston had written:

I feel guilty for being relieved at anyone's death, but the truth is that Gincie's way is clear for a return to California, should the two of you wish it. There is no one left who gives a damn about Mark Carrington or how he died.

Travis wondered at his own reaction to the news. Once he had wanted the dream of California to be restored, had wanted it more than anything else. But the purchase of Sunrise and the agreement with Alex regarding Wild Swan had changed all of that, and he had grown satisfied with overseeing the ranch in California at a distance, with putting his roots down in Maryland. But now Gincie was as terrified here as she had been in California; they were no longer living at Wild Swan; and as Boston had said, the way was open for their return as a family to the Far West.

He considered it. He imagined packing up the family and going west again to the sun-drenched acres in the Sonoma Valley. He thought of the warm, relaxed life there.

And then the images of Wild Swan flooded into his mind: images of Alex and Rane and the rest of the family; of the welcome the Culhanes had received when they had sought shelter; of the blacks and whites who worked together to glean the best from the land; of the green richness of that land; of the children wandering it with such joy; of the horses that were among the best in the country; of the swan necklace and earrings, so symbolic and dear to Alex, given to her by Rane, left to Gincie to wear when she was ready to admit herself sole mistress of Wild Swan.

Sole mistress of the Wild Swan he would rebuild if the family, his family now, would allow it, and most of all, if Gincie wanted it. Without her passionate involvement, there was no Wild Swan for him.

Much of what had burned in the house could be replaced, but some things were forever lost: the paintings of the horses; the trophies that had melted in the heat; the correspondence, ledgers, and breeding records that had been in the library (though Padraic still had his own carefully kept set of those records); and most of all, the chronicles of healing methods kept by Virginia Thaine, Alex's grandmother, and Alex's notes kept over a lifetime of tending to the sick. It was a loss of precious history, and Travis wondered if Gincie would ever adjust enough to that loss to view a rebuilt house as home.

At least he did not feel pressed to make a decision about Wild Swan immediately. Everyone in the family was still so shocked and struggling to find a new center now that Alex and Rane were gone, no one had yet raised the question of what to do next.

The first news of the horses came all the way from Louisville, Kentucky. Moonraker, Lady Lex, and two other horses had been offered for sale to a major Thoroughbred farm there. The horses were in sorry shape, but they were still recognizable, particularly Moonraker and Lady Lex, and even without that, since they had no papers attesting to their bloodlines, there had been immediate cause for suspicion. The men who had tried to sell the animals were such a ragtag lot, no reputable horse breeder would deal with them. When the one who seemed to be the leader of the group was questioned about the horses' origins, he had become very agitated and had left the four animals at the farm, promising to return on the following day with the necessary papers.

The men had never showed up again, but the farm owner wanted the Culhanes to know that the horses were being cared for and would be returned to them at their direction. He was apologetic about not apprehending the thieves, or those who had purchased the horses from the thieves, if such they were, but he had been sure they would not leave the horses there and had been prepared to have the men arrested on their return to his farm. He extended his sympathy for the losses suffered at Wild Swan.

The fact that four of the missing horses were going to be returned was good, and Travis made immediate arrangements for them to be shipped east, but the rest of the news was terribly frustrating. The thieves now knew they had stolen such distinctive and valuable animals that they had no access to the markets that would pay the full price. It must have stunned them to learn how widely the news of their crime had spread. Travis assumed that they would be even more careful than before, and he doubted that any of the other horses would be offered to qualified horsemen. He hoped his private detectives could follow the trail.

He tried to remind himself that it was an act of respect that was making it possible to get any of the horses back at all, but he knew that even more than getting the animals back, Gincie needed to know the identity of the thieves and who, if anyone, had hired them.

He read the reports from the detectives and longed for them to say more than they did. He had not told Gincie about the investigation or about the death of Mark Carrington's widow, and he hated keeping secrets from her; it was not the way of their marriage. Had she not been so withdrawn into her own nightmare, in addition to being faced with their current disjointed life, he knew she would have suspected he was keeping something from her.

The household staff had moved to Sunrise, but the horses at Wild Swan remained there with their attendants, a situation that caused an unnatural division in the employees, who were used to working in unison at Wild Swan. Mrs. Williams had resumed classes for the children, and those were held, as they had always been, in the little building constructed for that purpose at Wild Swan, but even this seemed odd now since Lexy and the twins were not just a skip away from the house where they lived; instead, they walked to school in the morning with the McCoy children and others from Sunrise. It gave Willy McCoy even more time to pay court to Lexy; he was happy only when she allowed him to carry her books and her lunch pail. The twins and Willy's brothers teased him mercilessly about this, but he persevered.

Blue was still tottery, but able to follow Tinker and the children around again, and it was worth all the care lavished on the dog to see how much his survival meant to the children.

To the children, the idea of death coming in the night and stealing life away while one slept was terrifying. None of the three was having nightmares as violent as their cousin Joseph's, but Tay spoke for all of them when he confessed, "I'm awful glad when the sun comes up."

When the four horses arrived from Kentucky, it was plain that they had been driven hard by the thieves, though the breeder who had taken them in had given them good care since. It hurt to look at the marks of abuse on their coats and to witness how skittish they had become when people approached them.

Saddest of all was Moonraker. Both his forelegs were swollen, his knees scarred as if he had fallen hard, and he was lame enough to make it doubtful that he would ever race again. The best they could hope for was that he would recover sufficiently to be capable of breeding mares.

Padraic clucked and crooned over his returned charges as if they were abused children. Padraic's world was as disrupted as everyone else's, and not only emotionally. He and the Culhanes decided to appear at the racecourses the next year for the simple reason that Alex would have had it no other way, but the horses that had already been entered in future races under the Falconer name as owner would now be ineligible for many of those races because changes of ownership after the time of entry were not allowed. The Culhanes' horses were still eligible and so were others for races whose entry dates were still open, but all in all, the situation called for changes in what they'd planned.

When Travis went to Baltimore to meet with one of the detectives, he didn't even have to use subterfuge to keep Gincie from knowing of his mission; she had no interest in going into the city and none in why he was going; daily life at Sunrise was all she could cope with for now.

The detective, a Mr. Timms, who looked more like a clerk than a man of intrigue, cautioned Travis not to get his hopes up, but the man's own excitement was palpable.

"Of the woman, not a trace, but I think I've found the boy, or the man, I should say. He goes by the name of Carrington. He's a doctor in Ohio. He has a wife, two children, and a country practice that pays more in foodstuffs than in money, but he's highly thought of. He served with the medical corps of the Union Army in the western theater; that's how I got on to his trail. He's the right age."

"It all fits," Travis said. "His stepfather was a doctor." He tried to keep his hope in check as Mr. Timms had suggested, but he had a feeling about this.

There had been a few other possible leads for Thurgood and Carrington, but they had been revealed to be false—the people proved to be the wrong age or had never been in Philadelphia where Nigel Carrington had practiced medicine, or had clearly defined family histories that had nothing to do with Gincie's lines. The detectives had even tried given names other than "Matthew," assuming that records were often inaccurate, so that "Michael," "Mitchell," and the like had been considered. There had been no trail leading to Mark Carrington, and for that Travis had been grateful. The detectives did not know the whole story.

But now this Matthew Carrington was found. Travis did not hesitate. He ordered Mr. Timms, who had not yet approached Dr.

Carrington directly, to go to Ohio and do exactly that. With him he sent a letter and instructions that all Dr. Carrington's expenses be paid if the man were willing to come to Maryland.

Lest the wrong person read it, Travis made the letter a plea, not a betrayal of family secrets, saying in part:

> *Gincie's half brother Mark caused her such misery over the years, it is important that she be reassured you have no part in it. If you are Mark's brother and Gincie's half brother, I beg that you come to us.*

He had no idea of how much Matthew knew of his brother's activities during the war and afterward, but if this were the right man, he would surely respond to the plea, out of curiosity if for no kinder reason.

The days after his meeting with Mr. Timms passed with agonizing slowness for Travis, and despite her preoccupied state, Gincie finally noticed how restless he was.

"Do you regret not going to California this year?" she asked. "Truly, if you think you should go, I can manage here." As she said it, she looked so apprehensive, Travis's heart ached for her.

He cradled her as if she were one of the children in need of comfort. "Next year will be soon enough for California. We have good people lookin' after our interests there." He did not attempt to explain his agitation; he just hoped Mr. Timms would report back soon.

When the detective came to Sunrise, he had Dr. Carrington with him, and from the moment Travis caught sight of him, his heart began to soar. Unlikely as he might look for the part, Matthew was surely the dragon slayer Gincie had needed all of these years.

Travis and Matthew shook hands while Mr. Timms stood by, beaming with his success. He then took his leave, knowing that Mr. Culhane would pay him well for this work.

Matthew looked around, asking anxiously, "Does Gincie know I'm coming? Whatever has happened, I don't want to make it worse for her."

It was exactly the right question for him to ask, and beyond that, Travis could see the faint resemblance to Gincie, legacy from their mother, though Gincie had the Thaine green eyes and the golden tints in her hair, inherited from her father. But they shared a certain structure of the face, the shape of the ears—small things that Travis nonetheless knew well in his wife.

"Gincie has no idea you're coming," Travis said as he led him into the house. "I haven't even told her I was looking for you. But I assure you, no other visitor on earth could mean as much to her."

Gincie was out helping with the harvesting of late vegetables, and Travis was glad to have time with Matthew before the two met face to face. He enlisted Della's aid, introducing Matthew to her and inwardly blessing the great self-control of the woman.

Della searched Matthew's face intently and then nodded, and she was warm in her welcome.

"I want to talk to Matthew for twenty minutes or so," Travis explained. "Then if you'd send one of the girls to get Gincie and let me know when she's here, I'll tell her what's goin' on so it won't be too much of a shock."

Della was only too happy to oblige. She had told no one, but she, too, had considered the possibility that Gincie's other half brother was responsible for the fire. But she could not believe it of the man she had just met.

Travis led Matthew into Sunrise's library, a much more modest room than the one at Wild Swan but now the center for the paperwork of both farms.

"We are still in disarray after a fire at Wild Swan," Travis said. He poured two glasses of whiskey and handed one to Matthew. "I know it's a little early in the day, but I think you're goin' to need this." And then he told the story of Mark's coming to Wild Swan at the end of the war and of how Mark had stalked Gincie in California until she had killed him, of the Culhanes' return to Wild Swan, and finally of the fire that had destroyed the house and killed Alex and Rane.

"I don't know whether or not you ever knew, but your mother was the one who burned down the barn and caused the death of the stallion Wild Swan all those years ago. Alex blackmailed her with knowledge of the crime to force her to leave Gincie at Wild Swan. Your mother came back only once, and I believe you and your brother were with her. She wanted money. But by that time, Nigel Carrington was dead, and Alex threatened your mother with exposure if she did not go away forever. You must see how the two fires are connected in Gincie's mind."

Matthew's face was white and drawn, but he was not too dazed to understand. "She thinks I or our mother had something to do with the most recent fire," he said slowly, not asking a question. "She thinks one of us might come back, to do more damage. Oh, my God! Poor Gincie! It must seem like a nightmare that never ends, but it ended in California. Mother died in Vicksburg during the siege, and I swear to you, doing harm to Gincie is the last thing on earth I would consider!"

Travis nodded. "I knew that the moment I set eyes on you, and I think Gincie will know, too." He thought of how extraordinary this man was. Not once had he proclaimed outrage at being judged capable of the same malice his mother and brother had shown.

Matthew took a good swig of whiskey and started to explain, "I loved my stepfather . . ." his voice trailed off as Della came to inform Travis that Gincie had returned to the house.

"Save it to tell Gincie," Travis said to Matthew. "She needs to hear everything. I'll bring her to you."

As soon as Gincie saw Travis, she peppered him with questions that betrayed how on edge she was these days, so much so that any break in the day's schedule sent her into a panic. "What is it? One of the children? Is everything all right?"

"Everything is more than all right," Travis answered. He put his hands on her shoulders, holding her steady. "I've found Matthew."

"Is he under arrest?" Her eyes glittered an eerie yellow-green.

"No. He's here to see you." He felt her shudder under his hands, and he pulled her against him. "He had nothin' to do with the fire, with anythin' Mark did. He's a doctor with a practice and a family in Ohio, and he has come all this way to reassure you. It's over, darlin'. Your mother died at Vicksburg; you know Mark is gone; Matthew is the only one left, and he wishes you no harm."

Gincie let him lead her to the library because she was too stunned to resist.

Matthew invaded her heart from the first moment she saw him. The ghost of the child she had known when she was so young was still there: Matthew, not Mark, a wholly different being. He looked so tentative, so apologetic, as if he were taking all the blame, as she had, for the "bad blood" in their veins. And yet she knew as absolutely as had Travis and Della that Matthew was not at fault for it.

His clothes were clean, painstakingly neat, but threadbare, and the leather of his shoes so worn, it could no longer be improved by polish. He was only four years older than she, but he looked more than that, worn by work and more, by caring. She knew he looked as her father must have looked when he gave too much of himself to his patients. She knew it though she had only the vaguest memories of her father and though Matthew had no blood tie to him. She knew it because she had seen the same in her cousins Nigel and Anthea, and in Max, but she also knew it from a source beyond them, from Matthew himself. As she had felt the twisted hate of Mark, so could she feel the warmth of Matthew. It radiated from him, filling the room, enfolding her.

Of medium height and build, with regular features, brown eyes, and brown hair receding at the temples, he was at first glance not prepossessing. But immediately the perception changed. His eyes did it; they were kind, intelligent, and most of all peaceful, despite his anxiety at their meeting. Whatever the burdens of his life, he was content with it. She doubted that her mother or Mark had ever been content with themselves or with anything or anyone else.

Matthew stood before her, not making any move to touch her, obviously being very careful not to frighten her, but his eyes asked that she trust him.

"Hello, Matthew. It was good of you to come." She brushed a tendril of hair back from her face and wished she'd done more than quickly wash her face and hands and dust off her clothes.

Her gesture broke the tension between them. Matthew grinned. "Even when you were a tiny child, you were always doing something, always trying to be in the middle of whatever was going on. It doesn't surprise me at all to find you do more than supervise at this farm." He paused, and then he said, "Your father was the best thing that ever happened to me when I was a child. I loved him. And in the brief time he was part of my life, he taught me that caring for other people is a fit way to live. It's why I took his name. I wish I'd gotten in touch with you long ago to explain."

She went to him then and put her arms around him. Her voice was muffled by tears. "I know my father would be so proud of you and so glad that he made a difference in your life."

Matthew's own arms came around her. "I'm sorry for the way Mother was and Mark, so sorry. Mother always wanted things she couldn't have, and that made her bitter. And her unhappiness, taught to Mark, turned to evil in him. He enjoyed making other people suffer. And he got the twisted idea from Mother that he was somehow entitled to Wild Swan. The last time I saw him was right before the war began, but I should have known he would try to harm you; I should have warned you."

She stepped back so she could see his face. "How could you? You are not like he was, not like Mother. And I am not like them. I'm not!" The words carried conviction and a blaze of joy for the unjust burden at last relinquished.

Suddenly, the words tumbled from both of them. She wanted to know everything about his life and he about hers. He told her of his early separation from their mother and her companion, the preacher who had had as little humanity as she, and from Mark. And he told of his determination to become a physician, first serving an apprenticeship with one and then taking formal training in time to serve with the Union Army. He spoke in glowing terms about his wife, Katlin, a native Ohioan and the reason he had settled there, and of their two children, James, ten, and Virginia, seven.

"I named Virginia in memory of the little sister I'd had for a while, but I remembered that you had insisted on being called by your nickname even then, so I hoped you wouldn't mind if you ever found out," he explained.

"Mind! I'm flattered. I hope I will meet my niece and my nephew as well as my sister-in-law someday." She smiled at the knowledge she had a whole new part of her family to meet, to meet without dread.

As avidly as she had listened to the account of his life, so Matthew listened to hers, his eyes steady on her face even when she faltered and then struggled on in telling exactly how she had killed Mark.

"I would have done the same thing," he said quietly. "I was tempted more than once when I was with him, but I didn't meet Katlin until the war was on, and we weren't married until it ended, so Mark never knew my wife or children, never had a chance to threaten them."

Gincie glanced around and discovered that Travis had left them alone.

"Your husband is a special man," Matthew said, and Gincie nodded, her throat suddenly too tight to allow speech. She thought of all Travis had gone through for her sake, how hard it had been for him to bear the fact that she had not come to him when Mark had first made his threats, how patient he had been with the terror she had felt about the blood she shared with her mother and Mark, how much he cared about her to go to such lengths to locate Matthew. Inwardly she resolved that, henceforth, no man on earth would feel better loved than Travis. She knew she was blushing while she considered all the ways she was going to prove her love, and she didn't care.

Gincie moved in a euphoric haze unlike anything she had ever experienced before. She could not mourn the death of her mother, years past, but only known to her now. So much misery and hurt had flowed from Piety Thurgood Carrington. Gincie was sure her father would have lived for years more had not Piety rejected every gift of love he offered. Piety had not even been able to accept the child they had created together.

Alex and Rane had raised Gincie, and she realized anew how fortunate she had been in their care. She was not sure she would have survived with the same spirit and intelligence that Matthew possessed had she had to spend her childhood with their mother.

She was free for the first time in her life, and the knowledge of it made her luminous. The children noticed the minute they returned from school.

"You look like you just got a present, Mama," Tay said, as she hugged each of them in greeting.

"I did receive a present, a marvelous present from your father. He found my half brother Matthew and arranged for him to visit us here."

"Half brother, that's a funny thing to be," Lexy said, and Gincie hastened to explain.

Someday the children might need or demand to know the full truth; already they knew that something was odd about their mother's background, but it had been explained in the most basic terms that Gincie had come to live with her grandparents when her father had fallen ill and then died, a slight twisting of the facts. And as for Piety, the children had been allowed to assume that she, too, had died long ago. It was a little more delicate to account for Matthew's existence, but Gincie simply added him to the previous story.

"My mother was a widow when my father married her, and she had two sons by her first marriage. They were my half brothers. But after I came to live at Wild Swan, they went to live in other places, and we lost track of each other. The older boy, Mark, died somewhere out west"—she said it without a catch in her voice—"but Matthew lives in Ohio with his wife and children, and he's a doctor just like Nigel, Anthea, and Max."

The children's curiosity about Matthew overrode any need they might have had for further details of the past, and Matthew proved himself more than equal to the occasion of their meeting. He adored children and was gravely patient in answering their questions and in asking his own about their favorite activities. They, in turn, were delighted with their new uncle and with the photograph he showed them of their aunt and cousins. Though the little rectangle showed a stiffly posed family group, Katlin's humor showed through in her barely restrained smile, and little Virginia had a definite look of mischief, though James was trying to look somber and grown-up.

Gincie wanted Matthew to meet the whole family before he returned to Ohio, and he agreed because he knew how important it was for her to be able to show that the curse had been lifted. He understood her attitude completely; it was reassuring to him to know that Gincie was not like his mother and brother. And he already felt that he would be comfortable with the doctors in the family. It intrigued him to think that their experiences in the war had surely been similar, though they had never met during the conflict. He wished that they had, that he might have reestablished contact with Gincie then and protected her somehow from Mark, sparing her years of suffering. But that time was lost, and the best they could do was to go on in the light Travis had brought to them.

Chapter 24

Travis watched Gincie in wonder. He had hoped Matthew would make a difference to her, but he had not known how profound and instantaneous that difference would be. Her joy shimmered around her. But even as he rejoiced with her, he acknowledged to himself that she had, in vital ways, suddenly become a stranger.

He had thought he knew how affected she was by her background; certainly he had recognized the terrible changes Mark had made in all of their lives. And Alex had warned him long ago that Gincie burned with a fire that came as much from her will to be the opposite of her mother as from her sense of justice. Alex had believed that even Gincie's commitment to the work and danger of the Underground Railroad had been part of both.

It was through that work that he and Gincie had met. He could not prevent the thought that her life might have gone in an entirely different direction, might not have included him at all, had her mother been able to find contentment with Nigel Carrington. He hated the idea that his marriage might have been possible only through misery, that perhaps this new Gincie would have made entirely different choices. He condemned the speculation as futile, but that did not lessen its impact.

Since the fire and the loss of their unborn child, they had held each other in the night for mutual comfort, but not for passion. Their sorrow and the grinding press of the days consumed by all the tasks necessary to reorder their lives had left no energy for sex.

Travis felt a growing emotional and physical need to possess his wife, but he mistrusted the motive of his need, fearing that it stemmed as much from wanting to refocus her attention on him as from love. And so he came to her warily, unsure of himself, and of her.

Gincie was aware of his unease; she was aware of everything. With the fear that had stolen so much time from her heart and mind banished forever, she found that everything, including the people around her, had a crystalline transparency, Travis especially.

The autumn night was cool, and the fire on the bedroom hearth added its flickering gold light to the glow of lamps. Gincie stared at the flames, considering one subtle approach to her husband after another, casting each one aside until she turned to him with the truth.

"I love you, Travis Culhane. The best thing that ever happened to me was meeting you. That's no less true now than it was then. Yourself, our children, Matthew—they are all gifts from you. You have been so patient though all my years of terror, the first and best thing about how I feel now is that I can come to you as I should have in the beginning, without that terror, without my mother and Mark standing in the shadows behind me. Knowing Matthew, knowing what kind of man he is, doesn't make me want to go away from you, quite the opposite."

Travis watched her as if he were hypnotized. The firelight silhouetted her soft curves through her nightgown, curves he had traced and held and fitted against his own harder flesh for the seventeen years of their marriage, curves that had sheltered him and cradled their three living children and the one who had died before birth. The light caught gold in her unbound hair, sculpted the delicate symmetry of her face, and pooled in her eyes.

Travis stood still as Gincie came to him. She framed his face with her hands and began to plant small nibbling kisses, clearly prepared to arouse him slowly and patiently.

His arms came around her. He lifted her off her feet and kissed her fiercely, probing her mouth with his tongue. When he put her down again, they were both breathless.

"Darlin', I'd like to see what you were goin' to do next, but I can't wait!" Travis confessed, his voice broken by passion and laughter, the hard evidence of his desire pressing against her belly.

They fell on the bed in a tangle of arms and legs and laughter. Gincie straddled him and began teasing him again with light, close-mouthed kisses that were belied by the sinuous rhythm of her pelvis rubbing against his.

Touching her breasts and anything else he could reach, he bore the enchantment of interweaving sensations as long as he could, and then with a groan, he lifted her up to free himself and brought her down on his shaft, holding her close against him so he could thrust deep before freeing her to set the pace.

She gloried in the hard, hot length of him sheathed inside of her. She rode him, feeling every inch of him slowly thrusting in and out, then faster until she fell forward on him, and he rolled her beneath him, his power melding with hers as he loomed over her, bringing her to pleasure that engulfed her entire body before he let himself go.

And through it all their voices blended as their bodies did—
each other's names, words of endearment and satisfaction, cries of
exultation—a song for two voices.

They rested in each other's arms and then sought each other
again for a slower, gentler coupling. This was a new beginning and a
reaffirmation of vows that meant more now than they had when first
spoken. They did not question, but were simply grateful for the
energy that continued to flow throughout the night, allowing them to
drift in and out of lovemaking as if they were still in the first years of
youth, as if she were seventeen and he twenty-four again, as they
had been on their wedding night.

They were justifiably weary when morning came, but it was not
trying, as the exhaustion from grief had been.

"I hope we get all the horses back and that the murderers are
found; of course, I do. But it doesn't matter the same way to me
anymore; it doesn't threaten my life not to know," Gincie explained
slowly as she considered it, and Travis knew it was time to tell her
the things he had been keeping from her.

"Mark's wife is dead, of natural causes," he said, and he told
her of Boston's letter and of his own reaction to it, and then he
finished, "I want to rebuild Wild Swan so that we, our children, and
generations to follow can, if they wish, live in the same beauty Alex
and St. John and Rane created there. But none of it makes any sense
unless you can live there joyfully again. If there are too many ghosts,
it is no place for you to be and, therefore, no place for me and the
children."

The future course of their lives hung in the balance of Gincie's
silence, but neither of them was uncomfortable with it. Gincie lay
with her head cradled against Travis's shoulder, his arms holding her.
She could feel the steady pulse of his heart. She gave herself the
time to assimilate what he had told her.

She was not angry that he had waited to give her the news about
Mark's wife. She would not have been able to cope with it when
Travis had first known. But now it was a distant echo of a horrible
time. She had always felt a vague pity for the woman, no matter
what her motives had been in marrying Mark. She could not imagine
that any woman deserved to be tied to such a beast. She had
recognized the woman's threat to her own legal standing in California, but she had never perceived her to be a physical danger like
Mark, or as she had come to believe Matthew also was. Finding out
that Mark's wife was dead was far, far less vital than knowing that
Matthew was a fine man.

She thought of what it would be like to live at Wild Swan again,
to live there with no possibility that her grandmother or grandfather

would ever again be there to advise her, to comfort her. And then she smiled to herself, understanding that they would always be there. She understood everything all at once.

"There will be ghosts. Every well-loved place has ghosts, traces left of what once was to help us shape what is still to come. I will welcome them when I feel them near. But life is for the living; Gran and Grandfather knew that better than anyone. To let Wild Swan become a sad place would be the worst thing of all. Sorrow and joy and everything in between, life at Wild Swan has always contained them all."

She propped herself up so she could see Travis's face. "And having said all that, now I'll tell you the most important thing of all. I don't care where we live—Wild Swan or California or somewhere else. You've given me my dream; I need never again fear that one of my blood will harm you or one of the children. My mother . . ." her voice broke a little, and she steadied it. "There will always be a child in me who wishes she could have loved me better, loved me at all, but the truth is that she was a cruel woman who had much to do with making Mark the way he was. I cannot mourn her."

She traced his face with her fingers, as if the sight of him weren't enough, as if she would absorb his image through touch. "So, I have my dream. Now let us have yours. If you truly mean it about Wild Swan, if it is for your own sake, then let us indeed rebuild, as soon as we can."

Travis's eyes were suddenly overly bright, and his voice was husky. "You'll have me weepin' in a moment." He studied her face as intently as she had been studying his. Despite the lack of sleep, her green eyes glowed, her skin was rosy, and her lips were slightly swollen from his kisses.

Her joy had become his, and it made him feel slightly drunk. He had to struggle to bring at least a shade of reason to their situation. "The family may not feel comfortable with our rebuildin' Wild Swan," he cautioned. "No matter what we say about the farm bein' a place for all of us, it will be different for them knowin' we rebuilt it."

"Perhaps, but I think they will be relieved," she countered. "They have known since Gran proposed her plan that we would eventually be in charge of Wild Swan; the only sorrow is that it has happened so soon."

They postponed any discussion of business with the others until after Matthew had left. To Gincie's great pleasure, the rest of the family welcomed Matthew into their midst. At first the warmth they extended was for Gincie's sake, but it was quickly transformed into a reaction to Matthew himself. All of them found him easy, intelligent company. The exchange was not one-sided; for Matthew, it was like discovering a whole new family through Gincie, a family full of people like Nigel Carrington, who was no less a hero in Matthew's memory than when he had been stepfather to the small boy.

When Matthew had departed for Ohio, Travis and Gincie sent word to the family that they would like to see everyone at Sunrise when their schedules allowed a meeting.

It was a golden day in November when they gathered. The nights had turned cold, but the days were like honey: warm, smooth, and rich.

Despite the temptation simply to enjoy the fair weather and being together, Travis came right to the point by announcing, "Gincie and I would like to rebuild Wild Swan. It seems the sensible thing to do, as we are the ones who have lived there and would again. But we realize that it must be a decision shared by all. It is a family home and should remain so. We won't do anything without your permission, and whatever you decide, not even Wild Swan is worth a breach in this family."

Travis couldn't gauge their reactions, but at least he saw no open rejection or animosity regarding the plan.

"We don't expect you to make the decision right now, but since you're all here, I think it might be a good idea if Travis and I absent ourselves for a while, so that you may discuss the idea without constraint," Gincie told them.

It was such a reasonable proposition, no one objected, but Gincie admitted to Travis that it did feel odd to know that there was a family council going on without them.

The children were playing happily with their cousins when Travis and Gincie rode off together, heading for Wild Swan.

"Still confident of their reaction?" Travis asked, and Gincie nodded. "I am. No one in the family is very proficient at hiding his or her feelings, except perhaps for Reid, who has mastered a certain look of neutrality when he's asking questions. But for the most part, everyone is very open, and I didn't see any shock, just interest and, yes, relief."

Padraic and the others greeted them on their arrival, and they were immediately engulfed in the business of the farm.

Though their racing calendar was truncated, they were still scheduling appointments for mares to be bred to their prize stallions. Some horse owners thought that due to the tragedy, all business was canceled, and others seemed to have made some illogical connection between the damage to the house and the value of the breeding stock. Gincie and Travis were doing their best to counter such

trends. They were advertising in *Turf, Field, and Farm* and other
agricultural and sporting journals, and they were writing to the farms
that had patronized their stallions' services in previous years. Padraic
was gallantly part of the process, as determined as they that all not
be lost.

Today he had the names of two more farms in mind to contact.
"They're not after doin' it on a grand scale," he admitted, "but
they've got some good mares, an' they've bred to our boys before."

"It's worth a try," Travis agreed.

They were all conscious of how precious time was in a racing
business that was increasingly favoring the running of younger horses.
It left little time for a bloodline to fall into disuse or disrepute. The
racing records of Wild Swan's horses had always been the best
advertising for breeding to their stock, and even a small gap in
attendance at race meetings was risky, though they were aided by
the fact that their reputation was long established and the bloodlines
widely distributed due to the breeding program and stock sold over
the years.

But as they discussed the business with Padraic, both Gincie
and Travis were focused on the charred remains of the house. It was
the center and symbol of the estate. They wondered how long they
would have to wait for the family's decision.

They had their answer on their return to Sunrise.

Blaine had been chosen spokesman, and he came right to the
point. "We don't need time to consider your plan; we are all agreed.
The idea of rebuilding Wild Swan is splendid. And you are the ones
to do it. One of the most generous and wise things Mother ever did
was to encourage each of us to do what he or she was most suited to
do. And she accepted the risk that that diversity might see the end of
Wild Swan. Fortunately, the two of you assure the rest of us that this
is not the case. We all look forward to seeing Wild Swan rising from
the ashes."

There were fine details to be taken care of, details that Blaine
enumerated in his quiet, matter-of-fact fashion, in particular that the
shares the rest of the family held would be owned almost entirely by
the Culhanes from henceforth, and wholly owned by them before
long, according to an adjustment of the pattern Alex had set up when
she offered the partnership to Travis and Gincie.

Though all the arrangements were vital, the words did not
matter to Travis as much as the feeling in the room. Far from being
offended by the notion that Wild Swan would become Culhane
property, they saw it as a good and natural progression. He knew it
had begun with the fact that he had married Gincie all those years
ago, but he knew as well that did they not find him worthy on his

own merit, not even his marriage tie would assure their approval of his possession of the farm. He had been grateful for a long time that he had these people in his life, but only now did he realize how much they returned the feeling. He felt more a part of the family than he ever had before.

With the formal answer given by Blaine, the rest of the family expressed their feelings without restraint, and Travis heard the relief Gincie had predicted. Portions of Alex and Rane's bequests could have been pooled to rebuild the house, but the truth was that there were other far more direct needs in their lives, because as Blaine had observed, each member of the family had followed a path away from the farm.

Flora and Philly always had plans for expanding the school and for numerous projects they supported to help poor immigrants and workers, and Blaine was one of their most faithful backers. Morgan and Adam dealt in very large sums of money to finance new ships and to buy cargoes to sell at various ports. New capital was always needed and welcome. And Sam's interests were at Brookhaven, not at Wild Swan, though the two farms and Sunrise gleaned mutual benefit in various exchanges of crops and stock. Anthea, Max, and Nigel, with Sally's enthusiastic support, wanted to increase their medical services to the poor and add additional qualified medical help; proof of that need was in the fact that Max had not accompanied the others because he had had to cover for the other two doctors. Reid and Larissa accepted the fact that they would be investing everything they could manage in the paper for some time to come. In addition, there were the children already born to the third generation and those yet to come; their parents intended that all should have the best education possible, and that was another investment entirely.

"Alex knew exactly what she was doing when she left the swan necklace and earrings to you," Sam told Gincie. "She knew what a fit mistress you would be for Wild Swan."

The words were a confirmation that no jealousy existed where it well might have, and Gincie was infinitely touched.

What had been planned as a simple family supper turned into a celebration so festive, Tay said, "It feels like Christmas even though I know that's a long time from now."

"You start waiting for Christmas the day after it's happened," Kace teased, but when the children were told about the cause for joy, Lexy supported Tay's view. "It does seem like Christmas!" She felt light and happy, as if everything inside were dancing.

"I hate how the house looks now, all burned and sad," she

confessed. "It will be wonderful to see it like it should be and to live there again!"

"Wild Swan rising . . ." Travis could see Blaine's words transformed into reality, and his mind was full of plans to obtain the workers and materials as soon as possible. Though winter weather would interfere with building now and then, he had every intention of pressing the work as swiftly as possible.

By the time the family gathered at Brookhaven and Sunrise to celebrate Christmas, the rubble at Wild Swan had been cleared, and vital structural work on the house had begun. Months of work lay ahead, but hope infused everyone who visited the farm, and no one had any trouble envisioning the restoration.

"You're doing a fine job," Morgan told Travis, having taken note of the lavish care that was going into every step. Morgan was in a good position to judge the quality since he demanded the same care in the building of Jennings-Falconer ships.

"My main job is hirin' men who know how to do the work," Travis admitted ruefully. "And the most difficult thing beyond findin' those who will be able to do the brick and plaster work is to convince everyone that we want the house to be built as it was in the last century, not with factory-made parts and medieval fantasies."

"Simplicity is always the most difficult thing to achieve," Morgan said, thinking of the clean, lovely lines of the sailing ships he would always prefer, as Rane had, to the steamships of the new age.

Lexy's voice rose clear and sweet over the friendly babble, "Oh, look, Gran's birds!"

Silence fell instantly as everyone looked up to see the wild swans passing overhead, part of the great flocks of swans and geese that had once again returned to the Chesapeake for the winter.

Gincie moved to stand beside Travis, slipping her hand into his. "Benediction in a season of swans," she whispered, knowing he would understand. Tonight she would wear the swan necklace and the earrings, fully accepting the duties and the strength, and Travis would understand that, too.

Travis thought of Hawthorn, so long lost to him, of California, with the heart ties relinquished, and none of it mattered. Wild Swan mattered. Wild Swan rising out of the ashes. Whatever the children chose for their futures, he and Gincie had come home.

Book Two

LEXY, KACE, AND TAY

Chapter 25

Wild Swan, Prince Georges County, Maryland, June 1885.

Lexy's smile grew wider even as her eyes prickled with tears as the house came into view. She leaned over on the wagon seat and kissed her father's cheek.

"Every time I come home, I realize again how beautiful the house is, how right it is. I'm so glad you and Mama decided to rebuild!"

The house loomed large, its main section flanked by the hyphens that connected it to the side wings, the five-part structure giving it a graceful dignity. The brick was warm rose in the sun, and the farm was lush with summer's green.

The house was a testament to Travis's relentless insistence on finding and hiring only the best glaziers, masons, plumbers, plasterers, and joiners. In some ways, it was probably sounder than it had been in its original state, and in certain instances, it was surely more convenient because Travis and Gincie had felt no obligation to duplicate the original plumbing, or lack thereof, or the original kitchen, but had instead made them as modern as possible.

But while Lexy admired the house, Travis admired her. His children enchanted him. That he and Gincie had produced three such extraordinary beings never ceased to amaze him; Lexy most of all because she was so like her mother. Tall, slender, with her gleaming golden brown hair and bright green eyes, she crackled with life even when she was quiet.

Gincie had been elaborately casual about sending him to pick Lexy up at the spur line rail station, along with various supplies destined for the farm, but Travis knew she had done it deliberately to allow him time alone to visit with his daughter.

"I hope you and Mama aren't missing important races by waiting here to welcome me and the boys home," Lexy said worriedly. "I mean, it's lovely of you to do it, but it wouldn't do to lose races for us."

Travis gave a shout of laughter. "Spoken like a true child of

Wild Swan! But we did well at Baltimore, and the horses are racin' at Jerome Park and doin' fine without us. Your mother and I couldn't miss welcomin' our first college graduate home. The twins are goin' to have to work very hard to match your record."

"Tay will do well because he never does any less," Lexy said, "and Kace will do exactly what he pleases, which will be more than most can do even when they try their best."

Their conversation ended as Gincie flew from the house, her joy at having her daughter home visible on her face before she said a word. "Oh, you look beautiful! How did the commencement go? Were Matthew and Katlin able to attend?" The questions and exclamations tumbled out until Gincie had to pause for breath.

"Mama, do you want me to tell you everything in five minutes, or may I have a little more time?" Lexy asked, and then both of the women were laughing as they hugged each other.

Lexy had just completed four years at Oberlin college in Ohio. She had chosen the school for its long record of just policies. Two years after the preparatory school had opened in 1833, the collegiate department, as well as a theological school, were in operation. It had been the first college in the United States to offer coeducation and had admitted students in 1835 "without respect to color." It had been a center of antislavery sentiment in the years before the war, with Underground Railroad connections close by.

Lexy had enjoyed her classes and the friends she had made, but Ohio was a long way from Maryland. She had come home for Christmases and had spent the summers at Wild Swan or traveling to California or England, but still, the months away at school would have seemed much longer than they had had it not been for her uncle Matthew and his family. They had been delighted when she had been admitted to Oberlin College and had offered her a home to visit when she could. They lived on a very modest scale because Matthew had many patients who could afford little beyond a few eggs or some other produce in payment of fees, but their household was a happy one. Lexy had, with the passage of years, gleaned most of her mother's history, and she was grateful not only that her mother's strength had allowed her to survive such a background, but also that her father's love had caused him to initiate the search for Matthew.

She chattered to her mother about Matthew, Katlin, James, and Virginia, giving her all the details of her most recent visit with them and of the last days at the college. She knew her parents felt some guilt for not having gone to Ohio for the commencement, but Lexy had meant it when she had dissuaded them clear back at Christmas. Her education had not been a matter of graduation speeches; it had been a progression of learning through the years. She had gone to college at sixteen with a good education behind her and had added to it, and her parents were responsible for having made it all possible. That was far more important than taking time from their many duties to travel to Ohio.

However, she also realized that she had given gifts in return for those from her parents. She would have preferred to have worked for Reid's newspaper for the past four years, but she had recognized the sense of her parents' argument that a college education could only enhance her journalistic skills. The delay in taking the job at the *National Witness* had been a bargain between her and her parents, and now the terms had been fulfilled.

"You're sure you wouldn't at least like to have the summer before you start working for Reid?" Gincie asked her at supper that night.

"Absolutely sure," Lexy said firmly. "A few days here, and then I'm going to Washington."

Gincie made no more protests. They would be futile. It was a choice Lexy had made years before and from which she had never swerved. And Gincie knew that Larissa and Reid would watch over her daughter. She suspected her lingering reluctance over Lexy's choice of employment was really a reaction to the measure of her own intensity that she saw in her daughter. She had hoped Lexy, living without the threat of war that had hung over Gincie's own generation and without the familial conflicts of her own life, would be able to have an easier time of it, would be able to remain younger for longer. But Lexy had long been impatient to get on with her work, surmounting all obstacles, including the years at college, with a competence beyond her youth.

Though inwardly she quailed at the image of Lexy associating with the rough-and-tumble types that many reporters seemed to be and with the even shadier characters who might provide the news, Gincie could not deny that she was proud of her daughter. It was surely better to have a child of such purpose than one who drifted without direction.

Though she was going to be nearby in Washington from now on, Lexy spent her first full day at home as she always did on her return to Wild Swan, riding its acres and those of Sunrise, visiting with the inhabitants of both farms, and generally reassuring herself that nothing had changed on the land. The continuity of the land was important because people could not stay the same; they changed, aged, died.

The losses they had suffered in the years since the fire at Wild Swan had been, in one sense, nothing more than the natural course of things, but in another, it seemed as if the deaths of Alex and Rane had severed the ties that had bound the rest of the generation to life. One by one they had begun to drift away.

Alastair Cameron had died the year after the fire. Mabel Barlow had passed away two years later, and Jed, unable to bear being in the place of so many memories of their lives together, had moved to be with the son and daughter-in-law who lived in Illinois, where the son was a horse trainer.

Polly and Cassie, the sisters who had worked for Alex for nearly all of their lives, were still as determinedly full of life as Della, but they had both lost their husbands. Della, with sad, wry humor, called them "the three black widows." Out in California, Rachel was also a widow, Boston having died five years before.

Though Padraic had been gone for two years now, he was the one, more than the others, that Lexy found herself looking for every time she came home.

After Samson had been killed, Padraic had been the one who worked most closely with Alex and then with the Culhanes when it came to anything concerning the horses, and it still seemed odd not to hear his Irish-softened voice about the place.

He had grown very vague and forgetful toward the end of his life, and the last time Lexy had seen him alive, he had mistaken her for a young Gincie. He had been heard to speak to his wife Katy, too, as if she hadn't been dead for many years. But he had never lost the slightest detail regarding the horses. And one early morning, after assisting a mare through a difficult birth, Padraic had gone back to his little house for "a bit a' rest." He had not awakened again.

In England, the Bettingdons had lost Angelica to the same kind of gentle passage from old age into death, but she had lived for seven years after her husband's death, her mind sharp though her body had grown increasingly frail, and Gweneth and Christopher were grateful for the extra years they had had with her.

Angelica was buried in England and Boston in California, but all the others, including Alastair, were buried at Wild Swan.

Often Lexy wished time would just stop, that there would be no more aging or death, but she could also see the beauty of the rhythm of life and death and the eternity of knowledge and memories passed from one generation to the next.

And always there was the pulsing life of the land. The variety of the yield from Wild Swan and Sunrise never ceased to impress her. Vegetables, fruit, flower seed, fruit tree cuttings, grain and hay for feed, eggs and dairy products enough to supply the farms with surplus to sell, cattle for milk and for beef, swine, poultry, honey from the hives, the list went on and on, and over everything in importance were the horses—horses for farm work, horses for road and field use, horses for jumping, and most of all, the Thoroughbred racers.

In a world of changes where more and more of the major racing stables were owned by men who bought and sold horses as if they were as inanimate as stock certificates, Wild Swan continued to breed, train, race, and sell its own stock with a steady reputation for producing some of the soundest and swiftest horses in the country.

At Sunrise, Lexy was given a hearty welcome by everyone except Willy McCoy, who blushed and stammered as he greeted her. Willy had grown to be quite handsome in his way. He was big and rawboned like his father, his ears didn't seem to stick out so much anymore, his hair had calmed to auburn, and his skin had weathered and toughened enough to make the freckles less noticeable. But he was still so openly adoring of Lexy, so apt to lose his normal self-confidence around her, that it was difficult for her to see the man instead of the gawky boy, and she wished they could just be friends, as she was with his brothers, without the burden of his devotion. He was a year older than she, and it struck her that it would be a great relief when he found a wife.

"So you'll soon be in pr . . . print again," he offered shyly.

"If Cousin Reid finds my writing good enough."

"It will be! Why, I've still got all . . . all the articles you wrote for his paper when you were just a kid."

It was Lexy's turn to blush. She wasn't embarrassed by the "Child's View" articles Reid had published over the years, articles written not only by her, but by other youngsters, and given a special place in the newspaper; she was embarrassed that Willy's adoration would lead him to save such things. Not only did she feel unworthy and inadequate in the face of it, but she also had a vague feeling of guilt that was never far from the surface when she was around Willy, as if somehow she had done something to cause his infatuation. She hoped she would never develop such an attachment for someone who could not return her affection.

Michael McCoy, observing how patient she was with Willy when he took her around to see all the new additions to the livestock at Sunrise, thought that it might be a good thing if Miss Lexy weren't so kind to his son.

Whatever chance there was for quiet was happily shattered the following day by the arrival of the twins, Kace from Harvard at Cambridge, Massachusetts, and Tay from Cornell at Ithaca, New York. They were seventeen, and not only was this their first year at their respective colleges, it was also the first time they had been apart for an extended time.

Lexy knew what an effort they had made in the past few years to be more independent of each other and how hard the struggle had been. Their personalities were quite different, and ironically, this was what made the separation more difficult. Kace was devil-may-care, intelligent, but apt to get by and to manage his adventures with charm and without much thought of the consequences. Tay, on the other hand, was more responsible. Together they were a perfect combination of fire and sense; separately they were still trying to feel complete without the mutual balance.

Kace was taking courses in science and the arts in order to be a "gentleman farmer," as he put it. Tay was much more focused, having committed himself to six years of study, four to achieve a bachelor of veterinary science degree, and two more to be awarded the degree of doctor of veterinary medicine. Only one student had thus far done the work required for the DVM degree because there were other institutions that offered the degree for far less time and course work, but Tay was not deterred. He wanted to study under the auspices of James Law, a Scotsman, professor of veterinary surgery and breeding of animals, trained at the Edinburgh Veterinary College, a man of high repute in both Great Britain and the United States. England and Scotland's training was still far superior to America's, and Professor Law was relentless in his campaign for the establishment of government veterinary schools, including a full veterinary department at Cornell. He believed that the facilities offered at a separate veterinary college would be invaluable, particularly in the area of the great plagues that periodically devastated cattle and swine, causing severe economic losses.

"Professor Law is a remarkable man!" Tay said. "He envisions a time when superstition will have lost all its power regarding the treatment of animal disease and scientific methods will provide ways of preventing or curing lung fever and Texas fever in cattle, swine plague, and all manner of other contagions."

Tay's family was accustomed to his enthusiasm. For years, he had been reading Dr. Law's *Farmer's Veterinary Adviser*, a textbook written for students and stockmen alike, with the fascination most young men reserved for tales of adventure. As far as Tay was concerned, the possibility of preventing suffering and curing sickness in animals was the greatest adventure of all.

But still Travis felt obliged to say, "While I certainly applaud his goals, endin' superstition among farmers is a little like endin' the weather."

"That's true," Tay conceded, "and I don't expect farmers to change for sentiment's sake, though many treatments based on superstition are cruelly painful to the beasts and ought to be stopped out of kindness, if for no other reason. But farmers will respond to almost anything that offers a chance of higher profits and fewer losses.''

Kace loved his twin too much to harbor personal envy of him, but he did sometimes wish he shared Tay's fervor for a single subject. Kace understood that his own course of education would, over a lifetime, provide benefits as valuable as Tay's, though different from them. But he often felt as if he were unconnected, drifting through his classes, and he hoped he would feel less restless and more settled in the curriculum as he advanced. He was grateful that he suffered no such insecurity when he was working at the farms. The land and what it could produce were real and precious to him, and he reminded himself that the science courses he was pursuing at college could only add to his proficiency on the land.

"I presume we'll have first call on your services when you've qualified, and the best rates, of course," he teased his brother, affection clear in his voice. Suddenly he remembered how Tay had mourned when Blue had died and Tinker had quickly followed, the horse refusing to form an attachment to any other animal, refusing to live without his companion. He and Lexy had been sad, but Tay had spent days trying to coax Tinker out of his decline.

It occurred to him that he and Tay were like Tinker and Blue. It had always looked as if the old hound were trailing the horse, but in the end, it was the horse who could not do without the hound. Tay was the faithful one, but he, Kace, was the one who could not imagine a world without his twin. He knew the choice of different colleges had been a good one, but he admitted to himself that missing Tay had been a constant theme in his days, not overwhelming him, but always there, making him long to share this or that incident with his brother, knowing the understanding between them could not be matched by other friendships.

He had missed Lexy, too, but in a different way. She had been away at school for four years now, so he and Tay had gotten accustomed to seeing her only at intervals. He smiled to himself, considering how she had been the voice of conscience for them for so long. As children, they had been able to plot any sort of mischief with the sure knowledge that Lexy would be there to caution them about consequences that even Tay had not considered. He doubted she knew that both of them carried her voice with them still, a constant inner whisper. He did not worry about her journalistic plans as he knew their mother did; he could not imagine a situation Lexy could not handle.

Gincie watched Kace's changing expressions and felt a swell of maternal tenderness. Though Kace and Tay were different in personality and clearly not identical, they both had gilded brown hair and their father's vivid turquoise eyes. She loved them for their own sakes, but she also loved the visible inheritance from Travis.

She thought of the tragedy and turmoil of nine years before and marveled that so much had healed since then. She still missed Alex and Rane; she always would, as she would always regret the child she had lost. But Travis had made the world come right. Wild Swan had risen from the ashes just as he had planned. And though Gincie had made two trips to California with him since the fire, she now knew, as surely as he did, that Maryland was where she belonged. Even the loss of the child had been tempered by having Matthew in her life; it was not an exchange, but a balance.

Two more of the stolen horses had eventually been returned, and though the Culhanes would never know for certain, they were fairly sure that a wastrel named Jimmy Bethune had been responsible for the theft and the fire. One of his companions, a slow-witted man named Harv, had bragged drunkenly that he and Jimmy had raided one of the best horse farms in Maryland, in the whole country in fact. Unable to shut him up, Jimmy, also in his cups, had stabbed him to death in front of the other saloon patrons. Jimmy Bethune had been jailed, but before he could come before the judge, he had died in an altercation with another prisoner. It had taken some time for the news to filter back to Wild Swan from Missouri and had required a combination of Travis's detectives and horsemen who had known of Wild Swan's losses. Gincie had not been sorry to learn of the deaths of the two, nor had she felt any special triumph. That Matthew had not been involved was all she needed to know. Random evil was frightening, but far less so than blood vengeance.

She studied the faces of her three children, and when Travis caught her eye, the smile she gave him was so radiant, he was flooded with affection and ardor in equal measure, and he wasn't sorry when the children confessed themselves wearily ready to surrender the day for sleep.

Lexy and her brothers spent hours talking and wandering the land in the next few days, reaffirming their ties to each other, enjoying the old ease of the triumvirate. They visited Sam at Brookhaven and also went to Baltimore for a day with the family there.

Lexy always felt a bit ancient when she saw her cousins again after the passage of even so little time as six months. Adam and Mercy's boys—Nathan, eleven, Zachary, nine, and Seth, six—were a lively bunch, as comfortable on ships as their parents, and already, including Seth, giving evidence they were going to be men of formidable size.

Joseph Edwards, at eighteen, was already a man. Tall, with dark hair and darker eyes, he was far more reserved than the rest of the cousins. Even when he tried to be part of a gathering, there was part of him that held back, always observing, not participating. He had trailed Anthea and Max on their medical rounds since permitted to do so, serving an invaluable apprenticeship, and now he was attending the University of Pennsylvania, where he would earn his medical degree.

Lexy supposed his detachment might serve him well in medicine now and again, but overall, it seemed it would cause him more harm than good. He had lost so much when he was young, he didn't trust love. To Joseph, loving meant losing, and being too involved with life or with other people was too risky. Lexy knew that the Kingstons worried about his reserve. Once, after Kace and Tay had perpetrated a particularly devilish piece of mischief, she had heard Anthea confiding to Gincie that she wished Joseph were inclined to such antics, that it would be more natural than his extraordinary self-control.

Lexy never knew quite what he was thinking, but she was nonetheless very fond of him and considered it an accomplishment that she could usually coax laughter from him. Joseph, she was sure, felt more for other people than his demeanor betrayed. Laughter might seem safe to him, but as far as she was concerned, it was a key; if you could laugh with others, there was no emotion you could not feel.

Lexy especially liked visiting Nigel and Sally because they were so content with each other, but she knew they had their sorrows as well. Since their marriage, Sally had been delivered of two stillborn babies, and though she seemed to have adjusted to the losses, the family knew she desperately wanted to give Nigel a child.

The Culhane children visited with the older generation, too. It was always reassuring to see Morgan because he looked so much like Alex and Rane, and he was so like Rane in personality, it was as if they still had a younger version of their great-grandfather with them.

Flora was the only one Lexy worried about, and it was not something she could define, just a greater delicacy than she had noticed before, though Flora's spirits seemed in no way diminished, and Marsh Whitcomb was still her constant companion.

But when Lexy asked Anthea about Flora's health, Anthea echoed her concerns. "I've asked her if something is troubling her, but she maintains she is doing remarkably well for a seventy-year-old, and I can't dispute that. I know my father is worried about her, too, but he hasn't made any more progress with her than I have, and if her twin can't make her confess to any problems, then I certainly can't.''

When they arrived back at Wild Swan, their parents were nearly ready to leave for the Northern racing circuit. Though there would be capable help from the staff at both Wild Swan and Sunrise, Travis and Gincie expected their sons to be their representatives in their absence. Lexy hid her amusement at the way her brothers preened with the responsibility entrusted to them, but she knew they would do twice as much work under these circumstances than they would do with their parents in residence.

More anxious than ever to settle into her job, Lexy moved to Georgetown. She had agreed to live with the Tratnors, at least at first. It was a reasonable request from her parents, but she had some reservations about the arrangement. She wished she got along as well with her Tratnor cousins, or rather, with one of them in particular, as she did with those in Baltimore. She had no real problem with Ben, at nineteen the oldest, though she found him very dull indeed. He wanted nothing so much as to be a banker and was already apprenticed to one, working as a clerk and teller. He was brilliant with figures, but in normal discourse, he was so pedantic, one could fall asleep listening to him. He had an air of pomposity that would have been better suited to a man twice or more his age. She wondered how Reid and Larissa had managed to produce a child so different from themselves.

She liked Joshua, at fourteen the youngest of the three. He was caught between child and man, grown gangly, and bedeviled by a voice that went up and down the register without his volition, but he was quick, full of fun, and easygoing.

Jilly was the problem. At seventeen, she was already possessed of a singing voice that had the range, power, and clarity to cause shivers down the spine. She was also lovely to look at, a slender, dark-haired, silvery blue-eyed combination of her handsome parents. And she was jealous of Lexy.

Jilly was too well bred to be open about her animosity, but Lexy always felt it in her presence, saw it betrayed in the coldness of Jilly's eyes when she looked at her, heard it in the way she spoke to her—seldom, unless forced to by the situation and always with a curt edge to her voice.

And Lexy knew why it was so. Jilly adored her father and resented the bond he had had with Lexy for so long, the bond of common interest in the newspaper. Jilly had no interest in journalistic pursuits, but that did not make her feel any more charitable toward Lexy.

Reid adored his daughter and admired her musical talent, and

Lexy wished Jilly could see that, but instead, her cousin seemed conscious only of the fact that the work closest to her father's heart was being shared with her cousin, not with her.

Lexy recognized her own temper and knew it was most apt to flare when she perceived an injustice. And she considered Jilly's treatment of her stupid and unjust. But she did not want to disrupt the Tratnor household, and she tried to understand how Jilly felt by imagining how she herself would feel if Jilly shared Travis's passionate interest in horses while she did not. She hoped she would be more gracious than Jilly, but she couldn't be sure, and that helped her be more tolerant of her cousin's behavior.

In any case, the newspaper quickly filled Lexy's days, leaving her little time to be at the Tratnor house or to worry about it when she was. She knew she had more to prove than most of the newspaper staff simply because she was related to Reid. She also knew she had much to learn, and she went to work with that attitude, determined to be patient no matter what the job at hand.

The *National Witness* had gained standing year by year and was now housed in a marble-fronted building and had an impressive list of subscribers, but Reid was never complacent. He paid reporters in various cities and regions as well as buying the work of independent journalists. The paper's telegraph bill ran to a small fortune each month. And one did whatever job was assigned, even to setting type. Lexy liked the old tradition, taking the type from the wooden cases that were divided into boxes, one for each character, and placing it in galleys, or brass frames, and then making the galleys up on the stones, as the flat tables were called. It was tedious work, and more experienced hands were far quicker than hers, despite her experience with her little press at Wild Swan, but she enjoyed the direct connection with building a newspaper.

Mr. Watts, who was in charge of all the presses, new and old, noticed her willingness and her enthusiasm and was the first to unbend a little from the aloof wariness with which most of the employees treated her.

"Appears you may have more 'n a smudge of ink in your veins," Mr. Watts told her, and Lexy took it as the highest compliment.

Her case was not helped by the fact that Reid had hired two women previously, both of whom had quit to be married after working at the paper just long enough to take up valuable training time. Lexy was continually aware that she had to do no less than her best on every assignment, no matter what it was.

When General Grant died at Mount McGregor, New York, Lexy was able to add background information she had gleaned from time spent at the Saratoga Springs races because Grant's home was close by and had seen a steady stream of visitors in past years, including everyone from other ex-soldiers and statesmen to Samuel Clemens, who wrote under the name of Mark Twain. Whatever mistakes Grant had made in his presidential years, the country remembered him for his leadership during the war years and paid tribute.

But aside from this upheaval, Lexy's routine consisted of a seemingly endless round of social reporting—who was received at the White House by President Cleveland, who had wed or was planning to wed, what entertainments would be forthcoming when the weather cooled in the autumn, what was worn by whom to this or that function.

The trailing scarves, handkerchiefs, and draperies that looked like medieval banners had been dubbed "Moyen Age" by *Harper's Bazaar,* and Lexy dutifully wrote detailed descriptions of various manifestations of this and other fashions, all the while conscious that she didn't give a fig about such drivel. But she reminded herself that if she could do this well, when she had so little interest in it, then when more compelling stories came her way, she would be that much more capable.

Part of the newspaper's strength was that it dealt with the trivial as well as the important, guaranteeing a broad readership. But that did not stop some of the reporters who considered themselves above such work from teasing Lexy.

In one sense, the teasing indicated a more relaxed attitude toward her presence on the staff, but Robert Jenkins, one of the newsmen, pressed the point too often for Lexy's temper to hold.

"What color is the most popular this week?" he asked with mock seriousness. "It's important for the nation to know."

Lexy studied him for a moment and then said, "I'm not sure what everyone else is going to be wearing, but you would look too lovely for words in a deep pink. It would bring out the roses in your cheeks and make your eyes sparkle."

Jenkins was a smooth-faced young man and as much of a dandy as his salary would afford, unlike most reporters who seemed to take a perverse pride in looking scruffy, as if to show how hard they worked and how worldly wise they were. Jenkins also fancied himself a ladies' man, and though he was fairly discreet because of fear of earning his boss's disapproval, he was not above winking at Lexy and employing other flirtatious affectations which he obviously thought made him very attractive.

At the moment, he wasn't the least bit attractive. His cheeks were flushed beet red, far beyond the roses Lexy had suggested, and the amusement of their co-workers was audible. His expression was thunderous, and Lexy regretted having taunted him, thinking that she really didn't need an enemy here.

His next action took her completely by surprise. He shook his head ruefully, saying, "My sister Edith would say I deserved that. She doesn't let me get away with teasing her, either."

It was a shock, albeit a pleasant one, to discover that her erstwhile tormentor had this human side and was connected to other people, including a sister named Edith. And because of Rob's willingness to accept blame for the exchange, what could have degenerated into an ugly scene became instead the beginning of friendship.

Once past Rob's posturing, Lexy found an amiable, quick-witted young man. She wished she could tell him that he was much more appealing without the facade of the dandy, but as they grew to know each other better, she didn't dare to do that. She realized that his confidence in himself as a man was very fragile, probably because he looked so much more like a choirboy than a romantic hero.

They shared meals when they could and never ran out of topics to discuss. Rob nearly worshipped Reid and shared many of his convictions.

"There might be some jealousy about your having a job on the *Witness*, but anyone who knows Mr. Tratnor knows that he would never hire anyone, relative or not, if he didn't consider that person a good writer and good for the paper," Rob told her one day shortly after their truce had been made, and his words went a long way toward boosting her confidence in her own abilities.

Lexy was fascinated by Rob's grasp of political situations; the complexities and repercussions of various pieces of legislation never seemed complicated to him.

When Lexy applauded President Cleveland's orders for the removal of illegal fences put up by white settlers on Indian lands in Oklahoma, Rob took the darker view.

"He warned the settlers to stay off the lands earlier this year. It's spitting into the wind. Short of shooting the settlers, there isn't anything to do about keeping them off Indian territory if they want to be there. It's exactly as Mr. Tratnor says. This country decided a long time ago that Indians have no rights beyond what white men grant them for the moment."

Reid had never ceased to plead the cause of a just settlement with the Indians, but the massacre of Custer and his men at the Little Big Horn had proved as disastrous as the family had feared; the country had been roused to furious demand that Indians, all Indians, be punished and at least contained on reservations, if not killed outright wherever they could be found. The slaughter of the buffalo in such vast numbers had had the deliberate sanction of the government and had proved a valuable tool in bringing the Plains Indians to heel by starvation. And in the Northwest, Chief Joseph of the Nez Percé had gone to war with the United States in 1877. For four months, he had, with only three hundred warriors and despite the handicap of traveling more than a thousand miles with women, children, and old people, opposed and eluded five thousand soldiers. He had done it so effectively that the newspapers had begun to call him "General Joseph," and the public had been forced to grant him grudging admiration. But in October of that year, he had had to surrender within thirty miles of the Canadian border, within thirty miles of freedom for his people.

Reid had printed Chief Joseph's words of surrender on the front page of the *Witness:*

> . . . *It is cold, and we have no blankets. The little children are freezing to death. My people, some of them, have run away to the hills, and have no blankets, no food; no one knows where they are—perhaps freezing to death. I want to have time to look for my children and see how many of them I can find. Maybe I shall find them among the dead. Hear me, my chiefs! I am tired; my heart is sick and sad. From where the sun now stands, I will fight no more forever.* . . .

Some months later, the chief had been allowed to visit Washington City to plead for better treatment for his tribe, who were being held in terrible conditions at Fort Leavenworth, Kansas. Reid had again given the chief's eloquence full exposure. Chief Joseph had protested the fact that none of the promises made to him and his people had been kept:

> *Words do not pay for my dead people. They do not pay for my country, now overrun with white men.* . . . *Good words will not give my people good health and stop them from dying. Good words will not get my people a home where they can live in peace and take care of themselves.* . . . *You might as well expect the rivers to run backward as that any man who was born a free man should be contented when penned up and denied liberty to go as he pleases.* . . . *I have asked some of the great white chiefs where they get their authority to say to the Indian that he shall stay in one place, while he sees white men going where they please. They cannot tell me.*

> *Let me be a free man—free to travel, free to stop, free to work, free to trade where I choose, free to choose my own teachers, free to follow the religion of my fathers, free to think and talk and act for myself— and I will obey every law, or submit to the penalty.*

Rob could quote Chief Joseph with startling accuracy, and in spite of his youthful appearance, he had a deep voice that gave the words their full power when he recited the passage beginning, "Let me be a free man."

"It seems to me that nothing Thomas Paine or Thomas Jefferson or any of the other men who founded this country said makes a better plea for dignity and freedom than Chief Joseph did," Rob said, "and yet it availed him nothing. It will be the same in Oklahoma. If whites want the land, they'll take it. Even the Apaches, as fierce as they are, cannot hold against our greater numbers."

Pockets of resistance in the Southwest were the last show of defiance from Indians in the United States, though there were small vestiges of resistant peoples, such as some Seminoles hidden in the swamps of Florida and other tribes in isolated regions. An overwhelming majority of the people of the various Indian nations now lived only where the white men allowed them to live. The Indians' defeat had been so thoroughly accomplished that they were now appearing as romantic subjects in paintings, a sure sign that the stinger had been removed.

Lexy and Rob went to an exhibit of such work and left in mutual disgust.

Lexy soaked up everything Rob had to teach her about the political intrigues of Washington, and though she judged it a small gift in return, she did have something to offer.

Rob, completely ignorant of the finer points of horse racing, was nonetheless captivated by the sport. And he viewed Lexy's mastery of it as close to alchemy.

Lexy had not considered that her upbringing in the world of horse racing would benefit her career, but Reid never wasted the expertise possessed by his staff, and he saw no problem in sending Lexy to cover the Baltimore and Washington meetings in October. Rob went with her when he could, and he absorbed her knowledge of this as she had his regarding politics.

The first day of the Pimlico meeting was Wednesday, October 14, and though the weather was fair, the track was heavy.

"It means the spectators can wear their finery without fear of getting rained on, but the horses have to watch their footing. The times won't be as fast," Lexy told Rob. "Wild Swan has an entry in the Dixie Stakes for three-year-olds, and my father has a good horse up for the Great Pimlico Handicap Steeplechase. The three-year-old is out of a mare of the Swan line and by Moonraker, so he's got a good chance. And Father's horse has speed as well as strength for jumping."

Rob was dazzled by the day because both entries won. It made no difference in his admiration that Wild Swan's horses didn't do quite as well for the rest of the meeting; his initial experience had been magic.

Travis and Gincie liked Lexy's companion and treated him cordially, but they had no illusions about any romantic interest in that quarter; they could see that the two were as casually at ease with each other as Lexy was with her brothers.

Travis teased Lexy for writing about the races and the horses entered with such objectivity that it would have been difficult for any reader to know how closely connected she was to the sport, but he was very proud of her.

Reid was well pleased, too. Lexy managed the various ingredients of the race meetings—the social conventions, the owners, jockeys, and horses—with lively skill. He thought it would be a good investment to send her to some of the major meetings in the new year.

Reid's plans for Lexy were far more calculated than she realized. Everything Lexy was doing, from covering social functions to attending the races, was not only adding to her self-confidence and her ability to write well about a subject even if it did not interest her deeply, but was also allowing her to establish connections to the most powerful political and social figures. Those people were learning that Lexy Culhane was a patient listener and a fair observer; they were beginning to trust her and to speak freely in her presence. Those connections would stand her in good stead for important stories in the years to come. Meantime, Reid made no point of the process, not wanting her to become self-conscious.

Oblivious of Reid's calculations, Lexy continued to learn day by day. Sometimes she doubted the treatment she had given this story or that and wished she could have written it better. Often she chaffed at the frothy nature of some of the subjects she was assigned. And only rarely did she have the sense of euphoria that came from knowing she had done a piece exactly right, the words flowing as if they had a life of their own. But never did she doubt that she had chosen the right profession, or perhaps it had chosen her. It wasn't difficult to believe that it had been born with her as much as the color of her eyes.

It did not matter how it had come to be. It was deep in her blood and bones, a reason for being. It was enough.

Chapter 26

Lexy had had little time off from work since beginning her job and had not wished for it, but she was happy to spend Christmas week at Wild Swan, especially because her brothers were home. And though she didn't want to dwell on it, she was also glad to be on her own ground rather than Jilly's. She thought of the Tratnor household as Jilly's territory because her cousin was a constant annoyance to her there, having grown so openly sullen in Lexy's presence that Larissa had noticed enough, without knowing the cause, to tell her daughter to stop sulking. That had not endeared Lexy to Jilly. At least at Wild Swan, Jilly would be there only for Christmas and New Year's Eve, and in any case, she was not likely to misbehave while Lexy was flanked by her brothers.

Though it was good, as always, to have the family gathered, there was a deep sadness underlying the festivities this year. Flora was dying. Denial was not possible. She had become so frail, every fine bone showed, and the great vitality she had once possessed was gone, her old spirit showing only in brief flashes. What had begun as a small lump in her breast was spreading to consume her.

Anthea made no claim to scientific detachment in the case of her aunt. Flora meant so much to her, she hated thinking of the time when she would be without her counsel.

"For vanity's sake, she would not even consider surgery while there was still a chance," she raged when Lexy asked her for details.

"Would the surgery have cured her?" Lexy asked.

"It would have given her a chance," Anthea answered, and then looking into Lexy's clear green eyes, she felt obliged to add, "Just that, a chance, and not a very good one. Most certainly a little more time, but also the pain of mutilation and recovery and almost always eventual recurrence, almost always death." She drew a deep breath to steady her voice. "It is her choice, and in my heart, I cannot condemn it. Medicine does not have enough to offer. She is living her last days with grace, and I will make sure she has enough opiate to die with dignity at any time she chooses."

Accepting not only what Anthea said, but also the fact that she judged her mature enough to confide in her, was a rite of passage. In that instant, Lexy felt as if she had left the last of her childhood behind and had been admitted to the ranks of the women of the family.

"My poor father, it is nearly unbearable for him to watch his twin die," Anthea added softly. "And for Marsh, the pain is no less. I think Flora has the easier task, though she is the one dying."

Lexy watched the two men, her heart going out to both of them. Never before had she appreciated just how courtly Marsh Whitcomb was. He was unfalteringly polite to everyone and attentive to Flora without smothering her. He was careful not to limit Blaine's access to her, always finding some excuse to step aside when Blaine was near. But he left no doubt that only death would separate him from Flora.

For Christmas, he gave her a diamond broach, an exquisitely crafted piece made to last for years and years, a defiant declaration of the endurance of his love, no matter what threatened.

Flora had tried to send him away as soon as she had known about her illness; she had tried to pretend that the affair had paled for her. But Marsh had not believed that for a moment. From the beginning, their love had been physical as well as emotional; he had discovered the lump in her breast almost as soon as she had.

"I am the one who has not wanted to marry; now you are the one who should go free," she had insisted during the long night when they had faced her dying and wept and talked as nakedly as either had ever talked to another human being.

"I would marry you now if you would agree," he told her. "The years are running out for both of us. I have no intention of relinquishing any of the time I might have with you." He did not doubt his ability to stay with her until the end; he doubted only that he would be able to let her go when it was time. He could feel himself pulling her back, urging her to live just a little longer, and he knew that must end soon.

It took a great deal of energy for Flora to be with all of the family, but she would not have missed it. Alex had always made Christmas a special time. And Flora felt very close to Alex now, could feel her presence, could see her in Morgan and even more in Gincie and Lexy, who were so much a part of her tradition.

Flora had come to say good-bye in her own way. She was slipping away day by day, and she wanted a clear picture of these people she loved so much to be in her mind when she had gone too far to come back.

Everyone tried to behave as if nothing were different, and yet they were all conscious that this was the last Christmas they would spend with Flora. It made the holiday more poignant, so that laughter, tears, and gestures of affection were even more easily exchanged than usual.

"Isn't it strange? Any one of us could die tomorrow from any number of causes, but because we know Flora is dying, life is suddenly infinitely precious," Gincie whispered to Travis as they lay in bed in the early hours of Christmas morning. "It ought to be precious always, without the reminder."

"It is, darlin', it is. Everythin' we do, from raisin' children to raisin' horses, says that we know life is precious. But we've got to believe more in life than in death to go on."

Gincie turned her head to kiss the warm flesh of his shoulder and felt the beat of his heart against her. His hand stroked her body gently, and she was comforted.

The Kingstons and Falconers now had two other doctors to help share the patient load at their clinic, and up to the last moment, Nigel and Sally had planned to be at Wild Swan for Christmas, but then one of Nigel's patients had shown signs of going into early labor, and since the woman had had difficulty with her previous delivery and trusted Nigel as her physician, he and Sally had remained in the city. But they managed to come for New Year's Eve, with the report that the woman and her new baby were doing fine.

"She is the loveliest child!" Sally said. "Though she was early, she's got a full head of dark hair, and she wasn't at all wrinkled. And her father stayed with her mother the whole time, so she was welcomed by both of her parents. She's a lucky little girl."

"And so would any child be who was born to Nigel and Sally," Joseph murmured to Lexy. Joseph remained very fond of Sally, who had taken such good care of him when he was young, and he knew it was hard for her to see newborns in other women's arms. And yet, she insisted on going with Nigel when she could help, and she never expressed any resentment of the women more fortunate than she. Joseph understood that for Anthea and Max, he was enough, though he was not their natural son. They were both consumed by the needs of their patients. And he did not think that Nigel needed a child as much as Sally did, because he, too, had an extended family through the people he treated. But for Sally, it was different. She desperately wanted to have a child of her own flesh.

"Maybe they will still have a healthy child," Lexy said. "Sally isn't thirty yet; there is time. But it must be awful for her to remember the two who were born dead." A shiver ran down her spine at the idea of carrying a dead baby inside one's body; it seemed the worst perversion of the womb.

No one was more conscious of Sally's burden than Anthea. She doubted that Sally had ever confided in Nigel about the guilt she felt. Despite Anthea's assurances that one thing had nothing to do with the other, Sally continued to believe that the pregnancy and abortion she had suffered at thirteen were responsible for her inability to bear a living child. And she took full blame, refusing to see herself as the victim. For Anthea, it was endlessly frustrating to witness Nature's savage caprice in granting one child after another to those who did not want them or could not feed them while withholding the gift from those who would treasure a child beyond all else.

Given the cynical turn of her thoughts, it did not particularly surprise Anthea when the baby was abandoned on the clinic's doorstep. The misspelled note simply confirmed her immediate suspicion:

Yu don hep me, so now yu got baby.
Ruby

The woman had come to her after the baby had quickened, and Anthea had refused to interfere in the pregnancy. Ruby already had three other children, each by a different man. Her "protectors" never lasted long enough to give her any real security, but that didn't deter her. Though she was beginning to show the effects of the years, she continued to believe a rich man would surely come along to support her.

Anthea would not have objected to anything Ruby wanted to do with her life if only the woman had made an effort not to conceive or at least had she cared for the children once she had them. But Ruby seemed incapable of connecting cause with effect, refusing to use any of the means Anthea prescribed to prevent conception. And if she wasn't overtly cruel to her offspring, neither was she attentive, letting them run wild and forage for themselves most of the time, depending on them to supplement her uncertain income by petty thievery. She had lost two children to fevers, but three had survived and now this one.

It was a boy, so thin and weak he could scarcely cry. He was feverish and crusted with his own vomit and excrement. Anthea doubted he would survive, but she set to work at once to at least make him more comfortable.

Sally found her when she was just beginning to bathe the child.

"Mrs. Rudrick is here to see . . ." Sally's voice trailed off as she saw what Anthea was doing. "Oh, the poor little thing! Whatever is his mother thinking of to let him get in such a state!"

"His mother left him here because she doesn't want him," Anthea said, keeping her tone quiet to avoid upsetting the baby, though she felt like shrieking in rage.

"Let me do that," Sally said, and there was so much tenderness in her eyes, Anthea had to look away. "I'd appreciate your help, but he's in awfully bad shape," she warned, suddenly afraid of Sally's fierce concentration on the child.

Sally hardly heard her. The baby drew her like a magnet. She barely noticed that he smelled vile or that his skin was a sickly yellow gray. His faint mewling cries went straight to her heart.

She washed him, wrapped him warmly, and coaxed him to take milk a drop at a time, crooning to him all the while. Anthea's warning was there in her mind, but she kept thrusting it away. She concentrated all her energy on the baby as if she could make him survive by the sheer force of her will.

Despite the kindness of his own heart, Nigel was as disturbed as Anthea when he returned from a sick call and discovered what was going on. The child was so ill and fragile, he dreaded what would happen when it died in Sally's arms.

"I know what you're thinking," she said suddenly. "You're thinking, 'Poor Sally, she's so delicate, she'll fall to pieces if the baby dies.' Well, it isn't true. I carried our own children all those months, only to deliver them dead into this world. I'll always mourn them. But I'm still here, and I'm not insane. And if I'm strong enough to live through that, then I'm strong enough to try to persuade this little one to live, or at the very least, to make sure his last knowledge is of kindness."

Under other circumstances, she might have laughed; Nigel looked so startled at her outburst. But then she considered that it was surely her fault as much as his that he reacted so. He had been protective of her from the beginning, growing more so with the loss of their babies, and she had allowed herself to lean on him, perhaps more than she should have.

"It's really 'poor Nigel,' isn't it?" she said softly. "I've let you take responsibility for so much, even for myself. But I'm strong enough to do this, I promise you I am, whatever happens."

She was as good as her word, steadfast in her care of the child even when it seemed that the feeble life was ebbing away. She lavished love and care on him as if he were the most beautiful child ever born. And after the first week, if he was not beautiful, he was not as homely as he had been. The cow's milk seemed to agree with him enough so that Sally gave up the idea of finding a wet nurse for fear the change in diet would not suit him as well. He was putting on weight, and his skin was turning a healthier hue. Even his cries were louder.

Sally named him Sebastian, explaining to Nigel that she wanted him to have a name of distinction, and Nigel, no less than Sally, thought of the name as Sebastian Falconer and liked the sound of it.

Nigel had meant to stay detached so that he could comfort Sally should the infant die, but it was no use. Within a few days, he was as enraptured as she; within a month, he felt as if Sebastian had always been their son.

Anthea didn't dare speak to Sally about Sebastian's parentage, but she felt obliged to talk to Nigel. "You do realize that Ruby is at best an inept prostitute, and she probably isn't even sure who fathered the child . . . Sebastian."

Nigel controlled the flash of anger that swept through him; he knew Anthea was speaking out of concern for them. "I don't care who his parents are," he met Anthea's gaze directly, "any more than I care about Sally's parentage. She had a hideous beginning, yet she is everything I could ever hope to find in a woman. I expect with love and care, Sebastian will grow into a fine man."

To his surprise, Anthea beamed at him. "Good. I just wanted to be sure you had thought it through; I should have trusted that you would. The next thing for you to do is to go to my father and make sure you have the legal right to Sebastian. I wouldn't trust Ruby to leave him with you if she thought he was giving you joy. She dumped him on the doorstep to punish me, not to benefit anyone."

Nigel did just as Anthea suggested, and Blaine, for the sake of the child, spared no particle of the formality of the law, making sure that Ruby understood how dire the consequences would be if she dared to consider trying to regain custody of her baby. Whatever fleeting impulse Ruby might have had to make a profit from her child was stifled by the stern authority Blaine exerted.

Sebastian Falconer had been welcomed by every member of the family by the time the redbud was showing in the woods of Wild Swan. Flora seemed to take particular pleasure in seeing the child with Nigel and Sally, as if it completed some picture in her mind, and Sally took Sebastian with her and visited Flora often, though she never stayed long for fear of wearying Flora. Death was very close now, and Sally treasured the defiance of it that tiny Sebastian represented.

One way or another, all the women of the family paid their tributes to Flora for the unending battle she had waged for most of her life to give women a better chance of equality through education. She was special to them, honored, and beloved.

Then she was gone. No one asked, but Marsh Whitcomb knew that Flora had at last taken enough of the drug Anthea had left always in her reach to sleep forever. Marsh knew because he had held her in his arms as she drifted out of his reach.

"What a lovely, unexpected gift you have been to me," Flora said before she closed her eyes.

Marsh was glad she would suffer no longer, but he dreaded the days without her more than he had ever dreaded anything before.

"It should go without saying, but I hope you won't disappear from the family now," Gincie said, approaching him after the funeral. One by one other members of the family made sure he knew how welcome he would always be.

It meant a lot to Marsh, but he knew that for his own sanity, he could not stay that closely connected to them, not without Flora. She had named him executor of her will and wanted him to help Philly with the administration of the school and various charitable projects she had established over the years. He had promised he would do as she wished, and he meant to keep his promise, but more than that he could not bear. And he knew he would not have to explain to Flora's family.

Anthea and Larissa were most concerned about their father; he looked so sad and lost. But their mother scarcely let him out of her sight, and they accepted the fact that as much as Blaine loved them, no one was dearer to his heart than Philly. She would ease his mourning as no one else could.

Lexy returned to Washington immediately after the funeral. She was discovering the odd truth of a journalist's existence—no matter what was happening in her personal life, there was a part of her that went on observing, recording, discarding, always considering which subjects might work for the paper, which not. In one sense it was eerie to have the rather cold-eyed observer inside, always there watching, no matter what the passion of the moment, and yet, it was comforting, too, a discipline that gave continuing order to her life.

One of Reid's main campaigns at the moment was to make people see the injustice of the growing resentment toward the Chinese in the Far West. In Washington Territory, there had been several ugly incidents wherein the "Celestials" had been attacked and driven out of their lodgings with no provocation. And there were stirrings of the same malaise in California where a large number of Chinese had settled, first during the Gold Rush and then during the building of the transcontinental railroad.

The harsh truth was that the Chinese had been useful when they had taken low-paid, menial jobs at a time when workers were in short supply and white men did not want or need such jobs. But now, with the influx of more white men and with the ups and downs of the economy and the periodic shortages of employment, the Chinese were being blamed for taking jobs from the whites. It did not help their cause that they were still willing to work hard for low wages and kept so much to themselves and their own way of life.

Reid wrote eloquent columns pointing out the larger issue, that no one was safe under the laws of the United States unless all were safe, no matter what the country of origin. And in this instance, the paper was firmly aligned with the White House. President Cleveland had issued a proclamation ordering that domestic violence in the Washington Territory stop or he would use military force to end it. By his proclamation, he was declaring the life and property of the Chinese as worthy of protection as any other.

"What do you think of this?" Reid asked Lexy one day, handing her a newspaper folded to yet another article about the Chinese problem.

She read the lines with growing puzzlement:

In face of demagogic bluster and of bitter sectional sentiment, the president's declaration stands alone, the protest of a just man against injustice, of an honorable man against dishonor, of a humane man against inhumanity, in the name of the nation whose reproach is his. Whatever the action of Congress in this matter, the attitude of the Chief Executive is unmistakable.

There can be no diversity of opinion among honorable and intelligent men in regard to the moral aspect of this question. It must not be forgotten that the Chinese were not only tolerated, but welcomed in the Far West thirty years ago. While cheap labor was necessary to the existence of the incipient industries undertaken then upon the Pacific Slope, no protest was heard from any quarter against the foreigners who supplied it. It is only when manufactures have become sufficiently profitable to pay higher wages to white men that the cry of unfair competition is heard. . . . We are under the most solemn obligation to protect them so long as their residences under the jurisdiction of our government establishes their right to protection. . . .

"It is exactly what you've said, but the writing style is just a bit different," she said as she unfolded the paper to discover that it was a copy of the San Francisco *Examiner* and that the article bore the name of the contributor, H. Mackenna.

Lexy hadn't long to wait for further details; Reid's enthusiasm was obvious as he explained. "I've been following his writing for some time. He's very good. I wrote to him some weeks ago, asking if he would consider contributing to the *Witness*, or better yet, coming to work for me here. It's not that I don't want competent reporters in the Far West, but I think his Western views applied to the Eastern Seaboard would make interesting reading. He hasn't consented to the move yet, but he will be sending articles to me. We'll see how it goes, but I have a hunch Mr. Mackenna will be on the staff of the *Witness* before too long."

Lexy greeted Reid's excitement with mixed emotions. H. Mackenna was obviously a man who dealt with serious subjects, and she couldn't help but think that if he joined the paper, he would automatically be given assignments that she, Rob, and others coveted. However, in fairness, she had to confess to herself that he was, as Reid had said, very good. The first article of his she'd read had not been a fluke. The pieces he did for the *Witness* in the following weeks were no less skilled. Most of them came across the country by rail, but when there was a particularly interesting and timely situation developing on the West Coast, Mackenna used the telegraph. For the sake of the paper, she could do no less than welcome the addition of Mackenna's columns, but she harbored the hope that the Western news would prove so compelling that he would stay put.

She formed a vague picture of the man in her mind, putting him at about Reid's age, in his fifties, but despite the fact that Reid was tall and athletic, she imagined H. Mackenna to be rather seedy looking, as so many newspapermen were, their less than prepossessing exteriors hiding the inner extravagance of their imaginations and prose. She guessed his name to be "Henry," "Horace," or such, but it didn't concern her enough to cause her to ask Reid if he knew what it was.

There were other, more important matters to consider. As the spring wore on, labor unrest grew throughout the country, strikes involved thousands of workers on railroads and the like, and the agitation for an eight-hour workday grew ever more strident. A weak federation of trade unions had set the goal two years before to achieve an eight-hour day by May 1, 1886. That organization was, as of this year, the American Federation of Labor, and the target date was drawing near. Demonstrations were planned for the first of May, and there were already editorials about the "communistic" tendencies of the organized workers. But Reid and most of the staff of the *Witness* took a less extreme view, without losing sight of how precarious the situation was.

"Workers ought to be able to lead decent lives," Lexy insisted. "And eight hours of the hard, numbing work so many do is enough. Not even horses or mules do more than that on a well-run farm; surely human beings ought to be treated at least as sensibly as livestock."

"But it is certain the masters will not give the men anything," Rob pointed out. "If labor is to have an eight-hour day or any other benefit, it will have to be taken from the employers."

Reid, playing the devil's advocate, asked, "And how do they

take what they want? By refusing to work? But that isn't very effective, is it? The masters can always hire other men. So the workers who strike must keep those other men from taking their places. Do those ends justify those means? And while it might not cause much harm to refuse to make a pair of shoes in a certain factory, who can foretell the damage that could be caused if the rail lines of this country were shut down by strikers? What of foodstuffs that don't get to their destinations? People in the cities depend on food shipped in from the country. What of mail and the vital information carried therein? What of strikes that stop the heart of communication? What of medicines that don't reach their destinations? It is the workers' organizations in California that are most against the Chinese, that are most apt to attack them. Do the ends justify the means? What of public meetings that turn violent and destroy property and even lives? Can anything gained by such tactics justify the losses?"

Lexy and Rob felt very young in face of Reid's wider vision. He made them see the awful possibility of anarchy. It was frighteningly easy to imagine the cities where most manufactures, and thus workers, were located becoming wastelands of violence if thousands of workers took to the streets. And yet, it was equally undeniable that too many of the wealthiest men of industry thought of their employees as less important than the parts that ran the machines. If a vital gear broke down, it might be difficult to repair or replace; not so a worker. There were so many who needed work, it was an employer's market. Lexy's observation was savagely apt; most of the industrial giants treated their race and road horses a thousand times better than they did their workers. The *Witness*'s policy was to ask for humane and reasonable discourse on both sides.

The first of May passed with large labor demonstrations in many cities, but without the widespread violence that had been feared. And then on the fourth of May, at Haymarket Square in Chicago, Illinois, nearly two hundred policemen were sent in to break up a workers' meeting. A bomb was thrown into the police ranks, and all hell broke loose. In the panic, many shots were fired.

The figures kept changing on the telegraphic reports coming in to Reid, but it seemed that six or seven policemen were dead or dying, more than fifty others were wounded, two or three civilians were dead, and scores more injured. Most newspapers carried violently antilabor headlines: "The Anarchists Provoke a Terrible Slaughter," "Now It Is Blood!" and the like.

But Reid had an inside source for the story. H. Mackenna was heading east and had purposefully planned a stop in Chicago.

Chicago had been courting hysteria for weeks. In April the

Chicago *Tribune* had labeled the participants in one labor union parade as "Mostly Communists . . . Nearly all Foreigners." And by that time, twenty thousand workers locally had triumphed in their fight for an eight-hour day while sixty-two thousand more were deemed ready to strike for it.

On the third of May, an outdoor meeting near the McCormick Harvester Company plant had been the scene of police intervention. A strike was in progress at the factory, which was being operated with the aid of police guards. When the strikebreaking workers came out, the strikers attacked them, and the police moved in. One striker was killed, and several strikers and policemen were injured.

The Haymarket meeting had been called by the radicals as a result of this incident. Mackenna did not condone the strikers' actions on the third, but he maintained that the Haymarket gathering had been quiet and peaceful with a crowd of only three thousand at its height, though the sponsors had looked for twenty-five thousand. And many of the three thousand had gone home when it began to rain.

The catalyst for the violence had been Captain John ("Black Jack") Bonfield of the Chicago police. He was violently antilabor, and he had marched his men to the meeting. With that, the bomb had been thrown and pistol fire had come from both sides. Leading anarchists and socialists were being sought for indictment.

Mackenna's dispatches did not argue that the violence was forgivable, only that it was avoidable. He argued that the right to free assembly was a precious one and must be granted even to those whose ideas were unsettling or unpopular. He argued that if such assemblies were met with open hostility from police or military forces, then not only would there inevitably be bloodshed, but the violence might gain such force that it could stop the very machines the factory owners were so determined to keep running. He argued that masters and men must find a more reasonable bargaining method than dynamite and pistols.

Mackenna was a sorcerer with his pen. Not only describing events but also supplying human details—the stark terror in the faces of the crowd and even in the eyes of some of the policemen when the shooting started; the pull and sway of panic as people tried to flee the danger. He made the reader feel what it had been like to have been caught in the riot.

Lexy no longer had any reservations about the addition of such a journalist to the paper. He could only add to the interest and prestige of the *Witness,* and that was to everyone's benefit.

Lexy was not at the newspaper offices when H. Mackenna arrived. She was covering the last day of the Washington, D.C.,

Spring Meeting. Rob Jenkins managed to join her in time to cheer Calaveras, Travis's entry in the steeplechase, to victory. Wild Swan's entries in a variety of races had not produced outstanding results, but there were few stables that could offer steeplechasers as fine as Travis's.

Larissa had joined Gincie and Travis to watch the race, and not even the bad weather that had made the course heavy going and had splattered them all with rain could dampen their high spirits.

Gincie asked Lexy and Rob to join them in a celebratory meal, but they declined.

"I have to go back and write about today's events, with particular emphasis on the steeplechase, of course," Lexy explained, and Rob made his own excuses.

They walked into the newspaper offices just as H. Mackenna was preparing to leave, having finished discussing terms and assignments with Reid.

Lexy, who never gave much thought to her clothes beyond wanting them to be serviceable and comfortable for her working days, suddenly wished she were wearing something extravagantly fashionable or at least an outfit that wasn't mud-bedecked at the hem and rain-splattered all over. She, who normally had little trouble in meeting people, found herself so tongue-tied, she didn't know what response she had made to H. Mackenna's polite greeting.

The "H" didn't stand for "Henry" or "Horace" or anything else so tame. His name was Hawk. And all the other speculations she had made about him were wrong, too, completely wrong.

Chapter 27

Hawk Mackenna wasn't Reid's age; he was just thirty. And there was nothing seedy about him. He was a good four inches over six feet tall, an immense man with broad shoulders covered by a coat that must have been tailored for him. His hands were long-fingered, lean and competent looking; Lexy had the unsettling thought that his whole body was like that, big, but lean, built for strength, usefulness, and agility not always found in men as large as he.

At first glance, his face looked as tough as the rest of him, but there were odd elements that made the impression shift and change. His hair was coal black; his skin had a bronze cast. Straight black brows, a blade of nose, jutting crescent cheekbones, and a strong chin added to the certainty that war paint and a swift horse would suit him. Though his features were sharper than a full blood, if he didn't have a good portion of Indian blood in his veins, Lexy was willing to eat her rain-wilted hat. And yet, his eyes were not the expected darkness; the brown was shot through with tawny gold. And his mouth—in such a rugged face, it should have been harsh, but like the eyes, it was unexpected—even, full-lipped, sensuous.

A small, white scar showed on his right temple when the dark, silky hair fell away; Lexy curled her fingers into fists to resist the temptation to touch the mark, as if she could ease the pain that had happened long ago.

The blood rose hot in her cheeks as she realized she was making a fool of herself, gawking like a lovestruck schoolgirl. In compensation, her voice was much cooler than she intended when she said, "Your observations of the Haymarket riot were very good, clear and vivid."

Hawk thanked her politely, letting no emotion show. He was skilled at hiding what he felt. He didn't intend to feel anything at all about Lexy Culhane, cousin to Reid Tratnor. Her sort were always trouble, and he had had enough trouble with women, with one woman in particular, to last for a long while. Surely Miss Culhane was one of those women who, relying on the kind offices of friends or relatives, arranged to do useful work just long enough to pass the time until they chose a spouse and retired oh-so-gracefully from the daily demands of a job.

But as Hawk was making these unflattering judgments, he was also observing things that didn't fit the image. She was embarrassed to have stared at him so openly; the blush still colored her cheeks, and embarrassment had undoubtedly added the ice to her voice, making the compliment sound like an insult. Nonetheless, there was something very appealing about her. He was amused by her disheveled appearance, which she was trying without much success to right with a pull here and a pat there. His nostrils flared slightly; the sweet smell of woman was mixed with the very earthy odor of horse. He wondered if she'd been thrown, but Mr. Tratnor's question dispelled that notion.

"Well, how go the Culhane fortunes today?" Reid asked, trying to put Lexy at ease. He was interested in her reaction to his new employee; he had never seen her so disconcerted by a male. He was also a little apprehensive; he did not know Hawk Mackenna well yet, but he was sure the man was far too sophisticated for Lexy.

Reid's ploy worked. Lexy pulled herself together enough to give a concise account of the day's racing, showing her pride in the steeplechase win, but admitting honestly, "It might just be that it's early in the season, but Wild Swan's crop of two- and three-year-olds just doesn't seem to be in top form this year. It happens, you know; no matter how carefully the horses are bred and trained, that certain something that makes a winner just can't be predicted. Perhaps things will be better in Baltimore. Wild Swan has a good entry for the Preakness, but he'll be racing against the Bard, among others, and I'm not sure he's fast enough for that."

If Hawk had allowed his emotions to show, surprise would have been uppermost. He took a closer look at Miss Culhane. He'd already registered the fact that she was lovely; that hadn't been obscured by the damage done by bad weather. But now he noticed that in addition to being a vivid green, her eyes were alive with intelligence and enthusiasm.

The comparison flashed through his mind against his volition; Caroline's eyes had been bright with schemes, with pleasure when she received a compliment or a present, but never, that he recalled, with any particular intelligence. He wondered why that had never occurred to him until now. Caro had also been small and voluptuous; Lexy Culhane was tall and hardly curved at all, certainly no pocket Venus. And she talked about horses and races with the expertise usually reserved to racetrack touts. Undoubtedly under those long skirts she was as clean-boned and leggy as the Thoroughbreds she praised. He'd never bedded so tall a woman; he wondered what it would be like to have that length matching his more nearly than any had before, long legs tangling with his own.

The jolt of pure lust startled him, and he rejected it with a savage will; finding Caro was all that mattered because only through her could he end his quest.

Having found her voice and having spoken sensibly about the races, Lexy felt less nervous, but she was very conscious of how closely Hawk Mackenna was observing her. The shuttered look in his eyes reminded her of Joseph; he had the same way of taking things in while giving nothing away. The next logical assumption was that Hawk, like Joseph, was afraid of emotional involvement with other people, afraid of loss. Swiftly, she reminded herself that her previous assumptions about this man had been wrong.

She wrinkled her nose and brushed at her jacket. "I was so happy to see Papa's Calaveras win, I threw my arms around him— the horse, not Papa. Obviously, I made the wrong choice. Papa would have appreciated the hug more, and I wouldn't have come back here reeking of the stables." She laughed, and Hawk liked the sound.

"Calaveras for 'The Celebrated Jumping Frog of Calaveras County'?" he asked, his smile so sudden and charming that Lexy had to stop herself from repeating her performance of idiotic staring.

"But of course! It was too fitting to resist."

"I wonder what Mr. Twain would make of that?"

"Oh, he thinks it's a fine joke, particularly since Calaveras wins so often," Lexy said.

Her voice was so matter-of-fact Hawk knew she was not speaking so to impress him; the famous writer was personally known to her and her family.

Her family. Reid had mentioned that Lexy was a cousin, but only with the mention of Wild Swan had the pieces slipped into place, including the old scandal in California. It had happened long ago, while he was still a child and before he'd even seen San Francisco, but there had been vague, secretive mentions of it when the Culhanes had visited San Francisco some years ago. Travis Culhane was no stranger to the area, but Gincie Culhane had not been in the city since 1870. The newspapers had been lavish in their welcome of her. If he had covered the story, he might have met Lexy then, or perhaps during subsequent trips Lexy might have made to the state. It was odd to consider it; Lexy Culhane was definitely having a peculiar effect on him.

He made himself take his leave because to stand there any longer would be awkward. And Lexy made herself proceed to her desk without looking after him.

The spring races at Baltimore started three days later, so Lexy was out of the capital for most of the next week, covering the races. She hoped by the time she had to see much of Hawk again, she would be able to maintain a businesslike facade.

By sheer will she did manage to do so at the newspaper offices, assuring herself that the involuntary jump her pulse took every time she saw Hawk was no more than a matter of his huge size and overwhelming presence. She noted with satisfaction that everyone seemed to respond to him with deference, even those who normally treated everything and everyone with careful cynicism.

She greeted him pleasantly when their paths crossed and offered information about the amenities of Washington when he asked for it, but she kept her distance.

That was much more difficult when she arrived back at the Tratnor house one warm June evening to discover that Hawk had been invited to dine with them.

In the intimacy of the family setting, it was impossible to

maintain her reserve without being rude, and Hawk was a perfect guest, not effusive, but warmly appreciative of the setting, the food, and the company. It occurred to Lexy that he was being deliberately charming, that it was still impossible to tell what he was really thinking, but at the same time as she thought it, she admitted the injustice of such a judgment.

Observing his attitude toward her Tratnor cousins, she could see why he was so good at his job. Twenty-year-old Benjamin, with his enthusiasm for dry figures and anything at all to do with banking, eighteen-year-old Jilly, with her interest in music, and fifteen-year-old Joshua, with his pleas for stories about the Far West—without apparent effort, Hawk drew them into easy conversation, learning a great deal about them while giving away little of himself.

However, he paid a price for his charm. Though he had shown no more favoritism to Jilly than to her brothers, she was smitten and began to blush and flutter her eyelashes every time Hawk looked her way. Normally Jilly's voice was melodious, but it grew shrill, punctuated by affected giggles, as she vied for Hawk's attention.

Lexy was acutely embarrassed for her cousin, and she couldn't help but wonder if she had looked just as foolish when she had first met Hawk.

"Jilly, I hope you'll sing for us after supper," Lexy said, trying to divert her cousin's attention, trying to remind her that she had talents more worthy than fawning over the guest.

But Jilly dismissed Lexy with a cold glance and turned her talent into part of the game, ducking her head and gazing up at Hawk. "I will if you enjoy such entertainment, Mr. Mackenna, but I wouldn't want to bore you."

"Things well done are seldom boring," Larissa commented with asperity. "It is only when one performs out of one's depth that trouble comes."

Larissa's reprimand to her daughter for her behavior was too obvious to miss, and Jilly subsided into a pout, which made her look very young. Reid exchanged a look of exasperation with Larissa.

Lexy suspected that Hawk hadn't missed anything, including Jilly's attitude toward her, an attitude that had worsened with the news that Lexy was to accompany Larissa and Reid to a reception at the Executive Mansion, while Jilly was considered too young to go.

Lexy felt as if they were all sitting there unclothed as Hawk inspected them with his light-filled eyes.

"Hawk's a grand name!" Joshua said, unconcerned about Jilly's behavior, since he thought his sister was always silly. "Is that 'cuz you're an Indian?"

"Joshua!" Reid barked, but Hawk forestalled the rebuke.

"It's a fair question," he said. He couldn't be offended by the boy, who was showing only admiration, and now he was informed enough about the family to know that Boston Thaine, Larissa's great uncle, Lexy's great-great uncle, had married a half Cherokee woman. Joshua was not likely to ask such a question out of malice.

"I've got Indian blood on both sides. My grandmother on my father's side was part Cheyenne and married a Scotsman; my grandmother on my mother's side was a Cherokee who married a man named Hawkins. My mother wanted me to have a powerful Indian name; my father wasn't so obliging. 'Hawk' for 'Hawkins' was as close to that as he'd allow."

He recited the facts dispassionately as if the complications of his heritage had been easy, but they hadn't. His grandparents on both sides had seen the mixing of blood as a noble thing, as had his mother, from what he could remember of her; but his father had been both attracted and repelled by his own Indian heritage and by his son's. He had had the aquiline features that had sharpened Hawk's own, rather than the broader lines of pure Indian blood, and his coloring had been lighter than Hawk's, so that he had blended easily with the mixed blood of the Far West.

Not so Hawk. His Indian blood was undeniable, and his father had alternately accepted and rejected it, as he had his own. Hawk wasn't sure whether the memory was accurate or not, but he thought that things had been better before his mother had died when he was just short of his fifth birthday. In any case, he had the scars to prove that most of his life with his father had not been easy. He also had the education to prove that whatever his father had felt toward his son, he had done his best to equip him with the best weapons, especially education, for survival in a white man's world. Hawk had made himself believe that his father had loved him; even now, he needed to believe that.

Lexy saw it, a flash of something in his eyes. She knew she was not mistaken. For that instant, he had looked vulnerable, years younger, wholly different. Something to do with his background. It reminded her that she, too, was an observer, though Hawk had a way of narrowing her perceptions to include little else but him.

As if to redeem herself, Jilly consented to sing after all. Whatever Jilly's faults, her voice was marvelous, with a purity and strength that raised it far above mere competence. And Benjamin was an adequate accompanist on the piano. Though he lacked creativity, he played with the same precision he gave to his accounts and provided a background for the soaring voice.

In a way, Hawk pitied Jilly for her talent. She was gifted, and he wondered what would become of her. She belonged to a social class that frowned on the kind of public appearances necessary for a stage or musical career. As modern as Reid and Larissa were, Hawk could not imagine them sanctioning their daughter touring to entertain audiences in various halls. And yet, he could imagine that were Jilly confined to after-supper singing in her own home and the houses of friends, she could easily grow bitter and discontented over time.

Hawk's attention shifted to Lexy, and he was startled to realize that this was the first time he had seen her face in repose. She was usually animated by some idea, moving in a flurry of energy, but tonight she had allowed the music to soothe and enchant her.

The still perfection of her face reminded him of a cameo, a cameo Caroline had worn at the throat of her blouse, a creamy, high-necked blouse that had set off her dark beauty and had made her look so innocent. If only he had known that appearance and reality could be so disparate, except that perhaps his lust for Caro had been so strong it would have made no difference.

Past experience made him doubt his own perceptions, but he did not think Lexy's innocence was a sham. It shone from her in a way Caro's pose had never done. It made him feel protective toward her, understanding how difficult it must be for her to endure Jilly's dislike while living in her cousins' house.

He shoved the thought away. Lexy didn't need his protection, and he didn't need to feel this way. Such feelings in Hawk were reserved for only one person, no one else. It was just as well that Lexy was scheduled to spend most of the summer at the races.

Lexy felt exactly the same way. The last thing she wanted to do was to behave like Jilly over Hawk Mackenna. And beyond that, her work was very important to her; she could not afford to dissipate her energy by indulging in a schoolgirl crush.

On June 2, President Cleveland, who was forty-nine, had married Frances Folsom, the twenty-one-year-old daughter of his former law partner. It was a private ceremony, but at the completion of the service, church bells rang all over the city and a twenty-one gun salute echoed from the Navy Yard.

Lexy had written about it, a subject which had the attention of most of the country since a wedding in the White House was a special event. And she reported firsthand the June 10 reception that formally introduced Mrs. Cleveland to society, a huge gathering of the socially, politically, and officially powerful of the capital, among them the Tratnors, Lexy being included because of them. And despite having reported on so many social functions, she had to confess herself awed.

Satin, velvet, crepe, brocade, tulle, lace—the variety and shades of fabric went on and on, elaborate gowns being paraded by the carefully groomed ladies of Washington through the rooms of the White House, which was itself dressed in flowers. Roses, white and purple hydrangeas, ferns, amilax, and many more filled the rooms and the lighted conservatories.

Lexy was hard-pressed to pay as much attention to the gowns as to the flowers, but her attention was caught by the diplomats and their ladies in their gorgeous apparel and court dresses. They had been given a separate entrance by means of the South Portico and into the East Room, and very early that apartment was filled with excited babble in several languages.

Lexy dutifully did her best to make the descriptions vivid enough so that the newspaper's readers could feel as if they'd attended the reception, but by mid-June, she was at the races, a setting much more to her taste, and she celebrated her twenty-first birthday at Sheepshead Bay on Coney Island with her parents and her brothers, who came to honor the occasion.

Coney Island had long been a favorite summer retreat for the theatrical and political folk of New York City, and interest in the resort had broadened over the years to include just about anyone who could manage to get away from the heart of the city to enjoy the amusements and the ocean breezes. The increase in vacationers and special events in the world of horse racing had led to the formation in 1879 of the Coney Island Jockey Club. The following year the course at Sheepshead Bay had opened to immediate success.

It was in the spring of 1879 that Pierre Lorillard's horse, Parole, had won a string of victories in England, culminating in the Derby. It was the best a horse sent from the United States had ever done in England, and it sparked a patriotic interest in racing in America more fervent than had ever been seen before.

The problems of entering American horses in English events were formidable. First, the horses had to be chosen far ahead of the races, and since the big stakes were for two- and three-year-olds, that meant making very acute judgments about very young horses, without having one's whole stable to back up the entries in case any of the chosen broke down. Then there was the problem of transport. No matter how careful the handling, sea voyages were hard on them. They could not throw up, but they could be miserably seasick. And what might be easily worked out of a horse who was used only for riding or in harness could be debilitating for an animal whose sole purpose was to run like the wind. Finally, even if the horses arrived in top shape, they had to become accustomed to climate and turf conditions different from those at home. The tracks themselves were different. Most of them in America had prepared surfaces, most in

England were grass; most in America were ovals, most in England ran more on the straight; and most races in America were run counterclockwise, in England clockwise. It was a lot for a young horse to adjust to, but Parole had done it with great flare.

This year the course held special interest for Lexy because a turf course had been added to other attractions, and there was such a program to beautify the grounds that the track was fast becoming the most popular racing ground in America. It was already notable for having offered, two years previously, the first course of more than a mile in America when it had remodeled the racetrack to a mile and a furlong. That same year had seen the inauguration of the Suburban, a handicap sweepstakes that had immediately become the most talked about race in the country due to the quality of the competition. This year Troubadour, owned by Captain S. S. Brown of Pittsburg, had won it, and the large field had contained other fine horses, including Himalaya, Joe Cotton, Lizzie Dwyer, and Ban Fox. Troubadour's career as a two- and three-year-old had been erratic, but at four, he was coming into his own. The Suburban this year had seen the heaviest betting on record, and Troubadour had won at four to one. Wild Swan's entry had not placed, but the Culhanes' disappointment was mitigated by the fact that they had not expected to prevail against such a field this year. Also, they had had some unexpected success in other races at Sheepshead Bay, and that helped.

Much of the talk was about the Futurity, to be run in 1888. There was certainly no greater game of chance than this type of race, for foals were nominated by means of their dams being named in the year they were bred, the produce to race as two-year-olds. Fees were paid not only on the nomination of the mare, but also in subsequent installments up to the time of the race.

Wild Swan's entry, made the year before, had been a mare of the Swan line bred to Moonraker. The resulting colt, born this year, had been named Pharaoh, not only in reference to the "sport of kings," but also in sly allusion to the card game faro.

"If there's a bigger gamble than this," Travis had said, "I don't want to know what it is."

The other big news of the summer on Coney Island was the opening of the Brooklyn Jockey Club's track at Gravesend (named by early settlers for its English counterpart). Since the Coney Island Jockey Club held races on Tuesday, Thursday, and Saturday, the Brooklyn Jockey Club claimed Mondays, Wednesdays, and Fridays, thus marking the beginning of continuous racing, Sundays always being exempted.

There was a third track, at Brighton Beach, run by the Brighton

Beach Association. It had opened in 1879, but the betting there had been limited to auction pools only, and the track had been rather slow in attracting the best stables.

Though there were scores of other subjects that Lexy was determined to write about someday, she put her best efforts into reporting the activities of the racing world. She observed the details of everything, from who attended the races and what they wore to the condition of the horses. She had the advantage of her background, and that gave her access not only to the leading owners, but to the trainers, grooms, and jockeys as well, who were tolerant of Lexy's presence because they knew she was not only as capable as they, but was also willing to help with the doctoring of a horse or whatever task needed doing around the stables. Lexy Culhane did not give herself airs.

Lexy understood that for all their openness with her, there were racing strategies the horsemen would not discuss with her, but they weren't likely to discuss them with anyone else, either, and if the horse had had several races, the pattern of its running was evident and limited the way it could be raced. Figuring out those patterns enabled her to write convincingly of racing campaigns even if no inside clues had been given to her.

Most mornings, she was at the track by dawn to watch the horses being exercised. She carried a stopwatch and made careful notes of the horses' times in practice runs and of their individual strengths and weaknesses. Though it was work, she was the first to admit it was also pleasure. She loved the way the early light poured like liquid gold over the horses and riders, illuminating every detail and picking up the dust motes stirred by the animals. And she loved standing by the rail and feeling as much as hearing the thud of hooves as a racehorse swept past, often with a stablemate running with him so that both would feel the press of competition. She loved the chatter of stablehands blending with the sound of the morning birds. She loved the various personalities of the horses that made them so different from each other even when they came from the same bloodlines.

One morning she neglected her own work to help find a cat named Honey, so called because of her color. There were always cats around the barns, welcomed by the stablemen as a means of keeping down the rodents that feasted on the horses' grain. But Honey was no ordinary cat. She was companion to a three-year-old colt, Excalibur, and traveled to every racetrack with him.

Excalibur was not the best of his year, but he was a competent and willing runner who often finished in the money—as long as he could see Honey. Their bond had started when he was a wobbly foal

and she a kitten, and though the cat seemed to need time off from
her duties now and then, Excalibur was inconsolable when she left
him. He sulked, refusing to eat or run or do anything else asked of
him.

Excalibur was supposed to race that afternoon, but his handlers
knew he would have to be scratched from the program if Honey
wasn't found soon, and they forsook all pretense of dignity in their
anxiety to find the cat.

Lexy had a hard time not laughing at the spectacle of grown
men prowling, and in some cases crawling, about, coaxing, "Here
Honey, here kitty-kitty."

Lexy had the honor of finding the cat, who was crouched with
feline patience in a shadowy corner of a barn, staring at a mouse
hole. "Unfaithful friend," she chided as she picked the cat up and
stroked her under the chin. Aside from a little growl of protest,
Honey allowed Lexy to carry her back to the colt and seemed to take
the cries of relief that greeted her as no more than her due.

Excalibur's head came up, and he whickered to Honey, all signs
of dejection gone.

"He'll race good as gold now, thanks to you, Miss Culhane,"
the trainer said.

"More thanks to Honey," Lexy corrected. "We had a horse and
a hound who were companions like these two; I know how close the
bonds can be."

When she left the pair, Honey seemed pleased to be back on
duty, and that afternoon, Excalibur won his race while the trainer
held the cat in his arms along the rail. Lexy wrote a humorous piece
entitled "The Colt and the Cat," describing not only Excalibur and
Honey but other racehorses that had everything from roosters to
goats and donkeys as companions.

But Lexy did not confine her writing to specific animals or
races; she also wrote of the broader trends in the sport. Some
publications, such as the widely read *Breeder's Gazette* out of Chicago,
were becoming virulently anti-flat racing, not only citing abuses in
the sport, but also attacking the very premise, claiming that there
was something intrinsically wrong in raising horses simply to run. On
the other hand, they claimed that horses raised for harness racing
were useful because horses that pulled carriages and wagons were an
important part of everyday life. Thus, any improvement in the breed
was useful.

There were abuses in racing, and they were growing as the
numbers of races and racetracks grew. Lexy did not attempt to
present the sport as being without fault. Any business that involved
such enormous sums of money was bound to attract a certain number

of unsavory characters and practices. But she knew that the vast majority of the people involved were honest men interested in honest sport. She was in a good position to argue this case, with her knowledge of the animals and the men.

Some of the men were so colorful, they were automatically good material for journalists. Elias J. Baldwin, nicknamed "Lucky" Baldwin, though he hated the inference that his wealth was due to luck, was always worth a story. Now approaching sixty, he had a trail of scandals behind him. He had been married several times and had been accused of compromising various young women, to the point that lawsuits had resulted, and a cousin of one of the women had shot Baldwin, wounding him, though not seriously. His current wife was some forty years younger than he. Even the major New York papers considered him good copy. In fact, his reputation as a ladies' man often obscured his reputation as a turfman. His stable was superb, and he was one of the few who had regularly shipped horses from the West Coast to compete in the East.

Lucky Baldwin had a finger in just about every pie in the Far West, from hotels to mining to land speculation. He owned vast tracts of land in Southern California and was the region's strongest booster. And like most of the self-made millionaires of the Far West, his fortunes fluctuated wildly so that sometimes he could afford his lavish life and sometimes he hadn't enough to pay the workers on his Santa Anita ranch. But his horses were never less than the finest.

Mr. Baldwin always treated the Culhanes cordially, partly because they had spent time in California, but also because he respected the horses of Wild Swan. Lexy had met Mr. Baldwin on numerous occasions and found him entirely unexceptional, not at all the scandalous monster many thought him. She did not discount his eccentricities, or his craftiness, but she acknowledged what he'd accomplished, and when she wrote about him, she wrote about his racehorses, not his personal life. In turn, he remained willing to talk to her, though he often refused any comment to other members of the press. Lexy suspected that his wild legend came, at least in part, from his unwillingness to respond when journalists interrogated him.

The Dwyer brothers were also a force to be reckoned with and very much part of the new trend in racing; they had little interest in breeding better horses. They simply bought the best, offering such high prices that few refused to sell to them. No matter what the bloodlines, the Dwyers wanted to see what a horse could do before they acquired it, so their purchases often won under other owners' colors before the Dwyers purchased them.

The Dwyers had inherited a butcher shop in Brooklyn from their father. They had expanded it to a successful wholesale meat business. August Belmont, a customer who had become a friend, had sold them their first good horse, Rhadamanthus. And Rhadamanthus had been followed by a long list of winners running under the Dwyers' red and blue.

The Dwyers knew how to divide their talents to make the most of their stable. Philip did the buying, scarcely ever showing less than the best judgment, and Michael placed the stable's runners in the races and did the betting for the pair. It was a system of management which served them well.

Though Lexy was fascinated by the efficiency of the Dwyers' system, she was enough of a traditionalist to be slightly uneasy about it, too. She did not see how the demand for better horses could do anything except improve the breed, but it was still difficult for her to accept the separation between breeding and racing the horses. She was more comfortable with the ways of such men as August Belmont with his Nursery Stud in Babylon, Long Island, and Pierre Lorillard with his Rancocas Stud in Jobstown, New Jersey.

Pierre and his brother George had been formidable figures in the racing world since the early seventies. But unlike the Dwyers, theirs had not been such a close association, as they had rival stables. George had been more fortunate in his American racing than in his English attempts, but Pierre had long been a power not only in America, but also on the other side of the Atlantic with his entries into various English races, particularly with Parole's triumphs in 1879. His Rancocas Stud was equipped with every modern convenience to make life healthy and productive for the horses. He had been one of the first to see the advantage of the lighter weight of aluminum instead of steel shoes for horses, and since such were not being manufactured at the time, he had ordered a set from Tiffany's, a measure of how far he was willing to go for the sake of his horses.

To Lexy's mind, Pierre Lorillard was the perfect blend of the traditional and the new turfman, for he bred, raised, and took a close interest in his own horses, and yet, he was willing to buy an outside horse if he thought the animal merited it.

Mr. Lorillard had astonished the racing world this year by putting his Rancocas stable up for sale. The news was of special interest to horsemen of means because it meant they would have a chance to purchase the Lorillard champions. Part of the stable had already been sold, and the Dwyers had bought the top four offerings for a total of $67,500, a record amount at the time of the sale.

The breeding stock was scheduled for sale in October. There was already much speculation about who would buy the renowned Iroquois or Pizarro or the famous brood mares. Gincie and Travis had not been interested in the horses in training, but they hoped to purchase one of the mares at the October sale.

Some publications, including the *Breeder's Gazette*, claimed that Mr. Lorillard was fleeing the racing scene due to the terrible dishonesty of the betting at the tracks, with bookmakers, owners, trainers, and jockeys conspiring to decide most races before they were run. Far from being the truth, Lexy knew that Mr. Lorillard was retiring from racing in order to dedicate his time and fortune to other enterprises, including improvements and expansions planned for his shooting and fishing club, Tuxedo Park, set on seven thousand acres in Orange County, New York.

But Lexy did not think he would stay away from racing forever; he was just too good at the game. She also completely discounted rumors that his brother's death had anything to do with the dispersal of the stable; George Lorillard had died suddenly a week after the announcement of it, not the week before.

The repeated charges of fraud at the tracks were serious enough to have resulted in some new laws about betting in New York State. And, again, Lexy was not so naive as to insist that all races were honest. But the more she dug for the truth, the more evidence she discovered to uphold her own belief that the vast majority of turfmen were honest and that the chicanery was being practiced at less popular tracks with less prominent horsemen and particularly with less popular jockeys—for jockeys were surely the most important factor in determining whether a race was run honestly or not.

Before the war, when the sport had been so Southern, most jockeys had been slaves and had been allowed little glory. But now the top riders were becoming as recognized and as well applauded as their famous mounts. They earned large fees for granting "first call" to certain stables and collected handsome wages for selling "second call" as well. It was legal, and it was a measure of how much the skill of the rider was being credited. Lucky Baldwin had purchased first call on Isaac Murphy for eight thousand dollars, and second call had been sold to Ed Corrigan for two thousand, Corrigan having the right to have Murphy ride for him when none of Baldwin's horses were entered in a race.

Lexy loved to watch the best jockeys at their work—men like Murphy, one of the few black riders left now that the job was so lucrative, a superb rider who seemed to have an almost mystical connection with the horses he rode; or Snapper Garrison, another of the high-priced riders, a white man whose riding style was the opposite of Murphy's. "Snapper" was the nickname given to the man for his violent activities in urging, with whips, spurs, and a forward lunge in the saddle, that last burst of speed at the finish line. Lexy did not like his style, but she had to concede that he was able to get the best from even the laziest horses.

And she could not imagine Murphy, Garrison, or any of the other top riders, some of whom worked for Wild Swan, agreeing to fix races. If their own honesty wasn't enough, the risk of being banned from an important track was too great.

Her father agreed. "But remember," he cautioned, "horse tradin' has always had its bad side. You get down to too many men just carin' about winnin' races and not about the breed, you're bound to have some cheatin'. It's just one of the reasons we need a truly national jockey club to regulate the sport."

It was a plea Lexy added to her articles, a reasonable answer to those who would ban the sport altogether. All the various tracks had their own jockey clubs, and while a bad rider or trainer might be banned at one track, he could simply change to another because there was no overall authority to see that he was out of the game entirely. Prominent trainers and jockeys who raced at major tracks were too well known to shift around, but there were many less established men who could get away with it.

There were other functions a national jockey club could perform, such as setting racing dates so that tracks did not run in opposition to each other. Some courses worked out reciprocal dates, but many did not, running in conflict with each other and edging the sport toward excess.

The most difficult thing to write about was the most basic. People would gamble. No matter what preachments or proscriptions, they would find a way to lay a wager on a horse, on the turn of a card, on the outcome of a football or baseball game. And horse racing could not attract the huge crowds if betting were eradicated. To Lexy's mind, the most sensible response to the impulse was to oversee the gambling, not outlaw it. If the betting were kept honest, everyone benefited. There were already fees and percentages paid by the bookmakers that helped in the upkeep of tracks, and Lexy saw no reason they should not continue to be collected.

But against the course that seemed so rational to Lexy were arrayed the self-appointed guardians of virtue—many of them fanatics who harked back to an older, darker time when the Puritans of New England had established their colony not to enjoy the freedoms of a new land, but to perpetuate the rules of a life so strict and joyless, England had rejected it entirely. The spiritual heirs of the Puritans—those who would outlaw all gaming, forbid most other pleasures and amusements, censor books, and prevent all discussion of control of conception and other sexual matters, and were too often the same people who were absolutely ruthless in their business dealings, who gave no quarter to their workers—those were always part of the fabric of the country, sometimes quiescent, sometimes seemingly omnipresent. And they always seemed to consider themselves on intimate speaking terms with God.

It was, to Lexy, not only an extraordinarily inhumane philosophy, but also ludicrous. She wondered why it never seemed to occur to the believers that a God so cruel would be unappeasable by anyone, even by those who were supposedly chosen. But she did understand how such people could view the pleasure and the passion of horse racing and of wagering on the races as being equivalent to the doings at Sodom and Gomorrah. She did not think she could change their minds by anything she wrote, but she hoped that by reporting the liveliness, ceremony, and beauty of the races, she could help to persuade the wider audience not to be swayed by the fanatics.

With Reid's approval, she submitted an article to *Turf, Field and Farm*, and it was accepted. It was printed under the byline "Lexy," with no surname, typical for sports articles, as many of the writers used a single pen name only. She wasn't the first woman to have been published in the journal, but nonetheless, it was a thrill to see her work there and more so to have the editors express interest in further pieces from her.

Though she had been glad to escape the oppressive heat of Washington, having spent most of the summer at racecourses in the North, in September she found it good to be back in the capital, back in the newspaper offices. But it was not so pleasant to be residing in the Tratnor household once again.

She did not consult anyone; she did not want to be dissuaded. She found rooms at a boardinghouse in Washington and moved out of the Tratnors' Georgetown house. She used the fact that she was now twenty-one and employed, and ought to be independent, as the excuse for the move, but the family wasn't fooled.

"I wish I could promise you that I could make my daughter behave," Larissa said sadly, "but I can't. I've seen how she treats you, and I thank you for being so gracious about it. But short of locking her in her room forever, I don't seem to possess the means to make her civil."

"She's accustomed to being the daughter of the house, and I'm just enough older than she so that she must feel she's being relegated to the role of younger sister by my presence," Lexy said, eager to offer an excuse because Larissa and Reid had been so generous in giving her a place to live. But inwardly she thought that if Jilly didn't find something useful to do soon, she was going to become so tangled in her own discontent, no one would be able to extricate her.

Jilly didn't want a job, and she didn't want to go to college. Worse, to Lexy's mind, she didn't seem to want to make anything of her musical talent. She sang willingly for small groups in private homes, but she seemed to have no ambition beyond that.

It was difficult for Lexy to understand Jilly's lack of ambition. To Lexy, the idea of being able to open one's mouth and produce perfect music seemed vastly more exceptional than her own talent for making one word follow another on a page. She herself possessed an adequate voice that would not shame her in the rendition of Christmas carols and the like; she could hit all the right notes, but her voice was soft, nothing like the soaring splendor of Jilly's.

Lexy expected Jilly to be openly triumphant about the move, but she wasn't. She evinced something closer to vague uneasiness mixed with guilt.

"You don't have to leave, you know," she said curtly, as Lexy packed the last of her things.

"I think I do," Lexy said quietly, not looking at her cousin, afraid that her temper might flare.

"You always get your way!" Jilly exclaimed in sudden fury.

"No," Lexy said, looking right at her. "I *make* my way. There is a difference. And once you understand what that difference is, you will certainly be happier than you are now." She took a deep, steadying breath before she added, "You are very talented, you know. You ought to think about doing something with your talent. Many, many people, and I'm one of them, would give a great deal to be able to make music as you do."

Prepared for a fight, Jilly was undone by the compliment. "You really believe that?" she asked.

"It isn't an act of faith; I've heard you sing. I know how good you are."

Jilly fled, leaving Lexy to stare after her, amazed at how uncertain her cousin was about a gift that was so obvious. It depressed her to know that no one was going to be able to convince Jilly of her worth until she was ready to accept the joy and burden of it herself.

Lexy had dreaded her parents' reaction to her move, but it was surprisingly mild.

"It's understandable that you want more independence," Gincie conceded, "and you are of age. But your father and I trust you will not hesitate to ask for help from us or from Larissa and Reid should you find yourself in difficulty."

Gincie saw no reason to confess to her daughter that she and Travis had gone through much to arrive at this calm point.

"I won't have it!" Travis had declared when he heard of the change. "She's too young and too beautiful to be on her own in

Washington. It's one thing for her to be under the Tratnors' roof; it's quite another for her to be at the mercy of every scalawag who haunts the capital!"

Gincie had found herself in the odd position of defending her daughter's move when she had been ready to condemn it just seconds before. "She's not planning to sleep on the streets! She's rented lodgings at a respectable boardinghouse. And Reid and Larissa will still see much of her. She hasn't complained, but you know as well as I that Jilly has made her life miserable. And Lexy has proved herself a responsible adult; it's only fair that we recognize that. We knew where she was this summer, but most of the time, she wasn't with us. If she can manage her life at the races without being turned from her work, she must be capable of living decently and safely in Washington."

"Why do I feel as if I've lost this battle without firin' one clean shot?" Travis asked ruefully.

"Because you're a reasonable man, and you must remember as clearly as I what I was doing at her age. I was already married to you and living behind enemy lines. And you were off most of the time standing a good chance of getting killed. The way Lexy is choosing to show her maturity and independence is vastly preferable to that and not nearly as dangerous."

Though Tay accepted Lexy's change of circumstances with his usual equanimity and with the knowledge that nothing he could say would make any difference anyway, Kace gave her more trouble than their parents had. He harrumphed and warned her about the slimy lounge lizards known to frequent Washington. He carried on until Lexy stopped his tirade with a peal of laughter.

"Honestly! When did you grow to be such an old curmudgeon?" she teased. "I'll have you remember you're my *younger* brother." She softened the rebuke by kissing him on the cheek. "I will be careful. You know I will. You're the one of the three of us who is most likely to get into trouble. Tay and I are witnesses to that!"

Kace continued to grumble, but it lacked force.

The strongest opposition to her new quarters came from a totally unexpected source, from Hawk Mackenna.

Chapter 28

The work she'd done during the summer and the new association with *Turf, Field, and Farm* had given Lexy extra confidence. And having decided to live on her own, she felt she was far more mature than she had been just a year before. As a consequence, she felt less ill at ease in Hawk's presence. She still found him a compelling man, but now when their paths crossed, she managed to treat him with the same offhand friendliness that characterized her relationships with the rest of the newspaper staff. And he seemed content to pursue the same course.

Therefore, she was stunned when he approached her one day and said without preamble, "I heard you've left the Tratnors' house. That's a damn fool thing to do, even if your cousin is an unpleasant piece of business. What in the hell is your family thinking of to allow you to move to a boardinghouse?"

For a moment, all Lexy could do was to stare up at him. He seemed even bigger than usual and certainly threatening, his features drawn in a ferocious scowl.

She started to defend herself and stopped abruptly, her own temper matching his. "What possible business is it of yours?" she demanded, clinging to her newly discovered sense of independence. "You are not my father, my brother, or my guardian, thank heavens!"

"Well, someone ought to be serving as your guardian!" he shouted, and then reluctantly, he let his anger go. He couldn't sustain it in face of hers. Her eyes were the brightest green he'd ever seen, and she reminded him of nothing so much as an infuriated cat, a beautiful cat to be sure, but still ready to spit and claw. They were standing outside the newspaper building, and passersby were regarding them with varying degrees of interest and amusement.

He cleared his throat, aware that he had crossed the barrier he had set between himself and Lexy Culhane. "I apologize. You're quite correct; it isn't my business, and you do have the right to live wherever you please. I am concerned only about your well-being, and I overstepped the bounds because of that."

His apology had the odd effect of making things less, not more, comfortable between them. His excuse sounded weak to his own ears. Being concerned about her well-being indicated a degree of intimacy they had been scrupulously avoiding; he knew that now, knew that she had set her own limits as he had.

To her amazement, Lexy saw Hawk's dark skin flush darker on his neck and cheeks. Inwardly, it pleased her, but she forbore mentioning it. It pleased her, too, now that she thought of it calmly, to know that he had spoken out of concern for her.

"Truly, it was time for me to leave my cousins' house, and not just because of Jilly. I've chosen a very respectable place, and Rob lives just a few doors down from me should there be any difficulties. It may not be exactly what my family wants, but they trust me to make the best of my new address. Don't you think you could do the same? I appreciate your concern, but it really isn't necessary." Her voice was gentle, the anger gone from her eyes.

Hawk felt that he had somehow lost the advantages of his superior age and experience in this exchange. He felt like a gawky boy. And he was not at all comforted by the idea of Rob Jenkins living in close proximity to Lexy. He had accepted the interest he had experienced at his first meeting with her, but he had vowed detachment. She was the boss's cousin; she was too young; after Caroline he didn't need anything more than casual involvement with women; and he still had a compelling personal mission of his own to pursue. All of those reasons were still valid, but now he knew that Lexy could blow his detachment to bits with little effort. It was a disconcerting lesson.

"I think it's a lucky thing I never had a sister," he said, trying to put what he was feeling on a less treacherous footing. "I would undoubtedly have been far too overbearing."

Lexy looked straight at him. "I already have two brothers, and love them though I do, two of them are plenty. Excuse me, but I must be going."

She left him staring after her, and the image of her smile—warm, but also touched with mischief—lingered. In the politest way, she had called his bluff. She knew very well that whatever his feelings were toward her, they were not fraternal.

Lexy was not surprised that Hawk seemed even more self-contained and distant than usual when next she saw him. He could not have said more clearly that he was interested in her had he announced it publicly. It gave her a peculiar feeling of power, but she knew it was double-edged; she was no less interested than he, though she wasn't yet sure of what she wanted or expected from him. She had always been able to treat young men as friends because, until Hawk, she had not met a man who engendered any feeling beyond that in her.

Hawk was different. She finally admitted to herself that when she looked at him, she did not envision a cordial, easy friendship. When she looked at Hawk, she wondered what it would feel like to have his hands touch her, what it would be like to be kissed by that sensual mouth.

She was impatient with herself. She wanted to be a journalist, had wanted to be that for as long as she could remember. She had no intention of being deflected from her course by a man. It was not that she didn't want a husband—she had grown up surrounded by too many good marriages to want to forgo such joy—but she did not want to be distracted by such considerations now. And thinking about it at all made her conscious of how differently she regarded Hawk compared to other men she knew.

She didn't know Hawk. Despite the little pieces of knowledge that were falling into place, the things she did not know about him far outweighed those pieces. He was only nine years older than she, but he was worlds older in experience. And though he was obviously well educated, whatever his background, and very controlled in most of his dealings with other people, there was an undercurrent of violence and danger. She was honest enough to admit to herself that that was part of what attracted her to Hawk; it also warned her away. If she were sensible, she would consider Hawk Mackenna treacherous ground best avoided.

That would have been more easily accomplished had they not worked together. Whatever personal currents she felt, Lexy had no doubt about her growing respect for him as a journalist. And while she did not denigrate the work she had done over the summer, she did not equate it with his.

Hawk had been out of Washington for part of the summer, too. He had gone to Chicago for some of the long-running trial of the Haymarket rioters. Of thirty-one people indicted, only eight were brought to trial. They were charged with being "accessories before the fact" and "accessories to each other" in the murder of Mathias J. Degan (the policeman killed by the original bomb), with murder by pistol shots, and with general conspiracy to murder. The identity of the person who had thrown the bomb had not been established, but in the end, the judge ruled that if the defendants had agreed to overthrow the law by force, and if the policeman had been killed "in pursuance of such a conspiracy," they were guilty. One of the defendants got fifteen years in prison; the others were sentenced to hang.

In his coverage of the trial, Hawk wrote that the end did not justify the means, that justice for working men and women could not be achieved through bombs and gunshots. But at the same time, he pointed out that the evidence against the defendants had varied greatly and that justice in the courts was in dire jeopardy if charges were not, in every case, substantiated by evidence. The lack of clear proof about who had thrown the bomb was, to him, a glaring weakness.

"I still believe that the whole mess could have been avoided had the police not marched in as they did, though that does not excuse the violence that followed," he said. "But the worst of it is that after so much upheaval, labor has gained little. Men have lost their jobs and their lives and have nothing to show for it, though all they asked for was reasonable working hours and wages."

"It won't end here; I'm sure it won't," Lexy said. "Labor may be weakened now by its failures, but with so much at stake for so many, I can't believe the movement will just stop."

Hawk thought of the earnest faces he had seen in Chicago before the riot had begun, and he had to agree with her.

By mutual, if unspoken agreement, they allowed themselves the common, neutral ground of discussing the stories they worked on and other events covered by the paper. It seemed such a safe course that it had become a familiar pattern before Lexy realized that sharing their ideas, their mental lives, was an act of intimacy in itself.

Lexy was fascinated by the dichotomy of Hawk's mind, coldly analytical on one hand, but also capable of fierce passion about the causes he believed in. Though he accepted the inevitability of the Indians' defeat by the relentless policies of the United States government, Hawk's sorrow had been evident when news came of Geronimo's surrender. There were other warriors more prominent than Geronimo, but the Chiricahua Apache had, by his long refusal to be tamed, captured a good deal of attention in the newspapers.

"Indians need symbols as much as anyone, and Geronimo was one of the last symbols of freedom," Hawk said, and Lexy thought he was mourning the loss of a symbol for himself as much as for the Apache and other tribes.

In October, though it meant missing the races in Baltimore and Washington, Lexy went north again on assignment, first to the breeding stock sale at Rancocas.

There were some surprises in the stallion sale. It had been thought the renowned Iroquois would bring twenty-five thousand dollars, but he went for twenty thousand, and the once mighty Duke of Magenta was sold for the pitiful sum of twelve hundred. However, the bidding on the brood mares, except for the very old ones, was lively.

Lexy took no part in the sale, but she shared the excitement of it as she watched her father bid. Gincie had stayed behind to be with their entries in the races at Pimlico, but she and Travis had already agreed on the mare they would like to add to their stable.

Gypsy was a four-year-old who had competed brilliantly as a two-year-old, had started well as a three-year-old, but had then fallen ill early in the season and had not raced since. Very rich men were bidding at the sale, but Gypsy turned out to be affordable due to her uncertain future. The Culhanes had great faith in her. Her sire was Falsetto, one of Leamington's sons. Falsetto had been nearly invincible as a three-year-old, though he had not fared well when Mr. Lorillard had sent him to England, and on return to the United States, Falsetto had served only a few seasons at the stud at Rancocas before being sold to A. J. Alexander for the Woodburn Stud in Kentucky. His misfortunes in England notwithstanding, his bloodlines were impeccable and so were Gypsy's.

The Culhanes were considering racing her again the next year, but their major intention was to use her as a brood mare. They did not think her illness or lack of performance in her third year were reasons enough to doubt her. Wild Swan had a long history of taking a chance and winning with horses others thought unworthy, a history that went clear back to the lame mare Leda, who had been brought by Alex and St. John from England and had been the foundation mare of the stable.

In addition to reporting on the sale, Lexy added a note about how, true to his announced intentions, Pierre Lorillard was lavishing great care on his sporting and social club, Tuxedo Park. The club had even set a new fashion trend when, at its first annual autumn ball, Griswold Lorillard had worn a tailless dress coat, a style that some now called the "tuxedo" and which was sure to gain favor since it had started at such an elite gathering.

Travis and the mare went back to Maryland, and Lexy went on to New York City where Rob Jenkins joined her so that the two of them could provide eyewitness accounts of the preparations and then the celebrations surrounding the dedication of Bartholdi's great Liberty statue. President Cleveland, other governmental officials, and the First Company and the Old Guard of the Union Veteran Corps came from Washington; various countries were represented by their ministers; and there were special delegates from France, among them Lafayette's grandson.

October 28, the day of the dedication, dawned in fog and drizzling rain which made it difficult to see the delayed marine parade or anything else clearly, but the thousands who had assembled to see the celebrations refused to allow the weather to ruin the occasion. There was an enormous humming energy that drove the day.

New York Harbor was crowded with vessels from rowboats to yachts, and seven men-of-war were anchored south of Bedloe's Island. Lexy was grateful that she didn't have to scramble for transport; Morgan had not only arranged for her to be aboard a Jennings-Falconer vessel, but had also used his naval connections to gain access to Bedloe's Island for her.

All morning, boats and ships of all sizes were busy in the water while Liberty stood on the quiet of the island, her face covered by the French tricolor and by great clouds of mist that obscured the statue to all except those who were at her feet. With her heart in her throat, Lexy climbed the four hundred steps to the head of the statue, trying to ignore the swaying of the dark staircase. It was worth it, she decided, the minute she had the view. From the head of the statue Liberty's immensity could be felt right down to one's bones. And Lexy felt as if she were flying, or so close to it that if she let go, she would soar away, over the mist and the sea.

The feeling stayed with her when she was on the ground again, while she listened to the speeches later in the day after the dignitaries had arrived amid whistles, bells, cannon salutes, and cheers. Count de Lesseps spoke, and afterward there were loud cries for Mr. Bartholdi, who came forward, bowed, and waved his hat to the audience, but didn't speak, whether from choice or from the fact he was not supposed to do so according to the program, no one knew. Senator Evarts spoke next but had only gotten through about two-thirds of his speech when the mention of Bartholdi brought such loud cheers from the audience that those in charge of unveiling the statue mistook the signal and withdrew the flag from the face of the statue, thereby signaling the steamer and batteries, which let loose a mighty salvo of cannonading and whistling. Helpless against the noise that went on for a full twenty minutes, Mr. Evarts took his seat.

When the thunder had ceased, the band played the "Marseillaise Hymn," "Yankee Doodle," and "The Star-Spangled Banner." Then President Cleveland gave a gracious speech and was followed by other speakers, including Monsieur Le Faivre, representative on behalf of the Republic of France.

Lexy tried to pay close attention to all of the speeches, but the mix-up in the order of things amused her and made, she admitted to herself, far better copy than an orderly procession. Nothing, however, could detract from the immense glory of Liberty with her strong, serene face, now unveiled. When Lexy looked up at her, the day was untarnished.

She and Rob had divided the duties of covering the events; they worked well together, but during the entire time they were in New York, Lexy wished it were Hawk who was with her. The thought made her feel guilty because Rob was such a good companion as well as an astute observer. But that did not stop her from feeling a start of joy when she saw Hawk again.

He, on the other hand, did not look so welcoming. "Did you enjoy your visit to New York with Rob?" he asked, and was immediately appalled at the jealousy he heard in his own voice. He'd already made up his mind that Lexy wasn't for him, and yet, he didn't want any other man to have her, either, an attitude he found no more acceptable in himself than in others.

"I'm sorry," he added abruptly, before Lexy had a chance to reply to his question. "May I begin again? I hope you enjoyed the time in New York; the stories you and Rob did were very good."

Lexy searched his face and saw nothing but sincerity there, replacing the earlier temper, and that was fine with her. She knew it was cowardly, but she didn't want any ill feelings between them, even when the problem was of his making. "Thank you," she replied. "Liberty is truly impressive! I don't doubt that she will be an enduring symbol for everyone who enters New York Harbor." But then her seriousness vanished in laughter. "Oh, Hawk, it was all very grand, but it was also very funny! I wish you could have seen the looks on the dignitaries' faces when the statue was uncovered ahead of schedule and all the cannons and whistles went off! I vow, I was not the only one struggling not to laugh. Actually, I think most public ceremonies would be much improved if the speeches were thus shortened."

Hawk laughed with her, and then he drew a grave face, though his eyes were still dancing. "I had to take an assignment that would undoubtedly have been yours had you returned in time. I hope I did it justice."

The article was entitled "Battle of the Reptiles" and concerned the fight between a newly arrived Gila monster from Arizona and a pet two-year-old alligator from Florida, both belonging to the Fish Commission. The reptiles had eaten within the past week or so and were in a torpid state, which caused the attendants to think them harmless. But while both animals were on the floor as their enclosures were being cleaned, one of the keepers inadvertently nudged the alligator into the Gila monster, and the lizard attacked the alligator. It had taken extraordinary means for the attendants finally to separate the animals; they had all but drowned the Gila monster and had used a spade and various other tools before they had been able to make him loose his grip on the alligator. But in the end, the alligator had perished of the poison.

It was, after all, only an incident between two rather ugly little beasts, an incident that would never have gotten into the papers at all had Hawk not heard of the Gila monster's arrival, wanted to see it, and gotten there in the aftermath, when the keepers were most anxious to tell of the battle.

It was the way Hawk had written about it that gave presence to the event. He might have witnessed a titanic clash between dinosaurs. The battle was described in great detail; the little alligator was given the role of innocent because the ground had been his and the keepers had been quite fond of him. Hawk had, with his words, made the small incident large, tragic, and comic at the same time.

"It's brilliant and devilish!" Lexy exclaimed, knowing how precisely Hawk had calculated the response of the readers. Her laughter bubbled over. "I can almost feel sorry for the Gila monster; no one championed his cause."

Hawk had meant to make her laugh and had counted on her understanding the mechanics of how the piece worked. In fact, he'd had her in mind when he wrote it. It was still a new experience to share his work with a woman.

"If you saw that little monster, you wouldn't plead his cause, either. It would be difficult to imagine an uglier creature! It seems excessive that he is also poisonous; his looks alone should be enough to kill his enemies."

When Hawk asked her out to supper, she accepted without hesitation. She expected it to lead to a new place in their relationship, but she was disappointed. Hawk was always interesting company, but he was careful to be no more. She suspected he regretted the invitation. She was growing very frustrated wondering what would happen next, wanting something to happen. As close as she was to her mother and to other women in the family, she did not feel she could confide in any of them. It was one of the few times when she thought having a sister might have been helpful.

She knew that Hawk was attracted to her, but he had already made it clear that he thought she was too young for him; his attitude about her living in the boardinghouse was proof enough. Exasperated with herself as much as with Hawk, she wished she could feel the same attraction for some other man that she felt for him. But it didn't seem to work that way. She knew a good number of "suitable" young men, but they held no interest for her beyond friendship. She was well aware that she was regarded as a challenge by some, as a hopelessly modern, working woman by others. She didn't care what they thought; she cared what Hawk thought. She wondered if she were writing articles about more serious subjects if Hawk would then see her as more mature.

It was dangerous speculation. It led her to take action in a way she might not have done otherwise.

She was pleased when Landon Tilitson sought her out at the boardinghouse. She had been fond of him and his twin sister, Lorna, when they had all been at Oberlin College. Because she had twin brothers, Lexy and the Tilitsons had shared an immediate bond as well as stories about the antics of the two sets of twins. Both Tilitsons were sunny-natured, intelligent, and pleasant to be with, despite the fact that they had been orphaned at an early age and raised by rather stern grandparents. Their way had been eased by a sizeable fortune left to them by their father, and if the grandparents weren't very outgoing, they had loved the twins and had done their best to make them feel secure.

Lexy had kept up a correspondence with Lorna for some weeks after graduation from college and knew that she had married, but the letters had ceased as each of them was swept into a new life. It had not seemed an ominous development at the time, just the natural course of things, but Landon's immediate outpouring of grief and fear changed that view.

"Lorna is in terrible trouble!" he said. "I came to help her, and I've just made things worse. I didn't like her husband from the beginning, and that put distance between my sister and me, but even I never suspected he would do this!"

"Lorna's here?" Lexy exclaimed, trying to make sense of his hurried words. It was one thing to have lost touch by mail, but it was quite another to learn that Lorna was nearby and had not gotten in touch with her. "What would you never have suspected?"

Landon swallowed hard, and his eyes slid away from hers. "Her husband is a brute! I think he beats her, though she never told me so. I've hardly seen her since her marriage, and then she stopped writing after she lost the baby."

Lexy asked precise, calm questions, exactly as she would have for any story she was going to write, all the while conscious that this was a friend they were talking about, not a stranger.

At first she wondered if Landon's suspicions might stem from jealousy, if perhaps he would have found no man worthy of his twin sister, but gradually her doubts disappeared and her horror grew as he offered one clue after another. Far from jealous, Landon had wanted his twin to be happy, wanted it to the extent that he had quieted his own doubts for her sake. But they had not stayed quiet. Lorna had not written to him about her marital problems, but he had read between the lines. He and his sister had always been able to confide in each other, and even given the new boundaries brought by Lorna's marriage, there was no comfortable explanation for her disquietingly bland letters. They had become little more than polite notes from a stranger.

Landon handed Lexy the packet to read. It did not take long; there was so little there. And what was there was utterly unlike the Lorna Lexy remembered. These sparse lines had none of the liveliness that had characterized the young woman she had known. The most telling of the missives was the last one, which ended, ". . . and now I have lost our child. Surely I am a failure on every count."

"I should have gone to her the instant I learned of the miscarriage, but I didn't. I did not want to intrude on her marriage, and the letters I sent to her were met with silence, or at best, rebuff. And then her husband answered my last letter." Landon handed her one more letter. It was a chill, dismissive note stating only that Lorna was "in need of special care," and would not be able to write to her brother for the time being.

"He committed her to an insane asylum," Landon stated flatly, and though by now Lexy was expecting something of the sort, it was still a shock.

Lexy knew of the place Landon named. It was near Alexandria, Virginia, but she did not know much about its operation other than that it was private. She had heard rumors of it being a place where the wealthy could discreetly handle problems of unstable relatives. No matter how well-run it was, it was horrid to think of Lorna being there.

Clinton Van Dyne, the man Lorna had married, had presented himself as the scion of a wealthy New York family, and he had seemed to possess all of the graces of that position, but Landon had discovered that he was far less than he pretended to be. He was the black sheep, long since disinherited, given to living on his wits and various forms of financial speculation involving other people's money. Even the letters, purportedly from various members of his family, welcoming Lorna as a new bride, had been forgeries. Unfortunately, Landon had not begun his investigations until his worry about his sister had grown so acute. And with their grandfather dead and their grandmother ancient and ailing, Landon felt the full weight of responsibility.

Clinton and Lorna had taken a house in Alexandria, but as Landon related what he knew, it became more understandable to Lexy why she had not seen either of the Van Dynes. Lorna had not, to Landon's knowledge, gone out in society at all, and Clinton, unable to bear close scrutiny, was operating behind the scenes, gathering investors for his latest scheme, which promised enormous profits for speculation in questionable railroad shares. And all the while, he was living well on Lorna's inheritance. That, Landon was convinced, was the key to everything.

Landon doubted that Clinton had known that Lorna's money came with strings attached. Lorna's father and then her grandparents had understood the dangers of being a young women of means. And because of that, they had made sure that she would retain control of her fortune even after she wed.

"I don't believe he ever considered it," Landon said in disgust. "Or if he did, he was sure that Lorna would never oppose any of his expenditures. But for all her sweetness, my sister has no trouble adding one column of figures with another, and she has never been one to squander money. She has always been conscious of the fact that our father worked hard and honestly for what he left to us."

Lexy didn't bother to point out that the same could be said of Landon himself. She had known they were well provided for, but not until now had she understood just how well. Neither of the twins had ever been ostentatious in the way they lived at college, but the truth was that they could have existed like royal heirs had they so chosen.

"There were two ways for her husband to gain control of her inheritance," Landon said. "One was to kill her outright, and I thank God that he has not had the courage to do that. The other was to prove her incompetent, to become her guardian and guardian of her fortune. That he has done, I fear, by having her committed for mental disorders."

He shook his head as if he'd sustained a blow. "I was so careful in uncovering his nefarious ways, but when it mattered most, I behaved like an idiot! I went to the asylum and demanded to see my sister. I made no attempt at subterfuge! Admission was refused."

"Oh, Landon! Do you truly think that made any difference? You and Lorna look so alike! No one who has seen Lorna could mistake your relationship to her. Undoubtedly, her husband has forbidden her visitors, and most particularly you."

The idea took hold with such immediate force, Lexy caught her breath. But when she made herself examine all the angles carefully, she was sure it would work.

"If I can get myself committed, I could find out about Lorna, about the whole place," she said.

Landon stared at her. "You sound as mad as they say Lorna is! God knows what might happen to you in such a place."

"But it wouldn't be for longer than a few days, a week at most," Lexy protested. "I would make sure that my 'husband' would come back to get me out in that time." She already had a good idea of whom she would enlist to help her with her plan. "And honestly, I don't want to do this just for you and Lorna. It would make a good story, an important story. And that matters because, if things are really wrong there, if innocent, sane people like Lorna are being held there, then it ought to be exposed!"

Her motives were good, but she also admitted to herself that this was just the sort of serious story she had been wanting to do for a long time, something with more import than the racing season and parades.

Landon's misgivings did not ease with her explanation, but he accepted anyway because he was so desperate. He had come to Lexy because he did not have important enough connections here to override the rights of Lorna's husband. He had not considered that Lexy would become so personally involved, only that with her job at the newspaper, she might be able to discover more about the asylum than he could. But now that she had proposed her plan, even with the obvious danger, it appealed more than anything else he could think of. Lexy did have powerful connections, and by her account, there would be someone to get her out after a limited time. Most of all, someone who loved Lorna would have a chance to get close to her.

Lexy had not doubted her ability to get Landon's agreement, but getting Rob Jenkins to play his part was surely going to be more difficult.

At first he simply refused. "No sane person goes to one of those places willingly! And I'm not going to help you go. There must be another way."

"There isn't," Lexy insisted. "Any other course might alert the attendants who have charge of Lorna; she might be put into even more danger than what threatens her now. I swear to you, there is no saner person than Lorna. I can't believe she's suddenly gone mad, not even over losing her child. She's my friend, as is her brother, and they deserve my help. And I want that story, Rob. I want it very badly."

"To impress Hawk Mackenna?" Rob asked without rancor.

Lexy felt her cheeks grow hot. "Perhaps it is partly for that, but there are other, more valid reasons. Lorna needs help, and I want to do the story. If you won't help me, I'll find someone else. And it won't be Hawk Mackenna," she added before Rob could suggest it.

She knew she was taking unfair advantage of Rob's friendship, but she did it anyway. He could not resist the blend of logic and cajolery she employed. But she felt even more guilty for lying to Reid. She told him she wanted to do a special story on Maryland and

Virginia horse farms, with an eye to those that were trying to retain a foothold in the racing world, as Wild Swan was, despite the migration of the business to New York and other points north and west. Since he had no special assignments in mind for her at the moment, Reid agreed. It was acutely uncomfortable for Lexy to witness how easily her lies were accepted. She had the habit of telling the truth, and so people expected nothing less from her. She wondered if Reid would ever trust her again after this was over.

She worked out the story of her supposed illness, figuring that a case as parallel to Lorna's as possible might help insure that she would see her friend in the asylum. She bought a doll with a leather body and bisque head. It had vapid blue eyes, blond human hair, and little teeth that showed like a fox's through the half-open mouth. Lexy practiced holding the doll and crooning to it, and she tried to look vacant-eyed, but since it is impossible to really look at one's own eyes in a mirror, she wasn't sure about the effect.

She made Rob go over and over his lines. At first, he was so stiff and hesitant, he couldn't have fooled a child, but gradually he warmed to it until he played the role of grieving but impatient husband quite nicely. Lexy had convinced him that if he didn't do well enough, the staff might suspect something amiss from the beginning and that that might make it even more dangerous for her.

Lexy was so busy with her plans, she did not feel any real fear until they were nearly at the institution. But when Rob guided the carriage over to the side of the road so that she could muss her hair and clothing, the first cold doubts touched her spine. For the first time she realized that it would not just be a matter of fooling the staff, it was also going to mean being with the truly insane. Surely a good many of the patients would be so rather than simply victims of greedy relatives.

"Ready to turn back?" Rob asked.

She thought of Lorna, and she shook her head. "No, I've got to do this. But I'm glad you'll be back for me. Five days ought to be enough. And I don't care what excuse you use, just make sure you get me out." They had discussed various ploys for that, including the death of a relative and Rob's supposed need to remove himself and his wife to another state.

Bellwood had the well-manicured grounds of the country estate it had once been. The main house and the outbuildings were all carefully kept—as was the great stone gate and wall that encircled the place.

Under Lexy's direction, Rob had written a note alerting the institution of his intention to bring his wife, so they were expected. He had also brought money, provided by Landon, because the one thing they were sure of was that the place would charge dearly for its services. Indeed, from the start of their "interview," it was clear that Rob's ability to pay was the main concern.

Rob was very convincing as the sorrowful husband, explaining that his wife, Abigail, just hadn't been the same since the loss of their newborn baby. "She just sits and rocks that doll all day long. And she gets very upset if you try to take it away from her. But she isn't violent," he hastened to add. "She just isn't part of this world anymore, and as much as I love her, I can't take care of her at home any longer." Without specifying, Rob made it sound as if there were more pressing things in his life, perhaps even another woman.

"We understand," the matron assured him, her voice soft and low.

Lexy noticed that everyone spoke in a near whisper and that no one looked at her with more than passing interest. No one addressed her directly or asked anything of her; everyone seemed content to accept what her "husband" told them. And why not, she thought cynically; he was the one who was going to pay them.

She tried to notice everything while maintaining an unfocused look. It wasn't so difficult. The soft voices and bland faces made her feel as if she were indeed drifting off into some separate place. It occurred to her that the staff even spoke to Rob as if they were addressing a small child. And they used a voice that small children detested, a voice implying great superiority and control. They did not make her feel as if they had her welfare uppermost in their minds.

When Rob took his leave of her, she could tell he was not comforted either. He gripped her hands while he murmured, "Now, my dear, you'll be safe and happy here; I won't allow anything less."

Lexy knew he intended the women and the one man in the room to take it as a warning. She stole a look at the man, Dr. Jarvis, the director.

Everything about Dr. Jarvis was small—his body, his eyes, his mouth, his hands, his contribution to the conversation. Beyond murmuring a few lines about "best of care," "see to her every need," and the like, he had little role in the proceedings. But his eyes were bright beads, and Lexy was sure he was very good at keeping the accounts. She doubted that he was a qualified doctor of medicine. He was there as the authority figure, the titular male. She shifted her eyes away quickly before she could be caught in a direct look.

For an instant, as Rob was leaving, Lexy had a sudden overwhelming desire to go with him, to abandon the entire plan in a burst of cowardice. She gripped the doll tighter and closed her eyes, reminding herself that Lorna was here somewhere; the story was here, too.

Chapter 29

Lexy had imagined several possibilities of treatment at Bellwood—among them violence—but she had not imagined the truth of it. There was violence, a quick slap or shove if patients did not obey instructions instantly, but the main attitude of staff toward patients was far more damaging than that. Dressed alike in shapeless gray smocks, the patients were treated like idiotic children—the attitude of the reception carried on. Addressed by their first names, they were herded from the second-story sleeping room, a huge room furnished with rows of beds, to the first-floor dining room of trestle tables and straight-backed chairs, to the room where they spent most of the day, a large rectangular space as bleak as the rest of the patients' areas.

The reception area where Rob had left Lexy had been furnished in elegance; the patients' quarters were as bare of color as a prison, as their days were bare. No diversions of any sort were provided, no books, no materials for sewing or knitting or making any of the home crafts that must have diverted many of the women before they had come here.

The food was starchy, greasy, and bland, so that many of the patients had a bloated gray look, while others were painfully thin from being unable to digest the fare, usually watery soup followed by lumpy potatoes drizzled with oily gravy for the main meal. Recognizable pieces of meat, vegetables, and fruit were virtually nonexistent.

The plumbing facilities were primitive, and baths were offered infrequently and without hot water. The smell of unwashed and undernourished bodies hung over everything; worse was the stench of despair from women who had surely been far more meticulous in better days.

Despair was everyone's companion here. The sixty or so inmates, ranging from one girl in her teens to the elderly, had been abandoned by their families in this awful place. Even the most mad seemed to know that.

There were patients who had clearly lost all contact with reality. One woman knew she was Jeanne d'Arc and babbled continually, in recognizable French, to her voices. Another thought she was not only a man, but a policeman, and spent most of her time wandering from one person to another, announcing, "I'm taking you in," and then repeating long lists of offenses. One spent only short periods in the company of the others because she was possessed by uncontrollable fits of violent rage that set her on the others with fists and teeth until she was hauled away. Many of the inmates bore bruises from her attacks as well as from not pleasing the attendants quickly enough, but even these were borne with a strange apathy.

There were a considerable number who talked softly to themselves, and others who mourned the desertion of a lover or, as Lexy was pretending to do, the loss of a child, but most of these, she was sure, were no more insane than she. Grieving and beaten, yes, but not mad. And surely this was the last place that would offer them any help. There seemed to be no treatment offered. Conversation amongst the sufferers was discouraged; most had given up any attempt at it. Lexy had considered that a doctor might discover she had not only not lost a child but was still a virgin, but there was little chance of that, and no need for her to stage an hysterical scene as she had planned should a doctor attempt to examine her.

After the first day, the next four stretched like an eternity before Lexy, and she had yet to find Lorna. As stealthily as possible she had searched every face. Even allowing for the horrible changes that the asylum could make in one's appearance, she was certain Lorna was not one of the women around her. And unless Lorna truly had gone mad, she would certainly recognize Lexy.

She lay on the lumpy bed listening to the whimpers and whispers and shuffling of bodies in the night. She tried to concentrate on everything she had seen and heard during the day, but she felt her mind slipping out of focus, drifting in the gray.

"God, what is the matter with me?" she murmured, not aware of speaking aloud, conscious only of a huge wave of panic beginning to edge in.

"What you drink, what you eat here, makes you tame. Drugs, you see." The voice whispered out of the darkness, raising gooseflesh on her skin.

"Sometimes I don't eat or drink anything for a long, long time, just to remember how it is to feel and think." The whisper came again, and Lexy tried to picture the woman who was in the bed beside her, finally recalling that she was a tiny, birdlike old lady called Maud. Usually Lexy's newspaper habits made it simple for her to record everything around her, but now putting one image together with another was nearly beyond her.

"Maud?" she questioned softly.

"The same. If you keep taking what they give you, you won't remember my name or yours either."

Drugs—Lexy grappled with the thought and understood how much could be explained that way. Opiates to make everyone docile and vague.

"Don't visitors notice when they come to see their relatives?" she asked. If any of her family saw her or spoke to her while she was in this state, they would know in an instant that something was terribly wrong.

"They don't come. People don't come here to visit, only to be hidden away. The doctor and the matrons tell the relatives that it is better if they don't come, and the relatives like to hear that."

Despite the eeriness of the hushed words in the dark, Lexy had no doubt that Maud was absolutely sane. She listened for a moment, wanting to ask her more, sure that the night attendants would regard a purposeful conversation as quite different from drugged babbling, and all the while fighting the mists in her own brain.

Finally, she decided to take the risk of telling Maud the truth. "I'm looking for a friend, Lorna Van Dyne. She lost her baby, and her husband brought her here."

Footsteps sounded down the row, and Lexy froze, her heart beating too fast with the terror that Maud would not notice the approaching attendant or would purposefully betray her. But Maud knew who her enemies were and stayed immobile and silent until the woman had passed by.

"She is here, but they've put her in the infirmary. She had a bad fever. But maybe she'll be back here soon. Maybe. They don't like us to die. It's risky for them to collect for the dead, even here."

"Maud, where is the infirmary?"

Lexy heard the old woman suck in her breath in fear before she answered. "You can't go there! They would be so angry if you tried, so angry!"

"I have to go there!" Lexy insisted. "And I'll be in far worse trouble if I don't know exactly where it is."

There was a long pause, but finally Maud said, "It's the door at the far end of the hall, behind the staircase. But some of the attendants have their rooms above and are always about; they'll find you!"

Lexy's mind wandered to the question of why the staff would be on the top floor and the inmates downstairs where surely escape would be easier. Then she understood. She had heard the main door thumping shut and being locked, and she had noticed that the casements were small-paned and nailed shut, with only small openings for air. It would take strength and determination to escape this place, and opiates insured that there was little of either. She wondered about the woman who had fits of violence; maybe she would be even more violent if she were not drugged.

She meant to go in search of Lorna, but her body gave up the struggle against the drug, and she slipped into sleep.

The first thing she noticed the next day was that Maud avoided all direct eye contact with her. She didn't blame the old woman, but it made her feel even more alone. Her desire to find Lorna dominated her entire being so that she knew she must indeed seem mentally deficient as she stumbled from one apppointed place to the next, muttering to the doll and trying at the same time to ascertain where various members of the staff were throughout the day. Apparently some of them, the doctor among them, lived in the outbuildings—not for them too close an association with the inmates—while the lower ranks inhabited the top floor of the house. But there was always someone about. Looking for Lorna under cover of darkness seemed the only option.

Now that Maud had warned her, Lexy ate and drank as little as possible. Perhaps they varied what was drugged, but she suspected the bitterness in the tepid tea was laudanum or something like it. It was ominous that none of the attendants seemed to care whether she ate her meals or not; proof of how little resistance there was from the patients. Their families had judged them and sentenced them, harsh actions that could break the strongest spirit, and many of these souls were very fragile.

By nightfall, Lexy was feeling a bit light-headed from hunger and fear, but it was preferable to the distorted way her mind had been the night before. She lay on her bed listening to all the sounds around her until her head ached with the effort.

"I watched you today. You're clever, as I am. You didn't take any of their medicine. You mean to find poor Lorna. After two o'clock in the morning until the dawn breaks, they aren't so careful. Not much chance, but a little one."

Maud's voice whispered over Lexy's skin. By now, she understood how much of a risk Maud perceived this sharing of cogent thought to be.

"Thank you," she said softly.

She waited, judging the passage of time as best she could, feeling the house settle into a deep stillness.

When she left her bed, she did so on her hands and knees, clad only in the plain nightgown she had been issued. Whatever clothes patients brought with them were locked away somewhere or disposed of, for all she knew; it was an important lesson that personal choices were not tolerated here. She took the time to stuff the doll far under the bed. The November chill seemed to seep into her bones; she wondered if they provided heat when winter truly came. But she stayed on her hands and knees, not only to avoid any lurking attendants, but also in the hope that the other patients would not notice or at least not call attention to her passage.

No attendant had checked on the sleeping women for some time, but Lexy realized little by little that she was not the only one awake. There was a waiting silence around her, a cessation of the regular breathing of sleep and of involuntary movement. There must be others besides Maud who avoided the drugs. And yet, no one called out, not even St. Joan. Just one small thread of sound came to her. "Good luck," the voice said, though the speaker could not possibly know what she intended. Perhaps they all thought she was trying to escape; perhaps others had tried.

She had the mad vision of popping upright should she be discovered and proclaiming her true identity and mission; she would then appear to be every bit as deranged as St. Joan. She bit her lip against the hysterical laughter rising in her throat.

A weak light came from the open door into the hall. When she reached the opening, she drew herself up along the dark shadowed edge, and holding her breath, she peeked outside the room. Dim lamps glowed in the hall, but she could see no one there. She listened for a long time, and then she ventured out, scurrying down toward the infirmary like some furtive creature of the night.

She was shaking when she reached the door beneath the stairs. The door was not fully closed, and soft light flowed around it, but she could not tell whether the room was guarded from within. For a moment, she was frozen in place, unable to take the final step into the room, unable to sneak back the way she had come. Hawk's face flashed before her at that instant; he would not approve of what she was doing, but surely he would disapprove even more if she didn't do it well. To have come this far and go no further was unthinkable.

Her knees nearly gave way with the relief of finding no attendant in the room. There were three beds, one occupied, but no one stood guard.

The figure in the bed stirred and moaned a little, and Lexy heard the rasp of her breathing. She moved toward the sound and stared down at a face so gaunt and pale with illness, if she had not been searching for Lorna, she would not at first have recognized her.

She called her name softly. "Lorna, it's Lexy, Lexy Culhane. I've come to help you. Lorna, please, wake up now. I haven't much time. Lorna, please."

Lorna's eyes opened slowly, and the first thing that registered was terror. She opened her mouth to scream.

Lexy put her fingers gently over Lorna's mouth. "Yes, it really is I. Your brother couldn't get in to see you, so I came. They think I'm insane, but I'm no more mad than you are."

She wondered if it were true as Lorna's dark eyes continued to reflect nothing but confusion and fear, but finally, acknowledgment began to dawn. Lexy took her fingers away. "I'm so sorry, I can't do anything right now. My friend won't be back for me for three more days. I've got to pretend to be unbalanced until then. But I'll get you out with me, I promise. Please, try to save your strength until then." Lorna looked so small and weak, Lexy almost said, "Try to stay alive until then."

She took one of Lorna's hands in hers and stroked the hot, dry skin. She wanted to stay here with her, but knew she had to get back to her bed. And then the decision was taken out of her hands. The door swung open, and she was discovered.

The woman was tall and heavy, but she moved with great speed, grabbing Lexy away from the bed and shaking her hard. "What are you doing here?" she demanded, and it didn't take any effort at all for Lexy to let her eyes glaze over in terror. "My baby, I've lost my baby. I heard it crying here," she mumbled, eyes searching the room frantically as if she were sure she would find the infant in some corner.

The woman shook her again, and then with the same casual violence that Lexy had already witnessed, she slapped her hard, giving the left side of her face such a blow with her meaty hand that Lexy could feel the flesh beginning to swell almost immediately. She heard a gasp from Lorna and prayed her friend would not betray them both.

"Can't have her bothering the sick, now can we?" the woman said, as if she were doing Lorna a favor. Lorna said nothing. Lexy kept mumbling about her lost child, hoping that it would be a further signal to Lorna that she knew the circumstances of her confinement.

The matron dragged her back down the hall, her grip so tight on Lexy's shoulder that she knew she was going to bruise there, too. It was all she could do not to retaliate. Though she would undoubtedly lose in the end, she could think of nothing she would rather do than drive her fists into this mass of cruelty. Bellwood was rapidly making her fit for an asylum herself.

Lexy thought the woman was returning her to the sleeping area, but instead she was taken to a much smaller room and shoved inside. She heard the door lock and the footsteps going away. She slid down the wall and sat on the floor, panting. She hoped the attendant would just leave her here for the night, but the hope was short-lived. The woman returned with another nearly as large as she. As soon as Lexy saw the straitjacket, she shot to her feet and cowered across the room from the two. Her mind was skipping wildly, and for an instant, she thought she had blurted out the truth of her presence here, anything to avoid restraint, and when she realized she hadn't, she clamped her swollen jaw so tightly, the dull ache turned to a sharp pain. She was suddenly more afraid of these two women than she had ever been of anyone in her life. And she was convinced that the truth, if they believed it, might put her in even more danger. They were strong enough to kill her and claim afterward that she had brought it on herself by her own violence.

She meant to be docile, to avoid more hurt, but when they bundled her into the loathsomely rigid material and straps, she could not be still. She twisted and struggled, appalled at the animal moans that came from her throat.

The women handled her as if she were a bundle of rags.

"We can't have her disrupting things," the first woman said. "Wandering around in the night. Upsets everything. Daft as she is, still, I'll warrant she'll remember this and behave herself."

The other woman answered with grunts of agreement.

Lexy spent the rest of the night and most of the next day locked in the room. The first hours passed with agonizing slowness as her cramped muscles burned as if they were on fire. And then her arms began to go numb. She was cold and then hot, but finally those sensations faded. For a long time, she thought she would give anything for a drink of water, but that need ebbed until everything began to fade away. That frightened her more than the pain and thirst had, so she started concentrating on everyone at Wild Swan, even on the horses, conjuring them in her mind one by one. And then she thought of Hawk, thought of him in such minute detail that she could imagine that his clean, masculine scent filled her nostrils. She was still thinking about him when they came for her toward evening.

She did not protest when they stripped her and sluiced her down with cold water; protest would have been futile, and she was beyond any claim to dignity. But when she tasted the bitterness of the draught they tried to make her swallow, her body rebelled, and she retched so violently that acid burned in her throat, and the matrons ceased trying to force anything down her.

"She'll be hungry enough tomorrow," she heard someone say, as if she were a dumb beast of no consequence. She didn't care; she curled in on herself on the hard bed and let Hawk's face drift through her mind again. Tomorrow she would be stronger; she would think of Lorna and the horrors of this place; she would hold to the fact that the day after, Rob would come to rescue her.

*　*　*

Lexy's enthusiasm and will to carry out her investigation of
Bellwood had swept Rob along until he had played his role of
distressed husband with some pleasure. But once he had left her at
the asylum, his own commitment to the project had begun to fade,
to be replaced by guilt and apprehension. To make matters worse,
Hawk Mackenna seemed to be taking an inordinate interest in him
and in Lexy's whereabouts. Rob kept reminding himself that what
he or Lexy was doing was none of Mackenna's business, but it was
difficult to convince himself of that when pinned by the intensity of
those dark, gold-flecked eyes.

"Do you know which farms Lexy was going to visit?" Hawk
asked first, and despite his best efforts, Rob's eyes slipped away
from the other man's. "Errrr . . . ah, no, not exactly. She's the horse
expert, not I."

Rob knew he had answered badly, looking guilty as sin, and it
was only the first day of Lexy's stay at Bellwood. And it didn't get
any better. Wherever he turned, Hawk seemed to be there, watching
him with eyes so piercing, his name seemed more fitting than ever.
"Has Lexy sent any messages?" "Are you sure she's looking at
horses?" The questions seemed to follow Rob everywhere, and he
couldn't get his impressions of Bellwood out of his mind. He, no less
than Lexy, had noticed how the staff had avoided dealing with their
new patient directly. He could not help wondering how long Lexy's
spirit and quick temper would submit to that kind of treatment. He
suspected five days were too many.

Hawk was running out of patience with himself as well as with
Rob. He kept repeating to himself that whatever Lexy was doing
should be her own concern, but his heart and mind kept telling him
otherwise. In the week before her absence from the city, she had
avoided him, of that he was sure. He'd become accustomed to
spending a good deal of time with her, both of them accepting the
boundaries he had set. But he didn't believe that the uneasy feelings
he had came simply from missing her. His journalistic instincts were
aroused. Lexy was hiding something, and Rob was helping her.
That, Hawk admitted to himself, bothered him greatly. If she had a
problem, or a special story she was working on, and needed help,
why hadn't she come to him instead?

On the third day, Hawk issued a supper invitation to Rob that
was more in the way of a command. Rob would have refused except,
by then, he was so worn down by fretting about Lexy, he no longer
knew what he wanted to do about her secret. He talked to Landon
Tilitson, getting more details about what Landon suspected in regard
to his sister's incarceration at Bellwood, and Landon had done noth-

ing to quiet his fears, even suggesting that perhaps the two men ought to go out there and take both women out by force. The prospect of gaining anything by force fit Hawk better than it fit himself or Landon, Rob knew, and that tipped the balance. Rob accepted Hawk's offer of a meal.

At first, Hawk played the genial host, so that Rob could almost believe that this was no more than a friendly gesture from one member of the staff to another. He knew he was drinking a bit too much, but somehow he felt that if he refused more, he would appear not only young and inexperienced, but a prig as well. Though not that many years separated them, Rob was always conscious of feeling at a disadvantage with Hawk. He put Hawk in the same league as Reid, and he had been fighting the beginnings of hero worship since the man had joined the *Witness*.

Hawk was at his most charming, telling anecdotes about his newspaper days in the Far West and questioning Rob about his own experiences. And then suddenly, Rob was aware that the bonhomie of the evening had vanished; Hawk was watching him with fierce, narrowed eyes.

"Where is Lexy, and what is she doing?" Hawk demanded.

Rob weighed his conspiracy with Lexy against his growing concern as well as his fuzzy mind would allow, and with a sigh of relief, he gave up the struggle, now so eager to confess that the words tumbled over each other.

Of all the things Hawk might have guessed, this was not one of them. "You're telling me that Lexy is in a madhouse with no proof of her true identity and you helped her to get inside?" he asked, his voice slow and deliberate in contrast to Rob's.

Rob gulped, stopped in midsentence, and then nodded miserably. "I know I shouldn't have done it, but Lexy is very persuasive. She . . ." his voice trailed off as he took in the blazing fury in Hawk's face.

"Come on!" Hawk snapped. "We're going after her and her friend."

Rob found that their bill had been paid and they were outside the restaurant while he was still struggling to understand what Hawk meant. "Tonight?" he asked. He was feeling more sober by the minute, and he welcomed the cold night air against his skin.

"Tonight," Hawk growled. "Do you think I would allow Lexy to stay in that place any longer now that I know she's there?"

It was not a question that required an answer, and it banished any lingering doubt Rob had about how Hawk regarded Lexy. Hawk had just staked his claim as clearly as if he had announced, "She's mine." This was something quite beyond concern for a colleague.

Hawk at rest was formidable enough; with a driving purpose, he was a force that knocked down all the obstacles in his path without seeming to notice they were there. Rob simply did as he was told.

Hawk took the time to find Landon Tilitson, at Rob's direction. He knew that Lexy would never leave Bellwood without her friend, and having Lorna's brother there would be useful. Hawk also made sure that the horses were fit and fresh and that the carriage he hired had ample room for passengers, and he paid the driver generously to follow orders.

Hawk gave little thought to the dangers of rocketing through the night. He could not conceive of anything that could keep him from Lexy. He had been a large man for a long time; he could hardly remember feeling real fear as an adult, but he felt it now, a living thing twisting in his gut. And he who prided himself on his ability to control his emotions in any situation felt barely in control of the rage building inside with the fear. If he found that harm had been done to Lexy, he wasn't sure he would be able to control his response to it. Finally, he was furious at Lexy for causing him to feel such an unpalatable mixture of emotions, and furious at himself for allowing it.

When the old man living in the gatehouse at Bellwood refused admittance, insisting that no one was allowed in at night, Hawk lifted him off his feet and suggested that if he wanted to live to see the sunrise, he would open the gate immediately. The man complied without further protest, eyeing Hawk as if he were confronting the Devil himself. And then he blinked in surprise at the money pressed into his hand. "Crazy man to go with th' crazy women," he muttered as the carriage continued on toward the main building.

Rob and Landon followed in Hawk's wake like faithful squires. When pulling the bell rope elicited no response, although the bell could be heard within, Hawk began to pound on the door and yell at the top of his lungs until the door was cracked and a woman's voice asked, "Who are you, and what do you want at this time of night?"

"We've brought the congressman's wife," Hawk lied, without specifying which congressman. "She's very ill, and her husband wants her in your care."

The words opened the door as if by magic. By the time the two matrons beheld the angry giant, his two followers, and no woman, it was too late for them to slam the door shut again.

"We've come for Abigail Jenkins"—he winced inwardly at calling her by Rob's name—"and for Lorna Van Dyne."

"That's impossible!" the older of the two women sputtered. "This is highly irregular! I won't allow it!" She was accustomed to getting her way, but her voice quavered a little as Hawk continued to stare at her.

"It's not only possible; it will be done immediately. Otherwise, I think I might break your neck," Hawk suggested. The pleasant measure of his voice made the words all the more threatening.

The woman stepped back a pace, and recognition dawned on her face as she got a second look at Rob. She had been there when Rob brought Lexy to Bellwood, and the other woman thought she'd seen Landon before and then remembered who he was when she saw how much he looked like Lorna Van Dyne.

"You will take us to them right now," Hawk ordered, still in that awful, pleasant voice.

The women exchanged glances, both of them thinking that the two patients were not in any condition to be seen.

"Mrs. Van Dyne has had a fever; it would not be wise to move her," the older woman said in a last attempt at regaining control of the situation.

Hawk advanced on her. "Now," he repeated, his outward calm belied by the wild pounding of his heart; to be so close to Lexy and still not have sight of her was made more frightening by the fact that the woman hadn't even mentioned her.

"The authorities will hear of this," the matron said, but she was already turning to lead the way. There would surely be a world of trouble for this night's work, but she didn't consider her salary adequate to risk any more delay with the enraged giant confronting her.

The next few minutes passed like hours for the three men. They got to Lorna first, and Landon groaned aloud when he saw her. But this time when Lorna opened her eyes, she was not afraid. Lexy had told her that Landon was close by; Lexy had told her that they were going to get her out of this place. For the first time since Clinton had brought her to Bellwood, Lorna smiled. She whispered her brother's name and made the effort to stretch her arms up to him as he bent to lift her from the bed.

"No one will hurt you again, no one," Landon murmured brokenly as he carried her out to the carriage.

"I'll go get Abigail," the matron said, but Hawk refused. "We'll go with you."

A last flicker of outrage rose in the woman. "You can't go with us! It isn't proper! The room is full of sleeping women."

"Nothing about this place is proper," Hawk countered. "Mr. Jenkins and I will go with you."

Hawk would never forget the glint of eyes caught in lamplight, eyes watching from the stillness. The room smelled musty, like a stable that had been shut up too long.

"Oh, my God, Lexy," he breathed when the light caught her. She was huddled in a tight ball of misery and did not awaken until he touched her gently, stroking the hair back from her face, and then she looked at him for a long moment. Finally she asked, "Are you really here?" her voice rasping in her dry throat.

"Yes, sweetheart, I'm really here," he said, not even aware of the endearment. She looked as frail and ill as Lorna, but when he gathered her into his arms to carry her out, she protested, "I can walk."

He continued to gather her up until she was against his chest. "You can prove how strong and independent you are later. For now, please just allow me to carry you off in the best tradition of knightly chivalry." He needed the reassurance of her pressed against him.

Everything was still very hazy for Lexy, but she was convinced that Hawk was here in the flesh and that he was carrying her out of this awful place, carrying her without apparent effort. Her mind wandered over the wonder of that; she was slender, but she was tall. She had not until this moment considered it possible that a man could carry her with anything less than great effort in an emergency. She started to giggle and couldn't seem to stop, until she suddenly realized that they were leaving Maud behind.

"We have to take Maud with us," she said. "I won't leave without her."

Hawk stopped in midstride. "Maud?" he asked cautiously, sure Lexy was delirious.

"The old woman in the bed beside mine. She's perfectly sane. I won't leave her."

"Get the woman named 'Maud,' " Hawk ordered Rob. The urgency in Lexy's weak voice touched him unbearably. He didn't want to fight with her or refuse her anything. He just wanted to get her out of here safely.

Rob shrugged and did as he was told, thinking that they were already in as much trouble as there could be. Maud, he discovered, was delighted to come with him, and he was relieved that every one of the women in the room did not get up to join the procession. He trusted that their stunned surprise would last until he and the rest of the party were away.

Even in the coach, Hawk did not relinquish his burden. He held Lexy to his warmth, his heart pounding against her in the aftermath of the raid on Bellwood. He fought against the violence still coursing through his veins; hitting a woman was taboo, but that did not prevent him from wishing he could have flattened the attendants with his fists.

He was not through giving orders.

Lorna would have good care from her brother, but that still left Maud. "Rob, find a place for Miss Maud to stay," he said.

Rob stared at Hawk through the dimness inside the carriage. The man had entirely motivated and dominated the rescue, and it would be difficult to wrench control from him under any circumstances, but for Lexy's sake, Rob felt obligated to try. "And what about Lexy? Are you taking her to her family?"

"You helped her to get into this mess; I helped her to get out of it. Mr. Tratnor doesn't expect her back for two more days. It will be her choice how she returns and what she tells him. In the meantime, I'll take good care of her." He knew what he was proposing was beyond the bounds of propriety, but he didn't care. Nothing could make him give up Lexy at this point.

Rob's own guilt for his part in the escapade worked against continued defiance of Hawk, but still he said, "She's already been hurt; don't harm her further."

"Never, never as long as I live," Hawk vowed, gathering Lexy closer to him.

Chapter 30

Hawk kept expecting Lexy to raise some protest of her own or at least to question him about where they were going, but she did not. That frightened him; he was accustomed to her high spirits. To find her so quiet and docile made him fear that she had some serious injury.

Lexy roused slowly to Hawk's insistent demand that she open her eyes. She looked up at him and then gazed around the unfamiliar surroundings. "Where am I?" she croaked.

"Here, drink this before you try to talk," he said, his own throat tight in response to the roughness in her voice. He lifted her up so she could sip from the glass of water he offered, and she drank deeply, thinking that nothing had ever tasted so good before.

"Whoa, there!" He held the glass out of her reach. "You can

have all you want, but slowly, slowly, so you won't make yourself sick. How long since you've had anything to eat or drink?"

"Only yesterday," Lexy replied after some thought. "But one has to be careful at Bellwood; they put opiates in the food and drink." She looked around without surprise or outrage. "Why did you bring me here?"

He looked down at her bruised face, at the circles under her eyes. "Because I couldn't bear to let you out of my sight, not yet. Christ, Lexy, I was so afraid!"

Hawk Mackenna had been afraid for her. Warmth flowed through her as if she'd drunk a shot of brandy instead of water. "I was afraid, too," she confessed, gazing up into his eyes, and despite her hunger and exhaustion, the words flowed out of her, vivid, horrifying images of Bellwood.

His own muscles knotted at the description of the straitjacket; he thought he would have gone truly mad to have been so restrained.

"Most of the women there are no more insane than I!" Lexy said, her voice shaking and tears beginning to stream down her cheeks. "It's wicked! And the people who abandon their relatives there are as guilty as those who run the place. I'm going to write about all of them!"

Hawk drew her into his arms again. For all her resolve, she seemed so delicate and hurt, he felt an overwhelming need to protect her.

"Hush now, save your strength. I want you to eat something before you sleep."

At the mention of food, she realized how ravenous she was, but there was something that sounded even better. "I want a bath," she said. "They washed me, but I still feel filthy." She shuddered.

"You will have both," Hawk promised and set about to provide her with all the comforts of his home.

Even in her dazed state, Lexy was charmed by his living quarters. She had never been here before and would have expected him to have rooms in a boardinghouse or hotel, but instead, he had rented a little house that was detached and down in a garden away from a much larger dwelling. It was a "granny" or "mother-in-law" house, and if Hawk seemed a bit large for the rather small configuration of the place, still it provided him with comfort and privacy.

She recognized as well as he that it was highly improper for her to be here, but she was not troubled in the least by that. After being at Bellwood, the finer points of correct behavior held little interest for her, and she felt utterly content and safe in Hawk's care. She was grateful, too, that she did not yet have to face Reid or Larissa or, worse, her parents. She needed the interlude to decide how she would tell her family about her investigation of Bellwood and, more, to decide what she would say in the article she was determined to write about the asylum.

She roused herself enough to inquire about Lorna and Maud and accepted Hawk's assurances that they would be well cared for by their respective escorts. He and Lexy shared a smile at the idea of Rob in charge of Maud.

"She's a remarkable old woman," Lexy said. "Despite the horrors of that place, she has managed to stay alert and," she searched for the right word, "complete. Bellwood strips everything away—dignity, identity, thought, emotion—but Maud refused to be robbed of anything."

Hawk made no attempt to guide Lexy's changes of mood. It was no use to tell her that her experiences at Bellwood were behind her now; they were very much a part of her and would never, he thought, be wholly gone. He was ready to listen to what she needed to say.

Like most bachelors in the city, he took many of his meals at taverns and restaurants, but he also kept his larder well stocked. He was accustomed to fending for himself, and he liked the convenience of being able to dine in his own quarters while he worked late, honing the words for an article or story. He was able to provide Lexy with a creditable repast of bread, cheese, cold roast chicken, and tart apples washed down with cider.

He marveled at the pleasure he got from simply watching her eat. She savored each bite as if it had been prepared by the best chefs in the city. And then she regarded him owlishly as she took another sip of cider. "Thise ish strong stuff, in'it?" She giggled and clapped a hand to her mouth at the sound of her own words, slurring despite her efforts to speak correctly.

He laughed with her while removing the glass from her hand. "Strong enough for you in your present state," he commented.

He put the water he'd been heating into the tin tub and then added enough cold to make it comfortable. He arranged a screen to give her privacy. "I'm sorry that the management doesn't run to ladies' nightwear, but one of my shirts and a robe ought to suffice." He put the garments over the screen as he spoke. "Tomorrow we'll decide what to do about clothes for you."

"Ish already tomorrow," she pointed out in the interest of accuracy.

"It depends on which tomorrow you're talking about," he teased, and after a moment of thought, she nodded solemnly.

In order that she not fall asleep in the tub, he kept talking to her when she'd stepped behind the screen, but his efforts were in vain; one moment Lexy was fairly coherent, and in the next she was sound asleep, as exhaustion, a good meal, potent cider, and a warm bath caught up with her all at once. Hawk rescued her just before she slipped under the water. He lifted her out of the tub and wrapped her in towels and then a blanket, chuckling to himself. He had meant for her to relax enough to sleep soundly, but his timing had been a little off.

He would have had to have been blind to have missed the contours of her body as he dried her off, and even then he would have traced them by touch. But as clear as the youth and beauty of her were the bruises on her arms and shoulders and the abrasions visible from her struggle to elude the straitjacket. The marks of her time at Bellwood effectively quenched any lust.

He dressed her in his shirt and covered her warmly, and then he sat beside the bed for a long time while a gray, overcast day broke over the city.

When Lexy awakened in the afternoon, it took her a moment to remember where she was. She called Hawk's name but received no answer. Then she found the note he had left for her. It told her to make herself at home and not to worry about anything; he'd see her later.

She took him at his word. There was little she could do, anyway, since her wardrobe consisted of the sacklike nightgown from Bellwood and Hawk's shirt. Her mind skittered away from the realization that Hawk must have seen her nude and dressed her in the shirt. The last thing she remembered was being in the tub.

She wandered around the house. Hawk was neat in his living habits and not given to random collections of things, but what he did have was obviously carefully chosen. Books were everywhere, but even these were displayed with order. And there were objects from various Indian tribes: a beautifully woven basket, a war club, a beaded vest, a pipe, a geometrically patterned blanket. Plainly, his Indian heritage meant a great deal to him.

She felt like curling up and sleeping some more to the sound of the rain that had begun to fall, but instead she found writing materials and began capturing the horrors of Bellwood on paper. She stopped after several pages, hating the distant voice of the article, convinced that it would be far too easy to set aside what was recounted there.

She began again, and this time, she used her own voice start to finish. "Last night I was rescued from the Bellwood Asylum for Insane Females . . ." She wrote furiously, ink splattering when her thoughts outran her pen. She made herself relive the sights, sounds, and smells of the place, the bleak cruelty of it. She wrote of the sane kept with the insane and of the utter lack of any diagnosis or treatment. And she did not spare those who condemned their relatives to Bellwood.

Hawk returned to his house while Lexy was writing the final paragraphs. He reached for the stack of finished pages, his hand hesitating over them, his expression asking permission without words.

She nodded vaguely, still caught up in getting the final sentences just right. When she had written the last word, she sat back and closed her eyes, emotionally exhausted in a way she had never experienced with a story before.

The rustle of the pages brought her out of her stupor, and she looked up to see that Hawk was engrossed in reading her article. He reached for the last page without looking up from the text. Lexy put the paper in his hand.

She cared very much about what he thought of the piece, but beyond that she had a sense of rightness about him sitting there concentrating on the pages, as if this were part of a long-established routine of sharing each other's work. She made herself reject the image. Their being together now was the result of extraordinary circumstances; there were still countless things she did not know about this man.

Hawk put the pages down. "It's powerful, Lexy. No one could read this and not be moved. Reid will publish it; he couldn't refuse. And the article will serve the further purpose of at least keeping the operators of Bellwood at bay, if not, as to be hoped, putting them out of business."

He went on to explain that so far there seemed to be no alarm raised by Bellwood about the missing patients, though he was sure Lorna's husband and Maud's relatives would be notified. For the moment, the two women were in good hands.

"Lorna has been seen by a doctor who says she ought to recover swiftly now that she's getting proper food and care. He's willing to testify that she has obviously been abused and neglected at Bellwood. And of course, her brother will see to her welfare from now on. Maud is another matter altogether. I think Rob is growing quite fond of her, though he claims she eats enough for five men, but some more permanent situation will have to be found for her."

Hawk's words of praise were still uppermost in her mind, but she made herself concentrate on the consequences of what she had set in motion. "Blaine is a fine lawyer; he ought to be able to help both Lorna and Maud if they need legal protection. And as for Maud, my great aunt Philly is very adept at finding places for people with problems." Lexy thought of how generously Philly credited Flora with having taught her that there were solutions, albeit they often took a full measure of work and time to find, for the troubles of those society too often threw away.

Rather than compromise Lexy's reputation by asking her land-lady to fetch clothing from Lexy's quarters, Hawk had purchased a skirt, blouse, underthings, and nightclothes. He presented her with the packages, and to her surprise, she discovered that everything seemed to be of the proper size.

"How did you manage it?" she asked before she considered the import of her words; for all she knew, Hawk was so experienced with women, he had shopped for their clothing countless times before.

"Just lucky, I suppose," Hawk said. He was not about to admit that he had had no difficulty in describing Lexy's height and exact proportions to a fascinated clerk.

Having suitable clothes in hand made Lexy aware of the fact that she was still dressed in Hawk's shirt. It hadn't seemed signifi-cant when he had come in and while she was absorbed by her writing, but now she was embarrassed.

She clutched at the clothes. "I'll go dr . . . dress, so I can go back to my . . ." Her voice died away as Hawk came to her.

He took the clothes from her unresisting hands. "Please stay, just until tomorrow. There's nothing you can do for Lorna and Maud tonight, and I would feel better if you were out of sight at least until tomorrow. I don't think the people at Bellwood will know who you are, not until the article is published, but just in case they've come into the city looking for their patients, I'd prefer that each of you is protected."

It had the semblance of reasonableness, but Hawk knew he had proposed it more because he wasn't ready for Lexy to leave than because he really feared the Bellwood people would locate her. He hoped his protective instincts would have quieted by the next day. And Lexy accepted it for parallel reasons. Hawk made her feel safe, and tomorrow seemed soon enough to face Reid and everyone else.

Having made the decision to remain at Hawk's house, Lexy found it strangely easy to let the rest of the world disappear. She did not even change out of his shirt. It no longer seemed important. This man had saved her from Bellwood and had cared for her as tenderly as if she were a child. It no longer mattered to her that he had seen her naked. She was floating in a space where only she and Hawk existed. It was as if he had always been part of her life and always would be. She had never experienced this singular focus on a man before. And even confessing her own foolishness to herself did not lessen the intensity.

Hawk provided a delectable supper complemented by a fine bottle of claret. He called it "a meal provided by intensive research of the city's wine and food shops." Lexy didn't care where it came from; it tasted ambrosial.

It took them a long time to finish the meal because they talked throughout about many subjects. Lexy found that Hawk was adept at drawing information from her. He wanted to know about her brothers and the other members of the family, but while he was forthcoming and even eloquent as he described the history of each of the Indian artifacts in his house, he had far less to say about the more intimate details of his life, and his eyes became so shuttered when Lexy pressed him that she backed off. She couldn't be sure, but she was beginning to suspect that his own childhood had been so bleak and painful in comparison to hers, that it was probably something he not only didn't talk about, he tried not to think about it. It made him seem lonesome and made her more willing to talk about her own family, as if she could offer it to him as comfort for his own lack. She understood the irony; his reticence now made her feel more, not less, intimate with him.

Listening to Lexy talk about her parents and the twins was like listening to a wonderful fairy tale about a family entwined in love and shared lives. It was too late for him, but not for the person Hawk cared most about.

Lexy didn't know what thought had intruded in Hawk's mind, but she felt the atmosphere between them change as if the temperature had abruptly plummeted.

She wanted to ask him what it was, but she knew it was useless; he had retreated once more into himself. But this time she felt little impatience. She had felt very close to Hawk tonight, and she would again.

Despite his protests, she helped him clean up the remnants of their meal, but she accepted his suggestion that she retire for the night. Suddenly she was exhausted again, the energy that had coursed through her while she wrote the article and later while she spoke with Hawk ebbing away. But she was worried about where he was going to sleep.

"Don't fret about it," he said. "I think if I added up all the nights I've slept on something other than a mattress, they would outnumber the nights in a bed." What he would really like to do, he confessed to himself, was to sit beside the bed again, watching her sleep, watching over her.

But he had told her no less than the truth, and he had no trouble falling asleep wrapped in blankets on the floor. He had not slept at all the night before, and worry about Lexy had taken its own toll.

The scream was so piercing, Hawk was on his feet before he even knew he had awakened. The sound came again, a long keening wail of terror.

She had left one of the gas jets burning low, and in the soft light, he saw that she was lying rigidly with her arms wrapped tightly around her as if she were still in the straitjacket.

He called to her softly, and when that had no effect, he touched her shoulder. "Lexy, Lexy, wake up now. You're having a nightmare, nothing more." Her cries tore at him. He gathered her into his arms, rocking her. "Lexy, please wake up! Please! It's only a nightmare. You're safe, you're safe with me."

Her body jerked violently as she awakened, and she panted as if she couldn't get enough air. Her arms went around Hawk, and she clung to him as if she were drowning. "Oh, God! I thought I was back at Bellwood! I couldn't move. It had been days and days, and they weren't ever going to untie me!"

He rubbed her back, conscious of how cold she was against his warmth. And gradually, he grew conscious of other things as well. The nightgown he had purchased for her was no disguise for her at these close quarters; he could feel every curve and line of her, and his mind supplied the image of how she looked without even that flimsy covering.

He had thought himself so capable of protecting her from everything and everyone, including himself, and now it seemed he had overestimated his own chivalry. He wasn't wearing much more than she, only his smallclothes, left on in deference to having her in the house, and his body's sudden reaction to her proximity was growing more evident by the second.

"Ah, Lexy, I'll . . . ah, get you a glass of brandy . . . or something . . . so you can sleep again, ah . . ."

The uncharacteristic hesitancy in Hawk's voice penetrated Lexy's consciousness as her terror began to fade in the reassuring warmth of him. And she began to be aware of other things, too. She could feel his muscles tauten, as if an invisible current were running through his body, until he felt rock hard. And his shaft was growing, swelling and hardening, too. She could not mistake that, pressed against him as she was.

She had never made love with a man, but unlike many of her contemporaries, she was not ignorant of the process. She had often witnessed the heroic coupling of the stallions with the mares, and her mother and Anthea had taken particular pains to answer her questions honestly. They had wanted her to know that while the basics might be the same as they were with animals, sexual relations between a man and a woman should have as much to do with the mind, the heart, and the spirit as with the flesh, that anything less was a sad and demeaning fraud that too often resulted in unwanted pregnancies.

She knew her mother would want her to wait until she had found the man she would love for the rest of her life. She did not know whether or not Hawk was that man, but she knew that she would never be indifferent to him; she had felt his impact from the first time she had seen him, and in spite of her attempts to deny it, it had grown steadily until he was part of all her days, even when they were apart. And she wanted him now with a hunger she had never felt before. She not only wanted him to banish the night terror, she simply wanted him.

The slow undulation of Lexy's body against his was making it difficult for Hawk to think clearly, but he made the effort, speaking harshly out of his own distress. "Lexy, this won't do. Another minute, and I'll have you flat on your back." He tried to untangle himself, but Lexy just wrapped herself more tightly around him.

"I want you, Hawk. Please, love me?"

The bold statement of desire paired with the soft question touched and delighted him. So much about her had delighted him from his first sight of her; that truth shimmered through him with the pulse of his desire.

"Good God, Lexy, you don't know what you're saying!" he groaned. "There are things about me you don't know, but I'm no seducer of young virgins!" But as he was saying it, he was inhaling the sweet fragrance of her and feeling the silk of her hair and skin.

"Every woman is a virgin until she has known a man, and while I may be younger than you, I am not a child." She pointed out the obvious in a slow, husky voice that made him feel as if she were suddenly as old as Eve and he the virgin. Her mouth sought his, tentative at first, but seeking to know the way to please him, and he was lost.

Lexy knew he still had reservations, but she felt his surrender, and she vowed the seduction would be so sweet for him, he would never regret it. It stripped away the last of her fear about how it would be for her the first time. She was determined only that she would not let her inexperience spoil it for him.

The sensual mouth that had struck her as incongruous from the beginning was, she discovered, marvelously skilled at lovemaking. He began with a touch so soft on her own mouth, she had to concentrate to feel it, but he gradually deepened the contact until her mouth opened to his and his tongue searched inside, though he took exquisite care not to hurt the bruised side.

Every sensation was new to Lexy. When his tongue probed and tasted her mouth, she felt heat begin to coil deep and low inside of her. Her little mew of surprised pleasure made Hawk smile as he turned his attention to the satin of her throat and the firm swell of her breasts. He had rid himself and her of their scant coverings, and the light still burned, but she did not ask for darkness. Everything about her openness made him aware of his responsibility to make this first time good for her. As his body drove him on, he accepted that he would regret taking what she offered, but he did not want her to regret the way of it, whatever else her misgivings might be when morning dawned.

Despite the bruises, her body was beautiful, and he took his time savoring every inch of it, arousing her with his hands and mouth, glorying in the ripples of sensation he could feel beneath her skin. Her years of riding and the quick way she moved to every task showed in the fine-honed lines of her.

He nuzzled his face against her stomach. "You're like a Thoroughbred yourself," he teased, "slender, strong, swift, but soft in all the right places." He stroked the curve of her hips for emphasis.

She smiled up at him as he levered himself above her so he could see her face. "It's the way they raise the women of Wild Swan." She said it with pride. She was offering everything she was to him, not just some creature she had become for the night. She traced the clear definition of the sinews in his arms and chest and then dropped her hand lower to touch the muscular plane of his belly, the delineations so different from hers, feeling the muscles quiver. "And you," she whispered, "you are like the stallions, all power and grace."

Suddenly they were both laughing at their shared fancy. They rolled together on the bed, nipping at each other, touching wherever they could reach. But the power of the image remained with them, too, and it was in both their minds when Lexy lay panting beneath him. She looked at the glistening strength of his body, at the jutting evidence of his desire, and she had no more words.

Hawk trembled with the effort to go slowly as he entered her, and he stopped when he saw her features tighten, though she made no protest.

"I'm sorry, sweetheart, sorry," he murmured, his hand seeking between them to stroke the tight bud of her desire again.

Lexy lay suspended between pain and pleasure, all her senses centered on the searing intrusion of his body into hers. For a panicked instant, she did not believe she could bear it if he went further, and then the pleasure began to sweep through her again, stronger than the pain, making her begin to move involuntarily. She was too inexperienced to know what her body was searching for, but suddenly she wanted him to move, too, wanted him to complete this. She looked up at him and the fear was gone. This was Hawk; he had saved her from Bellwood and cherished her; she trusted him now to take her from child to woman.

She arched her hips as he thrust deeper; there was a moment of sharp pain, and then the pain was gone, washed away in wave after wave of sensation that made her cry out in pleasure.

"That's it, love, that's it! Let it carry you!" Hawk felt her smooth, hot muscles stroking him. He wanted it to go on forever, but his body surrendered. He tried to withdraw to protect her, but she murmured a fevered protest and held him fast, her legs around his hips, her body keeping him captive inside.

Lexy was stunned by the mad frenzy that shook his body. At his most powerful, he seemed most vulnerable. He slumped against her and rolled to his side, taking her with him. She felt the pounding of his heart and the quick pumping of his lungs slow; she felt his manhood still within her, but nestled soft, wholly changed from the full, hard strength that had possessed her. Now she felt as if she possessed him, as if some essential part of him beyond his sex was in her keeping.

Lexy did not regret making love with Hawk, but she saw the complications. It had not been as simple as seeking the most basic comfort from her terror; she had trusted Hawk as she had never trusted another human being. And with the trust there had been love; there still was. But she did not attach expectations to it. She didn't know what she wanted from him, but she knew that he had his own demons, whatever they were, and she had no intention of making his life more difficult. It seemed to her that easing the way for the other was required by love, whether it be for a friend or a lover.

She stroked the soft waves of hair at the nape of his neck and the damp expanse of his shoulders. She suffered from no late shyness, but rather from a vast contentment. Because she had no preconceptions, no previous experience, each new sensation Hawk conjured in her seemed perfectly right. She felt him swelling again against her, and the sound she made was so like a purr, Hawk smiled.

This time he remained in control of his own passion long enough to nurture hers to the peak, so that he watched her eyes widen in shock at the force sweeping her body, and he caught her cries in his mouth, filled with a fierce need to possess her completely.

He had long regretted loving Caroline; for the first time he regretted that someone else was the center of his heart. As Lexy slept in his arms, he admitted to himself that were his life different, had Caroline never existed, he could love this woman well, could love her as she deserved. But as it was, he was less than heart whole for her. By the time he fell asleep near dawn, he was determined that he would somehow make it enough.

Hawk was still sleeping when Lexy awakened. Careful not to disturb him, she eased out from under the arm and the leg he had thrown over her in sleep. It was odd to realize there had been no feeling of strangeness in waking in his bed half pinned beneath him. But it was strange to see him in sleep, still and quiet. He was so vitally alive that his conscious presence was overwhelming.

He was lying on his stomach, his face half turned toward her, his lashes lying in dark crescents on his cheekbones.

She put her hand to her mouth to stifle a gasp of horror. Now she remembered feeling the slight unevenness in the skin of his back and buttocks, but she hadn't had a clear sight of it, and she hadn't, in the passion of the night, thought about what it meant.

They were faint, but unmistakable, lighter than the bronze of his skin, testimony to more than one savage beating. Tears blurred her vision, and without being aware of what she was doing, she reached out and stroked his back as if to ease the hurt.

She jumped when Hawk captured her hand in one of his. His dark, gold-flecked eyes were watching her. "Don't weep," he commanded softly. "It was over long ago."

"Who?" she asked, her voice trembling.

He hesitated for a moment, and then answered, "My father. He was a man who could not live with his own contradictions. He was incapable of contentment. And sometimes he accepted the Indian blood that ran in both of us, other times he wanted to beat it out of me, as if he could free me and himself of all that being a 'breed' means."

The matter-of-fact acceptance in his voice did not assuage her grief. "You were a child, just a child! It is a miracle that you have become the man you are and not some twisted, hate-filled creature. I cannot imagine what it was like for you. I have received only kindness from the hands of my parents." The tears overflowed.

The sight of them trickling down over the fading bruise on her cheek hurt Hawk far more than the memories of his father's abuse. He sat up and pulled Lexy into his arms. "Where is that tough journalist who took on the devils of Bellwood?" he coaxed. "Look, I don't condone what my father did, but there were also people who were good to me along the way. My grandparents were among them, always patient, always kind. And for all his meanness, my father gave me an invaluable gift. Whatever else we were doing, wherever we were, he insisted that I never neglect my studies. If there were no school available, he got the books and made sure I read them. He meant education to be a way to be less Indian, but I found it was a way to escape, to travel to exotic places for hours at a time, a way to think about things and dream dreams I never would have otherwise. So whatever his motives, the result was of benefit to me."

Lexy pulled away so that she could see him. She cupped his face in her hands, studying the strong bones. The little scar at his temple had new significance for her now; she was sure it, too, was a token of his father's "education." "You are wise to view it as you do, but I don't have to do the same. I will always mourn for the little boy who was treated so cruelly."

She kissed him gently, without passion, as if she were offering solace to his younger self.

Hawk had expected that no matter what the intimacies they had shared, morning would find Lexy burdened with second thoughts, regrets, and renewed modesty. It stunned him to see that none of this was true; she was as open and loving as she had been the night before. He wanted nothing more than to make love to her again, but the day and his life were catching up with them.

He meant to somehow soften the words, but he couldn't find the way, and he heard the harshness of them in his own ears. "Lexy, I'm not sure what we ought to do next, but you have to know, I have a son, Jared. He's six years old, and as soon as I can arrange it, I'm going to have him with me."

Feeling as if she were made of glass, Lexy got out of bed very carefully and donned first the nightgown and then the robe that Hawk had gotten for her. With meticulous attention to detail, she made sure every ribbon was tied in a neat bow.

"And how does your wife, or is it ex-wife, fit into all of this? Or is the child with someone else?" Her words were as careful as her actions.

Her cold withdrawal hit him in a wave, and he groaned. "Ah, hell, Lexy, it's bad enough, but it's not what you think! I haven't left a string of wives, or even one, behind me." He rubbed his face, suddenly feeling a hundred years old, though what he had to tell her could, in his opinion, only happen to a young and extremely foolish man.

"I was never married to Caroline, Jared's mother. I wanted to marry her, but she kept making excuses—she was afraid of her family's disapproval, she was afraid of this, or that—but the truth was that she was already married to a much older man. I don't know for certain, but I think she chose me for stud service. Everything that seemed so much the work of kind fate then, now seems wholly calculated."

He told the story without sparing himself, of how a supposedly chance meeting on a foggy San Francisco street had blossomed into a romance with the woman named Caroline, at least on his part, of how captivated he'd been by her dark beauty and her air of mystery. He had been twenty-three years old and had already achieved some recognition as a journalist. He had felt very mature and worldly, but nothing had prepared him for a woman like Caroline. She was well practiced in all the social graces. She was accustomed to the very best in everything due to a father who had built a fortune on selling supplies to miners rather than trusting his luck to the metals in the ground, though Hawk had not discovered who her father was until after the affair was over; Caroline had used neither her true maiden name nor her married surname. All Hawk had known was that Caroline was not the sort of young woman with whom a man had a casual affair, and he had been anxious to marry her and sure that they could since she was twenty-one. Then the affair had ended with nothing more than a short note from her saying that she had changed her mind about her relationship with Hawk and had fallen in love with another man.

"I was frantic to find her, to convince her that I was the right man for her, but she seemed to have vanished without a trace, and eventually I had to accept that she had no intention of being part of my life again. After a time, it seemed for the best; it's doubtful that I could ever have provided her with the luxuries to which she was accustomed."

His voice took on a peculiar flatness, as if he were trying to distance himself from the rest of the story, but his eyes burned with the pain of it. "I didn't know about Jared until last year. And that time it *was* just a chance meeting on a street in San Francisco. Caro was horrified to see me, but her little boy—our little boy—was happy to tell me that his name was Jared Fordyce and that he was five years old. Caro was clever in her choice of me. She has dark eyes, dark hair, though her skin is very fair, and her husband, when he was younger, must have had dark hair, too, for his eyes are so and his skin is swarthy. The child could be theirs. But he is not! He is my son. If you saw us side by side, you could not doubt it."

Lexy was so mesmerized by his story, she settled on the bed again without knowing she'd moved. Sitting so close to him, she could see the light changing in his eyes. And she saw the sudden softness there as he continued to talk about the child.

"I find myself wondering odd things. Though his Indian blood is less than mine, I wonder if Jared will learn he hardly needs a razor when he comes of age." He touched his nearly smooth cheeks reflectively, and Lexy's eyes stole to his chest as well, loving the almost smooth expanse, thinking that she was truly lost if his sparse body hair contrasted with the luxuriant hair on his head was enough to distract her with images of their lovemaking.

Hawk's voice changed again, sharpening with barely suppressed rage. "What will they tell him if his round, childish face matures with bones like mine?"

"What if it doesn't happen?" Lexy whispered. "What if you're wrong, and Jared is not your son?"

"He is. The timing was perfect for the birth of my son. But beyond that, beyond the fact that he looks so like me, I just know."

"All right, if that is accepted, what do you plan to do, steal the child from his mother? She is married, and you did not say the child appeared to be mistreated. In fact, your description of your meeting with him makes him sound like a happy, well-cared-for little boy."

Hawk fought against his own memories that insisted, no matter how hazy the images, that things had been much better in his childhood while his mother had still been alive. He reminded himself, as always, that he had no intention of being harsh like his father. All he wanted was a chance to cherish and raise his son.

"She lied to conceive him; she has no right to him," he said. "Jared is my son."

Hawk, normally so logical, was completely illogical on the subject of Jared Fordyce. Lexy wanted to hate Caroline; instead, she felt a sneaking sympathy for the woman. She doubted very much that Caroline had had no feelings for Hawk; she could not imagine any woman being immune to his attraction, let alone to his lovemaking. And whatever Caroline's motives had been, whoever had fathered her child, Hawk's brief descriptions of the boy showed a confident child happy to be on an outing with his mother. Lexy could not see how having Hawk in vengeful pursuit could bring anything but harm to both mother and child.

She felt as if she were picking her way along a steep cliff. "Does Caroline know you intend to take her . . . er, your son?"

"I expect she does," he answered grimly. "The Fordyces left San Francisco within twenty-four hours of my meeting with Caro and Jared. I admit they were, by all accounts, only passing through in any case, but I'm sure they hastened their travel plans. It took some time, but I discovered a lot about Caroline and her husband after they left. They'd gone east right after Caro ended her affair with me; they were back in San Francisco because her husband still had business interests there, and I suppose Caro risked it because she had no intention of running into me or thought it would make no difference if she did. From California they went east again and then on to tour Europe, but they are due back by next spring."

"Due back where?" Lexy could hardly form the words because she suspected she knew the answer.

"Here, in the capital. Sylvanus Fordyce's business includes a good many government contracts. He has a house here, as well as those in various other cities, but the best bet is that he plans to settle here for a while."

"So your coming here, uprooting your life in California, everything has been for the sole purpose of lying in wait for Caroline and Jared? This house," she gestured with her hand, and her voice strengthened with dawning anger, "it's small, but there's plenty of room for a man and a child, and it's much better than a boarding-house. And your job at the paper, your friendship with all of us, they're all just pieces of your scheme to establish a place for Jared. But it doesn't quite make sense that you have planned to take him and then stay in the same city as his parents." She used the word deliberately. "Unless, of course, you've assumed all along that Caroline will come with Jared, will come to you."

It was one thing to be with Hawk, to trust him as one independent person to another; it was quite different to find that none of them, including herself, meant anything to him compared to his plans for the boy who might or might not be his son and the woman who might be persuaded to leave her husband.

Though she was sitting close beside him, Hawk could feel the great distance between himself and Lexy "It isn't like that!" he protested. "You are all very, very important to me, you in particular. I've made a new life here. But I admit, I have also made sure it would have room in it for Jared. I have no intention of spiriting him away and spending the rest of his childhood running and hiding. Caroline's husband is a powerful man; he could afford to hire an army to pursue us. He will have to know that I am Jared's father, that I have a right to the boy. And Caro is Jared's mother. I no longer love her, but if it is necessary, I will provide for her."

"You mean, if you destroy her marriage, her husband turns her out, and her wealthy father refuses to offer her assistance. My God, when you plot vengeance, you make it complete!"

"It isn't like that!" There was despair mixed with the anger in his voice. "There is no easy way for this to be done, can't you see that? But the child is mine. I can't just let him grow up apart from me, never knowing that he is my blood. I want him to know that I love him, no matter how he was conceived. Hell, I want him to know that I loved his mother when he was conceived, that I wanted to marry her."

"You want to be the father your own should have been. You

want to share the kind of love you always wanted and never had."
Her own anger was dissipating, leaving cold sorrow in its wake.

Hawk mistook the softness in her voice, assuming that with understanding had come agreement. "It is all more complicated than I would wish for us, but I think we ought to get married."

Since marriage had never been one of her major goals, Lexy had done little speculating about how she would react to a proposal or how such an offer would be made, but not even habitual imagining would have prepared her for this. She buried her face in her hands, torn between the desire to weep and the urge to laugh. The laughter won, causing Hawk to make worried noises as he tried to draw her into his arms.

She pushed him away. "I may be slightly hysterical, but this whole situation is absurd, as insane as anything I witnessed at Bellwood," she said when she got control of her voice. "I seduced you, Hawk Mackenna, not the other way around, and I am not going to propose marriage to make it right. Even so, I am not Caroline. I don't have a husband in hiding somewhere, and I'm not going to disappear." She drew a deep breath. "I care about you a great deal. I would never have made love with you had I not known that I felt something for you deep inside. I would never have trusted you so much. But I don't have any plans for marriage to you or to anyone else. And I would never even consider it with a man whose life is in such a mess! You call it love for your son, and I know that's what you believe it is, but your plan involves destroying a little boy's security and what may well be a very happy home now, no matter how unfaithful Caroline was seven years ago. Hawk, you don't have room for me or for any other woman in your life."

Marriage to Lexy would complicate his life immeasurably, and what she said was undeniably true, but Hawk did not feel any relief at her refusal to consider his suit, and that confused him. Jared had been the center of his goals and thoughts for so long, it made him very uneasy to know that the circle had expanded to include Lexy Culhane.

"What if you are with child?" He had to ask the question.

"I am not Caroline," she repeated. "If I am carrying your child, we will decide what to do about it, but there is no sense in worrying about it if it doesn't exist." She felt curiously numb about the possibility of being pregnant; at the moment there were too many other things to consider.

Hawk broke the silence that stretched between them. "I could have said no last night."

"Could you?" Lexy replied, and there was a world of ancient and newly gained knowledge in her wide green eyes.

"Perhaps not," he conceded, and there were inward concessions, too. Though she might falter now and again and need support, as he would, their relationship, whatever it was to be, would be built on equal ground. Before Lexy, it was not the way he had ever imagined it could be with a woman. Now he wondered if anything less would ever again satisfy him.

Chapter 31

At first Reid was so furious at the risk Lexy had run by having herself committed to Bellwood, he threatened to fire her.

"Relative or not, I won't have reporters who engage in wild schemes to make up a story!" he snapped.

"I agree with you," Lexy answered calmly. "But that isn't what I did. The story was there; I simply went inside to report it."

Though Lexy had been willing to face Reid alone, Hawk had insisted that since he had played a part in it, he should be there for the interview.

"Mr. Tratnor, please read Lexy's article before you make a final decision." Hawk could easily have been on a first-name basis with his employer, but he had deliberately refrained from presuming, and though his words were quiet and reasonable, he was openly siding with Lexy. And that impressed Reid; whatever feelings Hawk had for Lexy—and Reid suspected there was something there—Hawk was one of the most astute journalists he knew. If Hawk judged a story worthwhile, it was.

Though Reid could not banish the knowledge of the danger Lexy had been in, it did not blind him to the power of her words as he read the pages. He understood immediately that this story had come from the guts and the heart, as had his own best writing. But there was a difference. When he had written from the battlefields of the war, when he had written about the aftermath of Custer's massacre, he had done so because he felt he could do no less and might influence a few people, though he had not had any true hope that anything would really change. But with the right publicity, Lexy's story could put Bellwood out of business, or at least gain improved treatment for the patients.

"It's damn good!" he growled when he'd finished reading it. "I'll probably never approve of the way you got this, and I'll leave it to you to explain to your parents, but I will put it on the front page."

Reid was all business after that, ordering extra copies to be run of the next day's edition, suggesting a few but important changes to Lexy, and dealing with the possible consequences of having taken Lorna and Maud out of the institution. He agreed with Lexy that Blaine ought to be called upon to sort out the legal ramifications, and to that end, Lorna, Landon, and Maud were spirited away to Wild Swan where they would be out of view and could meet in peace with Blaine.

Lexy's article was published under the name "Abby Adams." She and Reid decided it was fitting; one of her real names was, after all, Abigail, and very few readers would miss the reference to President John Adams's wife, who had admonished her husband to "Remember the Ladies" when it came to the new code of laws that would have to be made for the infant nation. Abigail Adams had been very clear about what she wanted:

> . . . be more generous and favorable to them than your ancestors. Do not put such unlimited power into the hands of the Husbands. Remember all men would be tyrants if they could. If particular care and attention is not paid to the ladies, we are determined to foment a Rebellion, and will not hold ourselves bound by any Laws in which we have no voice or Representation.

The pen name was suitable on many counts. It would hardly do for the article to be signed with her usual "Lexy," since the subjects she had previously dealt with had been, for the most part, the races and social events. Nor did Reid want her to use her real name.

"I have a mixed feeling of hope and dread that this will not be the last article of this kind that you do. You have the power and the insight, and now you know that you do. It would be safer if you were not so easily identified with the work," Reid pointed out bluntly, and though Lexy had an instant of regret that "Lexy Culhane" would not be printed boldly at the end of the piece, she agreed with him. It was safer not only for her, but also for her family. And "Abby Adams" was fitting for her, for the legacy given to her by the women in her family who never ceased to strive for women's rights. The sorrow of it was that the original Abigail Adams had written her words a full hundred and ten years ago, and yet, so many rights were still denied to women. Lorna's incarceration at Bellwood was a clear case of a husband's tyranny. The more Lexy thought of it, the more she liked the idea of trying to live up to the name.

Though Reid was tempted to give Rob Jenkins hell for helping Lexy with her scheme, he knew it would be unjust. Reid saw a lot of Alex and Gincie in Lexy, as well as elements from Travis; Rob Jenkins was no proof against that kind of determination.

Rob knew he'd gotten off lightly with only a few curt words from his employer, and having spent considerable time in Maud's company listening to stories about Bellwood, he could not dispute that Lexy's cause was just. He felt just a bit heroic himself for having done his part.

In addition to being grateful for his help, Lexy was thankful for his discretion. He was the only one who knew that Hawk had taken charge of her after the escape from Bellwood, and whatever he suspected about what had followed, he did not question or comment.

Lexy found that she could handle everything connected with the Bellwood story with great calm—everything except the inner turmoil from her brief, hidden time with Hawk. Even the session with her parents paled beside that.

Gincie and Travis were upset, angry, and not as shocked as they wished to be.

"It's hard to be firm with her when I remember that my first sight of you was of a young man named 'Gentry' riskin' his life to guide slaves north," Travis admitted wryly.

Gincie made a face at him. "Are we to be forever haunted by our youth? I want to say that what Lexy has done is not the same, but it is, it's just the same. She saw a terrible injustice, and in her way, she went to war."

It helped Lexy's case that by the time they saw her, the bruises had faded, and they had also met Lorna and Maud, hearing firsthand from them how hellish Bellwood had been.

"You must know that your mother and I are horrified by the risk you took," Travis told her, "but we're also very proud. And that puts us in the position of bein' able to do little more than to ask you to take very good care of yourself if you decide to fight other battles. No story on earth is worth your life."

Lexy thought they could not have chosen a more effective way to make her consider her actions; hurting them was the last thing she ever wanted to do. Hawk's image slipped into her mind, Hawk quite splendidly naked, his eyes both dark and golden in passion. If hurt was to come from her involvement with him, it must be her hurt alone. But in spite of her resolution, she wished she could confide in her mother. She was accustomed to understanding and encouragement from that quarter, and it made her feel more than a little lonesome to accept that, having chosen a course different from the one her mother would have approved, she could not expect support from her. In many ways, sleeping with Hawk had been a more profound step in setting the course of her own life than going to work for the paper had been.

"We owe a debt of gratitude to Mr. Mackenna," Gincie said. "Please tell him he is welcome at Wild Swan. I should like to meet the man someday soon. I've enjoyed his work in the *Witness*. If you are going to put yourself in dangerous straits, it's reassuring to know there is someone bold enough to help you out of them."

Lexy felt the blush climbing in her cheeks. It took all her self-control to meet her mother's eyes steadily. "I think you will like him, and he would be interested in Wild Swan. He's interested in everything, I think."

Despite her best efforts, Lexy knew she had betrayed something because she saw the sudden sharpening of interest in her mother's eyes, felt her waiting for further information.

She heard herself chattering about how much she liked Hawk, Rob, and her other colleagues, running them all together in an attempt to make Hawk seem no more than the rest, but though her mother did not question her further, Lexy did not think Gincie was diverted, and she knew she was going to have to be very careful lest she betray herself.

Considering all the careful planning she had done to achieve her journalistic goals, she had been singularly remiss in attaching so little importance to the effect a man could have on her life. Hawk loomed so large in her mind, everything, everyone else, appeared smaller, less significant. And though she was sure he was conscious of her presence in his life, she doubted very much that he was as obsessed as she was. She wondered if that were always the difference between men and women in affairs of the heart. She skirted around the admission that she was in love with Hawk Mackenna. She tried to call it caring, concern, intellectual compatibility, even lust, anything but love, but in her most honest moments, she admitted to herself that she could not imagine feeling more for a man than she had come to feel for Hawk. And that was perilously close to the only definition of love that made sense.

She made no effort to avoid Hawk. She was determined to go on as before; it would be too obvious if she changed her behavior around him, and more important, she did not want to forgo his company, nor did she think he would allow it if she tried. She felt as if they were in a strange dance, both of them moving with care, listening for the music to tell them what to do next. And the most frustrating part was that the rhythm was being set more by the absent Caroline and her son than by Lexy and Hawk.

Lexy listened to her own inner rhythm as well, and her body told her she was not carrying Hawk's child.

She was straightforward when she told him she had not conceived, but she did not see what she expected.

"Surely you are relieved!"

"All good sense says I must be," he agreed slowly. "My life is complicated enough as it is and is complicating yours, but somehow, it is not difficult for me to imagine having and loving a little green-eyed boy or girl—and you, having you." His eyes flared with the sudden light of passion, the night they had spent together reflected there.

Because of his obsession with Jared, Hawk knew he had no right to press any claim on Lexy, and by unspoken, mutual consent they had been discreet since she had left his house, seeing each other at work, sharing meals in restaurants, occasionally going for walks or to exhibits in the city when they could, spending a good deal of time with each other but not alone and certainly not in a place that might give them the opportunity to make love again.

It was the wisest course, but it did not stop Hawk from desiring Lexy with a constant ache. The scent of her, the texture of her hair, the green of her eyes, the shape of her that his hands and body remembered too well: everything about her conspired to arouse him when he was with her and to haunt him when he was not. But he was practiced at concealing his feelings, and most of the time he knew he did very well at hiding what he felt for her. He did not think she knew the power she had over him now. More than ever he wanted the Fordyces to return from Europe and Jared to be with him. Of the confrontation that was bound to come between himself and Caroline and her husband, he thought as little as possible; it was necessary and would have to be dealt with when the time came.

He was as interested as Lexy in the outcome of the revelations about Bellwood, and he was deeply impressed by the help offered by various members of Lexy's family. Blaine Carrington, who would, Hawk was sure, never use his considerable reputation for personal gain, was relentless in pursuit of the best outcome for Lorna and Maud.

Lorna's husband was predictably enraged by the release of his wife from the asylum, but he was also a man who could not stand to have his business dealings brought to light. Blaine used his connections to force Van Dyne to agree to a divorce and to return to Lorna that part of her inheritance that remained. The alternative, her husband was told in the bluntest terms, was arrest and certain imprisonment for a long list of illegal schemes, schemes that had involved men who would be only too glad to have a piece of his hide.

Much of the evidence had already been gathered by Landon Tilitson, and Reid used all the resources of the paper to add to the list.

Maud's case was different. Her family was coldly aloof, unwilling to have the old woman living with them, for Maud was set in her ways and outspoken. But for all of that, they were not malicious enough to sanction abuse and were embarrassed to have been taken in by the Bellwood staff, who had convinced them that the old lady would receive good guardianship in gracious surroundings. To save what face they could, they were willing to pay for Maud's expenses in her new situation in Baltimore, a place found for her by Philly. Two widows had combined their possessions and lived quite pleasantly in a large house. Once they had met Maud, Philly had little trouble persuading them to expand their household to include her.

A considerable number of the patients at Bellwood were taken home by their families in the wake of the scandalous revelations, but many remained, some of them suffering from severe mental disorders. The "doctor" at Bellwood turned out to be, as Lexy had suspected, no doctor at all.

"No one knows enough about sickness of the mind to cure it. Sometimes patients just seem to get well; too often they wander in and out of the darkness," Anthea told Lexy. "But any sensible physician must surely agree that they must be treated with kindness, kept clean, well fed, and where it is possible, occupied by some task. Those things are necessary for anyone's physical and mental health."

Anthea was willing to do more than talk. She enlisted Max, Nigel, and a few other physicians in the project to provide some supervision at Bellwood. It wasn't a perfect solution, but it was one that enabled the owners of the institution to keep the place running with an improved reputation. The owners had denied that they knew of the abuses there. No one believed them, but as Anthea said, "It doesn't matter whether they're telling the truth or not about the past; the present and the future at Bellwood are going to be much improved."

Anthea's enthusiasm for the project was enhanced by the fact that she and the other physicians had, in exchange for charging very modest fees for their services, gotten the pledge of a certain number of beds to be reserved for indigent patients who would be recommended by them and who were to be treated with no less dignity than those who had full fees paid for them.

Gincie and Sam had their own contributions to make, having decided that the asylum could do with a flower and vegetable garden. They would oversee and finance the initial labor, plus making sure that the project continued. Patients would not be required to work in the garden but would be encouraged to do so, and the flowers and produce would be used at the institution.

"Sam and I think a few fruit trees would be a good idea, too," Gincie said, envisioning the first green shoots that would appear on the young trees and in the plots when spring came. "I'm sure there were once all kinds of plantings at Bellwood. Gran always drew such peace from her gardens, as her grandmother had before her, as Sam and I still do. Maybe those poor souls at the asylum will find peace there, too."

Hawk heard about the family's involvement from Reid, from Rob, and sometimes from Lexy, but he sensed the lessening of her euphoria over the success of the campaign to change Bellwood. It seemed so natural, he wasn't even aware that he was growing increasingly sensitive to Lexy's moods.

"You must be pleased by what's happening at Bellwood," he insisted. "You could scarcely have hoped for better results."

She hesitated, trying to find the words to frame her mix of emotions. "That's true, and I realize it could all have turned out much worse, perhaps even with legal action against us for taking Lorna and Maud away. And I know that with Anthea, Nigel, and Max involved, patients will be treated well. But there's part of me that keeps pointing out how many other such institutions still exist to prey on the helpless. Of course, I am not the only voice asking for humane treatment of the insane, but altogether, it's a small chorus. I fear real changes won't come in time for most of the people trapped in such places." She shifted restlessly and looked at her hands instead of at Hawk. "And though I'm grateful for everything they're doing, I didn't mean for my story to demand so much from my family. It makes me feel less competent."

Now it was Hawk's turn to search for the right words. "I don't really know your family, but I am learning more about them day by day. You haven't made any of them do anything they don't want to do. They are in the habit of being involved in civic duties. And whether it's your family or other citizens who respond to the call to make things better, that's the whole point of writing articles like yours about Bellwood, isn't it?"

She could find no fault in his logic. "It is," she conceded, realizing he had made her feel better about the whole situation. She also realized that from the little she knew of Hawk's father, community involvement had not been one of his endeavors. Whenever she thought of the deprivations of Hawk's childhood, it made her newly grateful for her own upbringing. And beyond that, it made her want to share her family's warmth with Hawk, a risky proposition since it would entail having her family, particularly her mother, see her with him. She wasn't sure that she could conceal how she felt about him in front of such a discerning audience; she wasn't even sure she wanted to hide her feelings. He was an intelligent, handsome man. If he were not obsessed with the past, with Jared, she could imagine it would be very pleasant to appear at Wild Swan with Hawk. But as she envisioned it, she wondered where her independence had gone.

She felt as if the decision had been taken out of her hands when she received the note from her mother inviting Hawk to spend Christmas with them, if he had no other plans. Gincie had deferred to Lexy by enclosing the note to Hawk with the one to her daughter, but that did not stop Lexy from feeling as if she were obligated to extend the invitation to Hawk. Her parents had already expressed a desire to meet him, and her mother had discovered, though not from her, that Hawk had no family in Washington—at least not yet, Lexy amended grimly, not until the Fordyces returned. Having had no previous experience of trying to keep secret a special interest in a man, Lexy could not judge whether she was being too sensitive or whether her mother really did suspect something and was using this civilized method of learning more.

When she gave him the invitation, Hawk was aware of her unease. He read it and then studied her face. "I won't accept if you'd rather I didn't," he said bluntly, and then added, "Perhaps it would be better to refuse. As generous as the invitation is, Christmas is surely no time for strangers to invade your home."

Perversely, his willingness to forgo the visit made Lexy determined to pursue the opposite course. She recalled how warm and festive Wild Swan was at Christmas, and she doubted that Hawk had ever experienced anything like it.

"Christmas is exactly the time when strangers should be made welcome," she corrected him. "And anyway, you're not really a stranger to them. They know you from your writing and from your rescue of me. And the Tratnors know you personally."

She smiled at him with wry candor. "However, I warn you that I think my mother suspects you are more than a friend to me, and the rest of the family, my father and my brothers in particular, won't be far behind in their speculation. It's both the strength and the weakness of my family that everyone knows everyone else's business most of the time. What makes it bearable is that when things are bad for someone in the family, he or she has everyone else ready to offer help and support."

It was a way of life Hawk could scarcely imagine, and for a moment, he felt desperately hungry to experience, just once, what it would be like to share such warmth, even as a stranger at the feast, but then he considered the full implication of what she'd said.

Before, he'd only been thinking of the surface discomfort of her having to take responsibility for him as a guest in her home; now he thought of exactly what she'd said.

"More than a friend." Indeed, he was. He doubted he and Lexy could ever be anything as uncomplicated as just friends again. He could not imagine a time when he would look at Lexy Culhane and not feel desire for her. And while he trusted his circumspection, and hers, with strangers, he was far less sure about her family. If he felt the current of excitement that always seemed to run between himself and this woman, would not those who knew and loved her so well also feel it?

"Oh, hell," he swore with sudden weariness, "I don't want to compromise you in the eyes of your family. I'll meet them some other time."

It was a red flag to Lexy.

"Compromise! In this context it is a hideous word!" she snapped. "And it does not suit. By using it you denigrate yourself and me. You keep trying to take the blame for what happened between us, but there is no blame, and it was my choice, more than yours. I don't know what the future holds for us, but I refuse to be ashamed of the night we spent together! And I have just realized that I hate the idea of spending Christmas at Wild Swan while you spend it alone here. If you can bear the scrutiny of my family, then I certainly can."

Hawk was a little dizzy from the circular course they had just taken, but he could not back down from the challenge in Lexy's eyes. Though he had no intention of telling her, Hawk suddenly saw that he had an obligation to her family. He, no more than Lexy, knew what was to become of the two of them, but it was increasingly difficult to imagine a life without her. Her family had the right to know what kind of man he was.

Hawk had, in spite of his background, or perhaps because of it, developed a fair amount of self-confidence at an early age and had been acting on it for a long time. But it wavered noticeably when he put himself in the place of Lexy's parents and viewed himself through their eyes. He was a good journalist and gainfully employed, and the Culhanes were not the sort to object to his Indian blood. But on Lexy's behalf, they would certainly condemn his past involvement with a married woman (no matter that he had not known she was married at the time) and his present determination to claim Jared, at whatever cost to himself and to Lexy.

By the time he arrived at Wild Swan with Lexy, he was as nervous as he could ever remember being. He knew his responses were too stiff and formal to the warm greetings he received, but he couldn't seem to help himself.

Even when he had been blazing with anger over her peril at Bellwood, Lexy had not seen Hawk look as formidable as he did now. The bones of his face seemed carved in stark relief, his eyes were dark, seeming to have lost the golden light, and his lips were set in such a tight line, his beautiful mouth looked entirely different. He greeted each person he was introduced to with the briefest acknowledgment.

Finally Lexy muttered to him, "Chief Hawk, you are not here for treaty negotiations; this is a Christmas party!"

Her teasing took him unawares, and he smiled down at her. "I'm having a little trouble convincing myself of that."

Gincie's first impression of Hawk Mackenna was of a man so stern and withdrawn, she was sure she had mistaken her daughter's interest in him, but she saw the smile transform his face; she saw how Lexy looked at him; and she knew that for the first time in her life, Lexy had met a man who could not be kept at a safe distance by the casual familiarity of friendship. Actually, for all the restraint Mr. Mackenna was showing, Gincie doubted the man could ever be described as "safe." As long and as satisfyingly married as she was to Travis, still, Gincie was not blind to Hawk's appeal; he was so big and so male, he more than held his own among the family's men.

Gincie was reassured by the fact that Reid regarded Hawk with high esteem, but she was also conscious of the fact that that was based on their professional relationship and on the personal contact Reid had had with Hawk since Mackenna had come to Washington. Reid freely confessed that he had never made any attempt to investigate Hawk's past.

"It did not seem necessary for my purposes," he told Gincie when she asked, "but I presume you are interested because of Lexy—yes, I've seen that there's something between them, no matter how discreet they are trying to be. If you wish, for Lexy's sake, I'll try to find out more about the man."

Gincie was sorely tempted to take him up on his offer, but then she thought better of it. Nothing anyone could have told her about Travis would have changed her mind about him; she was sure Lexy was equally steadfast. Beyond that, it seemed a violation of trust to subject Hawk to such a search, and she told Reid as much.

"I'm relieved," he said. "I really do like him, and I would bet more than I could afford that he is honorable."

Gincie hoped he was right, but she planned to keep an eye on Hawk Mackenna so that she could make her own judgment. However, she had scarcely decided that when she found herself defending him.

She had always suspected that when the time came for Lexy to choose a man, Travis, for all his kindness and logical approach to things, was going to be no less difficult than most fathers who adored their daughters. They had never discussed it, and Travis would have denied it anyway, but Gincie knew that as much as he loved the twins, Lexy had a special place in his heart. Unlike many men who wanted only sons to carry on the name, Travis had wanted a daughter for their firstborn, and it touched Gincie still that he had wanted their little girl to be like her. But now he was going to have to understand that Lexy was enough like her mother to make her own choice.

Lexy and Hawk had arrived two days before Christmas, and the first night of their visit, Gincie could almost hear Travis thinking before he said, "He's a grim one. Can't understand what Lexy sees in him."

"You're not supposed to see what Lexy sees," Gincie told him, continuing to brush her hair. "But wait until you see him smile. I think even you could notice the change."

Travis was not pleased with the course of the conversation. He had meant to be subtle and wanted Gincie to assure him that their daughter had no romantic interest in Hawk Mackenna. "You invited him, not Lexy. Maybe she's just bein' polite."

"Maybe," Gincie agreed, trying not to laugh.

"Well, damn it all! It doesn't help anythin' for you to pretend to agree with me when you really don't!"

Gincie put the brush down and gave him her full attention. "What do you want me to do? You wouldn't be so worried if you didn't already know that Lexy has some special interest in the man, so it isn't going to matter whether I deny it or not. I'm not sure Lexy has admitted it to herself yet, but I think she's in love with him. And no matter how uneasy he has been today, I don't have much difficulty remembering that he's the one who charged into Bellwood and rescued our daughter." She shuddered involuntarily. "For that alone, I am willing to grant him much."

"Includin' our daughter?" Travis growled.

"She isn't ours anymore, my darling. Lexy will give herself when she chooses a man, just as I gave myself to you and took you for my own."

Travis opened his arms, and Gincie went to him, nestling against him. "Everythin' you say is true," he sighed, "and I reckon that if I'd just met the man without any connection to Lexy, I'd judge him an impressive fellow. But none of that helps when it's connected to my little girl. That's what she's always goin' to be to me, no matter how many times I tell myself she's a woman grown."

"I don't think she'll mind you thinking of her that way, as long

as you don't make her choose between you and Hawk Mackenna,"
Gincie said, a question in her voice. After a long pause, Travis
replied, "I may be havin' trouble with this, but I'm no fool. Just like
her mother: tell her no, and she'll say yes, no matter what."

"And aren't you glad I did?" Gincie said, nuzzling his throat,
coaxing him to forget the problems he couldn't solve anyway.

The more he saw of them, the more Hawk liked Lexy's family,
but he still felt ill at ease unless Lexy was right beside him. The
atmosphere at Wild Swan made him acutely conscious of how unaccustomed he was to a sense of family. The little taste of it he had
had when very young did not compare with this busy intertwining of
lives. But his emotional unease did not prevent him from appreciating
the impressive organization of Wild Swan, Sunrise, and Brookhaven.

Lexy took him riding over the farms, pointing out the various
enterprises. He was a good rider, and he enjoyed watching Lexy's
easy competence in the saddle. Even more, he liked the way the
people who worked at the farms greeted her. She was obviously held
in great affection by everyone, and her manner toward them was
warm and friendly as she asked for personal news of each of them or
related something of interest. At Wild Swan and Sunrise, the horses
were always the center of concern, and Lexy's pride was evident
when she showed them to Hawk and pointed out strengths,
weaknesses, and the hopes invested in the racing animals. It amused
and fascinated him to listen to her and the horse handlers discussing
the details of the animals' care and training.

Lexy's position as favored daughter of the house was unassail-
able at Wild Swan, and when the Tratnors arrived, Hawk thought that
was what accounted for Jilly's unusual benevolence toward her cousin.

"I see Miss Tratnor doesn't care to challenge you on your own
ground," he said.

"Well, that's generally true, but you should have noticed she
isn't flirting with you, either, and that can only mean something of
greater moment than being here has distracted her," Lexy teased.
She was able to be much more tolerant of Jilly's whims now that she
no longer lived in the Tratnor household. "I'm not sure of it, but
family rumor has it that Jilly is engaged to be married. If that's the
case, we won't have long to wait to be told," she added with wry
amusement.

She was quickly proved correct. Jilly was engaged to Dermot
Hargrave III, scion of a New York family prominent in the world of
finance. Her brother Benjamin had met the man through his banking
job and had brought him home to meet the Tratnors some months
before. According to Jilly, she and Dermot had immediately recog-

nized each other as soul mates, but after listening to her for a while, Lexy and Hawk thought it sounded more like a meeting of pocketbooks than of souls. Jilly was very impressed with Dermot's wealth, with the diamond ring he'd given her, and with the position she would have in New York as his wife.

Privately, Hawk rather pitied Dermot Hargrave III. He could imagine few things worse than being married to a woman whose abiding interest was in the riches the man could provide. Still, he worried about Lexy.

"Is it difficult for you, having Jilly announcing her engagement, and having . . . well, having me here with things the way they are between us?" he asked. "Nothing's changed; I intend to have Jared with me, and I know how you feel about that, but I would still like you to marry me." It occurred to him that he wanted it even more now than when he had first asked her.

"I hope you do know how I feel about Jared. I expect I would love him without any effort, your child or not. My objection is to your determination to have him no matter what the cost to him, to his mother, to Mr. Fordyce," Lexy reminded him. They had not spoken of marriage since the first time, and suddenly it was important to her that Hawk truly understood her position.

"Jared is not the only stumbling block," she said softly. "I don't know that I want to be married, at least not yet. I care as much about my writing as you do about yours; I don't intend to give it up."

"I wouldn't ask you to," Hawk replied instantly.

"Perhaps not," Lexy said, but she was far from convinced. She feared that because Hawk had so little experience of family, he might well have even more traditional ideas about it than most; she could not see how her desire to continue in journalism would fit in with that. And neither of them had said anything about love. They were mentally and sexually compatible, which was more than could be said for many couples, but Lexy would not even consider making such a commitment without love being clear on both sides. And since she didn't yet know exactly how she felt about Hawk, she could hardly ask him to declare his feelings.

"I think we will just have to be patient with each other and the situation," Lexy said, thinking that her own patience would not be so sorely tested if she didn't have the disconcerting tendency to see Hawk naked when he was fully clothed. She reminded herself that that was lust, not love.

Hawk was having his own struggle with the same problem. When the winter sunlight caught the gold in her hair, when her face tilted up to him just so and her eyes glowed green, when he heard her laugh or watched the animation in her expression as she discussed this idea or that; there were countless things about her that made him want to take her in his arms and make love to her. Since that wasn't possible, he took scrupulous care not to touch her, not to make temptation worse. He reflected grimly that frustrated though he was, at least his behavior was proper enough by any measure, even that of Lexy's parents.

Or of the twins. They arrived on Christmas Eve, and while Hawk had been prepared to like them for Lexy's sake, he found it wasn't difficult in any case. They were appealing young men, full of enthusiasm and openly glad to be home. They were transparent in their attitude toward Hawk, too, both of them extremely grateful that he had gotten Lexy out of danger, but also curious and wary about what role he now played in their sister's life.

The differences in the twins' personalities were plain in the way they approached Hawk about Lexy.

"We really appreciate your helping Lexy," Kace told him, "especially because we're both too far away to keep an eye on her."

Hawk had to hide his amusement at Kace's assumption of the role of protective brother when it was far more likely that Lexy had ridden herd on Kace than the other way around. But Tay was another matter, more reserved and thoughtful. There was a certain purity about him that made Hawk think it would be very uncomfortable to disappoint him, particularly in the matter of his sister.

"Lexy is very special to us," Tay said in his quiet way, but the tone conveyed a warning.

"Lexy is special to everyone who knows her," Hawk said, meeting Tay's eyes squarely, but he wished there was more he could say to reassure him.

Envy was so foreign to Hawk's nature, it took him some time to identify it in the flood of other emotions that crowded Christmas Eve. It was the first time he had been part of a celebration that was so full of laughter and tenderness that the joy of it was near pain, everything underlaid with the knowledge that it was a precious, fleeting time set aside for the whole family to acknowledge the love that bound them together. And even feeling the welcome from the family, Hawk was acutely conscious of being an outsider. He envied not the occasion itself, but the ease with which the family marked it, their shared assumption that this was as natural a part of their year as planting on the farms and business in the city. Even the dead, particularly Alex and Rane Falconer, were included, remembered and mentioned gently now and then, not in mourning, but as part of the collective memory.

Hawk's memories of his father, the person who had had the

most to do with raising him, were such a mixture of abuse and love, there was no comfort to be found there, only conflict.

The one clear thing he knew was that he wanted Jared to have childhood memories like these people had, not like his own. Just how he was going to manage that, he wasn't sure, but once he had Jared, he would find a way.

Though engulfed in the festivities, Lexy was continually aware of Hawk. It didn't matter that he was so big and male, he reminded her at odd intervals of a polite, shy child at a party, wanting to join in but not quite sure how. Her heart ached for him, and then the gifts undid her entirely.

She had wondered at the amount of his luggage, since his normal mode of dress called for simple, well-tailored garments. She had had a momentary fear that he was going to become a peacock for the visit to Wild Swan, but had discarded that possibility as ridiculous. And now the mystery of the extra luggage was solved. Hawk had brought a gift for every member of the family and for Della, too.

It had not occurred to her that he would do such a thing. She had made it very clear that he was to be an honored guest and had no obligations beyond being there. But that had obviously not suited him. In addition to what she had told him about the family, he must have questioned Reid, because everything he had chosen was perfectly suited without being so lavish that it might embarrass the recipient.

For Gincie and Travis, there was an old print of Sir Archy, the stallion whose get had dominated American racing for so many decades before the war and to whom mares at Wild Swan had long ago been bred. For Kace and Tay, there were books from England on the latest developments in the agricultural and veterinary sciences; for Della, a fine paisley shawl; for Morgan and Sam a book of engravings of the old clipper ships, some of which had been built at the Jennings-Falconer yard; for Adam and Mercy, it was a work on navigation; on and on, including gifts for the Tratnors, Philly, Blaine, the doctors, Sally, Joseph, and the children.

Lexy's hands shook as she opened the heavy package that was labeled simply, "To Lexy, from Hawk."

It was a lady's lap desk, its gleaming dark wood finish inlaid with mother-of-pearl. Inside, it was fitted with small bottles for ink and sand, a mother-of-pearl pen handle with a metal nib, and compartments for paper and other writing instruments. Embossed leather padded the slanted writing surface.

The writing box was not only an object of beauty and convenience, it was a clear acknowledgment that her work was important to her and so to Hawk.

She looked up at him, her throat so tight, she was barely able to murmur, "It is exquisite! Thank you so much."

She saw that Hawk was having his own difficulties with emotion. Her parents had given him a set of Mark Twain's books, made special by the fact that they had gone to the trouble of begging a favor from Mr. Clemens, sending them to him for his autograph, explaining whom the books were for. Difficult, eccentric, and cutting as Samuel Clemens could be, he was also capable of great generosity and kindness. And he had shown both in the matter of the gift for Hawk. As it happened, he was familiar with Hawk's work and approved of it, and he had signed the books as one writer to another.

Lexy remembered her mother asking what sort of books Hawk liked, and she knew her parents could not have chosen a more fitting gift to express their gratitude to him.

She had chosen her gift to him carefully, too, but now as she watched him open it, she was so assailed by doubts, she wished she could snatch the package back from him.

She had looked at scores of pocket watches until she had found the one she wanted. There had been countless examples of elaborate scrollwork and floral designs of stags' heads, hunting scenes, and the symbols of various professions, and finally there had been the fanciful engraving of a knight in armor, mounted on a destrier, and bordered by a twining forest that concealed a dragon. Inside the watch case, she had had engraved: "To Hawk, Dragon Slayer, from A. Adams." She had wanted him to have it as a symbol not only of his rescue of her from Bellwood, but also of his part in the birth of Abby Adams, that part of her that had always wanted to write stories that might make a difference.

When she had found it, it had seemed the perfect gift, but now she wondered. Its elaborate pattern was unlike any of his possessions, unlike anything he would have chosen for himself. And yet, in her family the gift of a watch had a significance she was facing only at this moment. Her mother had given her father a special watch in gratitude for the care he had given her after she was wounded. For gratitude and so much more. Gincie had wanted Travis to have something from her, something he would wear close to his body and look at often, something that would remind him of her constantly. Lexy faced the fact that she wanted the same things from Hawk.

"It is beautiful," he said, his voice low and gruff, his eyes suddenly overbright. His long fingers closed over the watch as if he would never let it go, as if he feared it might somehow disappear because it wasn't something he deserved in the first place.

Lexy thought of all the carefully chosen offerings he had made to her and her family with no expectation of anything in return; she thought of how patiently he had borne the close scrutiny here, despite his unease; she thought of how good he was with the children, treating them with interest and dignity that charmed them; she thought of how strong, intelligent, and enduring he was, and of how vulnerable.

And finally she knew what love was. It was wanting to shelter and reassure Hawk so that he would learn to believe he didn't have to stand outside of celebrations of the heart, that he deserved to be part of them as much as anyone else did. She also wanted to take from him as much as give, for while he was vulnerable in some ways, he was strong in others, possessing mental and physical courage in full measure.

She loved Hawk. He teased her senses, delighted her mind, and tugged at her heart. Suddenly she could not imagine a life without him. And yet, admitting she loved him changed nothing; Hawk was still centered on gaining custody of Jared, and he would not have room in his life for a woman until he had resolved the matter of his son.

She didn't say the words aloud and neither did he, but the current ran so strongly between them, the rest of the gathering faded away until a simper from Jilly made them aware that they were beginning to attract attention by their stillness.

Lexy tipped her chin up defiantly. "Happy Christmas, Hawk, and many more."

"And for you Lexy, happiness always."

"Well, that does it," Travis drawled to Gincie, as they watched from across the room. "He thanked us very kindly for the books, but the watch went right to his soul, just like the one you gave me." He patted his pocket where Gincie's gift still ticked merrily.

Gincie thought how strange it was that now that the love was so visible between Hawk and Lexy, Travis was accepting it while she herself was feeling a dreadful wrench. She knew how her grandmother must have felt when Alex had seen her with Travis that Christmas twenty-seven years ago.

She put her hand over his, imagining she could feel the pulse of time and his heart. The pain of witnessing Lexy entrusting her love to Hawk eased. Travis's fingers were warm as they curled around her own, and she thought, "This is what I want for my daughter, a shared life with a good man."

Hawk glanced across the room to find Gincie's eyes on him. For an instant, he felt caught and pinned by the intensity of her gaze, as if she were stripping away all of his defenses and seeing him exactly as he was. And then she smiled at him with such kindness and understanding, he felt as if she had touched him in some kind of benediction. Nothing could have made him more conscious of his responsibility to love Lexy without hurting her.

Chapter 32

Lexy spent New Year's Eve at Wild Swan without Hawk. They pretended it was because he had work to do and also because he thought she ought to have this time with her family, without worrying about how Hawk was faring with them. But the truth was a paradox; in moving closer to admitting that they loved each other, they had lost the ease they had cultivated so carefully. Now desire shimmered between them constantly.

Lexy was at once fascinated and appalled that she had reached the point where merely looking at Hawk was enough to cause her body to react with tightening nipples and a throbbing ache low and deep inside of her. She suspected, and sometimes saw, that it was worse for Hawk. She wondered how they would bear continuing to see each other at work, even if no place else.

Constant mention of Hawk at Wild Swan made it impossible to be free of thoughts of him. In one way or another, every member of the family wanted to let her know that he or she had liked Hawk Mackenna, and she was grateful for the approval, while she ached to be with him. It was the first time a visit home was less than satisfactory.

Her best intention had been to refrain from any interference in Hawk's dealings with the Fordyces, but her hunger for information outweighed everything else.

"Did you ever know a man named Sylvanus Fordyce in California?" she asked her father. "He seems to be quite a powerful man, and since he and his wife are due to arrive in Washington in the new year, I expect the paper will print some sort of announcement." She made herself stop explaining, fearful that she'd already said too much, but her father accepted the explanation, whereas she was sure her mother would have seen right through the too-casual inquiry.

Travis thought for a moment, and then nodded. "Actually, I do know a little about the man, not firsthand, mind you, though I did meet him a couple of times, but on general rumor. He's very well regarded. You know how much cheatin' there's been on supply contracts, probably since the first ones for boots at Valley Forge, but certainly since the comin' of the railroads. But Mr. Fordyce is known for doin' honest work for the government and for private business for honest fees. There was some talk when he married a woman much younger than he, but that seems to have been a good match, and I believe they have a young son, though I never met the wife or the child. I don't think the Fordyces have been much in California these past years, at least I haven't heard so on my visits there."

"They will be returning from an extended tour of Europe, but I don't know where they were living before that," Lexy said, proud of the calm tone of her voice.

"Isn't it goin' to be difficult for you to write society news after your adventure?" Travis asked, his apprehension for her future plans plain. He had no suspicion of the Fordyce connection to Hawk.

"Well, I can't claim it's what I want to write, but all of us at the paper have to do some of it. And I do plan to cover the races in the coming year. But I also have some plans for more Abby Adams pieces, though they will not be as dangerous to pursue as Bellwood," she hastened to add at the look of dismay on her father's face. She kissed him on the cheek. "I promise, Papa, this time Reid will know what I'm doing."

New Year's Eve had always been a special, tender time at Wild Swan, but this year, Lexy felt set apart, as if all of her emotions were suspended when Hawk was not present.

It made her feel even closer than usual to her cousin Joseph, who for all his congenial manner, never seemed to allow himself to be a real part of family festivities. But she recognized the difference. Joseph was removed from his own life, not allowing himself emotional risk of any kind; she, on the other hand, seemed to suffer every emotion one right after another when she was near Hawk and found only partial respite when she was away from him.

She escaped Wild Swan relatively unscathed except for a gentle warning from Tay. "I like Hawk Mackenna," he said, "but I think something's wrong. I don't need to know what it is because it's none of my business. But please, don't get hurt if you can help it. I'd hate to have to challenge Mr. Mackenna to a duel; the outcome would undoubtedly be messy and not to my advantage."

Despite his attempt at levity, he was serious, and Lexy was touched by his concern. But she refrained from telling him that it was she who had seduced Hawk, not the other way around, and contented herself with a laughing assurance that no duel would be necessary.

She meant for her conversation with her father to end her search for information about the Fordyces, but it was only the beginning. For Hawk's sake, she wanted the glowing reports of Sylvanus Fordyce to be false. She checked not only the archives of the *Witness*, but of the *Post* as well, and every reference she found presented a citizen of the highest caliber. Worse, the mentions of Mrs. Fordyce were even more flattering. She was described as "beautiful," "vivacious," "gracious," "cultured," "accomplished," on and on until Lexy thought she really despised this paragon of virtue. The lines about their son were scarce and brief, but each one described a happy, well-mannered child, adored by his parents.

Every word she read confirmed Lexy's original fear that Hawk was going to destroy a happy family, and not even his conviction that he had fathered the child could make her accept that. For her, everything was made worse by the fact that she could not discuss it with him. It was forbidden territory; he would be furious if he knew about her research.

She decided she needed to focus on her work, and to that end she discussed her story ideas with Reid, received his approval, and only then told Hawk that she was going to Baltimore for a while. She told him about the investigations she planned, and he had to concede they were intriguing, but he was not fooled.

"Running away," he said, and it wasn't a question.

"It is better than doing nothing more than waiting for the Fordyces," she flared, and then with anger and frustration still coursing through her, blasting away caution, she added, "I asked my father about them, and I've been reading about them. Unless everyone has been fooled, they are fine people and a happy family!"

She regretted the words as soon as they were spoken, but she faced his fury without flinching.

"You have no right to go behind my back!" he snarled, looking as if he'd like to hit her.

Her anger drained away, leaving her feeling more sad than anything else. "No, I suppose I don't, and that says a great deal about what is between us—or rather, what is not."

The light faded from her eyes, and her expression was coldly withdrawn, giving nothing away.

Hawk felt the chill down to his bones and wanted to call her warmth back, but he had nothing to offer as long as he pursued his son.

"Lexy, please, take care of yourself."

His voice had gone soft and gruff with concern for her, and she was glad they were outside in a public place; otherwise, she thought she might have thrown her arms around him and begged him to reconsider his plans for confronting Caroline Fordyce. Instead she put her hand in his for just an instant, promising, "I plan to be very circumspect, and I'll be taking jobs, not getting myself committed." She swallowed against the lump in her throat. "I'll see you when I get back."

She left him standing there, but she could feel his eyes following her as she walked away.

In Baltimore, Lexy stayed with Anthea and Max. Anthea was the perfect person for consultation because Lexy intended to find out everything she could about the lot of working women in the city, and Anthea's practice was mainly among them. Anthea was both enthusiastic and realistic about Lexy's project.

"It will take laws and enforcement of those laws to truly change things," she said, "but at least, your articles have a chance of making people aware of what is going on. Because of the strikes last year, many are even less sympathetic to workers than before, and women are always the forgotten ones, anyway."

Anthea had practical advice about the investigation, suggesting that Lexy begin with some of the employment agencies. "They charge fees for finding the jobs, but I've heard that too often they send their clients to unsuitable positions, and all the while they're charging those fees."

Lexy had learned a valuable skill during her short stay at Bellwood; she had learned how to render herself nearly invisible. By casting her eyes down and never meeting any gaze directly, by forsaking her normally upright carriage for an inward roll of the shoulders, by adapting uncharacteristically nervous gestures such as rubbing her hands together and plucking at her skirt, she relinquished the power to command attention and respect. It was frighteningly easy, not even requiring much makeup, just a little too-light face powder and slightly unkempt hair. And no one questioned the name "Mary Jones." Her only problem was to remember to answer to it.

For the first few days, the greatest impediment to her plan was her own spirit, which threatened to rebel against being a victim, but then the pose grew easier to maintain because the ill treatment by others began to assume its own relentless logic.

Anthea was right about the employment agencies; they had no concern for the women seeking positions, only for the fees they could collect.

Lexy presented herself as a gentlewoman who had fallen on hard times. She had thought she was going to have to create an elaborate excuse, but there was not only no personal interest in her, there was no interest in which jobs she might be suited for, which not. She was viewed simply as a warm body desperate for work.

She was sent to a clothing manufacture where, though the work was fairly simple and repetitive, she proved inept. The women who had been there for some time could cut the materials and speed the pieces through the sewing machines with great dexterity; for Lexy, it was as if all of her fingers had become thumbs. She was told that since she had so much to learn, she could expect no wages for the first two weeks and would only be paid thereafter if she proved she could do good enough work.

The place was cold, damp, and badly lit, and the women worked ten to twelve hours a day, six days a week. Some of them were no more than children, and others were far too old and frail for such arduous days. Not all of them spoke English. There was a scattering of Eastern Europeans who kept to themselves for the most part. They were treated even more harshly than the rest by the woman who was the immediate overseer. In turn, she was answerable to a deceptively jovial-looking man who never had words of praise for anyone, so it was easy to see how the woman found the immigrant workers a suitable target for her own frustrations.

It was a thoroughly miserable place to work, and yet, Lexy experienced a certain camaraderie amongst the women, a ripple of shared gossip and giggles now and then, and help offered to the less skilled. They were united by the oppression of their jobs. But the young ones were bound by something more, by the hope that this would not be their lot forever. The ones who were married dreamed of their husbands and themselves somehow achieving a better life, if not in time to enjoy, then for their children. Some of them who had husbands who left visible bruises dreamed that a better life would make kinder mates. None of them seemed to dream of ridding themselves of brutal spouses, and most of the unmarried women were so conscious of how difficult it was to make enough to support themselves, they were willing to settle for any man at all as long as he received regular wages.

Their dreams and fears were so different from Lexy's own that she understood for the first time the vast gulf created not only by having a family of some means, but more by having been educated so thoroughly from such an early age and having been assured that she could achieve the very best life had to offer as long as she was willing and capable of working for it.

She spent a week at the clothing manufacture and then got a job at a laundry where the problem of cold working quarters was replaced by the discomfort of scalding water, harsh soap, clouds of steam, and hot, heavy irons. Many of the workers had deep coughs and other complaints from going from the overheated rooms to the winter cold outside.

Within a few days of working there, Lexy hardly had to play a role. Her hands were scarlet and sore, her body never quite adapted to the contrast between the suffocating interior and the cold outside, and her muscles were strained from lifting heavy loads. Work here went from seven in the morning until six at night and paid two dollars a week, a little more if one were skilled at fancy pressing.

Most working women lived with their families, all members contributing their wages toward the rent and expenses. Those who had no families were in worse condition, despite their independence, and tended to form their own little families by seeking lodgings together at boardinghouses. Only the most naive stayed in places that advertised themselves as "homes for females," since such establishments were known not only for giving poor value for the rent paid, but also for sometimes being little more than brothels.

Lexy went to one boardinghouse after another on the pretense of wanting to rent a room, but living in the squalor of such places was a step she was unwilling to take. She was so exhausted after her workday, she could not face trying to sleep amid the noise and vermin, and she admitted to herself that she needed the sanctuary provided by returning to the Kingstons' house at night.

Though she had supported the project wholeheartedly in the beginning, Anthea was beginning to have her doubts. "Don't you think you've seen enough?" she asked. "You look quite unwell, and you've certainly learned enough of working conditions to write a coherent piece."

But for a variety of reasons, Lexy wasn't ready to stop. She was fascinated by the world she had discovered, fascinated by the way the women went on working at jobs that would drive her to despair if she believed she were trapped there for more than a week or so. And she was fascinated by the adversarial positions of employers and employees. She could see that just a little effort and expenditure on the part of the employers could create far better working conditions. But the employers had one goal—to obtain the highest productivity for the lowest outlay of capital. Employee loyalty was not a consideration; at least not in the sort of work Lexy was seeking. She was paying fees to agencies for the jobs, and there was no shortage of impoverished women who were doing the same. She thought of how things were run at Wild Swan, Sunrise, and Brookhaven, with everyone cooperating for the common good; the farms were utopias compared to the factories.

Her other reason for continuing was Hawk. Collecting information for this project was proving so exhausting mentally and physically, she was able to hold thoughts of Hawk at a distance most of the time. It made her feel as if she were in possession of herself again. It seemed vitally important that that be so because no matter what Hawk thought, she could not imagine he would be able to separate Jared from Caroline. Mothers who loved their children belonged with those children; Hawk would see that in the end. And that meant that there was a good possibility that he would take Caroline with the child, not only for the child's sake, but also for his own. He had, by his own admission, been deeply in love with the woman when the child had been conceived. There was no guarantee that the old feelings would not be rekindled, despite Caroline's perfidy.

Lexy reminded herself that she had never really possessed Hawk in any profound way; gaining custody of his child had always had priority over her place in his life. She needed to know that she would still be able to function when Hawk was gone from her. So willingly she gave fierce, passionate attention to her writing, taking copious notes at night even when the day's work had left her weary to the bone.

After the laundry, she worked in a spice and coffee factory where, though her work was a dull, meticulous matter of weighing and packaging, the atmosphere was redolent of the sharp scents of exotic places, and the working conditions were much better than she had previously experienced. The company was owned by a family whose knowledge of the spice trade went back generations. They were proud of the products they offered, and they were generally kind to their employees. Anthea and Max teased Lexy that they could smell her before she appeared.

"It's like Christmas coming down the street at night," Max said, and Lexy thought the cinnamon, cloves, and other strong oils must have penetrated her skin so deeply that the scents would never go away.

Her next job was nauseating in comparison. The factory made wigs, hairpieces, brushes, and other similar products, and the stench from the bundles of animal and human hair being treated in various ways was enough to make Lexy lose her appetite entirely and remember the spice factory with longing. The making of the hairpieces required some training, and this was another job where wages were withheld until a certain level of competence was reached—a good way to get free labor.

Lexy had not judged herself particularly squeamish, but handling human hair disgusted her, almost as if she were working with the dead, though women who sold their hair were alive and trying to stay that way. She didn't want to, but she kept imagining the desperate straits that must have driven many of the women to such a transaction. She preferred to work with the animal hair that went into shaving brushes, hair mattresses, and the like, but it was still unpleasant work.

Her next job was in a factory that made boxes. It was the worst of all. The little rooms were so dark that gaslight had to burn all day, and the workers were locked in, making it certain that if there was a fire, they would have little chance of escape. The place was filthy, and the work itself dirty. Many of the workers were consumptive, few ever got enough to eat, and some were as young as twelve years old. As Lexy sat there making box lids, she thought of this setting multiplied by countless thousands, women and children locked away like prisoners, punished for being poor and uneducated. Three days of it, and she could hardly drag herself back to the Kingstons'.

The sun had long since set when she reached the house. The soft glow of light from the windows beckoned, and there was nothing in the world she wanted more than a hot bath. The door opened with a flood of light, silhouetting the figure standing there. She mustered a smile, assuming it was one of the doctors leaving on a call, but her smile faded as she recognized the tall, broad-shouldered shape before Hawk breathed her name.

For a moment, she was so dizzy, she swayed where she stood, unaware that the light on her face showed him the depth of her shock.

"What are you doing here?" she asked, but it was more accusation than question.

Hawk thought of all the casual excuses he had considered, and he abandoned them all. "You've been gone for more than a month. I love you, and I was dying for the sight of you."

The fact that he said the words with such quiet despair somehow made them more shocking than if he had shouted them at her. And the lack of joy told her that nothing was yet resolved regarding Jared Fordyce.

Nothing had changed, and everything had. This man, so self-reliant and self-contained, had step by step opened himself to her until he had taken the ultimate step.

He made no move to touch her. He just stood there, his truth clear between them.

She should send him away, deny him, deny the risk of loving a man who was not free. She could not do it. She went to him, putting her arms around him, nestling against his chest.

"I love you, too, Hawk," she whispered, and then she repeated it more strongly.

His arms came round her, wrapping her so tightly against him, she could scarcely breathe, but nothing mattered as much as seeking the warm, strong comfort of him. All her assurances to herself that she had controlled how badly she missed him were revealed as lies in that instant. And finally she understood that it wasn't as if he had taken possession of her, but rather, that she had given herself into his keeping and taken him into hers by the simple fact of loving.

Her work was not separate from the rest of her life; it was an intrinsic part of it, of her, and so was Hawk, everything woven into the same fabric. She could not tell what the pattern would eventually be because the Fordyces were an unpredictable part of the weaving. But to be with Hawk, she would give up claim to the future and live with the pattern they discovered together day by day. It had to be enough because the alternative—living without him—was now unthinkable.

Hawk led her into the house, one arm around her waist because he wasn't ready to relinquish physical contact with her. With the stronger light indoors, he could see how tired she looked. She had lost weight, and there were violet shadows beneath her eyes. Her cheeks were smudged with dirt, and her hands were worse, filthy and rough with cuts and half-healed scorch marks. He wanted to hug and shake her at the same time. He was arrogant enough to understand that part of her state was surely due to missing him, but he also understood that halfway measures would never satisfy her when she was after a story. He would have liked to forbid her to ever put herself in any kind of jeopardy again, but he knew he didn't have the right and had to content himself with fussing over her about minor things, telling her there was a hot bath waiting, asking if he could offer her some supper, assuring her that Anthea had already told him where to find everything.

Lexy felt as if she were the victim of a benevolent conspiracy. Anthea and Max had obviously told Hawk exactly when to expect her home, but neither of them was in evidence. It wouldn't have mattered if they were there; Lexy's world was filled by Hawk. Even the mundane chore of washing away the grime of the day took on its own erotic glow, reminding her of the time she had spent with Hawk in his house, reminding her that he had seen her nude for the first time that night when he had rescued her from the bath. With a giggle, she suppressed the impulse to call out that she thought she was falling asleep.

She felt like laughing or singing or dancing; she felt all the grim fatigue of the day easing away.

She ate the food Hawk put before her with a better appetite than she had had in weeks, until finally she had to protest, "Please, no more! I feel like a stuffed turkey. You ought to be careful or I shall grow to expect this pampering.''

Hawk's face was suddenly serious, and he reached out to take one of her sore hands in his, touching it gently. "That would be fine with me. You could use some pampering now and then, but you only allow it when you're too tired to protest."

She couldn't help it; she thought of the phantom Caroline, who by all accounts enjoyed being the cossetted wife of her wealthy husband. "Would you prefer that I was a more helpless sort of woman?" she asked.

Hawk's first inclination was to laugh at the suggestion, but then he saw how much it mattered to her. "I didn't meet you in a hat shop. I met you as a fellow reporter. You'll have to take my word for it that your fire and your intelligence have attracted me as much as your big green eyes from the very beginning. I couldn't stand you if you played the helpless miss, but that doesn't mean you have to be strong all of the time."

He couldn't find the words to explain that the very fire that drew him frightened him for her sake. He feared she was capable of allowing it to consume her when her interest and her passion were engaged by a story. He knew he could not change that, but at least he could be there for her when she got too close to the flames, where safety and health were sacrificed for an idea.

"What are we going to do now?" she asked softly.

"Whatever you want. You know I still want to marry you, and I know you will not as long as the matter of my son is unresolved. But I love you, and I want to be with you, any way I can." He raised her hand to his lips, and the little kisses he placed there ran as in a current down her arm and flickered through her whole body.

Lexy had always had goals and a set plan of how she would accomplish them, but she cast aside the old way in that instant. She would love Hawk day by day for as long as they had.

"I want to be with you, too," she said, and it was as if they had exchanged vows.

She went back to Washington with Hawk and wrote a series of articles about the plight of women in the factories. She did not spare the readers any of the details, wanting them to experience the squalid conditions, wanting them to see the cuts, the burns, and the hands that had fingers mashed or even missing from working with various pieces of machinery. She wanted them to know how one long grueling day followed the next, and most of all, how even small changes could greatly improve the conditions for the workers. Reid was generous in his praise and support of the series, and Lexy labored over every line, but now, in addition to her work, there was her life with Hawk.

They saw each other when their paths crossed at the newspaper office, and they did their best to be discreet, maintaining a facade of easy friendship. But away from the newspaper, their world was entirely different.

Lexy was determined that their time away from work would be spent as they pleased, not as convention demanded. Hawk had offered marriage, and she had refused. While she did not intend to flaunt their relationship so boldly as to give the gossips ready fuel, she also refused to skulk about as if she were ashamed of their affair. They went to galleries together, to restaurants for quiet suppers, or just for walks about the city that was growing more elegant with each passing year, and everywhere she went with Hawk, Lexy carried herself with pride. It was easy to be proud in his company.

But their time together at Hawk's house was best of all. In the first of their nights when they returned to Washington, they were ravenous for each other, spending feverish hours learning how to share pleasure. Lexy marveled that what had seemed alien the first time—the long glide of Hawk into her body—now seemed as natural and necessary as breathing. The flexing of his muscles under his sleek skin enchanted her; the coiled power that was always there enthralled her.

And for Hawk it was no less. Though he was far more experienced than she, he had never, not even with Caroline, felt this combination of lust and tenderness. He hungered for her body, but he cherished the person inside. Love had never been more than an abstraction for him; now it was the reality of his days. His blind passion for Caroline seemed no more than a crude imitation of this, but that did not change his feeling of obligation and connection to Jared, and because he knew it threatened what he had with Lexy, he took infinite care in loving her, seeking to bind her to him as he was bound.

Hawk had always been so essentially alone, he had never imagined how comfortable it could be to have someone so intertwined with his life. When the first frantic hunger of their passion had been sated, he found new delights in just spending time together. They discussed the stories they were writing and the news in general and never seemed to run out of subjects of mutual interest. And often they shared silence, each of them writing, or reading, or just thinking, separate, and yet together in the room so that a glance brought the reassurance that the other was still there. He quickly came to hate the days and nights when Lexy was not with him. Sometimes the absence of her warmth in his bed made it impossible for him to sleep, and he would spend the hours until dawn working.

Lexy fared no better when she was apart from him, but she kept her lodgings at the boardinghouse. Fortunately, the landlady knew that Lexy had relatives in Georgetown and apparently assumed that she spent a lot of time with them. In any case, she did not express any disapproval or curiosity about Lexy's absences.

Despite her joy at being with Hawk, Lexy needed a place of her own. No matter how strongly she felt about her choice to be with Hawk, she did not want to inflict the social consequences of that choice on her family. They knew there was something special between her and Hawk, but that was far different from knowing that she and Hawk were living together much of the time.

She was also determined that there would be no unwanted pregnancy, and now Hawk was no less determined that she not conceive. He wanted them to be married, but he did not want pregnancy to be the reason. He had to face the fact that his life was already hopelessly complicated by the existence of a child he had not planned for, whatever Caroline's intentions had been.

Lexy was grateful that Anthea had always been so open in her campaign to educate men and women in the methods of avoiding conception, always answering questions with honest practicality.

Lexy had questioned Anthea at length while she was in Baltimore. At the time, she had thought she was doing it because she saw it as part of the factory women's dilemma—how to care for children, often too many of them, while having to work long, dreary hours— but now she wondered if it had not been as much for her own benefit, arising out of some inner conviction that she would make love with Hawk again.

She would have liked to take Hawk to Wild Swan to see the redbud blooming in the woods in first token of spring and to view the new crop of foals, but she resisted the temptation. If she had worried about revealing too much before, now she was certain she looked exactly like what she was—a well-loved woman. She was sure Reid knew, and she was thankful that he was not making it his business to interfere.

Each day with Hawk was a gift made more precious by the knowledge that sooner or later the Fordyces were going to arrive in Washington. But the sharpness of the knowledge was blunted by the passing days of the quickening season.

March flowered into April, and Jilly was married with all of the pomp she desired. Lexy was one of the attendants, Jilly's feelings of triumph at the status she was achieving by becoming Dermot's wife having translated itself into general benevolence. Hawk was at the wedding, too, with the rest of the newspaper staff. And though Lexy made the effort to treat him as no more than a good friend, she felt as if she and Hawk were an old married couple. It was growing more and more natural to have a life with him, more and more difficult to imagine some outside force being strong enough to end it. And when she did make herself believe it, she envisioned some sort of violent confrontation because nothing less would be fitting.

May brought gardens full of flowers and increasing activity at the racetracks. Social events in the capital grew more numerous, too, as people sought to take advantage of the fair weather of spring, before sultry summer days made any activity strenuous.

Though she covered important stories as Abby Adams, that did not excuse Lexy from continuing to share the duties of reporting the social scene. And it wasn't always a frivolous occupation; often the political pulse of the nation was easier to monitor there than anywhere else.

There were rules to the ritual. If a hostess made a member of the press welcome, she expected to receive a glowing, or at the very least, kind report written about her party. It wasn't the most honest kind of reporting, but interesting information gleaned at the gathering could be used carefully in columns apart from the social news.

Hawk teased Lexy about the way she fussed over what to wear to these events when normally she dressed for practicality and didn't worry beyond that.

"It's much easier for you," she retorted. "But I have to make sure I look businesslike, though not too businesslike, feminine, but not too feminine."

"You're pure female, no matter what you wear," Hawk said, his eyes taking appreciative inventory.

"Fortunately, everyone does not look at me as you do, as if I'm not wearing any clothes at all." Lexy went to him, pretending to straighten his jacket as she purred, "Just the way I see you." She tilted her head for his kiss.

The exchange flashed through Lexy's mind as she arrived at the Pattersons' garden party. She hid a smile and tried to look properly impressed by the lavish scene before her, the grounds of the Patterson mansion having been bedecked with ribbons and rainbow displays of flowers. The women attending the affair were no less colorful, their bright gowns catching the afternoon sun as they moved about on the arms of their escorts. Tea, punch, and a wide array of dainty foodstuffs were set out on tables attended by servants in livery. Mr. Patterson had begun to amass his money by supplying meat to the Army during the war and had continued to enlarge his fortune by various merchandizing schemes on a grand scale, and Mrs. Patterson was herself the daughter of a shopkeeper, but she did not allow that to deter her from adopting a style of living that would have befitted European royalty. But despite their pretensions, Lexy liked the couple. Under the finery, they remained both well intentioned and shrewd, and Mrs. Patterson seemed to know what was happening in the capital before anyone else. It was also she, rather than her husband, who followed the races, and that made Lexy a favorite in her eyes.

When she had first started working for the paper, Lexy had felt uncomfortable when she received special attention because of her family and Wild Swan, but she had learned to accept that her heritage was as much a part of her as anything else and that if it helped to get a better story, it was foolish to object.

As her hostess was greeting her effusively and asking questions about Wild Swan's racing prospects for the year, Lexy noticed that some of the men were looking distinctly more flushed than the gentle warmth of the afternoon allowed, an indication that beverages stronger than punch and tea were being offered. The Pattersons knew how to keep the gentlemen from protesting too much about attending a garden party, and for Lexy it meant that some tongues would be loosened. Judging by the number of senators, congressmen, and other government officials present, there might well be some interesting slips before the afternoon was over.

She focused her attention on Mrs. Patterson again as the woman said, "There's a couple here I particularly want you to meet. Though they haven't been there for some time, they once lived in California. Your family might even know them."

With no more warning than that, Lexy found herself face to face with Sylvanus and Caroline Fordyce. Mrs. Patterson rambled through the introductions, including information that came to Lexy in broken fragments.

". . . been traveling in Europe with their darling son, Jared . . . Lexy is one of our modern women, works for the *National Witness* . . . you might be familiar with her parents, Gincie and Travis Culhane . . . wonderful horses . . . good ones nearly every season . . . Fordyces are just back . . . so pleased to have learned of their arrival when scarcely anyone else knows. . . ."

At first Lexy was sure she was going to faint, and then she wished she could. She couldn't get enough air, and her cheeks had the unpleasant drawing sensation that usually presaged throwing up.

"Are you all right, Miss Culhane?" Caroline Fordyce asked, her throaty voice and beautiful face filled with genuine concern, and by sheer will, Lexy pulled herself back from disaster.

"Perfectly all right, thank you," she lied. "It's just a bit warm this afternoon."

She heard herself asking the proper questions about their sojourn in Europe, about their plans for settling in Washington, even about their child. "Mrs. Patterson mentioned your son. Has he enjoyed your travels?"

"We can surely be judged as overly indulgent parents, but we are blessed in Jared," Mr. Fordyce answered. "He is such a quick-witted, adaptable little chap. I think he enjoyed Europe as much as or more than we did. Very impressed he was by the castles and such, always wanting to know exactly how old everything was."

"Sylvanus has such patience with our son," Caroline said, with a smile for her husband. "If he didn't know the answer to Jared's questions, he soon found out for him."

They were a handsome couple, Sylvanus above medium height with an erect bearing, white hair, and a weathered face that looked rather forbidding until he smiled or looked at his wife, and Caroline— Caroline was exquisite. She was small, and she had a heart-shaped face dominated by large dark eyes and framed by lustrous dark hair. Her skin was fair, her features even except for the surprise of a sultry mouth.

Lexy didn't want to think of it, but she did; she thought of how that mouth must have kissed Hawk's mouth, which was so sensuous in his otherwise harshly sculpted face.

Mr. Fordyce was speaking of Travis Culhane with the same respect her father had given the man, and he was saying how much they had enjoyed some of the races they'd seen in England, though the French version of the sport was not so fine.

Lexy gave the proper responses, and all the while, she was seeing Caroline and Hawk together, making love as she herself and Hawk made love.

Caroline was everything she herself wasn't—small enough for a man to cradle easily, with the contrast of pale skin and dark hair delineating her beauty so clearly, no one could fail to see it. And though there was nothing overblown about her, she had a voluptuous figure. By contrast, Lexy felt she looked like a tall, slender boy. Hawk could not have chosen a woman more different from Caroline, and with her self-confidence rapidly crumbling to dust, Lexy wondered if that were precisely what had attracted him to her, making her nothing more than an anodyne for the pain he had felt from loving Caroline.

"I know you must be very busy in getting your household resettled here, but I wonder if you would have time to allow me to interview you in the next day or so. I would like to meet your son and have a little more leisure to gather impressions of your time in Europe."

It was like riding a horse too fast, feeling the barely controlled wildness getting closer and closer to a full bolt: the impending calamity was as compelling as it was terrifying.

There was little time. It would be very noticeable if she made no mention of the Fordyces in her account of the Pattersons' party; Mrs. Patterson was certainly expecting her to do so. And even if she did not, the news would appear in other local papers. The Fordyces were important people; their arrival in Washington was more than social news, due to Mr. Fordyce's status in the business world.

And Caroline would see Hawk's name in the *Witness*, or someone would mention one of his articles; Hawk wrote the kind of pieces that made people talk and define their own positions.

For her own sake, for what she was surely going to lose, Lexy wanted to be as clear as possible in her judgment of the Fordyces.

Caroline and Sylvanus graciously agreed to grant the interview on the following afternoon.

The rest of the party was a blur to Lexy, though she tried to keep coherent notes. People were talking about a wide variety of subjects, but none of it seemed as important as the Fordyces' arrival in Washington.

The day had started out so gently and had been scheduled to close the same way, with a quiet dinner and the night spent with Hawk. Now she was torn, still longing to be with him, but conscious of how everything had changed. She had no intention of telling him that Caroline and Jared were here, not until she found out more. She was going behind his back in a way that he could only interpret as betrayal.

In the end, she went to him because she couldn't make herself stay away. And she kept telling herself that if she could act the madwoman at Bellwood, then she could play a calm sanity she did not feel with Hawk.

But Hawk was not the callous staff at the asylum; he was the person who was more attuned to her than anyone else had ever been, and he was aware that something was wrong.

"If you continue to eat like that, I estimate you will disappear altogether in less than a week," he said, eyeing her nearly untouched dinner.

Every time she attempted to take a bite, she found her throat unwilling to cooperate. "Mrs. Patterson provided a feast this afternoon," she said. It was true, though she hadn't eaten any of it.

But Hawk wasn't convinced. "What's wrong? You're nervous as

a cat even if you are making a great effort to appear otherwise. Does Abby Adams object to having to cover the social calendar?"

"She does, though she shouldn't," Lexy said, seizing the excuse to talk about her work at some length.

She felt she'd done a fairly good job of diverting him, but her own mind was still filled with images of Caroline Fordyce.

She knew she ought to spend the night at her boardinghouse, but she couldn't make herself do it. Everything seemed to be moving at once very quickly and very slowly. She wanted the night to last forever; she wanted dawn to break immediately. She wanted Hawk to hold her and make her believe it was going to be all right for them.

She watched the play of soft lamplight on his skin. She thought of how the muscles felt when she rubbed his back; she thought of the faint tracings of his cruel childhood that never ceased to move her. She thought of how their bodies fit together, and yet, when he took her in his arms and started to touch her in the patterns that had pleased her so much before, she suddenly felt suffocated.

"What the hell!" Hawk swore in angry concern, feeling her body tense, but Lexy didn't want to face any more questions. She kissed him frantically, twining herself around him until his arousal was hard and hot between them, and she reached to guide him into her.

But even driven by his need to possess her, Hawk could not mistake the dry, unwelcoming tightness of her.

He rolled away and lay panting as he fought to gain control of his body.

"God damn it! What are you trying to do?" he ground out when he could manage his voice. "Rape doesn't interest me."

She couldn't explain that she felt as if all the connections between them had been severed, as if she were in Caroline's bed.

"I'm sorry," she sobbed. "I'm sorry."

He gathered her into his arms as she wept, his anger dissipating in worry. He murmured words meant to comfort as he held her. He knew Reid would have told him if anything had happened to one of the family. With no information from Lexy about the source of her misery, Hawk felt helpless. He held her throughout the night even after she had fallen into an exhausted sleep. And with all of the catastrophies he imagined, including that she might be pregnant despite their mutual efforts to prevent it, he did not consider the possibility that the Fordyces had at last arrived in Washington. He was so consumed by his love and concern for Lexy, he acknowledged no other claim on his heart or soul this night.

Chapter 33

Lexy's last hope died the moment she met Jared Fordyce. She had no doubt that he was Hawk's son. It was not just a matter of coloring, including gold flecks in the dark eyes, or of the hint of Hawk's strong features hidden in childish softness; it was a certain turn of the head, the way he stood, myriad small things that became enormous in proving the father in the son.

And he had the same steady confidence of his father. When he and Lexy were introduced, he looked right at her, inspecting her closely. "Pleased to meet you," he said dutifully. But then he grinned and added, "You're awfully tall an' pretty!"

Caroline smiled ruefully but did not criticize her son for his forthright observation, and Lexy thanked Jared for the compliment.

"Do you have any little boys of your own?" he asked.

"No, not yet," she answered. She kept at bay the sad thought that now it was very doubtful she and Hawk would ever share a life and children, and she could not imagine bearing children by another man. It was difficult enough for her to think of herself in the role of mother; impossible if the children were not Hawk's.

Everything about the Fordyces bespoke a happy family. Earlier in the interview, Sylvanus had been there, patient and intelligent in answering Lexy's questions. And yet, he had continually deferred to his wife, making sure that her opinions got the same consideration as his own. When he had excused himself due to obligations elsewhere, even Lexy felt the loss of his presence, and it was hard to credit that Caroline had ever had another man in her life; she was so connected to her husband, so obviously in love with him.

It would have been easier to resist the pull of Caroline's personality if she had been nothing more than the indulged young wife of an older man, but there was far more to her than that. Whatever she had been when Hawk knew her, she was now a well-read, thoughtful woman who was also a startlingly talented painter. It was Jared who informed Lexy of that fact, showing her his "Europe book."

"Mama made it for me," he explained, opening the sketchbook

to reveal page after page of watercolors, each with a short caption scripted below it.

A faint blush tinted Caroline's cheeks, and she gave a self-deprecating shrug. "It's the toy of the moment because I just finished it for him."

"It is extraordinary!" Lexy countered, unwillingly enchanted by the skill and delicacy of the work. "The colors, the composition, everything about the paintings is dazzling! You could very easily be a professional artist."

"No, I couldn't," Caroline said firmly, and she met Lexy's inquiring look steadily. "It pulls me, you see, too much. It is all right as long as I understand that it is only a diversion, as long as I don't allow it to be a compulsion. Oh, it is not that Mr. Fordyce objects," she hastened to explain, not wanting there to be any misapprehension. "He is as enthusiastic as Jared about my work, but he would be hurt if it took all of my time. And it could, as much as I love my family, it could take all of my time. . . ." Her voice drifted off, and then she collected herself and regarded Lexy anxiously. "I must sound quite addled. You are dangerously easy to talk to."

"You don't sound the least unbalanced to me; I do understand," Lexy assured her. "I feel the same way about my writing. I am not at all sure I could divide time fairly between it and a marriage. But it seems a great waste that women seem to have to make the choice while men do not."

Caroline nodded in agreement, but then she straightened her shoulders. "Everything in life is barter of one sort or another, one thing given for another, and I am happy with the exchange I've made. I love my husband and my son dearly."

Lexy did not doubt the sincerity of Caroline's words, but for her own part she still felt a keen sense of loss. She could not judge, even if she had the right, whether or not the uninterrupted domestic tranquility the woman provided for her husband and child was worth the loss of the paintings that would never be done, but she could judge what her own course must be. Her previous hesitation vanished. She could not bear that Caroline should lose the very thing for which she had sacrificed so much.

"May I have a private word with you?" she asked, glancing at Jared who was still engrossed in the sketchbook.

Caroline looked puzzled, but not alarmed, and she suggested to her son that he go see if cook had any gingerbread for him. "I'll engage a nurse when I find someone suitable," she said, watching him leave the room, "but I refuse to put him in the care of some grim old dragon. We had a nice young woman while we traveled, but she married in England, and . . . oh, I'm sorry to prattle on when you have something to tell me."

Lexy made herself look at the other woman as she confessed. "I do work for the *Witness*, and I do plan to write an article about you and your husband, but nonetheless, I came here under false pretenses." She took a deep breath. "Hawk Mackenna works for the paper, too. He believes Jared is his son, and he wants him."

All the color drained from Caroline's face. "It can't be!" she gasped.

"I'm sorry, but it's true. And it's true that Jared is Hawk's son; he looks too like him for it to be otherwise. You see, I know well the subtleties of how Hawk looks, how he moves. I love him very much, and he says he loves me. But this fixation about his son stands between us. Though I have had doubts since he first told me about Jared, I might have come to support his cause had you and Mr. Fordyce proved unfit parents. But you are not. You are as warm and loving as any child could ever wish, and I have never met a happier child than your son. Hawk has no right to threaten these bonds, no matter how Jared was conceived."

"We'll go away again. I'll tell Sylvanus that we must leave Washington immediately; I'll think of something. I'll . . ." The terrified words tumbled out until Lexy put up a hand to stop them.

"No, you can't keep running from him. You must know Hawk well enough to know that he will pursue you until this is settled. It is why he came to Washington, to wait for you. He thinks he was used for stud service," she could think of no polite way to phrase it, "and I think that has blinded him to reason."

The silence stretched taut between them, and Lexy could almost feel Caroline weighing how much to tell.

Finally the other woman bowed her head in a gesture of surrender. "You have risked your own love to warn me; you deserve the truth from me."

Her eyes looked blind as she gazed inward. "Love can be a terrible tyranny as well as a gift. My parents always wanted children, but I was not conceived until my mother was more than forty years old. I will never know for certain, but I suspect that my father may have wanted my mother to rid herself of the risk of pregnancy so late in life. Obviously, she did not follow that course. She had me, but at the cost of her own health. She never recovered, and she died when I was three. I think I remember her, or at least a sweet voice, but perhaps it is only what my father told me, not memory. He loved her very, very much. And I think he felt guilty that because of that, he might not love me enough. But that was never, never the case. If anything, he loved me too generously. He had had few advantages and almost no education in his own youth; he made sure I had the best of everything. But still he worried about what would happen to me when he was no longer there to protect me. Sylvanus was the final protection, a widower, mature, but in good health, a trusted friend and wealthy in his own right. Father made it very clear that he favored the match, and I knew that Sylvanus was fond of me." The words stopped abruptly, and she clasped her hands together so tightly, the knuckles gleamed white.

"I was so innocent, so stupid!" she declared. "I should have known that Sylvanus would never have contemplated marrying me had he not loved me. Friendship with my father would never have been enough. But I didn't know that, I didn't know! I accepted all of his gentleness, his adoration, as if I were entitled to it.

"Oh, we slept together as man and wife," she admitted bluntly, "but Sylvanus soon discovered how much growing up I still had to do. The tyranny of love again, this time his for me. He felt guilty for marrying me. And though his intentions had been good, he began to believe that I deserved a younger man, a different life, whatever it required to make me happy. And his greatest guilt was that he did not believe he could give me a child. He had been married and widowed before, and he took full blame for their childless state. He didn't lie about it; he told me before we married. I didn't feel any great maternal yearning for a child, so it did not deter me from marrying him, but he added it to the list of his imaginary sins. He became humble, hesitant in his dealings with me. All I knew is that he had changed, and rather than compassion, I felt contempt. I began to believe, as he did, that the marriage had been a mistake, no matter how much my beloved father had desired the match. I spent my time painting and going about with my friends, anything that took me away from Sylvanus. And then I found Hawk. It was a dangerous time for me, and he was a dangerous man."

She studied her hands intently as her fingers pleated the material of her dress. "A woman would have to be blind or dead not to want Hawk Mackenna," she said softly, "and I was neither. I was a discontented young woman who was tired of being well behaved and protected. And poor Hawk, for all his beauty and his strength, he has had so little love in his life, he wanted more than I could give. But I didn't know that. I didn't know what Hawk needed, what Sylvanus needed; I didn't even know what I needed. I was used to being cared for by men, not to understanding that they, too, need care. Hawk was a wild, wonderful way out of my safe, boring life. And God help me, I enjoyed every minute of the affair! I enjoyed risking the danger of discovery; I enjoyed going to Hawk as a mysterious woman with no past and no future; I enjoyed making love with him." She checked abruptly, and Lexy knew her own pain was clearly visible.

"Please go on." Lexy made herself say it; she needed to know all of it, though she wished none of it had ever happened.

"He didn't know you then," Caroline reminded her gently. "And he didn't know me. It wasn't for stud service, I swear it wasn't! I loved him more than a little. But I was also more married than I knew. When I discovered I was pregnant—and heedless, stupid woman that I was, I had not thought it would happen to me—all I could think of was Sylvanus, not Hawk. Whatever he thinks now, Hawk was not ready to be a husband or a father then. It would have been a disaster for both of us, and for Jared.

"I grew up very quickly, and suddenly I could see not only how I had abused Sylvanus's love and trust, but how much I needed both, how much I needed him. Hawk was excitement; Sylvanus was home. I went to him and told him what I had done and that I was with child. I never told him who the father was, and he never asked. He told me that because the child was mine, it was also his. He has never faltered from that course. He cherished me during all the days of my pregnancy, and he has cherished me and Jared ever since. I love him so much, sometimes I lay awake at night praying that he will live longer than I, despite the difference in our ages, so that I will not have to be here without him."

She bowed her head and covered her face with her hands. "I hurt him so much, I never want to hurt him again. And knowing who fathered Jared would surely wound him terribly. Sylvanus is such a just man; it would be like him to believe that Hawk does have some right to Jared. Oh, God, what am I going to do?" Tears leaked through her fingers.

In the strange intimacy created by their mutual involvement with Hawk, it seemed perfectly natural for Lexy to put her arms around Caroline, though the comfort she offered was not easy. "You trusted Hawk once, enough to make love with him. You're going to have to trust him again, to meet with you, to listen to your version of the story before he draws your husband into any of this. And if he still insists on involving Mr. Fordyce, then you must warn your husband. I don't underestimate how hard it would be for him to put a face to your infidelity, but I've seen the love between you, and I don't believe anything on earth could kill that."

Caroline sat there, considering what Lexy had said, and finally she roused herself to ask, "What will you do?"

"I will tell Hawk about this visit; I can do no less than that. And then I think I will go away for a while."

"Hawk is going to be terribly angry with you. I am grateful for the risk you've taken for me, but I don't really understand. Why didn't you just let things happen as they would? I think that's what I would have done," Caroline confessed.

"Somehow I don't believe that's true," Lexy countered, "not with a child involved. Jared's welfare comes first with you and with me. And it's really quite selfish. I don't want a man who is so tied to his past that he can't see a future with me. It would be different if he truly had a right to the child; if Jared really needed him, then Jared would become part of my life, too. But that isn't the case. Jared belongs right here with you and Mr. Fordyce, and until Hawk accepts that, he hasn't room in his life for me."

"I hope Hawk comes to his senses, not just for my sake, but for his own," Caroline said slowly. "If he loses you, he will have lost far more than he ever had with me, more, I think, than he's ever had with any other woman. It's odd, but at this moment I pity him as much as I fear him."

Lexy took her leave of the other woman, hoping she would continue to feel that way rather than being driven to intemperate action by her dread of what Hawk might do to her happy family. For her own part, Lexy wished she could feel like the heroine of the piece, but she felt curiously numb.

She went back to the newspaper office and sought a meeting with Reid.

"England!" he barked when she'd presented her idea, and she went on quickly. "Yes, you've mentioned that you'd like more firsthand accounts in the year of Queen Victoria's jubilee. I'd like to be there for a while, and with our family connections, I would be able to see a wide variety of things, not only the races and activities at court, but a view of the working people, too. Abby Adams could go along with Lexy, though the Abby pieces would have to be published with some discretion, else I might find my welcome in doubt."

"Whoa," Reid said, putting up his hand. "I'm not dismissing the idea, I'm just . . . ah, puzzled about why you have this sudden interest in going so far away." He looked at the ceiling for a moment and then pinned her with his dark blue eyes. "Work and private life ought to be separate, I suppose, but they often aren't. I assume this means you and Hawk have had a falling out?"

She could not resent the question; she and Hawk were important to Reid and the operation of the paper. He had a right to know if their private problems were going to cause trouble for the paper.

"We haven't had a falling out yet, but we're going to," she answered steadily. "And that's all I can tell you about it, except to assure you that it isn't his fault. We both have some decisions to make, and it would just be better if I weren't here for a while. I know it will leave you short of coverage of the races here, but I promise that the work I do in England will be worth it."

It was hard for him not to press her for further details about problems between her and Hawk; his journalistic instincts hated not knowing all of the facts about any story, but he had to concede that it was none of his business as long as Lexy and Hawk continued to do good work for the paper. And he did not doubt that she would send fine material from England. "All right, England it is, but as with Bellwood, I leave it to you to explain to your parents that this is your choice," he said.

Telling her parents seemed an easy task when compared with breaking the news to Hawk. She stayed to write the piece about the Fordyces, and she thought that if Hawk came in, she would tell him here, on neutral ground. But in the end, she had to confront him at his house.

He smiled in welcome and put his arms around her, hugging her in welcome. "I was beginning to worry about you. I've got the fixings for an adequate supper, but if you'd rather, we can go . . ." Suddenly conscious that something was very wrong, he put her away from him so that he could see her face clearly. Whatever had been bothering her had obviously gotten worse. "What is it?"

For a moment, she was tempted to steal one more quiet meal, one more loving night with him, and she looked at him with all of that yearning in her eyes, but it was too late for that. The blessed numbness crept over her again. "I spent the afternoon with the Fordyces, with Caroline, Sylvanus, and Jared. They've just arrived; I was introduced to them at Mrs. Patterson's party. I went there under the guise of wanting to interview them about their travels in Europe, and I did ask questions about that. Then when I was able to have time alone with Caroline, I told her you were here; I told her what you want. I told her to trust you to meet with her before you involve her husband. I told her because they are a complete, loving family. They deserve to be together. You must come to see that!"

He gazed at her in shock that turned swiftly to rage as the full import of her confession dawned on him. "How could you do that?" he snarled, and for an instant, Lexy was physically afraid of him.

He saw her flinch, and his own misery grew to equal his anger. "Christ! I'm not going to beat you."

"No, it isn't that easy, is it?" Lexy said. The distance between them was physically so small, but in every other way it was a vast chasm growing wider by the second. She could bear his rage more easily than the vulnerability she saw beneath it. As Caroline had said, Hawk had had so little love in his life, and now she, Lexy, had joined the list of those who found someone or something more important than he. The fact that she believed he had brought it on himself did not help.

"I think I'd better leave now," she said, and he nodded, hoping that with her out of his sight, he might be able to stem the tide of desolation that was surging through him. Caroline and Jared were shadowy figures at the moment; Lexy filled his mind.

He found a cab to take her to her boardinghouse, and he watched it out of sight, the rich sounds and scents of the spring night rising in mockery about him.

Lexy left for Wild Swan the next morning. She had not slept at all; the image of Hawk's face, suddenly gaunt with sorrow and anger, would not go away even when she closed her eyes. She longed for the seasonal order of the farm, for the settled, old-fashioned feeling of the place that had yet to know gas light or the newer electric light or the ring of a telephone. For all her protestations about being a mature woman with a responsible job, at this moment, she longed for the privilege of being a child again, of having someone else making the important decisions and protecting her. She longed for it, but she knew she had gone far beyond that point; only an adult could have inflicted such deep wounds on Hawk, and only a woman grown could feel the pain of loss she was feeling.

She thought she was quite composed when she greeted her parents, but Gincie took one look at her and asked, "Are you ill?"

Her mother's alarm steadied her. She resisted the impulse to crumple and seek shelter; she had made her own decisions about her relationship with Hawk from the beginning, and she was still doing that.

"I'm just tired," she said. "I've decided to go to England for the paper, and I'm having to make plans quickly."

"England! For the paper?" Travis said, his skepticism plain, and Lexy could see he was already planning to go do battle with one Hawk Mackenna.

"All right, I admit there are personal reasons for doing this now, but I don't want either one of you to blame Hawk. I'm the one who caused the rift, and I think it will be better for both of us if we're apart for a while."

Gincie was the first to realize that there was nothing they could do to change her mind. Had Lexy broken down and played child to the parent, it would have been another matter, but since she obviously had no intention of doing that, she deserved to be treated as an adult making adult decisions. It was also reassuring to remember that the Bettingdons were in England and would keep track of her.

Gincie was relieved to see that Travis's mind was following the same course; the light of battle was fading from his eyes, replaced by resignation.

"Well, darlin'," he said to their daughter, "just don't stay away too long. The American turf needs you to write about our races. And we need to see your face now and then," he added softly, giving her a hug that was a blessing on her plans and a promise that he would not go after Hawk in anger.

Once she had informed her parents of her plans, things began to move very quickly. There were definite advantages to being a member of her clan. She barely had time to pack before she found herself in Baltimore, boarding a Jennings-Falconer steamer bound for Liverpool. Though she told Morgan and Adam that any available accommodation would do, they made sure she had the best, a royally outfitted cabin rich with teak, brass fittings, and velvet upholstery and crowded with books, flowers, and baskets of fruit from the family. She left with news of them, too, word from Adam and Mercy that they were expecting another child and that Sally was also pregnant. She was happy for both couples, though she shared the family's unspoken concern that Sally and Nigel might suffer another tragedy. Surely this time they would have a healthy baby.

She took with her other, less momentous bits of family news, too, immediacy to offer the English branch, though voluminous letters crossed the Atlantic regularly.

But of Hawk, she had had no news at all since the night she had left his house. She had not seen him during her brief return to Washington, and she did not even know whether he was aware of her plans.

After other visitors had left the ship and sailing was imminent, Rob Jenkins arrived in a flurry, and Lexy felt an instant start of remorse that her first thought was not of Rob himself but of the possibility that he brought word from Hawk. But he soon disabused her of the notion.

"I just found out from Mr. Tratnor about your trip," he exclaimed. "I couldn't let you leave without saying good-bye. Oh, Lexy, I don't know what's going on, but it's got to have something to do with Hawk. He's acting like a bear with a sore paw, and you're leaving the country. I've felt responsible for your involvement with him ever since the night we got you out of Bellwood. Is there anything I can do?"

He looked so worried, so dear and familiar, that Lexy gave him a peck on the cheek, causing him to flush with pleased embarrassment.

"You're a good friend, and there *are* some things you can do for me. In the first place, quit feeling guilty. Whatever lies between

Hawk and me is of our own doing, not yours. In the second place, don't blame Hawk for any of this; we just need to be apart from each other. And in the third place, you'd better get off this ship unless you plan to work in England for a while, too."

She spoke with such calm assurance that Rob brightened visibly, and he was smiling as he hurried off the ship. But Lexy's smile was shaky as she watched the figures of her parents, other relatives, and Rob grow smaller and smaller. She had been to England before, but never without at least her brothers going with her. And more than that, she was leaving Hawk so far behind.

"Rane ran off to England once, but he came back to Alex just in time," Della had told her while she was at Wild Swan, and then she had added, "Gwenny went to England to be with someone; that's quite different. But I expect you know why you're going and what your trip will bring."

It wasn't difficult for Lexy to translate the gently spoken words into an admonition that she be honest with herself about the journey. But then, Della didn't know about the ties that pulled Hawk back to his past.

Thinking about Della made her think about everyone else at Wild Swan whom she loved and who loved her and about not being there when the twins came home from school, and she felt a wave of homesickness so strong, her eyes filled with tears. She opened her eyes very wide to keep the tears from overflowing in front of the other passengers crowding the rail, and she thought that if she felt like this before the ship cleared Chesapeake Bay, she had no business claiming maturity. She decided she would just have to endure the crossing and count on the excitement of writing articles from England to lift her spirits.

The captain and crew had other ideas. Lexy Culhane was one of "the family," and the chance to please her and thus to please Morgan and Adam Falconer, was an opportunity worthy of concerted effort. Two days out, Lexy realized that she would have to be much ruder than she was to continue to sulk in face of the crew's efforts to make the journey pleasant. They were so relentless and so anxious in their attentions, she could not resist them.

By the time she arrived in England, she had managed to reduce Hawk to a constant but manageable ache in her heart and mind. As long as she surrounded herself with other people, she could keep memories of Hawk at a distance.

Chapter 34

England and the Bettingdons engulfed Lexy the moment she landed. Alerted of her arrival by transatlantic telegram, Gweneth and Christopher had not only made arrangements for her to travel by the best rail accommodations, but they also sent her cousin Nicholas to escort her.

Lexy had not meant for her English relatives to bear the burden of her visit; she had not only money she had saved from her salary, but also the security of the legacy from Alex. She had planned to use it to supplement her newspaper salary in England if that were necessary, but the Bettingdons wouldn't hear of her making her own arrangements. They pointed out that whenever any of them visited Maryland, they were treated like royalty, with the way smoothed at every turn.

"But Gwenny, Wild Swan is where you were born! It's your home," Lexy protested.

"The Falconers and the Carringtons came from this country," Gwenny reminded her. "You have ties of blood nearly as strong as my own to this country. Christopher and I would be very hurt indeed if you did not consider our home your own," she added as an irrefutable final point.

In the case of the Bettingdons, "our home" meant a country mansion, several smaller properties, and an elegant London residence. And more, being related to them meant an automatic entree into the highest social circles and an acceptance not usually granted to "colonials."

Lexy felt honor bound to confess that she had brought her dual identity with her, explaining that while Lexy would be doing inoffensive reports about the races and other social events, Abby Adams might write articles that were not so flattering. She planned to be careful so that no one would discover that the two writers were the same person, but it was always possible that someone might find out. The Bettingdons already knew about the Abby Adams pieces Lexy had done in America because Gincie had sent them copies, but it was different for them to know Abby was going to be loosed on England.

But the family treated Abby Adams as their own delightful secret. It quickly became the habit to ask, "And what would Abby think of this?" about various news reports in the English papers or about rumors spreading around the country. Even for Lexy it was easy to imagine Abby as a completely separate person, so that when she wore a particularly fanciful hat to the races, she could observe, "I'm not sure Abby would quite approve of this; it's a bit extreme for her taste."

The Bettingdons were still closely involved in the turf world, and with them Lexy went to such famous races as the Derby, the Epsom Grand Prize, the Oaks, and the Ascot Stakes. When she had been in England before, she had been too young to attend the races, and now she was entranced by the ceremony and color to be found at the English courses. As with racetracks anywhere, the chance to risk a small wager or a fortune brought a broad mix of people, so that it was possible to observe everyone from princes to pickpockets in the same small area. The roads to the courses were crowded with luxurious equipages, many of them driven by their owners, who were reviving the old showmanship of being notable whips, particularly with the four-in-hand arrangement whereby a skilled driver controlled four horses. Well-bred, highly trained teams of horses were prized and expensive to buy and maintain. And their beauty was hard to resist as they flashed by in a blur of chestnut, bay, brown, gray, and more rarely, black.

Christopher and his sons were skilled drivers who won Lexy's approval by always considering the well-being of their animals more important than a flashy show. Since coaching was also enjoying a revival of interest as a sport in America, Lexy added descriptions of the English horses and drivers to her racing news.

To her amusement, Lexy found that her male relatives provided a service she had not considered. In addition to proudly introducing her as their American cousin and as a writer of the sporting and social news, they kept a sharp eye on which gentlemen were allowed to approach her. Though she treasured her independence, she welcomed this action. A certain set of Englishmen were becoming notorious for searching out American heiresses as a way of shoring up sagging walls and fortunes, and she had no desire to be pursued because of mistaken assumptions made about her value on the marriage market due to her relationship with the Bettingdons. Bruised from the loss of Hawk, she had given no thought to the possibility that other men might show interest in her. And now that they did, they seemed so young and untried compared to Hawk, she felt more embarrassed on their behalf than anything else. She was sure that most of them would be genuinely shocked if they knew of her past history, for all that they already judged her rather wild and unconventional for being an American and a journalist besides.

Lexy was aware that there was a class of men in the United States who did little useful work, but it was not the same as the institutionalized ennui she found amongst the younger members of the noble class in England. To be sure, there were exceptions such as Christopher and his sons, who were involved in the daily business of running various enterprises, but many more avoided such involvement as if honest industry were a contagion of the middle class and not to be risked. She did not envy their irresponsible style of living; instead, it made her uncomfortable and heightened her awareness of her own heritage, which taught little could be had without effort.

As far as Lexy could see, the lives of women of both the upper and the middle classes were similarly unproductive.

Gweneth had come to England as Christopher's bride, but she had brought Wild Swan's pattern of independence and action with her. She had maintained it as well as she could ever since, and she had achieved even more stature after the death of her mother-in-law had made her the matriarch of the family, though she still missed Angelica's wise advice.

But it was not the same for Christopher's sister, Amelia, long married with children and grandchildren of her own, for Hugh and Nicholas's wives, or for Lexy's cousin Eveline. She liked all of the women, admired the children they had produced, and could see that their marriages were happier than most, but still she found their lives stifling, their days such an endless round of social obligations and costume changes that finding time to think was nearly impossible. Even she, who had never cared much about what she wore, was spending an inordinate amount of time, not to mention money, just to maintain a wardrobe that would not disgrace the women of the family when she accompanied them. And that in turn required the attentions of the army of servants who peopled the various residences, servants who went so far as to iron the morning edition of the London *Times* and everything else that might have the slightest wrinkle, including boot laces. Lexy was accustomed to servants, but not to the tyranny they exercised in English households. She soon gave up trying to do things for herself in order to ease their workload; in quiet and seemingly subservient ways, they made it clear that they required things to be done in a predetermined manner. They upheld the rigid class structure as strongly as anyone and were more impressed by titles than the family itself.

For that reason, they also seemed more worshipful of Queen

Victoria than were members of her court, who, at least from the sampling Lexy was meeting, were not overly impressed by their monarch's glorification of middle-class values, though they were respectful of her power and the stability of her government.

The Bettingdons offered to arrange for Lexy to be presented to the queen. But in the end she felt obliged to refuse the opportunity. If it did become known that she wrote as Abby Adams, it might prove an added embarrassment to the Bettingdons had they arranged a meeting with their sovereign.

Her cousin Eveline assured Lexy that it was not an experience to be envied. "Everything is done so formally; what one may wear, say, and do are calculated down to the smallest detail. It's all foolish, really. And the queen looks rather like a tortoise, a tortoise in a black shell and a white bonnet."

Eveline's eyes grew round as she considered what she'd said, and then she and Lexy began to laugh.

Lexy wiped her eyes. "Oh, dear, now I could never meet her face to face. I would probably burst out laughing and be judged the rudest of Americans."

But even with her cousin's irreverent image in mind, Lexy was impressed by the celebration on June 21 of the fiftieth anniversary of the queen's accession to the throne. Enormous crowds of adoring subjects lined the streets from the palace gates to the Abbey of Westminster, where the court and the royal family attended a religious service. Lexy was with the Bettingdons and therefore got a clear view of the queen in her characteristic bonnet and a lace-trimmed black silk dress, details that would undoubtedly fascinate the readers of the *Witness*. The roar of the onlookers along the parade route as well as the inscriptions displayed left no doubt about the subjects' enthusiasm for their ruler, and there were additional celebrations and great displays of fireworks for days afterward.

It touched Lexy that the poor of London seemed as happy to celebrate their queen's long reign as those who were more fortunate. It made her see that while the upper class might view askance Victoria's rigid moral preachments and sentimental insistence on what she saw as family values, for the lower classes those same dictates gave her rule a common touch they could understand and a standard to which they could aspire.

The poverty in London not only appalled Lexy, it terrified her. Despite some renewal accomplished during Victoria's reign, there were sections of the city that were like kingdoms of the underworld, so dark, dank, disease and crime ridden, they seemed to exist on a planet separate from the one that provided flower-laden parks, tempting shops, and all manner of amusements for those who could afford them. And the darkness seemed impenetrable, ruled by its own language, customs, and lords.

Trying to get a clear view of life where some of the worst slums existed was not only hazardous, it was frustrating. Lexy was not so foolhardy as to risk prowling about by herself. Nor was she willing to involve Christopher, Hugh, or Nicholas, since the territory was nearly as foreign to them as it was to her, for though they had diverse business interests, these were not centered in London.

But Christopher had a suggestion: "Michael Winterbourne could take you safely into the depths of the city."

At first, Lexy could not put a face to the name, and then she remembered the aloof blond man she had met on a couple of occasions at the Bettingdons' London house. He had never been part of the racing set or any other social gathering, but had been there for meetings with Christopher. He had been courteous when they were introduced but nothing more. She imagined that time spent in his company would not be comfortable.

Much of what she was thinking showed on her face, and Christopher nodded. "I see you remember him. Sir Michael is a bit stern. He does not offer his friendship easily, but once you have it, it endures. And he has more connections in London than anyone else I know, connections at every level."

Christopher considered that an adequate description of the man, but Gwenny did not, and she proceeded to tell Lexy more details about the man. "Sir George, Michael's father, was a wily man by all accounts. He inherited a minor title and a fortune which had been much diminished by his own father's and grandfather's gaming habits. Sir George discovered he had a talent for business, and he did not consider it beneath him. He invested in railroads, factories, land, all sorts of things, and usually he came out better than he went in, until he'd become very wealthy indeed.

"He and his wife had three sons, and Michael was the youngest. I know he seems older, but he's only thirty-three, the same age as Nicholas and Hugh. As the youngest son, he was not to inherit the title or the estates that went with it, but since the family was by then so well off, he also did not have to seek a position in the army or elsewhere. I suppose he was rather spoilt—there are some tales of wild days at Cambridge—but he was also, by all reports, quite scholarly and possessed of his father's keen head for business, even at an early age, much more so than his brothers. In the normal course of things, I expect he would have pursued his own interests as well as being a business agent for his father and then for his eldest brother. But poor Michael, nothing has been 'normal' since shortly after he reached his majority."

Gwenny's green eyes filled with tears, and she sniffed audibly. "Oh, he would hate it if he knew how sorry I feel for him, but I do. He lost so much so quickly! First his parents were killed in a coaching accident, and then within a year of that, both of his brothers were gone, the heir by a fall on the hunting field, and the middle brother from a lung complaint. By that time, Michael was engaged to the daughter of a mill owner. He had met the family through his father's business interests. Of course, the old cats said that since Michael had now inherited the title, he would surely choose someone more worthy. But Michael went right ahead and married the woman he loved. And within two years, his wife and the child she carried were both dead in childbirth."

"My God!" Lexy exclaimed. "It is a miracle that the man was not driven mad!"

"It did not do that, but it certainly drove him inside of himself," Gweneth said. "More than a few people call him 'Icy Winter' behind his back. I'm sure he knows, but they are not people who matter to him, anyway. He has not forgiven those who condemned his wife because of her origins, and he has little tolerance for people he judges frivolous. I know it is a sore trial to him to attend court functions, but he does when he must. He is too canny to give up the benefits he can glean there. I do not want you to mistake the man because of what I've told you. He is one of the most astute men of business in the realm, and he is known to be ruthless in gaining his ends. But he is also the man who personally makes sure that scores of children in the East End and elsewhere have enough food, clothing, and education to survive far better than they would otherwise. That is why he would be the perfect guide for you; he knows the poor as they are."

It was high praise because the Bettingdons had always understood that being fortunate carried with it the obligation to help those who were less so. If they were impressed by a man's charitable acts, that man's compassion and generosity had to be out of the ordinary.

"Sir Michael sounds as if he would be the perfect guide," Lexy said, "but if he is as complicated and self-contained as you say, why should he take the time to indulge me?"

"At first because I will ask him to," Christopher said calmly, "and then because even Michael Winterbourne is no match for one of Wild Swan's women."

Lexy had reason to doubt Christopher's statement when she first went into London's darker regions with Michael Winterbourne. Without verbally violating the bounds of civility, he made it clear that his kindest estimation of her motives was idle curiosity, his worst that she was one of the satin and bows contingent of female writers and wanted nothing more than the notoriety of being able to claim she'd visited the dangerous districts, much like those who used to visit insane asylums or prisons to gape at the inmates.

Michael Winterbourne was tall, leanly built with thick golden hair and sharply cut features that were saved from any feminine cast by the high-bridged imperiousness of his nose.

"Icy Winter" was an appropriate nickname. The man's eyes were deep blue, a color that could be warmly alive, but in his case, the brightness was frozen over with distaste.

He greeted her with cold propriety when they set out in the cab, but before they reached their first destination, he turned to her and said, "I can't begin to understand your motives for wanting to go on this expedition. I don't have to understand them. His Grace is a steady friend. He sees some purpose in this, and that is enough. But the people we are going to see are just that, people. I won't have you staring at them as if they're part of a zoological exhibition."

Under other circumstances, Lexy would have gotten out of the carriage and made it a point not to see him again, but she needed his help. She curbed her temper and met his glare with her own level gaze.

To his own surprise, Michael heard himself asking, "I wonder what you are thinking?"

Lexy considered for a moment, and then she said, "I am thinking that while the English can be the most civilized and courteous people on earth, they can also be the rudest." He was so proper; surely he could be shamed into better behavior.

Michael stared at her, and then he gave a bark of laughter. "I deserved that," he admitted. "I beg your pardon."

He was intrigued in spite of himself and beginning to see there was more to this American cousin of the Bettingdons' than he had first supposed. He wanted to laugh again when he found that he was chiding himself inwardly with the reminder that because a woman was beautiful did not mean she must also be devoid of intelligence.

Lexy could feel the softening of his attitude toward her, and the sudden light in his blue eyes changed them dramatically, but she knew she was still on trial and must guard her behavior carefully. She had considered telling him about Abby Adams, but had decided the fewer people who knew the better. Now she stayed with the decision out of stubbornness and the conviction that this man wouldn't be impressed by her credentials, anyway. American newspapers would mean little to him, she guessed. He was going to judge her on how she comported herself while in his company, and that was fair enough. With that in mind, she clamped down on her emotions for the rest of the day.

It was well that she did. Winterbourne did not spare her. He took her to tenements that were so filthy and crowded, she had to swallow repeatedly to keep from gagging. Scrawny children with blue-white faces clung to their mothers' skirts or scratched at their heads and bodies in a desultory manner, as if they had been vermin-ridden for so long, they were hardly aware of it until a particularly nasty bite or a migration of the small creatures from one site to the next caught their attention.

Communal outhouses, few in number for the population packed in the flats, reeked of excrement, and fetid puddles made walking hazardous. And often, these primitive sewage arrangements were contiguous to the pumps used for drinking and to the tubs and lines used for laundry. In such surroundings, it amazed Lexy that laundry was ever done.

She resisted the impulse to hold a handkerchief to her nose or to betray any other sign of her revulsion. She knew Michael was watching her closely, and that steadied her. But beyond that, she did not want to offend the people they were visiting.

Though there were some sideways looks and muttering, for the most part Michael was received with dignity and, on the part of the children, with affection. These were people he knew well and cared about. He asked specific questions:

"Has William recovered from his fever?"

"Is Dolly still going to school?"

"How much coal do you think you'll need this winter?"

On and on, and though Lexy could hardly understand some of the answers, Michael seemed to have no such problem.

She hung back, listening and watching everything, trying not to disturb the people by her presence, but she knew they were acutely aware of her and wondering exactly what Sir Michael meant by "friend," which was how he introduced her.

At one stop, a Mrs. Cranner, in the midst of squalling babies and piles of fancy hand sewing she did for a West End shop, proudly offered her guests a cup of tea.

The cup was chipped and dirty, and the tea was little more than brown-tinted, tepid water, but Lexy was prepared to down it rather than risk giving offense. With a slight shake of his head, Michael signalled her not to drink it. Then he asked Mrs. Cranner about her work, and while her attention was diverted he took Lexy's cup and tossed the contents out on a particularly stained bit of floor. Mrs. Cranner had long since given up the struggle to keep the dirt at bay except for a miraculously clean island that existed to keep the soil from the cloth that would go back to the shops.

Lexy noted that Michael drank his own tea while Mrs. Cranner watched.

"Why did you do that?" she asked after they had left the place.

"Because I found I could not face the possibility that you might contract some contagion while under my care," he answered.

"But you drank the tea," she protested.

"Well, yes, but I seem to be immune to whatever fevers exist here." And then he added with a smile, "Besides, as usual, Mrs. Cranner added a large swig of gin to my tea. I'm sure it's lethal enough to kill almost everything, including me if I visited too often."

This smile so transformed him that Lexy looked away. She felt as if she had caught a private glimpse of a younger, more innocent man, the man who had existed before life had extracted such a price from him.

As much as the columns by Lexy and Abby Adams were different, so now were Lexy's days. Sometimes she was involved in the social rounds that went on, though Ascot had ended the official season and many of the aristocracy had taken themselves off to the country. The Bettingdons left for the country, too, but Lexy still had the comfort of their London home and the company of some of the friends she had made through the family, people who were also staying in the city. No matter how liberal-minded the Bettingdons were, she knew that they felt some trepidation in leaving her there, but they had to acknowledge that she was an adult, and they trusted Michael Winterbourne.

Lexy was sure that under normal circumstances, Michael would have left the city as well, but when she mentioned it, he dismissed the idea with a curt, "I assure you, I am not being held in London against my will."

Increasingly her time was spent with him. He showed her the lives of the costermongers who dealt in fish, fruit, and vegetables, and the other hawkers: piemen, muffinmen, Irish cats'-meat dealers, old women with pickled whelks and cress for sale, boys with oranges and nuts, on and on. He showed her the street entertainers who swallowed snakes, walked on stilts, and displayed other exotic talents before begging coins. He showed her the legions who still lived by what they scavenged from the streets and sewers, everything from rags, bones, and bits of coal and wood, to copper and silver coins, pieces of iron, and even serving ware and jewelry recovered from the drains. Those who worked the sewers, called "toshers," formed an elite of their own for the hazards they faced. They never worked alone because the older tunnels were liable to collapse, the noxious fumes could kill, and there were fables of men, feet stuck in the slime, being eaten alive by rats. Even if the rats were not man-eaters, the threat of being drowned in the incoming tide was certainly real.

And everywhere were the children, many of them selling bits of everything from the time they were barely out of leading strings. Many boys had their own carts and their own women by the time they were thirteen or fourteen.

Michael was not foolish about their explorations. He carried a heavy walking stick, and he kept a good distance from any situation that looked as if it might be dangerous. Sadly, the most threatening were often the children: children who ran in packs like dogs, graduating from petty offenses to more serious crimes as they got older and stronger. They lived in a world where no one cared about them except their pack mates, so it was not difficult to understand why their loyalties lay only there. Though it might seem harsh that boys should have the obligation of running their own barrows or stalls from an early age, these were far better off than the children who ran wild.

Michael made no mention of her continued reserve until they had witnessed an especially vicious attack by bigger boys on a smaller one who tried vainly to retain possession of a bundle he was taking to a rag-and-bottle shop to sell. There was nothing Michael could do to stop the attack; there were too many of the bullies, and he had Lexy's safety uppermost in his mind. The best he could do was to pick the little fellow up when it was over, check him for serious injury, and finding none, send him away with far more coin than he would have gotten for the oddments he had collected from the streets. But though the little boy took the money, he looked no less terrified of Michael than he had been of the bigger boys, and he slunk away like a whipped puppy.

After it was over, Michael studied Lexy's face and could detect no sign that the incident had affected her at all.

"I am curious," he said. "Do they seem like human beings to you, or some species apart?"

With images of the abused child still in her mind, Lexy lost patience and her temper. "Sir Michael, you have made it clear from the first day that you assumed the onerous duty of escorting me only because Christopher requested it. And I have known from the first day that if I dared so much as wrinkle my nose, let alone shed a tear, you would consider it reason enough to judge me inadequate to this task, and thus you would feel justified in ending these excursions. Frankly, I don't know anyone else in London who could show me the same things. So I have betrayed no feelings at all. It isn't entirely your fault; journalists are not supposed to show emotional involvement. But the truth is that I wanted to strangle those bullies and take that little one home. I've wanted to scrub out the rooms, stock the larders, provide decent jobs for the adults and schooling for the children. I've wanted to change everything. I've wanted to choke over the filth and weep over the waste." She took a deep breath to steady the tremor that had begun to shake her voice. "Is there anything else you want to know?"

"Only how you have managed to be so patient with my boorish behavior," Michael said, making no effort to hide his distress.

At that, Lexy protested. "You took on a task that you didn't want, and you've performed it admirably, despite your reservations. I could not have seen half as much without you as my guide." She hesitated, and then she asked, "Do you think we could go on as friends?"

"I think I would like that very much," Michael said, and then he had a question of his own. "How will you write about what you've seen?"

"Not like Mr. Dickens wrote about the United States on his first visit there. He was still apologizing twenty years later. I do understand that there is no useful purpose in condemning a whole society for its inability to be perfect in all things. And the United States is not so virtuous that I could use it as a pulpit from which to preach. But it is different there. People are not quite so fixed in their places by education or the lack of it, by the way they speak or who their parents were. There is an optimism, not just in the small pleasures that might be gleaned day to day as the people do here when they clap for a juggler on the street or find they have enough for a few ounces of meat for the Sunday meal, but in a larger way, in the belief that no matter what their origins, they can, with work, patience, and, yes, luck, go as high as anyone. They believe it even if it isn't true for them, because it does happen for some."

She sighed, considering it. "I don't think the poorest believe that here. I don't think it's true here. And that's what makes the conditions they live in so frightening." She added with grim honesty, "As it must be increasingly so for the freed slaves in my country. So many promises were made when the war ended. But all the fire went into the war and burnt itself out. There was none left to keep the promises. In that way, the freed slaves in my country are becoming like the poor in yours, devoid of hope of real change."

"So what will you write?" Michael persisted, fascinated by her insight and her honesty.

"I am not wholly sure yet," she admitted. "But surely a cautionary tale would make more sense than a diatribe."

She hesitated, and then she squared her shoulders in a gesture Michael was coming to recognize as characteristic when she was summoning an extra measure of resolve. "If we are truly to be friends, there is something I ought to tell you. Perhaps you should have known from the first, but it didn't seem necessary then; it does now," she said, and she told him about Abby Adams.

She expected him to be angry, but he was not. The fact that in England only her relatives had known until this moment made her confession an act of trust that touched him. And he had his own revelation to offer in return.

"I read your articles on the insane asylum, and about the lot of working women in Baltimore. They were very fine. I should have guessed you were the person who wrote them. Not that I haven't enjoyed Lexy's commentaries on the turf," he added with a grin, amused at her look of astonishment. "Didn't you think that Englishmen read American newspapers? Of course, the *Witness* came highly recommended by the Bettingdons, though they never betrayed your dual role."

The sharing of the secret and Michael's acceptance of her journalistic goals forged a bond, a bond that strengthened the others that had been subtly weaving between the two of them ever since the first antagonistic day.

And now that the antagonism was gone, they spent even more time in each other's company and never ran out of topics of mutual interest.

Through Michael's eyes, Lexy saw that the problems of the poor in London were part of a complex pattern of causes, one building on the next. Attempts had been made, for decades, to improve conditions, but in Michael's opinion, most of these attempts had been wrongheaded.

"There has been such a distinction made between the 'deserving' poor and those who are 'undeserving,' meaning a class of people who make a profession of begging and have no desire to work. I admit, there are some like that, but there are many, many more who simply cannot find enough work at a high enough wage to sustain them. There is such a vast world of casual laborers in this city, people whose work is cyclical or seasonal, from dock work to housebuilding to jam-making; people who have no security in their jobs, no guarantee that work will be there for them from one week to the next, or even from one day to the next.

"London is an odd city. It's a port whose shipbuilding and other industries have been declining for years. It's the capital, and it's where much of the court spends at least part of the year. But the business of running the government and attending the royal family does not produce the same number or kind of jobs as does intensive industry. Most of the employers in London are employers on a small scale only, and most of the inhabitants of the West End have little contact with the laboring class, not beyond servants. So what charity there has been from the truly wealthy has been given with little understanding of the poverty it means to cure. And there has usually been some measure of punishment in it due to the fear that giving alms too easily will encourage pauperism.

"For instance, at one time it was determined that many children did not receive any education because they had no boots to wear to school. Boots distributed to the children would seem to be an easy solution. But then it was pointed out that if such charity were widely known, poor parents would certainly begin to keep their children home even more often in order to obtain free boots. Who knows? Perhaps there is some truth in that, but it seems cruel and ridiculous reasoning."

Lexy could not suppress a shudder as she recalled the pinched white faces of the children peeking from behind their mothers' skirts, and worse, the children who belonged to armies of their own, swarming from one dangerous pursuit to the next. "Do you see no way of improving things then?" she asked.

"Oh, yes, there is a way," he said slowly, and in that instant, despite his fine-boned aristocratic blondness, Michael was like Hawk, fierce intelligence pooled in his eyes, and a certain grim satisfaction showing in his face at the thought of justice made inevitable. "What charity will not do, fear will. In the seventies, things were not so bad. Winters were mostly mild, and the economic situation was not so clearly dire. It really was possible to put the poorest of the poor out of mind. And it was also possible to extend Mr. Darwin's theory to them, to believe that they were, after all, the mistakes of the species and that sundry disasters befalling them and thinning the ranks were nothing more than Nature's way of pruning the branches. But now, now it is different. The winters have turned severe again; the depression that really started more than ten years ago has only been fully felt in the past few years; and the discontent is spreading to 'respectable' workers, even to skilled artisans. Last February, there were riots that brought the denizens of the East End to the West End. Windows were broken, shops looted, and fear unleashed, fear that the poor will not stay forever in their kennels like obedient hounds."

"Do you want a revolution?" Lexy asked bluntly, too caught up in the passion of his words to be subtle.

He shook his head impatiently. "No, I don't! I want sane decisions to be made, sane measures to be taken before revolution is unavoidable."

Though the long summer twilight was falling over the city, and they were both weary, Lexy did not refuse when Michael said he had something else to show her.

He took her to Trafalgar Square and then to St. James's Park, and he pointed out the many people still there in the fading light.

"Who do you think they are?" he asked.

"People who are enjoying the exceptionally fine summer weather," she hazarded, though she knew that Michael would not have asked the question if the answer were so simple.

"They are doing that," he agreed, "but when darkness comes, they will still be here. They are spending the nights here and not spending a shilling for rent. If the weather continues so fine for the rest of the summer, they'll manage well enough. But winter will come, and they will have to find rooms again, crowded unsanitary quarters, if they can find the money to pay for such."

The figures in the park changed for Lexy, appearing entirely different now that she knew they had no shelter to go to. She shivered, though the air was warm.

"Just so," Michael said. "And here they are right at the gates of a more privileged world, close enough to strike fear into privileged hearts when they are finally noticed. The poor are easy to ignore when they are confined to a place apart, much harder when the boundaries blur."

"A cautionary tale indeed," Lexy said. "I think I know what I am going to write now."

She spent the next week writing about what she had seen, what Michael had taught her. She made the observations as vivid and personal as she had in previous Abby Adams pieces; she made it a tale of people and of what they owed each other for their mutual welfare, rather than a recital of failed governmental and charitable policies. She was shameless in pulling at heartstrings with descriptions of the children, believing that no matter how stubborn people were in their righteous conviction that the poor deserved their lot, few could ignore the suffering of the young or the threat of what might happen if those young survived to grow up full of bitterness and despair. All the while she wrote, she was conscious that her words would probably have little effect, no matter how eloquent she was, but the whole purpose of Reid's paper was to bear witness, as the masthead proclaimed, and that often had to be enough.

There was no reason for Michael to escort her anymore, and facing that, she also faced the fact that he had become very special to her. She had not come to England to find a substitute for Hawk, and Michael was too proud and complete a man to be a substitute for anyone. But he was, in his fierce independence, in his intellect, in the flashes of humor and tenderness, like Hawk. And he had, she discovered, begun to fill the empty spaces in her heart.

She had not heard from Hawk since she had arrived in England, and she had not written to him. Nor had anyone from the paper or her family sent news of him. She had read his reports in the paper when the editions arrived ten days or more out of date, but that had proved no substitute for his physical presence. And now she found that when she tried to picture him, his dark visage was often eclipsed by Michael's golden one.

She didn't know how she felt about Hawk's fading image. Rationally she knew it was healthy. By interfering in Hawk's past, she had, at least to his mind, betrayed their future. She had loved him; part of her would always love him; and she had learned a great deal about loving from him. But by his silence since she had left, he surely felt well rid of her.

She did not feel the same wild compulsion for Michael Winterbourne that she had felt for Hawk. She wasn't sure she ever wanted to feel that again. Now that she had so many weeks' distance from Hawk, it seemed as if he had existed in another lifetime and as if he had been some sort of opiate that engendered its own craving.

She could not imagine feeling so about Michael, but she recognized the value of what she did feel for him—enormous warmth, intellectual and physical attraction. Had she not been with Hawk, she would have thought these constituted love at its fullest. Perhaps they did. But if she were ever to love a man again, Michael or someone else, the magic would be to forget how it had been with Hawk and to accept these quieter manifestations of love not just as adequate and sensible, but as the best there could be.

She did not expect she would have to make a decision about what she felt or didn't feel about Michael, but she was grateful that at least he had awakened her to the possibility that there might be someone else in her life besides Hawk.

Having convinced herself that she would not see Michael again except when he visited the Bettingdons, her surprise showed when he presented himself.

"Did you think, or was it a hope, that our association would end when the work was done?" he asked, and despite the even tone of his voice, his face showed how much her answer mattered to him.

"I hoped I would see you again," she answered honestly, "but I wasn't sure you would desire it."

"I do, and a great deal more. We are a good match for the serious side of things; I would like to know if we are the same for the lighter side."

He spoke with a smile, but his eyes betrayed his intensity. She suspected it had been a very long time since Michael had considered his own joy and pleasure to be of any importance. Perhaps as long ago as before his wife and child had died.

Suddenly she could not bear that anything less than the truth should exist between them. "I left the United States because of a man. He was my lover. He is a good and honorable man. We simply had problems we could not solve. With you before me now, I cannot imagine that he will ever be part of my life again. But I don't know what would happen if I should see him again, and I surely will because he works for the *Witness*, too." She shook her head in bafflement. "I just don't know. I'm a rational human being, but I can't explain this adequately. He is like an addiction for me. You deserve far better than this."

"No one deserves better than this," Michael said. He cradled her face in his hands and kissed her gently. "I'll take the risk. Surely you must know that despite my trangressions against society's expectations, I am still considered a marriage prize." He stated the case with cynical weariness, not arrogance. "If I wanted one of society's offerings, I could have her. But I don't. I want a certain American woman who has a brain and a heart and knows how to use both of them."

He kissed her again, and Hawk faded back into the shadows of memory.

Chapter 35

For the first week after Lexy confessed to her meeting with the Fordyces, Hawk felt such rage, he was glad she was staying out of his sight. He assumed she was at Wild Swan or with the family in Baltimore.

By the second week, the rage had faded enough for him to recognize the pain he was feeling, but he shoved it away from his consciousness. What mattered now was that Caroline knew his intentions. What mattered was Jared.

His first impulse was to simply go to the Fordyces and demand custody of his son. But even in his agitated state, he recognized the intemperance of such an action, and further, though reluctantly, he recognized that this view was Lexy's and had become his own.

He wrote a polite and proper note to Mrs. Sylvanus Fordyce, stating that he believed they had met in California and that he wished to call in order to extend his best wishes for the family's settling in Washington. And then he schooled himself to wait for an answer, still doing it Lexy's way, though he thought it more likely that Caroline would bolt with the child than that she would agree to see him.

However, within a few days he had not only a proper answer to his missive, but an invitation to tea in the afternoon.

She was even more beautiful than she had been the last time he had seen her. Added maturity and responsibility had given her a luster no young girl could possess. Only now did he know, by comparison, how young and giddy she had been when they had had their affair. Images of their passionate lovemaking flashed through his mind, but he was disconcerted to find that they were only memories. No response stirred in him. He could look on her beauty and remember stroking her body, and all the desire he felt was for Lexy, for the tall, slender strength of her, for the golden brown hair and green, green eyes. He had imagined many things about meeting Caroline again, but not once had he considered that his mind and heart would be filled with another woman. It gave him an air of detachment that Caroline noted with relief.

"It was a very long time ago, wasn't it?" she said. She was watching him closely, and she looked apprehensive, but she was also self-possessed, prepared to defend her own.

It occurred to him that she might have sent Jared away so that he would not be able to see him. "Is he here?" he demanded.

"Yes, he is. And you will meet him. But first I want you to understand that I will not let you have him. There is nothing you can do that will make me give him up. Even if you tell my husband, I will keep my son." Her voice didn't falter, and she looked straight at him. "I am sure you want to exact some revenge, but remember, whatever you do to me, to this family, you do to Jared. No matter how much you hate me now, I cannot believe you will hurt a child for it."

"My child," he reminded her harshly.

"Your seed," she flashed back, and then her face softened. "Spoiled, foolish, young—despite all the things I was then, I did love you, Hawk. You were handsome, dashing, intelligent; you still are. But I loved Sylvanus more; I always will. I'm sorry I discovered that too late to spare you hurt, but I will never be sorry I had Jared, never!"

"Yet you expect me to give up all rights to him?"

"I do, because there is no way that you can share him that will not destroy the very family that keeps him safe and happy."

In spite of the intimacies they had shared and in spite of her protestations that there had once been love, the boundaries were drawn between them, and there didn't seem to be any point in wasting time in meaningless attempts to cross the distance.

"You give your word you will not tell Jared, at least not today?" Caroline asked, and Hawk nodded.

When Jared was presented to him, Hawk felt such a rush of emotions, for a moment he was unable to answer the little boy's polite greeting. Far more now than when he had had the brief glimpse of the child in San Francisco, he could see himself in Jared. It was as if he were looking at himself far back in time. And yet, it wasn't so. He had been bruised and afraid most of the time; Jared glowed with confidence and contentment. If this child had ever been afraid, it had only been from the night shadows every child conjured as he tested the limits of imagination. And Hawk doubted that Jared had ever been struck, for any reason.

He could hear Lexy's passionate defense of Jared's security more easily than he could recall the words Caroline had spoken to him this afternoon.

Caroline Fordyce. Not "Caro" anymore, not even in his mind.

Suddenly Lexy seemed so close, he wanted to share the sight of his son with her. But it was impossible; these were two parts of his life that could not be joined.

He became aware that Jared was watching him, not with any personal involvement, but with the curiosity of a child observing an adult acting in an odd manner. He pulled himself together enough to greet the boy with the same respect he would have accorded an adult, and Jared responded happily.

"Mama says you're from California, an' you write things for newspapers. I'se been in California, too, but I don't 'member it so good. I think I might like to write things when I get big, but maybe I'll be a cowboy or a soldier instead."

They talked about other subjects, but inevitably, Jared became restless, too polite to say so but wanting to get back to his play.

Watching him leave the room was like suffering an amputation. It was no less drastic than that because there would be no going back. For honor, for love, for Jared, for himself, even for Caroline and her husband, this was the way it had to be.

Hawk waited until he was sure he could control his voice. "You have done a fine job with him. I will not jeopardize that. I won't try to see him or you again, but promise me that if you ever need anything for him, you will let me know."

Caroline nodded, and then she closed her eyes and tears leaked from under the lids. "Thank you, Hawk, oh, thank you!" she breathed. "In turn, I promise you that he will never lack for anything, most of all for love."

Where once he had considered ruining her for what she had done, now he found himself anxious for her sake. "The servants might well have noted the resemblance. Will you be all right for having me here?"

Her chin came up. "The servants will keep their speculations to themselves; they are well paid, and I doubt they would risk their jobs for gossip. But even if Sylvanus sees you, and he might because this city is not so large, he will not ask. He could not love Jared more had he fathered him, but he knows he did not. If he had wanted to know your identity, he would have asked years ago. As long as he does not have to fight you, he will let it be as it is."

She paused, searching for the right words. "Married people make truces about many things, some important, some not, but the truces are all designed to make it possible for men and women to live together in contentment. Will you offer Miss Culhane a truce? I liked her very much, and I will always be grateful for what she risked for me and Jared, and for you."

Hawk took his leave without giving her a response, and Caroline was sorry for the shuttered look that had descended over his face at the mention of Miss Culhane. The woman had had much to do with ending Caroline's long nightmare that Hawk would find her and take Jared, and she prayed that Hawk and Lexy would find a way back to each other.

After Hawk left the Fordyce house, he walked for hours. Every once in a while, some site would register as a place he and Lexy had visited together, but most of the time he wasn't conscious of his surroundings. He felt more adrift than he ever had in his life. He had been driven by the single goal of claiming Jared ever since he had seen him in San Francisco, and now it was over. And it had not finished with dramatic action. A quiet, rational meeting with Caroline and Jared, and the pages of that chapter of his life had fluttered closed.

His body ached for action, as if it had been denied a fight. He would have liked an excuse to punch someone. Instead he kept walking until sheer fatigue began to calm the swirling energy, and then he went back to his house and drank until he passed out.

He awakened in the morning with ample evidence of why he seldom overindulged. He couldn't remember the last time he had felt so ill and hoped he would not know the feeling again for the rest of his life. But his physical pain was nothing to the inner hurt he suffered when he caught sight of Lexy's belongings. He had meant to send them to her boardinghouse the day after their confrontation. Now he understood that his failure to do so had been deliberate. The lap desk he had given her was there and articles of her clothing. He touched the soft weave of a shawl and wanted it to be her soft skin. Suddenly her essence seemed to be everywhere around him, but it was ghostlike, slipping away as he reached for it.

He was still angry with her although he longed for her.

"God damn it, Lexy! I don't know whether to celebrate or curse the day I met you!" he growled. His words echoed around the empty house, but just for an instant, he could see her standing there, squaring her shoulders and facing him head on.

He waited for her to return to Washington, thinking that somehow he would know the right thing to do when he saw her again.

It did not improve his patience or his temper when he began to realize that everyone at work was treating him with elaborate care, a process which included making no mention whatsoever of Lexy. But no one seemed condemnatory either, least of all Reid, so he had to assume that whatever Lexy had said had exonerated him of all blame. He supposed that should have been a relief, but instead it infuriated him.

Finally he could bear the suspense no longer. He went to Reid. "Is Lexy at Wild Swan or in Baltimore? When is she coming back to the paper?" he demanded in a tone he had never before used with his employer.

Far from reacting in kind, Reid's sympathy was evident as he said, "I'm sorry. She sailed for England some time ago, shortly after you and she had your . . . er, disagreement. She didn't explain what the disagreement was about, but she made it plain that it wasn't your fault," he hastened to add.

"England," Hawk said as if the word were entirely unfamiliar. "For how long?"

"I'm not really sure," Reid answered. "She is going to do some articles from there. We didn't set a date for her return. After all, part of the family still lives there, and . . ." Hearing how inane his explanations sounded to his own ears, Reid switched course in midstream: "Well, that's all true enough, but it isn't as true as the fact that she went to put some distance between herself and you."

Watching Hawk's reaction, Reid felt as if he had just participated in an execution. For a moment, the younger man's face was naked and drawn with pain, and then every trace of emotion was gone.

"It's probably for the best," Hawk said. "Thank you for telling me. I know this has been uncomfortable for you."

Reid judged that Hawk would henceforth exert rigid control over showing any interest in Lexy, and he was soon proved correct. When Lexy's first reports began to come in from England, Hawk read them, as did everyone else at the paper, but he neither praised nor criticized too much, giving the impression to most of the staff that whatever had existed between him and Lexy was over and had ended amicably. Only Rob Jenkins and Reid knew that the situation was far more complicated than that, but neither of them wanted to press Hawk about it.

For Hawk it was an exercise in extreme self-discipline to have no more of Lexy than her work sent from so far away and to pretend it meant little to him. The truth was that when he was alone at his house with copies of the *Witness*, he read Lexy's words over and over, trying to picture her in the settings she was describing.

It was much worse when the Abby Adams pieces began to come in. Hawk knew Lexy would not and could not have written about London's dark side without being there. It didn't reassure him that she had relatives to watch over her; if she were going to dangerous places, he wanted to be close enough to defend her. He knew how impatient that attitude would make her, but that didn't change it.

He was angry with her. He missed her. He loved her. He was glad they had this time apart to straighten out how they felt about each other. He hated every minute apart from her. Sometimes he came close to hating her for fleeing to England instead of staying to face him. Yet, at other times, he understood how intolerable it must have seemed to her to be near him when their last meeting had ended so disastrously. She could not have foreseen that he would carry her in his heart when he went to confront Caroline. He wanted Lexy back. He wanted to be free of wanting her.

The only thing he knew for certain was that he had never been this confused in his life, not even in the aftermath of his affair with Caroline. He decided that he would simply wait Lexy out. She would have to come home eventually, and surely by then they would know how they felt.

That plan granted him a small measure of peace that was broken when Lexy began to be the news in addition to writing it.

The reports started to appear in papers other than the *Witness*, and not only in Washington and Baltimore papers, but in the sporting journals and the New York papers, too. At first they were just notes that recorded the presence of the "beautiful Miss Culhane" at various social and sporting events. Polite note was made of the fact that she was employed by the *Witness*, but much more was made of her connections to Wild Swan and to the Bettingdons in England. It made good copy to be able to tell of an American woman who was cutting such a dashing figure amongst the aristocracy. Inevitably, the coverage expanded as it had when Leonard Jerome's daughter Jennie had married Randolph Churchill, or indeed, as it had when Gweneth had married Christopher.

In one report, Lexy had been asked about her knowledge of Abby Adams, who had written so movingly of the plight of the poor in London:

> *Miss Culhane acknowledged that she is acquainted with Abby Adams and expressed admiration for her fellow journalist. But she observed that their choice of subjects is quite different, and with the smile that has charmed more than a few people in England, she confessed that their styles differ in more than the written word. "Miss Adams does not approve of my hats," Miss Culhane said.*

The staff at the *Witness* thought it a good joke and applauded Lexy for it and for providing the paper with free advertising in other publications. Hawk made himself smile with the rest of them, no easy task when he was wondering who the "more than a few people" were whom Lexy had charmed.

He hadn't long to wait for an answer. The gossip about Lexy soon began to link her name with that of Sir Michael Winterbourne. The papers made much of Winterbourne's tragic past and of the fact that he had been quite reclusive in recent years, but not so since meeting Miss Culhane. Now he was seen in her company at all sorts of gatherings.

Next came the incident of the gray horse, reported with great relish as yet another example of the intrepid Yankee being equal to any challenge the Old World offered.

Miss Culhane had been asked to join a riding party at a country estate and had been given a spirited gray mount. The sporting set instantly recognized the significance of the horse's color, for only a very stupid or very capable rider accepted a seat on a strange gray, a color that would stand out in a field of mostly dark horses and make the rider's skill or lack of it all too evident.

Gossip had it that the hostess of this particular outing had had her eye on Sir Michael for one of her daughters for several years and was furious that an American had achieved such an obvious place in his affections. Not having seen Miss Culhane ride, she had assumed that the rumor that American women were wild and unmannered in the saddle and could only ride astride was true, and she had meant to show her up. Instead, Miss Culhane had coolly thanked her for the loan of the horse, had explained that her training at Wild Swan had included riding astride, riding bareback, and riding sidesaddle, and had proceeded to enjoy the ride while proving herself up to the best standards. But Sir Michael was reported to be furious with the hostess for daring to endanger Miss Culhane, and it was certain the woman's marriage plans for her daughter were in the basket. The story concluded with the coy observation that wedding bells were certainly possible from another quarter.

Being in the newspaper business, Hawk knew that such tales were often woven out of the barest scraps. But he drew no comfort from the knowledge, because in this case he feared the story was true.

Once the idea had taken hold, he was shaken by the ferocity of his jealousy. He wanted to kill the man named Winterbourne.

The irony of it nearly overwhelmed him. He was the one who had taught Lexy how to make love, how to enjoy all the delights of the flesh. He recognized his arrogance: he had not really considered Lexy loving another man. He had thought of the two of them being apart, but not of her being with someone else. He had no interest in other women, so how could she be interested in another man? And then, with a sinking heart, he recalled that Lexy had feared he wanted not only Jared, but Caroline as well. No matter how he had assured Lexy of his love for her, the evidence had been that anything concerning her came second to his goal of getting custody of Jared and, perhaps, of Caroline.

He had thrown Lexy out, and she was doing the sensible thing in establishing a new life that did not include him.

Suddenly he saw the future as it would be without Lexy. He might see her when she returned to visit her family, but it would only be in passing, two civilized people denying by their polite smiles and distant greetings that there had ever been anything except brief friendship between them. She would never again turn with a glad smile at the sound of his voice. He would never again have the delight of sharing ideas with her, of laughing with her, of comforting her when she was frightened or sad, or of having her comfort when he was troubled. He would never again feel her body against his, never make love to her again, never experience her tenderness or her fierce possession of him again. Never.

The last vestiges of his anger for her interference, of his pride, of any lingering doubts about their suitability for each other—everything was washed away in this stark knowledge.

He went to Wild Swan, counting on the fact that if the Culhanes kept to their regular schedule, they would be back from New York now that it was September, preparing for the autumn harvests and for the last of their races in Washington and Baltimore.

To his great relief, he found that Lexy's mother was at

Brookhaven, though Travis was at Wild Swan; Hawk wasn't sure he could face Gincie Culhane with any control because Lexy looked so much like her.

Travis greeted him pleasantly enough, but his surprise and curiosity showed plainly in his eyes. Hawk felt pinned by those turquoise eyes, and with a mixture of relief and horror, he heard his own confession flowing out of his control.

"Lexy left because of me. I was furious with her, and she had no way of knowing I would ever feel any differently." He did not spare the details of his past, though he didn't use Caroline's name or Jared's. "Lexy told me I had no right to the child, but I wouldn't listen, and I didn't understand that she was right until I was face to face with him and his mother. They have nothing to do with my life now; there is nothing I can give my son that would make his life better than it is, too much that I might do to harm his happiness. But I don't want you to think that because of this, Lexy is second choice. She is the first. When I went to see the woman and my son . . . her son . . . Lexy was more clear in my mind than the people before me. And she's haunted me every day since. I am stubborn and slow to know my own heart, and pride got in my way, too, but I swear to you, I love your daughter more than I have ever loved anyone before, more than I will ever love anyone again."

Unconsciously he curled his hands into fists. "Am I too late? Is she marrying that Englishman, that Winterbourne?"

Though his face did not betray it, Travis was more than a little unnerved by this encounter. He wished that Gincie were here, but then he thought better of it, understanding that Hawk was in enough pain without having Gincie witness it, too. Travis doubted Hawk had ever talked so honestly of his feelings to anyone before, except, perhaps, to Lexy.

The man had been direct; Travis felt he could be no less. "Lexy has written to us about Sir Michael. He is the one who served as guide and guard when she explored London for the Abby Adams pieces. Thank God, he is by all accounts a competent man! I respect my daughter for the work she does, but that doesn't mean I don't fear for her. The Bettingdons hold Sir Michael in high esteem. They are the ones who introduced the two, and they would never have done such a thing without complete confidence in the man."

Travis paused, but found no way to soften the blow. "Lexy has grown very fond of Winterbourne, maybe even fond enough to marry him, though she hasn't said so yet. But she's clear-sighted about what it would mean to become an Englishwoman. No matter how American and how free she is now, she knows that being Sir Michael's wife would mean makin' changes and compromises. I don't know whether she's willin' to do that or not.''

He hesitated again and then went on. "She hasn't blamed you, not from the first." He saw no need to add that his own feelings had not been so generous. "But she did write to her mother and me that she didn't expect to hear from you again. That was in the same letter that told us how generous Michael Winterbourne was bein' with his time. I think there's a good chance that she's learnin' to see her life without you in it. And maybe she's beginnin' to see Michael Winterbourne in it."

The silence stretched between them, broken only by the heavy ticking of a clock. Hawk uncurled his fists, finger by finger, surprised to find he had clenched his hands so tightly, they ached.

"Sir, why are you being so pleasant to me?" he asked.

"I've wondered the same thing," Travis admitted, "ever since you arrived today. But it really isn't such a mystery. I worry about Lexy, and she'll always be my little girl in some ways, but I also know she's a woman grown. A lot of thought and care and love went into raisin' her, and she hasn't disappointed us yet. She's a fine, strong woman, just like her mama, and just like her mama, she's no fool about people. She chose to love you, there's no doubt about that; she was shinin' with it when she brought you here for Christmas. So, if she chose to love you, there've got to be good reasons for it. And one of the most important reasons must surely be that she knew you would let her grow as a journalist, even if you worried about her methods for gettin' a story. That's something beyond appreciatin' her because you find her beautiful and desire her. I would not like to know that Gincie loved me only for the physical pleasure she finds in me; I know she loves me for a score of other things, as I love her, as you love Lexy."

"As Winterbourne must love her since he's already helped her with her work," Hawk muttered.

"Exactly so," Travis agreed. "So what do you plan to do about it?"

"I plan to go to England and ask her to marry me," Hawk said, a great peace settling over him now that he had allowed himself to commit to the only action that made sense. "I should have gone weeks ago. I did ask her to marry me before, but I can see that it wasn't much of an offer." He looked at Travis expectantly, and Travis couldn't help but grin.

"If you want my permission to court Lexy, you've got it, but you must know the only permission you'll need is hers."

When Hawk attempted to thank him, Travis stopped him. "This isn't a selfless act. She may be all grown up and independent, but I don't fancy the idea of my daughter livin' so far away. If she can be happy with an American, I'd just as soon she married one.''

Hawk did not see Gincie. She arrived home from Brookhaven shortly after Hawk had departed, and she wasn't as surprised by Hawk's visit as Travis had been. "I wondered how long it would take him to come to his senses," she declared.

Travis was more surprised by her reaction than he had been by Hawk's appearance at Wild Swan, but Gincie's explanation was to the point.

"Lexy looked at him the way I still look at you. It's not that I don't believe she could find contentment with another man. But I want her to have the fire and the joy. I'm not sure anyone ever has more than one chance at that, and some people never have the chance at all. Hawk is Lexy's chance as much as she is his. It's all very simple, really. I just hope Hawk is in time. Lexy wouldn't be the first woman to settle for a comfortable marriage."

"That's true enough," Travis said. "But I don't think being married has ever been a special goal of Lexy's. That should give Hawk Mackenna the edge; he's very forceful, even when the situation is hardly to his advantage."

Travis told her about Hawk's past and the child, and he was relieved that while she wished Hawk did not have such a burden to bring to his relationship with Lexy, she did not condemn him for it. But both of them agreed it was not information the twins needed to have.

Hawk's confidence lasted all the way across the Atlantic and as far as London, but it was considerably shaken when he saw the grandeur of the Bettingdons' town house. It took insistent persuasion on his part, plus the presentation of his press credentials and news of the American family, to convince the staff to divulge Lexy's whereabouts. At last he was directed to the country estate of Sir Michael Winterbourne, where, he was told, the duke and duchess and Miss Culhane were visiting.

Although he had obtained the information he sought, Hawk was aware that these servants who were caring for the house in the family's absence were viewing him as if he were a wild man, or a wild Indian. He was not aware that in his anxiety to get to Lexy, his normally impassive facade had slipped. To the servants, he looked so fierce, they wondered long after he'd gone whether they should have given him directions.

The British rail system was the best in the world, but it seemed far too slow as Hawk traveled to Winterbourne's estate, slow enough to show him the excruciating neatness of the countryside. He stared out at the precise hedgerows, fields, and cottages, at the little villages with their church spires, at the fat cattle and sheep, and he felt more alien than ever before. Not even being part Indian in a country that didn't like Indians had made him feel this out of place. At home he was taller than most men; here he felt like a giant. He had towered over people at the rail station, and looking out at the little houses, he thought he'd have to duck his head in most of them to avoid mortal injury. There seemed to be no in-between; to his eyes, it was a country divided between very small houses and very great ones. The small houses made him feel too large physically; the great houses, if they could be measured by the attitude of the Bettingdons' London servants, were going to make him feel small inside, and inadequate.

He had first met Lexy as a fellow journalist, and though he had been impressed when he had finally visited Wild Swan, her family had been warm and welcoming, and she had been with him, assuring him that he belonged there with her. The differences in their backgrounds had been very clear from the beginning, but only now did he see how vast those differences could be.

Lexy was related to English nobility. That didn't matter in the offices of the *Witness*, but it mattered here. Lexy, for all her forthrightness and the freedom of her American spirit, had learned all the graces. If she wished, she would have no trouble fitting in as the wife of a titled Englishman.

He hired a trap at the station, and when he arrived at Winterbourne, all of his worst fears were confirmed. The grounds were immaculate, the house enormous, a collection of wings added through the ages yet somehow managing to retain a unique harmony. It sat there in serene grandeur, claiming the dignity of past generations and those yet to come. It took no leap of the imagination to see Lexy running all this, infusing it with her own bright life and style.

The servants here were as disconcerted by his unannounced arrival as the London staff had been, and they were glad to turn the problem over to the duchess.

Gweneth Bettingdon looked so much like Morgan Falconer, Hawk would have known she was Lexy's great-aunt without any introduction. And she placed his name immediately.

"I've read your work in the *Witness;* you're a very good writer," she said.

Under normal circumstances, such an accolade was the best thing a journalist could hear, but nothing felt normal to Hawk at the moment, and he would have preferred to hear her say, "Oh, yes, Lexy has mentioned you."

Gweneth's expression was friendly enough, but she was puzzled by his presence and waiting for an explanation.

He thought of several excuses and discarded them all in favor of the truth under the steady gaze of Gweneth's green eyes. "I've come to take Lexy home, if she'll go with me."

Despite years of experience in tempering her reactions, Gweneth could not hide her shock at his announcement. Though she had suspected heartbreak might be the cause of Lexy's extended stay in England, Lexy had never said a word about it, and none of the letters from the American branches of the family had mentioned it either. Now she was staring at the largest and best-kept secret she had ever known. This was certainly not a business matter concerning the newspaper.

He was properly, even somberly dressed, and neatly groomed, but he was unmistakably American, and further, unmistakably Western. His Indian heritage was as plain to Gwenny as if someone had handed her a copy of his family tree. Suddenly she was more homesick for the United States than she had been in years.

"Ah . . . does Lexy know you're here? That is, is she expecting you?" Gwenny asked, though she hadn't much doubt about the answer.

"No, she doesn't."

"Oh, my!" Gwenny sighed, thinking that what had been a pleasant afternoon had been instantly complicated by the arrival of this man.

"Has she accepted a marriage proposal from Winterbourne yet?" Hawk asked abruptly, and Gwenny just barely prevented herself from uttering another "Oh, my!"

She knew she was reacting in a fluttery manner wholly unlike her normal style, and she realized that for a long time she had been dealing only with people who knew the rules and kept to them, from the lowest-ranked servant to the members of the court. Observing the social conventions kept this small country "civilized," kept things moving at a measured pace. But Hawk Mackenna was not bound by such restrictions. She could feel his explosive energy as if it were ricocheting off the walls.

"I don't think Sir Michael has asked her yet—he has been very careful in his suit—but I am quite sure he means to," she said, deciding honesty was the only thing that would serve. And as much as she liked Michael Winterbourne, she could not help but be sympathetic when she saw the relief in Hawk's face.

"Where is she, please?"

Gweneth hesitated a moment, and then she said, "She's out riding with my husband and Sir Michael. They should be returning shortly. If you watch out of that window, you might see them coming in." Offering him refreshment or expecting him to sit and wait quietly seemed too foolish.

"I love her very much. I hope I'm not too late." The soft words drifted to her from where he had taken up his post by the window.

As soon as he caught sight of the three riders, he was gone.

"Oh, damn!" Gwenny swore because she felt she was entitled to the satisfaction of hearing the imprecation said aloud. She wished she could hide inside until the initial meeting was over, but she decided Christopher did not deserve to be the sole witness to the meeting of the triangle. She followed Hawk outside, her face serene in denial that she knew the entire household staff was avidly monitoring the afternoon's developments.

Lexy's riding habit was crisp black with a white stock. Her hat was tipped slightly to one side—no straight-on propriety for Lexy—and the sun caught the gold in her neatly dressed hair. She moved in easy rhythm with her mount, and she was laughing with Christopher at something Sir Michael had said.

The unrestrained joy of the sound rippled over Hawk's skin as if she were touching him, and he wondered how he had survived without it, without her, for so long. Everyone and everything else faded away.

Still looking at Michael, Lexy wasn't aware of anything amiss until his attention shifted from her and he said, "I wonder who that fellow is?"

Lexy followed his gaze and jerked so hard on the reins, her mount snorted and sidled in protest. As she moved to settle the horse, Hawk plunged forward to grab the bridle. He was gentle enough with the animal, stroking its nose and soothing it, but he wasn't going to let it make another misstep.

Lexy stared down at him, blinked, and saw that he was still there.

"Hawk." His name was scarcely more than a whisper because she couldn't seem to get any air into her lungs.

For a while she had been haunted by various images of how it would be when she saw Hawk again, whether it would be a scene of anger or regret or reunion. But then without word from him and with more and more time spent with Michael, she had ceased to speculate about it. She had thought her affair with Hawk was firmly in the past.

But even when she had considered it, she had never imagined this. She thought she had seen Hawk in every mood, but she had never seen him like this. His feelings were etched clearly on his face for all to see—hope, fear, and love blazing in the golden light of his eyes.

And then he said it aloud, stripping away all of his defenses, though they were not alone. "Lexy, I love you so. Am I too late?"

"Jared?" she asked because she had to know.

"Is with his mother and his father, as he ought to be," he told her without flinching, and then he added, "I should have come after you right away, but I let my pride and a lot of other useless things get in the way."

The three riders and the man on foot were frozen in a strange tableau until Christopher's horse whickered plaintively at being held in check when he was so close to the comfort of his stall.

The sound broke the spell, and Lexy turned to Winterbourne, tears shining in her eyes. "Michael, I am so sorry!"

At that moment, Michael Winterbourne would have liked to leap from his horse and pound the big, dark American into the ground. He would have liked to throw his head back and howl against the injustice of losing Lexy so soon after he had found her. But he was unable to shed the generations of good manners that had been bred into him.

"No apology is necessary," he said. "You were ever honest with me, and there are some things in our lives we cannot predict or control."

He dismounted and put out his hand. "I am Michael Winterbourne."

The world moved back into its normal motion because of his civil gesture. Hawk offered his name and shook hands with him. Grooms seemed to materialize from nowhere to take the horses. Christopher and Lexy dismounted, and Gweneth came forward from the point where she had frozen when Hawk confronted Lexy.

"I expect you have a great many things to discuss," Michael said. "Please join us for tea when it suits you." Deliberately he turned his back on the couple and walked away, Christopher and Gweneth trailing behind him.

Hawk looked at the grand house, at the manicured grounds and the fields of the home farm stretching away. What he was asking Lexy to give up was in sharp focus.

"I won't ever be able to offer you anything like this," he said, "nor will I ever be as gracious as that man, not when it comes to a rival for your heart. But I will love you as well as I can until the day I die. Is it enough?"

Lexy was still in shock from the mere fact of his presence, and while he seemed to be moving ahead at great speed, she struggled in his wake. But she did not doubt her love for him. She was coming alive, her senses stirring as if from a long sleep. She had convinced herself that everything was all right without him. She had nearly convinced herself that life with Michael would be perfectly accept-able and fulfilling. Now she saw the lie. Hawk was in her blood and her bones, in her heart and her soul and her mind; in every essential part of her, Hawk abided. But there also abided a last doubt.

"I want to believe what you say, but please, be very, very sure. I will not be a substitute for Caroline Fordyce and Jared. I am not even sure I want children and certainly not right away."

"Lexy, you saw Caroline; you know that she is a beautiful woman. And you met Jared. It would be a cold heart that did not recognize what an appealing child he is. And for me, there was more because I could see myself in him. But even so, even with all of that, even face to face with the two of them, you were more real than they. Looking at Caroline, I wanted you. Looking at Jared, I saw what you had tried to make me understand, that I am not connected to him as a man must be to be a true father to a child. Am I too late?" he asked again, and then he simply waited for her to make her judgment.

She saw the truth in him, and she saw her own. Despite his vitality, the record of their time apart was marked in the deeper hollows that made his cheekbones more prominent.

She pulled off her riding gloves and reached up and traced the lines of weariness etched in his skin. And then she touched his mouth, his beautiful, sensual mouth that somehow fit perfectly in his lean, fierce face. The heat of the memory of how his mouth could make her feel traveled into the center of her, to a place that Michael had never touched and never would.

"You aren't too late. I love you, Hawk Mackenna," she said, and his control broke. He kissed the fingers that had danced with butterfly delicacy over his skin. Then with a groan he wrapped her in his arms, and she could feel him trembling, betraying the fear he had carried that he had lost her.

"It's all right now, love, it's all right," she crooned.

Inside the minutes ticked by too slowly for the Bettingdons and Michael while they went through the ritual of having tea, all three of them resolutely staying away from the windows that would have given them a view of the couple outside.

But Gweneth felt the prickle of tears at the sorrow in Michael's face, and finally she could not bear the social pretense that nothing was wrong.

"I am so sorry," she said. "You are a chivalrous man to behave so generously."

Michael's eyes strayed toward the window. "Not so generous;

greedy, in fact." His gaze swung back to meet hers. "I saw how he looked at her; I saw how she looked at him. Because I have seen it, I would be greedy all my life to have her look at me like that. And she never would. Never."

Chapter 36

Lexy and Hawk were married in a little stone church near the Bettingdons' principal country estate. With Christopher and Gweneth in charge, there were no problems with obtaining a special license or with making the other arrangements. Though Hawk would have waited for a wedding at Wild Swan if Lexy really wanted it, she did not insist. She knew the world would swallow them once they returned home, and marrying in England allowed them to honeymoon on the voyage back to the United States. Being with Hawk was the important thing, not where they married.

Their courtship had been so unorthodox from the beginning, Lexy would not have protested being his mistress until they returned to Maryland, but Hawk seemed to need everything done properly now that they were to be married. She reminded herself that she had been the one who had initiated their lovemaking in the first place. She found it touching that he needed the structure more than she, but she understood. He had grown up with his family in such disarray, he needed careful signposts to reassure him that he was proceeding the right way.

The wedding was small, but Michael Winterbourne was there to toast the bride: "Alexandria Abigail Culhane Mackenna, may you be joyful all the days of your life."

She wished the same for him, but their time for speaking intimately was past, and though she had been honest with him, just as he had said, there were debts of the heart she would never be able to repay. He had courted her with honor and gentleness, and she had coaxed him out of the winter season in his heart. And now she was leaving him to be alone again. She hoped he would not be so for long, but there was nothing she could do to ease his pain.

Hawk's jealousy over Lexy's obvious tenderness for the man

was mitigated by the fact that she was Mrs. Mackenna, not Lady Winterbourne. It made a vast difference.

They had come to England separately on the Jennings-Falconer line, but they steamed home together in style, sharing a richly appointed cabin that they scarcely left during the voyage.

"Everyone on the ship knows what we're doing," Lexy said, nuzzling against his shoulder, inhaling the musky spice of his scent, and wondering if she would ever have enough of him. The more they made love, the more she wanted to lose the boundaries of her own body and become part of his.

"Do you mind?" he asked.

"Mind what?" She had forgotten what she had said.

Hawk's chest rumbled with laughter beneath her. "Mind that everyone knows what we're doing," he prompted, his fingers playing in her hair and tracing the shell of her ear.

"No, of course I don't mind," she declared, as if she had never mentioned it in the first place. "We're married, you know." She spoiled her own self-righteous tone by giggling, and then her laughter turned into a purr as Hawk reversed their positions and loomed over her, one hand sweeping down her body in a gesture as possessive as his voice murmuring, "Lexy Mackenna, I love you."

His fingers teased the hollows behind her knees, the curve of waist to hip, the fragile line of her neck, circling softly and slowly until she was lifting her hips off of the bed begging for an even more intimate touch. He complied, his fingers stroking between her legs and sinking inside her as his mouth nipped and suckled at her breasts until all the currents flowing through her met and crested in a huge wave.

She did not mind that he had such power over her; she could see her own over him. As he worked magic on her flesh, his own was consumed by the spell. His eyes glowed in a face starkly sculptured by passion, and he cried aloud when he thrust into her at last, her hands guiding him home.

They had been apart for long days, and they were newly married, so their physical hunger for each other was natural, but only in being together again did they discover how much they had missed each other's companionship.

For days the words tumbled out of both of them—details of the stories they had worked on while apart, discussions of the political situations in the United States and England, plans for future articles.

"I read every word you wrote from England," Hawk confessed. "You did fine work, but I worried about where you had gone to get a lot of the information. I know I have to be grateful that Winterbourne was there to . . . ah, guide you."

"Protect me, you mean," Lexy said. "Despite my misadventures at Bellwood, I am not a fool. I know there are places I can't go without help. But I hope you aren't going to prove a dictator about this. I'm a journalist, and that wasn't changed by my wedding ring."

She spoke evenly, but challenge made her eyes very green, and Hawk swallowed his objections. He would have liked to forbid her to ever put herself in danger again, but it would be a useless exercise, and beyond that, he had no right to demand it. Both of them had agreed to omit the phrase "to obey" in their marriage ceremony, and Lexy had never pretended that she would suddenly become meek and helpless because she had become a wife. Rationally, he knew he would not like it at all if she did, but he also knew that he would never be easy with her risk-taking.

"I don't want you to change," Hawk said, "but I can't promise not to worry. I only ask you to remember that when you put yourself at risk, you risk everything I hold most dear."

"Someday I am going to write about how dangerous it is to marry a man who can spin a silken web with words," she teased, but then she leaned against him in surrender. "I'll be careful, Hawk, I promise, as you must be. I don't want to lose you, either, not ever."

She understood as she never had before the sorrow that underlay the joy of loving like this. Nothing was forever, not even the stones of the earth, and how fragile and small was a human lifespan, even one that went to old age.

"Not ever," she repeated, her voice barely above a whisper for the lump in her throat.

Hawk understood because the fear of loss was even sharper for him. He had never, not even when he had thought himself passionately in love with Caroline, expected to have this kind of closeness with another human being. And having more meant having more to lose.

"We won't take any of our time together for granted!" he announced with sudden vehemence. "We can't make the allotted days more in number, so we'll just make each one mean more."

Both of them felt as if they had exchanged vows all over again and would for the rest of their lives, learning along the way how the vows had to change and grow to contain their loving.

Within a few days of docking in Baltimore, Lexy and Hawk were recalling their days aboard ship with longing.

Travis and Gincie had been informed of the wedding by cablegram and had sent their congratulations, and Gincie accepted the fact that she wasn't to have the fun and worry of planning for Lexy's wedding at Wild Swan, but she was sweetly insistent that there be a party for the couple.

"It's only fair," she pointed out to Lexy. "The family and many friends care about you. They couldn't share the joy of your wedding, but at least they can celebrate your homecoming and toast the future happiness of the Mackennas."

Though Hawk had even more reservations than Lexy about being the prime exhibit, the party turned out to be enjoyable for everyone, and the couple found an unexpected benefit in being able to answer the questions about their courtship and wedding in one session instead of having to repeat it over and over in the ensuing days. The staff of the *Witness* was there, as well as friends from Baltimore, Washington, and the surrounding countryside. The twins were at school, but Hawk confided to Lexy that that suited him just fine.

"I'd like them to have a little time to get used to the idea of my marrying their sister."

One of the first things Lexy had done on arriving home had been to hug her father. "Thank you, Papa, for sending him to me."

Travis was profoundly grateful that it had worked out so well for his daughter; he would have hated to have had a part in making her more unhappy than she had been when she left for England. But in fairness, he felt obliged to share the credit.

"I might have been able to delay him, if I'd had a mind to, but that's about all. He was on his way."

Though it was difficult for Travis to accept that his daughter was a married woman now, he believed she had found a man to match her in intelligence and heart, and there was nothing better he could wish for her.

The Culhanes' gift to the couple was a lot complete with a trim little house in the West End of the capital where more and more luxurious homes were being built. It was one of the properties Travis had invested in years before, and it had grown steadily in value since then.

At first Hawk didn't want to take the gift. "It is just too much," he insisted.

"Too much for our only daughter?" Travis asked mildly, and then Gincie offered, "If it will make you feel better, we can arrange to have it be solely her property."

Lexy opened her mouth to protest this idea but closed it again when she saw the relief in Hawk's face. "I would much prefer that," he said.

As long as she knew that whatever they owned was for both of them, it was enough, and having their own home would be a great improvement over paying rent on Hawk's quarters.

"Thank you, it's a wonderful gift!" she said.

As Lexy had been news while she was in England, so her marriage to Hawk was judged fair game by papers on both sides of the Atlantic. The match was touted as a wildly romantic blend of the old and the new, a reference to the fact that both husband and wife were journalists and that the wife had announced her intention of continuing to work.

"Isn't it odd that you are never asked if you intend to continue at your job?" Lexy remarked waspishly to Hawk, after answering yet another set of questions from a New York reporter. But then she was instantly contrite. "It isn't your fault, I know it isn't! Do you think you are going to be able to bear being married to an advocate of women's rights?"

"I think my wife's belief in justice, no matter what sex or skin color or belief is involved, is one of the things I love very much about her," Hawk told her, and her love for him shimmered through her as it did so constantly these days.

Too many of the papers identified Sir Michael Winterbourne as the rejected suitor, but there was nothing Lexy could do except to continue to name him a friend and to remind the reporters that Sir Michael had been at the wedding. Her life was with Hawk. Every day gave further proof of how much they belonged together.

Once they were back in Washington, their hours were consumed by catching up with work, planning new projects at the paper, and moving into their house; so many nights they tumbled into bed too tired to do anything except sleep. But that brought its own reassurance. They had each grown accustomed to the security of another warm body in the bed, though neither of them knew just how much until Hawk left for Illinois to cover the executions of the Haymarket conspirators who had been held in prison since the previous year.

"Why do you have to go?" Lexy asked, her concern for the pain that was already in his eyes winning over her professional instincts. "Those men are going to be hanged. That's the brutal truth; everyone knows it. Why do you have to be there?"

Hawk was tempted to tell her it was a stupid question and that she ought to know better, but under her harsh assessment he could hear her worry for him.

"The name of the paper is the *National Witness*," he reminded her patiently, "and Mr. Tratnor has meant it to be that since the beginning. I've followed this story from the start; it would be negligent and cowardly for me to avoid the end."

"I do understand," Lexy admitted. "It's just that it is such a grim business. I'm sorry you have to go." There was no use in offering to go with him; it was his story, and she had work of her own to do.

On November 2, Governor Richard J. Oglesby commuted the sentences of Fielden and Schwab to life imprisonment, but on November 11, the other conspirators—Parsons, Spies, Engel, and Fischer—were hanged. Hawk had seen his share of rough justice during his youth in the Far West, but nothing could lessen the impact of such ugly deaths. Anyone who thought hanging was a clean way to kill had never watched the process, the choking and jerking and the involuntary evacuation of the bowels and bladder.

One other man would have been hanged with them, but Louis Lingg had committed suicide in his cell, using a bomb.

The grim irony of that was difficult to write about. The easiest and most probable answer was that this was final proof of the truth of the bombing charge made at the time of the arrests. But Hawk knew he would always wonder if the man had ended his life that way as a gesture of defiance, taking credit for something he might not have done at all. He wondered where the prisoner had gotten the explosives. He wondered if perhaps someone else had killed the prisoner in this way to justify the arrests and the hangings. But he had to accept that he wasn't going to get the answers and that his job in this case was to report the executions and go home.

He didn't just want to go home; he wanted to *be* home. He had known he would miss Lexy, but he was stunned by the depth of his need. He had hated sleeping alone, had awakened all through the night each night, searching for her. And now the clicking of the train's wheels seemed intolerably slow, though he had once liked the sound. He was beginning to understand why poets claimed that love made a man insane.

In his absence, Lexy's thoughts were as parallel to his as the rails. Though she was busy during the day, she was ever conscious that Hawk was not in the city, not there to share a quick meal or to exchange ideas on this or that. And he was not in bed at night to make love or simply to share his warmth.

She had always, even when she was growing up amidst a loving family, had a part of her that was separate, alone, and pleased to be so. It was the part of her that had decided so early that she would be a journalist, the part that had directed all of the major decisions she had ever made. Indeed, it was this solitary, interior person who had finally known she would not be happy without Hawk. But still, despite accepting that, she had believed that that inner shadow would somehow remain intact, still guiding, still making decisions independently.

Now she was not so sure. She worked, ate, slept without Hawk, but everything was slightly out of focus, as if she had lost her center. The result was that she was at once exhilarated at finding someone who fit so closely with her own soul and terrified that there seemed to be no private places left within her. It was, she realized, what she had always feared about marriage, though she had not known its true dimensions until it happened.

There was some comfort in acknowledging that it was like being on a horse sailing over a jump: the course was set, and there were no more decisions to be made, not, at least, until the ground was reached once more. And at the bone, she admitted that nothing, not even losing part of herself, would be as terrible as losing Hawk.

When he walked into the newspaper office on his return from Illinois, Lexy forgot that there was anyone else in the place and flew into his arms with a glad cry. He hugged her so tightly, she was half lifted off of her feet.

"I missed you so much!" Their voices blended in the silence that had fallen around them. Only when Hawk had kissed Lexy thoroughly did either of them come to their senses enough to realize that they were providing a show for an admiring audience. Lexy blushed, but Hawk looked calmly around the room until everyone remembered something else to do besides gawk.

Reid congratulated Hawk on the solid work he'd done on a grim subject, and Hawk appreciated the praise, but beneath his joy at being home and in having done good work, Lexy could feel how weary he was.

When they were alone at last in their house, Hawk collapsed into a chair and closed his eyes, letting the solace of homecoming wash over him.

Lexy stood behind him and ran her fingers through his thick dark hair and then began to knead the tight sinews of his neck and shoulders. Hawk groaned in pleasure.

"It was very bad, wasn't it?" she said softly. "My poor darling. But Reid was right and so were you to go. No one could have done a better job of reporting the executions than you did."

She couldn't erase the horrific images from his memory, but her voice and her touch cut through the painful loneliness of spirit he had suffered in doing the story. He pulled her around and tumbled her into his lap and just held her wordlessly for long moments, absorbing the warmth and scent of her.

Finally she felt his hold loosen, his breathing deepen as he fell asleep. She had planned a different sort of activity for his first night home, but she found this infinitely satisfying. More than just weariness, it was an act of profound trust that he could so completely let go and sleep like a child because he felt safe with her.

She was learning that it was not so hard to allow someone into the most private recesses of her spirit when he, in turn, allowed her the same privilege.

In some ways, for Hawk the experience of being married was even more of a change than it was for Lexy, because in marrying her, he had also acquired a large family. He was learning that the joys and sorrows that affected one branch rippled through to everyone else. And though the family members made an effort to respect each other's privacy, privacy became in that manner a gift rather than a right. Lexy had made every effort to avoid placing any blame on Hawk when she had fled to England, but the family had known that he was the cause. The knowledge was not the question, only how it was used, or ignored.

Even his job had been changed by marriage. In spite of the fact that he continued to address Reid in formal terms as his employer, there was no avoiding the fact that he was now related to the man by marriage and would have to perform very badly indeed to put his job at risk. He was glad that he had established his journalistic reputation before coming to work for the *Witness* and had worked for the paper for some time before marrying Lexy; otherwise he might have had to spend far too much time and effort in proving himself to the other reporters at the paper. Now he understood better than he had before how hard Lexy had worked to establish herself as a writer on her own merit. He understood why she felt compelled to take chances.

But he was also learning the compensations for relinquishing privacy and for having to tread carefully. Within a week of each other, Dinah Falconer was born to Adam and Mercy, and Joy Falconer was born to Sally and Nigel. The arrival of both babies was greeted with general rejoicing, but there was an added poignancy in welcoming Joy to the family. She was a beautiful baby and a healthy one, and Adam and Mercy, no less than the rest, celebrated the special triumph of the birth because Sally and Nigel had suffered such sorrow in their previous attempts to have a child.

After watching Hawk with the babies, holding them with such tender reverence, his huge presence such a contrast to the tiny bundles, Lexy had no trouble imagining how he would be with his own.

"Do you mind that I don't want children right now?" she asked.

Hawk chose his words carefully. "I confess, I would like to hold our son or daughter someday, but no, it doesn't bother me that that time hasn't arrived yet. I'm still getting used to being married, as you are. And I still want all the time I can have with you, just you. Our lives are crowded enough at the moment without the complication of children."

Lexy wondered if the time would ever come when she wanted them. The image of a little boy or girl who was a blend of both of them was attractive in an abstract way, but the realities of having a helpless creature so entirely dependent on her as the new babies were on their mothers made her feel claustrophobic. She thought the new additions to the family were as pretty as any babies she had ever seen, but they did not fill her with longing to have one of her own. She did not, in fact, find babies very appealing generally and wondered at the looks of adoration she saw on other people's faces when they viewed an infant. She wondered if there was something essential missing in her nature, or whether it was a matter of that nurturing instinct being turned to her writing. For that, she did feel protectiveness, even tenderness—a direct connection that ran from her brain to her heart when the words were just right.

She hoped if she and Hawk ever did have a child, she would discover that her feelings about her own would be different from the detachment she felt from other people's infants. And she was somewhat reassured that she found older children fascinating. She loved the way their minds worked, fixing now on one thing, wanting to know everything about it, then skipping on to something else with lightning speed and endless curiosity. But she saw the danger there, too. How would it be possible to be responsible and giving enough with such a being and still have the time, dedication, and energy for her work?

She understood why so many of the women who campaigned for women's rights found the issue of children so complex. For many, the answer was to have no children; for some, it meant having children and forsaking all else for years on end in order to devote themselves to those children; and for others, it became a matter of a delicate balance between the demands of a career and the demands of a family.

Lexy had no illusions about how difficult that balance would be to achieve, nor did the paradox escape her. She could not imagine that Hawk would think it reasonable to have to forgo a story because of some problem with the children. Would he have missed finishing his coverage of the Haymarket riot because of colic at home? She doubted it. Yet a woman who made the same decision would be judged unnatural.

Her anger at the injustice of it was tempered by the fact that Hawk, far from pressuring her to have a child, was scrupulously careful to do his part to prevent her becoming pregnant. He was the kind of husband Anthea wished many of her patients had. And he never mentioned Jared, never tried to use the child as a weapon to urge her into pregnancy.

She was sure he often thought of his son, but she was equally sure that he did not seek him out. The Fordyces were still in the city, but for Hawk, it was as if they had vanished. They were not part of his life anymore. For that alone, Lexy would have thought her husband one of the strongest men she had ever known.

There seemed to be no final conclusions to be drawn from many of her internal debates. She was learning that perhaps that was the whole point, that there were no final conclusions as long as a marriage existed.

Hawk was learning and adjusting, too. She noticed it most of all when the family gathered. He clearly wanted to be part of it all, but it was so new for him to be connected to so many people, she could often sense his withdrawal, as if he continued to question his right to be there. During Christmas at Wild Swan, she made sure she was beside him most of the time.

"Afraid your brothers are going to throw me out?" Hawk teased.

"I have been hovering, haven't I? Would you prefer I didn't?" she asked.

His answer was heartfelt. "No, I wouldn't! I need all the support I can get." He drew her close for a quick hug, and Lexy caught sight of Kace grinning at them from across the room.

"Kace and Tay approve; they told me so," she said. She batted her eyelashes at him in her best imitation of a demure maiden. "They just wanted you to make an honest woman of me."

"Honest—you have never been less than that, my love," Hawk said, suddenly serious. And he was as grateful as she that the twins had accepted him so readily as a brother-in-law. Though the siblings' lives had gone in different directions these past few years, they were still very close, and he knew how unhappy Lexy would have been if the twins had condemned her choice of a husband. But her happiness was the whole point among the three men, and since she was so obviously joyful in her marriage, the twins took that as proof enough of her wise choice.

For Lexy, the one sour note in the celebration was having Jilly and her husband there. Within moments of their arrival, she wished fervently that they had stayed in New York. She thought that she and her cousin had made peace, but it seemed that her marriage to Hawk had changed all of that.

"My, my! Trust you to make news with your marriage. I thought you only reported the news," Jilly said when she first greeted Lexy. Her voice sounded playful enough, and she was smiling, but Lexy saw the old look in her eyes, the kind of baffled rage a child experiences when she sees that another child has something she wants and doesn't understand how such a thing could have happened.

"I assume the social news was very sparse when the papers wrote about me," Lexy replied with a smile as insincere as Jilly's.

Being around Jilly made her feel off balance. It seemed no one else noticed the friction between her cousin and herself. Jilly was elegantly dressed and bejeweled, the wealth conferred on her by marriage to Dermot Hargrave III clearly visible, but her laughter was just a shade too shrill, her movements agitated, like a windup mechanical toy.

Lexy was prepared to dislike Jilly's husband, suspecting that perhaps he wasn't as civilized as he had seemed at the wedding, but observing him, she came to realize that he, at least, shared her worry about Jilly's behavior. He watched his wife anxiously, his eyes both puzzled and hurt, but he was too reserved by nature to be overt in his affections. Lexy could not imagine Jilly and Dermot ever being as intimate mentally or physically as she and Hawk were. And that strengthened her. She did her best to avoid her cousin, and she resolved not to let the digs go too deep. But her patience fled when Jilly turned her venom on Hawk.

"Your husband is so . . . so large and so Western," Jilly purred as she sidled up to Lexy, her eyes on her own husband and Hawk where they stood talking a short distance away.

Lexy wished she had kept to her program of staying at Hawk's side, but she steeled herself to patience. "Yes, he is. I noticed both of those aspects the day I met him. Aren't I fortunate?"

Jilly failed to heed the note of warning in Lexy's voice. "After all, you had the chance to become a member of the British nobility, and by all accounts, Sir Michael Winterbourne is a very special man. Certainly you must wonder if you made the right decision."

Lexy stared at Jilly until the younger woman's eyes slid away from hers. "Your parents are such wise people, I wonder where they got such a fool for a daughter. I've put up with your nastiness for years, but I will not put up with a single word against Hawk, not a single word. He is large, Western, intelligent, kind, humorous, romantic, and a host of other marvelous things. And I love him with all my heart. I can't help it if you don't feel the same about your husband. You know, the mistake you always make is in believing that if other people are happy, they have somehow stolen that happiness from you."

"I do love Dermot!" Jilly protested, tears filling her eyes at Lexy's unexpected ferocity. "Oh, Lexy, I'm sorry. I don't know why I am so disagreeable. Well, yes, I do. I am jealous of you. I can't help it; you have everything!"

Lexy regarded her with a mixture of pity and exasperation. "You chose to marry Mr. Hargrave. You are dripping with diamonds and have, by all accounts, a notable house in New York and a fine country home. You seem to have everything you ever wanted. Surely your discontent is misplaced. I think you ought to look for the seeds of it in yourself, not in others." Her voice was quite gentle, for the habit of placating Jilly was an old one, but the censure was plain, and Jilly suddenly looked so young and sad that Lexy relented. Searching for a safer meeting ground she asked, "How is your singing these days? Do you have enough time for practice?"

It was not such a safe topic, after all. Jilly's face went very still, and the youth was gone. "My days are very full. Being Dermot's wife means meeting many social obligations. There isn't much time for silly hobbies, though sometimes a friend will ask me to sing at a party, when there is a lack of other entertainment."

Words about squandering such a precious talent welled up in Lexy, but she restrained herself and said none of them aloud. She and Jilly were on shaky ground already.

This time it was Hawk who came to her side, lending his support to her as she had been doing for him. He was friendly to Jilly, but she drifted away as soon as she could.

Hawk watched her go, a frown creasing his brow. "For someone who seems to have everything, she doesn't appear to be very happy. She's been behaving like a crazed butterfly ever since she got here. Her husband's worried about her. He didn't say so, but the whole time I was talking to him, he was watching her as if he were afraid she was going to explode. He invited us to visit them in the new year. I think he really wants us to come; you understand, relatives but not as close as Jilly's parents or her brothers. I think he wants someone to see Jilly as she is in her daily life, maybe to see what's wrong. He truly seems to want her to be content, though he isn't a very demonstrative man. I told him we would do our best to go to New York."

"You told him that without consulting me?" Lexy hissed.

"Yes, I did," Hawk said, staring at her as if she had just changed shape before his eyes. "Don't tell me that Jilly still has the power to upset you with her petty sniping? I would have thought she'd have grown out of doing that, and anyway, it certainly can't matter anymore."

Lexy was so angry, it was all she could do to keep her voice low enough so that everyone wouldn't be party to their quarrel. "Of course, it can't matter anymore. After all, Jilly has Dermot, and I have you, and now that we're both married women, everything that ever was in our lives before must be entirely changed. And since you are my husband, it's perfectly fitting that you commit both of us to whatever obligations you deem worthy. And it shouldn't matter to you one bit that I've just spent a miserable time with Jilly and can't wait until she goes north again!"

"You are behaving like a spoiled child," Hawk observed coldly.

"You pompous ass," Lexy said, smiling sweetly for the benefit of any onlookers, though her eyes were slitted with anger. "Jilly thinks you're 'large and Western' and little else; petty sniping, indeed!"

The air between them crackled, and it was agonizing to maintain the pretense that all was well. Lexy caught her mother looking at them curiously and wondered how successful the pose was, but at least Gincie didn't ask any questions.

It seemed the evening with the family would never end, but it was worse when they were alone. They undressed in silence and staked out separate territories in the bed, each clinging to a side in order not to touch the other.

Though it was one of the mildest winters in years, neither of them could remember feeling quite this cold in bed before.

Lexy tried to hold on to her anger—after all, she had been defending Hawk to Jilly—but it seeped away, leaving her with a picture of how it had seemed to Hawk while he spoke with Dermot: a friendly invitation with a plea behind it and Hawk believing so much in his wife's strength that he couldn't imagine that she could still be vulnerable to her cousin's attacks.

Hawk fared no better. He hated the distance between them in the bed, and he hated the distance between their spirits even more. If anything were needed to underscore how far he'd come from his days of self-sufficiency, this was it. And in the awful quiet, he heard Lexy repeating Jilly's words and finally understood what she had been telling him.

"What did you say when Jilly called me 'large and Western'?" he asked.

"I said you were, and that you were also 'intelligent, kind, humorous, and romantic.' " The words whispered back to him in the darkness. "And I told her that I love you, very much. I do, you know."

"Oh, Lexy, I love you, too! I'm sorry I didn't understand about Jilly. I'm still getting used to being part of the family, and I don't always understand all the complexities of it." He reached for her and was infinitely relieved that she came into his arms without resistance, shaping her body to his. She was shivering, and when he touched her face he felt tears.

"God, don't cry! I can't bear it!" He stroked her hair and held her close.

"It's why I don't handle Jilly very well. I don't like to fight with people I love, and I do love her even though she makes me angry more often than not," Lexy sniffed. "But fighting with you is much, much worse."

He understood what she meant. He had seen her fight for an idea, for justice; for those things, she would do never-ending battle using all the weapons she could muster. But bickering with those close to her heart was not in her nature.

"I don't want to fight with you, either," he said. "But perhaps you have something to learn about families, too. You shouldn't be afraid of being angry, at least not with me. I won't like it, and I'll probably be angry in return, but I won't stop loving you."

She thought about that for a moment, and then she sighed. "That's all very well, but I think I'm too old to learn how to be comfortable in combat."

Hawk had to laugh. "I've just realized how peculiar this conversation is. Most men would give a great deal to be married to women who preferred peace in the home, and yet, here I am urging you to do battle." He was rewarded by her giggle, muffled against his neck.

Then he sobered. "But we're not like most other married couples, and I don't expect or want us to be. However, we're bound to have problems finding enough time to be together when we're working on stories that take us out of the city. We haven't talked about it, but I presume you'll be attending the major race meetings once the season starts, and I'm sure I'll also be traveling. I confess, when Dermot invited us to New York, I wasn't thinking as much about you having to be with Jilly as I was about the two of us going away together for a little while before the racing season starts in earnest."

Lexy thought about all the days they would be apart. It was a subject she had been avoiding since she had discovered how much she missed Hawk when he had gone to Illinois, but now she faced the fact that if she wanted to maintain her reputation with the sporting journals, she had no choice but to follow the horses. And as much as she liked doing the Abby Adams pieces, her major work was still in the racing world, and she didn't want to lose the gains she had made there.

The New York trip took on an entirely different aspect. They would be doing something for Dermot, and indirectly for Reid and Larissa, but they would also be stealing time for themselves. As for what Jilly would think of the visit, Lexy no longer cared.

Chapter 37

Whatever Jilly had thought initially about having the Mackennas visit, she welcomed them quite cordially when they arrived in early March.

Lexy quickly understood why; this was Jilly's territory, where she was recognized as one of the social elite. Here she could display all she had gained through marriage to Dermot.

Even Hawk, who was inclined to be more indulgent in his view of Jilly than Lexy was, had to share her cynicism.

The Hargrave residence in the city was on Fifth Avenue, the neighborhood favored by the Astors, Vanderbilts, and other wealthy families, and everything in the Hargrave house proclaimed the ability to buy anything that was desired. And what seemed to be desired was all of European origin: paintings in ornate frames, furniture sporting every kind of decoration but offering little comfort, vases and statuary depicting ancient myths, heavy yards of brocade, velvet and silks covering the furniture and draping the windows, Italian marble framing the fireplaces and paving many floors—the inventory went on and on.

The house was decorated with an abhorrence for any serene, empty space, and within a short time, Lexy longed for the spacious, uncluttered rooms of Wild Swan and for her own sparsely furnished house.

"My God, a guest could suffocate in this place, and no one would find him until the smell got too bad," Hawk whispered, and Lexy smothered a nervous giggle. The house made her feel as if she were tiptoeing through a museum. Even the servants seemed like strange furnishings as they crept about, intent on doing their duties with as little human disturbance as possible.

"Dermot allowed me to redecorate most of the house," Jilly gushed and then paused.

Lexy thought, "I could have guessed that," but she said, "What an enormous task, and you've done so well!"

Hawk gave her hand a squeeze of approval, but Jilly looked at her closely, as if she suspected the praise was false. Or perhaps some last vestige of her parents' good taste remained in her. If it did, she must surely have flashes of knowing how horrible this house was.

Before they had come north, Lexy had spoken with Larissa, but only now did she understand what Jilly's mother had meant when she said, "You'll find they live in opulence, and of course, that is their choice, but. . . ." Larissa had frowned, searching for the right words, not wanting to be disloyal to her daughter. "Well, I am probably old-fashioned, but I would not like to live in quite so much clutter. Expensive clutter, mind you, but clutter nonetheless. Jilly has everything and more than anyone could want, but I do wonder if she's really happy. When her father and I visit, we are always kept so busy that we don't seem to be able to find time to talk."

It had been clear that Larissa hoped Lexy would have a chance to have intimate chats with Jilly, and Lexy hadn't had the heart to point out that despite the fact that she and her cousin were fairly close in years, they were distant in everything else.

And now, even with so brief a glimpse of how Jilly lived, Lexy could not imagine that achieving intimacy of any kind was easy in this house. No wonder Reid and Larissa visited so seldom.

Lexy shuddered at the thought of how it would be when the Hargraves had children. She did not envy any child who would have to grow up in this stifling atmosphere. She was sure Jilly viewed producing an heir for the Hargrave name as part of her social duty. She hoped that Jilly would have grown up considerably by the time she had children. To her, it seemed that Jilly had stopped maturing some years back, so that she was more willful child than woman, always swaying to the whims of what others wanted of her, yet not ever quite measuring up because she had no idea of what she wanted of herself.

Though she felt like a coward, within a few days, Lexy was determined to spend as little time as possible in Jilly's world, which consisted of nothing more than shopping expeditions and gossip over tea, worse than the rounds in England.

Like her mother and the other women of the family, Lexy viewed shopping as a chore to be undertaken and accomplished as swiftly as possible when something specific was needed. To spend hours doing nothing more than looking at gloves, hats, gowns, and such to see if something caught one's fancy was, to her, not only a frightful waste of time, but also boring.

The gossip sessions were worse. The women were strangers to Lexy, and she felt as if she were being displayed not only as Jilly's cousin, but also as an example of that odd breed—women who had careers. And further, having lately brushed against the English aristocracy and having been mentioned in the society news of major newspapers gave her enough notoriety to make her welcome in various parlors and drawing rooms. But if the women there looked at her as an oddity, she found them no less alien. They reminded her of bright-plumaged, chattering birds.

Conversation was not easy.

"Servants are such a trial these days, don't you find it so?" one woman asked.

"No, not really," Lexy answered. "But then, my husband and I lead a fairly simple life."

"Of course," the woman continued, "you're down there where there're so many Negroes."

"Did you meet the queen?" another woman asked.

"No, I didn't think we'd have anything to say to each other," Lexy replied, adding inwardly, "any more than I have anything to say to you."

The woman looked at her suspiciously, as if she sensed there was a joke that she didn't understand.

Their bigotry, social pretensions, and general empty-headedness made Lexy want to turn into Abby Adams before their eyes and tell them exactly what she thought of them, but she restrained herself out of consideration for Jilly.

Hawk rescued her. He took the blame on himself and was gently insistent that they really did have some business to conduct while they were in the city.

"Both of us are published in papers other than the *Witness*," he reminded Jilly, "and it's helpful to meet the editors face to face to discuss future work."

"If the truth were known, I expect Jilly will be happily rid of me," Lexy told Hawk. "I've done my best, but I don't think it was good enough. Jilly has surely known that I haven't enjoyed these little excursions."

Being with Hawk was entirely different. With him she could slip back into her role of journalist.

Hawk had a wide variety of friends among the New York press, so that Lexy met editors and reporters from the *Tribune*, the *Herald*, the *Morning Telegraph*, the *News*, and Mr. Pulitzer's *World*.

At the *World*, Lexy was introduced to Elizabeth Cochrane. Two years younger than Lexy, Miss Cochrane was also inches shorter, dainty, with reddish-brown hair and hazel eyes set in an oval face. But her eyes were shrewdly intelligent, and there was nothing dainty about what she wrote as Nelly Bly. Her pieces were about the same things that concerned Abby Adams—the injustices suffered by the poor and the helpless. But the editors knew Lexy as a horse racing expert, and many would have had a difficult time reconciling that with the reforming Abby Adams, and so, Lexy did not tell Miss Cochrane. Therefore, while the woman was polite, she obviously did not think she and Lexy had much in common, though she questioned Hawk closely about several subjects.

But it was Lexy's turn to have center stage when they visited with turfmen. Hawk was interested and proud as he listened to her answer questions and discuss the upcoming season, not only with some of the most notable writers in the field, but also with the old guard of racing enthusiasts, the ones who had, like Alexandria Carrington Falconer, always regarded racing as an art as much as a sport. Though she was a generation or more younger than most of them, she lamented with them the increasing dominance of men who seemed to feel no basic love for the animals themselves but only for the profits they could generate.

Lexy continued to believe that the better aspects and participants in the sport would prevail, but she had to agree with some of the doomsayers that the new developments were opening the way to increasing abuses: horses that were run too often and run with injuries, jockeys who did not care as much about a clean ride as they did about winning, and bets that were climbing so high, fouling another horse was growing more profitable.

The saddest aspect of the changes was that the elders of racing were reaching the age where illness and death were thinning their ranks. William R. Travers had died just the year before, and he was still mourned. Lexy had written a memorial piece about him, and his friends appreciated the fact that her emphasis had been on his quick wit and verbal acuity, despite the fact that he had stuttered.

The same men who mourned him also continued to mourn Alexandria Carrington Falconer. Lexy had proved her writing ability to them, and she did not mind that it only helped her cause to have had such an illustrious great-grandmother. Alex had been a legend while she lived; since her death, her fame had acquired mythic qualities; she had become in memory more daring, more beautiful, more compelling than any human being could possibly be.

Lexy understood the logic of the myth. Alex had competed with and often bested these men in the sport of kings. And while they truly admired her, it was also salve to bruised pride to make her larger than life in order to explain her success. Talking about her in this light, Lexy could see her clearly again, and much of what she saw was not the legend, but the loving woman who had welcomed the Culhanes to Wild Swan when they had fled from California.

They discussed the increasing need for a national governing body for the sport and how it should be empowered to declare tracks, riders, and stables outlawed if they did not conform to the rules.

But most of all, they discussed the coming season and the Futurity to be run at Sheepshead Bay. They all knew that Wild Swan had an entry, and they wanted to know just how good Pharaoh was.

Lexy smiled when she thought of the two-year-old black by Moonraker. Powerfully built for his youth, and fast, very, very fast, he was a horse who loved to run. She smiled, but her only comment was, "He is the best Wild Swan could produce for the race. Gentlemen, you will have to decide what that means matched against the fact that other fine stables are as determined as my family is to win that race."

She was glad she had never considered keeping the identity of Lexy a secret by choosing another name as she had with Abby Adams, because she enjoyed every minute with the turfmen and the writers of the sporting press.

But she and Hawk did not confine themselves to business. They went riding in Central Park; they went to exhibits and museums; they dined in fine restaurants; and they made love despite the forbidding decor of their ornate bedroom.

However, they were, after all, guests of the Hargraves and could not, without rudeness, avoid every social engagement Jilly and her husband invited them to attend.

Even without additional guests, dinners at the Hargrave house were so formal, the Mackennas dreaded, but could think of no graceful way out of, an invitation to another Fifth Avenue residence. They knew they were supposed to feel honored to have been asked, but all they wanted was for the evening to be over.

They wanted that even more once it had begun. The house they were visiting was so elaborately decorated, it made Jilly's efforts look quite restrained. The Talfords had made money in railroads and had connections with the Vanderbilts and other robber barons and their families. The guest list that night could have been used for a who's who of New York's upper crust. Servants in livery anticipated every want, the rooms overflowed with hothouse blooms, and the women overflowed with jewels. Most of the people here cared far more for Lexy's family connections than for anything she had accomplished on her own, though she was relieved to see a few familiar faces, members of the racing fraternity. But in this setting, the easy give-and-take of racing information would have been deemed improper, at least until the ladies withdrew to allow the gentlemen their port and cigars, a convention Lexy detested.

It amazed her that any private citizen could own enough matching silver and fine china to accommodate so many guests, but the Talfords did, and their French chef had overseen the preparation of an extravagant feast. Lexy lost track of the number of dishes offered: fish, fowl, and meat in many varieties, accompanied by all manner of sauces, breads, side dishes, and condiments. And following the main part of the meal, there were desserts of every description, from ices to puddings to tarts and cakes.

If the opulence of the food made Lexy feel slightly queasy, the gifts offered to the female guests shocked her so that when she realized what they were she nearly exclaimed aloud.

Each woman had been provided with a little silver bucket and a tiny shovel, the sets specially ordered from Tiffany's. Down the center of the tables ran artfully carved wooden troughs filled with sand. And hidden in the sand were sapphires, rubies, emeralds, diamonds, and pearls. The ladies were invited to dig for a trinket or two, and with expressions of appreciation for the clever idea, they did so, except for Lexy, who felt as if she were paralyzed.

The paradoxes of this social class had never hit her as hard as they did now. These men were the ones who kept the country moving and growing, who built railroads and shipping lines, who made steel and pumped petroleum from the ground. They provided countless jobs, and increasingly, out of civic duty, they gave to cultural institutions and to charities desperately in need of their support. But they were also the men who gave little thought to the welfare of their workers, who fought viciously against any labor organization that asked for safer working conditions, more humane hours, or better pay. They savaged their own kind as well, claiming the natural "survival of the fittest" when they forced men with smaller holdings out of business. They were the men who could provide these jewels in the sand for women who didn't need them while people starved and lived in the most wretched poverty not far away.

Jilly was staring at Lexy, knowing how she would feel about this ostentatious display, daring her to make a scene. Across the table, Hawk was gazing at her too, but in empathy, as appalled as she, and then he said, "I hope you find a beautiful stone, perhaps a diamond. And then you can show it to Philly."

She understood. As clearly as he could, he was telling her that there was nothing to be done, except that she could at least give the jewel to Philly for the school.

She made herself smile, and she dug deliberately until she found a diamond and put it in the little silver bucket. The bucket she would keep forever, to hold her pens, to remind her of the waste that more than matched the want in the world.

The next morning was Sunday, and on Monday, they would be

returning to Washington. They had been in New York for ten days, but it seemed twice as long.

"I am so homesick for our house and for the paper, I can hardly bear it," Lexy confided to Hawk, who was in perfect accord.

They had been favored with glorious early spring weather during their stay. Crocuses had appeared, backyard gardens were tinted with green, trees were budding in Central Park, and when the Mackennas had ridden there, they had seen robins. The winter had been so mild and the spring weather so early, out in the countryside, farmers had been planting for some time.

But Sunday reflected their mood. It was damp, drizzly, and cold. It obviously suited Jilly's mood as well. She couldn't wait to pounce on Lexy.

"Are you going to write about last night?" she demanded. "Are you going to tattle on the nasty rich people?"

Lexy was so weary of Jilly's attitude, it was an effort to summon the energy to answer. Hawk saved her the trouble.

"You should know your cousin well enough to know she would not betray you in that way. But I suspect you ask only because you yourself feel some unease about such excesses. Perhaps you should question yourself instead of Lexy."

He did not raise his voice, but Jilly's shock was plain. Intent on Lexy, she had not noticed that Hawk was in the room, and she was chagrined that he should call her to account. She opened her mouth to reply and then closed it again. Her eyes filled with tears, and she whirled from the room.

Lexy expected Hawk to go after her, but instead he said, "It is past time for that girl to grow into a woman. I do not envy Dermot. Lord! I hope your uncle doesn't question me too closely about this visit. I don't relish telling him that his daughter is a spoiled brat who lives like Marie Antoinette."

"Surely he and Larissa already know," Lexy said sadly. "After all, they've visited here, too."

Though Dermot continued to treat them cordially, the atmosphere in the house was strained as Jilly stayed in her rooms, pouting.

The Mackennas used part of the time to pack in preparation for leaving the next day, but as the afternoon wore on, Lexy noticed that Hawk was spending an inordinate amount of time peering out of the window. She had been ignoring the weather, but Hawk's preoccupation with it made her notice that it was raining very hard. Still, she didn't see any cause for alarm. But when he went to the window yet again, she asked, "What are you finding so fascinating in a wall of rain?"

"Not just rain, sleet and wind, too. We may not be leaving

tomorrow." He spoke with his back to her as he continued to look out. She went to his side and still saw nothing more than a blustery rainstorm.

"I can't explain it," he admitted, "but this storm feels like something very big. I don't know how the weather stations missed it, but they did." He moved his head to ease the tension in his neck. "It feels like storms I've experienced in the West—sudden, powerful, and capable of doing a lot of damage. If it is like that, it's going to be worse that there was no warning."

"I hope you're wrong," Lexy said. "Being trapped here by the weather for the next few days is a nightmarish thought."

By morning the world was white with wind-blown snow. Hawk was incredulous when Dermot announced his intention to visit his office despite the weather.

"Can't you forgo it for a day or so? It's going to be very dangerous out there. It's not just snow; it's also ice and wind," Hawk pointed out.

But Dermot was a New Yorker, born and bred, and he was not about to allow "a little weather" to interfere with his daily routine.

Hawk did not let Dermot's sangfroid alter his own plans. "We are not even going to try to leave today," he told Lexy, and she made no attempt to change his mind because she was beginning to share his apprehension. Though Jilly surely wished they would leave as much as they wished they could, she managed a halfhearted acquiescence. "Of course, you must stay until it clears." But her expression said that if her husband could go to his office, then the Mackennas should be able to travel.

They dressed as warmly as they could, Hawk having the temerity to ask for and receive some heavy outerwear from the Hargraves' closets. They both wanted to see what it was really like outside, and Hawk did not try to dissuade Lexy from going. He could feel the change in her as much as in himself. Whatever alteration the storm had made in their personal plans, they were slipping into their roles as journalists. If this storm really were as big as Hawk judged, then there was a story to cover.

Within a few blocks, there was ample proof that the storm was even worse than Hawk had imagined. The wind was sweeping south sidewalks clear and piling ever-increasing drifts on the north side of the streets. Trees were being uprooted; telephone, telegraph, and what electric lines there were were down, felled by the weight of the icy snow. Gas lines also ran above the ground and were in jeopardy. The cold was lung-searing; it could not have been much above zero. The elevated trains, horsecars, omnibus stages, coaches, cabs, and carriages—every form of transport was grinding to a halt.

Hawk and Lexy watched in horror as a huge van overturned, the horses slipping on the ice and going down in a tangle of legs and harness.

Moving on the snowy, icy pavements with the demon wind countering every movement was agonizingly slow, but they went to the rescue of the horses, Hawk lending a hand to help the driver untangle the traces as Lexy did her best to grasp headstalls where she could, all the while talking as soothingly as possible under the howl of the storm.

It was horrible, because one of the team had broken both forelegs. He kept trying to get up, his eyes wild with terror because his legs would no longer obey him.

The driver had no gun, but he produced a heavy hammer, and Hawk held the injured animal's head steady as the man slammed the hammer into the beast's temple. It took more than one blow. Lexy didn't know she was crying until she discovered the tears freezing on her face.

Hawk dragged her away from the horses and the overturned van. "It's enough! We're going back to the house."

She leaned into his support gratefully. She could not remember being afraid of anything in nature before, but she was terrified now. The storm seemed like a living creature, huge and powerful, with a voice, sometimes low and rumbling, sometimes a high-pitched wail, but constant.

Buildings were adding to the hazards, with toppling chimneys, falling cornices, and glass from broken windows. Lexy and Hawk stopped their slow progress once to pull a man out of a snowbank and again to offer what aid they could to another who had been cut on the cheek by a piece of falling masonry. He was dazed by the cold and the injury, and Lexy thought they were going to have to haul him with them, but Hawk found a policeman who promised he would get the man to medical aid.

The officer shook his head and frowned at the Mackennas and the injured man. "I don't know where common sense has gone today! Nobody should be out in this, but too many people are tryin' to go to work, just like nothin's happenin'." He had to lean very close for them to hear him.

The Mackennas had seen proof of his statement all along the way, and they were both thinking of Dermot while they forged their way back to the Hargrave house.

As soon as they were inside, Hawk said, "I'm going out again to see if I can find Dermot. I went with him to his office, and I'm sure he takes the same route every day. But I'm also sure he couldn't have gotten all the way today; he must be trying to get home."

"Then I'll go with you," Lexy said, squaring her shoulders.

"No, you won't," he countered. "If you go with me, I'll have to worry about you as well as Dermot."

The logic was inescapable. She was no match for the strength of the storm; Hawk had hardly been able to maintain his footing. But she felt like a coward because the last thing on earth she wanted to do was to go outside again.

Hawk whispered so none of the hovering servants could hear, "As bad as it is outside, I'd rather brave the elements than Jilly."

Lexy managed a weak smile, but then she warned, "I'll give you two hours. If you're not back by then, I don't care what's happening outside, I'll come after you. I don't want to lose you!"

He kissed the tip of her cold nose and then her mouth. "I'll be back in time," he promised. And then he was gone.

The door had scarcely closed behind him when Jilly appeared, and Lexy thought that if Jilly wanted a fight now, she would have one. But instead, her cousin approached her timidly.

"It's very bad out, isn't it?"

"Yes, it is," Lexy agreed.

"Where is Hawk?" Jilly asked, looking around vaguely as if she expected him to appear out of the walls.

"He's gone out to find Dermot. He doesn't think your husband could have made it to his office. All transport is stopped. Hawk thinks Dermot must be trying to come back here by now."

Jilly stared at her for a long moment, and then her face twisted and tears ran down her cheeks. "Ever since Dermot left this morning, I've been trying to tell myself this is no more than a late winter storm that won't amount to much. Not much," her laugh was jagged, "only enough so that when I look out the window I can see it piling in small mountains against some of the houses. Dermot could be buried in one of those mountains, and no one would find him until the snow is cleared away. And now Hawk has gone out after him. I should have persuaded Dermot not to go; I could have done it!"

Her mood veered to defiance and then shifted again. "Maybe I could have, maybe not. Dermot is set in his ways, and he doesn't think I have much sense. We're not like you and Hawk, not at all. You discuss things. He treats you like an adult."

"Yes, he does, but he also does what he thinks best. He wouldn't let me go out with him again," Lexy offered, trying to stave off the hysteria building in Jilly, causing her emotions to veer this way and that so that Lexy had trouble anticipating where they would go next. She kept expecting Jilly to pounce on her with the usual frustrated anger, and with Hawk risking his life to find Dermot, Lexy had no intention of putting up with that.

But instead, Jilly suddenly crumpled and spoke more rationally than she had in a long while. "I don't know what I'll do if something has happened to Dermot. I do love him, but I've gotten myself into an awful mess since I married him. I wasn't much use before, but since I've become his wife, I haven't had to be competent in anything that matters. Oh, I've chosen furniture and what not," her hand gestured vaguely, as if to encompass all the gaudy rooms, "but it wasn't really a choice, it was an imitation of other houses around here."

She looked squarely at Lexy. "I'm not so devoid of taste as it seems. I know how ugly all of this is compared to the simplicity of Wild Swan and of the house I grew up in. I just didn't have the courage to be different here. It's the same with my music. It is socially acceptable to dabble in the arts, but wholly unacceptable to be dedicated or professional about it. So I hardly ever sing anymore. I hate the silly shopping and tea parties, and I'm as appalled as you are by such displays as the Talfords' party. But I'm not like you; I don't know how to change it, how to change myself!"

There was so much despair and panic in her voice, Lexy could not help feeling sorry for her, but neither could she see an easy way out of the web of Jilly's life.

Finally she said, "I suppose you must weigh how much you want to change against how much society's adverse judgment might mean to you and to your husband. And perhaps you ought to find a way to use your music more." She brightened as a new thought occurred to her. "What about giving charity performances? Even if people wanted to object, they couldn't very well, could they? It would make them seem meanspirited. At first, I expect, the tickets would have to be sold to your own circle, but Jilly, you really are very, very good, and that ought to be enough to expand your audience after a time."

Jilly didn't say anything for a long interval as she considered Lexy's proposal, and then her eyes began to shine. "It will work! I know it will! And Dermot has never cared half as much as I have about what people think. He truly is dear. He's always said that what makes me happy makes him happy. Poor man. He's given me everything, and I've still managed to be miserable. A change will be to his good as well as mine." Her smile faded, and she whispered, "None of this will matter, nothing will matter if Dermot is lost in the storm . . . or Hawk."

"I gave Hawk two hours. After that I'll go looking for him," Lexy said.

"And I'll go with you," Jilly said.

The two women were at that moment closer to each other than they had ever been.

At first Hawk was confident that he would find Dermot very soon. He reasoned that the man must have been fighting his way home for some time by now. But as the minutes ticked past, his self-appointed task grew more difficult. All considerations of proper attire had been sacrificed to the cold, so that people were bundled to the ears in odd assortments of garments, including blankets and buffalo-skin robes. Hawk thought that Dermot had set out in his usual conservative suit with the addition of a stout topcoat, but he wasn't sure that was all he would be wearing now, and certainly his scarf would be wound around his face against the cut of the flying ice. The result was that Hawk had to approach every man who approximated Dermot's stature. The going got progressively rougher, so that he, fit as he was, was soon gasping for breath, the moisture freezing on his scarf. It made him worry more about Dermot, who was not particularly athletic. It was too easy to imagine him toppling over from a heart seizure.

Landmarks, signs, even massive buildings, were, like the people, losing their identities in the snow, and Hawk picked his way with extra care; getting lost was the last thing he needed to do.

It amazed him that even in the face of the storm's ferocity, which isolated each person in layers of clothing, news and rumors managed to make their rounds, most of them probably true. All the ferries were shut down; passengers in huge numbers were stranded in the ferry buildings. Trains that had been heading for New York must have been stopped on the tracks out in the countryside since they had not arrived in the city. God only knew what was happening to the passengers immobilized in the cold. No mail or newspapers had been delivered, but more important, no fresh milk had come in from the farms. There was also talk of shortages of meat and produce.

Hawk reflected grimly that there was no doubt that the poor, who bought their food day by day as they could afford it, would suffer the most. They, too, would be the most vulnerable to the lack of heat in the tenements. Coal prices were already said to be going up. Most tenement dwellers got their milk by hanging tin pails on the doorknobs to be filled by the milkman with a dipper from his bucket, and they purchased coal in nickel and dime quantities from the grocer. It was too easy to imagine thousands of people huddling in vermin-infested buildings with no access to food or heat.

Not all business had come to a halt. Saloons, bars, and dining rooms in big hotels had more than they could handle as many people decided that being stranded where there was warmth, food, and drink was a better fate than braving the storm. Hawk wondered if Dermot was safely sheltered in such a place while he staggered along looking for him.

He found him by sheer good fortune. He saw an edge of cloth protruding from a snowbank, and he went to give aid as he already had several times to strangers. But this time when he pulled the man out, it was Dermot.

He felt elation and dread simultaneously. He'd found him, but he wasn't sure he was in time.

Dermot was dead weight, and when Hawk uncovered his face, the skin was blue white. He slapped Dermot's cheeks sharply. "Come on, man, come on! You've got to help me. Jilly's waiting at home for you. Dermot, can you hear me? Dermot!"

"Too tired." The words were faint, but they were sane.

"You can't be too tired," Hawk yelled. "Your wife and mine are waiting for us, and Lexy will be out looking for us if I don't get back. Now, come on!"

Dermot was solidly built, and the two of them reeled drunkenly as Hawk set them in motion, supporting most of Dermot's weight until Dermot began to move under his own power, muttering, "Jilly's waiting, Jilly's waiting."

Whenever Dermot faltered, Hawk shored him up and kept going. Harder than the physical labor was the fact that he was no longer able to offer aid to anyone else. He tried to ignore the distress around him, but he saw it all—not only people who needed help, but also horses standing or lying down in frozen misery, cut from their traces and abandoned by their drivers when the vehicles could go no further. Some lay dead of gunshots used to put them out of their misery.

By the time they got to the block where the Hargrave house was, Hawk thought they might both end up freezing in a snowbank. His arms and legs were so leaden, he had to think carefully to take one step after another. But he kept imagining Lexy plunging out into the storm to find him. Indeed, when they finally reached the steps leading up to the house, the door opened to reveal not only Lexy, but Jilly as well, both women shapeless but determined in multiple layers of wool.

Lexy cried out Hawk's name, and Jilly, Dermot's, and then the women were helping their husbands inside.

"Dermot needs a jolt of brandy and a warm tub immediately; he's frozen to the bone," Hawk said, unaware that his words were slurred, his own teeth chattering, but he did not protest when Lexy subjected him to the same treatment he had prescribed for Dermot.

To everyone's relief, neither man seemed to have suffered any permanent damage from exposure to the cold, but Dermot stated flatly that he would have died if Hawk had not found him.

"I knew I was going to die, but it just didn't seem to make any difference. I was so cold, but once I'd fallen, and the snow was drifting over me, I felt so peaceful, nothing else mattered except resting. If there is ever anything I can do for either one of you, you have only to ask," he told Hawk and Lexy.

And Jilly, still clinging to Dermot's hand as if afraid he would disappear into the storm again, added her own fervent thanks.

The two couples shared a rare camaraderie, survivors of the storm, and the men talked openly of what they had seen.

Dermot was still shaken by his own stubborn stupidity. "Despite all the evidence, I would not believe the severity of the storm," he confessed, shaking his head. "And there are legions like me. What arrogance! We think of this as the most advanced city in the world—to think less is treasonous for a New Yorker—and so, it is as if even Nature cannot prevail against us. What folly!"

"I wonder how they are faring at home?" Lexy mused. "Such a storm must extend a good distance up and down the coast."

It was frustrating to speculate because with all communications cut off, there was no way to glean any information. Lexy and Jilly tried to comfort themselves with the sensible thought that things must be at least a little better further south where the weather was almost always warmer.

The snowfall slowed early on Tuesday and stopped in the afternoon, but the temperature failed to climb much above zero. And though the winds had lessened, drifts were still piling up, and whirling snow filled the air.

Thoroughly chastened by the storm, at first only the boldest souls ventured out, but then sleighs began to appear, the sounds of their bells ringing on Fifth Avenue, Broadway, and most other main streets. It was decidedly odd to look out and see snow piled to second-story windows in some spots and sleighs riding high.

The most bizarre event was the ice floe that floated out of the Hudson River and into New York Bay and then up the East River until it wedged itself between the Brooklyn and Manhattan docks. It was six inches or so thick and nearly a quarter of a mile wide and a mile long. The ice blocked the river, thus stopping the ferry which had just resumed spotty service. Before long, men and some women were daring to make the crossing from shore to shore on the ice. But the fun nearly ended in tragedy when the ice, broken up by tugboats, disintegrated so quickly that the last six adventurers, who had ignored police warnings, had to be rescued from an ice block by one of the tugs.

Hawk and Lexy got out of the house as soon as they could, intent on covering the story, particularly after Dermot suggested a way they could relay the news to Washington. Dermot had a representative in London, and he pointed out that the oceanic cables ran well below the surface and must be operating. Therefore, messages could be sent to the *Witness* via London. It was undoubtedly the most expensive way of filing a story, but the news was major, so Hawk and Lexy decided to do it, and then they discovered that no messages were getting through to the capital, even by such an elaborate route, because apparently the lines carrying all four hundred circuits were out there. A message could be sent to Boston via London, but that was all.

Along with the more lighthearted attempts of the citizenry to make the best of the storm by sleigh riding and playing in the snow, there were more sinister aspects to the story. There had been a huge supply of freshly butchered meat in the city, but that had not stopped the prices from being raised, and milk and coal had likewise been made dear. There had been some fires in poorer districts, and now adding to the hazards, garbage and sewage were being cast out into the snowbanks with no thought of what would happen when the snow melted. Transportation was slow to resume.

But by Wednesday, after a few small snow flurries, the wind ceased, the temperature began to climb, and in early afternoon the sun appeared. Trains began to arrive at Grand Central Station, and passengers who had made it in from their frozen siege in the countryside had their own tales to tell. A few people had died because they had left the trains in order to find shelter elsewhere, but most of the travelers made it safely to the city.

Bridge and ferry traffic resumed, too.

It was obvious to the Mackennas that the rapidly melting snow was going to create additional stories of flooding in the city, but they did not stay to cover them. By the same tortuous cable route through which they had tried to file their reports and which was now restored enough for patchy service, they received word from Reid, addressed to both the Mackennas and the Hargraves:

MORGAN DIED AT SEA. COME HOME AS FAST AS YOU CAN.

Chapter 38

The storm, formed of two systems that had merged, had struck the Eastern Seaboard from north to south. Washington had been nearly as isolated as New York. But if the elements had been harsh on land, on the water they had created instant, swift-moving chaos. Even Baltimore's harbor had seen the wind blast most of the water out, stranding steamers on mud flats. There had been no time for the ships at sea or, indeed, for those close to the coast, to seek shelter. Many had suffered damage and casualties; some had been lost altogether. Hundreds of people died.

Morgan had been taking a yacht for its maiden voyage, sailing the ship to New York for its owner, a financier with a keen interest in the sea and ships. The man had wanted the finest craft available and had chosen the Jennings-Falconer yard for that reason. He had been aboard for the voyage. And the ship had proved herself yare in every way, riding out the terrible storm with nothing more than a slightly damaged mast.

Those on deck during the worst of the blow had been, at Morgan's orders, secured by lines to the ship. But one of the younger sailors had gone overboard anyway. It had happened so quickly and in such poor visibility, no one was exactly sure what had happened, whether the line had given way, the knot had come untied, or the sailor had unfastened himself for a fatal moment in order to move further than the line allowed or to go below.

Everyone was exactly sure of what had happened next. Morgan had seen the man fall into the sea, and, without hesitation, he had untied his own line and gone after him. Like many sailors, the youngster couldn't swim. But Morgan got to him and held him up until a line could be thrown into the roiling sea. It had taken a long, treacherous time to haul both men aboard.

Though waterlogged, the sailor suffered no lasting effects, and at first, those aboard the yacht had thought Morgan had fared as well. He had opened his eyes and had asked very clearly after the welfare of the boy. And then with equal clarity, he said, "Sam sails to China with me. I promised. All the way to China . . ."

Those were his last words. His eyes closed as his exhausted heart stopped beating.

The ship that had started out so bravely survived the rest of the storm to return to Baltimore bearing her sad cargo.

Sam had long known her only rival was the sea. And in the end the sea had won. But Sam had her own victory. Morgan would lie beside all of the others at Wild Swan, and someday she would lie beside him. At least the sea had not kept his body. It was important somehow. She had always hated the idea of a sailor's burial. The body sinking down to be consumed by creatures in the dark water, to be dispersed by the currents.

There were good things. She clung to them. Morgan's bouts with malaria had often threatened his life. But he had not, after all, died a weakened old man. He had been straight and strong and true to his passion when he had set out on the new ship. And he had perished quickly on the liquid world he had loved more than the land.

And there were the children and the grandchildren. Her Seth was years gone, but Adam and Nigel were still part of her world with their wives and their children—people who loved her and whom she loved. They mourned with her; they would stand beside her in the lonely days to come, they and the rest of the family.

There were so many people who had to suffer loss with no one to comfort them, and she was grateful she was not one of those. And she knew she would survive. The younger generations still needed her; the acres of Brookhaven needed her. And beyond that, her obligation to Morgan and the love they had shared had not died with him.

But none of this altered the fact that she had loved Morgan Falconer since she was eight years old. She had borne his children and shared his triumphs and tragedies as he had shared hers for all of these years. Once they *had* sailed all the way to China together and back again.

He would never touch her body with love again, and she would never stroke the brave lines of bone and sinew so different from her own. They would never again turn to each other in the night or share the days. They would never worry or celebrate together over the doings of their sons. Never again. She had a lifetime of memories of Morgan locked in her mind, her heart, her soul, and she could produce them at will, but they would never be the same as having him beside her.

She wasn't sure what she believed, but she hoped that somehow Morgan and Seth were together now, with Alex and Rane and all the others who had died. She understood too well why people clung so tightly to the belief in an afterlife. It was so bitter to think this was all. For a moment she was fiercely envious of Alex and Rane, who had died together.

> They that go down to the sea in ships, that do business in
>   great waters;
> These see the works of the Lord, and his wonders in the deep.
> For he commandeth, and raiseth the stormy wind, which lifteth
>   up the waves thereof.
> They mount up to the heaven; they do down again to the
>   depths: their soul is melted because of trouble.
> They reel to and fro, and stagger like a drunken man, and are
>   at their wit's end.
> Then they cry unto the Lord in their trouble, and he bringeth
>   them out of their distresses.
> He maketh the storm a calm, so that the waves thereof are still.
> Then are they glad because they be quiet; so he bringeth them
>   unto their desired haven.

The ancient psalm joined Morgan to all the men who had so perished, and more, they joined him to Rane, to his father who had come from the sea people of Clovelly in England.

To lose Morgan was a double loss, for he had not only been his own man, but had also become, with Blaine, one of the patriarchs of the family and the one most like Rane. The older he had grown, the more he had resembled his father, not only physically, but also in spirit.

Lexy, standing with Hawk at the graveside, was not aware of how desperately she was clinging to his hand, and he did not try to ease her grip. He did not know the elder Falconers as well as he knew the Tratnors and the Culhanes, but he felt the same ripples of selfish terror that were running through Lexy; given the way of life and of death, one day one of them would stand over the grave of the other. And Sam and Morgan had known each other since they were children, had loved each other for that long; it made Hawk feel as if he had already lost precious years from his time with Lexy.

He understood that night that she wanted something more than lovemaking from him when she pressed herself so closely against him, as if seeking to merge their bodies so that one could not be lost without the other.

"It's all right, love. It's a tragedy that Morgan died, but he and Sam had many years together, and we will, too, we will!"

Her skin was cold from the fear of loss. Hawk held her and stroked her, sharing his warmth. "You can't live in dread every minute," he chided gently. "People who do have no joy at all."

She responded not to his logic, but to the overwhelming reality of his physical presence. His scent was all around her, soothing her, and the lean strength of him protected her own softer flesh.

When they finally joined their bodies, they moved with deliberate slowness, defying time, defying death, loving each other as if they had years far beyond the span of a human life.

Both of them clung to the memory of that special interlude in the weeks that followed as their work consumed and separated them.

It was an election year, and for Hawk that meant following the ins and outs of policy and politics even more closely than usual. Cleveland, the first Democratic president elected since the war, had overcome not only the virulent opposition of Tammany Hall, but also the disclosure that he had fathered an illegitimate child. His tactic of admitting that he had had appealed to the public, and he had beaten James G. Blaine by a narrow margin of the popular vote.

However, there was one enormous problem Cleveland had been unable to surmount. When he had taken office in March 1885, the treasury had been filled to overflowing, and during his term money had continued to accumulate until the president saw such a crisis that he had made it the subject of his State of the Union message in December 1887, saying that the public treasury

> *becomes a hoarding place for money needlessly withdrawn from trade and the people's use, thus crippling our national energies, suspending our country's developments, preventing investment in productive enterprise, threatening financial disturbance, and inviting schemes of public plunder.*

"Having too much money with which to run a government must surely be one of the world's oddest problems," Lexy mused when she and Hawk discussed the situation, but she understood the complexity as well as he. The surfeit of funds came mainly from high tariffs charged on imported goods. There had been attempts to lower the duties, but they had come to naught. The protectionist forces of the manufacturing states were very strong, stronger than the sparsely settled West, and stronger than the agricultural South, which had had little external political power since the war, though internally it was doing far too good a job of negating every political right and freedom granted to its black citizens in the aftermath of the war.

An increase in expenditure on public works might have provided at least a partial answer, but the president had a horror of the waste and dishonesty that too often plagued such projects. And because of the far-reaching powers President Lincoln had assumed during the war, the country had been relieved to return to a less pervasive central government. That attitude had been made only too plain in the withdrawal of federal forces from the South and in the dismantling of the reconstruction that was to have changed the political face of that region.

It was going to be an interesting election, but Lexy confessed to Hawk, "I feel unpatriotic thinking it, but I wonder why anyone would want to be president. Lincoln was assassinated, and Garfield was, too. There is always the chance that another madman will seek to change history in the same way. And beyond that, there is the daily scrutiny by the public, and there is all that power connected with the office, no matter how it is tempered by the rest of the government."

"That power is the point," Hawk said. "No matter how diligent and decent, a man who wants the highest political office must also want the power."

"Would you?" she asked curiously.

"For the good I might do, yes," he answered. "But for the daily burden of the office and for the compromises that must be made, no."

"It's just as well, because I would make a terrible First Lady. I can think of nothing I would rather not be." Her expression of disgust made Hawk smile, but then she demanded, "How would you like to suffer most of the burden, the compromises, and none of the power?"

"I wouldn't like it at all, and I suspect many of those women haven't liked it, either," Hawk answered. "But can you imagine if I were president that you would not still be closest to my mind and my heart? Who knows how much or how little the First Ladies have to do with presidential policy?"

"The women themselves; they are the only ones who know!" She counted on her fingers. "And there are seven of them living. I wonder what they would tell me."

Hawk recognized the absorbed look on her face and sighed inwardly, knowing that she was going to add this story to the list of subjects she wanted to explore. Only two of the women, Mrs. Cleveland and Harriet Lane Johnston (James Buchanan's niece), lived in Washington, which meant that Lexy would be out of the city even more than the races demanded, which in turn meant that, coupled with his own schedule, they would have less time together. He loved her intellect as much as he loved anything else about her, but that did not make it any less painful to face the extra days alone. Nor did it help when he had to admit to himself that he was not willing to reduce his own coverage of the news to give them more time together. The reality was that they both worked at demanding jobs and would have to make sure their marriage survived in spite of that.

At first it was not difficult, since their initial assignment on returning to work was to finish coverage of the blizzard, writing more details of what they had seen in New York, as well as correlating reports from other regions.

News of the storm damage filled every paper. Ironically, in January, Dakota and other parts of the West had suffered a horrible blizzard that had killed livestock and people, but that region was not a population center like the Eastern Seaboard, and so the storm had not been so extensively reported. Reid had followed the Western news because it seemed to prove what old Jericho had told him years ago about the land being fit only for the nomadic Indians and herds of wild game, not for domestic cattle and their keepers. And he had felt duty bound to make note of the fact that most Indians in the region were now confined to reservations, unable to travel and hunt with the seasons, made more vulnerable to the elements than they had ever been before.

Reid shook his head as he read the latest casualty figures before giving them to Hawk. "Maybe Nature doesn't want anyone living here, either."

But man and the land were resilient. The cities cleaned up their messes, and New York in particular began to talk about having utility lines and even trains below the ground so that no storm could ever again knock out communications and power. Early planted fields were replanted. Spring returned.

Lexy and Hawk began to see less and less of each other, but because they had discussed it, they did not allow the physical separations to become divisions of the heart. They sent notes to each other, and when possible, they arranged to meet and spend time together in cities other than Washington, though their schedules were dictated by the news they were seeking.

It wasn't the easiest way to run a marriage, but it was possible, and in some ways, it was very romantic.

"I feel as if I'm still being courted and still courting you," Lexy told Hawk. "I don't feel like an old married woman at all!"

"You're not an old married woman; you won't ever be. Whatever aging we do, we'll do together. That way neither of us will ever notice that we're growing older." Hawk said it with a grin, but his eyes were serious, and Lexy took his words as another vow in the series that had only begun at their wedding.

Still, nothing erased the loneliness of being without him. She missed him most of all late in the night, and she missed him as much for the comfort of his presence as she drifted into sleep as she did for their lovemaking.

Hawk confessed himself in similar distress. "I see a woman who walks a certain way; I see the sun on golden brown hair; I hear a special note in a voice, and I think that by some happy chance, you're there. I'll probably come to a bad end, stabbed to death with a hat pin wielded by a woman I've mistakenly accosted, thinking she was you."

They laughed together, but Lexy had to wipe her eyes more than once when she took a train going one direction and Hawk left in another.

In addition to attending the races, Lexy pursued her idea of interviewing the former First Ladies: Mrs. John Tyler, Mrs. James K. Polk, Mrs. Harriet Lane Johnston, Mrs. Ulysses S. Grant, Mrs. Rutherford B. Hayes, Mrs. James A. Garfield, Mrs. John McElroy (who, while not quite a First Lady, had assumed certain duties at the behest of her brother Chester A. Arthur, who had lost his beloved wife just the year before he succeeded Garfield in the presidency), and Mrs. Cleveland.

Tracking the ladies down took stamina. Mrs. Polk lived in Nashville, Tennessee, and two of the women, Mrs. Hayes and Mrs. Garfield, lived in Ohio. But they knew of the *Witness*, and they were gracious when Lexy requested interviews with them.

She was fascinated by their distinct personalities. Julia Gardiner Tyler was thirty years younger than the widowed president she had married in 1844, making Tyler the first president to marry in office. Mrs. Tyler had been a much-courted favorite of society before her marriage, but she had adored the president and "reigning," as she called it, as First Lady. When Tyler had died in 1862, she had been heartbroken. At sixty-eight she was still beautiful.

Mrs. Grant, too, spoke in glowing terms of her years in the White House. Despite having come from a Southern, slave-owning background, there had never been any question of her loyalty to her husband and thus to the Union, and with the complicity of the cabinet wives, she had entertained lavishly, proud of her position.

For Mrs. Garfield, memories of her time as First Lady would always be darkened by the assassination of her husband by an embittered attorney who had failed to get a consular post. She had been ill and convalescing at a seaside resort in New Jersey. She had returned to Washington by special train to be beside him during the torturous three months of his battle for life. When he lost the fight, she had gone home to the farm in Ohio, but she was unrelenting in her efforts to keep the records of her husband's career alive.

Before Lexy had done half of the interviews, she knew the public would love the articles and that she herself would always be dissatisfied. Each of the women she spoke with was willing to give her some little humanizing tidbit. Even Mrs. Polk, who at eighty-five had led a long life as a devout Presbyterian and disapproved of horse racing, among other amusements, and who knew of the Culhane connection to the sport, was willing to relate how much she had enjoyed helping her husband with his speeches and other correspondence. But there was a barrier Lexy could not cross.

She felt naive and presumptuous for not having anticipated it, but not until she spoke with the women did she realize how bound to the demands of history they all were. They were unelected, in place only through the office of their husbands, or uncle or brother, as in the cases of Harriet Lane Johnston and Mary Arthur McElroy. But each one of them had a sense of duty to the man who had made her hostess to the nation, and each of them was determined that she would do no less than enhance the man's legend.

The self-effacement was not, she understood, an entirely selfless act. By keeping the flame for the men, they shared the reflected light. But that did not ease Lexy's conviction that precious history was being lost in the censorship and gilding of memories.

The one of the seven whom she was never able to interview was Mrs. Cleveland. The current First Lady proved completely inaccessible, proof perhaps that she was even more afraid of betraying some confidence than were the others, who were further removed from the presidency. Lexy considered using family connections to force the issue, but in the end decided against it. She did not want to treat any of the women as a hostile witness, and more, in this case, she judged it an unworthy method to gain her ends.

"They're well written, and the readers will be fascinated, but I suspect Abby Adams isn't satisfied," Hawk said when he read the stories. He eyed her apprehensively, not entirely sure that the truth as he saw it would be welcome.

But for Lexy, his honesty was proof of respect. "Don't ever be afraid to tell me what you think. I could not have borne it if you had patronized me or, worse, if you had underestimated me so that you could not see that I would be disappointed with the material I got. But I'm glad I went as Lexy Culhane and not as Abby; I think she would have made it even more difficult for the women to be honest."

Hawk thought it was surely a measure of how married he was to Lexy's mind that he could understand how she perceived Abby Adams as a separate entity and that he did, too. And it was a good thing they were so attuned mentally, he reflected sadly as they said good-bye again, because their bodies were certainly not enjoying the same continued closeness.

Though he appreciated good horseflesh, formal race meetings didn't hold the same fascination for Hawk that they did for the Culhanes. But now he found himself looking forward to the Futurity at Sheepshead Bay at the end of summer. It would be enjoyable to be with the whole Culhane family, but most of all, he would have a few days with Lexy in a resort atmosphere.

"We'll do some riding of our own," she had promised, her innocent expression in direct contrast to her salacious suggestion.

In addition to the personal complications in her life due to separations from Hawk, this season's racing presented unique journalistic challenges to Lexy. Wild Swan always had entries at most major courses, but this year was different. This was Pharaoh's year.

The black colt was splendid, a running machine so powerful for his young age that every horseman in the country was watching him. And though Wild Swan's history encompassed a long list of champions, Pharaoh was a phenomenon because the stable's horses still tended to mature later than their two-year-old season, as they had from the beginning of Wild Swan's history, when endurance for the longer races of the era had been as important as speed.

Pharaoh had a deep chest, a long, coordinated stride on clean legs, and quick action—all visible virtues—but the invisible aspects of his character were equally important. He was sweet-tempered, even playful, off the track, acting like a large pet dog, following his favorite people around, nudging them for treats and attention, but once he was set to run, he was ferocious in his will to get to the front and stay there. The danger was that he would exhaust himself in his refusal to temper his speed, but because he did have endurance beyond most two-year-olds, the risk was worth it.

Pharaoh faced a formidable field of rivals, a potentially explosive crop of two-year-olds that included Proctor Knott by Luke Blackbrun out of Tallapoosa; Salvator by Prince Charlie out of Salina by Lexington; and Tenny, son of the French horse Rayon d'Or out of Belle of Maywood.

Travis and Gincie did not want to overwork Pharaoh in his first season, but by the time the Futurity was to be run, the colt had won five of six races, including the prestigious Junior Champion Stakes at Monmouth Park, and the race he had lost had not been for lack of trying, but because he had been cut off and hemmed in in a large field, and his jockey had made a wise decision not to force the horse through a jam that could easily have resulted in serious injury.

Throughout the season, Lexy tried to be impartial in her reporting of Pharaoh's races, but it grew increasingly difficult as the colt's fame spread and his name and image began to appear on everything from handkerchiefs to cigar boxes.

Periodically, the public's fancy was caught by a racehorse, though usually not until the horse had run and won more races than had Pharaoh, but in his case, the combination of beauty, spirit, and early victories proved irresistible. And strangely, though the Culhanes had bred and trained him, references were not to them, but to the legendary Alexandria Carrington Falconer.

"I'd rather attention was not fixed on us," Gincie confessed. "Anything to lessen interference in Pharaoh's training."

Though Lexy was inevitably doing her own part to fix attention on the colt, she understood the problems public scrutiny caused. It was a good thing Pharaoh was so even-tempered, since large crowds of people had begun to come to see him, and transporting him from one racecourse to another meant trying to outmaneuver the public in order to keep impromptu reception committees down to manageable size. But worst of all, such interest made it nearly impossible to maintain any secrecy regarding his training schedule and his general condition, factors that influenced the racing strategies of other stables as well as the betting odds.

Despite the fact that the swelling enthusiasm for Pharaoh made good copy, Lexy refused to fill all of her columns with the obvious and continued to write about other horses and other aspects of the sport, particularly the antibetting measures that were beginning to creep into the legislation of northern states.

In the previous year, New York State had passed a law limiting betting to the dates between May 15 and October 15, a boon to Baltimore and to the National Jockey Club in Washington, D.C., which held race meetings earlier in the spring and later in the fall. Since the Northern tracks had long wanted to expand their season, the legislation was to the more southerly jockey clubs' advantage. Lexy approved of that, but she also saw the danger of laws being passed against the very thing that kept racing alive.

In her columns, she argued that the people that were most involved—the breeders, trainers, owners, track officials, and the gambling fraternity—must police their own sport, keeping the races clean, the betting honest, and the calendar reasonable enough so that horses were not overraced and the segment of the public that did not approve of racing in the first place could not claim that there was too much of it. She championed the cause of a truly national and powerful jockey club, hearing her parents' voices advocating the same with every word she wrote, but she felt as if she were spitting into the wind. Pharaoh fever continued to sweep the country, and not enough of the racing world recognized the danger that the legislation presented.

In order to maintain her own objectivity, she withstood the frenzy over Pharaoh as long as she could, but when she joined Hawk and the rest of the family at Sheepshead Bay, she succumbed. It was impossible to resist. Her parents and brothers were trying to be very calm, but their excitement was palpable. Pharaoh was in top condition, the end of summer was soft on Coney Island, and through the colt, Wild Swan had a chance at the richest purse in the country. Even Hawk added to the madness by presenting Lexy with a jewel box that had Pharaoh's image inlaid on the top.

"It's a reward for not taking advantage of your position as an intimate of the Culhanes," he said.

"I did try," Lexy insisted virtuously, and then she spoiled the effect by giggling. "But now I am surrendering to the madness! I'll put my jewelry in the Pharaoh box, blow my nose on a Pharaoh handkerchief, secure my stockings with Pharaoh garters, cover my . . ."

"Stop!" Hawk commanded, holding up his hands in mock horror. "I don't want to search through horse blankets to find my wife."

"I was thinking more of silk," Lexy said, looking at him from under her lashes, but then she sobered. "I know it is really just another race, but I do hope he wins! Mama and Papa would be so pleased! It's not just the money, though heaven knows it is a fortune; it would be a vindication of the talent they have for breeding and training horses, of the talent great-grandmother Alex had, and of the hard work all of them have done for so many years."

The upcoming race was quite enough excitement for the family, but Kace added more in the person of Rosalind Cunningham. She came to Coney Island properly chaperoned by a widowed, middle-aged cousin, Edith Chapman, but neither Rosalind nor Kace made any secret of the fact they were in love.

Rosalind was nineteen, a year younger than Kace. She came from a respectable merchant family and had cousins at Harvard, which accounted for Kace's introduction to her at a skating party hastily arranged to celebrate surviving the great blizzard before the ice could melt again.

She was, by current standards, extraordinarily beautiful, with big blue eyes, neat features framed by shining blond hair, and a shelf of bosom and curve of hip which, even demurely clad, rivaled Lillian Russell's celebrated attributes. Kace's eyes were not the only ones that followed her every move, but Rosalind betrayed no interest in any male other than Kace.

Lexy thought that if her brother expanded his chest any further in pride, he was going to pop all of his buttons off his shirt. She thought a good deal more than that, but she managed to keep it to herself until she and Hawk were alone.

"Do you think it is possible to remove the brain surgically and still leave such a pretty face?" she asked and was immediately appalled at how malicious she sounded. "Oh, Hawk! I'm not usually such a cat. But I tried, I did try, and I didn't get one intelligent response from her. From what I could tell, she reads nothing other than novels of romance and cookery books. She's genuinely kind and good, I think, but . . ."

"But she is everything you detest in a woman," Hawk finished, quite gently, for her. "She believes it is sufficient to be an ornament, like a china shepherdess on a mantelpiece. And while you might forgive a preference for that kind of woman in a stranger, it is hard to forgive in your brother because it seems as if he is rejecting everything you are."

"Yes, it does!" she snapped defiantly, but her eyes filled with tears. "How can he love a woman . . . no, a girl, like her?"

Hawk rolled his eyes heavenward and groaned. "Words are my business, but I don't think I possess an adequate supply to explain to you how foolish a young man in love can be. It's a form of insanity. Not only do all practical considerations cease to exist, but every word and motion of the beloved becomes embarrassingly precious, and the rest of the world simply vanishes." He paused and then added thoughtfully, "I believe I have just described my own behavior regarding you."

Though privately Lexy thought it probably described his behavior with Caroline more than with herself, she was amused, as Hawk intended her to be. And being amused made it possible for her to understand her own reactions more honestly.

"I'm jealous," she admitted with wonder. "Kace, Tay, and I have always been very close, and in some ways, because I'm older, I feel as much their mother as their sister. I've wanted what I think would be right for Kace, and for Tay, and that is not necessarily what either of them will choose. I've heard Tay teasing Kace about his romantic escapades, and I've seen how popular both of them are with local girls, but this is the first time either one of them has presented a young woman as being so special."

"You needn't look so guilty," Hawk said. "You were perfectly civil to the fair Rosalind, and unless she's hiding her mental light under a bushel, she *is* extremely stupid."

Lexy stared at him for a moment, not sure she'd heard him correctly, and then she laughed, relieved that jealousy had not completely undermined her judgment.

But to compensate for her uncharitable thoughts, she went out of her way to be kind and attentive to Rosalind. In the process, she noticed that the rest of her family was doing the same thing. Even her mother, who was usually so calm, appeared flustered and baffled after spending time with Rosalind. And Tay, who was surely the kindest of the three Culhane children and who was unfailingly cordial to Kace's ladylove, finally confided to Lexy, "It's like making friends with an overbred lap dog; it's so soft and pretty, but it hasn't a particle of practicality in its nature."

"It is heavy going, trying to have a conversation with her," Lexy said, and then she asked, "Do you think Kace is really serious about her? I mean, marriage serious?"

"I think so," Tay answered. "He's utterly besotted, and he's very protective in his way. Oh, I know I'm the one who always brought home strays, but Kace likes to shelter people with his strength, as you do, and he's much more romantic than either of us and a lot less practical.

"You see, I think he senses that she's been made defenseless by training, if not by nature, though who could ever know what she might have been if she'd been raised differently, and he wants to protect her from the consequences of that. What he doesn't know is that in the end, she won't be enough for him; she can't be enough."

"We're spoilt," he said, and his expression was so earnest, Lexy wanted to hug him as she had when he was a little boy wrestling with a particularly complicated idea. "Kace and I are accustomed to women who think, women who do things. We're so accustomed to that, we don't even question what it adds to our lives. Kace doesn't know how much he will miss it if he marries Rosalind, but he will know eventually, if he does marry her. And the saddest thing is that even poor Rosalind will know that something is amiss, that he's losing interest, but neither one of them will know how to change anything."

"You're so wise sometimes, you frighten me," Lexy said.

"Not wise enough to make Kace see any of this," Tay said regretfully.

"Wise enough not to try." This time, Lexy did hug him. He sounded so desolate, and she realized that if the situation was difficult for her, it was nearly impossible for him. He and Kace had shared a special bond since birth, and while it would probably have been a major adjustment no matter which one fell in love first, Kace's choice made everything much, much harder.

The most ironic part of the whole situation was that Kace viewed the cordiality offered by his family to Rosalind as her due, earned by her charms, rather than as a gift to himself. He was so blind to her shortcomings, he could not imagine there were any.

Among other vast areas of ignorance, racing was a blank in Rosalind's mind. She had never had any interest in horses, and her family frowned on racing, a prejudice they were trying to overcome now that their darling had fixed her affections on Kace Culhane. Mr. Cunningham, with little effort, had discovered that the Culhanes were people of property and prestige, even if he did wish they were involved in something less remarkable than horse racing.

True to her nature, though Rosalind knew how important racing was to Kace, she had made no attempt to learn anything about it, confident that Kace or someone else would tell her anything she had to know.

"Though it grows a bit wearying, it is rather amusing to have to explain everything to her," Lexy admitted to Hawk. "It makes me see the sport with new eyes."

"Ah, but does she remember anything you tell her?"

"Well, no, not so that you could notice, but she seems to enjoy it anyway." There was a small part of her that envied Rosalind for the childlike enthusiasm she possessed. The horses were "oh, so big and fierce-looking," the silks were "so pretty, such bright colors," and the races themselves were "so thrilling, just like a circus without the tent!" Apparently, anything with animals reminded Rosalind of a circus.

But for Lexy, the races were as much business as pleasure, and she continued to try to write sane copy in the midst of Pharaoh madness. There were other races besides the Futurity, but it was hard to direct attention to them because the Futurity's purse was the largest ever offered. The betting was heavy, too. Pharaoh was the favorite, but there were plenty of people who were willing to risk wagering against him on the principle that no race was certain until it was over.

Early in the morning of the day the Futurity was to be run, Lexy went with the twins to the stable where Pharaoh was being kept. Rosalind did not favor early hours, and Hawk had deliberately decided not to accompany Lexy because he wanted her to have this special time with her brothers.

The colt nuzzled each of them in turn, making contented little snuffling noises. He looked so calm, almost sleepy with his eyes at half mast, it was hard to imagine how changed he would be in the afternoon when he was led onto the course.

"It's your big day, boy," Lexy crooned, "but it's probably just as well that you don't know that. For you, it's just another race."

"Pardon me, but you're the Culhanes, aren't you?"

Lexy swung around at the sound of the husky voice with the traces of an English accent, and she recognized the figure before them. She had even mentioned him briefly in one of her articles about gambling at the races.

Of medium height, very slender, dark-haired, and smooth-skinned, the young man was known simply as George, with no surname. Standing not far away was his constant shadow, a huge black man, a mute, known as Charlie.

The racing world contained more than its fair share of characters, but George was among the oddest of these. He didn't look older than fourteen or fifteen, but he was a well-established "beard," an agent for those who desired to place bets but did not wish their business known, often because they were well-known "plungers" and didn't want others copying their bets and thus changing the odds. George and his silent companion were a common sight at the major racetracks, and George, for all his youth, had a reputation for absolute honesty in his work.

"We're the Culhanes," Kace confirmed. "How can we help you?"

"I think it's the other way around; I think I can help you," George said, and there was no mistaking the nervousness in his eyes as he glanced around.

Lexy noticed that Charlie's eyes were also moving constantly, staring at each shadowed space before moving on to the next, and she shivered at the sudden cold that ran down her spine as she tried to tell herself that this peculiar confrontation was probably no more than George wanting to solicit a little business, wanting to know if the Culhanes would like to place an anonymous bet on their colt.

George's next words dispelled that notion.

"They're going to nobble your nag," he said abruptly, the culture of his earlier words eclipsed by racing cant.

For an instant, the two sides simply stared at each other, and then Kace snarled, "What in the hell are you talking about?"

Lexy put a placating hand on his arm when she saw his fists clench. "Give him a chance to tell us," she cautioned.

George's eyes, a bright unsettling combination of amber, brown, and gold, flashed to hers, and then his attention shifted back to Kace.

"I overheard it last night. I didn't see who was talking, didn't recognize the voices. I hope they didn't see me. They were too far away for me to hear it clearly, so perhaps I'm mistaken, but I think they mean to drug Pharaoh—not to kill him, mind you, but to make him lose. Word is that there is a lot of money, too much, being privately bet against him."

They were all frozen in place again. The young man's words conjured the worst aspect of racing, the shady dealings that, if practiced enough, would be the death knell of the sport. And such dealings, while not unknown, were very, very rare at tracks as prestigious as Sheepshead Bay. But then, races with a purse the size of the Futurity's were also very rare.

"An opiate, a stimulant, there are all sorts of compounds. . . . Arsenic, that's what I expect they'll use," Tay said calmly. "It's used medicinally as well as for poisons, and it's easy to buy. In the proper dosage, it can make a horse behave erratically without killing him; it can throw him off just enough without anyone suspecting anything. In the wrong amount, it can kill him."

George's sigh of relief that someone believed him was audible, but Lexy, her journalist's instincts rising above all else, still felt obliged to play the skeptic. "Why should you risk telling us?" she asked. "You could just as well use the knowledge to your own advantage and bet against Pharaoh."

With a low, rumbling growl, the big black man started forward, but without even looking at him, George motioned him back. "I don't bet on the races. No matter how lucky you are one day, on most days it's a fool's game. My job is to place the bets for those who want to play, not to change the odds by betting their hunches. I'm honest, and I want the sport to be honest, too." He paused and then added, "It's not just the gaming; it's the horses themselves. Most of them are fine and strong and true. And Pharaoh is one of the best I've ever seen. He deserves the chance to run a clean race. Drugging a horse is always dangerous; as your brother said, they could just as well kill your colt as throw him off his stride. It wouldn't be what they wanted, but Pharaoh would be just as dead."

Lexy put her hand out. "Thank you for taking such a risk to warn us."

George shook hands with her, his own hand narrow and fine for a man's, but strong in its grip.

The worst of it was that there was no way they could determine who was behind the plot. They agreed with George that even if they knew the identities of the thugs he had overheard, it was likely that they were only hirelings. And they were equally sure that the instigators of the plot were not from the ranks of the owners, trainers, or jockeys who were involved in the Futurity. It was unthinkable that these men, who were among the most respected in the game, would stoop to such tactics.

"My bet, were I a betting man, would be that the whole thing has been hatched by someone from one of the outlaw tracks," George said. "I know most of the betting men from the major courses, and I think, though I can't be sure, that I would have at least recognized a voice if any of them had been familiar to me."

It was at once a comforting and a chilling thought; comforting because nothing could be worse than having to accuse a trusted member of the racing fraternity of such treachery; chilling because it gave them very little to go on.

The so-called outlaw tracks were those that made no effort to coordinate their calendars with other courses, were lax in enforcing the standard rules of racing, and often looked the other way in matters of foul riding and shady gambling practices. The good stables shunned them, but they managed to attract enough action from inferior horses and humans to do a lively business. They, more than any other factor, threatened legitimate racing by practicing abuses that gave fuel to the moralistic forces that wanted to shut the sport down entirely.

Even Lexy, with all of her diligence and her myriad connections to the racing world, had found the outlaw tracks impenetrable. She had tried to investigate one of the most notable, a track in New Jersey, but she had not only learned little, she had felt physically threatened. It was a world completely different from the legitimate tracks, where respectable women were increasingly pampered in order that they might feel as comfortable there as their husbands. Lexy's excursion to the other world had yielded little information and had resulted in pinches and proddings, which she had, in some cases, fended off with the judicious use of a hat pin. It was an episode so demeaning, she hadn't told even Hawk about it.

The faces there came back to her now. She knew the images were little better than caricatures, but still, they all seemed ominously similar—unkempt, belligerent, many intoxicated, and greedy, greedy for winnings gotten in whatever way. She could not believe that more than one in ten of those men had any love for the sport itself or for the horses. It was the gambling that interested them; they would have been as happy at a ring where dogs tried to tear each other's throats out or fighting cocks spurred each other to bloody death.

She thought of a few of those brutes gathered together, plotting Pharaoh's downfall, and she shuddered.

"There is one more thing, but I don't know what it means," George said. "I'm not sure I heard correctly, but I think they mentioned 'the kid.' It might have been 'th' kid'll do it,' " his voice was suddenly a low, indistinct rumble, "but it might also have been 'th' bid'll do it,' meaning something to do with the money they put up." Again his voice was muffled in mimicry of what he had heard. "I just don't know. And even if it were 'the kid,' what does that mean? It could be a plunger who goes by that name; it's not unusual. Anyone who's young in this game is called that at some time or another; a lot of people call me that."

"Maybe it wasn't a nickname, maybe they meant a child," Tay said slowly, thinking it through. "A stableboy, a newsboy, a vendor— there are all sorts of children underfoot every day." His gaze swept the area around them where more and more activity was beginning as the morning advanced.

George and Charlie glanced about, too, more conscious than ever of how exposed they were in their meeting with the Culhanes.

"I haven't anything else to tell you," George said abruptly. "Just watch your horse. Keep every stranger away from him, even children. Good luck. I hope he wins."

"Wait!" Kace said, and he turned back, but before Kace could say more, George held up his hand to stay him. "Don't offer me money. I already gave you my reasons for coming to you, and none of them has to do with getting one bribe higher than another."

They watched him walk away with his companion. "What a strange fellow," Kace muttered.

"Because he's honest?" Tay inquired with a rueful grin, but then his expression sobered. "All we have to do is keep everyone and everything away from Pharaoh until the race."

"If what he said is true, George could be in great danger for telling us. I hope he and Charlie will be all right," Lexy said, still staring in the direction the two had taken, though they had disappeared from view. She knew it was only a trick of the imagination, but the figures at the outlaw track loomed very large in memory, many of them bigger than Charlie, all of them bigger than George.

"They seem to be able to take care of themselves," Kace pointed out, but then he spoiled the observation by adding, "but we'd better keep an eye on them, particularly after the race if Pharaoh wins."

Now that George and Charlie had gone, the whole affair seemed extremely unlikely, making them wonder if they were being played for fools. Nonetheless, they took the threat seriously and informed Gincie and Travis as soon as they arrived.

Travis considered what they told him, and then he said, "I hope it isn't true, but until Pharaoh runs this afternoon, we and our people are the only ones who go anywhere near him."

Gincie and Travis looked as grim as their offspring had ever seen them, and their parents' reaction underscored their own determination that no attack be made on Pharaoh.

When Hawk got there, he too joined the vigil. During his Western years, he had seen some savage ways of deciding various contests, so he was less skeptical than the others. Even Rosalind reacted soberly to the situation, recalling how awful it had been when a neighbor's dog had been poisoned.

"At least she can connect one event with another," Hawk whispered to Lexy and won a brief smile from her.

They did not ask for assistance from the track stewards or the police for fear that such action would make it even more dangerous for George, but with Travis, Kace, Tay, Hawk, and their stable hands, they had a small army of large men to guard Pharaoh.

People who wanted to see how the colt looked before the race were turned away, but though they were disgruntled, most of them could understand such measures when the stakes were so high. Those who couldn't understand that had no difficulty understanding the implacable men they faced.

But in the end, the agent of destruction was indeed "the kid," a small, scrawny boy named Simon who walked horses and did other odd jobs at the track. He had been allowed to help with Wild Swan's horses because he was good with the animals and obviously in need of the coins given to him for the work.

With a big grin, Simon started toward Pharaoh's stall, his hands digging into his pockets. Without George's warning, he might have gone unnoticed, but as it was, Kace and Tay were on him in an instant.

"Whoa, there! Where do you think you're going?" Kace asked.

Simon looked up at them with big brown eyes. "I was jus' gonna give Pharaoh some apples, fer good luck," he said, clearly puzzled by the adults' action.

"Well, today we're not letting Pharaoh have any treats," Tay said. "You know how he is; if we'd let him, he'd eat everything in sight, maybe so much that he couldn't run."

Simon nodded vigorously. "That's right, he likes to eat! But he likes apples 'specially." While he talked, he dug several small apples from his pockets.

"But those aren't apples you got for him, are they?" Tay asked gently, staring at the fruit that looked decidedly the worse for having been in the little boy's pockets.

Simon gazed in wonder at Tay for the magician's knowledge, but he answered readily, "Nope, they ain't, but they'se apples jus' th' same. A man give 'em t'me t'give to Pharaoh, fer luck he said. An' he give me a dollar, too."

Tay's face suddenly paled visibly. "You didn't eat any, did you?" he asked urgently.

Simon was insulted. " 'Course not! They'se fer Pharaoh!" But then the color faded from his own face, leaving a splash of freckles in high relief. "Hey! They'se somepin' wrong with these, ain't they?" He dropped them on the ground as if they were venomous spiders.

"We think someone is trying to poison Pharaoh," Tay confirmed, gathering the dropped fruit. The apples had been neatly cored, and then the stem plugs had been replaced. Tay pulled one of the plugs out and gingerly tasted the residue of white powder inside. Most of it had been absorbed by the apple. He could smell nothing except apple, and a tiny taste was nothing on his tongue. Nearly odorless and tasteless; in the circumstances, these characteristics were definitive. "Arsenic, I'd stake money on it," he said. "And Pharaoh would have eaten every bit of the apples."

"I didn't know, I didn't! I wouldn't hurt ol' Pharaoh!" Simon's eyes filled with tears, and he glanced around as if he expected the rest of the Culhanes to attack him in rage.

Travis knelt beside the little boy. "We know you wouldn't. The man who gave you the apples knew you were a friend of Pharaoh's, that's why he did it. Do you know who the man is? Is he around here now?"

Simon surveyed everyone within sight and then shook his head. "Never seen him afore, an' he ain't here now." Color touched his pale cheeks, and he hung his head. "I bragged t' 'im that you let me be with Pharaoh whenever I wanted. He knowed I could do it." His voice dropped to a whisper as the full weight of what he might have done descended on him, but when he would have scrubbed at his eyes with his hands, Tay stopped him.

"No, Simon, we don't want any of that stuff to get in your eyes or anywhere else. First thing we do is clean you up."

Ignoring Simon's squeamishness at being fussed over by them, Gincie and Lexy helped, even to sewing his pockets shut so that he could not inadvertently put his hands back in where the apples had been. The equipment they had on hand to repair saddlery and racing silks did not run to an extra pair of pants for Simon. They could have clad him in racing silks, but the last thing they wanted to do was to draw attention to his connection with them.

"They are so sure of this, I doubt very much they've considered failure. If you hadn't gotten the tip about this whole mess, you never would have suspected Simon," Hawk said. "If he's not handy, I doubt they'll search him out, even when the plan fails, so why don't I take him home, if he has a home."

When asked, Simon was quick to tell that he did have a home where he lived with his mother and her friend, not like some kids who "don' have no place t' go of a night," but he wasn't so quick in agreeing to leave the racecourse with all this excitement going on.

Quietly Tay reminded the boy that the men who had given him the doctored apples were probably going to be very angry when they discovered that their plan hadn't worked and that it would be much smarter for Simon to be at home than here when that happened.

On further consideration and with ten dollars given to him by Travis, Simon went with Hawk. Simon had never had eleven dollars all at once, and the fortune did much to ease his sorrow at missing the rest of the adventure.

When the horses were called to the post for the Futurity, it seemed to the Culhanes and Mackennas that the day had been ten times as long as a normal one, but Pharaoh came out looking magnificent, dancing a little now that he was with other horses gathering for the race.

As the horses lunged forward at the starter's signal, Pharaoh immediately claimed the race for his own, going to the front and staying there. Proctor Knott got close at one point, with Salvator coming up behind him, but Pharaoh was unbeatable, flowing over the course as if he were more of the wind than of the earth. In the brief span of the race, he was the embodiment of all the centuries of breeding that had gone into the creation of the running horse.

The Culhanes and Mackennas stood for a moment in absolute silence as the roar of the crowd engulfed them, and then Gincie breathed, "My God, he did it!" and threw her arms around Travis, releasing them all from the spell so everyone was hugging and kissing everyone else.

In 1885, 752 horses had been nominated through their dams; fourteen had made it to the post today, three years later; and now Pharaoh had won $40,900 in one race, the richest purse ever in America.

Chapter 39

The press of people who wanted to talk to the Culhanes after the race was enormous, but the twins managed to slip away.

"It will probably be impossible to find him, and he's already said he doesn't want anything from us, but the least George whatever-his-name-is can accept is our gratitude," Kace told his father.

Travis was in full agreement. "If you can, offer him ten percent of the purse; it's not so much that it should embarrass him, considerin' that we probably wouldn't have won at all without his help."

"We might well be a lot worse off than just losing the race," Tay said. "People think that since horses are so large, it must take an enormous amount of any drug to affect them, but it doesn't. The effect depends on the drug or poison and on how it hits a particular animal. I'm sure the apples are full of arsenic, but only a teaspoon or less of the pure form would have killed Pharaoh."

The three men shared the vision of how Pharaoh looked now—

hardly tired from his effort and full of himself for winning—and how he might have looked writhing in agony until all of the life was gone.

The twins tried the betting ring first, but saw neither George nor Charlie, so they went on checking one area after another.

"Maybe they left the track," Tay suggested hopefully.

"I don't think so," Kace said. "Somehow I don't think George is the kind to turn tail. He wouldn't have come to us if he were."

Finally they had nowhere else to look but the stabling area, which was busy with preparation for the rest of the afternoon's races.

"At least we ought to be able to see Charlie, and then we can find George," Tay said, but it wasn't the big man he caught sight of first.

"Uh-oh!" He grabbed his brother's arm. "Isn't that George going into the barn at the far end?"

"Yes, and Charlie isn't with him, but someone else is!" Kace finished for him, and they both broke into a run, dodging horses and stable men.

They halted at the entrance to the barn, where light gave way to sudden darkness. The building was used mostly for storage of feed and equipment and should have been quiet, but instead there were ominous thuds and voices howling in rage.

"I knew it was you. I saw you . . ."

"Spoil our game, will you . . ."

"You little . . ." Obscenities filled the air.

"Got the nigger, now it's your . . ."

It was four to one, and George was fighting viciously, kicking with his feet and slashing with a knife. But the circle was closing in on him, and two of his attackers had blades, too.

Kace and Tay jumped in, going for the armed men first. The twins were fit and knew how to defend themselves, but the men they were fighting had a lifetime of violence behind them as well as the two knives.

The only and brief advantage they had was surprise. The man Tay went after lost his grip on his knife just long enough for Tay to chop at his wrist, making him drop the weapon. But Kace, trying the same maneuver, received a slash across his upper arm that burned like fire for an instant and then went numb. He changed tactics, kicking the man hard in the shins and then smashing his nose as he bent forward. The air whooshed out of his lungs from a hard blow to his ribs from one of the other men, and he narrowly avoided a knee in the groin.

Tay was battling just as hard, but he had the presence of mind and enough desperation to gulp air and shout, "Keep on, Kace, George, the others are on their way."

He'd never know whether his yell had done it or whether the thugs had finally realized who they were, but one of the men yelled, "Shit! It's th' Culhanes. They got an army!"

The last blow was an uppercut to George's chin that slammed him back against a post and crumpled him to the floor, and then the four attackers were fleeing the barn, their gaits showing some injury, Tay noted through his good eye, the other eye blurred and rapidly swelling shut from contact with a fist.

The twins were glad to be alive; pursuit didn't enter their befuddled minds as they turned their attention to the unconscious George.

"There's blood on his jacket," Kace observed anxiously as he knelt beside the still figure. "After all this, I sure hope we saved him."

"He's still breathing, and there's blood on all three of us, especially on you; that arm's going to need stitches," Tay observed, his habitual calm taking hold again, but it fled entirely and his hands froze once he'd peeled the jacket and shirt away.

Layers of cloth and the angle of the knife thrust had limited the wound to a long, shallow scratch that was already beginning to clot. The scratch ran from the shoulder to the top of the cloth binding George's small but definite breasts.

"What the hell is this?" Kace swore, and without thinking about it he ran a hand over George's trousers. "My God! It's female!"

Despite the circumstances, Tay would have laughed aloud if his lip hadn't been swelling as quickly as his eye. "This is the first time I've ever seen you at a loss with a woman." He peered more closely at George's face, and very gently he wiped at the rather heavy eyebrows and at what looked like a faint shadow of whiskers. Both smudged on his fingers. "Well," he said, and then "well," again, and he and Kace knelt there for a long moment, ignoring their own injuries and even George's as they tried to assimilate their new knowledge.

George stirred, groaned, and her eyelids fluttered a few times and then opened, "Charlie?"

Kace touched her cheek softly. "No, sweetheart, it's Kace and Tay Culhane." He wasn't conscious of the vast change in his address, but George was. She frowned at him and looked down at her open shirt.

"Damn," she muttered. She blinked a few more times, trying to dispel the fuzziness in her head. "I suppose you're going to tell."

"Tell whom?" Tay asked mildly. "We're still trying to recover from our own er . . . surprise. But one thing we all ought to do is get out of here now. Those men might stay around and discover we haven't any reinforcements after all."

"You go on. I've got to find Charlie," George said, concentrating on getting up on legs that seemed to have lost all their muscles.

"Wait here. Neither you nor Kace is in any shape for extra walking. I'll check the rest of the barn, and then we can get out of here." Tay deftly used a piece of Kace's own shirt to bind Kace's arm so that the bleeding would at least slow. He considered it a measure of how wobbly Kace was feeling that he allowed his brother to take charge.

George straightened her tattered clothing as well as she could while Tay searched the barn. "I appreciate the help, but I'm not going anywhere with you," she said firmly.

Kace didn't have the energy to argue with her, so he just ignored her announcement, thinking he'd let Tay convince her.

But when Tay came back, his face was bone white. "I found Charlie. He's dead. They slit his throat." He couldn't think of any way to soften the blow.

George lurched to her feet with a terrible cry, and Tay accepted that he had no choice but to take her to her friend. He put his arm around her to support her, and she did not refuse his help. Kace went with them, his legs gaining strength from necessity.

It was a grisly scene. Charlie's face was battered, as if he had put up quite a fight before they had subdued him, tied him up, and cut his throat.

"That's why those men already had some bruises. I noticed them," George said matter-of-factly, as if she were commenting on the weather.

Kace and Tay flanked her, unable to look away from the body.

George collapsed to her knees and stroked the battered face. "Oh, Charlie, you deserved better than this, so much better," she crooned, but then, instead of weeping, she began to curse, using words that shocked the twins, though up to that time they would have considered their own knowledge of profanity extensive.

"Now we have to tell the police," Tay ventured, and then winced at how insensitive that sounded, but he was totally undone by the strange combination that was George—the soft expression and the slender hands stroking the now grotesque face while her husky voice spewed curses.

She looked up at him. "Of course, the police must know. And how much they will care about the murder of a mute black man who frequented racetracks!" Her gaze shifted back to Charlie. "He was born in slavery, but when freedom came, he learned to read and write; he learned to believe all of the promises. And worse, he believed he could speak out for justice. So they cut out his tongue; white men in white robes cut out his tongue. That was in the South, but do you think that Northern, white policemen will treat him with any more kindness?"

"No, most probably not," Tay said honestly. "But we have to report the murder, anyway. And my brother is about to fall on his face; you don't look much better; and I for one do not want to be here if those men do come back."

George took one more long look at Charlie, and all the fight went out of her. "All right, whatever you say."

All the way back to their family, Kace and Tay expected someone to accost them, but aside from a few odd looks for their disheveled appearance, they were ignored. There was a lot of celebrating going on over the Futurity, and who cared if a few people got too enthusiastic? In fact, a lot of onlookers assumed that the Culhane boys had had a little altercation with George over a bet they'd placed but had settled it amicably, if roughly, since the three were staggering along together. And though the twins thought everyone would now know, because they themselves did, that George was a girl; with her hat back in place and her masculine attire pulled into some kind of order, no one saw anything except what he expected.

However, the appearance of the three was not greeted so cavalierly by the Culhane party, summoned from the clubhouse by a servant who couldn't quite manage to look disinterested in the state of the twins and George.

But aside from Rosalind's shriek of dismay at Kace's wound, the family reacted with admirable calm, and the twins were more than willing to relinquish control.

Travis served as liaison with the authorities, both the track stewards and the police, while Gincie was entirely focused on seeing to the medical needs of the twins and George.

"Kace needs stitches, and all three of you need patching up," she declared. "Travis, you can tell whoever needs to be told while I take these three to the hotel. The police can talk to them after a physician has seen them."

The plan made as much sense as anything else on this mad day. Travis, Hawk, and the other men would fan out to look for the four attackers, who were marked by signs of battle, but they had no great hope of finding them. Despite the close combat, Kace, Tay, and George had only general descriptions to offer: big men in ill-fitting suits with hats shadowing their faces except in the thick of battle. George said one of the men had a misshapen nose, probably from repeated fighting, and Kace added that he had taken care of another profile by smashing it.

The problem was that none of them believed the men were still at the track. That had seemed a possibility even after Tay had found Charlie's body, but now on reflection, it was clear that the attackers, having failed to kill George, would want nothing so much as to be away from the area. Though the victim was a black man, they had committed one murder already.

"Even if they hadn't killed George's friend and tangled with you, there must be other people looking for them," Travis reasoned. "I doubt they're cautious in their bets. Surely they must owe a goodly sum somewhere. And if someone put them up to it, they're answerable to him or perhaps to a group, too."

Travis and Hawk stayed behind to handle matters at the track while Gincie herded her patients and Rosalind and Edith to their hotel where she arranged for a doctor to attend the wounded.

While they waited for the doctor, Tay decided he had to tell, since Kace and George weren't volunteering. "Uh, Mama, there is one more thing."

George roused out of the lethargy of shock enough to give him a hard look of warning, but then the hopelessness of the whole situation washed over her again, and she subsided. Kace was paying no attention to either of them as he suffered Rosalind's anxious fussing, playing the stoic for her while he wished that he could just pass out until various parts of his anatomy stopped hurting. Hazily he wondered how it could be that his bruised ribs hurt more than the knife wound.

Gincie caught the byplay between Tay and George. "Well?" she asked and waited.

"Well, the fact is that George is a girl," Tay said in one quick breath, and the room went still. "It seems it ought to be known before the doctor arrives," he added defensively.

All eyes were suddenly focused on George, trying to match the truth with the illusion that had fooled them up to now.

George's cheeks were suffused with color that added to the rainbow effect of the growing bruises.

Gincie had accepted the fact that someone had tried to poison Pharaoh and had controlled her shock at seeing her sons so battered, but Tay's revelation stunned her so that sheer nerves made hysterical laughter rise up in her throat, and she had to bite her lip to keep it back. And then she saw how utterly miserable and stripped of self-confidence George was, and compassion replaced the hilarity.

She went and knelt beside the chair where George huddled, and very carefully she took one of the slender hands in both of her own, holding it loosely so that George could pull away if she wished.

"It's a bit out of the ordinary, but not so much as you might think in this family. The first time my husband saw me, I was dressed as a boy." She was gratified by the flare of interest in George's eyes and by the hand that rested quietly in her own. "Both of us were working on the Underground Railroad, and sometimes it was just safer for me to be a young man than a young girl. I can certainly see how in your business the same disguise would be necessary." She had recovered her poise enough to say it as if it really were not that uncommon to find a young girl working as a beard at racetracks. "But I must admit, it is rather awkward to continue to call you George. Might we know your real name?"

The girl considered the request for a long moment, and then she said, "Georgiana Victoria Cheney." The offering was hesitant, as if she hadn't thought of herself by that name for some time. And then in an even fainter voice, she added, "My father used to call me Georgie."

"Would you permit us to call you 'Georgie'?" Gincie asked. "I think it might be a bit easier for us now that we know you're a girl."

Georgie shrugged in acquiescence and winced at the pain the motion caused her. She couldn't see what difference it made what they called her. She had no intention of seeing any of them again after this day. She wished she'd never gotten involved with the Culhanes, but she knew she would do it all again the same way. At the very least, the memory of her father would have haunted her forever had she not done her best to prevent an attack on an animal as fine as Pharaoh.

But when she thought of going on without Charlie as her guardian and her friend, her mind went blank. She had not felt this vulnerable since her father died.

Seeing the sorrow, feeling it as if it were her own, Gincie lost her heart to the woebegone child in that instant, but sure that Georgie would not welcome any more overt signs of mothering, she refrained from offering them.

The doctor came, cared for the trio, and departed without, much to his credit, turning a hair over finding that one of his patients was a female dressed in male attire.

"Georgie thinks she's just going to go back to her life the way it was, but she won't be safe. I think she ought to go back to Wild Swan with you," Tay said. He was clearly prepared to argue his case, but Gincie took away his thunder. "I agree, but she's not going to. How do you propose to accomplish this? We can't kidnap her."

He was so relieved that his mother was on his side, he told her his plan without hesitation. "It isn't fair, but it will work. Lexy can make sure that George's name—not her real name, just 'George' and the fact that 'he' was a beard—gets into the papers. If what Georgie did to save Pharaoh is made public, it will be that much more impossible for her to go back to her old life. I believe the men who went after her today will come after her again, anyway, but she'll believe it, too, if the report is in the papers. I'm certain she's alone now that her friend is dead. Living a lie the way she was doing, there couldn't have been too many people who were very close to her, though maybe some at the tracks know and have just looked the other way."

"If Lexy or Hawk won't do it, we'll find another way to get the story out," Gincie said. "But you do understand how angry Georgie's going to be?"

Tay nodded. "I know it will take time, but I hope she'll forgive us when she finds a better life at Wild Swan."

Gincie looked into her son's eyes and felt her heart skip a beat. "Oh, my dear, go carefully. She's had such a strange life; even from the little we know of her, that is plain. You can't expect her to want the same things you want."

Tay didn't bother to deny that Georgie had touched him in some special way, and he was relieved when Lexy went along with his plan without protest.

"I'll do it myself. It's up to me to write the article rather than letting someone else report what happened and get it wrong. Hawk will help; Pharaoh's fame makes this more than sporting news. I agree with you; Georgie can't stay here." Briefly she told Tay about her visit to the outlaw track. "I've never seen such a collection of rough types in one place, not even in some of the worst parts of cities. I cannot bear to think of Georgie being hunted down by brutes like those."

"You know she may never forgive you or Hawk," Tay persisted.

Lexy shrugged. "At least she'll be alive to dislike us. Papa has taken care of Simon. He made sure the police talked to the child, and then he gave Simon's mother a thousand dollars and told her that even though he didn't think the men would come after her son, it would be better if she and the boy went away for a while. He said she looked as if she'd witnessed the ecstasy of the Second Coming, and he doesn't think she'll be taking her friend with her. Simon didn't say much about him, but he doesn't seem to like the man, so perhaps something good has come out of all of this."

"A new life for Simon and his mother, and a new life for Georgie," Tay mused, and he missed the sharp look Lexy gave him. She noticed the special note in his voice, the softness in his eyes when he said Georgie's name, and like her mother, she feared for him. Tay had always collected the helpless and the hurt, but this was different. This was not a broken-winged bird or a child no one else would play with; this was a very complex young woman who had already found her way into Tay's heart, even if he weren't aware of it.

Because of their inside information, Lexy and Hawk managed the story not only for the *Witness*, but for major New York papers, those of other cities, and for the sporting gazettes. They did it with the same professionalism with which they approached any story, but they admitted the strangeness of it.

"At one moment, I feel as objective as the words I'm writing, and in the next I realize all over again that this is my family I'm discussing," Lexy told Hawk.

"I'm in no better case," Hawk confessed. "I might have been able to consider them dispassionately once upon a time, but certainly not since I married you. And what a story it is! There are thousands of people out there who normally don't give a damn about racehorses, but they care about Pharaoh. I doubt very much that the villains of this piece are going to want their identities known, and that's all to the good. If they have to stay in hiding and mind their own skins, they will be less able to go looking for Georgie, at least not right now."

"If Mother and Tay prevail, it won't matter anyway because George is going to disappear under Georgie's skirts."

For Georgie, everything narrowed to a nightmarish tunnel where there was no light, no sign of where she had entered or of where she was going to get out. She just seemed to be marching along at the Culhanes' direction, their kindness and concern muffling her in a soft darkness she could not combat.

She consented to stay at the hotel with them because she knew if she tried to leave, she would collapse. The blow that had knocked her unconscious had left her dizzy and disoriented, but clear enough to remember that Charlie wouldn't be waiting outside for her. The Culhanes so obviously wanted to help, she decided reluctantly to let them because she had no choice.

But she had every intention of returning to her life, even without Charlie, as soon as she could. She had no doubt that the public concern would be for the attempt on Pharaoh, not for the murder of Charlie, but she appreciated the fact that Lexy questioned her closely about the man, wanting to know everything possible in order that she could write about him.

Georgie repeated the story of how Charlie had been rendered mute, and then she said, "It robbed him of his voice, but not his heart. He was so big and looked so dangerous, but he was a gentle man. He never wanted to hurt anyone, but he would have given his life for me." She stopped, swallowing hard. "He did give his life for me. I shouldn't have let him out of my sight, but we weren't always together. He would never take a room in a boardinghouse; he always found some place to stay at the racetracks. Here, he was staying in that barn. The owners and trainers liked having him around because he was so good with the horses and because he kept things settled down just by his presence. Charlie has watched over me ever since my father died nearly five years ago." Her voice trailed away as images of her friend tumbled about in her mind.

Lexy wrote at length about the man called Charlie. He reminded her of the stories about Samson at Wild Swan. Both had been hideously maltreated; both had returned kindness and loyalty instead of hate; and both had given their lives for others. The tribute she wrote was as much for Samson as for Charlie.

Georgie was still with the Culhanes when the first pieces by Lexy and Hawk were published, and she recognized the betrayal immediately.

"I wanted people to know about Charlie, but not about me!" she gasped. Lexy and Gincie were with her, but it was Lexy who received the brunt of her anger. "You knew! You knew when you wrote this what it would do! I can't go back to my life now!"

"You can't go back anyway," Lexy said. "The men who killed Charlie surely lost a fortune because of you. Do you think they will just leave you alone? You couldn't even go to Charlie's burial."

Travis had arranged for that, as he had arranged for so much else, and Georgie had had to accept that she couldn't be there. But she had trusted that within a reasonable amount of time, the killers would cease to plot revenge against her and move on to other mischief. Now she saw how childish that hope had been. Even if the killers were to disappear from the face of the earth, she could still not go back. Though she had done the right thing in going to the Culhanes with the information, and though the vast majority of the men she dealt with as a betting intermediary believed in fair races, they also relied on the absolute discretion of the beards. And she had violated that trust.

Lexy knew exactly what she was thinking. "The police know of your involvement, and so do the track stewards; you spoke to them. Do you think word won't get around about how you helped us?"

"Lexy and Hawk wrote about you, but Travis and I approved," Gincie admitted. "We can't just leave you here! We want you to come with us to Maryland."

Georgie stared at first one woman and then the other, at the faces that were so alike. At that moment, she thought they were both crazy women. Going to Maryland with them had never occurred to her.

"The racing season in Maryland is very short. I make my living at racetracks," Georgie said flatly.

"I am not asking you to go to the racetracks," Gincie countered. "My husband and I want you to go home with us to Wild Swan."

"To do what?" Georgie asked, her voice still dead.

"To do whatever suits you, but most of all to allow us to repay as well as we can what you did for us." On further consideration, she and Travis had decided not to offer Georgie money for fear she would take it and bolt into danger. Instead, the money would be there for her later, to do with as she wished. "Wild Swan has some of the best racehorses in the country. Pharaoh has proved that, and you helped him to do it. It would not be such a different world for you." And then very gently she added, "Even if nothing untoward had happened, your disguise could not have lasted forever, you know. You are a young woman, not a young man."

Georgie opened her mouth to protest and then closed it again. And in the end she went with the Culhanes because she was too bruised, dazed, and disoriented to think of what else to do.

Help for the project of getting Georgie away undetected came from an odd source, from Rosalind and her chaperone.

Gincie was resigned to the bad report Edith Chapman, the chaperone, was surely going to carry back to Boston. The small, neat woman had been a silent ghost at Rosalind's side, saying little despite Gincie's attempts to draw her out, but her dark eyes had been taking everything in, and Edith was beside Rosalind when the young woman offered her services.

"Georgie can hardly go out shopping the way things are, and she can't leave in the clothes she's got. She needs another disguise. Well, not really a disguise," she giggled, "since she's really a girl. Anyway, Cousin Edith and I are altering a few things of mine for her. They'll do until she's safely at Wild Swan. It was really Cousin Edith's idea."

"And because her hair is a problem, as short as it is, I took the liberty of purchasing a wig for her," Edith said. "I don't think anyone would ever suspect it wasn't for me. I played the part of a vain old woman quite well, if I do say so."

She laughed aloud at the look of surprise Gincie wasn't able to hide, and then she sobered. "Mrs. Culhane, I appreciate what Rosalind's family does for me, but nonetheless, my life is normally very, very dull. I regret that there has been violence connected to your splendid horse, but I don't regret being part of the adventure, and you may be assured that Rosalind's parents will hear only good of the Culhanes from me."

When Gincie related this conversation to Travis, he asked with wry humor, "Are you sure that's what we want?"

"Rosalind isn't so awful," Gincie protested, "a bit dim, but very, very kind. Kace could do much worse." As she said it, she wondered if her son could really bear the constant companionship of a woman who did so little thinking.

Georgie was more horrified than pleased when the clothes were presented to her. Up until then she had gotten by with her suit of clothes, brushed off as well as possible, with a shirt lent to her by Tay, and by washing her smallclothes at night. She had assumed that somehow her clothing would be fetched from the boardinghouse; she had refused to think of dressing as a female.

In fact, Hawk had gone to her quarters and, under the guise of pursuing the story, had bribed and sweet-talked the landlady into leaving him alone in the room. He had then pocketed the few personal items he was able to find, such as the photographs of Georgie's parents and Charlie. Georgie had had to trust him enough to ask him to bring the volumes of Shakespeare and the Bible where she had hidden her money, confident that the landlady was not the sort to search books. Hawk had managed to smuggle the books out, but he had brought no clothes, and now Georgie had to face the truth that the Culhanes truly intended she leave her identity as a young man behind.

She felt suffocated by the women—Gincie, Lexy, Rosalind, and Edith—watching her so anxiously, and she glared at Lexy with particular venom, wanting to blame her for her predicament though something inside of her insisted that she herself had precipitated the whole mess by overhearing the poison plot. But Rosalind was her undoing.

"Of course they aren't as nice as things you would choose for yourself, but Cousin Edith and I have tried very hard to make sure they'll fit you. Without being able to measure you, it was a little difficult, you see. But we hope they'll do just until you get to Maryland," Rosalind offered nervously.

Rosalind was everything Georgie had never been and wanted never to be—helpless, fluttery, soft. But it was those very characteristics that made Georgie feel protective toward her. To her mind, Rosalind was so unfit for survival, she would always need people to help her along, and in return she would give cheer and kindness. It wasn't the best exchange Georgie could think of, but it wasn't the worst either, and at the very least, Rosalind was not the sort deliberately to hurt anyone.

It did not occur to Georgie that her attitude stemmed from Kace Culhane's. Kace treasured Rosalind; therefore, Georgie would do the same. The first thing she had seen when she had come to had been Kace bending over her, calling her "sweetheart." It had given her a peculiar feeling, something beyond dismay that her disguise had been discovered, but which she had no frame of reference to understand. It was as if everything had suddenly slipped into a foreign tongue she could not decipher.

Despite her pose, Georgie did not think of herself as a young man. Her own body was a constant reminder that she was not, no matter how she dressed. But denied all the attention most young girls received simply because they were female, Georgie did not think of herself as a woman, either. She was accustomed to being an observer of all the foolishness between men and women, not a participant in the game.

She did not puzzle out the reasons. It was enough that Kace's lady wanted her to wear these clothes.

With Rosalind's help, she donned a blue dress with a fitted bodice that curved down below her waist in the front while the softly draped skirt was extended in the back by a small bustle. It was, by Rosalind's standards, a very simple day dress. But to Georgie, it was so heavy and complicated, she could not imagine why women allowed themselves to be so imprisoned. But she stood patiently while Rosalind danced around her.

"You look lovely! You're so slender, you don't even need a corset. This blue is a little pale for you—you have the coloring to wear stronger shades—but still, it becomes you."

Georgie looked at herself in the mirror and blushed in embarrassment. In her own eyes, she looked like a child playing grown-up in clothes borrowed from her mother.

It was some comfort that the others did not seem to perceive her that way when she was presented to them. Their looks of astonished pleasure seemed genuine.

Her cheeks turned deeper rose when Kace exclaimed, "Goodbye, George! Hello, Georgiana!" and swept her an elaborate bow. She didn't notice the stunned look on Tay's face. She found she was sorry that Kace would not be going back to Wild Swan with his parents but would instead be returning to Massachusetts and college. Tay would also be going back to school.

For honor's sake, Tay had explained to Georgie that it had been his idea, not Lexy's, to include the information about "George." It had been an ordeal for him to tell her because he desperately wanted her to like him. But to his relief, her reaction had been mild.

"Your family is very good at getting what they want," she had said. Actually, even her resentment toward Lexy was easing, impossible to sustain in face of such relentless care for her well-being.

She realized that she was giving her life into the Culhanes' keeping for the time being, and seeing no sensible alternative, she ceased to battle against it.

The most haunting thing about her departure from the state of New York was the ease with which it was accomplished. With Charlie gone, there were no close ties to break. Eventually the landlady would clean out her room and sell what was left there. There would be some grumbling among the bettors when their dependable agent did not reappear, but that was all.

Georgie was too honest to ignore the comparison between the indifference of her old life and the welcome the Culhanes were offering. Dressed in the finery that continued to feel utterly strange, she went south on the train with them with more anticipation than she had felt in years.

Chapter 40

Georgie fell in love with Wild Swan at first sight. She had heard of the legendary farm for years, but nothing had prepared her for the reality of it. The white fences and well-kept buildings, the harmony of the workers, black and white, the air of serenity that pervaded the place, and most of all the horses—the glorious heart of the farm— everything conspired to steal Georgie's heart.

Gincie and Travis had expected to deal with a resentful young woman for some time to come, so they watched in wonder as Georgie blossomed by the day. And in exchange for their care, she offered them her trust, and they learned more about her than anyone had since her father died.

Her parents had brought her with them from England when she was seven years old, but her mother, never very strong, had died two years later. Georgie had adored her father, but she was clear-sighted about him. He had been a miracle worker with horses and jockeys, able to train both to perform to the best of their abilities. But he had a fatal flaw. He was unable to control his thirst for strong drink, and his binges had made him so unreliable that he had moved from one job to another.

It had not been quite so bad when his wife was alive, but once she had died, he lost all control. He had tried to do the right thing for his daughter by placing her in the care of a woman who had children of her own, but when he had returned for a visit, he had discovered that Georgie was being treated worse than a scullery maid, spending her days scampering from one chore to the next and receiving little more than harsh words and harsher blows for her trouble. By then Charlie was with him, and the two men took the thin, bruised little girl with them.

The three had benefited from each other's company. Georgie's father had tried harder to stay off the bottle in order to care for his child, and Charlie had been there to do his own work and what he could of Mr. Cheney's when Georgie's father succumbed to temptation. They worked at various horse farms and at the tracks, and Georgie became George because it was easier and safer. People got used to seeing the little boy with the two men, and they often tossed him coins for the odd jobs he did around the stables. If they had any comment to make about the child, it was that he was nearly as handy with horses as his father and a good deal more reliable.

But Randall Cheney had destroyed his health, and when Georgie was twelve, he died.

"I know he loved me," she said softly. "And he was always very kind to me. But he missed my mother terribly. He always said she was the only thing that ever made sense in his life. He was the younger son of a good family, you see, and my mother was a parson's daughter. By his own admission, Papa was a wild youth, but he fell in love with Mother, as quiet and proper as she was. Both families forbade them to marry, so they ran away. And though Papa had spent some time at university, horses were really all he knew or cared about besides Mama. I think he tried to stay alive for me, but without her, it was just too hard for him."

Charlie had continued to watch over Georgie after Mr. Cheney died; it was a perfectly acceptable situation because no one knew Georgie was a girl. And Georgie, who had long acted as a messenger for the horsemen, fell quite naturally into carrying their bets for them, too, at first because it amused them and then because they grew to depend on the youngster's honesty. And though they would never admit it, quite a few of them came to think of the boy as lucky for them. They paid him to place their bets, and sometimes, when they did very well, they gave him a bonus. The racing season in New York State was usually lucrative for Georgie, but the money didn't always last through the months when the tracks weren't operating. During that time, Georgie and Charlie usually found work at various stud farms in the Northeast.

"My grandmother Alex would have liked you," Gincie said, and she told her the story of Alex and St. John, whose marriage had been greeted with the same lack of parental support, plus a problem with the law. She did it deliberately to make Georgie feel at home and to make it seem more possible for the girl to enjoy being female. It was the one area where progress was uncertain at best.

Georgie considered dressing as a girl to be part of the price she had to pay for being at Wild Swan, but it remained just that—a price, not a pleasure. She was going to be seventeen in November, and she had had no close female companionship since her mother had died when she was nine. In her view, being female meant a loss of freedom and no advantage. She wore feminine garb when she had to, but she continued to walk with the long stride of a boy, a habit that frequently tangled her legs in her skirts.

Her hair was growing out, but it had a way to go before it was going to look decent.

She was happiest when she was allowed to don boy's clothing and work with the horses. There, no one could fault her. She had the magic. If she hadn't been a girl and too tall now, she would have made a good jockey.

Once they had tested her skill, Travis and Gincie allowed her to take the horses out for training. It was the best reward they could offer her for her efforts to acquire the feminine graces.

Gincie was willing to admit that men had many advantages in society and before the law. But she wanted Georgie to know that it was possible to live a full, intelligent, and productive life as a woman. She was proud of the proof she had to offer, not only in her own role as mistress of Wild Swan and Sunrise, but in Sam's management of Brookhaven, Anthea's practice of medicine, Philly's teaching, and Lexy's role as a journalist. Even Sally and Mercy, whose lives were more traditional, were partners in all the major decisions made regarding their families.

At first Georgie was painfully shy with the women, unused to such company and, beyond that, afraid they would question her right to be at Wild Swan, but each of them went out of her way to praise Georgie's saving of Pharaoh and then to treat her as if there were nothing unusual in how she had come to be part of the family.

Georgie had had no formal education, but she was well read in the classics. Both of her parents had insisted that she study as much as they knew to teach her, and whatever else their backgrounds had lacked, it had not been access to books. In this, her upbringing was like Hawk's. She could read Latin at a fairly high level, though she confessed regretfully that she had made little progress in Greek.

"It wasn't Papa's favorite subject, and Mama hadn't studied it at all, so I never got very far with it."

Though her reading was varied and included everything from Shakespeare to newspapers to veterinary manuals, her wandering life had not allowed for the encumbrance of a library to be transported from one place to another, so the privilege of reading anything from Wild Swan's extensive collection was one she enjoyed as much as working with the horses.

In the domestic arts, Georgie was not so learned. Whatever her mother had taught her of sewing, cooking, and the like had slipped from her memory. In this she found a rueful ally in Philly.

"I've always been hopeless in such matters," Philly admitted. "When I first married Blaine, I felt inadequate all of the time because I couldn't cook even a simple meal without destroying it. Bless his heart, he never complained. But I have gotten somewhat better since then; not much, mind you, but a little. And I do think there is good reason to learn how to do those things, tedious though they may be. I am fortunate that I don't have to run an enterprise like Wild Swan."

"Why would that make a difference? There are people hired to do all of those things," Georgie reasoned.

"That's true enough. But what sort of influence could one have on such a staff if one didn't begin by knowing how the job ought to be done? It's not the same as my little household; the farms are like small towns."

Georgie conceded the point, and she did her best to pay attention to Della's instructions in the kitchen. Most of the cooking was now done by younger workers, but Della, ancient as she was, still carried herself upright, her mind was clear, and her word was law in the kitchen and elsewhere when she had a mind to exercise her seniority.

The cooking lessons were made bearable to Georgie by the friendship that quickly developed between herself and Della. The old woman's long history at Wild Swan fascinated her, and Della was equally captivated by the young girl. As far as Della was concerned, it didn't matter where the Culhanes had found her: the child belonged at Wild Swan.

Georgie's sessions with needle and thread were not so felicitous. At least when she cooked she could enjoy the results because Della was there to keep them from going too wrong. But since she cared so little for clothing, she could muster no interest in setting one stitch after another, whether by hand or by machine. Still, she kept at it doggedly to please Gincie.

Despite what Philly had said, Georgie did not really believe that the domestic arts were going to figure in her future life. She let herself drift from one day to the next at Wild Swan, but she did not for an instant assume that this was to be her life from now on. It was a splendid but temporary refuge, and someday she was going to have to leave and get on with her own life.

The family did not feel that way, but they tried not to smother Georgie with their growing love. It was difficult. Though she did not view it so, in their eyes, Georgie had been deprived of much they could so easily give her—a sense of security and family. She seemed so alone, it was hard not to hug her close and shower her with promises that from now on she would have roots in this particular place with this particular family.

For Lexy, Georgie was a unique experience. Lexy had expected that the younger woman's resentment would take some time to fade, but Georgie was too fair-minded for that, and once she had seen that the Culhanes were truly concerned for her welfare, she had relinquished her anger. Georgie had had to adjust to so many things in her life, she had long since learned to be adaptable. Lexy admired that trait in her and wished she had more of it herself. There were a lot of things about Georgie that charmed Lexy, and before long she found she was regarding her as a little sister.

There had been a few girls among the children of the workers on the farm, but most of the offspring had been male, and the children she and the twins played with most often had been the McCoy brothers. Even as children, she and Jilly hadn't been the best of friends; she was much closer to her cousin Joseph. She had had some good female friends in college, such as Lorna Tilitson, but she had never had a female counterpart of herself in the family. Now it was as if she had a sister six years younger than she—a perfect gap in their ages that allowed for caring without rivalry.

She was able to see Georgie in an entirely different light, as well, as a sister-in-law, married to Tay, but she kept that thought to herself. Tay was a long way from considering marriage, and Georgie wasn't convinced yet that she wanted to be a woman, which made the chance that the two would become romantically involved remote. And to that she added the fact of Kace's choice of Rosalind. If one brother could fall in love with such a piece of fluff, why not the other?

Georgie was never going to be a Rosalind. She was too curious, too intelligent, too used to being responsible. And she was never going to look as decorative as Rosalind, either. But in her own way, she was beautiful and was going to grow more lovely with the years. Lexy had noticed her strange eyes even when Georgie had been disguised as a man, and now with her face scrubbed clean of the heavy brows and mock shadow of whiskers, the eyes dominated the fine-boned face. The combination of amber, gold, and brown was much lighter than Hawk's eyes and definitely more feminine, protected as they were by thick dark lashes and set under softly arched brows.

Everything about Georgie was delicately attenuated, belying the strength she displayed when she was working with fractious foals in the nursery or keeping an overly anxious racehorse in check.

Lexy tried not to make the comparison, but she could not deny that it was much more interesting to be in Georgie's company than in Rosalind's.

She spent more time than usual at Wild Swan because Hawk was gone much of the time, covering the contest for the presidency. As Abby Adams, she wrote a few columns about the parallel campaign of the Equal Rights Party and other movements dedicated to gaining political rights and power for women, but at best, what supporters of these parties demanded would not be granted for decades, and at worst, the agitation drew the cruelest kind of derision, scorn that questioned the right of the campaigners to call themselves women at all. The inescapable truth was that those in power would not give up power easily.

Georgie, with her heritage of respect for the printed word, enjoyed talking to Lexy about her reporting, and she had the added advantage of understanding the sporting news as well as the political. But these days it was often the latter that interested her the most.

"You report it, so you must see it more clearly than most; men have so many advantages over women," she argued.

"I can't deny that, but things are changing, albeit very slowly. There are parts of the West where women can vote, and little by little, women are entering the professions. But no matter what injustices there are, being a woman is not a choice; it is the way I was born, the way you were born," Lexy reminded her. "To pretend otherwise is to deny the birthright of being part of half of the human race and means an uneasy pretense of being part of the other half. You couldn't have done it forever, you know; you are too beautiful. You would have become more and more odd as a man."

She saw the flare of panic in Georgie's eyes and understood that the girl still had some hope of going back to her old way of life.

"You don't want to accept it yet, but you are a beautiful woman," she repeated. "And I swear to you, being a woman is no bad thing. I am not less capable of rational thought and productive work because of my sex, and thus, it is enough to be a human being, male or female. But were I not a woman, Hawk and I would not be together. Loving a good man and being loved by him is surely one of the benefits of being a woman, though not the only thing to do with one's life."

"For you, because of the way Hawk is, that is true, but from what I've seen, many men want women who do not think at all," Georgie said. The words were without rancor, sad and resigned.

Lexy had expected more panic at the topic, and so it took a moment for the full import of what Georgie was saying to dawn on her. The girl was attracted to one of the twins, to the wrong one, to Kace. Her stomach did a turn at the thought. Kace was clearly attracted to women of an altogether different sort. And Tay, Lexy was sure, was already developing a crush on Georgie that had nothing to do with brotherly love. She nearly groaned aloud, considering the contrariness of love.

The grave face of Michael Winterbourne appeared in her mind. He would have made a wonderful husband, and she could have been a good wife to him, but there was Hawk. For her, there had always been Hawk from the day she had met him.

And to her joy, she had more time with Hawk once the presidential election was over. Cleveland won the popular vote by more than a hundred thousand votes, but Benjamin Harrison, a rather dull Indiana lawyer, won by sixty-five votes in the electoral college and thus won the election. As Hawk and others had predicted, the issue of high tariffs and an overflowing treasury had defeated Cleveland. His mild attempt to lower tariffs had been labeled free trade, and dire predictions had been made about how American workers would be overwhelmed by the "pauper labor of Europe" if tariffs were not high enough to keep foreign products out, or at least to make them prohibitively expensive.

But with a touch of guilt for her lack of civic concern, Lexy found she didn't care nearly as much about the election as she did about having Hawk home again.

November also brought the celebration of Georgie's seventeenth birthday. The family tried not to overwhelm her, but they still managed to make the day hers. And the day after that, Travis had a rather formal interview with her during which he set her wages and informed her that he and Gincie were not willing to listen to any protests unless Georgie thought the figure too low.

"It isn't too low, Mr. Culhane. You know how generous you are being. But it isn't necessary; it isn't even fair. Mrs. Culhane and the other women have filled my wardrobe with clothing; I pay nothing for food and lodging, and I still have my earnings from the season."

"You wear the clothes to please my wife," Travis said bluntly. "And food and lodgin' are normal provisions for kidnap victims, if the captors have any decency at all. Your earnin's from previous employment have nothin' to do with your work here. And work it is, though you enjoy it. You're one of the best horse trainers we've ever seen. That alone would make you worth what I am offerin'. But you're absolutely right to suspect it goes beyond that. Gincie and I, and the rest of the family, have grown very fond of you. We don't want you to leave us. But you are used to workin' and bein' paid for it, and it seems reasonable that that apply here." He did not mention the prize money set aside for her, but he did add, "I know you don't care to be reminded, but Pharaoh ran his race and won nearly forty-one thousand dollars. It's a pretty sure thing that wouldn't have happened without you. More'n likely Pharaoh would have died."

Georgie knew that she would not have let anything sway her if she had wanted to leave Wild Swan, but she didn't, so she allowed everything he said to make sense. She put out her hand, and Travis offered his just as gravely so that they could shake on the bargain. But when she had left the study, he allowed himself a tender smile. He, like Gincie, was finding it easier and easier to think of Georgie as their fourth child.

It was even easier to imagine at Christmas when the twins were home, and Lexy spent as much time as she could at the farm. Rosalind was visiting, too, again with her cousin in attendance, and Hawk was there part of the time, but the twins, Lexy, and Georgie were the ones who never tired of talking farm business or of riding out on the crisp winter mornings, saluting the swans when they flew over.

The exchange of Christmas gifts was telling. While Georgie gave each of the twins carefully selected books—generous gifts, but ones which could not be misconstrued as being too personal—Kace gave her a shawl of brightly patterned silk. On the surface it appeared to be a personal gift, but it wasn't. It had been chosen by Rosalind, and it suited her idea and Kace's of what a young girl should want, having little to do with Georgie's taste, though she was gracious in her thanks. On the other hand, Tay gave her the latest edition of Dr. Law's *Farmer's Veterinary Adviser*, the noted textbook used by veterinary students and stockmen alike. Wild Swan's library included the book, but this was for Georgie's own use, to study and to write in as she wished. It was a perfect and intensely personal gift because it indicated how well Tay understood her and how much he approved of Georgie just the way she was.

It made Lexy want to weep for her brother's thoughtfulness, and she felt as sad and touched for Georgie, who took special pains during the holidays to dress as femininely as possible, though she could not bring herself to give up her breeches when she was riding or working around the horses. Lexy gave thanks for that; she didn't think she could bear to see Georgie trying to accomplish her work in a prim riding habit or such just so that she could feel she was living up to Kace's standards.

Georgie continued to treat Rosalind with patience and kindness; her code of honor demanded no less, and so little threat did Rosalind see in the younger woman, she was perfectly happy when Kace rode off with Georgie and the others; anything, as long as she herself did not have to climb aboard a horse. Kace insisted that she would eventually come to see the pleasures of riding, but Lexy doubted it. Rosalind regarded horses as if they were fire-breathing dragons.

The group went often to Sunrise, where the atmosphere had been enlivened by Willy McCoy's marriage to a young woman named Lizzie Carson. She came from a farming family in the western part of the state and knew as much about livestock and crops as the McCoys did. She was a small, lively woman whose laughter rang out often. Willy was more than content, and now he could greet Lexy without the constraint that had characterized their earlier relationship.

"Are you jealous now that your first beau has found another?" Kace teased.

"No, infinitely relieved," Lexy shot back. "For a while, I thought I might have to find a wife for him myself. It's difficult to be around someone who cares too much when you haven't any feelings in that direction." She was instantly sorry she'd said it, and she winced inwardly at the identically closed, thoughtful looks both Georgie and Tay wore, but there was nothing she could do about calling the words back. And then she told herself that becoming overly cautious in their company wasn't going to improve matters. Hard as it was, she had to accept that everyone, even her brothers and Georgie, about whom she cared so much, had to make his or her own choices. For her own part, she was profoundly grateful that Hawk was her choice.

Jilly and Dermot had come home for Christmas, beaming with the news that they were to be parents in the new year. Lexy no longer worried about what kind of parents the child would find. Jilly was singing for charity and giving lessons, and even the prospect of having to suspend her activities for childbearing did not infringe on her new serenity.

"I'll find a way to do both," she announced confidently. "And it will be lovely to have a baby to sing to."

Jilly was not so naive as to believe she would ever experience the full use of her talent, but she was also aware of the benefits of her compromise. She wanted, more than ever, to be Dermot's wife and to bear his children, and she had matured enough to understand that she could never have done these things while appearing on a public stage, no matter how indulgent Dermot was.

For Lexy, it was much easier to be with Jilly now that the old animosities had been wiped away by the shared disaster of the blizzard. But for Hawk, it was not quite as comfortable. Both Jilly and Dermot continued to treat him as if he were a knight from a storybook.

"You are their hero, you know," Lexy told him when he complained that he could hear his armor clanking. "Without you, Jilly would be a widow. Instead, she and Dermot are happy and expecting a child. You're my hero, too," she sighed, batting her eyelashes at him and pretending to swoon.

"Lord, don't do that! I'll think I'm married to Rosalind," Hawk laughed.

Lexy laughed with him, but she thought again of choices. Michael Winterbourne had not yet married, but Lexy had been glad to hear through Gwenny that at least he was seeing a woman of whom the Bettingdons approved and that he was no longer as coldly alone as he had been.

Lexy saw no reason to discuss this with Hawk, nor did they talk about the Fordyces, who were mentioned in the social columns in December because they were leaving the capital to go back to California. Lexy trusted Hawk enough to know that he had had no further contact with Caroline and Jared, but she wondered how he felt about his son moving so far from him; she wondered whether he allowed himself to think of Jared at all. In some ways, Hawk was more disciplined than she. It was possible that he had simply closed that chapter of his life for Jared's sake, and for the sake of his own sanity. Lexy tried to do the same, telling herself it was Hawk's past, not hers, but Jared's existence made her feel guilty, as if she should be having children to fill his place in Hawk's life.

Rationally she knew that was no reason to have a child, but there was a world of things about loving and marriage that had little to do with what was rational. Hawk was not pressuring her to have children, but she knew he would like to have them someday. He was endlessly patient with Adam and Mercy's and Nigel and Sally's children. But no matter how good he was with them, she knew it would be her own life which would be changed the most by additions to their family. She wasn't ready for that to happen. She cared passionately about her work, even about the social and sporting news, which might seem frivolous to some but which reflected a good deal about the age. And she cared passionately for Hawk.

It made her uneasy when she examined it too closely, but there was a fear deep inside her, a fear that children would separate her and Hawk in some fundamental way, rather than drawing them together. Their work required that they be physically apart, but because their minds were engaged in the same activity, the inner distance was never that great. They remained intimately linked mentally, and when they were together that translated easily into physical intimacy. She could not at this point imagine expanding the close circle of their loving without breaking it.

As much as she loved her work and could not think of living without it, she could see the advantages of her parents' way of life. Living and working together on the land allowed room for young, growing things, including children. Though Travis was away in California occasionally, and though he had also gone to the races a few times without Gincie, most of their days were spent together.

When she considered it, Lexy remembered that her father had had as much to do with raising her and her brothers as had their mother. And there had been the large staff of Wild Swan, and the staff in California before that, to share in the burden of making children feel secure and loved.

But her life with Hawk was not the same. They didn't live on land where the children could run wild, and they weren't ever going to have a large staff. Ironically, if they were suddenly gifted with such a life, they would have to spend their time managing everything as her parents did, and their lives as journalists would be over.

While Lexy could find no easy answers, Rosalind seemed to have no similar problem. She loved being with the children, and she was so childlike herself, they whispered their secrets to her and played with abandon in her company.

"I want a big family," she announced, smiling demurely at Kace, who grinned back and said, "That's an idea that deserves some work."

They were so openly adoring of each other, their New Year's Eve announcement that they planned to marry as soon as Kace graduated in the coming year was no surprise. Kace had already obtained Rosalind's parents' permission, and he had spoken to his own parents before telling everyone else.

There was little Gincie and Travis could say. They wished Rosalind were a little brighter, a little more capable, but she was from a good family, was sweet natured, and loved Kace. Nor could they object that the couple was too young. Kace would be turning twenty-one, finishing college, and taking over the management of Sunrise; he was surely man enough to take a wife, and Rosalind was not a child, at least not chronologically.

So the couple was toasted with fine champagne. Georgie was there with everyone else to wish them all good things, and Tay did not allow his smile to falter as he hugged his twin and clapped him on the back.

Chapter 41

In February, Hawk and Lexy went south together, and Joseph went with them.

The initial idea had been Lexy's, born of the notion that much that had been right about the South before the war had been because of the women and that much that had gone wrong since was also in their domain. Before the war, they had been the ones who had been most closely tied to the daily lives of the slaves, most likely to doctor the illnesses and injuries inflicted by the system. Despite enjoying the life provided by slaves waiting on them every moment of the day, they had expressed their unease to each other in letters and in journals which had, in some cases, reached a wide audience by being published.

But since the war, a collective loss of memory seemed to have developed so that how terrible slavery had been was forgotten and an impossibly golden kingdom full of perfect knights and gentle ladies was remembered. And women seemed to be the keepers of the dreams, the ones who wrote endless letters to newspapers begging for tribute for the multitude of dead who had worn the gray. It was the women who formed the societies, raised money for monuments, and mourned past glories.

"It doesn't seem that harmful, just a way to ease the awful loss of brothers, sweethearts, cousins, husbands, fathers—so many men and a whole way of life—but I think it *is* harmful," Lexy said, sounding out the idea for the story with Hawk. "It's as if the surface gentility gives permission for the darker things underneath, for the abuse of blacks and the denial of progress and justice. It's nearly twenty-five years since the war ended."

"I don't disagree with anything you say, but I think you need to know exactly what you seek to accomplish by writing about it," Hawk cautioned. "The relationship between the North and the South is still strained."

"Responsibility," Lexy said softly. "If women are to have the rights and privileges of full citizenship, then they must also bear the responsibilities. You know all the stories about how slaves used to undermine their work, slowing it almost to a standstill when the overseer looked away, making a simple task complicated and time-consuming to protest in the only way open to them. Well, I think women do it, too, in various ways, some of them self-destructive. Anthea sees countless women who are so addicted to patent medicines full of alcohol and opium, they haven't had a sober day in years. I understand that poor health or sometimes lives that are just too constricted drive more than a few to it, but I think many are simply willing to pay any price rather than take responsibility for their own lives. It is seductive, the idea of being cared for as if one is a child or an exotic plant. I think part of what Southern women are trying to preserve is the right to that kind of coddling. But in doing that, they also send the South backward, impeding progress at every turn, progress for blacks and whites. One certainly sees no agitation for women's rights in the South, or indeed, for rights for anyone who is not white and male."

"There are aspects of Southern politics, particularly on the local level, that I would like to see firsthand. Perhaps we can make this journey together," Hawk said, and was rewarded by her instant enthusiasm for the idea.

He did want to do the story, but his primary motive for accompanying her was something he had no intention of discussing with her. Though the South was supposedly notable for its chivalrous treatment of women, he did not want Lexy to go there alone. Abby Adams was not the type of woman who was welcome in the South, and he hoped that Lexy would be less likely to betray that side of herself if he were with her.

Reid listened to their proposal with grave attention. "It's never going to be easy." His voice was weary, devoid of its usual energy. "The South fired the first shot, and they were beaten. But it isn't as if the conflict were between foreign powers, so that the vanquished could be sent away, or borders drawn between us and guarded. They were Americans before the war and afterward, our brothers always. Family fights are always the most vicious, particularly when neither side admits fault or defeat. And there has surely been fault on both sides. The failure of Reconstruction is proof that the North did not, in the end, care enough about the fate of the freed slaves to insure justice for them. That's scarcely different from the women in the South who once spoke of slavery's abuses and yet were not, after all, willing to give up its benefits. It's always a question of whose ox is gored."

He thought about the paper's policy toward the South, and he wasn't entirely pleased. There had never been a conscious decision made to placate that region of the country; Reid had reported and condemned the most vicious acts of the night riders, but generally, the *Witness* had followed the path of other papers by turning a blind eye to the willful, daily violation of federal law. It was no less than a policy of appeasement designed to allow the disparate halves of the country to coexist. And the most basic justification of it was that no one wanted another war.

Reid still had nightmares about what he had seen as a correspondent on the battlefields. And now he had sons, and he didn't doubt that there would be grandsons, perhaps beginning with Jilly's first child. The generation born and those yet to come were compelling reasons to avoid further conflict.

But he wondered what the cost for this avoidance would eventually be. A country that denied rights to so many people, not just to blacks, but to Indians, Orientals, and women, too, would surely have to pay a high price someday. As each generation before the war had hoped to be spared the carnage of it, so he found himself hoping his children would not see a bloody harvest as the result of justice unfulfilled in his lifetime.

He did not delude himself about changing the paper's policy regarding the South. It would go on reporting and protesting major outrages, but it would not harp on the daily oppression. He regretted his sensible cowardice even as he admitted it. And he gave the nod to the Mackennas in admiration for their refusal to accept the status quo.

"I know you'll do a good job, but have a care; they've been known to hang people they don't like down there."

"Or to burn them," Lexy said quietly.

A short while later, she had the eerie sense that just alluding to the fate of Phoebe and Aubrey had planted the idea in Max's mind, though he had not been there to hear her words. As soon as word spread through the family about the Mackennas' planned journey, Max came to them.

"I haven't spoken to Joseph yet, but I ask you to consider allowing him to go with you, if he will."

"I would think it is the last place he would want to go," Lexy pointed out.

Max's homely face held none of its usual good humor. "I am sure it is, but I think he needs to go. Anthea and I could not love him more were he our own son, and I know he loves us. But for all the years he has been with us, I believe there is still a greater part of him that is locked back in the child who saw his parents murdered. He never speaks of it, but it's there. It's there in his eyes, in his mind, and in his heart; it's there between himself and the rest of the world. I don't expect him to forget what happened. It wouldn't be healthy if he did. But I want him to view it with the eyes of a man, not through the terror of a child."

Joseph had just finished his formal medical training, taking less time than most and staying at the top of his classes. He had already begun to practice medicine with the Kingstons, Nigel, and the others at the clinic. And Lexy understood why Max deemed this trip important enough for Joseph to leave his work.

She had always been aware of the distance Joseph kept between himself and everyone else. That sort of remove from other mortals was consciously cultivated by some physicians as being appropriate to their lofty station, but that was not the way Max, Anthea, and Nigel practiced medicine. They were of the school that believed sympathy and empathy for their patients were as important as any nostrum they could prescribe. Though he did not state it aloud, Lexy understood that Max believed that unless Joseph allowed himself to be more involved, he would never be a truly fine physician, despite his brilliance.

She looked at Hawk, and he agreed. "If Joseph wishes to come with us, he will be welcome." In fact, Hawk thought it a grand idea because it would mean Lexy would have two men to escort her.

Joseph agreed to go, not because he wanted to, but because he could not imagine refusing anything Max or Anthea asked of him, not even this. They had given him so much and asked so little, if they had bid him go to Hades to fetch a bucket of water, he would have tried.

And the South was hell for him, instantly different from Maryland, for all that state's Southern characteristics.

They traveled under their own names—Mr. and Mrs. H. Mackenna and Mr. J. Edwards—but they cloaked their true purpose in a vague tale of being interested in investing in a large farm or perhaps a lumber business. When asked, Hawk was forthright about being a Westerner, though not about anything else, and Lexy was ready with vague references to the fact that her father had been a Virginian who fought for the Confederacy. She felt a twinge of guilt for making it sound as if Travis had died in the war and for the tears she manufactured, but she didn't want to be questioned too closely about her father or his military career; there were still enough horse breeders left in the South so that the Culhane name and everything that Wild Swan meant were known.

Gaining the information they wanted was horrifyingly easy. Since they were posing as investors, it was logical that they would ask about the availability of workers.

"Ain't like th' old days, but you kin get yoahsef a passel a' nigras fer little enough pay. 'Course they cain't work like white men, but you set 'em in th' right direction an' keep at 'em, th' work gits done."

". . . gotta watch 'em, else they'll steal ya blind."

". . . like children, they just can't think for themselves."

The voices blended in various accents, betraying regions and education or the lack of it, but the idea was the same, a denial of the blacks' basic humanity, a view of them as something between beasts and humans, perpetually childlike. And if there had been moral doubt toward the end of the war about defending a culture built on slave labor, that doubt seemed to have vanished from most white minds in the years since. Every soldier who had died had gained near sainthood. Over and over the Mackennas and Joseph were told that the Negroes had really been better off as slaves, cared for and guided. Slavery in white memory was an institution that had provided an industrious, protected life for the African savages. The current state of destitution and ignorance in which most Southern blacks now lived was used as proof that they were unfit for freedom or citizenship. The fact that they were denied education, decent jobs, and wages at every turn was not part of the equation.

And the sense that the good old system had been betrayed was most acute among white women who were old enough to remember how it had been in the days of slavery and how it was now. Though the black women who had cared for them or for their children and for their households had been slaves, most of the white women believed they had had a close personal relationship with their servants and were still baffled, all these years later, at how those slaves could have left them when emancipation became law. The women might be adept at manipulating things behind the scenes, but they enjoyed the pose of being delicate, helpless creatures, and maintaining that appearance required men who indulged the behavior and servants to cushion the days by doing the work. It had been far easier when the servants had been slaves.

Many of these women spoke openly with Lexy when she approached them on the basis of wanting to know how difficult it would be to staff her mythical household and when she questioned them about social opportunities. With her Confederate father, she had the proper heritage and by complaining dolefully about how difficult it was to be a good wife when efficient help was so hard to find, a household so difficult to run, she fit right in. She became one of them, a fluttery creature whose narrow life was defined by small problems enlarged in order that they might be important. Such an existence would drive her mad, but she realized it wasn't confined to the South, though it was made worse here by the old connection to slavery. Rosalind would fit right in with these women. Lexy wished the comparison between these women and her sister-in-law to be did not occur so readily.

The freed black women and their female descendants interested Lexy just as much as their former owners and their families did, but her own color was no help in this direction. Black women were no more inclined to risk telling what they were really thinking to a white woman now than they had been in the days of slavery. Lesson after lesson about the cost of getting uppity had been taught too well and often violently.

Hawk fared a little better because he concentrated on the male side, and he did find black men here and there who were willing to talk to him, usually ministers who wanted to assure someone interested in settling in the community that there was no shortage of men who needed work.

The South was still basically rural, and the land was still basically white owned, with black tenant farmers doing much of the labor. Some of the black spokesmen were willing to articulate the need for more jobs and better wages, but that was as far as they would go. The status quo was as important to them as it was to the whites, perhaps more so, because it was blacks, not whites, who were called out in the night and flogged or burned out or hanged.

In North Carolina, Hawk found one man who spoke more candidly than the others. The meeting was not by accident. Hawk searched out Jonas James because the man had served in the state legislature right after the war, before Reconstruction had failed entirely, and he had been quoted a few times in Northern newspapers as a voice of reason in that tumultuous time.

White hair framing his dark face in tight coils, Mr. James was a man of quiet dignity, and when Hawk requested an interview, he told the man his true purpose in the South. After some thought, Mr. James agreed to talk to him.

And he was forthright. He stared at Hawk for a moment, and then he said, "What you really want to know is the only thing of importance I have to tell you: why Reconstruction failed. The answer isn't complicated. There were some abuses, some black men and some white men, too, who grabbed power and made trouble with it in those days after the war, but the truth of the matter was that the South had lost the war but had had no change of heart, and the last thing on earth white Southerners wanted was to be told by Northerners how to run their states. It would have taken federal troops stationed here for generations to change that."

He paused, gazing blindly into the past. "The North never loved black men that much. And now the story going about is that it was all the fault of ignorant freedmen and greedy carpetbaggers and scalawags." His dark eyes caught and held Hawk's. "It wasn't that; there were only rare, brief times and only in the Deep South when the state legislatures were controlled by black men and Yankees. The white men who had been in power before the war were the ones who were in power again afterward, just as soon as their citizenship rights were restored. It was the heart that never changed," he repeated. "Few want to hear the truth of that time; no matter how well you write about it, there will still be few. But I thank you for listening to me."

"The honor is mine, sir," Hawk replied. What the man had told him was not new information to Hawk, but he would hear it henceforth in his mind in Jonas James's deep, soft voice, which, despite the man's beginnings in slavery, showed the precision of years of study and a deliberate movement away from the speech of the quarters. What was new was Hawk's realization of loss. He had thought in terms of what had been denied to blacks, but now he was conscious of how much was lost to whites, to everyone, by the refusal to allow an entire race to learn, progress, and contribute to society.

It made him think of his own mixed blood, of the Indians who had been so decimated since the war. He thought of the lessons those dead might have taught; he thought of the knowledge of how to live with the earth without destroying it, knowledge that was drifting away with bones turned to dust. He thought of how insane it was to be willing to lose so much because of bigotry and fear of those who are different.

Hawk was obviously not of pure Anglo-Saxon heritage, and yet, it was equally clear he was not of Negro blood either. He was also well spoken and well dressed, an outsider supposedly seeking to invest money in the South, and he, Lexy, and Joseph were treated with courtesy throughout their trip. If one were the right color, there seemed no end to the graciousness of the hospitality offered, from delicious food to impeccable service, usually provided by blacks, to comfortable hotel rooms.

Even the Georgia town where Phoebe and Aubrey had been murdered offered what it could, though in this case it was a boardinghouse run by an elderly widow.

The trio went to the town specifically for Joseph's sake, but by the time they got there, the Mackennas' dread was no less than his.

"We don't have to go there," Lexy had offered, but Joseph said, "I do have to go there. Max is right, only it's taken me this long even to begin to understand that while I've grown up, become a man, become a physician, part of me is still a small child in that place, watching my parents die."

The old images were such a nightmarish jumble in his mind, Joseph wasn't sure what to expect, but he thought at the very least there would be the memory of a guilty secret held by the town. The cruelest thing of all was that his family's tragedy seemed to have figured so little in the community's history. His name caused no stir of recognition.

He remembered clearly the location of Mr. Crowper's store, but the old man was long gone, and a different name decorated the sign.

They hired a buggy, and the Mackennas went with Joseph to where the Edwardses' house and school had been.

The land was overgrown with weeds. Nothing new had been built, and the old charred timbers were still visible here and there through the dry brambles of winter and the first touches of green spring.

Joseph stood silently for a long time, fighting back the night, and then he surrendered, letting it come to blot out the sun. Though he stood where the house had been, he saw everything as if he were small and hiding in the woods again. He saw the shrouded riders, demons in the flickering light of torches; he heard their voices and knew who they were even all these years afterward. He watched his father fall to the ground with part of his face blown away; he saw his mother run into the flames screaming his name so that the men would think that he had died, too.

He didn't know he was weeping until his throat closed, and he had to struggle for breath. He fell to his knees and pounded the earth with his fists, struggling to release the terrible flood of rage and grief.

Lexy made a movement toward Joseph, but Hawk stopped her. "Let him be."

She buried her face against Hawk's broad chest, seeking the warmth and comfort of him, trying to blunt the empathetic pain that made it too easy to imagine how it would be had her own parents perished here.

None of them was aware of how long it had been, but finally Joseph got up. His eyes were red, his face haggard, but he had found a weary peace.

"In my nightmares, the flames filled the world, and the men on their horses were larger than any mortals could be, huge man-beasts that would have crushed me like a gnat." Though the images were horrific, Joseph's voice was quiet.

"Nothing will ever change the truth that murder was done that night, but I see it now as it was; ignorant, hate-filled, frightened, and dangerous men killed my parents. But for all their ugliness, that is all they were, just men."

He stared at the blackened piece of timber. "The hardest thing now is to accept that they died for nothing. Nothing changed here. If anything, blacks have fewer rights and fewer opportunities than they did when my parents were here."

"You can't know that! There is no way to measure what effect your parents might have had on the people they taught," Lexy protested, but her voice sounded weak to her own ears.

As they were getting back into the buggy, two black men came walking down the road, red dust swirling in their wake. They cast swift glances at the three whites but did not break stride until Joseph called, "Wait, please!"

Reluctantly the two men halted and stood with their heads down, as if a direct look might be mistaken for aggression.

"Please, do you know what happened here?" Joseph asked. "We were just curious about what burned down. Seems like a nice piece of land; strange that nothing has been done with it since the fire, which must have been some time ago."

One of the men mumbled, "Doan know," and continued to study his feet, but the other one, after some hesitation, shrugged and said, "Schoolhouse be burn down by night ridahs all dem yeahs back. Bad times den, an' de teachahs be white from de Norf, teachin' negras. Dem teachahs be kilt dat night." He shrugged again. "Long time back dere."

Joseph was tempted to betray who he was by asking about the people he had known, about Rufus and Beulah and others, to ask if at least the teaching his parents had begun had been carried on, but then the impulse died. The man who had spoken obviously regretted that he had said so much; he was trying to sidle away.

"Thank you," Joseph said, and he turned away from them so that they could go on. He didn't want to search and find only that his parents had vanished without a trace. If he did not ask, he could believe that at least a few of their former pupils had gone on studying reading and figuring even after their teachers had been killed. It was not impossible; after all, slaves had risked death to learn how to read.

When they went back to town, he saw that though Mr. Crowper was gone, the store was still the gathering place, and the regulars had taken up their positions.

The faces had changed, aged, weathered, and wrinkled around the bones, or puffed out from too much whiskey and food, but he recognized the voices; even with the raspiness of years, he recognized two of the men, and possibly others, but two for sure—Beau Corey and Hank Willet.

His father had called out those two names first and then the others. Beau Corey had howled in outrage at being identified; Hank Willet had wanted to kill the child as well as his parents.

At that instant, the images of that night were clearer than they had been out where it had happened, but his vision was clearer, too.

He did not deny the hate coursing through him, the boiling desire to beat them, choke the life out of them, burn them alive. Terrible ways to kill them spun through his mind in lurid detail. And then other images superimposed themselves; images of all the years he had spent with the Kingstons, years during which he had watched them turn all of their energies to healing the sick, to alleviating suffering wherever they found it.

Suddenly more vividly than he could see the night of the murders, he saw the strong serenity of Anthea's face, and he saw Max's homely features, which were handsome to all who knew him.

For an instant, the images were strong enough to blot out the aging features of Hank, Beau, and the others. Even when he focused on them again, they were just men, as he had realized in the clearing, just men, little men. Violence to match theirs, vengeance for memories—it was all futile. They would never know it, and it would make no difference in their bleached hearts if they did, but he knew, and it was enough. The best revenge could be had by being the best doctor he could be, by treating black and white, rich and poor, as he had been trained to do, as Anthea and Max had shown his soul long before his formal education had begun.

"Are you all right?" Lexy asked him softly, worried by the stark paleness of his face and the rigidity that had frozen his limbs.

Joseph jerked, as if startled from sleep, and then he nodded. "I am now."

He looked at the group on the porch and then back at Lexy. "Some of those men were the ones who killed my parents. But it doesn't matter anymore."

Lexy shivered, and it took all her self-control not to stare at the men, but she had no doubt that Joseph meant what he said.

"I think it's time we all went home," Hawk said. He shared Lexy's horror, but more than that, he was chafing under the constant awareness of the violence that lurked beneath the slow, seemingly innocent rural way of life, violence he could do nothing about. The men on the porch enjoying the warmth of the sun, talking among themselves, spitting and scratching now and then like contented dogs—they were the same men who found it reasonable to wrap themselves in sheets and sweep like a killing wind through the night in the name of ignorance and bigotry.

On the journey home, Lexy and Hawk spoke little of what they would write, but they both knew the words would be tempered. In their separate ways, they would plead for greater justice for all citizens in the South, but under it all would lie the same acceptance Reid had come to long since, that nothing, not even injustice to an entire race, was worth another war, a war that would have to end with no quarter this time because allowing the whites to go home to their lands after the last war had left the blacks dispossessed and powerless.

For the Mackennas it had been a disheartening journey, but at least they had the satisfaction of knowing that Joseph had, after so many years, faced the demons of his past. It would take time for him to adjust to the changes, but already there was a difference in him, a subtle relaxation of the guarded stance with which he had always faced the world.

And for Lexy there was a personal gain as well in a new understanding of her father. She had always adored him and still had much of her child's view of him as a man of extraordinary strength, wisdom, and love. But now she saw more clearly than ever before the torment of his heritage; he had been born and raised a Southerner, had fought for the Confederacy, and then he had had to leave the land for which he had nearly died.

Shortly after returning to Washington, she went to Wild Swan to see him, compelled to tell him what she had felt while in the South. She tried to describe it objectively, but Travis easily heard the frightened voice beneath the careful words.

"You don't have to make it softer for me, darlin'," he chided her gently. "I know what you saw."

Her control broke, and she took shelter in his arms, no longer the controlled journalist. "Papa, it was horrible! It is a different country. The war didn't make us one. It is as alien there as if it were a world away."

"It is a world away," Travis said, hugging her as if she were a tiny child again. For the first time in years he let himself see the sweet acres of Hawthorn again, let himself feel the ferocious love he had had for that land, let himself mourn anew for a birthright relinquished.

"It will stay locked away, secret and separate for my lifetime and probably for yours. I couldn't wait for it to change. But someday it will. I have to believe that."

Gradually the sounds and scents of Wild Swan came to both of them, familiar reassurance of continuity.

"Your mother and I were so much luckier than so many," Travis said. "We had this place to come to; we had Alex to take us in."

Lexy appreciated her mother at that moment as much as her father. Her mother hadn't asked her why she needed to talk to her father; she had simply told her that he could be found in the barn with the brood mares.

And Alex was the one who had taught Gincie to be so generous in her loving. Alex was the one who had made Wild Swan a refuge from the beginning.

"Your great-grandmother was a special woman," Travis said, affection and amusement in his voice. "She could match the most elegant ladies in the land when the occasion called for it, but I can see her here just as well, takin' care of the mares and makin' the foals feel that bein' born wasn't such a bad thing after all."

"I can remember her very clearly," Lexy said.

They stayed there for a long time, feeling Alex's presence in the twilight of the barn, letting her comfort them as she had all who had come to Wild Swan in her lifetime.

Chapter 42

In March, Hawk reported on the political implications of Harrison's inauguration while Lexy accounted for the gowns the wives of the dignitaries wore to the various receptions. Having just returned from the Southern expedition, Lexy didn't mind doing such frivolous work. It not only underscored a definite division in readers' minds between Lexy and Abby Adams, it was a relief to be doing something that did not continue to haunt her after the day's work was done.

In April, Lexy and Hawk were in Indian Territory, sent by Reid to report on the opening of public lands there.

Over the years, the *Witness* had reported the problems with land ownership in the Indian Territory, or "Oklahoma," as it had been named in 1866 by Reverend Allen Wright, principal chief of the Choctaw Nation. The name was a combination of two Choctaw words, "okla" meaning people, and "humma," meaning red.

At first, Indians from a wide variety of tribes had been removed to these Western acres because few people could imagine that whites would ever want to settle on such desolation. It was to this area that Boston had gone with Rachel and what was left of her family when the last of the Cherokee, forced away from their green farms in the East, had traveled the Trail of Tears.

No one could have predicted the enormous Western migration that had begun after the war and that had continued unabated. No one could have foreseen the appetite for land, any land, a hunger shared by railroad builders, miners, ranchers, and farmers.

Vast tracts of Indian Territory were not assigned to any specific Indian nation, but were reserved for Indian use, mostly for the grazing of livestock in country that was too arid to support many head of cattle or horses to the acre. But over the past few decades, with the ever-increasing pressure from white settlers, the concept of the use of unassigned lands had eroded. And since the war, the Indians of the Southwest had had even less power at the bargaining table than before because many of them had supported the Confederates. It mattered to few outside the Indian nations that that support had had some very practical aspects, the main one being that federal protection had been withdrawn during the war, leaving the Indians open to Confederate activity. In fact, the territory had suffered at the hands of both Union and Confederate troops.

Now through a series of reassignments, laws, treaties, and bargains with the Indians, some of the land was to be opened to white settlement. And in the end, how it had been accomplished mattered little against the reality of white pressure for settlement.

The process had already begun in Sioux territory in South Dakota, where the Indians were restricted to a few reservations while the rest of the land was open to settlement, but Reid was sure, due to information from various trusted sources within and outside of the government, that the run for land in Oklahoma was going to be phenomenal.

Not even Reid's certainty prepared the Mackennas for the madness they found. Thousands upon thousands of people were prepared to race for one-hundred-and-sixty-acre homestead plots when the official signal was given at noon on April 22.

They spent the time before that day talking to as many people as they could, Lexy recording the women's points of view, Hawk the men's.

The overwhelming motivation was a new start in a new land, a leaving behind of businesses, farms, lives that had lost their appeal or had failed utterly. And many were, regardless of the success or failure of their present lives, simply compelled by the pull of Western lands that had, from the country's beginning, drawn the population across the continent, and some were undoubtedly evading the consequences of trouble at home. But everyone shared the fever of the gathering.

It was like a huge circus with thousands of tents and a continual hum of activity. Lexy was fascinated by the way the women, despite the dirt and chaos, managed to create some sort of order so that they could feed their families.

Though many women were there only because their husbands had decided that this was what the family would do, there were others who were as anxious as their spouses to claim a homestead, and some who were there on their own account, most of them widows determined that they and their children would benefit like everyone else.

Some people, dubbed "Sooners," had already stolen into the territory, but most were gathered to run at the signal on April 22. They were mounted on horseback or prepared to drive a wide assortment of vehicles, from wagons to buggies to carts. Some were on foot, unable to afford better.

Lexy and Hawk paid exorbitant prices for inferior horses, but they deemed the expense worth it as a way truly to experience the event.

The best estimate was that fifty thousand people had gathered. When the signal was given, Lexy felt as if every one of them were right beside her. The press of people, animals, and vehicles was tremendous, the air shattered by the roar of voices and obscured by thick clouds of dust.

She and Hawk had planned to ride together, but the maelstrom of horses and vehicles made hanging on and going forward more than enough to cope with. She had never been so glad of her riding skill. Like some other women, she was riding astride, but there were women on sidesaddles as well, and their skill in staying in the saddle was remarkable.

Her horse, as unprepossessing as he was, was caught up in the herd instinct to run, and she let him, not pulling him up until he began to falter from exhaustion. She guided him steadily away from the center until she was on the outskirts of the crowd, and the race swept away from her, with stragglers bringing up the rear.

Broken-down vehicles, lame horses, and bruised riders littered the landscape, making it look as if there had been a battle. The thunder of hooves faded in the distance.

Lexy started to laugh. She knew it was a reaction to the exhilaration of the day, to the danger of the ride, but she couldn't stop. Covered with dust, breathing the odors of horse, hot leather, and sweat from the multitudes, with heart still pounding and knees shaking, it felt wonderful to be alive.

"Didn't find a plot to your liking, lady?" Hawk's voice was muffled by the bandana he wore over his nose and mouth, but his eyes were golden with his own excitement and with relief at finding Lexy unhurt.

"All kinds of plots, enough for several farms or articles," she replied to his pun, still laughing as she leaned precariously in her saddle so that he could give her a hug and a kiss.

He wasn't going to confess it to her, but as soon as the run had begun he had been frantic for her safety, cursing himself for allowing her to participate. But as soon as he had caught sight of her, he had also recovered his sanity. "Allowing" her had nothing to do with it. And the truth was that though he was competent in the saddle and much stronger than she, she was a better rider.

Lexy was not fooled by Hawk's teasing. She could feel how concerned he had been for her in the tension of his body when he hugged her. And that night, he showed his concern in the exquisite care he took in making love to her, his mouth and his long, strong fingers tracing every line and hollow of her body until she lay open to him, her hands urging his entry, her voice crying her joy aloud when he came into her.

Their quarters were makeshift, part tent, part shack; the sounds of celebration were all around them; and neither of them cared.

When they lay quiet, drifting toward sleep, Hawk's body was curled protectively around Lexy's so that she could feel his warmth cradling her spoon fashion, one arm draped across her waist.

"Thank you," she murmured sleepily.

His laughter rumbled against her. "It seems to me the credit is shared."

"For that, too, but more, for everything you are," she said, and he understood.

After sharing the work and the experience of two such intense stories and each other's company, it was difficult for them to separate, but Lexy had the comfort of knowing that at least she would be with her parents in Louisville for the Kentucky Derby on May 9.

The Kentucky Derby had more local interest than anything else these days, as there were Eastern events of far more importance and with far larger purses, but nonetheless, it was a good early test for three-year-olds. Even among the best of the breed and even without injuries, performance from one year to the next could vary widely, particularly from the two- to the three-year-old form. And this year because both Pharaoh and Proctor Knott were among the Derby entries, interest was keener than usual. The chance to test against Proctor Knott early on made it worth it to the Culhanes to miss the spring meeting in Baltimore.

Pharaoh had wintered well and had taken to spring training with a will, but the Culhanes did not underestimate Proctor Knott or the others in the field. And although there was little chance that another attempt would be made to drug Pharaoh, particularly in the small world of Kentucky racing, they took no chances, making sure someone was with the colt at all times.

The day of the race was clear and the track fast, and because of the draw of the two famous colts, twenty-five thousand people were. in attendance, the most in the history of the Derby. In the crowd were such notables as the flamboyant financier "Diamond Jim" Brady and Frank James, brother to the outlaw Jesse. Mr. James made the Culhanes think of Georgie because he, too, sometimes acted as a "beard" and was known for his honesty in placing bets for others. They knew how much Georgie had wanted to come with them, but she had agreed to stay away from the racetracks for at least a while longer. She could not argue with the Culhanes' insistence that the longer she stayed away from her old haunts and people who had known her as George, the harder it would be for the thugs to trace her. Gincie was not so forthright about her real plan, which was for Georgie to become so accustomed to life at Wild Swan and to being a woman, she would never want to go back to her previous existence.

Indeed, Gincie doubted that Georgie's enemies would recognize her even now, less than a year since she had foiled the poisoning attempt. Of course, the longer hair and the woman's clothing caused much of the transformation, but Georgie herself could play any part she wished if she put her mind to it, changing her naturally long stride to small mincing steps, changing everything about the way she moved, and changing her voice most of all. Not only could she drop her own faintly English and educated way of speaking for the cant of the racetracks, but she could also imitate anyone's speech within minutes of hearing it.

The extremely shy and feminine young woman horsemen met when they came to do business at Wild Swan might have had little to do with the real Georgie, but she had been convincing enough so that no one had recognized her as George from the New York courses.

Despite the young woman's cheerful disposition and her willingness to put her hand to any task, Gincie was well aware that none of them really knew what was going on in Georgie's head most of the time. It made Gincie wonder how much of Georgie's seeming contentment at Wild Swan was an act staged for their benefit.

But she had no doubt that she would have enjoyed attending the Derby if for no other reason than that there were three ways of betting—auction pools, bookmaking, and mutuels—being offered to the public.

When she shared the thought with Travis, his grin was rueful. "I've considered the same thing. I wouldn't admit it to Georgie, but it must be excitin' to be so involved with the gamblin'. She was respected enough to be trusted with large wagers; she must have known most of the time where the big money was comin' from and where it was goin'. I hope Wild Swan isn't too tame for her." He paused for a moment and then said wistfully, "And I wish Rosalind were just a little more like Georgie."

Gincie didn't scold him for the disloyal thought because she shared it. With each day's passing, Kace's wedding drew nearer, making his family confront their doubts about his choice. Someday he would be the one bringing horses to such meetings as this one, and it was difficult to imagine Rosalind being any help at all.

"'At least she will enjoy the socializing and the display of finery at race meetings," Gincie said, and added, "and if that's not 'damning with faint praise,' I don't know what is."

"Ah, well, they'll probably manage well enough. We aren't the sort of parents who choose spouses for their children, and our children aren't the sort who would accept our choices, anyway." Travis's eyes found Lexy where she stood in earnest conversation with another horse owner. "She did fine all on her own," he observed softly, and then he gave Gincie a hug. "And worryin' about Kace or Georgie isn't goin' to help Pharaoh to run today."

They tried to convince themselves that this was just another race, but it was useless. If Pharaoh was to maintain his claim to being "colt of the century," there was little margin for loss. Thousands more than those watching the race today would be awaiting the results and taking them as a measure of how Pharaoh was going to run as a three-year-old.

The day had grown hot and dusty by post time, but the Culhanes hardly noticed. All their concentration was on Pharaoh and his chief rival, Proctor Knott.

Pharaoh came out looking alert and businesslike, ready to run, but behaving well, in sharp contrast to Proctor Knott, who was wild at the barrier, breaking away twice to expend his energy uselessly in lunging and racing more than an eighth of a mile before the race even began. More than once, his rider nearly came out of the saddle.

Lexy, watching beside her parents, said, "He'll lose the race right here if he doesn't settle down." She couldn't help but be partial, and she was filled with pride for the beauty and discipline Pharaoh showed as he waited for the race to begin.

Despite his misbehavior, Proctor Knott broke along with the field. Hindoocraft was the early leader, but Pharaoh was right behind him. Then near the first turn, Proctor Knott rushed to the front and led by three lengths entering the backstretch, with a sudden shift that put Sportsman second, Hindoocraft third, and Pharaoh fourth.

There was no denying the speed and power of Proctor Knott, but all through the backstretch, he was fighting for his head.

Travis muttered, "Careful, careful," knowing that Pharaoh was not going to tolerate being behind any other horse for very much longer, but not wanting him to overrun himself. His jockey was doing a good job, working with the colt. Pharaoh's speed increased, and he began to move up.

Leaving the backstretch, Proctor Knott was five lengths in front, with Pharaoh moving into second place, but when they took the turn for home, Proctor Knott's jockey was unable to control the horse as he raced to the outer rail, thereby losing many lengths. Rather than lose more ground by going back to the inside fence, the jockey, even when he had Proctor Knott straightened out and under control, chose to ride the outer rail.

With Pharaoh hugging the inner rail and Proctor Knott on the outside rail, the horses crossed the finish line so close in order that the judges had to deliberate the outcome.

"It's Pharaoh!" Lexy announced with conviction. "And look at the difference! He could still run another race; Proctor Knott is ready to fall over."

Still, it was agonizing to wait as the minutes ticked by, but finally the judges awarded the race to Pharaoh by a nose. It didn't matter to the Culhanes that Proctor Knott's backers were claiming he'd won, or that even if he hadn't, he would have had he not gone to the outer rail; as far as they were concerned, how a horse responded to his jockey was as important as his speed.

And Pharaoh vindicated their faith in him when he beat Proctor Knott again, this time in the Clark Stakes on the fifth day of the meeting, when he showed Proctor Knott his heels and left him with every stride on the homestretch.

Although there was a long season of racing ahead, the return to Wild Swan from Kentucky was triumphant, and no one was more appreciative of Pharaoh's performance than Georgie. She curried him and played with him until Travis teased that she was going to make the colt too soft for racing.

"Not Pharaoh!" she protested. "That's the lovely thing about him. He knows the difference between work and play."

Georgie was truly excited about Pharaoh's winning and his prospects for the rest of the season; she was still enchanted by every day at Wild Swan—and she dreaded going to Kace's wedding with every beat of her heart.

She was so much a part of the family now that it wasn't as if she were a guest who could offer an excuse for not attending; Kace and

Rosalind expected her to be there as much as they expected it of Lexy and Tay.

There was no one she could talk to about it; she had no reasonable excuse not to go to the wedding except for the truth, and she cringed at the thought of anyone knowing that she was so presumptuous as to want Kace for herself.

She judged herself a complete fool. Kace treated her like a little sister and was in love with Rosalind. And to make matters much more complicated, Georgie feared that Tay was growing too fond of her and that his feelings were not those of a brother. He was such a kind, intelligent man, she wished she could fall in love with him. But she didn't think it would ever happen, and the last thing she wanted to do was to hurt him.

Being a woman was a very complicated business, but though she might wish she had never been so changed by the Culhanes, she knew she could not quiet her heart now that it had awakened.

She had two choices. One was to leave Wild Swan forever. She did not fool herself that it would be easy. Charlie was no longer around to watch over her. And while she did not doubt she could shed the outward trappings that made her a woman—the longer hair and the clothing that fit over the slight curves regular meals had added to her figure—she had changed inwardly as well.

Day by day, she had learned to think of herself as a woman and to accept that at Wild Swan that was no handicap. It meant no lessening of responsibility, and it allowed living in harmony not only with the land, the livestock, and the people, but also with her own body. Until she had come here, she had not realized how difficult it had been to bind her breasts and to hide all evidence of her monthly courses. Now she was with other women who acknowledged the inconvenience as well as the promise and went right on with their lives. What had at first seemed like a loss of freedom now seemed exactly the opposite.

Her other choice was to remain at Wild Swan, to accept Kace's choice, and to be the best possible sister to him and to Rosalind. There was no middle ground in this; she could not stay and pout like a child.

She could hold the conflict at bay during the day because there was always work to be done, but at night she was haunted by visions of Kace making love to Rosalind. Unfortunately, having lived in a world where young men around the stables had been quite explicit about their sexual experiences and had had no idea that "George" was female, her visions were graphic in spite of lack of practical experience.

Unable to discuss her dilemma with the living, Georgie found strange comfort from the dead. It wasn't just the fact of generations buried at Wild Swan, it was the way they were remembered, referred to often with love, respect, and humor, as if they were still part of the fabric of the days.

To be born, to live, to learn, to love, and to die in one place where a community of people shared their lives with you and remembered you when you were gone: she liked the idea very much, much more than her previous existence, which had never had any roots.

In June she went with the others to Kace's wedding in Boston.

Rosalind's parents made it easy to understand her. Well meaning and well off, they played their roles as precisely as if they were on a stage. Mr. Cunningham, a man of expanding business interests and an expanding waistline, was the perfect patriarch who doted on his family while expecting them to heed his direction. Mrs. Cunningham was as fluttery as her daughter, accustomed to being shielded from life's more unpalatable truths, spending her days attending social functions and donating a precise percentage of her husband's income to the proper charities. She still showed vestiges of a beauty that must once have been as great as her daughter's, but it had faded and blurred with too much food and too little exercise. Her vapid manner might have passed for coy charm when she was young, but it was now vaguely embarrassing to watch. Still, she had the same genuine sweetness as Rosalind, so it was possible to at once like her and pity her while knowing that she would never understand the cause for pity.

Georgie wondered how Kace could look at Rosalind's mother and not be terrified for his own future. She suppressed the thought; if she were going to continue at Wild Swan, such observations were useless and destructive. And to be fair, though Rosalind knew of Georgie's origins, she had obviously not told her parents. Nor had her cousin Edith, so Georgie was accepted as presented, as part of the Culhane family without a specific definition of her relationship.

They were too civilized to betray themselves, but the Culhanes were no more comfortable with the Cunninghams than Georgie was. The Cunninghams were so dull, long silences punctuated by nervous throat clearing characterized attempts at conversation. And though nothing was said openly, the Culhanes were aware that Rosalind's parents were shocked by their association with horse racing. At the same time, they could not deny the success the Culhanes had made of that and other ventures, and they approved of the family's connections to shipbuilding, the law, finance, English nobility, and even the newspaper business, although points were lost there for Lexy's involvement.

"I rather fancy being the black sheep," Lexy whispered to Hawk after a particularly stilted conversation with Mrs. Cunningham.

"I expect you're really beyond the pale, having married a wild Indian," Hawk growled in her ear. It was too foolish to mind, but the way the Cunninghams eyed him, as if he were suddenly going to jump up and scalp someone, made him nervous.

But for all the uneasiness of the two families mixing, no one could deny that Rosalind was a lovely bride, her blond beauty ethereal in satin and lace, and Kace was the perfect bridegroom, tall and strong, eyes alight with love, voice clear as he made his vows.

Her face devoid of expression, Georgie watched the ceremony. This was what Kace wanted, and so it had to be all right. She felt as if her heart were breaking, but she knew it wasn't true. Losing her mother, her father, and then Charlie had been worse than this, and she had survived.

Because her own nerves were raw, she could feel Tay's hurt as if it were her own. Outwardly he betrayed none of it. He played his part as best man to his twin, and at the reception for the young couple afterward, no one seemed more pleased than Tay. But in the brief instants when his face was in repose, his eyes were infinitely sad.

Though Georgie had none of her own, she realized that when siblings were close, marriages would always mean adjustment, more so in the case of twins. But she also knew that Tay was too generous of heart to begrudge his brother happiness. It was quite the opposite problem; Tay feared that his brother had made a choice that would bring him sorrow.

"We might both be mistaken," she murmured softly as she stood beside him, watching the newlywed couple lead the first dance.

Tay did not pretend to misunderstand. "I hope you're right. I've always known that Kace and I are different, that we want different things, but not this different." He paused and then very gently turned the tables on her. "And it is as hard for you to witness this as it is for me, isn't it?"

"Of course not!" she answered too quickly. "I mean, I care about all of you. You have taken me in and made me feel like I'm part of your family, so I naturally want all of you to be happy. But I don't know Kace well enough to know what will or will not make him so."

"Oh, I think you know all of us very well indeed," Tay corrected her, still studying her face. "Would you honor me with this dance, Miss Cheney?"

His smile belied the formality of the request, and Georgie accepted the invitation to join the other couples on the floor. She wasn't overly confident of her dancing ability, but she welcomed the chance to distract Tay from his knowing pursuit of the truth, and she trusted his social grace to make up for her lack of it.

And when Kace asked her to dance, delivering Rosalind into his brother's arms at the same time, she did not refuse the exchange. If her breath came with difficulty, as if she had been running, if she couldn't quite meet Kace's eyes, it didn't matter. Unlike Tay, he was so intoxicated with the joy of the day, he didn't notice.

"Rosalind looks so beautiful; I can't wait until we leave!" he groaned, just as he would have to Lexy, his other sister. Georgie shared his wish for escape, though not for the same reason.

"My God, this seems to be an extraordinarily long day!" Hawk muttered to Lexy.

He was finding the day a peculiar mix of celebration and disaster. He had recently reported the aftermath of the devastating flood in Johnstown, Pennsylvania, where heavy rains had filled the Conemaugh Reservoir, collapsed the dam, and killed more than twenty-five hundred people in the valley below.

Hawk's articles had been printed not only in the *Witness*, but in several other papers in various cities. He was proud of the work and knew that it had, along with other journalists' efforts, helped to stir the sympathies of people everywhere so that help was flooding into the valley at nearly the same rate the murderous waters had. But he hadn't expected to be questioned about the gory details on Kace's wedding day.

The approaches to the subject were all variations on the same theme, obligatory words about how nice the ceremony had been, how beautiful the bride was, a slight hesitation, and then, "Was it really so awful at Johnstown? Were there really bodies lying right where the water left them?"

"Yes, ma'am, Rosalind is a lovely bride, and yes, there were bodies everywhere, carcasses of cows, horses, and other livestock, too, lying in the mud," Hawk had just said to the overdressed matron who had questioned him and who now looked satisfyingly horrified. She was bustling away to share the grim report as Lexy returned to his side.

"You're not the only one who thinks this day is too long," Lexy said. "Georgie and Tay are miserable."

She said it with such certainty that Hawk took a close look and decided she was probably right, though the two were doing their best to smile.

"It's just as well that Rosalind and Kace will be gone for most of the summer; that will give Tay and Georgie time to adjust," Hawk suggested.

Lexy looked up at him for a long moment. "I might have married Michael Winterbourne; I might even have had a good life with him. But not in a thousand summers would I have forgotten you or ceased to love you."

Among the proper Boston matrons who observed Hawk Mackenna soundly kissing his wife in public, reaction was equally divided between outrage and envy.

Chapter 43

Besides Pharaoh's continuing triumph throughout the summer, the biggest racing news was the opening of Morris Park.

Jerome Park had been endangered by New York City's plan to acquire the land for a reservoir. Mr. Jerome had approached John A. Morris, a noted financier and horse owner, and had asked that he consider building a new racetrack for the New York Jockey Club. The result was Morris Park in Westchester County.

It had taken twelve months and $1,500,000 to build, but when it opened on August 20, 1889, it was deservedly called the most beautiful racetrack in the world. The clubhouse was five stories high and had an outdoor roof lookout porch. All the buildings were of iron, brick, and stone in a Pompeian villa style. Red-tinted concrete decorated many of the sidewalks and paths. There were nearly ninety buildings spread throughout the grounds, and the stables had one thousand stalls. There was even a special spur on the railroad to convey public and private coaches to the track.

Pharaoh made opening day his own by winning the race for three-year-olds, cheered on by thousands.

No one was more pleased to be among the spectators than Georgie. Tay had escorted her north to join the Culhanes and Lexy. Georgie knew that the Culhanes still feared for her, but with each passing minute, it grew more evident that her appearance was too changed for old friends or old enemies to recognize her. Even those few who might have remembered that Cheney was "George's" sur-name did not make the connection. Miss Cheney was presented as a

Culhane cousin; she was beautifully dressed and soft-spoken; the men who gave her a closer look did not do so because they suspected they had seen her at the racecourses before.

At much as Georgie was flattered by the attention, she was also amused. She was no hand at flirting, but she found it easy enough to smile timidly and look away shyly, which seemed to be all that was required. And much of the time she had to hold back laughter at the idea of how these same men would have reacted had "George" made such gestures at them.

Georgie had wondered if she would feel pulled by her old life once she was back in that world, but she wasn't. She was too realistic to paint her previous existence in false colors, and comparing it now to her life at Wild Swan, it seemed both dangerous and lonely. Charlie had been a good guardian, but he could not make it possible for her to live as a female. Her only regret now was that Charlie had not somehow been able to find shelter at Wild Swan as she had. She had no doubt that the Culhanes would have welcomed him.

She would never lose her love for the Thoroughbreds or for the sport of kings, and being part of Wild Swan assured her that the connection would not be broken as long as she stayed there.

She reminded herself of that frequently as the time drew near for Kace and Rosalind to return from their sojourn on the Continent and in England. She reminded herself, too, that they would be living at Sunrise, not at Wild Swan.

She had spent a companionable summer with Tay, but she still felt only sisterly affection for him.

She had shared, with everyone else, the letters from the couple. She had made herself picture them together because thinking of Kace without Rosalind was forbidden. But, strangely, the letters hadn't helped that process. Wherever they went, Rosalind seemed wholly concerned with shopping and social events. She was the one who did most of the letter writing, so her view was the easiest to ascertain. She didn't mind the time Kace spent at various European stables and racecourses, as she saw this as part of his work, but she confessed to finding the treks through cathedrals and ruined castles "quite tiresom."

"They are all very alike," she wrote, "and so dingy with horrid liting that makes walking about trecherus. Can't think what makes Kace enjoy them so, but then, he's good about my visits to shops, so I must be good about the old stones."

If Rosalind's spelling was a bit primitive, it was adequate for the meaning, but the meaning kept giving Georgie images of the couple wandering across Europe, tolerating each other's tastes, but finding no common ground. The minute she thought that, she reminded herself that there was common ground in the bedroom. She knew that was true, but for herself, she could not imagine being physically intimate with someone whose mind was not similarly attuned.

There was no question that she was far too attuned to Kace. She sensed the difference in him the moment he and Rosalind arrived home. They both looked fit and, on the surface, happy, but the pieces didn't fit in quite the same way as they had. Kace had certainly been indulgent toward Rosalind before, but now the indulgence was not that of an ardent lover; it was more like that of a generous uncle or guardian.

Rosalind, however, didn't seem changed at all, and that in itself was a puzzle. It was not as if she had moved on to the role of wife and lover; it was as if she were still an innocent girl being courted. She was so much that way that Lizzie McCoy, who had worried that her own way of running the household at Sunrise would change with the advent of the new mistress, quickly discovered that things were to go on exactly as before. Rosalind's idea of her own duties was to arrange flowers and figurines and to approve menus if guests were expected for dinner.

Georgie's assumption that she would not be too closely involved with the couple's lives at the neighboring farm was soon proven false. Having few duties at home, Rosalind often came to visit. And though the older women at Wild Swan were kind to her, it was natural that she preferred the company of Georgie.

Rosalind was perfectly willing to work at some simple task such as repairing racing silks while Georgie went on with her own work, but more often, she simply chattered away about the months abroad, about how different life in Maryland was compared to what she was accustomed to in New England, and, hazardous from Georgie's point of view, about Kace, about how sweet he was to her and how much she wanted to have his children.

"He's so . . . so courtly," she said. "I thought the boys at home had manners, but Kace makes them seem so young and clumsy. He's so sure of himself. He'll be so good with our children, I just know it! He'll be stern but loving with our daughters, and he'll teach our sons everything they need to know about all sorts of things. Of course, a woman has to put up with . . . well, that, to have children."

The minute Georgie heard those words she knew she should have stopped all mention of Kace in the beginning, but she hadn't known how to do that, and she had been both attracted and repelled by the little confidences.

Rosalind was perceptive enough to notice that Georgie had frozen in place. "Oh, I know I shouldn't speak of such things to a maiden," she said, a blush coloring her cheeks in contrast to Georgie's loss of color. "But you seem so . . . I don't know, so matter-of-fact, and I don't have anyone else to talk to about it. I know it is my duty, and it isn't as bad as it was at first, but it is so . . . so messy and embarrassing. My mother warned me, but I didn't think it would be like that." The words poured out in a rush, and Georgie was horrified, suddenly understanding far too much.

"Poor Kace," was her first thought, and then "poor Rosalind."

She kept her eyes and her hands busy with the leather she was plaiting while she searched desperately for something to say. The safest thing would be to say nothing at all, but that seemed cowardly, and more, she feared her silence would be taken to mean assent.

"Rosalind, you've seen a good deal of Kace's parents, of Lexy and Hawk, and the other couples in the family. Surely you have noticed the delight the husbands and wives take in each other's company. I think that must reflect how they love each other physically as well as in other ways. Maybe after you have been married for a while longer, you will feel differently," she suggested.

"I don't see how! Men's bodies aren't at all beautiful like women's. Even with no light at all, I know how big and hard and hairy Kace is." Rosalind made a moue of distaste.

It was beyond Georgie to contradict her. Though she had avoided potentially embarrassing situations as much as possible, her life as a young man had meant seeing naked males now and then, particularly the slight, mostly young, bodies of the jockeys. Far from finding them offensive, she had thought them handsome in the clean sculpture of bone and muscle. And if she had thought that about the riders, who were miniatures, she could well imagine what her reaction to Kace in the nude would be. She had seen him a couple of times without his shirt, had seen his smooth-muscled back and his chest furred with golden brown, and had crept away from the sight, not because she found it offensive, but because she had been afraid the warm spreading tension she felt inside would somehow be visible on the outside.

Kace would be beautiful without clothes; all of him would be beautiful. She would never want darkness to steal away the sight of him. All of him would bespeak power, but also tenderness; she had no doubt of that.

"You have a most peculiar expression on your face," Rosalind said, stopping in the middle of prattle that Georgie had missed altogether.

"I'm sorry, I was thinking about Pharaoh's chances as a four-year-old. He's been eating his head off lately; we're going to have to watch him or it will be very difficult to get him into racing form for next spring." She knew Rosalind would believe the lie; Rosalind believed everyone at the farms was wholly obsessed with the horses all the time.

It was difficult enough having to deal with Rosalind, but it was much, much harder for Georgie to see so much of Kace, who began spending more and more time at Wild Swan.

At first Georgie assumed that Kace was coming over because his wife was there so often, but then she realized that that wasn't really it. Kace was starved for intelligent conversation about the horses, about politics, about books, about a wide variety of topics that he was used to discussing with his family and friends, topics in which his wife had no interest.

Georgie doubted that he was aware of his hunger, but she knew his parents were; she saw the worried looks they bestowed on Kace and Rosalind.

For her part, she tried at first to avoid Kace when he was about, but he sought her out so that she could not stay away from him without making it obvious. He missed his siblings and considered her one of them now; she knew it was no more than that, but that didn't make it any easier. She could recognize his footstep and the warm man scent of him without turning around. His deep voice could touch her as if his long fingers were stroking her skin. She turned eighteen and still felt like a foolish schoolgirl when Kace was around, a true irony since she had never been a schoolgirl, much less a foolish one, before.

Sometimes she was tempted to bolt, but always the enchantment stopped her. Each day her roots grew deeper, entwining her heart and her soul with Wild Swan's acres.

She was not used to things coming easily in her life, and so she came to accept that having to live closely with Kace's marriage to Rosalind was not the worst thing that could have happened to her. Instead of running from it, she began to spend even more time with the couple, being there for each of them when they needed her, playing the roles they had assigned her.

But Lexy and Tay were not as accepting of the changes as Georgie because they had not witnessed them day by day. Tay had been away at school, and Lexy had not spent much time at the farm during the fall. But when everyone gathered for Christmas, both of them were aware of the baffled sadness underlying Kace's affable demeanor. And they were both handicapped by the fact that they hadn't thought Rosalind was a good choice in the first place, so they felt they had to tread very carefully now.

Tay waited for his twin to confide in him and was torn between hurt and relief when Kace did not.

Meanwhile, Lexy assumed that if Kace talked to anyone it

would be to Tay, and so she was shocked when he chose her instead. The only warning she had was that he was uncharacteristically nervous, talking about inconsequential things in staccato bursts until he paused for a moment, took a deep breath, and asked, "Did you . . . er . . . did you like having Hawk . . . er . . . touch you from the beginning, or did it . . . did it take time for you to become accustomed? . . ." His voice trailed away in misery.

Lexy's heart ached for him. She had never known him to be so hesitant, and she understood immediately what was behind his question. And though they had never discussed such matters, she did not hesitate to answer him, feeling he deserved no less.

"I wanted Hawk to touch me before he ever did. I seduced him the first time, not the other way around, and it was before we married." She saw her brother's eyes flare in surprise, and she nodded. "Hawk would insist that it was his fault, or at the most, a mutual seduction, when in fact, he tried very hard to protect my virtue. But I was very determined. I wanted him then; I want him now. I love his mind, his heart, his spirit, and I love his body, too. I love being touched by him, and I love touching him in turn. If you and Rosalind don't have that, I am very sorry."

It had been years since she had seen Kace weep, but there were tears in his eyes now. "She allows me my 'rights' because she wants a child, but she is afraid of me when I make love to her. Oh, God, Lexy, she was afraid the first time, and she still is! It is as if I become a beast when . . ." He covered his face with his hands.

"My dear, it isn't your fault!" Lexy said. "Most of the time it's wonderful to be part of this family, but sometimes it complicates things. It's easy to forget that most people aren't nearly as open and accepting as Mama and Papa have taught us to be. I'm sure Rosalind's mother taught her that 'good women' don't enjoy making love; most girls are taught that. So poor Rosalind, she's probably more terrified of feeling pleasure than she is of anything you're doing. Surely with time and patience, she will understand it shouldn't be that way. Damn her mother, anyway!"

At least her enthusiastic curse brought a faint smile to Kace, but Lexy doubted Rosalind's ability to change, time and patience notwithstanding. Rosalind liked being a carefree little girl in a woman's body. It occurred to her that perhaps having a child would be the best thing for Rosalind; it would surely force her to grow up and to accept her body as a woman's, not a child's.

There was no doubt about Rosalind's interest in children. Jilly and Dermot were visiting as the proud parents of Dermot Hargrave IV, born in June and bearing the middle name Hawkins in honor of Hawk's rescue of Dermot. There was no lack of people who fussed over him, but Rosalind not only held him and cooed to him for long stretches, she was perfectly willing to change and bathe him as well. For someone who was so dainty regarding daily chores, it was a wonder to see how little fazed she was by the messes a baby makes.

And while Rosalind spent her time with the baby and the other children of the family, Kace enjoyed the company of the adults, transparently glad to have people to talk to.

Much of the talk was about Nellie Bly, the journalist, Elizabeth Cochrane, whom the Mackennas had met in New York, who had set out on November 13 to beat the travel record of *Around the World in Eighty Days*, which had been written by Jules Verne in 1872. Though the book was fiction, Nellie Bly was determined to better it in actuality, to prove that a woman could do it and to increase circulation for her paper, the *World*. She was filing her reports as she could, by cables and letters that were growing more irregular as she caught large and small ships, trains, and various other conveyances that were carrying her into increasingly exotic countries, traveling east all the while. There were times when she was out of communication for long enough to worry the public that some awful fate had befallen her. But then the next report would come.

"It's a marvelous feat! I wish the *Witness* was the paper getting all the additional readers, and I envy Miss Cochrane her courage and initiative," Lexy confessed when asked her opinion, "but I wouldn't want to be in her shoes. I like traveling well enough, but racing around the world without having time to really stop and explore things is not my idea of a good journey. Besides, I wouldn't want to leave Hawk for that long," she added, smiling at him. She didn't know until later, when they were alone, that her comment had caused Hawk consternation, not pleasure.

"Do you feel that being married to me holds you back?" he asked bluntly. "You could be doing this 'round the world trip as well as Miss Cochrane. And if not this, other things like it."

"Are you utterly mad?" She stared at him, her eyes wide. "I adore you! I cannot imagine my life without you! And I am doing what I want to do, with your full support; so few women have that from the men they love, so few! I meant what I said about the trip around the world. It's a stunt, a wonderful one, I admit, but not the sort of thing I'd do well. Hawk, you know me better than anyone on earth. Can you imagine that I could just pass by all the stories Miss Cochrane will only catch a glimpse of on her way?"

That brought a slow grin from him. "No, I can better imagine you disappearing into the hinterlands of China or the like."

Lexy cupped his face in her hands. "Do you feel . . . ah," she searched for the right word, discarding "imprisoned" as being too harsh, "limited by our marriage? I mean, I know you consider me when you make decisions about what stories you will do that will keep us apart, and we don't spend as much time together as most married couples do." She could not rid herself of the feeling that the ground she depended on was beginning to shift beneath her feet.

Hawk felt the need to tread carefully, too, and he knew that Lexy needed more than easy assurance. He took her hands in his own, kissing one palm and then the other. "When I come home, and you are not there, I miss you, often quite desperately. And if you had asked me these questions years ago when I was a young and foolish man, I would have told you that, of course, wives belong at home awaiting the pleasure of their husbands. And back then I might have married someone like Rosalind, God help me! I can see how unhappy Kace is. He has a wife who is always in place for him, but he is learning that a beautiful body and an empty head is a poor combination, while I learn every day what it is to make love to your mind as well as your body. It is worth the time apart; it is worth the unconventional in our marriage; it is worth anything to have that."

Lexy wasn't aware of her tears until Hawk wiped them away, his fingers tracing the contours of her face. They felt so close at that moment, it was as if they crossed the boundaries and flowed into each other's flesh and spirit.

Kace could see the closeness between his sister and his brother-in-law; he could see it between his parents, between all the couples in the family. In despair, he even saw it between Jilly and Dermot, though he had once thought Jilly too spoiled and pinch-hearted to be lovable.

Rosalind was lovable; he was certain of that. But this time with the family was making him see that the physical disharmony of his and Rosalind's marriage was affecting everything about their relationship.

He suddenly felt lonelier than he ever had in his life. Despite what Lexy had said, he accepted the blame for what was happening, or rather not happening, between himself and his wife. He was far more experienced than she; therefore, he should be able to make things better for both of them. He reminded himself that they had not been married for that long; surely in time they would learn how to shape their lives more gracefully to each other.

He could not allow himself to think that Rosalind was content with things exactly as they were.

He welcomed the increasing demands of work in the new year as their mares foaled and others were brought in to be bred to Wild Swan's stallions. He did not have to question the fact that he was spending more and more time away from Rosalind, more and more time with his parents, the farm workers, and Georgie in various combinations, at Wild Swan and Sunrise, depending on who was watching over the mares on the nights when births seemed imminent.

"I wonder if she will run like her brother?" Georgie mused, watching the newly born filly take a few wobbly steps and then find its way back to its mother's swollen milk bag. The foal was of the same breeding as Pharaoh, though she was a bay, not a black.

Outside the air was chill, made colder by a fitful wind. But inside the barn, it was warm and ripe with the scent of horseflesh.

"This filly is as much a gamble as Pharaoh was, for all the shared blood." Kace's voice was as lazy as Georgie's. She knew as much about horses as he did, knew that no matter how good the blood or the precedent, each foal was a new game.

Mare and foal were both fine now. There had been a tense stretch when the mare had been laboring too hard with too little progress, but Kace had not felt it necessary to call extra help. He and Georgie had delivered the foal together.

Georgie's hair was pulled back in a single braid; she was wearing a shirt and breeches stained from the night's work; there were faint smudges under her eyes; the lantern light cast shadows that sculpted her facial bones in high relief; and for an instant, Kace understood that she was the most beautiful woman he had ever seen in his life.

He blinked, rubbed his eyes and saw that it was just Georgie, his other sister, but the shock of the vision was still coursing through him when he said, "They'll be all right now. I must be getting home. Rosalind will be waiting for me."

It was a lie. There were only a couple of hours until dawn; Rosalind would be sound asleep and would stir only if he awakened her. He couldn't imagine why he found it necessary to lie.

Georgie took no offense at his gruff tone; she assumed it was because he was as tired as she. "She'll be pleased to know everything went well; she dotes on the new babies."

As expected, Rosalind was asleep, but he awakened her because it seemed desperately important that she share his world.

He told her about the foal, about how lucky they were that what could have been a very tricky birth had been so satisfactorily resolved. He waited for her to share even the tiniest bit of his enthusiasm, but there was no answering spark for his fire. She was patient at being awakened, tolerant of his excitement, but that was all. There was none of the communion he had shared with Georgie.

He drew Rosalind into his arms, kissing her, stroking her, needing more than ever to validate the bond between them.

She didn't fight him; she even spread her legs to accommodate him, but he could feel her going away, not coming closer to him as he entered her, and he knew, though there was not enough light to see her face, that her eyes were strangely vacant.

"Please, please be with me now. Let it happen for you, too!"

He hated the frantic note of pleading in his voice, but Rosalind gave no indication that she had heard him. If she had, she did not understand or respond.

Nothing was changed for her, but he thought if he were not very careful, everything would change for him.

Chapter 44

To great fanfare, Nellie Bly arrived back in New York on January 25, having made the journey around the world in seventy-two days, six hours, and eleven minutes.

In May, Lillian Russell made the first long-distance telephone call from New York to Washington, D.C., singing to President Harrison and other government officials over the line.

Oklahoma Territory was officially established, and Wyoming was to enter the Union as a state, as North Dakota, South Dakota, Montana, and Washington had the year before. But there was a difference. As a territory, Wyoming had had women's suffrage, and as a state it intended to keep it.

Though they knew it was nothing more than an arbitrary division of time, Lexy and Hawk shared the sense that there was something special about entering the last decade of the century, as if the country were setting the course it would take for a long time to come.

Some of it was worth celebrating.

The new states would have a voice in government that was far more audible than they had had as territories.

While no claim could be made for equality, still there were ever-increasing opportunities for women in higher education, in medicine, in law, and in a host of other fields. It continued to require extraordinary dedication and courage to break out of the ornamental mold, but now it could be done in ways that had been unthinkable at midcentury. Anthea was particularly encouraged by the new rage for sport among young women. Riding, bicycling, archery, boating, and all sorts of other outdoor pursuits were growing more and more popular for those who had the leisure and the means, and they were the ones who most often suffered from overindulgence in food and drink and from inactivity. As Anthea inelegantly stated it, "I'd approve of anything that will get them off of their bottoms and onto their feet."

The increasing use of electricity for light, for transportation, and for power, the expanding network of telephone and telegraph lines, the improvement of water and gas systems, benefited many in the cities, though rural areas were far less affected.

There seemed to be no limit to the inventiveness and productivity of the United States, both in manufactured goods and in farm produce. It was heady stuff to feel such power when only thirty years before they had faced a war that threatened to destroy the nation forever.

But if some of the chosen course was worth celebration, some of it was also worth mourning.

In the mills and factories of the Northeast, far too many men, women, and children worked too hard for too little and lived in squalor. Yet workers who organized and demanded better treatment were met not only with accusations of being communists, anarchists, traitors, and the like, but with brute force where factory owners thought necessary.

On the Western Plains as more and more land was opened for white settlement, the Indians had less and less. Their plight was so hopeless, they so powerless, thousands had taken up the "Ghost Dance" proclaimed by the Paiute messiah Wovoka to be a way to dance and sing away the white men, to make the earth the way it had once been for the Indians, and to bring back the departed members of the tribes. It reminded Lexy of the stories of people who had danced themselves to death while the plague ravished Europe in the Middle Ages. To the Indians, the white man was a never-ending pestilence.

In the Far West, mining continued to be a major industry, and arguments over gold versus silver as the basis for the nation's wealth were constant. And there were other problems as well. Jobs were still not as plentiful as they had once been, and that made it easy for workingmen to despise the Chinese and the native Californios as being a threat to white economic well-being. The Chinese were subject to exclusionary laws, and the Californios had been stripped of land and wealth by court cases regarding land claims that sapped their resources and seldom ended in their favor.

In the South, blacks were losing political ground year by year, damned by one high court ruling after another which said that discrimination in the private sector was not in violation of the Fourteenth and Fifteenth Amendments to the Constitution and by the federal government's reluctance to punish discrimination in the public, governmental sector of the states. More and more regulations were being used in the South to make sure that blacks did not vote or hold office. The dread of another war continued to be the South's best weapon in pursuing its own repressive course.

The lines were drawn not only between regions and between races; perhaps the clearest division was between the rich and the poor. The promise was that anyone who worked hard had a chance to amass a fortune; the reality was that most of the nation's wealth rested in the hands of a very small group of men who controlled transportation, steel, oil, communications, and other major industries. By some estimates ninety-nine percent of the wealth of the nation was controlled by one percent of the population. And money substituted for royalty; most of these men truly believed themselves superior and unaccountable to the laborers they employed.

"I wonder how often it occurs to them that if they would be kings, they might also lose their heads," Lexy said to Hawk while he was writing an article about some fixing of prices on Western railroads, a practice that hurt farmers who depended on the rails to ship their produce to market.

"I think it occurs to them quite often," Hawk replied grimly, "otherwise they would not be so willing to hire private armies to guard their properties and to keep workers in check." He paused, rubbing his brow wearily in a gesture very like Reid's. "I am no seer, but it doesn't take mystic powers to predict that there will be another financial panic, and probably fairly soon if the historical pattern continues: 1819, 1837, 1857, and 1873—sixteen to twenty years between them in this century. But this time, I fear it will be uglier than before because so many people are now dependent on the factories, the mills, and the few men who own them. Men and women who would never hurt anyone under normal circumstances will turn violent when they are deprived of the means to feed and shelter their families. It remains to be seen what the owners will be willing to sacrifice to avoid that."

It was hard for Lexy to believe they'd be willing to sacrifice anything at all, but she hoped her cynicism would prove unworthy.

She was increasingly interested in the woman's voice in the labor movements. If women were not among the leaders, they were close behind in the symbol they provided. The images of women being overworked were much harder for people to swallow than those of men in the same state. But paradoxically, women were generally paid much less than men and had fewer resources to sustain them in times of economic upheaval. And most depended on the wages of the men in their lives to help support them and their children. Lexy did not doubt that they would be there right beside the men if a time of confrontation came.

As Abby Adams, she continued to report the details and opinions of working women's lives, but as Lexy, she moved in the circles of great wealth. She was seldom free of the double view the two parts of her professional life gave her. And she remained determined that she would continue to be a good reporter on both counts.

Racing was suffering from its own excesses. The racing calendar was growing too full, the seasons blurring into one another and making the racing year too long for riders and horses, though this did not apply to the horses of owners like the Culhanes who avoided outlaw tracks and entered their beasts only in a carefully selected program of races. But they and others like them could afford such care because their animals were among the best in the country. There were hundreds of owners and thousands of horses which were not members of the elite; men and beasts raced where they could. If there were few incidents of foul riding on the better courses, they were now legion at the inferior tracks. Fixed races, drugged horses, and fiddled weights in handicap races were commonplace at these courses.

Though there was reciprocity among some tracks over setting racing dates, it was not enough, and worse, there was no overall system to make sure that a horse or rider banned at one track would be banned at the others, so the wrongdoers simply moved from one place to another.

There was also no standard for the naming of horses. Every horse of any merit soon gave rise to scores of namesakes, which led to endless confusion.

There had been talk of a national jockey club since long before the war, but now the idea was being given new power. Lexy knew this from the inside because Pierre Lorillard, currently the major advocate of the proposal, had contacted Travis to ask if he would be interested in participating, and Travis had not hesitated to agree.

Wild Swan had various entries for the 1890 races, and Travis's steeplechasers were in particularly fine shape this year, but Pharaoh was still their best hope. At four years old, he was far more mature than he had been just a year ago, a sleek, powerful stallion who had lost none of his zest for racing. But his record of winning was as much of a hazard as a benefit because in handicapped races he was given top weight to carry. In two instances during the summer, Travis protested the weight assigned, but though he lost the arguments, Pharaoh did not. Pharaoh went on winning.

Lexy was privy to the knowledge that this was the stallion's last season. Gincie and Travis had decided that the risk of injury was not worth it. Pharaoh had already proven himself time and time again; the next step was for him to prove that he could pass on his speed and steady temperament to his progeny. Their plan was to let him have his fifth year off, with only light work and plenty of freedom in the pastures to keep him in shape. Then he would stand at stud as a six-year-old.

Moonraker was commanding higher fees than ever and was being listed as one of the top stallions, his popularity as a stud having been enormously enhanced by his famous son and by his other get which raced so well. Pharaoh's stud fees would be even higher.

Lexy kept the plan a secret through the season, although she was to have the privilege of printing the news first when the season ended.

This year Georgie went to several of the race meetings with the Culhanes, but while the danger to her seemed far in the past, she found she preferred to stay at Wild Swan. She loved to see Wild Swan's horses run, but she felt more useful at the farm, where she could pitch in and do her part. At the races, her role was to be as decorative as Rosalind, and though she could play the part with little effort now, it would never suit her for long. She envied Gincie, who was Travis's equal in all the decisions they made while at the racecourses.

She didn't examine her feelings too closely, but it was also easier not to spend too much time with Kace and Rosalind at the racecourses, where it was more difficult to stay apart than at the farms. Kace had been keeping his distance since the night of the bay filly's birth, making sure he was not alone with Georgie again, though she still saw much of Rosalind. She accepted the blame for it, suspecting that she had betrayed her feelings for him somehow, perhaps by a look, by the way her voice sounded, by something—she wasn't sure. She thought he was being very civilized to handle it so gently.

She tried to do the same for Tay. He, too, spent most of the summer at Wild Swan. He never stepped over the boundaries of propriety, playing the good companion and brother. But if she had betrayed herself to Kace, so Tay betrayed himself to her. His voice softened just so when he spoke to her, and when he caught sight of her, his eyes lighted up in a way quite different from when he saw Lexy.

She didn't have any personal experience with men falling in love with her, but she knew she was not mistaken about Tay.

He was warm, intelligent, humorous, kind, and a very handsome man. He was tall like Kace, though of a slighter build, and he had the same bright turquoise eyes and golden brown hair. But he wasn't Kace. She damned herself for a fool for being unable to love such a special man, for loving his married brother. But no amount of rational thought could change the direction of her heart.

Though races were still going on in New York State, the Culhanes, both the younger and older couples, came home with the horses in September, before Tay returned to school.

The last race meeting they would attend would be in Baltimore the following month, but the pause in the schedule did not mean a lack of work. The fall harvest of various crops and other tasks associated with readying the earth for winter were just beginning, and the work with the horses was never done.

Georgie had ridden racehorses since her father had first boosted her into the saddle at a young age, but she had had no experience with jumping until she had come to Maryland. She was a fine rider, had a superb sense of balance, and was in as close harmony with the horses as any rider Travis had ever seen, and so he had been more than willing to teach her jumping. Hampered on the ground by his lame leg, he felt complete freedom when he was taking a horse over the jumps, leaving the earth to soar for those few precious seconds, and he knew that Georgie felt it, too. Not even at the beginning had there been any fear in her, just concentrated joy.

The jumpers and the practice courses were at Sunrise, and though it inflicted her presence on Kace, Georgie could not stay away when she had a chance to take the horses out. But it was not much of a problem, since Travis was nearly always with her, checking her form and the horses's, often riding the course with her.

Fox hunting was becoming increasingly popular in Maryland and elsewhere, and Travis's horses were prized in the field because he trained them not only to clear all sorts of obstacles but also to share the field civilly with other horses.

Unfortunately, it was not always possible to convince every horse that good manners were essential. Black Moon was a case in point. Sired by Moonraker out of a mare noted for her fine jumping ability, Black Moon had speed and talent, but his temper was erratic. Some days he was a perfect gentleman with other horses or by himself; other days he wanted to fight not only the other horses, but himself. He had proven himself equally uncertain in competition, either winning steeplechases with ease or fighting every obstacle and losing miserably; he seemed to have no middle ground.

Despite the problems, Travis hated to give up on him, and Georgie was in complete agreement. She loved riding Black Moon and could often coax him out of his sulks. She rode him as often as she could, hoping that behaving would become a habit with him.

However, now Travis had a good offer for him from Mr. Simmons, a man who rode with a hunt club in Maryland and who had had his eye on the horse since seeing him win a hurdle race in Baltimore the year before.

Travis was torn, not sure he wanted to sell the horse, though the offer was generous. He was considering keeping Black Moon as a sire, and it was also a matter of what a new owner would do if the horse misbehaved too badly. Black Moon's breeding was too promising to be lost by gelding, but there were far worse fates than that. Travis had seen too many fine animals consigned to the drudgery of dragging carts behind them, beaten and starved into submission.

Travis felt it was as much his responsibility to judge the man's ability as it was to inform him of Black Moon's idiosyncrasies, and his plan was to have Georgie take Black Moon around the course first and then allow the man to try the horse.

The September day was hot and muggy, and Black Moon was sweating before Georgie put him to the first jump. She was only vaguely conscious that the potential buyer, Travis, Kace, and Tay were watching from the sidelines. Her concentration was fiercely centered on Black Moon. She would be sorry to see him go, but at the same time, she wanted him to show how splendid he was.

Black Moon fought the bit a little at the beginning of the ride, but Georgie clucked and crooned to him until he gave her his full attention, and then he attacked the course perfectly, all his power disciplined into a measured pace, his form superbly collected as he sailed over the first jumps.

She heard the sound and saw and understood even as everything went wrong. And eerily, she could hear her father's voice saying very clearly, "Horses can only think of one thing at a time. It's the best and worst thing about them."

Black Moon had already gathered himself to go over a high, white painted section of fence when the wasps began to whine angrily around his face, and when one landed and clung near his right eye, he forgot everything except that he was being attacked. He lashed out in midair and crashed into the jump, tumbling over.

As she kicked free of the stirrups and flew out of the saddle, Georgie kept hold of the reins, hoping desperately that she could somehow keep Black Moon from injury. She hit the ground with her left shoulder first; the air went out of her lungs, and the world went dark, Black Moon's high-pitched scream echoing in her ears.

The group watching the demonstration saw the accident as if it were happening very slowly, and then they were running toward the fallen horse and rider. But no one was as swift as Kace.

He wasn't aware of his father or brother or the buyer or even Black Moon; there was nothing and no one in the universe except Georgie.

"Please, Georgie, please be all right! Oh, Christ! Open your eyes!" He was hot and cold, wild with terror. He had never wanted anything in his life as much as he wanted her to be all right.

She heard Kace's voice and struggled to open her eyes and to draw air into her lungs. The ugly gasping noises seemed to be coming from someone else until Tay said, "That's it, just take slow deep breaths."

When she got her eyes open, faces swam before her until she got them into focus enough to see that the three Culhane men were kneeling around her.

She remembered there was something important she had to tell them. "Not . . ." the word came out too faintly, so she concentrated on inhaling more air and tried again. "Not his fault, wasps." When the men continued to regard her anxiously, not sparing any attention, her worry about Black Moon intensified. "Is he all right? Is he?"

Travis glanced over at Black Moon, who was on his feet, in the care of Mr. Simmons and two stable hands who had seen the accident.

"He . . . er, she's right. He's got a big lump under his eye. A wasp must have stung him." Mr. Simmons was looking as stunned as everyone else, not just because of the fall he had witnessed, but because he hadn't known that the rider was a girl until he had seen her on the ground with her cap off and her braid spilled out.

"Black Moon is solid on all four legs," Travis said. "How about you?"

Georgie thought she was all right until she tried to move and pain speared through her shoulder. Biting back a cry, she slumped back down, right hand clutching at the pain.

"Easy now." Travis opened her shirt, revealing the bulge of the dislocated shoulder. His eyes met Tay's.

It steadied Tay to have something specific to do.

"Your shoulder's out of joint, but if you can stand to be treated by a horse doctor, I can put it back in place," he told her gently, ignoring the hiss of protest from Kace. A brief glance at his brother's face showed him muscles so tense, Kace looked as if he were in as much pain as Georgie.

"Just do it, please," Georgie whispered. If the pain didn't ease soon, she was going to disgrace herself by throwing up.

Knowing that delay would only cause her further suffering, Tay and Travis worked with swift efficiency, Travis holding her still while Tay used steady pressure and then a quick hard pull to snap the joint back into the socket.

Only when the fiery agony had died to a dull throb did Georgie become aware that her head was cradled against Kace's hard thigh and that she had clamped her teeth on the rough material of his pants and the flesh beneath.

"I'm sorry," she choked.

"Hush, love, hush," Kace soothed. "Just lie still until you feel a little better." He stroked the little tendrils of hair back from her damp face, his fingers still trembling from shock.

As blurred as everything was, she knew she was not mistaken. It wasn't brotherly affection she saw in his eyes, heard in his voice. Once she would have given anything to have him love her as a woman; now it only made everything more difficult. He was married to Rosalind, and Rosalind was her friend.

Tay and Travis exchanged a look, needing no words. Kace's feelings were as plain to them as to Georgie, and more, Travis saw Tay's pain as well. His sons were grown men now, and there was nothing he could do to make this easier for them or for Georgie. He felt desperately sorry for all three of them, and yet, he trusted each one to do the honorable thing.

When Rosalind arrived on the scene, she fluttered and exclaimed over Georgie's injury, but she was sensibly insistent that Georgie stay at Sunrise until she felt stronger.

With an effort, Georgie kept the panic out of her voice. "Thank you, but honestly, I will be much more comfortable in my own bed at Wild Swan. Due to the Doctors Culhane, I already feel much better." She managed to smile and to be more insistent than Rosalind. She could not imagine anything worse than spending the night under Kace's roof. In her weakened state, she was afraid she would betray herself to Rosalind. Tomorrow, tomorrow she would be better able to deal with all of this, she assured herself.

Travis and Tay added their voices to Georgie's plan. Kace kept silent, torn between wanting to care for her and recognizing the danger as clearly as she did. So Georgie, shoulder and arm immobilized, went home to Wild Swan.

Mr. Simmons was direct about his reasons for deciding not to buy Black Moon. "He's magnificent; there's no doubt of that. And the accident was not his fault or the rider's. But frankly, he is more horse than I want. He isn't a beast to be neglected and then taken out when it's convenient. I suspect he would make his rider pay for that."

"You're right; he would," Travis agreed.

"If I might make a suggestion?" Mr. Simmons said and went on at Travis's nod, "I don't think you're that anxious to sell Black Moon in the first place, and it seems to me that he already has his perfect rider."

"Yes, I think he does," Travis said. He waited until the next day when Georgie had a little color in her cheeks before he offered Black Moon to her.

Her reaction was exactly what he had expected; she looked forward to riding the horse again as soon as her shoulder healed, but she was shocked by the idea that she own the horse.

He held up his hand. "Whoa, now, before you give me all the reasons why not, remember, this isn't an outright gift. I'd like to use him for stud and for competition, too, and Sunrise would get part of the profits to pay for his upkeep and his entry fees. If you ever wanted to sell him, we'd have first bid and the right to top any other offer."

"You're not blaming him for what happened yesterday, are you?" Georgie asked anxiously. "Truly, it was not his fault!"

"I know it wasn't, but just the same, he's a lot of horse, a lot of talent, and a lot of temper. Watchin' him yesterday, I got to thinkin' that we can surely manage a cross that will produce the talent with a little less of the temper. I was relieved when Mr. Simmons said he didn't want him." He paused and then added, "You know you can ride any horse on either of the farms—that isn't going to change— but it's different, havin' a horse that belongs to you; you just naturally pay it more attention. Black Moon needs that."

He knew it was the right tack to use with her; Georgie could be very stubborn about doing what she considered right, but present it properly, so that she saw it as a way to do something for someone, or in this case for a horse, and her objections could be overcome.

"All right, I accept your much too generous offer, and I promise, by next year Black Moon will be the best jumping horse you've ever seen." She said it like a solemn vow.

"I wouldn't be surprised if Black Moon knows how to fly by next summer," he teased as he left her.

Gincie understood that there was more to Travis's gift than putting the horse in the right hands, and when Travis didn't volunteer, she asked him about it. "I know Georgie will make a good job of Black Moon, but I also know that isn't the only reason you gave her the horse. For some reason, you felt she needed a new cause to stay with us. Why?"

He hadn't discussed what he'd seen with Tay and certainly not with Kace, and he had hoped to avoid telling Gincie, but he found it a relief to share the burden. He told her exactly what had happened when the horse and rider had fallen.

"There's no mistakin' it. Kace was a crazy man gettin' to her, and when she came to, it was on both of their faces. Kace loves Georgie more than he's ever goin' to love Rosalind, and Georgie loves him back. And to make it all more miserable, Tay loves Georgie, too. Hell! What a tangle!"

"And you chose the very best way to let Georgie know that it is not her fault, that her place with us is as secure as that of our sons," Gincie said slowly and swallowed hard against the sudden lump in her throat. "Solomon Culhane, my wise husband." She smiled at him, but her eyes were bright with tears, and she wrapped her arms around him, holding on tightly. "I love you so much, and I wish my sons and Georgie could each know what that is like. I wish Rosalind could know, too, but I doubt she ever will because it isn't in her nature to love like this."

The remembrance of Georgie's pain was clear, an angry purple bruise on Kace's thigh, but Kace did not have to offer Rosalind any explanation; she never looked closely enough at his unclothed flesh to notice even so vivid a mark. But when it faded, the knowledge remained: he loved Georgie. He loved her intelligence, her grace, her courage, her kindness. He loved everything about her. He loved her with a passion that made him feel as if he had grown up in the instant he had seen her crumpled on the ground. And in growing up, he was forced to see his relationship with Rosalind for what it was, an infatuation that should never have come to marriage.

He accepted the blame as entirely his own, and he resolved that Rosalind would never suffer for it. But of how he would ease Georgie's hurt and his own, he had no idea.

Chapter 45

By November, Lexy knew it was only a matter of time before Hawk left to pursue the story of the Ghost Dance among the Sioux.

She had seen him deeply committed to stories before, but this was rapidly becoming an obsession. He read and reread every news story concerning the Indians in South Dakota and the followers of

Wovoka elsewhere. He used Reid's government connections and his own to pursue every bend of official and unofficial policy.

Wovoka had lived with white ranchers who had given him the name Jack Wilson. His sojourn with them had exposed him to Christianity, and that, mixed with his own background, had given his vision a specific moral code which emphasized honesty, kindness, avoidance of the evils of alcohol, and, above all else, no violence. The resurrection of the beloved dead, the reappearance of the buffalo and other game, the disappearance of the white men—all were to be achieved by divine intervention, not by war.

But for the Sioux, this was not enough. The past several years had brought one disaster after another upon them. The disciples who brought the Ghost Dance back to them wrought a major change in it. "Ghost Shirts" began to be worn by men and women. Like those of other tribes, they were decorated with the symbols of the wearers' personal visions, but unlike the others, these shirts were believed to be proof against bullets and weapons of all kinds, most specifically the guns of white men.

To most whites living near the Sioux, this was proof that the Indians were planning an uprising. Images of the old massacres were becoming terrifyingly fresh, and relations between the races were degenerating by the day. There was a rising chorus of demands from the whites for more soldiers and for military action that would stop the trouble before it began.

Added to this already volatile mix were the Indian agents, two in particular. James McLaughlin, in charge of the Standing Rock Agency, was by most accounts an honest, well-intentioned man, but he was also a longtime enemy of Sitting Bull and generally ascribed any trouble from the Indians as having been initiated by the old chief. The other man was Daniel F. Royer, put in charge of the Pine Ridge Reservation only a month before, an outstanding example of how unwise it was to award such stewardships as payment for political debts. Venal, untried, nervous, with no understanding whatsoever of the Indians and their problems, he was the worst man imaginable for the post.

Reid had this assessment from trusted sources, sources he had cultivated ever since his trip to the region in the aftermath of the Battle of the Little Big Horn. His interest in the fate of the Sioux and other Indian nations had never flagged, and even now, at fifty-eight years old and with his responsibilities at the paper tying him down, he still wished he were the one going to South Dakota.

Hawk considered all that they knew, and then he asked, "Do you think Sitting Bull believes in the Ghost Dance?"

"I doubt it very much," Reid answered. "He is a mystic in his own right, but he is also a realist. I cannot imagine that he believes flimsy shirts will stop bullets. But the worst of this is that it doesn't really matter what Sitting Bull believes or does not believe. What matters to the government is that he is a symbol of the unregenerate Indian. He has never admitted that white men or their government have any power over him, even when he has been forced to do as they dictate."

Hawk rubbed at the tense muscles in his neck and stared blindly at the notes before him. Vague images from his childhood swirled before him, images of his grandparents, white blood mixing with the red in a rare harmony that had touched him with a kindness his father could not manage. "Is there no good way out of this?"

"I never lose hope," Reid replied, "but the memory of what happened to Custer and his men is not far enough distant to be safe. Hysteria, incompetence, and fear—fear on both sides—make a bad brew."

He studied Hawk's face, and belatedly, he realized as Lexy had earlier, that there was a quiet but terrifying intensity to Hawk as he contemplated the story that was beginning to unfold. "Are you sure you want to do this? I can send Rob Jenkins or one of the others." He was trying to be delicate about it, but he felt like an insensitive fool because he had simply not taken Hawk's Indian heritage into account. It had never been an issue between them, but this was a different case. And he remembered only too well the haunting effect his own trip to the region had had on him, he who had not a trace of Indian blood.

Hawk did not raise his voice, but his face was set in rigid lines. "I am very sure I want to do this. Can you think of anyone better to do it than a man who is from both worlds?"

Reid did not attempt to dissuade him further.

"I will try to be home for Christmas," Hawk promised Lexy, "but if not, believe that I'll be thinking of you." He knew how important that family holiday was to her, and through her, it had become important to him as well.

"Just come home in one piece," Lexy said, holding back tears. This parting felt different from the others they had endured in the course of their work, and that frightened her. It was as if some vital part of his spirit had already traveled away from her.

"I'm not marching off to war," he chided, hoping it was true.

The cold wind sweeping across the plains was a shock after the mild November weather Hawk had left in Washington. It matched the winter that quickly began to chill his soul.

He bought the best horse he could find, and after a week, he felt as if he'd never be able to straighten his legs again. He had not spent so much time in the saddle since his boyhood, but it was worth the long, weary hours because piece by piece he was putting the puzzle together, talking to Indian agents, soldiers, white settlers, and when they would allow it, Indians. But the Indians he talked to were among the "friendlies," so called because they were remaining close to the agencies, trying to distance themselves from the "hostiles," who were said to be gathering in a distant northwest corner of the Pine Ridge Reservation near the southern border of the state. The friendlies did not wish to talk about the Ghost Dance at all. They were terrified by the increasing number of cavalry and infantry gathering at the Pine Ridge and Rosebud reservations. They wanted it known that they were "good" Indians. They tore at Hawk's heart.

Some of the very old and some in their twenties were willing to speak, sometimes in English, sometimes through a translator, but they did not wish to speak of things of the spirit; they wanted to know why the white people in Washington had decided to cut the Indians' beef rations in the past years, why they couldn't understand that the Indians were starving.

It was bad enough to know that Congress had severely cut rations for the good of the budget and that the Indians had suffered droughts and epidemics of influenza, measles, and whooping cough among the undernourished children; it was far worse to see the results before him. Despite the deepening cold, many of the people were dressed in little more than rags, and hunger was carved into their faces. Hawk wondered how they could survive another winter on the increasingly barren and ever-diminishing acreage allotted to them.

Though he wished he had Jericho Baines to guide him, he was glad the old man had not lived to see this. Reid's account had made the man vivid to Hawk, and he felt as if he knew how deep the wound would have been had Jericho had to witness this. He denied the growing intensity of his own pain, pain welling from wounds inflicted long ago, wounds he had thought well healed.

One old woman peered at him for such a long time, it was as if she were stripping the flesh from his bones to stare into the very center of him. She gabbled to herself and finally nodded, having settled some internal argument.

"Stay!" she commanded, and Hawk obeyed. She left him only briefly, and when she returned, she thrust a beaded strip of buckskin into his hands. It was old, but the flowers and designs so intricately wrought were still bright. It had probably been worn as a sash crossing the chest from shoulder to waist. Hawk was completely baffled as to why the woman had put it in his hands.

She stared at him, nodded again, and said, "For my husband, long time 'go, make it in freedom, no freedom here, you take, make free again."

Her face was creased by countless lines; her gray hair straggled in its braids; her dark eyes were faded by age; and she was dressed in a motley of buckskin and white man's cloth, and yet, she possessed such dignity, Hawk did not consider refusing the gift. Instead, he felt humbled by the honor, and he felt a host of other things.

He folded the band carefully and tucked it inside his shirt. "It will be free always," he promised. It was as if she had not only seen his dual nature, both Indian and white, but had also approved it. He took it as a blessing in a land that was growing short of grace. But if the old woman had blessed him, she had also, Hawk soon discovered, burdened him.

The images from his childhood had been vague during his meeting with Reid, but after his encounter with the old woman, they became clearer, more insistent, particularly the faces of his grandmothers, the primary source of his own Indian heritage. His father had been only a quarter Cheyenne, his mother half Cherokee, but in himself, both tribes and the blood of whites flowed together. For his father, the mixed inheritance had brought unending conflict as he alternately accepted and rejected what he could not change until there was nothing left except bitter, useless rage. But for himself, it had been different. He had felt pain, even as a small child he had felt it, but not hatred against himself, in response to the cruelty of those who felt free to treat people of mixed race as less than human.

Hawk had always accepted himself for what he was; despite his father's attitude and the pressure from outsiders, he had never wanted to be all white. Even when he had been quite young, he had understood that to be wholly white would mean relinquishing all of the love and kindness and magic his grandparents, particularly his grandmothers, had given to him during the brief periods he was with them. But only now did he fully understand that they had also given him the only sense of community—a belonging that went beyond immediate family—that he had known until he married Lexy. Along with the games, stories, and songs had come the knowledge that everything was connected to a way of life shared by many people. For the first time he understood that while it was possible to be alone and successful as a white—indeed much of what was considered valuable in white society concerned individual ownership of self, home, and business—to be solitary as an Indian meant being an outcast. The traditions of Indian life were not written down to be contemplated alone; everything, from worship to work to play, required communal effort. To take an Indian away from his community or to destroy the structure of that community was to destroy him utterly.

Bit by bit, everything that made life whole and possible for the Indians had been stripped away over the years, and in Hawk the conviction grew that he was witnessing the final dissolution not just of the Sioux, but of all Indians in the United States. And in the bleakness of that vision there was not only the observation of a journalist recording a disaster, there was also the risk of his own heart and sanity, because the best of both had come from this world that was being vanquished. It was not that he had ever lived for long as an Indian or that he ever intended to live so again—he was, in truth, less than half Indian, and his life was in the white world —but still, it was immeasurably important that the strength and symmetry of the ancient cultures survive as more than myth and memory.

He began to hear the music of his own Ghost Dance, the steady beat of the drums and the steps woven with the haunting flute notes, the dancers circling and circling until their minds were set free to roam with all the spirits that made the earth and the life on it harmonious. He had seen the dances and heard the music in his childhood, but he had not known then that the drums were his own heart beating.

He had to remind himself constantly that he was there as a reporter for the *Witness*, but he understood that to stray from that fixed point was to risk succumbing to total despair.

James McLaughlin would undoubtedly have preferred not to grant Hawk an interview, but the reputation of the *Witness* was such that he did not dare to refuse, and though it would have been easier had Hawk found no redeeming qualities in the man, it was not that simple.

Despite the miserliness of the government, McLaughlin was doing his best to see to the physical needs of the Indians. Unlike too many Indian agents, he felt the full weight of his stewardship. But his flaw was that he truly believed that Indians could only improve as human beings by becoming like white men; nothing in their own culture was worthy in his eyes. He was not alone; most of the white population of the country believed as he did—how could there be any more acceptable state than that of a white Christian?

And because his belief ran so deeply in his heart and his mind, he was genuinely hurt that the Indians did not appreciate his efforts on their behalf. He saw Sitting Bull as the major obstacle in the way of steering the Sioux away from their backward and heathen ways.

"Do you have proof, then, that Sitting Bull supports the Ghost Dance?" Hawk asked.

"It isn't necessary to have proof," McLaughlin answered angrily. "Whatever stirs the Indians up, whatever causes trouble amongst the Sioux, you can be sure Sitting Bull has a hand in it! He could have stopped all of this—they think that highly of him—but he hasn't! They've performed it right in his camp! No one will ever convince me that he isn't behind this. If we can just remove him from the scene, everything will settle down."

"How do you plan to 'remove' him without provoking violence?" Hawk kept his voice calm, but inwardly he despaired, and the drums sounded louder. Pure evil would be easier to combat than this good heart going in what Hawk judged a very wrong direction.

The agent was at least aware of the potential for disaster in the situation. "It must be done in the right way," he admitted, "and I hope the government will allow the agency, not the Army, to handle it."

Hawk took his leave, knowing there was nothing more to be gleaned from talking to the agent except a rise in his own temper. He thought of the added soldiers being sent to South Dakota, too many of them Indian fighters from way back, and he thought of how jealously various departments of the government guarded their powers and privileges. It wasn't difficult to foresee squabbling over who was to "remove" the chief. And with squabbling came bungling.

He felt as if he were watching the cast of a Shakespearean tragedy assembling on a stage, with the plot of betrayal and murder already laid out before them.

He had assumed that getting to talk to Sitting Bull would be the most difficult thing of all, but it was surprisingly easy, and he soon discovered that the audience had been granted not because he carried Indian blood in his veins, but because he represented the *Witness*.

Sitting Bull might be living simply in his cabin at his camp on the Grand River, but the ways of the world outside the reservations were familiar to him. He had traveled under the auspices of the showman Alvaren Allen and then with Buffalo Bill Cody's Wild West Show, performing in some of the largest cities in America, and he had always known the value of powerful allies. His memory was long, and it included the fact that the *Witness* had dealt fairly with Indians since its inception.

He was a showman, a chief, a medicine man, a warrior, and an implacable foe of the government in Washington because he had always known that no compromise was possible with an enemy who took everything and was still not satisfied.

When he had learned of yet another relinquishing of Sioux lands to the whites, he had named himself the "last Indian."

He was such a powerful presence, he made Hawk feel as if he were back at the beginning of his career, uncertain of how to approach the subject. Suddenly he remembered Lexy telling him that she had decided not to be presented to Queen Victoria because she could not imagine that anything useful would have come of it.

Lexy's image steadied him. He could think of no one, including Sitting Bull, whom his wife would not face if she thought justice might be served.

Sitting Bull was nearing sixty, and the years were written plainly on his seamed face with its broad, flat cheekbones, aggressive nose, and the long slash of mouth. His eyes showed his age, too, the dark irises slightly filmed and the whites discolored from a lifetime of exposure to the elements, but the cool intelligence was still there. And the pride, pride that had not been broken despite his being stripped of power, land, and freedom by the white men, year by year.

Hawk did not presume any easy familiarity with the chief, treating him with the same ceremony and deference he would have given to the president or a king, recognizing him as the political and spiritual leader of his people, recognizing him beyond that as part of the secret kingdom he was discovering in himself. Here the interior music was not strange.

Though Hawk had a young Indian man with him as a translator, Sitting Bull spoke mostly in English, a language he commanded with stark eloquence.

"The land I have under my feet is mine. I never sold it; I never gave it to anybody," he told Hawk. "White men steal the land more and more each day and kill all the creatures on it. There is no beast of earth or sky or water who is more greedy than the white man."

Hawk listened to and noted the chief's complaints, though both of them knew that all these grievances had been listed before, and that it was improbable that anything new would come of making them public again. But that did not detract from the validity. Hawk had seen such clear evidence of hunger, disease, and poverty that the images were burned into his brain.

Not all of the talk was so grim. There were white men whom the chief held in high esteem. He remembered his days with Buffalo Bill Cody as good ones and Cody as a good man. Before Hawk left him, Sitting Bull showed him the gray circus horse Cody had given him when the chief had left the Wild West Show. His face creased in a broad smile of affection as he patted the old beast and demonstrated a few of the animal's tricks.

Hawk found himself curiously reluctant to leave the old man. Sitting Bull seemed to him at once enormously powerful and yet vulnerable. He had a sudden mad wish to beg him to come away from the trouble, out of the soldiers' reach. But he saw the insult of even suggesting such a course.

They had both avoided talk of the Ghost Dance during most of the meeting, but in the final moments, though Hawk knew he was violating the code of decency that forbade one man questioning another about the state of his soul, he asked anyway. "Do you believe in the Ghost Dance?" He winced inwardly at the harsh demand of his own voice.

Rather than taking offense, Sitting Bull looked faintly amused, as if he understood even better than Hawk why the question had to be asked.

Hawk was acutely uncomfortable in the silence that followed, while Sitting Bull's serenity seemed unaffected. But when the old man answered, it was in his own tongue, and the translator softly supplied the English words, "It is impossible for a dead man to return and live again."

It was whites who had named the ritual "Ghost Dance" because of the emphasis on the resurrection of and reunion with the dead. As far as Hawk was concerned, Sitting Bull's answer was definite. It was as Reid had suspected. Though the chief might allow his people whatever comfort the new religion offered, he did not himself believe in it, nor was he its high priest.

As he rode away, Hawk thought how naive it was to think that the Ghost Dance was strong enough theology to appeal to Sitting Bull, a man so much a part of the old religion of his own people that he had experienced visions from an early age and had participated in the bloodletting of the Sun Dance, now forbidden by the government. He had "seen" Custer's troops before they arrived. He had warned his people against looting and mutilating the bodies of the soldiers and prophesied doom when they did so anyway. And surely doom had come to him and his people.

A shiver ran down Hawk's spine. The young translator had told him that the chief had been warned by a meadowlark that he would be slain by his own people. It was unimaginable that such a revered figure could so perish, but still, the messages Sitting Bull had received from the spirit world had previously been proven devastatingly accurate.

However, Hawk's pessimism lifted dramatically when he learned that Buffalo Bill Cody was arriving to coax Sitting Bull away from the area. Cody was not only a man the chief trusted, he was genuinely concerned about the chief's well-being. For him, Sitting Bull just might "remove" himself from the area. It seemed to Hawk a near miracle that such a sensible plan was to be employed in the general madness that prevailed.

Buffalo Bill arrived with three friends and a host of newsmen, some of whom Hawk knew. He welcomed the added press coverage because he hoped it would help check violence on both sides.

But Hawk's hope soon turned to ugly suspicion. Instead of letting Cody get on with the plan, the commander of nearby Fort Yates insistently extended the hospitality of the officers' club to the visiting celebrity. Access to the club and Cody was blocked, but rumor was that there were relays of officers assigned to drink with the visitor. On the surface, it could be taken as no more than a gesture of hospitality offered to a famous man visiting a bleak Army post, but Hawk suspected the more sinister motive of delay.

He also suspected that Agent McLaughlin might be behind it since he wanted his own forces at the reservation to handle the matter of Sitting Bull. Cody had a notoriously hard head for drinking, so at best, the delay would be short. Hawk wanted to know what use McLaughlin planned to make of that time, but if the agent had been accessible before, now it was impossible, short of a violent confrontation with reservation police, to get to him.

McLaughlin used the time well, telegraphing Washington to gain reinforcement for his own plan and a change of mind about Buffalo Bill playing any part at all. In this he was aided by the military, who were also opposed to Cody playing a role in the dealings with Sitting Bull.

The refuge of the hostiles was being called the "Stronghold," and now word went everywhere that Sitting Bull had accepted an invitation from Short Bull and Kicking Bear to join with the dancers there.

Hawk thought that if this rumor were true, it would be because the old chief meant it as a gesture of defiance against the cavalry and infantry pouring into the Pine Ridge and Rosebud reservations. But nothing concrete developed in the following days except that Hawk grew increasingly frustrated by his inability to find out what was really happening. He was treated politely but firmly by both military and reservation authorities and kept away from the people he most wanted to talk to, including Sitting Bull.

The rhythm of the phantom drums was changing, growing so loud and ominous that sometimes even filling his mind with images of Lexy did not stop the sound.

On December 14, a new rumor had it that Sitting Bull was ready to set out for Pine Ridge.

On December 15, the days of prophecy ended.

Hawk got the best account from the young man who had served as translator.

During the night, Sioux police, called "Metal Breasts" because of their badges, had gathered at Sitting Bull's Grand River camp. At dawn they had surrounded his cabin and had gone in to drag him out. He asked to be allowed to dress first, but the police, fearful of losing their prize, manhandled him, trying at once to dress him and to keep him captive, until one of his wives protested. Meanwhile, a crowd gathered outside.

When the chief was pushed outside by the police, he suddenly shouted, "I am not going." A shot was fired at the police chief, who fell, but even badly hurt, he managed to wound Sitting Bull. And the man who had been pushing Sitting Bull put a bullet in the Indian leader's brain, killing him.

When the battle was over, there were dead and wounded on both sides, including Sitting Bull's seventeen-year-old son, Crowfoot.

The meadowlark had told Sitting Bull, "The Sioux will kill you," and now it had come true.

The young man's voice was rigidly controlled as he related the events of the chief's death to Hawk, but then his words broke over the strangest detail.

"His horse . . . the gray horse who knows tricks . . . when his master was shot, the horse sat on his haunches and began to do his tricks . . . as he had in the Wild West Show. You see, he was trained to gunshots." His face twisted for a moment in a rictus of grief before he disciplined himself to impassivity once more. But his eyes widened when he heard the stream of obscenities Hawk let loose, some of which he understood, some of which he could only guess at.

Hawk dredged up every foul curse he had ever heard, and still it was not enough. He was so filled with regret and grief, he hurt inside, and the drums only he could hear pounded in his ears. At that moment, he wanted more than anything to go home, to crawl into Lexy's arms and forget that he had ever been to South Dakota. But what he had to do was telegraph the news of Sitting Bull's death to the paper and then continue to cover the story.

It was far from over. There were still an estimated three thousand hostiles at the Stronghold, and there were troops of soldiers anxious to deal with them. There was also increasing hysteria, continually encouraged by Agent Royer, among the whites, based on the assumption that the murder of the chief would surely mean that the Indians would go on the warpath.

In fact, as near as Hawk could determine, the Indians who were on the move, including some of those from Sitting Bull's camp, were fleeing further violence from the whites and were hoping that some miracle of the Ghost Dance would save them.

He did manage to meet with Royer face to face, but it was not only a waste of time, it was a nightmare. The man was just as incompetent as Reid had portrayed him, and he stank of fear. Indians were no more human to him than grizzly bears, and every bit as dangerous. Viewing Hawk as only a thin cut away from the other savages, he treated Hawk as if he feared he was going to attack him, and Hawk was more than a little tempted. Royer kept repeating over and over that the "matter had to be handled in the proper way."

And then suddenly Hawk was as irrational as Royer, for he saw before him not the Indian agent, but a nameless storekeeper from decades past. He could see himself as he had been then, a raggedy little boy for whom visits to a general store were still the stuff of wonder. But as rare as such expeditions were in his life, he knew the rules. He was not to touch anything or say anything, and he was to stay out of the way. But he could look. Even if he couldn't see over the counters, there were all sorts of things piled on the floors of such places. And if he were very, very lucky, his father might buy him a stick of candy. It had happened twice before, so it was not impossible that it would happen again. He stole glances at his father, trying to judge his mood, satisfied that if there was no obvious emotion on his father's face, at least that hard visage was not twisted with rage, an expression with which he was all too familiar.

It all came back to him—the warmth of the late spring day, the way the light had caught in the dust motes near the entrance to the store, the delicious odors that had permeated the place. Before he had even seen them, he had identified coffee, spices, cheese, rope, and leather, just from the smells. He could even see the marmalade cat that had been lying in a patch of sunlight, lazily cleaning its fur with its small pink tongue.

He caught sight of the candy jars perched in all their glory on a high counter, and he concentrated very hard on which flavor he would choose if he were given a chance. When it had happened before, it had come with a brusque, "Well, choose one, boy," with no warning either time, and he had known that if he didn't make the decision immediately, the chance would be lost.

He was concentrating so hard on the candy, he was scarcely aware of the people in the store, except to keep out of their way, but he heard what the storekeeper said and the silence that followed.

"Don't serve Injuns, big or little, so you jus' get along now." The words were made worse by the fact that they were spoken in such an offhand way, as if what the man was saying was so commonplace and acceptable, no special emphasis was needed.

Hawk remembered how dark his father's face had become, dark and twisted with rage, his big hands knotted into fists. In that instant, he had been more afraid of his father than ever before. He remembered how the customers in the store had looked, their faces blank as they pretended nothing was amiss, except for one woman. Her face came back to him, ethereal in the delicacy of features and pale coloring. She had not come to their defense, but after flashing one angry look at the storekeeper, she had regarded Hawk with such apology and compassion, the expression was still clear in his mind.

And then his father had drawn a deep shuddering breath, muttered, "Come on, boy," and they had left the store. That night his father had gotten very drunk and had beaten him so brutally that he had been ill for days, and many of the scars on his back were from that episode.

Staring at Agent Royer, he felt his father's rage and hate coursing through him, and he wanted to grab the man and strangle the life out of him. The blood and the drums throbbed in his head, but abruptly, he pulled back from the darkness. What the little boy had sensed was still valid. He had watched his father destroy himself with self-hatred and with hatred for others; he had suffered terrible pain at his father's hands; and somewhere deep inside he had always known that to become the mirror of his father would be to lose himself forever. No one, not the storekeeper from long ago or the man before him now was worth that. But he did not deny the satisfaction he felt from the fact that when he left Royer, the man was breathing as if he had run a hard race—or had nearly collapsed from fear.

Hawk questioned everyone he could coax or bribe to talk to him. He had no compunction about persuading some of the younger soldiers to say more than they should have. The problem was, no one yet seemed to know exactly what was happening.

Logically he knew that, given the violence that permeated the land, he stood as good a chance of being picked off by an Indian as by a white man, but it was the latter he feared more. He did not deny the duality of his nature, but on most days now, he felt wholly Indian.

He knew he was losing weight, and he had developed a racking cough, but he pushed himself relentlessly, unable to shake the feeling that he would somehow be able to prevent further death if he could just put all the pieces together properly. He recognized the fevered hubris of the idea, but he could not stop.

He spent Christmas Eve in a haze of misery, drowning the fire in his chest with some of the worst whiskey he had ever drunk and suffering nightmares of Lexy reduced to the poverty and illness he had seen in so many of the Indian women.

And in the end, there was nothing he could do to stop the slaughter.

Some of Sitting Bull's people had joined with Big Foot, who

lived one hundred miles to the south. He and his people were heading to agency headquarters near Fort Bennett on the Missouri River to get rations.

But the reservation authorities had decided that Chief Big Foot was another troublemaker and ought to be taken into custody. When the cavalry intercepted the chief, he assured them that his people's intentions were lawful, and when he was asked why he had allowed hostiles from Sitting Bull's camp to join with him, he pointed out that he had only taken in thirty-eight men and women who were weary, hungry, badly clothed, and suffering from the cold.

Colonel E. V. Sumner of the 8th Cavalry was not impressed by this explanation. He ordered Big Foot's band, numbering over three hundred, more than two hundred of them women and children, to go with him westward to Camp Cheyenne where he could watch them.

Though they felt they were being badly treated, the Indians complied with this order until they neared the region of their own village. Then they decided they would go no further.

Big Foot informed the colonel that they had been going only to procure food in the first place, had done nothing wrong, and would therefore return home. But during the night, alarmed by word that more troops were coming from the east, they fled, heading toward the Badlands, where they hoped to find refuge.

Orders went out that they were to be apprehended, and on December 28, another cavalry unit caught up with them. Big Foot surrendered under a white flag; his people were in no condition to fight even had they wished to.

The troops harried the tattered band southwest to Wounded Knee Creek and set up an armed ring around the Indian camp.

By morning, four more cavalry troops had arrived to swell the number of soldiers to close to five hundred. The commander of the additional troops at least had the decency to provide a camp stove for Big Foot, who was ill with pneumonia.

In the morning, decency fled. The order was given to disarm the Indians, but when only a few weapons were produced, the soldiers began to invade the tipis and paw through the Indians' possessions. The women began to wail at this trespass, and the fury of their men grew at this further outrage when they had been innocent of wrongdoing in the first place.

Yellow Bird, a medicine man, exhorted the men to resist, and when the soldiers attempted to search the man, the situation exploded.

A young Indian, by some accounts a deaf man who was even more terrified and confused than the others by what was happening, pulled a gun from under his robe and fired wildly. The troopers returned fire instantly, at point-blank range, felling nearly half of the warriors. The survivors drew the small number of weapons they had and charged the soldiers.

On the hill overlooking the camp, the Hotchkiss guns opened fire on the women and children who were pouring out of the tipis, and when they and the few remaining warriors fled away into a ravine, soldiers pursued them, firing on them until the guns were repositioned and could rain shot on everything that moved in the ravine. Some Indians ran as far as two miles before dying of their wounds.

When it was over, there were thirty-five dead white men and thirty-nine wounded, and it was probable that most of them had been hit by their own weapons in the crossfire. Of Big Foot's people, nearly two-thirds had been mowed down. There were at least one hundred and fifty dead, at least fifty wounded. Big Foot had been killed early on by a volley of gunfire when he had raised himself up from his pallet in a wagon bed. And most of the other chiefs had been killed behind him. The shooting, stabbing, and clubbing at close range had been bad enough, but the cold precision of the Hotchkiss guns delivering fifty rounds a minute had been worse, flattening everything in range, filling the air with deadly shell fragments.

The army had done its work without the oversight of the press, but Hawk pumped every detail he could from a young trooper who was in shock from what he'd seen and what he'd done. He drank too much of the foul whiskey Hawk offered, and he kept saying, "Big holes, there were such big holes in the women and children. It happened so fast, so damn fast!"

The boy's confusion and pain were palpable, but Hawk was beyond caring. This soldier was alive; Big Foot and most of his people were dead or dying. If nothing else, Hawk would record it accurately, right down to the fact that the cavalry unit that had intercepted Big Foot's people on their flight toward the Badlands was part of the 7th Cavalry, Custer's old regiment. In his fevered state, it was easy for Hawk to imagine that this was also part of Sitting Bull's prophecy of the doom that would come from looting and mutilating the dead at the Battle of the Little Big Horn.

The Indians were incensed over the massacre, and they ambushed the 7th Cavalry at Drexel Mission the next day, but the black cavalrymen of the 9th rescued the 7th before the Indians could inflict more than slight damage.

The truth was that the Sioux were too hungry, too tired, too divided amongst themselves to face the huge and well-equipped military presence. And General Miles, long experienced in the Indian wars, knew just the combination of threat and promise to bring them to heel.

On New Year's Day, 1891, Hawk went with the soldiers and civilians, who had been hired for two dollars a day, to bury the Indian dead at Wounded Knee.

A blizzard had swept the area, and the bodies were dusted with snow and frozen in place. Chief Big Foot lay slumped where he had fallen early in the battle, a trooper's bullet in his head. He appeared old and feeble in death, his head wrapped in a scarf as if yet to keep the cold out, his hands gnarled and curled.

Hawk stared at him for a long time and at the twisted bodies of the women and children. He saw himself there and his grandmothers; even his father was surely there among the twisted corpses with the black frozen blood marking them in great patches, with limbs mangled or missing. When the photographer he had hired would have fled the grisly scene, Hawk turned on him in such fury, the man subsided and did as he had been paid to do.

Sitting Bull had been buried in a homemade coffin filled with quicklime in a corner of the military cemetery at Fort Yates. Hawk wished he had photographs of that, too.

He wanted a tangible record. Nothing seemed real to him anymore. He was seeing everything through a fever of illness and grief. But he stayed through the complete surrender of the Indians on January 15, and through the grand review of the troops on January 21.

While the Sioux, still as statues in the winter wind, watched from the hills, regiment after regiment paraded before General Miles. A band played "Garry Owen," Custer's old battle air, as the 7th Cavalry passed by. Sabers caught the light, guidons stood out in the wind, rifles were presented, and the Hotchkiss guns, their carriages scarred by bullets, came last. The Indian wars in the West were over.

As Hawk witnessed the colorful, aggressive display before him, another image was stronger—Sitting Bull's gray circus horse performing with dumb innocence while his master died.

And inside of Hawk, the ancient music ceased, the beat of the drums and of the dancers' feet and the sinuous curl of the flute fading into a silence so lonely, he tried desperately to call the music back. But the silence held fast.

It seemed to Hawk that it had been years, not months, since he had seen Lexy. But now, at long last, he could go home.

Chapter 46

Lexy knew she was far more fortunate than the majority of people in the world this Christmas. She was healthy, she was employed, and she had most of her family around her. But she was miserable without Hawk.

Once word had come from him of Sitting Bull's murder, she had understood that it would be long days before Hawk came home. And it was not just that she missed him; she was terrified for his safety, physically because his Indian blood was bound to make him suspect to some, and mentally because his involvement had gone way beyond the normal even before he had left, and with Sitting Bull's death, Lexy feared Hawk was losing his sanity. The letter she received right before Christmas assured her that Hawk missed her and that, while the situation was grim, she was not to worry about him. But the message was short, the handwriting uneven, unlike his usual bold, regular script, and the best she could do in return was to send letter after letter and hope they reached him at the various places he was staying.

She was grateful that her family did not try to assure her that there was nothing to worry about, and she in turn tried not to burden them with her fears. But she nearly lost her hard-won control when Reid gave her the little box Hawk had entrusted to his care until Christmas. Inside was a gold locket on a chain, the face of it engraved with the same motif—two swans with necks bent to form a heart—that decorated the necklace Rane had long ago given to Alex and that now belonged to Gincie. Inside the locket were miniature paintings, one of Hawk, one of Lexy. The artist Hawk had commissioned was very skilled. Though he must have worked from photographs, he had captured the coloring and expressions of his subjects perfectly, so that though the images were small, Lexy felt as if she were looking in a mirror at herself and as if Hawk were right there. The locket was proof of how early and carefully he had planned the Christmas gift.

Reid put a comforting hand on her shoulder. "I feel some guilt for putting Hawk in this position," he confessed, "but the dispatches he's been sending—no one could be doing a finer job."

Lexy knew that was true, and she reminded herself of it over and over, trying to use it as a shield against the pain of Hawk's absence.

Kace and Rosalind were also missing from the Christmas celebrations, as they had gone to New England to spend the time with Rosalind's family.

In her overly sensitive state, Lexy observed that the couple's absence was having a good effect on Georgie and thus on Tay. In recent weeks when Lexy had visited the farms, she had been aware not only of an underlying restraint and sadness in Georgie, but also of a change in Kace. Kace was too careful around Georgie now, and though no one had told her the finer details of what had happened after Georgie had fallen off Black Moon, Lexy was, despite marriages and separate lives, still close enough to her brothers to read them quite easily. She saw that Kace's feelings were no longer so innocent toward Georgie. And she accepted, as her parents had, that she couldn't do anything for Kace, for Georgie, or for Tay, which only added to her general feeling of helplessness.

She was grateful to Joseph for his perspective. He did not try to mitigate the danger or the complications of what Hawk was doing, but he said, "Maybe he had to go, as I had to go to the South. I know that none of us thinks of him in the context of his Indian blood; he is just Hawk to us, to you. But to himself he might well be someone quite different."

He drew a deep breath and looked away for a moment before he went on. "As I was quite different. I grew up with Anthea's and Max's love surrounding me. I grew up and looked like a man. But inside I was still the child who was afraid of the monsters who came in the night. I couldn't see the truth until I stood in that clearing. Maybe Hawk is standing in his own clearing now."

"I wish I were with him," she whispered.

"Oh, but you are," he assured her. "And you will be the one he comes home to."

Although she had nothing pressing at the paper, Lexy went back to Washington immediately after Christmas, promising her parents she would return for New Year's Eve. She wanted to be close to the newspaper office in case of further word from Hawk, and she wanted the comfort of being surrounded by his things in the house they shared.

It was Rob Jenkins who brought her the news of Wounded Knee.

"It just came in on the wire," he said, handing her the text written in his slapdash hand. His manner was so tentative, his face so worried, she knew it was dreadful news before she read it.

She turned so white as she read that Rob exclaimed, "Lexy! Remember, he sent this report! That means he's all right!"

She looked at him with eyes gone pale yellow green with shock. "It just means he's alive; it doesn't mean he's all right." She crumpled the paper in her hands. "I'll wait; I'll wait in our house until he comes home."

Rob unclenched her fists and took her hands in his. "He won't be back tomorrow or the next day or the day after that," he reminded her gently. "It won't make him come home any faster for you to mope by yourself. Go to Wild Swan as you planned. I promise you, if there's any further word, I'll bring it out to you."

She did as he told her because suddenly she could not bear to be alone. Their house no longer had any comfort to offer; now it seemed to contain Hawk's nightmares.

She had reason to be glad of Rob's advice, for the old traditions observed on New Year's Eve at Wild Swan settled her, and the presence of the older generations reminded her that these people had experienced much good and bad in their lives and still functioned as complete human beings.

She thought particularly of the courage it must take for Sam to be surrounded by all the couples who must make her remember every minute that Morgan was gone. But Sam remained serene in the midst of all the celebrations, playing with her grandchildren, discussing various subjects with the adults, and generally participating in everything that went on around her. There was no doubt that she missed Morgan; she referred to him frequently, and most often with a special smile of memory. But she had resolutely gone on with her life since his death.

Lexy felt nothing but blind panic at the possibility of going on without Hawk.

Gincie, as concerned for the state of her daughter as for the absent Hawk, urged Lexy to stay with them until he returned, but Lexy once again returned to the city.

She had imagined herself to be so self-sufficient—she and Hawk were often separated by the demands of their jobs—but now she discovered that her well-being depended on knowing he, too, was all right.

She moved from one day to the next in a fog, and even her work, which had always before offered solace, was affected. She was relieved there was little of importance to report, most of the news being nothing more than stories of society's attempts to fight the doldrums of winter by planning various festivities, lectures, and exhibits, despite the fact that the Christmas holidays had just ended. It was also time to begin predicting which horses would be the top runners in the coming season and to report the prospects for the Board of Control. Travis was to be part of its organization, so once again Lexy had access to inside information, which, with her father's permission, she could use judiciously. For the present, the Board of Control was the best hope for regulating Thoroughbred racing in the United States, but it wasn't exactly a national jockey club, and already there was worry that the track owners were going to have too much power, a situation that did not please horse owners.

Lexy dutifully noted the sporting news in the column, but she didn't give a damn about any of it.

Even when she got the telegram telling her he was on his way home, she had to survive the days it took him to travel, and she didn't know exactly when he would arrive.

Most nights she could not fall asleep in their bed because she found it too lonesome, so she curled up in a big chair that Hawk usually occupied in the room that served as their combination study and living room.

Hawk found her asleep in his chair on the night late in January when he finally arrived home.

A lamp cast soft light on her, and he stood looking down at her, his throat working with the swell of emotions that the sight of her unleashed.

She blinked awake before he said anything and stared at him uncomprehendingly. Then she cried aloud in distress, rising from the chair and throwing her arms around him. She could feel him trembling, could feel the fever when she touched his face.

"Oh, my darling! You are so ill!" Of all the homecomings she had imagined, this was not among them, and for a moment, she was paralyzed, not wanting to let go of him, while knowing she had to pull herself together. Hearing the rasping in his chest brought everything into sharp focus.

"Don't fret," Hawk mumbled, but he was docile as she led him to their bedroom and began to undress him.

She brushed his hands away when he tried to help with the buttons.

"Don't fret, indeed! I've been half out of my mind with worry about you for weeks, and now you show up in a fever, thin as a rail, ready to fall over, and you tell me not to fret. I love you, Hawk Mackenna, and I'll fret just as much as I want to!" Tears were beginning to run down her cheeks, but she went right on with her task until she had him stripped naked and tucked in their bed.

With a little sigh, Hawk surrendered to her ministrations, but when Lexy began to sponge him down with cool water, he caught her hands and held them still. "I love you, too. Everything will be all right, now that I'm home with you." It sounded more like a question than a statement. He let go of her hands, and his eyes closed.

Though Hawk had insisted it would serve as a convenient link with the newspaper office, Lexy had never much cared for having a telephone in their house because it seemed intrusive, but she was grateful for it now.

She left Hawk just long enough to put a call through to Reid, explaining the situation and asking him to find a physician he trusted because it would take too long to summon one of the family's doctors from Baltimore.

Reid not only found the doctor, he came with him. The doctor's diagnosis of the physical ailment was reassuring because while he said Hawk was suffering from fever and inflammation of the lungs, he added, "Your husband is young and strong. Rest, good food, and plenty of fluids should set him right before long."

The doctor hesitated, searching for the proper way to approach a delicate subject, finally deciding to be direct because Mrs. Mackenna's clear gaze required no less. "His mental state is not so predictable. He seems so . . . so angry and disheartened." He did not want to be so rude as to say that the patient's surly attitude was not what he was accustomed to; most of his patients were grateful for his help.

"If you could cheer him, it would certainly help his overall condition."

The doctor meant well, so Lexy refrained from telling him that witnessing the massacre of a people was likely to weigh on any sane, sensitive man's spirit. Instead, she thanked him for his advice and for coming to them in the night.

She thanked Reid, too, and asked for an additional favor. "I know the whole family will want news of Hawk and to help in any way they can, but I think we need some days alone. Would you fend them off for me?"

"Consider it done," Reid said.

Hawk slept exhaustedly through the first couple of days, rousing only to partial wakefulness when Lexy urged him to drink broth or water or sponged him off to lower his fever.

He had seemed invincible to Lexy from the day she had met him. There was pain from his childhood, and it would always be part of him, but even that he had controlled. To see him so defeated, physically and mentally, was terrifying.

And then the nightmares began. The bodies at Wounded Knee were at one moment frozen in death, but in the next, he was sure he saw signs of life, and he shouted, "Get up, get up and run! Run away! Hide, hide, before they kill you!"

When he dreamed of Sitting Bull, it was always the same. "I should have gotten through; I should have warned him; I should have taken him away!"

Lexy wiped his face and crooned reassurance to him, but this time, instead of falling more deeply asleep, he awakened fully, hearing his own words. "I know what I'm saying."

Lexy cradled his head and gave him a drink of water, and then she answered him out of her own fatigue and worry. "If you know what you're saying, you ought to know how foolish it is. You are not God. You're not even the president. What happened was none of your doing!"

He closed his eyes and turned his head away. In the following days, she grew to dread this reaction. He ate and drank what was offered to him, suffered the care that was given to him, did as he was told, and remained all the while apart. It was as if he had not come home after all. And the saddest part was that Lexy believed Hawk was as miserable about that as she was.

She was right. Hawk kept gathering himself to travel back to her, desperate to share the warmth of their old closeness, but he could not leave behind the images of misery, betrayal, and death, and he did not want to bring them to her.

He hated being confined to bed and was relieved when he regained enough strength to do more for himself, but he also grew restless, impatient with himself, and snapped at Lexy when he didn't mean to.

He wanted to go back to work immediately, and Lexy, feeling that everything she said or did was wrong, asked Reid to persuade him to take it more slowly. Reid was a better choice than she knew.

Reid was the owner and managing editor of the paper. The easiest way would be simply to tell Hawk that he was not to return to work for a month, period, but instead, he approached him on a far more personal level.

Reid had been a frequent visitor recently, trying to lighten Lexy's load, so he caught Hawk unawares when he shifted the conversation, no longer talking about various news stories unfolding in the capital.

"You may find this difficult to believe, but I know exactly how you feel," Reid said, ignoring Hawk's expression of weary skepticism. "During the war, I went to the battlegrounds. I saw what was happening, and I reported from there. I was a good correspondent, a damn good one! But I can't tell you the number of times that wasn't enough. I saw men, so many of them years younger than I, shot and hacked to death, or wounded so severely they would never be healthy again, or rotting away inch by inch from one of the countless diseases that ran wild through every camp. And I felt responsible; I felt as if there had to be something I could do to stop it; if not the war, at least the carnage right before me."

He paused, slipping so far back in time that he wasn't aware that he had caught Hawk's full attention. "Ideally, being a journalist means always being able to observe and record events, no matter what those events are. But the ideal isn't always possible. I wanted to make the dying and the suffering stop, just stop. I wanted all those boys to go home. And it took me a long time to understand that it wasn't only because I hurt for their pain; it was also because I hurt for myself. The agony, the death, all the violence I could not stop made me feel small, unmanned, too mortal. I lost faith that life would ever have any worthwhile pattern again; I guess I lost faith in life generally. When I was wounded and ill, I made it back to Larissa, as you made it back to Lexy, but I didn't return with my faith intact. Before, I had wanted desperately to marry her, but I no longer trusted myself to be her husband or even to come back to her alive the next time."

Hawk watched in fascination as Reid's grim look eased, to be replaced by what he could only call bemused delight.

"Larissa had enough faith and trust for both of us," Reid said softly, remembering exactly how she had looked when she had come to seduce him on his last night of convalescence at Wild Swan, her body glowing under the long gown, her hair unbound, her eyes looking at him with love and with fear that her offering would not be accepted.

"Larissa had already lost one husband to the war, but she was willing to go on. Lexy loves you with the same faith, the same trust, and she has seen her share of inhumanity. But she can't reach you if you won't allow it. I think the two of you ought to go to Wild Swan for a while. It's a healing place." His eyes were suddenly piercingly direct. "I suspect you are feeling very foreign right now, more Indian than you have ever felt before. There's nothing wrong with that; it's natural. But don't underestimate Lexy or the rest of this family. Your mixed heritage is the last thing that would make a difference to any of us. When I met Larissa, I was a brash young newspaperman from New York; I assure you that was as foreign as you can imagine."

He smiled and then added very gently, "Let Lexy mourn with you."

He was gone before Hawk could think of what to say.

When Lexy came into the room, Hawk saw her with the sharpened vision Reid had given him. He saw that she was worn from her ceaseless care of him, but worse, she was so wary, her shoulders were braced stiffly as if she expected to be hit. His sharp words of the past days had surely fallen like blows.

He put out his hand. "I'm sorry I've been such a bastard. What do you think about going home to Wild Swan for a while, if your parents will have us?"

She took his hand and cradled it against her cheek, and he felt her tears on his skin.

More than his admission of apology, his calling Wild Swan "home" touched her unbearably and made her want to be there so badly she could almost smell the rich scent of spring on the land.

"I'd like that above all things," she said when she could control her voice. "I know how hard it has been for you, and I know that you've tried to spare me, but nothing can be worse for me than being shut out of your life."

She leaned down to tuck her head into the familiar hollow of his neck, his arms came around her, and for the first time since his return, Lexy felt as if she were touching both his body and his spirit.

The land was only beginning to show the first shoots of green, but the foaling season was well under way, and the farm bustled with activity.

Hawk understood the wisdom of Reid's advice more clearly with each passing day. Wild Swan radiated life and the endurance of generations of man and beast. The violence and death in South Dakota *had* made Hawk feel small, insignificant; in a way, Wild Swan made him feel the same because it contained so many cycles of birth, life, and death in its history, but here there was hope. Each life contributed to the whole, and even when there was violent death, the rest went on to reassert the value of life. Wild Swan made him understand what had so darkened his soul in South Dakota. There, he felt as if he had witnessed the final destruction not only of the Sioux, but of all the Indian nations whose ways of life had woven continuously through centuries until they ran up against white culture.

Finally he was able to talk openly with Lexy about the intensely personal experience South Dakota had been for him, about the things he had not been able to write in his articles. He explained about the beaded buckskin band, telling her what the old woman had said.

"The old woman accepted what I was, but I felt as if one part of me were being murdered by the other. I am white as well as Indian, and I've had my own war going on inside."

He told her about the phantom music, as compelling now in its absence as it had been when it filled his head; he told her how confronting Royer had tumbled him back into his childhood; and he told her his nightmares.

"I cannot get the bodies at Wounded Knee out of my mind. I

see them when I sleep—men, women, and little children lying where they fell, and old Chief Big Foot with his head still wrapped against the cold. And God help me, I must be mad, but when I think of Sitting Bull, I don't see him, I see that poor gray horse doing his circus tricks while his master dies."

Hawk's eyes glittered with tears, and Lexy's overflowed and rolled down her cheeks. "Then I must be mad as well," she said, "because of everything you wrote about the horrors, that image has stayed with me most clearly. And I swear to you, we are not the only ones. Hundreds, perhaps thousands, of the people who read what you wrote have also surely, through your words, seen one thing at least that will haunt them for a long time to come. It won't change what happened or make it right—nothing can do that—but it might make them think more carefully about what happens in the future. That is the only thing we can ever hope to accomplish."

The awful tension of anger and grief began to uncoil inside Hawk as he was reminded daily that he had a wife who understood and cared as passionately as he for the work they both did. The beautiful woman in the store all those years ago had cared but had been unwilling to act on her kindness. For Lexy, mute testimony would never be enough, and for that Hawk was infinitely grateful.

And he was made doubly glad in his own marriage by the negative example of Kace and Rosalind. He and Lexy saw a good deal of the younger Culhanes during their time at Wild Swan, and Hawk wondered how Kace could tolerate being married to a woman who shared so little of his life. He had assumed that with time Rosalind would take notice of the work on the farms, particularly at Sunrise where she lived, at least enough notice to be able to converse on common ground with her husband. But he could see no signs of that. Rosalind was as pleasant-natured as she had always been, but she never had anything to contribute to conversations beyond the latest fashions or society gossip, subjects which held little concern for the rest of the family. Hawk observed how gently everyone treated her, and he thought how awful it would be to require the same indulgence one gave to a pet.

And though Georgie was as kind to Rosalind as anyone, perhaps even more so, Hawk noticed how careful she and Kace were to avoid being alone.

"Do you think Rosalind suspects how they feel about each other?" Hawk asked Lexy.

"I don't believe Rosalind thinks of such things," Lexy said. "If she considers it at all, she probably believes that every woman must be in love with Kace, at least a little bit, but as far as seeing any threat, no. Rosalind is too childlike to respond like a woman. And in this case, it's just as well; Kace and Georgie won't betray her trust, so there's no reason for her to worry about it."

Hawk hoped she was right, but the more he saw of Georgie, the more he wondered how long Kace would be able to resist. In her intelligence and humor, in her strength and compassion, she was far more like the women Wild Swan had produced than Rosalind would ever be. But as strong as Georgie was, he doubted she would be able to refuse Kace long if he pursued her in earnest.

That night Hawk made love to Lexy with such concentrated tenderness, she relinquished all control, even her concern for his pleasure, until the only rhythm in the universe was the pumping of his powerful buttocks, the thrusting of his body into hers.

When at last it was over, neither of them had to speak aloud the thought they were sharing—that they were infinitely fortunate in their match compared to Kace and Rosalind.

Chapter 47

The Mackennas had long since been back in Washington when, in early April, word went through the family grapevine that Rosalind was pregnant. And with the news came the hope that the child would strengthen the young Culhanes' marriage and that Rosalind would mature at last.

No one hoped more than Kace did that the child would make a difference in his marriage. He had felt himself drifting further and further away from Rosalind. He had learned to block out her chatter so that it ceased to annoy him. He had quit trying to interest her in the horses or other aspects of farm life. And he had felt increasingly guilty about his own dissatisfaction because Rosalind really demanded very little of him and managed to be happy even though farm life in Maryland was vastly different from what she had known before.

Kace's guilt was magnified a thousand times by his feelings for Georgie. He was excruciatingly cautious in his behavior around her, with the ironic result that more than once Rosalind chided him for not being kinder.

"I know her background was decidedly odd, but she has blossomed into quite a young lady since your parents took her in," she said, "and she is such a good friend to me, I do wish you could be less gruff with her. I think you hurt her feelings when you growl so. You expect her to work as swiftly as the men; you forget she's just a slip of a girl."

Kace had no complaints about Georgie's work or about anything else to do with her. She seemed utterly perfect to him. But he doubted his own perceptions. Rosalind had seemed perfect to him, too, and now he wondered how he had thought they could ever content each other.

Being careful never to be alone with Georgie was not enough. He dreamed of her, and too often when he made love to his wife, his mind held Georgie's image, not Rosalind's. In his guilt and confusion, he was still resolved about one thing—that Rosalind would not suffer for a mistake that was essentially his. She had not changed; he had.

And now there was to be a child. He was happy for Rosalind's sake because she had wanted one. In fact, he had come to understand, belatedly, that having children was really the only point Rosalind saw in marriage. Loving a man for his own sake and her own pleasure was an alien concept to her. A child was an interest they could share.

But it was more than that. He discovered that he wanted the child, too. A little boy or girl, it didn't make any difference to him. He looked forward to teaching him or her all the wonders of living in the country and raising fine stock. Sometimes he got so carried away by his visions of the joys to come, that he was amused; he was already having to remind himself that he must accept it if his son or daughter chose some other way of life.

He didn't want to think about it, but he could not help wondering how Georgie felt about Rosalind's pregnancy. He was relieved when he observed that if her manner had changed toward Rosalind, it was only to the extent that as the days passed, Georgie was the one who was most patient with her whims.

At first Kace accepted Rosalind's growing fancies as natural to her physical state because he didn't know any better, but gradually he began to fear that her reactions were excessive.

It was not that she was developing peculiar tastes and aversions toward various foods or that she slept at odd hours; tentative questions to his mother had elicited the information that these were indeed normal symptoms. But there were other things he could not bring himself to ask Gincie about.

He had hoped that the child would bring him and Rosalind together even before it was born. He would not have insisted on lovemaking now, knowing that she had never overcome her aversion to it, knowing that once she had conceived, it had served the only purpose she saw for it, but he would have liked to have held her close at night, cradling her and their unborn child. But she no longer wanted to be touched by him at all.

The first night after Anthea had confirmed that Rosalind was quite likely about three months pregnant, though confirmation would not be certain until quickening, Rosalind gazed at Kace blankly when he started to get into bed with her. And then she said, "But surely you do not expect to share my bed now? You might harm the baby!"

"Is that what Anthea told you?" Kace asked, trying to hold on to his patience.

"She didn't have to tell me. Women know these things."

She stated it with such an air of complacent superiority that for an instant, Kace wanted to shake her, but then his temper died as swiftly as it had risen, and his pride rose in its place. He was not going to beg her for a place in their bed.

They were staying in Baltimore with Nigel and Sally. Kace spent the night uncomfortably cramped on a chaise, unwilling to admit to the Falconers that he had been banished from his marital bed. But when they returned to Sunrise, he moved to another bedroom, and the secret was out. Everyone at the farm was very discreet about it, but Kace was aware of more than a few pitying glances cast his way. He was also sure that what Rosalind regarded as normal would seem very odd to the other married couples on the farm.

Lizzie and Willy McCoy already had an infant son and were expecting another child in June, and Kace would have been willing to wager a fortune that the couple hadn't slept apart since their marriage, except when Willy had been away on farm business.

But he knew if he said as much to Rosalind, she would take it as proof that the "lower classes" were predictably unrefined in their personal habits.

Kace was glad that Anthea was willing to be Rosalind's physician because Rosalind would not have considered being intimately examined by a male and because Anthea was so calm and sensible in her approach to medicine and everything else, Kace hoped Rosalind would absorb some of her common sense. But he also knew that there was only so much Anthea could do for her patient.

No one was more conscious of that than Anthea herself. As the weeks passed, she discussed the case frequently with Max because she trusted his medical expertise more than anyone else's.

"She's always perfectly pleasant and nods agreeably at whatever advice I give her, but somehow, I don't believe any of this is real to her. Her morning sickness was mild and passed quickly, but she seemed to take it badly, as if the baby inside her wasn't supposed to have any effect on her body at all. And yet, when I've cautioned her against overeating and growing too fat, she reminds me that she's eating for two. And no matter how often I tell her that it is not possible to know the sex of the child by the way the baby lies or the way a ring on a string sways or any other superstitious method, she goes on asking which way works the best. It's as if she picks and chooses the facts and fictions that please her, and most of what pleases her is fiction. She knows so little about her own body and doesn't want to learn."

"And you've never come across such willful ignorance before," Max stated with deceptive innocence.

Anthea's smile was rueful. "Only with about ninety percent of the women in Rosalind's class. Their mothers teach them ignorance and aversion right along with embroidery and proper manners. At least Rosalind lives in healthy surroundings and will have good care. If nature will cooperate, that ought to be enough. But I do feel sorry for Kace."

Georgie felt sorry for him, too, more so by the day. At first the news of Rosalind's pregnancy had both shocked and reassured her, shocked her because it made her confront the image of Kace making love to Rosalind, and reassured her because that was the way it should be, and the child seemed the best possible safeguard against any indiscretion from her or Kace. She wanted to trust Kace's honor and her own never to betray his marriage vows, but since merely being around him was enough to make her feel wholly unlike her normal self, she judged that anything which emphasized the gulf between them was to the good.

Because of that, she was resolved to be supportive of Rosalind, no matter what fits and starts the woman displayed. However, she found the practice of her program increasingly difficult, regardless of the soundness of the theory.

Georgie knew far more about mares dropping colts than about the human equivalent, and admittedly there was a difference, but that didn't stop her from thinking that if Rosalind were a mare, she would be a risky prospect.

As the pregnancy progressed, Georgie quickly learned that Rosalind's moods were so changeable the best thing to do was to wait until she had an inkling of which way they were veering before she offered any comment.

Sometimes Rosalind was deliriously happy about the coming child, spinning out endless plans, plans which, Georgie noted wryly, were completely different for a boy or for a girl. A boy was to go to

Harvard and take his place among the leading businessmen in the country—no mention of being a horse breeder or a farmer—while a girl was to learn all the graces.

"But shouldn't a girl be well educated, too?" Georgie felt compelled to ask. "She would then be better able to survive if her husband should die or if they should have hard times and need her to help support the family. Or perhaps she should be educated just so that she can know more about the world, have more to interest herself and share with her husband." She was sorry as soon as she said it, but Rosalind saw no connection with her own state of ignorance.

"I believe it makes females discontented to be too educated," Rosalind said with such finality that Georgie subsided, biting her tongue against pointing out that it was a good thing Anthea and various other women in the family were well educated enough to make Rosalind's life easier at every turn.

But if Rosalind's happy moods were sometimes difficult to bear, her depression was much harder to cope with.

She complained about her increasing girth until Georgie could not resist asking in real puzzlement, "But surely you did not expect to stay the same shape while you carry your child?"

Rosalind twisted a strand of her golden hair and pouted. "Well, I knew it would show, but I didn't think I'd get as ungainly as Lizzie McCoy!"

Instead of pointing out what a stupid bit of snobbery that was and that in any case, Lizzie had been far more sensible about what she had eaten all along, Georgie reminded Rosalind that Lizzie had just produced a healthy little sister for the boy she already had. And then she added, "I'm sure Kace thinks you're beautiful just the way you are because he loves you and you are carrying his child."

Rosalind waved her hand dismissively. "Oh, I know Kace doesn't mind, but I do."

Far worse than her worries about losing her girlish figure were the nightmares. "I dream that the baby is just a lump with no arms or legs," Rosalind told Georgie, and there were various versions, all of them grotesque, and all related with real fear. And though she never said it aloud, Georgie suspected Rosalind was also having nightmares about her own death.

"I'm sure every woman in your condition suffers such megrims," she offered gently, avoiding the word "pregnant" because Rosalind disliked it, and feeling wholly inadequate against the woman's terrors. "But I'm not the one to give you comfort. Have you talked to Kace about your fears?"

Rosalind looked faintly shocked. "Men, even those as kind as Kace, can't be expected to understand such things."

Georgie did not try to change her attitude because it seemed so impossible. Nor could she understand how any couple could be intimate enough to create a child while being so distant in every other way.

Most of the time she found herself making the same pacifying, nonsensical sounds she would to a restive mare, and they seemed to calm Rosalind in the same way.

The one person she could talk to about the situation was Tay. At last, his training was complete. He was modest about it, but the fact that he was one of a very few students who had ever taken the full veterinary course at Cornell made him one of the best-trained veterinarians in the country.

He would take over the medical care of the livestock at Wild Swan, Sunrise, and Brookhaven, and then he would add client farms in Maryland, Pennsylvania, Virginia, and even further afield as the occasion arose.

He had not only the benefit of the best education available in the United States, but also his close association with Wild Swan. While it was true that many farmers refused to call a vet until their beasts were near death, people who owned high-priced, purebred livestock tended to be more advanced in their thinking and to want the best care available to protect their investments.

Tay was not too proud to enjoy the advantages his family connections gave him. While he had insecurities about his personal life, he had studied hard for his profession, he loved the work, and even where he could not help, he was confident that his patients would suffer far less at his hands than in the care of those who used arcane, cruel, and useless methods of treatment.

It was natural for him to discuss his cases with Georgie. She knew a great deal about horses; she had learned about other livestock since coming to Wild Swan; and she was always interested in better ways to treat illnesses and injuries.

Despite their size and strength, the Thoroughbreds were high-strung and delicate, prone to all sorts of problems. Wild Swan's racing entries this year were a disappointment before the season was well under way. There had been no catastrophes, but enough strains, sprains, bruises, and fevers to greatly reduce Wild Swan's chances of being in the money, though the Culhanes would attend the season anyway.

Georgie helped Tay in applying poultices, in other treatments, in setting up special feeding and exercise schedules; whatever there was to be done, she did with such a gentle, sure touch, Tay preferred her assistance to anyone else's.

The truth was, he preferred her generally to anyone else. He accepted the special spark he had seen flare between her and his brother, but he allowed himself to believe that with time and patience, he could win her affections. As clearly as Georgie did, he saw the coming child as a healthy barrier between her and Kace. But beyond that, his love for his twin was deep and enduring; he wanted Kace's happiness every bit as much as Georgie did; and so, Rosalind's erratic behavior disturbed him, too. Despite Kace's pretense that all was well, it was obviously not. He looked continually anxious around his wife, trying to please her, though she held him at more than arm's length.

Gincie and Travis had already gone north to the races without him because once Rosalind had announced that it would be highly improper for her to appear at the racetracks in her condition, Kace could not make himself leave her. His mother had resisted making any comment about Rosalind's ideas of proper behavior, but Kace knew how ridiculous she thought they were. The best he could do was to will himself to patience day by day.

And Georgie and Tay did their best to help ease his way by dancing attendance on Rosalind, who grew increasingly heavy and discontented as the muggy heat of summer settled over the land.

In July, Rosalind abruptly decided she would go to Boston to spend time with her family while she could still travel. Kace obligingly escorted her there, spent a few days with the Cunninghams, and then joined his parents at Saratoga.

Georgie and Tay breathed a mutual sigh of relief when the couple left. Georgie had already decided that this was not the year for her to go to the tracks since Rosalind needed her company, and now, with the new situation, there was the added reason that Kace would be at the courses without his wife. In addition, her main work interest was in Black Moon, and as hurdle races and steeplechases were falling out of favor at the Northern tracks, he would not be competing until the fall in Washington and Baltimore, which gave Georgie that much more time to work with him. She had made a promise to Travis about the horse, and she meant to keep it.

"Maybe Rosalind will stay with her family until the baby is born," Tay suggested, and though Georgie had secretly longed for the same thing, she protested, "But that would make it very difficult for Kace. He would have to stay up there, too, at least most of the time."

"Rosalind is very difficult for Kace right now," Tay retorted. "Maybe her own family can make her happier than we can."

"I do worry about her, even when she's out of sight," Georgie said. "She's a child herself, having a baby."

"Stop it!" Tay commanded. "You worry far too much about her.

She is not your responsibility!" And then ignoring his inner warnings, he added, "And neither is Kace. Georgie, I . . ."

He got no further. Georgie put her fingers against his mouth. "Please, please don't say it!"

But it was already too late. They stood frozen, both of them hearing his declaration of love and her rejection of it as if they had been spoken aloud.

Georgie was usually so calm and controlled, but at this moment she was as fragile as crystal, ready to shatter with the wrong words. She could bear to live with the knowledge that she loved Kace and could not have him, but she was horrified at the idea of having to refuse Tay's love because she did not want it.

She knew that he would marry her and love her for all of their days, and she cursed her own heart for being so unmoved by the knowledge.

Tay saw it all clearly, and rage and hurt unlike any he had ever experienced coursed through him. He wanted to rail at her that his brother had already made his choice, a wrong one, that it was a crime for four people to be miserable when at least two of them could be happy together.

But then sorrow and his normal compassion and good sense took over. Georgie could no more dictate to her heart than he could to his, and the last thing on earth he wanted to do was to drive her away.

"Today never happened," he said quietly. "Never."

His eyes searched hers, and she brushed impatiently at the tears that had overflowed. He looked so much like Kace and yet so different.

"Friends?" he asked, and she nodded, fully aware that without his generosity of spirit, she would have felt obligated to leave Wild Swan. Though her life here was growing more complicated by the day, she could not face leaving, not yet.

Rosalind returned from Boston within a few weeks, sooner than anyone, including she herself, had expected. Kace brought her home, having been summoned from Morris Park, where the Monmouth Park Association was holding its races this season.

Listening to Rosalind's account of her stay with her family, Georgie felt genuinely sorry for her.

"I don't belong there anymore," Rosalind wailed, her bewilderment plain. "Oh, my parents were kind enough, in their way, but though they want grandchildren, they acted as if my condition should be a dirty secret. They didn't want me to go out at all!" She twisted her hands together restlessly. "I suppose I would have thought that was proper before I came here, but now, now I don't belong there, and I don't quite belong here, either. I thought I was so grown-up when I married Kace, but I don't think that anymore. I thought all I wanted was a child, but I'm not even sure of that any longer."

"I doubt anyone is ever all the way grown," Georgie said. "If we don't learn and change as we go along, don't you think we'd be rather dull? And as for the baby, why, once it arrives, I'll wager you'll wonder how you ever existed without it! And with you and Kace as its parents, it's bound to be a beautiful child."

She was deliberately appealing to Rosalind's vanity, but she hoped her voice didn't sound as hollow to the woman as it did to herself. She couldn't shake the worry of how awful it was going to be if Rosalind did reject the child once it was born, and she was growing increasingly weary of being Rosalind's confidante. She scolded herself inwardly for harboring such uncharitable thoughts, but she was frustrated because it didn't seem as if any of the comfort she or anyone else was trying to offer Rosalind was doing any good.

The Mackennas shared Georgie's distress when they saw Rosalind in September. They hadn't been out to the farm since June, so the changes in her were very apparent to them.

"My God! She can't be healthy, looking like that!" Hawk said to Lexy as soon as they had seen Rosalind and Kace.

Lexy heartily agreed. Rosalind's slender blond beauty was now obscured by fat and bloat so that even her hands looked as if they could be punctured like balloons, and her color was gray. Lexy noticed that she wasn't wearing her wedding rings, undoubtedly because she could no longer force them on her swollen finger. Somehow that little detail seemed ominous.

Lexy spoke to her mother as soon as she could get her alone and was disconcerted to find that Gincie had no more answers than anyone else.

"The last thing I want to be is an interfering mother-in-law, and I don't know what I would do if I were to interfere," Gincie confessed. "She's not carrying the baby well, and she refuses to do most of what Anthea tells her to do. But then, some pregnancies are just difficult. Perhaps she is carrying twins. I must say, I was awfully large toward the end of my term when I was carrying the boys. But not like she is. Oh! It's such a muddle! I will be glad once she is safely delivered of this child. And I don't know what we would do without Georgie; she is the one who has the most patience with Rosalind, and Rosalind has grown dependent on her."

"It must be difficult for her," Lexy said. "How is Tay taking all of this?"

"With patience and kindness, as always," her mother answered. "I cannot wait until your father returns; everything seems better, or at least more bearable, when he is with me."

Travis had gone to California to check on their investments there as he did periodically, and Gincie's words reminded Lexy that her mother was also a wife and lover. Lexy felt a rush of tenderness and understanding toward her mother as a woman.

Though Lexy could speak honestly to her mother, the old ease with her brothers was gone. She could think of no comfortable way to approach either one of them. She felt sorry for both of them and for Georgie. And she could see no decent way out of the triangle. When she and Hawk returned to the capital, she had her mother's promise that she would be summoned back immediately if there were anything she could do.

"That's one of the advantages of working for family; Reid will understand if I'm needed here," she assured Gincie, but as she said it, she felt her own inadequacy to help her brother or his wife, and she was grateful that at least Anthea was Rosalind's physician.

Anthea maintained a calm demeanor, but her sense of helplessness was more than a match for everyone else's. She wanted Rosalind to stay away from hysteria and to produce a healthy child. She wanted Kace to be a contented father. She wanted Gincie and Travis to have the joy of their first grandchild. She wanted all of these things not only as a member of the family, but also professionally. And yet, she knew the case was getting away from her. She neglected her Baltimore practice to visit Rosalind out in the country, but even when she ordered her to spend the last few weeks in bed and to follow a specially ordered diet, she did not feel confident about the outcome. Rosalind was growing less and less forthcoming about how she felt, more and more reluctant about being examined.

"This is the sort of case that makes me feel as if the practice of medicine is little better than witchcraft," she told Max. "Or perhaps not as good. At least witchcraft might carry the power of belief for the patient."

"Do you think Rosalind is willing herself into disaster?" Max asked. He knew, as she did, that a patient's state of mind could affect the state of health.

"Well, she's not helping," Anthea answered. "But that's not the whole story. Her pulse isn't as steady or strong as it should be, and I worry about her general condition. Labor is a lot of work for a healthy woman and that much harder for one in a weakened condition. She's promised me she will tell me if she experiences any unusual symptoms. I hope she abides by that."

"I hope she recognizes them if she has any," Max said.

Rosalind had been put to bed at Wild Swan, not Sunrise, so that Gincie, Della, and the other women could care for her, and Anthea planned to go out and stay there when the delivery date drew near.

It was the most sensible plan for Rosalind to be at Wild Swan, particularly because she had declined not only her mother's offer to come south, but also Cousin Edith's willingness to do the same. Kace did not press her to accept either offer. He knew that her mother had little comfort to offer her, and he suspected that she did not want her cousin's practical advice.

But sensible though the arrangement was, it made everything harder on Georgie and Kace because now they were in each other's company continually. They did not acknowledge it openly, but they were both grateful for the balance of Tay's presence.

All three of them spent as much time as they could with Rosalind, reading to her, playing silly card games, talking—anything they could do to help the hours pass. Rosalind, never overly fond of her own company, now didn't want to be alone at all.

The change was radical for Kace. He went from being treated as nothing more than a bystander to his wife's pregnancy to having her fuss if he were gone from her side for more than a few hours. More than ever, he felt as if she were a child, refusing to grow up, but unable to avoid adult terrors.

It required too much effort to pretend for the others that the marriage was normal and happy, although at Wild Swan he and Rosalind shared a room once more, if not the bed, because she wanted someone there even while she slept.

Kace tried not to think about what their lives would be like after the baby was born, but the images came to him anyway, images of years and years of living with a woman who would never grow up, never share any of his interests or he hers. He rejected his self-pity angrily: the marriage was his fault. And at least they would have the child in common. That he might have spent his life with Georgie instead was a thought that brought such intolerable guilt and pain, he shied away from it as fast as he could whenever it slithered into his mind.

One night as Kace was getting ready for bed, Rosalind called him to her and quite deliberately took his hand and placed it on her distended abdomen covered by her nightgown.

"You can feel the baby kicking, can't you?" she asked. "I'm sure it's a girl, a lovely little girl with blond hair and your eyes."

In the past months, Kace would have given much to have been physically linked with the child. He had wondered what it felt like for Rosalind to have the child growing inside of her; he had wanted to run his hands over the growing evidence of it. But Rosalind had avoided all physical contact, and now he regarded her change of mind suspiciously as his hand rested where she had placed it. He could feel how tight and hard the mound was, but he felt no movement at all.

"There! Feel her kick!" Rosalind exclaimed. There was hectic color in her cheeks, and her eyes were too bright, and Kace still felt nothing.

Despite his lack of knowledge about human pregnancies, he was certain he ought to be able to feel something with the baby so far along.

"Are you sure she's kicking right now?" he questioned gently.

She looked at him for a moment, and then her lashes fluttered down, shielding her eyes. "No, I think she's gone back to sleep now, just as her mother intends to do."

She seemed to go to sleep immediately, but Kace stayed awake, listening to her heavy breathing and her little whimpers. Finally he got up and went to her. When he put his hand on her face, she did not stir, but he could feel the warmth of her skin. She wasn't burning up, and perhaps the heat was just the flush of sleep, but she did feel warmer than normal.

He hardly slept, but when Rosalind awakened in the morning and he asked her if she were feeling all right, she assured him that she was.

"If there is something wrong and you can't tell me, at least tell my mother or Georgie, won't you?" he said.

"Of course I will." She giggled. "I feel quite fine actually, but you look awful! I've heard that sometimes husbands suffer their wives's symptoms. What a delightful exchange!" She was so coy and flirtatious, for an instant she looked as she had when he had first courted her, lovely and full of life.

She fooled them all. She was gay and talkative for much of the day, though she slept on and off as if just being awake was tiring.

It was Gincie who discovered Rosalind's deception. After Della told her that Rosalind had scarcely touched her supper tray, Gincie went to ask what might tempt her appetite. Though she didn't want Rosalind to overeat as she had through too much of her pregnancy, Gincie was equally concerned that she not skip meals.

But all thoughts of food vanished the minute she saw her daughter-in-law. She could feel the fever before she touched her face, and she could see how glassy her eyes were.

"How long has this been going on? Why didn't you tell someone?" Gincie heard the frantic note in her own voice and willed herself to be calm.

Rosalind stared up at her uncomprehendingly, and then she said, "She's kicking; my baby is still kicking inside of me."

Gincie stripped away the bedclothes and put her hand on the hard swell of the baby. Her eyes held Rosalind's. "How long has it been since you've really felt any movement?"

Rosalind's eyes slid away and then came back, and Gincie could see the effort she was making to focus.

"A few days," she finally admitted, and the words were slurred. "But I've been having some cramps today. Maybe she's just sleeping until she's born. I want to call her Evangeline. Evangeline Culhane, isn't that a beautiful name?" Her voice trailed away.

"Yes, darling, it's a beautiful name. Everything is going to be all right, just rest now, and we'll take care of you," Gincie crooned.

But nothing was right again.

Rosalind's periods of lucidity were increasingly rare and brief as her body labored to expel the dead fetus and consumed itself with its own poisons. Anthea, summoned as quickly as possible, felt as helpless as the rest of them; there were no magic potions to battle the infection raging through Rosalind, nothing to make her kidneys function properly or to make her heart beat regularly enough for life. The drugs Anthea had were no match for the malady. It didn't matter whether the child had poisoned the mother or the other way around; the baby girl was born dead, and the mother was dying.

Once Rosalind opened her eyes, looked directly at Kace, and asked, "Is the baby all right? Is Evangeline all right?" and he answered, "She's fine, a beautiful baby girl."

"That's good." Rosalind's mouth curved in a smile, and Kace kept his tears back until her eyes closed again.

She did not recognize him again. In her delirium she was a little girl, just as she had always been inside, anxious to please her parents and in turn pleased with small simple things—a pet cat, a new dress, a skating party—innocent pleasures from the time which had suited her far better than adulthood.

After three tortured days and nights, Rosalind died.

Chapter 48

Kace wished someone would blame him. But not even Rosalind's family obliged. They had received the call warning them that their daughter was gravely ill, but they had not arrived at Wild Swan until after her death. They were shocked, but more, they were as polite and controlled about this as they were about everything else in their lives. It was a tragedy, but then, childbearing always carried risk and was the lot of women. If there were passionate displays of grief, they were private. Even Cousin Edith, who was more direct, only patted Kace's arm and said, "You were very kind to her. She couldn't have had a better husband."

Anthea and Gincie carried their own guilt for not having discovered the seriousness of Rosalind's condition until it was too late, but Max reminded them that though there had been a chance that inducing labor earlier might have helped, it was far more likely that Rosalind would have died anyway because the infection had been so widespread, affecting so many organs. Or perhaps kidney failure or her faltering heart had given the infection the opportunity to take over.

"A patient's cooperation is at least half the treatment," he reminded them, "and Rosalind did not cooperate." Max mourned the loss of Rosalind, but he did not want to see Anthea torment herself with undeserved guilt.

Neither Gincie, nor Anthea, nor Max, nor any other member of the family blamed Kace either. They viewed him as a man who had been trying to make the best of a difficult marriage and who had now lost not only his wife, but also his child. He thought their sympathy and compassion would smother him. Even Lexy and Tay were no help, treading around him with such careful concern.

But nothing could change the truth as he saw it. He had ceased to love Rosalind long before he had fathered their child; the love Rosalind should have had from him had been withheld from her as soon as he had known he loved Georgie.

He could scarcely bear the sight of Georgie now, not because he blamed her, but because he felt as if he had somehow corrupted her innocence as he had betrayed Rosalind. That he had never made love physically to Georgie did not ease the burden. He had loved Georgie in every other way, in the enjoyment of her spirit and her mind, in thinking about her constantly, in finding, even while he tried to avoid her, that a day was not complete unless he had seen her. All that he had taken from Rosalind he had given to Georgie.

He got through the preparations and the long day of the funeral by letting himself drift and not concentrating on anything or anyone. He supposed his responses were proper because no one looked unduly shocked, but he had little idea of what he had said throughout the day.

He watched the last of Rosalind's family and the other mourners leave Wild Swan in the late afternoon, and he knew it was time that he went home to Sunrise. But he couldn't quite face the house he had shared with Rosalind; he corrected the thought—occupied, not shared.

He wandered out to the brood mare barn and then wondered at the bitter irony of his choice of refuge. Most of the mares were already in for the night, comfortably settled in their stalls, their expanding bellies evidence of the foals they would produce in the new year.

The barn smelled of warm horseflesh and life, and Kace felt dead inside.

Georgie watched Kace go into the barn. His head was bowed, his gait slow like an old man's, and he looked so alone, she could not bear it. She stood frozen with indecision, wishing that Tay or Lexy had followed him out, and then she squared her shoulders and went after him.

If they had been careful not to be alone together before Rosalind died, since her death they had avoided all contact, and Georgie knew they could not go on this way. It would be intolerable not only for their own sakes, but for everyone in the small, closely woven world of Wild Swan and Sunrise.

She found him sitting on a bench, motionless, with his hands clenched so tightly on his knees that the knuckles gleamed white in the last light of day that filtered into the barn. His face was carved in such tense lines, he looked older than his father. But his eyes were dry. He had not wept since Rosalind had recognized him for the last time and had asked about the baby.

Georgie would have preferred wild weeping to this stony despair, but her own grief and guilt were locked as tightly inside her. She could not banish the idea that by loving Kace she had stolen something from Rosalind. Nor could she avoid thinking that with all the time she had spent with Rosalind, she should have been able to make her behave more sensibly, that somehow she had failed because of loving Kace.

She touched his shoulder as she breathed his name and felt the jolt of surprise that ran through him as he became aware of her presence. She drew her hand back quickly.

She thought of a thousand things she wanted to say to him, but all she could manage was, "Oh, Kace, I am so sorry!"

He turned his head, and for a moment, they stared at each other with all the barriers down.

Kace's eyes glowed blue green as if there were light behind them, and Georgie felt as if he were touching her everywhere. Tendrils of warmth curled through her, thawing the cold that had settled around her heart when Rosalind died.

And then the fire went out of Kace's eyes, and the shutters came down again. "Go away. Leave me alone, please," he said with great precision, and Georgie felt even colder than she had before.

But it was Kace who went away. Travis was still in California. He had been informed of Rosalind's death, but Gincie had also telegraphed him not to return on account of it. She would have loved to have him home, but he could not arrive until days after the burial, so there was no point. She decided it would be far more useful for Kace to go west for a while. She sent word to Travis before she talked to her son.

At first he protested that he had too much work to do at Sunrise, but she brushed aside his objections. "You mean you think it would be running away. It might be. But everyone needs to run away sometime. I see a certain justice in it. I ran away from California all those years ago. Now you can seek shelter there, at least for a while. Michael McCoy and Lem Washington are perfectly capable of managing Sunrise in your absence. That's why you pay them well."

When he thought of his mother's family at all, it was of the people of Wild Swan or of her half brother Matthew, with whom Gincie kept in touch by mail. He seldom considered the old history of violence that had resulted in his mother's shooting of Mark. It was a shock to recall that this wise, compassionate woman had executed a man. If she could survive that, then she could survive this. He was on his way to California by the next day.

Gincie mourned Rosalind, but she was nearly as sorry that Kace had ever married her as she was that Rosalind had died. There was nothing she could do for the dead Rosalind anymore, and her concern now was for her son and for Georgie.

Gincie hoped that a little time away would give Kace a new perspective. She knew he was blaming himself for his wife's death and for loving Georgie. She wanted to tell him that time was too short to waste in useless recriminations, that he and Georgie had the right to find happiness together, that Rosalind's untimely death did not alter the fact that her refusal to grow up and accept responsibility for herself might well have been what had set the tragedy in motion. But Gincie could not tell him what she thought, at least not yet. If anyone could get through to Kace right now, it was Travis, and Gincie hoped their time together in California would help to heal their son.

Georgie was no easier to approach than Kace. To say anything overtly was to acknowledge that her love for Kace was no secret. Gincie didn't think the young woman could bear that now. Her plan was that with Georgie at Wild Swan and Kace in California, they would each have time to think and to miss each other. But two days after Kace had left, Georgie was gone, too.

The letter she left thanked everyone for all the kindness they had shown her, apologized for her cowardice in not saying good-bye face to face, and promised that she would be back to see everyone someday. The letter did not say where she was going, and as far as Gincie could tell, most of Georgie's feminine wardrobe was still in place. She could have ridden away on Black Moon, but instead, she had written out a precise document stating that she was relinquishing the legal rights to the horse in exchange for the half-bred saddle horse she had taken. The brown gelding was dependable, but he had none of Black Moon's flash or fire, and he would not be noticed in passing as Black Moon would.

Gincie could hardly bear to look at Tay's face when he learned that Georgie had fled. She knew it was a mirror of her own heartbreak, heartbreak shared by everyone on the farms, by all the family.

At first no one could quite believe she was gone. But her absence was so tangible, soon no one could deny it. And there seemed to be nothing they could do about it. They did not know where she had gone, and more, she had chosen to go. They could not drag her back even if they could find her.

No one said it aloud, but they all found themselves mourning Georgie's going as much as Rosalind's death. And because Georgie had become so much more a part of the pattern of their days than Rosalind had, they were reminded of her more often. Chores she normally did, horses she was helping to train, people who were accustomed to her willing competence: there were so many ways of missing Georgie.

Tay was not willing to accept Georgie's absence without a fight. He was certain that wherever she had gone, it had something to do with horses, and most probably she had gone back to her old disguise, which would be much more convenient for traveling alone and finding work.

His veterinary practice was expanding, so his days were busy, and he was away from Wild Swan more and more. Wherever he went, he asked about "George," whether anyone had seen or hired a young man of his description lately. He could not bring himself to betray her by telling everyone she was female. But as he asked the questions, he doubted he would receive any answers. He was sure Georgie would have gone beyond the range of his normal travels. But he couldn't stop looking, and he dreaded the day his brother would come home.

Gincie had decided against sending word to the men in California. They could do even less from that distance than those at home, and she didn't see any purpose in distressing them before it was necessary.

They arrived home toward the end of October, just in time to see Black Moon compete. It was as if Georgie were with them because the credit belonged to her; she was the one who had worked so hard to train Black Moon to control his flighty temper while he was performing.

When Gincie had broken the news to Travis and Kace, Kace had asked, "Gone where?" his mind refusing to credit that she meant anything more than a visit somewhere.

"We don't know. She promised to come back to see us sometime, but we haven't heard from her since she left Wild Swan two days after you did, or rather, two nights."

It was obvious that his mother expected a strong reaction from him—his father had complied by swearing soundly and looking as distraught as if one of his own children had run away—but Kace felt numb, unable as yet to envision Wild Swan or Sunrise without Georgie. It was as if someone had told him that all the people or horses or buildings had simply disappeared.

He had made no decisions about Georgie while he was in California because he had realized he had so far to go in coming to terms with his guilt over Rosalind. He had wrestled nobly with the idea that having ruined one woman's life, he must be very sure he would not ruin Georgie's by loving her. He wasn't even sure he was capable of loving a woman long enough and deeply enough to make a life with her. Common sense told him that life with Georgie would be entirely different from the one he had led with Rosalind. But common sense did not seem to have much to do with love, as far as he could tell from his own experience. If he had had any plan at all, and it was vague at best, it had been to just see how things went once he was back in Maryland. But Georgie had ended all possibility of that.

It did not help to feel his siblings' pity so strongly, to see it in their faces. He even felt a stirring of anger toward Tay. He was quite sure Tay loved Georgie, too, so he thought it would have been far more natural had his twin punched him in his nose rather than showing such empathy. He thought he would be apt to do that were the situation reversed.

But not even the possibility of a battle with his twin ruffled the unnatural calm that enshrouded him.

He came alive the day Black Moon won the steeplechase at the Washington, D.C., Jockey Club Fall Meeting. The weather was fair, the course fast, and Black Moon won the event by two lengths, never missing a stride.

Kace hardly noticed the sympathetic murmurs mixed with varying degrees of shock that he was attending the races so soon after his wife's death. It didn't matter; the Culhanes and the Mackennas were there to watch Black Moon win for Georgie.

Travis had entered the horse, but he had listed the owner as G. Cheney, and he and Gincie still considered the animal Georgie's. Along with the sorrow of coming home to find Georgie gone, Travis also regretted that they had never told her of the share of the Futurity purse that was still hers to claim.

"At least she would have had no worries about finances," Travis fretted.

"But she might have gone very far away then," Gincie said, and she answered his inquiring look. "I'm sure she's not that distant. She loves Wild Swan and Kace and the rest of us. I cannot believe we've seen the last of her. She'll return; she must."

"Well, if she does, I hope Kace has sorted out what he is goin' to do about it by then. We talked about a lot of things out in California, but not a word about Georgie, and that told me as much as any speech. Damn! Guilt is such a waste of time!"

Guilt was not in Kace's mind as he watched Black Moon soaring over the fences. At first he stared at the horse blindly, and then the perfect, fluid motion of the animal collecting himself and flying over each obstacle became the rhythm of his own will and heart. The vivid life in Black Moon was his own, flowing back into him with such a rush of power and light, for a moment he reeled under the onslaught. And then the world steadied. He cheered with everyone else for Black Moon's victory, cheered for the skill, patience, and care Georgie had invested in the animal, and he was resolved that he would find Georgie.

He remembered too clearly telling her, "Go away. Leave me alone." He faced the fact that he might have hurt her too much for forgiveness; he even faced the possibility that she had decided she did not love him after all. But he was determined to have it out with her. The only thing he did not consider was that her burden of guilt was as heavy as his own. It simply did not occur to him.

Lexy noticed the change in him immediately. As the excitement of the race died away, she studied her brother's face, and then she said, "Welcome back."

"I'm going to find her," he said, and Lexy did not allow any of her doubt that he could do it to show. Instead she suggested, "Why don't we place an advertisement in the *Witness*, something discreet that will let her know we want her to come home?"

Kace thought it a fine idea, but he did not stop there. While Tay had asked after "George" wherever he went, Kace became obsessed with expanding the search to neighboring states, and he drove himself relentlessly to keep up with his work at Sunrise while spending all the time he could looking for Georgie. The one measure of restraint he imposed upon himself was in keeping Georgie's true gender secret, as Tay had done. He drew some comfort from the fact that if she were again disguised, she could hardly be courted by another man.

He had it in his mind that he would find her by Christmas, but the weeks passed, his deadline arrived, and there was still no clue to her whereabouts. And when the family gathered, Georgie's absence was keenly felt.

"All in all, it's been a rough year," Lexy said softly, her hand in Hawk's, but her eyes on her brothers. "You fought your war in South Dakota. Kace lost both Rosalind and Georgie, and Tay has lost, too." She didn't say it aloud, but she thought in some ways she had lost Hawk, because part of his soul was forever in the West with the Sioux, living and dead. But she was learning that no matter how much one loved another, complete possession was never possible, or even desirable. And what she and Hawk gave to each other was as much as either would ever be able to give to another human being; that was more than sufficient to make the gift complete.

"Tay cannot lose what he never had," Hawk said, "and I think he knows that already, as Michael Winterbourne knew when I charged into his world to take you back. And now Winterbourne is marrying a woman of whom the family in England heartily approves. Surely, Tay will have the same chance."

Not only had the Bettingdons sent word, but Michael himself had written to Lexy, telling her his plans, asking her best wishes, and sending her his own. She had smiled as she read, because he had sounded so young and happy. If Michael could find someone to fit his heart, then Tay, who was so much more open, could, too.

"But that still leaves the problem of Kace finding Georgie," Lexy said, and Hawk had no answer for her. They were all hoping that when the racing season began in New York once again, they might find her. It had been more than three years since she had come home with them, so it was probable that she would no longer be in danger from the men who had tried to tamper with Pharaoh, but it was hard to imagine her slipping back into her old life after going through such a metamorphosis at Wild Swan.

On New Year's Eve, Hawk shared a private toast with Lexy. "To 1892: may it be a better year for the country and for all of us. And may it see Georgie home."

But the first foals were born at the farms and the first signs of spring were showing before there was any word, and then it came in a letter about her, not from her. The letter was nearly illegible, but Kace finally deciphered enough to understand that she was at Silverwood Farm in Pennyslvania and that her friend Tobias Jefferson thought she'd be better off at Wild Swan because she'd gotten into some trouble at Silverwood.

"She don no I rites an mos here don no she be a wuman," was one of the clearest lines in the missive, and there was a lot of information missing, but one thing was clear, whatever kind of trouble she'd gotten into, she herself hadn't decided to ask for help from Kace or anyone else at Wild Swan.

It didn't matter; he was going to bring her home. He had the perfect weapon: she would not want to put Tobias Jefferson's job at risk, and since the man was already worried about the situation, Kace was confident that he could use this to his advantage and thus to Georgie's.

He had to give her credit for her cleverness. Mr. Catlett, the owner of Silverwood Farm, had once raised racehorses, and Tobias had been his trainer. Undoubtedly it was during that period that Georgie, and surely her friend Charlie, had come to know him. But when Catlett, a widower, had remarried five or six years before, he had married a woman who had strong objections to horse racing and the gambling attendant on the sport. However, Mrs. Catlett, like many other people, did not place trotters in the same category because they were, after all, raised for practical road work, and any improvement in the breed ultimately meant better animals to pull various conveyances. So Mr. Catlett had sold his Thoroughbred racers and had been building his trotting stable ever since.

By going to ground at Silverwood, Georgie had managed to find a place where she could still use her expertise about horses while avoiding contact with the Culhanes and most other people of the flat-racing set. There were a few exceptions, but most breeders and owners specialized in one sport or the other, and the racing events were quite separate.

Travis immediately offered to accompany Kace on his journey to Pennsylvania, but Kace refused.

"Papa, this is between Georgie and me, and the sooner we settle it, the better it will be for everyone. I feel responsible for her running away, and I ought to be able to get her out of whatever trouble she's in."

Travis did not press the point, and neither did Tay. Kace knew he could not have refused if his brother had insisted on going with him, and he recognized what Tay was offering in letting him go alone. But when he tried to thank him, Tay cut him off.

"We both love her; we both want her to be happy. Just bring her home."

Kace traveled north feeling as if he were carrying Tay's heart to Georgie as well as his own.

Chapter 49

Kace went as far as he could by train and then rented a horse to go out to the farm. It wasn't far from the station. Georgie would want to bring the half-bred horse back with her, so they would ship the animal by rail. He tried to keep his mind occupied with all of these little details in order to control his rising excitement.

When he arrived at the farm, he expected to see Georgie right away, and he expected her to be very angry that he had found her. But instead he was intercepted by a burly black man who peered at him anxiously. "Mister Kace, I'se pleased t'see you, yes, I am!"

"Tobias," Kace acknowledged, as he dismounted and held out his hand.

Tobias shook it and went on anxiously, "Dat Georgie, she say she all right, but I doan know. She got hit hard, an' she be hurtin' bad even iffen she say no. She gonna be right mad wid me fo' sendin' fo' you."

"Slow down, please, and tell me what happened," Kace said with forced calm, his own heart beginning to race. He had assumed "trouble" meant some sort of scrape over her pose as a young man; physical injury was not what he had expected to find.

Tobias did his best to comply, feeling better by the minute that this tall young man had come for Miss Georgie, seeing that the concern in Kace's eyes was far more than casual. Tobias had been born into slavery, but had come north at the end of the war as a free man, twenty years old and skilled in the care of horses. He had worked for various stables, but his job with Mr. Catlett had lasted for fifteen years now, and though Georgie's father and Charlie had both been trusted friends and he wanted to help the girl in any way he could, he did not want to jeopardize his job or his family's security any further. He had acquired a wife and children in his years at Silverwood. Mr. Catlett was a good man in his way, but he was also a severe one, and he would never countenance a black man giving shelter to a young white woman. Free or not, Tobias understood that white men still controlled his destiny.

"Dat stallion, he kill dat boy, iffen Georgie doan hep like she done. Trouble be, he already movin' fas' when she grab him away from de boy, so's she be hit hard up 'gainst dat wood. She say she jus' gots bruises, an' she doan want none a' de womens knowin' her secret. But I 'spect she got ribs dat's broke an' mebbe mo'. She . . ."

"Take me to her!" Kace was suddenly beyond politeness or patience; the picture of what Georgie had done was too vivid. It was typical of her to have intervened, sparing the stableman but not herself.

She was sitting on a stool, laboriously trying to polish the metal buckles of a headstall. Her lower lip was caught between her teeth in the fierceness of her concentration on what was normally an easy task.

Nothing was normal about the way Georgie was now. She was trying to do the polishing with her left hand because her right hand was nearly useless, the fingers not even strong enough to get a firm grip on the leather straps.

Her hair was cropped again, as it had been when Kace had first seen her, but now with the years of knowing, there was no way he could ever mistake her for a boy.

His breath hissed out through his teeth, and when she slowly raised her head at the sound, he got a good look at her face. The bones stood out in high relief, and the whole right side was bruised, her eye still nearly swollen shut though the accident had happened days before. The marks of injury were in stark contrast to the chalk of her skin. Her amber eyes had lost all of their light; they were sunken and staring, as if she were some small animal patiently enduring the hurt.

"Jesus, Georgie!" he barked, his distress at her condition making it a curse. She flinched and her face twisted with the pain even so small a movement cost her.

He was on his knees beside her without being aware he had moved. With infinite care, he took the polishing cloth from her and cradled her left hand in his, afraid of touching her further before he knew the extent of her injuries.

"Sweetheart, I want to take you home, but I need to know how badly you're hurt. The truth, please."

She focused on him with difficulty, not sure he was really there. She had tried, without success, not to think of him from the moment she had left Wild Swan. And then she had sought comfort by talking to Tobias about Wild Swan and the people there, most of all about Kace, though she had tried to make him no more important than the others. Since the accident, everything had passed in a haze of pain that had brought its own hallucinations of Kace and Wild Swan. And now Kace or his apparition was kneeling before her, calling her "sweetheart" as he had after the fight at the racetrack nearly four years ago.

She stared at him, noting the familiarity of the strong features, the thick, tawny hair, the startling turquoise eyes. It was not the same floating images of the past few days; this was flesh and bone and the reassuring man-scent of her beloved.

She felt as if she'd conjured him from fantasy to reality, against his will. "I didn't mean for you to come here," she whispered, trying not to draw too much air into her rib cage.

Gently he brushed his fingers against her uninjured cheek, feeling the fever. "I know that." He swallowed the lump in his throat. "But Wild Swan is home for you, as it is for me. It's home for you now especially because there are people there who love you and can take care of you. The truth now."

A spark of defiance lit her eyes and then died. "All of it is on my right side, ribs mostly. I think a couple of them are broken. It isn't that bad. It will just take time."

He remembered how his bruised ribs had ached after the fight when he and Tay had battled Georgie's attackers. And none of his ribs had been broken. He hated the idea of her suffering that kind of pain.

"I don't know what to do," he admitted honestly. "I think you know you can't stay here without putting Tobias's job at risk. And I know you'd be far better off at Wild Swan, but I don't want to injure you further by taking you there. Do you think you can bear the trip?"

She tried to think logically with a mind that was barely functioning. Despite her determination to heal quickly and without bother, things were not going well. She seemed to be getting stiffer by the day, and this morning she had awakened to a world even more blurred by fever than before. Worst of all, it was becoming increasingly difficult to breathe. If she remained at Silverwood and grew sicker, Tobias would suffer for it. He had taken her in and kept her secret. And now, she could not even do enough work to be useful, let alone to justify the risk Tobias was running.

Suddenly she longed to be at Wild Swan with a fervor that stunned her. How had she thought she could leave the people and the place forever? They formed the only real home she had ever had. And Kace was part of all of it, the greater part for her, no matter what role she was to play in his life. And he had come for her.

"I can bear the trip," she said, trying to make the words forceful, though they emerged as no more than a thready whisper.

"Are your ribs bound?" Kace asked, picturing all too clearly the possibility of a broken rib piercing inward due to a jolt on the journey.

She nodded her head slightly, but then he realized she must have bandaged herself and could hardly have had the strength or leverage to do a good job. He glanced around and discovered that Tobias had left them alone.

Without asking permission, he began to unbutton her shirt. "I'd better wrap you again before we go," he said, as if such intimacy was commonplace between them. She was too weary and ill to feel embarrassed.

Kace knew it had to be bad because no slight injury could so diminish Georgie, but nonetheless, it took all of his self-control not to betray his full horror when he gingerly removed her shirt and unwound the length of cloth binding her ribs.

Her side was a mass of black and purple swelling that extended from her neck down beyond the waist of her breeches. Even her shoulder and collarbone looked distorted. Her left side, though unbruised, hardly reassured him. She had grown so thin in her time away from Wild Swan, she looked terrifyingly frail against his own large hands.

"I can't ask any more help from Tobias," she said, as if she heard his unspoken thought that she shouldn't be moved after all.

He studied her face for a long moment. "All right, then home it is."

It was difficult to tell who was paler when Kace had finished rewrapping her ribs. Though he was as gentle as he could be, he heard every change in her breathing as she fought against crying out. He wished he could put his arms around her and take all the pain away.

There was no question of Georgie being able to ride a horse. Kace left her briefly and went in search of Tobias, finding that the man had anticipated his needs by hitching a team to a wagon. He had even packed Georgie's few belongings.

Georgie insisted on walking to the wagon, not only because she dreaded the pain of being picked up and carried, but also because she wanted to reassure whichever hands who were watching, and one in particular, that her injuries were not so serious.

Her limping progress was so slow, it was all Kace could do to abide by her wishes, and he stayed close beside her.

Georgie saw young Wilson watching, just as she had known he would. He approached, every line of his body rigid with concern for her, and she stopped walking, gathering her strength to speak to him.

"It wasn't your fault or the stallion's. He's young and skittish, but he's a good animal. Handle him firmly, gently, and he'll do as you ask." She couldn't get enough breath to speak strongly and could only hope he heard her clearly.

"You saved my life, George. I'll never forget," Wilson mumbled, and Georgie had no more energy to soothe him. Though only a few steps, the remaining distance seemed to stretch away forever as she made herself cross it. But when she stood beside the wagon, she realized there was no way she could climb in by herself. She looked up at Kace and surrendered responsibility for herself to him.

With infinite care, Kace lifted her into the wagon bed and got in beside her, and Tobias tied Kace's mount and Georgie's half-bred to the back of the vehicle.

Though he gave the word for Tobias to start the journey, Kace wasn't aware of the wagon moving. All his concentration was centered on Georgie. Her eyes were tightly closed, her face drawn in a grimace as she waited for the pangs of being lifted to ease. The motion of the wagon came to him only when he moved instinctively to cushion her against the bumps.

Georgie had never been dependent on him before. He saw that with sudden clarity. Even when he and Tay had joined the fight with her, she had been battling on her own and would have gone on doing so no matter what the outcome. And in all her days at Wild Swan, she had maintained that resilient core that never let her forget her survival was her responsibility, no matter how much care and love surrounded her. It was a lesson she had learned very early. And it had made it easy for other people to depend on her, including Rosalind, including himself.

He did not mistake her surrender now. Her physical condition was the catalyst, but her trust in him went beyond that and was very specific. It made him feel humble and more fearful than he wanted to admit even to himself.

Georgie opened her eyes and concentrated until she could see Kace clearly. His expression was so filled with tenderness and concern, she closed her eyes again. She wanted to reassure him, but it was taking all her energy to fight the pain. She felt as if a huge fist were crushing her chest; she could almost see each breath she took as a flash of red fire, flaring against her ribs.

"Just hold on, and you'll be home before you know it. You'll be feeling better in no time. I love you, and I'm going to take care of you." He hadn't meant to tell her quite like this, but nothing had gone as he had planned, and he needed to say it aloud, as if it were a spell to keep her safe.

Georgie tried to cling to the comfort of his voice, tried to sort out what he had said, but the wagon lurched, and her mind emptied of everything except the fight to stay conscious.

She used the last of her energy in thanking Tobias for having sheltered her for all these months.

The train journey was a nightmare. Kace managed to persuade her to drink water now and then, but she couldn't eat, and most of the time he simply held her, trying to cradle her from the motion as he had in the wagon. There were odd looks from other passengers at the sight of one man holding another, though it was obvious that the smaller one was ill. Kace ignored them all.

Having to change trains made everything worse, and by the time they arrived in Baltimore, Kace relinquished all pretense that he could take her as far as Wild Swan. He hired a cab to take her to the clinic, leaving her horse to be taken to a local livery stable.

She cried out when he lifted her down from the train, and when he got her into the cab, she was unconscious.

Kace didn't know that tears were running down his cheeks. It occurred to him that his father had brought his mother home gravely injured when she had been shot by the slave catchers. He wondered if his father had been as terrified as he was now; it was difficult to imagine Travis this afraid of anything. But Kace knew how much his father loved his mother. And now he knew that love could generate more terror than any other emotion. The brutal truth was that he could imagine life without Rosalind and the child he had never gotten to know; he was already adjusted to it. He could not imagine life without Georgie. The idea that he might go on existing while she was buried beneath the earth was intolerable.

The terror swept through him in an enormous wave. She was so hurt, even the best of care might not be enough.

"A while longer, just a little while, love," he murmured.

She stirred and whimpered but did not rouse fully even when he carried her into the clinic.

To his great relief Anthea, Nigel, and Sally were there, and their expressions of shock were instantly eclipsed by professionalism. But Kace would not leave Georgie when the two doctors suggested he wait outside the examining room.

"She might be afraid when she comes to; I want to stay with her."

Nigel and Anthea allowed him to stay because they thought they'd have to throw him out bodily otherwise, and in fairness, he was the one who had rescued Georgie and brought her to them.

They cut her clothing and the rib binding away to reveal the bruising and swelling that ran from her face down to below her knee on the right side, grotesque evidence of how hard the stallion had slammed her into the boards of the stall.

She did not react when Anthea palpated her abdomen or when her swollen knee was touched, but when Nigel probed her ribs, she came to, struggling violently to get away from this increased agony.

Kace moved swiftly to hold her immobile, and it was his voice she heard. "Georgie, easy now. Nigel and Anthea will make you feel better. We're at the clinic. Please, hold still so you won't hurt yourself further. Please, love, please!"

Kace was asking her to do something. For him she would do anything. She focused on his eyes that were looking down so anxiously at her. And when Nigel touched her again, she did not fight. She looked into Kace's eyes until the light faded from her own. The rasp of her breathing was loud in the room, though she was taking only short, shallow breaths. There was blood at the corners of her mouth.

Anthea and Nigel conferred briefly in low voices, and then Nigel asked Kace to step outside with him. Kace went reluctantly, not wanting to leave Georgie at all.

Nigel did not mince words. "I'm quite sure the collarbone's cracked, and the hip and knee are badly bruised and swollen, painful injuries, but not a threat to her life. The ribs are another matter, three broken, one badly. I think it's damaged the lung. And everything is made worse by the infection she's developed and her generally, debilitated condition. That makes surgery doubly risky. but . . ." He hesitated, the calm in his voice wavering before he got control of it again. "I think there's a sliver of rib that needs to be removed."

"And if you don't?" Kace asked.

"She might get well anyway," Nigel conceded. "But I don't think so. I think the internal wound will fester."

"Did I make it worse by bringing her here?"

"The damn horse is what injured her, not you," Nigel snapped, not wanting the idea to take hold in Kace's mind. "What kind of medical help do you think she would have gotten where she was, and when? She was already in dire straits when you found her."

Kace had to admit that was true. "Will you perform the operation?"

Nigel shook his head. "No. If they agree with the diagnosis, Max and Joseph are the ones to do it. Joseph is brilliant at this sort of work. You couldn't find better anywhere."

Only peripherally did he notice that his responsibility for Georgie's welfare was being accepted as if it were of long standing.

He went back to Georgie and stayed with her as Anthea, Nigel, and Sally organized everything, altering their own schedules as much as they could, sending word to Max and Joseph, who were out seeing patients, sending the news to the family. Anthea and Nigel, their focus still on the patient, had renewed cause to be grateful for the efficient way Sally dealt with the externals of any crisis, as it was she who did most of the arranging now and kept the clinic running smoothly despite the doctors' preoccupation, which included making sure one or the other of them stayed with Georgie in case she took a turn for the worse. The situation was also aided by the fact that they now had other doctors working for the clinic so that they could shift their patient loads somewhat.

"Can't you give her something to make her more comfortable?" Kace asked, as Georgie moved restlessly and whimpered, stilling only momentarily under his touch and at the sound of his voice.

"Not until it's time for surgery. Opiates depress respiration and everything else, and she's not breathing well as it is." It was a sensible, scientific explanation, but Anthea's eyes were soft with pity and regret.

Joseph and Max agreed with Nigel, and Kace waited outside the room during the surgery, but he did not wait alone. Blaine, Philly, Adam, and Mercy were all there. He gave them the bare bones of the story, and they didn't demand anything more from him. They simply surrounded him with their love and support.

While he waited, he thought about another time, about Tay undergoing surgery after he had been shot accidentally by Willy McCoy. He remembered the vast emptiness and dread he had felt at the idea his twin might die and be gone from him forever. He felt the same way now. But Tay had lived, and Georgie would, too; he would not have it otherwise. But he could not shut out the images of Rosalind and the baby, both of them dead.

Georgie survived the removal of the rib fragment, but the best that could be said about her condition was that she was still alive.

"We can't lose her!" Anthea exclaimed. "We just can't. Kace has lost so much already. He will go mad if Georgie dies."

Max shared his wife's desperation, but he was as worried about her as he was about Georgie and Kace because he knew Anthea continued to blame herself for not being able to do more for Rosalind. "We're doing the best we can," he reminded her.

Anthea had nothing to say to counter Max's words, but he knew by the stubborn set of her mouth that she was not going to be beaten by the odds against Georgie's survival.

The Culhanes and Sam came in from the country, and Reid, Larissa, and the Mackennas from Washington as soon as they could. Only Tay was missing, having been called to a farm in Virginia to treat a prize stallion that was ailing. But word had been sent to him to come when he could.

Kace saw them all as if through the wrong end of a telescope, tiny figures, far away. Georgie filled his vision. He spent hours holding her in his arms so that she could get more air into her lungs than was possible if she were lying down. He talked to her until his voice was hoarse, telling her to breathe deeply, terrified every minute that she was going to stop breathing altogether. When the coughing seized her and she cried out, he could feel the agony in his own chest.

Gincie understood his need to be with Georgie, but seeing that he was growing as pale as the patient, she was determined to temper his devotion with logic. "You cannot keep this vigil without rest," she told him. "We all care about Georgie and want her to heal. But it won't help her if you fall ill."

Kace knew his mother was right. He was concentrating so entirely on keeping Georgie alive, he felt as if his own life were flowing into her in a continuous stream. He feared that when she most needed him, he would be too empty and exhausted to aid her. He had come to understand that the ordeal was not going to be over soon. He wanted to believe he could see small signs of improvement, but she had scarcely opened her eyes since the operation, and when she had, they had been fever-glazed and uncomprehending.

"I'll sleep during the day and be with her at night," he informed his mother, his voice polite but brooking no argument. Night and the dark early hours of the morning, those were the times when Death visited most often.

With a twist of inward sorrow as well as pride, Gincie noted that he sounded more like his father every day. The threat of losing Georgie was maturing Kace more profoundly than his marriage to Rosalind ever had.

Kace was particularly grateful for Lexy's presence as he became aware that she was the one who had food ready to tempt him when he left Georgie; she was the one who was there when he needed someone beside him but didn't want to talk. Lexy had accepted Georgie as a sister from the beginning and had never evinced the slightest jealousy. It helped Kace to know that she would be devastated if they lost Georgie.

While she sat with her, Lexy talked to Georgie. "I don't know how you feel now about Kace, but I don't have any doubt about how he feels. He loves you, loves you a lot more than he ever did foolish, pathetic Rosalind. He's a good man, my brother. You could do a lot worse. But first you've got to get well. If you don't"—she couldn't bring herself to say, *If you die*—"Kace's heart will break."

She wiped angrily at the tears running down her cheeks. She didn't want Georgie to see her weeping if she regained consciousness, but she didn't come to while Lexy was with her.

Kace had grown so accustomed to Georgie's lack of response that when she finally opened her eyes and looked directly at him, he did not react. And then, struggling for the breath for each word, she said, "I didn't want Rosalind to die. I tried so hard to make her live!"

Kace was so startled, for a long moment, he couldn't speak, and then he found his voice. "I know you did. My God, Georgie, she lived as long as she did only because of you!"

It was true. Rosalind had certainly made no effort to live for him. During her pregnancy, it was Georgie she had trusted, and as she lay dying, lost in her childhood, it had been Georgie's voice that she heard, not his; Georgie urging her to drink, to rest, to get well.

"How could you think I blamed . . . ?" His question trailed away as he saw her consciousness fade again.

Suddenly he saw her in sharp focus. She had seemed to be resting more quietly, the bruises fading on her face, her coughing less violent. But now it seemed indicative of failing strength rather than recovery. Her face was skeletal, and when he held her hand, he could feel every separate bone and sinew. Now he understood that the increasing tension he saw on the doctors' faces, particularly on Anthea's, was not because they were tired—they often fought fierce battles for life—but because they were losing a patient they cared about very much.

"She isn't going to die," he murmured very low. And then he spoke louder. "You are not going to die!"

"No, you're not, Georgie. We're responsible for you, have been since the day of the fight, even if you didn't know it," another voice declared.

The relief of having Tay there swept through Kace. No matter the attempts they had both made to be totally separate, they remained bound to each other in ways only other twins could understand. But in this instance, from the moment of his arrival, Tay was dominant. It did not occur to either of them that their usual roles had reversed. Kace was desperately in need of reassurance and strength, and Tay was ready to support him in any way he could, not only for Kace's sake, but for Georgie's.

Georgie started to cough, and Tay watched as Kace sat on the bed and lifted her up against him in a practiced gesture to ease her breathing.

Tay was no less appalled by Georgie's condition than was his twin, but he allowed his fear no room to take root. What he had once wanted for himself he now wanted for Kace with equal fervor.

He repeated Kace's words. "She isn't going to die!" And then he added, "But maybe she needs a good reason to live. Have you told her how much you love her?"

Kace stroked Georgie's short hair, settling her as she stirred restlessly against him. "I've told her, but I'm not sure she understands, or maybe she just doesn't want to accept it now. She seems to think I somehow blame her for Rosalind's death." He told Tay about Georgie's brief period of consciousness earlier in the night.

Far from puzzling Tay, it confirmed his own guess about why Georgie had fled. "For a man who once had a reputation with the ladies, you are obtuse! She blames herself, not you, because she loves you, because she feels that that love was a threat to Rosalind. I know it sounds farfetched, but it's how you've felt, too, isn't it? Between the two of you, you've manufactured a heavy weight of guilt that neither of you deserves. Rosalind never suspected anything amiss, never! It's time for both of you to stop thinking you took something from her. And the least you can do for my wise advice is to make me best man at your wedding."

For the first time since the nightmare had begun, Kace smiled. Nothing had changed; Georgie still lay near death. Yet everything had changed. He believed what Tay said because Tay believed it.

Tay talked to Georgie not in a hushed, sickroom voice, but in his usual vital way as he alternately cajoled and scolded her. "I know you're tired, you're hurting, and you want to rest, but Georgie, you're slipping away, and we're not going to allow that."

Georgie had finally found a comfortable place to be. She drifted where it was neither too hot nor too cold, where the light was soft, sounds muted, and where there was no pain. Vaguely she sensed that she shouldn't be here, but she couldn't seem to fight through the layers of calm. Figures from the past hovered around her; she saw her father more clearly than she had in a long time. At one moment, he beckoned to her and in the next moved away so she could not tell what he wanted of her. Charlie was there, too. But it didn't matter; she was an observer, not a participant. It was the same with scenes and people from Wild Swan; they swirled around her like echoes. All her senses were muffled against the full impact until one voice grew more and more insistent, penetrating the haze— Tay's voice, Tay calling her, demanding that she respond.

Tay, not Kace. Then Kace's concern, his presence, had been a dream all along, shadowy like the other figures. Suddenly she had to know. She gathered her strength to swim to the surface of her mind, trembling with the effort, feeling all the injuries again as she struggled against the tide that would pull her back down.

When she opened her eyes, nothing was clear at first, and then she heard Tay's crow of triumph. "That's it, Georgie! You belong here with us. No matter how hard it is right now, you belong with us."

Us. Kace was holding her, his solid warmth bracing her, her head cradled in the curve of his neck, holding her as he had through all the fevered nights; the image came to her as if she had been floating above herself, watching all the while.

"You have to get well because I'm going to be the best man at your wedding to Kace." Tay said each word deliberately, wanting her to understand that he was giving up all claim to her.

It was an absurd time to be asking her to make such a decision, but Tay's course of summoning her to the present and treating her as if the future were not in doubt was working, and Kace was willing to try anything. He didn't even mind that this was turning into a joint marriage proposal.

"Tay might get over it if he didn't get to play the role of best man, but I wouldn't. I love you very much, and I'd like to have the next hundred years to prove it to you. Will you marry me, Georgiana Victoria Cheney?"

"Yes . . . love you." There were a thousand other things she wanted to say to him, but she hadn't the strength for any more, and she fell asleep as he shifted her to a more comfortable position, knowing exactly how to ease the aching.

Tay slipped out of the room without either of them noticing. He closed the door behind him and leaned against it, closing his eyes and letting the tears come.

He started at the touch on his arm and opened his eyes to see Lexy, white-faced with terror.

"It's all right," he said, putting his arms around her. "She's going to be fine. She just agreed to marry Kace."

Lexy didn't know the details, but she was sure Tay had had more than a little to do with it. "You are one hell of a man, brother mine," she said.

"The best man," he said, and he managed a grin. "Now, let's go tell everyone there's a wedding to plan."

Kace and Georgie were married at Wild Swan on a fair day late in April with only the family in attendance, in deference to the fact that Kace had been widowed less than a year.

Georgie was still painfully thin, but her short hair was decked with a wreath of flowers, and happiness made her face ethereal.

Georgie had been deeply moved when she learned that the whole family had been part of the vigil while she was sick. Nothing could have proven more graphically how much they considered her part of the family.

And because Travis and Gincie had insisted the money they had set aside for her was legally hers and no one else's, she was not coming to Kace without something to contribute to Sunrise. She would not have touched the money for herself, but it was a different matter to keep it in the family by using it for the farm.

Still, had she not thought she could give something special, beyond money, to Kace, she would not have married him. She would have been his lover, but not his wife; she understood far better than Rosalind ever had what being part of this family of bright, forceful people entailed. And the last thing she wanted to do was to enter into a marriage where Kace was always the giver, she the receiver of gifts. But she possessed the secret of what she could bring to Kace.

Rosalind had made Kace doubt himself as a man because she had been unwilling to accept the joys and responsibilities of being a woman in their marriage. Georgie had listened to Rosalind enough to know how distasteful she had found the physical side of marriage, and she had watched Kace go from an eager bridegroom to a man who was overly wary and too anxious to please his wife.

Georgie was going to make very sure that Kace realized he had a partner for his body and his mind and his spirit, not a china doll he had to keep on a shelf and not touch. Since he had already seen her mucking out stalls and training horses, she didn't think he'd be too apt to make the mistake. But she had reckoned without the effect her brush with death had had on him.

Because the doctors still wanted Georgie to take it easy and because the newlyweds would be traveling to New York for the summer races soon enough, Kace and Georgie had decided to spend their honeymoon at Sunrise. That suited Georgie perfectly. Coming home to the farm and the horses had yet to lose its enchantment; she doubted it ever would. She now included Sunrise in that as much as Wild Swan. And if she and Kace were to be happy in the house he had shared with Rosalind, they had to lay claim to the place together and establish their own patterns.

She was tired on her wedding night when Kace brought her home to Sunrise, but not nearly so weary as he seemed to think.

Lexy had given her the gossamer white nightgown. It was of finest lawn trimmed with French lace, and Georgie hoped it would help to make up for her lack of a figure and her lack of knowledge in the art of seduction.

But Kace gave her only one quick glance before he looked away. "It's been a long day, and I think it would be best if you get a good night's sleep, so I'll bid you good night." He didn't touch her, but moved toward the door, clearly intending to sleep elsewhere.

For an instant, she was immobilized by her own insecurities as a woman, seeing herself as so lacking in feminine allure that she could easily pass as a boy, but then she remembered the boundless tenderness he had showed to her through all the days of her illness, and she remembered all the endearments, and she said, "No! I won't have you leaving me unless it is because you really can't bear to be with me, here, in this bed. Is that the truth?"

The truth was that Kace could see every curve and line of her through the thin gown, could see the dark nipples of her breasts and the dark nest of curls at the apex of her thighs. The truth was that he couldn't look directly at her without feeling himself swelling hard and hot under his robe. The truth was that he was terrified. In the most basic of ways, Georgie was as innocent as Rosalind had been on her wedding night, and that night had seen the first of the frost that had blighted the marriage. He could not bear having to face that again. He loved so many things about Georgie, he would rather never approach her sexually at all than have to live with that coldness that once begun, withered everything else.

Georgie saw the fear in his eyes, and she saw the desire as well. She went to him and cupped his face in her hands so that he had to look at her.

"I love your intelligence and your wit. I love your kindness. I love the way you train horses, and the way you handle the staff, and the way you repair fences and pitch hay and drink coffee, and . . ." He could not resist sharing her smile as her list grew sillier, so her sudden shift in mood caught him off balance.

"I am not Rosalind," she said. "I love a thousand things about you, your body no less than everything else. I love what I've seen already, and I want to see the rest. You'll have to teach me how to make love, but I learn very quickly."

She was so earnest and eager, so different from Rosalind, he felt like weeping. And then as she pressed herself close against him, he felt a host of other things.

He kissed her softly at first, then with more demand. "Open your mouth for me," he murmured, and she complied. He felt her little shiver of surprise when his tongue entered her mouth, but there was no revulsion, only acceptance as she savored the new sensation, and then she was caressing his tongue with her own and a little purr trembled in her throat.

He cupped her bottom and lifted her against him, rubbing his groin against hers, shuddering with the sensation. She could feel him swollen and hard against her, but instead of pulling away, she melted closer.

It was he who set her from him and stepped back.

She opened her eyes and blinked at him, dazed by the rush of her own blood. "Did I do something wrong?" she asked.

He ruffled her hair and kissed her on the tip of her nose. "No, you're doing everything so perfectly, I'm going to explode if we don't slow down." He loved the blush coloring her cheeks; he loved everything about her. "Nothing we do with each other that pleases us both is wrong."

"Then I expect the possibilities are infinite," Georgie said, and she looked so entranced with the idea that Kace laughed aloud.

"If not infinite, at least enough to keep us busy for decades." The lightened mood helped to ease his tension. He picked her up and carried her to the bed, and then setting her on her feet beside it, he started to unlace the ribbons of her gown, his eyes asking if it were all right.

She gave a little nod of acquiescence and stood still as the gown puddled around her feet.

He ran his hands down her body with exquisite care, breathing, "Oh, you are lovely, so fine and sleek," and her fear that her body would prove too meager for his taste vanished.

"Not fair," she whispered, and her hands tugged at his robe until it too was on the floor.

She drew in her breath sharply, and for a moment, Kace was afraid that the sight of his nude body with his manhood swelling again toward full erection was too crude for her, but she quickly dispelled that notion.

"You are beautiful," she said, and she meant it. She loved the supple fit of his muscles over the bones, the slope of his waist from broad chest to narrow hips, the long strength of his legs, and the jut of his manhood. She was fascinated by that because she was causing the rising. She had never felt so female or so powerful. She reached out and touched him, feeling the hot strength. "Beautiful," she murmured again.

He groaned and sank down on the bed, pulling her with him, heating her with his own fever as he used his mouth and his hands to explore the taste and texture of her, trying at the same time to be mindful of the lingering soreness in her ribs. But she twisted against him with her own strength.

"I won't break," she said, her own hands busy stroking his skin, her mouth savoring the salt and sweet of his skin.

He loved the soft cooing sounds she made when he teased the sensitive folds between her legs, loved the deeper notes when he explored her virginal passage with his fingers, stroking and stretching her. He loved not only her acceptance of what he was doing, but also her acceptance of the pleasure it brought. Her eyes gleamed amber behind half-closed lids, and her face was etched with passion.

She rubbed against his hand, her body clenching around his fingers, and he could wait no longer.

He settled himself between her legs and entered her slowly.

Her eyes opened fully, and she stared at him. "I love you," they said in chorus, and then she arched her hips up, taking him deeper, feeling no pain as the ecstasy he had conjured in her body swept her away to a place she had never been before, and Kace followed her.

When it was over, so that his weight would not be too heavy against her rib cage, he used the last of his strength to roll to his side, taking her with him.

"Are you all right?" he asked, not even sure he was since he had never felt quite like this before.

"I don't think 'all right' covers this. 'Splendid,' perhaps, or 'glorious,' or 'extraordinary,' or some word I've never learned."

He felt as much as heard the laughter that rippled through her, and then she pulled back enough to kiss the knife scar that still marked his arm from the racetrack fight.

He had not known until this night how much of his confidence in himself as a man had been stripped from him by Rosalind's disgust for the physical aspects of marriage. But Georgie had known. And tonight he and Georgie had made love without a stitch of clothing between them and with lamplight and candlelight spilling over both of them; light against the dark image of his wedding night when all light had had to be extinguished in deference to Rosalind's modesty, when what he had taken for her inexperience had turned out to be revulsion that had never ended for her.

There was no revulsion here with Georgie; there was passion, joy, laughter, and most of all contentment and companionship that allowed him to imagine them years and years from now still together, still delighting in each other. Despite his infatuation with Rosalind, he had never envisioned them growing old together; they had both been too young and heedless for that in the beginning, and then the loneliness of their marriage had grown, day by day. He felt as if that had been in another lifetime.

"Georgiana Victoria Cheney Culhane," he spun the names out with relish, "you are going to make a magnificent old lady, and I am going to love you as much then as I do now, probably more."

"Splendid, glorious, extraordinary—no, indeed, the words aren't adequate. Maybe by the time we're both ancient, there will be a new one to describe exactly how we are together now and as we will still be then." Her voice was low and lazy, as she curled closer against him and fell asleep.

The last of the desolation Kace had felt with Rosalind was gone.

Chapter 50

Though she begrudged the newlyweds none of their joy, Lexy was envious. Kace and Georgie were together at Sunrise, and they would be together at the racecourses during the summer, while she and Hawk seemed to be spending less and less time together.

1892 was an election year, so Hawk was quickly consumed by stories dealing with the various political parties and causes that would shape the contest. In addition, Reid was slowly easing himself out of direct control of the paper. He wanted time to write a book about the war, the book that had haunted him ever since the war's end, and he wanted more time with Larissa. But the paper with its increasing staff, recently acquired Linotype machines, and ever-expanding circulation was a demanding mistress, and after all his years of effort, Reid wanted to be sure that it was turned over to someone he trusted, namely Hawk. Even Frank Faber, who might have wanted the position, agreed with Reid's choice and professed himself content in Baltimore.

Hawk had mixed feelings about becoming the managing editor of the *Witness*. While it was as prestigious and challenging an offer as was possible in his profession, it would inevitably mean that he would spend less and less time in the field directly reporting on stories that interested him. He just wasn't sure that his journalist's instincts would be satisfied by the new order of things. At present, he was feeling pulled both ways, and trying to take on more responsibilities for Reid as well as covering various stories left him little time for anything but work.

One of the continuing stories he worked on was the growth of the fledgling People's Party, or as it was now widely known, the Populist Party. The party's platform was concerned with agrarian interests, advocating the free coinage of silver and government control of monopolies, measures intended to help ease credit for farmers and to decrease the power of the railroads to charge exorbitant rates for hauling agricultural products to market. The party claimed that these measures would also help factory workers and other laborers in the East, but so far, the appeal was more to Westerners than to Easterners.

When Hawk left in June to attend first the Democratic National Convention in Chicago to be followed by the Populist Party's convention in Omaha, Nebraska, in early July, it never occurred to him that while he was headed west, Lexy was headed for trouble.

Lexy was also reporting on the political scene, trying to explore what influence, if any, women were having on politics. She had dutifully followed the proceedings of the Twenty-Fourth Annual Woman Suffrage Convention, which had been held in Washington, for three days in January. Twenty-six states had been represented by seventy-six delegates, and the leading women of the movement were there. Mrs. Stanton, now seventy-six, was permitted to retire, and Susan B. Anthony, who was herself seventy-two, was elected in her place. Lucy Stone was also there, and she was seventy-four.

These three women in particular were examples of women who had campaigned for women's rights for most of their lives, and Lexy held them in high esteem, but at the same time, what many politically active women were doing made her uncomfortable because they were directing so much energy toward trying to legislate moral issues, agitating for laws against drinking, gambling, and the like.

It was not that Lexy doubted the honesty of their belief that such statutes would improve family life for many, but she did doubt that their energies were directed in the most constructive way. It seemed to her that the basic need was for suffrage, and that every kind of power and privilege associated with citizenship and being able to exert some influence on one's society had to begin with the right to vote.

In addition, it was impossible to ignore that many women who were among the most ardent in the fight for rights were so bizarre in their other beliefs as to add clout to the claims that women were not mentally or emotionally stable enough to be trusted with the full rights and responsibilities of citizenship.

Finding that most organized religions had no word for women beyond bidding them to be humble and obedient servants to their husbands, women went to mountebanks and spiritual mediums who made outrageous claims of being able to influence the present by communing with spirits from the past. Finding that there were too few regular doctors who treated women as more than half-witted children, the women turned to odd systems of health and healing.

Because the false prophets and the charlatans of miracle diets and medicine expected full recompense for their efforts, their clients were most often from the socially elite.

Lexy was becoming convinced that real change, if it were to come, would have to grow from a source other than the formal conventions, from which issued fine rhetoric but little power.

Organized labor was as male dominated as other institutions, but there was a difference: there was room for women in the ranks. Women worked in the factories and were married to male factory workers, mill workers, mechanics, and laborers; and in the past few years of increasing strike action, the women had frequently been beside the men, demanding the same things—primarily higher wages and decent working hours. They attended union meetings and produced their own heroines, such as Mary Harris Jones, "Mother Jones," who was a familiar figure at various strikes, particularly among miners whom she helped to aid, enlisting their wives in her activities. Her motto was, "Pray for the dead and fight like hell for the living."

Lexy began to follow the news of strikes more closely, and though she had not intended to neglect her role as a sportswriter, July found her at the Homestead Steel works near Pittsburgh, Pennsylvania, instead of at the races in New York.

Reid was dubious about her going because strike grounds were dangerous places, but he could not hold out against her insistence that she had the same right as any good reporter to work on a worthy story, and he could not deny that her idea of approaching the subject of women's rights from the standpoint of what the women at Homestead were doing was an interesting one. In a year filled with political conventions that would entertain more than they would enlighten, stories with another slant were always welcome. And he had to concede that she was uniquely qualified on the basis of her past record. She had done a good job of investigating the lot of working women in the past, and he had every reason to believe she would do well this time, too.

"I haven't any rational arguments against your going," he confessed, "and I planned to send someone to Homestead soon anyway, but frankly, even discounting the rest of the family altogether, your husband is a formidable man, and I would not like to answer to him for endangering you for a story."

"Of course, it is utterly different from sending Hawk into a similar situation because he is a man," Lexy said silkily, and Reid threw up his hands in surrender. "I apologize and beg you not to tell the women of the family, especially my wife, about my lapse."

He sobered as he added, "But I trust you will not take any unnecessary chances."

She nodded her agreement, fully intending to comply, but since Hawk had already left for Omaha, she did not feel obliged to send him word about where she was going. She had already been in New York State for some of the races before returning to Washington with her story proposal, and she knew Hawk would assume she was still at the races, at least until he read the first of the pieces she would be writing about the Homestead strike.

The air in Homestead was probably as clean as it had been for a long time; the lack of smoke coming from the works was immediately noticeable, but everything was covered with a thick layer of oily grime, evidence of the work that was normally done here. The streets were wretched, the buildings shabby, the sidewalks treacherous, and Lexy felt as if the grit had begun to work its way under her skin the moment she arrived.

Andrew Carnegie had bought the Homestead works in 1883, and with the purchase he had acquired workers who were members of the National Amalgamated Association of Iron and Steel Workers, one of the strongest unions in the country, though unions generally were as apt to lose their fights as to win them, and even when they "won," it was often a case of preventing a cut in wages rather than gaining anything new.

At present, Carnegie was off in Scotland, basking in his reputation as one of the wealthiest men in the country and a benevolent one besides because of his civic and charitable donations, based on his belief that a rich man had an obligation to give away much of his wealth before he died. But his benevolence did not seem to include the men who worked for him. He had left Henry Clay Frick, his partner and another self-made millionaire, whose coke empire had fit neatly with Carnegie's steel, in charge at Homestead, and Frick was an avowed enemy of unions.

The union represented the plant's skilled workers and had enrolled only about one fifth of the men at Homestead when a notice, sent from Carnegie to be posted by Frick at the plant, announced that after the July 1 expiration of the current agreement with the union, the Carnegie Steel Company would operate as a nonunion shop. In late June, when negotiations with the union broke down, Frick declared he would close the mill on July 1 and reopen it on the sixth with nonunion men. It was a ploy designed to divide the unskilled, the majority of the workers, from the organized elite.

Lexy's interest had been caught by the news of the faltering negotiations, but by the time she got to Homestead, not only was the plant shut down, but it was also surrounded by a high board fence topped by barbed wire. The fence had portholes for observation posts as well as platforms with searchlights. It reminded Lexy of a prison, but in this case, the prisoners were being kept out.

There were rumors that Frick was going to bring in a security force to insure reopening of the plant with nonunion men, but before he had a chance to do this, the workers took over the plant; indeed, they secured the whole town. The unskilled majority, most of whom were illiterate immigrants, had joined ranks with the union, ending Frick's hope that he could divide the men.

Lexy wanted to be objective, but she was quickly caught in the tension that pervaded Homestead. On the surface, there was euphoria among the laborers for having taken control of the situation, but underlying it was the knowledge that Frick was not likely to allow them their way for long. And in any case, the men wanted their jobs and a decent wage, not control of Homestead.

The union's three-year contract had provided a wage scale based on the price of steel billets. The union had resisted wage cuts on several grounds, the main one being that Andrew Carnegie's strategy of flooding the market with cut-price billets to ruin the competition also had the effect of lowering wage rates while the company continued to prosper.

Lexy had arrived with the determination to see both sides of the story, but management did not seem, in her opinion, to have much justification for their actions unless one conceded that workers had no right to organize. It was particularly ironic that several years before, Carnegie had advocated peaceful settlement through arbitration. "To expect that one dependent upon his daily wages for the necessaries of life will stand by peacefully and see a new man employed in his stead is to expect too much," he had said. And yet, Frick wanted nothing more than to break the union, and he was acting in Carnegie's name.

Management would not speak to Lexy at all. She didn't know if it was because she was from the *Witness* or because she was a woman; she suspected it was a combination of the two. Labor had no such reservations. They knew the paper's reputation for fairness, and when she, deciding the truth would be more useful here than disguise, admitted that she was the author of the pieces by Abby Adams, several of the union leaders recognized the name.

It was liberating to be working openly as Abby Adams, but she tried to make it as clear as possible that while she was in sympathy with the strikers' aims, she had every intention of writing honestly about the situation, and that that might not always be to the union's liking.

Utterly certain of their moral right to be taking the action they had chosen, they were not daunted by this announcement.

Lexy had rented a room in a dilapidated boardinghouse, but she spent most of her time with Jake and Mae Bolton. The couple was middle-aged, and Jake was a staunch union man, proud of his status as a skilled worker and of the fact that his two older sons had followed in his footsteps. The Boltons' two other sons would do the same shortly.

"If there are still jobs to be had," Mae murmured, anxiety surfacing from beneath the optimism. But despite misgivings, she and other wives were strongly in support of their husbands and the strike.

Mae's blond hair was streaked with silver, and her face and slight form showed years of hard work, but she had obviously been a beauty in her youth, and she was still beautiful when she gazed at her husband or her sons. Everything in their small rented house was kept as clean as possible with the black grit filtering in.

Jake was a big, hard-muscled man with a surprisingly soft voice and an ugly puckered scar down the right side of his face, legacy of splashing molten metal.

When they were working, most of the men put in twelve hours a day or more, with holidays granted only on the Fourth of July and at Christmas. Fatigue, plant speedups, and the absence of safety equipment added to the hazard of work that was dangerous under the best of circumstances. Mangled limbs, savage burns, and death by accident were frequent occurrences. Immigrants were assigned the riskiest and most backbreaking jobs, were paid only nine dollars a week, and were often worse off than they had been in Europe.

And yet, Lexy heard Jake, Mae, and countless others assert that Carnegie himself was a good man. The union officers even sent him a cable in Scotland that read: "Kind master, tell us what you wish us to do, and we shall do it for you." They did not want to believe that Carnegie approved of what was happening to them, but evidence was to the contrary as he continued to enjoy his yearly sojourn in his native Scotland, where he lived in baronial style, a sharp contrast to the poverty of his early years, poverty that had driven his family to seek a better life in the United States. By allowing antiunion Frick to make the decisions, Carnegie was granting approval of his actions. It was as if the deprivations of his youth had taught him nothing about compassion and everything about greed. The term "robber baron" took on new meaning for Lexy, and she was haunted by memories of the dinner party that had included silver shovels and buckets and sand filled with jewels.

Since she ate most of her meals with the Boltons, Lexy used that as an excuse to bring gifts of food to them. When Mae tried to refuse, Lexy said, "I'm as proud as you are. If you refuse the food I bring, then I can no longer eat with you."

She suspected Mae was sharing the food with some neighbors who were in dire financial difficulties, and that was fine with her. She had just met these people, but the circumstances were creating an intimacy that would normally have taken years to develop.

It pleased Lexy in the sense that the Boltons and many of the others were people she would have liked to know under any conditions because they were interesting, hardworking survivors who had managed to build islands of love in the middle of such bleak surroundings and unrelenting toil. But she also knew that the swift friendship and trust were products of the siege that gripped Homestead.

No one believed that the quiet would continue. Lexy went with Mae at night to take coffee and food to Jake and other sentries who were clear proof that the workers expected Frick to do more than simply starve them out. Frick had said he would reopen the plant on the sixth.

The night of the fifth hummed with tension.

It was foggy, and though it was warm, Lexy shivered as she and Mae went on their rounds.

"It's the waiting as much as anything," Mae commiserated softly, and Lexy was grateful for her understanding. She thought this must be exactly how soldiers felt on the eve of battle, every nerve stretched too tautly, every sense concentrated on detecting any change so as not to be caught unawares.

Lexy could hear nothing unusual, but in the early hours of the morning of the sixth, word spread swiftly that the enemy was coming. And though the three hundred Pinkerton agents towed up the Monongahela River in two covered barges made their approach in near silence, the strikers were ready for them. When the barges tied up at the company wharf at 4 A.M., shots rang out from the shore and were answered from the barges, and the battle was joined.

To her great relief, Lexy found that once the fireworks had started, she was calm, her mind too taken up with trying to observe and record everything that was happening to worry about her own skin, even when bullets whined close by.

Early on, the tug that had towed the barges steamed off, so the Pinkertons were stranded on their barges at the wharf, but they were armed and determined not to give in to the strikers.

The strikers were well armed, too, including cannon in their arsenal, and the shooting continued hour after hour.

Lexy kept reminding herself that she was obligated as a member of the press to watch rather than to take direct action, but she could not include offering help with the wounded in that category, and she pitched in with the other women where she could.

She did not see Jake fall; she heard Mae's high-pitched scream of his name, and by the time she got to them, Jake was dead, his shirt drenched in blood from the bullet in his chest, Mae cradling his head in her lap.

"He only wanted just pay for a just day's work," Mae whispered, over and over, and then she was silent, and the noise of the battle washed over them.

For Lexy, everything seemed to slow down after that. She knew it wasn't so, but she couldn't make her mind comprehend. She had only known Jake and Mae for these short days, and yet, she felt as if she had lost a beloved member of her family.

Suddenly she longed desperately for Hawk, and he had never seemed so far away. But the thought of him strengthened her. She had a job to do, the only thing she could do that might make a difference—to bear witness.

The battle went on until, at last, when the barges, reinforced with steel plates, remained afloat despite cannon fire, the strikers poured oil on the water and set the oil ablaze. The Pinkertons were trapped in the inferno and raised the white flag to save their lives. The workers didn't want to accept the truce, but the union leaders intervened. The Pinkertons surrendered their arms and ammunition and started coming ashore.

Earlier Lexy had seen Mae leave with Jake's body carried by their sons and escorted by a cadre of women. She had started to go with them and then had stopped; as close as she felt to the Boltons, she did not think her place was with Mae at that moment of mourning. But now she saw that Mae had rejoined the ranks of the workers and their wives who were watching the Pinkertons, their loathing written plainly on their faces. Pinkertons had been used against strikers before, and their ranks included ex-convicts and many men who simply enjoyed a brutal fight wherever they could find one.

As if all motion had slowed, Lexy saw Mae pick up the rock, heard her own voice screaming, "Mae, no!" even as the stone sailed forward to hit one of the agents on the shoulder, but her voice was a useless whisper against the rising cries from the crowd as men and women loosed their rage, stoning and clubbing the Pinkertons as they were led away. Flesh split open, and blood poured from cuts on their faces.

There had been casualties on both sides, but this attack on men who were leaving under a flag of surrender was terrible to behold. Lexy wanted to close her eyes, but she made herself see it all, acknowledging that it was as much a part of the story of Homestead as the rest.

An eerie calm settled over the town. The strikers tended to their wounded, buried their dead, and waited for Frick to make concessions to them for their victory.

Lexy divided her time between listening to the union leaders discussing what concessions those might be and being with Mae, trying to help with the constant stream of people who came to express their condolences. In place of the open, giving woman Lexy had met at first, there was now a small shrunken figure with glazed eyes. It was as if Mae had died with Jake. It was too easy for Lexy to imagine cradling Hawk just as Mae had done with her man when he had died, and when Lexy imagined that, she understood how Mae and the others could have attacked the Pinkertons, but it was still horrifying. It was evidence of how quickly a mob could form from a group of otherwise sane people. She was never going to forget the sight of Mae picking up that rock and throwing it at the men.

Frick made no concessions. Six days later, eight thousand National Guardsmen marched into Homestead, sent by the governor at Frick's request. The town was put under martial law. The works were reopened with strikebreakers. The union had been vanquished.

Hawk arrived at the same time the guardsmen did. Lexy had no warning. One moment she was standing with the workers and their families, watching in silence as wave after wave of uniformed men swept into the town, and in the next, her shoulders were caught in a hard grip, and Hawk's voice was harsh as he swung her around to face him, ignoring the press of the crowd.

"God damn you, Lexy Mackenna! What in the hell do you think you're doing here?"

She was so stunned, for a moment she could only stare up at him, and then the angry murmurs around her pierced her consciousness, and she realized that Hawk was in danger of being attacked by her new friends.

"Please, it's all right," she said. "He's my husband." With that, everyone made an elaborate show of looking elsewhere, as if to give the couple privacy despite the crowd.

She felt she had every right to be furious with him, as he was with her, particularly since he had been so public about scolding her, but his hands were trembling, and beneath the anger, she saw how worried he was.

"Not here," she said, and his hands dropped away. He followed her when she led the way to a more secluded spot.

"I know how you're feeling," she said, controlling her own temper with an effort. "You are behaving like a parent who has just seen his child escape hurt. You're glad to find me in one piece but furious that I caused you worry. But I am not your child! I am your wife, but I am also a journalist, a very good one. I saw a chance for a story here, and I took it. I have a right to do that, just as you do."

Hawk thought he could hear the wind leaving his sails. Common sense had told him that Lexy could hardly be submitting additional columns to the paper had she been seriously hurt and that had she been injured at all, Reid would have sent word to him in Omaha. But common sense had had nothing to do with his reaction to having a fellow newspaperman hand him a copy of the *Witness* with the comment, "Abigail Adams seems to be covering a more interesting event than this."

The man had just arrived in Omaha and had several issues of the *Witness*, as well as other papers. "Keeping up with the competition," he explained, but his voice had trailed off as he read Hawk's expression, and he quickly found business elsewhere.

Hawk had cursed his own carelessness in not making more of an effort to obtain copies of the *Witness* in Omaha; he had cursed Reid for allowing Lexy to go to Homestead; and most of all, he had cursed her for putting herself at risk. He had not been this terror-stricken about her safety since he had rescued her from the insane asylum, and he hadn't been married to her then, hadn't known he could love anyone as much as he loved Lexy.

They stood facing each other on the dirty, deserted side street, neither one sure of what to do next, both of them caught between feeling justified in anger and yet unhappy with it.

The image of Jake dead in Mae's arms flashed into Lexy's mind again and with it the longing she had felt for Hawk.

She squared her weary shoulders and gazed at him steadily. "I did know you wouldn't approve of my coming here, but that was not enough to stop me. It can't be if I am to be a good, honest reporter. I couldn't know how ugly it would get, but I would have come anyway. It is so sad here! They have lost everything! Oh, my love, can't you understand; these are my Indians! I feel about them as you felt about the Sioux in South Dakota, as you still feel about them. And I couldn't stop the destruction here any more than you could there, but I can be a witness."

She reached up and touched the hard planes of his face. "That doesn't mean I don't love you and need you, because I do, so much. And I am sorry I made you afraid. I won't promise it won't happen again, but I am sorry just the same."

Suddenly he was so hungry for her, he could have taken her right there on the street. He wrapped his arms around her and hugged her so tightly, she squealed in surprise. But she didn't pull away, she rubbed against him, wishing their clothing wasn't between them.

"I have a room," she murmured against his chest.

The boardinghouse was empty, its inhabitants out with everyone else watching the troops arrive. It was just as well Lexy and Hawk had the place to themselves because they were too absorbed in each other to notice much about their surroundings. Once the door to her room was closed, they came together roughly, not even bothering to undress fully, Hawk unfastening his pants and Lexy pulling up her skirts and pulling down her drawers just enough so that he could thrust inside her, both of them gasping and moving in a frenzy that lacked all of their usual care in lovemaking.

Afterward, they lay stunned, neither of them quite sure about what had happened.

"Are you all right? Did I hurt you?" Hawk asked, and Lexy banished his anxiety instantly with her throaty laugh.

"I think I should ask you the same questions." She nuzzled against his neck, reassuring him with her touch, but then she moved away reluctantly and began to straighten her clothing, a blush coloring her cheeks as she realized how wanton she must look.

"I'd like to stay here and do that again, more slowly this time, but I've still got a story to write. I need to watch outside for a little longer."

The way she was looking at him left no doubt of her continued desire, but he didn't mistake her determination to finish the task she had set for herself.

There was no battle from the strikers to retain control of the mill and the town; they knew they were hopelessly outmanned and outgunned.

Hawk did not interfere with Lexy's movements, but when she did not protest his presence, he stayed close beside her, and he began to understand the involvement she had with these people. She greeted many by name and introduced Hawk, and though some of the union leaders recognized him for his own journalistic reputation, he realized that most of the people he met were interested only in sizing him up in order to determine if he were a fit husband for Lexy.

When they returned to the bleak little room for the night, Hawk saw the tension in Lexy's shoulders and began to knead them gently.

She rolled her head and groaned, "Oh, that feels so good!" For long moments, she gave herself up to the ease he was giving her, and then she said, "It's over here. Frick has won on every count, and he's going to punish the union and those who supported it by replacing them with new workers." She poured out all the details of the Boltons, of Jake's death, of Mae's assault on the Pinkertons, her words making Hawk see everything in vivid detail.

Abruptly he understood this afternoon's frantic lovemaking. On Lexy's part, it had been release from the harsh emotions and risk of the past days. On his part, it had been relief at finding her unhurt, still with a tinge of anger that she had put herself in danger, but more, it had been jealousy. He hated to admit it, but it was true. Before he had even gotten to Homestead, he had felt some part of her slipping away into her work in a way that hadn't happened before during their marriage. Now he understood how it had been for her when he had brought the ghosts of the Sioux back with him from Wounded Knee.

He understood, but it was still hard. No matter how much he believed in Lexy's talent and independence, he would never be easy while she was endangering herself for a story, even though he was willing to do the same with his own safety.

It was sobering to discover that he believed in the equality of men and women more in theory than in practice when the practice involved the possibility of his wife being killed or wounded by a stray bullet or an angry mob. But he had to accept it because to do less would be to risk losing what he did have with Lexy—the mutual respect and shared intelligence that made their union so much more than physical.

"There has to be something I can do once I've left this place, something to keep them from starvation. The family will help; I'm certain they will. We can start a fund for the workers, something!"

Hawk listened to her anxious spate of words, and he even added suggestions of his own, but both of them knew it was more like a child whistling against the dark than a real possibility of helping the strikers.

Finally sheer exhaustion overcame Lexy, making her body feel leaden, making her mind cloud and slow, but she fought sleep long enough to say, "I am very, very glad you are here," and Hawk took the admission for the gift it was.

Chapter 51

Because the Pinkertons were widely known and despised as hired thugs, the attack on them did not cost the strikers general sympathy, and they continued to be supported by many newspapers across the country. Even people who mistrusted organized labor on principle thought that the workers at Homestead had been treated badly.

But the sympathy evaporated on July 23, when Alexander Berkman, a young Russian-American anarchist, shot and stabbed Henry Clay Frick. The assassination attempt failed. Frick immediately announced that the nonunion policy would not change, went home to recuperate, and then carried on as if nothing had happened. Berkman was imprisoned.

It didn't seem to matter that while Berkman had been associated with radical labor groups in New York, he had had no direct connection with the Homestead strikers; he quickly became a symbol for the darkest suspicions about unions—that they harbored the worst elements of European revolutionary movements, that they would use immigrants and their dangerous ideas to destroy the order in the United States, to start a war between rich and poor.

The nation had been born in revolution, but only a fanatic fringe wanted another one. Image of the bloody excesses of the French Revolution and of subsequent European upheavals were more than enough to fill the majority of the populace, native and foreign-born, with dread.

Lexy was no more in favor of severed heads in baskets and gutters running with blood than any other sane person was, but she found it unbearably frustrating that people could not make the distinction between the strikers' legitimate complaints and the mad actions of someone like Alexander Berkman.

After Berkman, it was difficult to obtain contributions for the strikers, but Lexy kept at it doggedly, managing to send some money to be used by the union leaders for the most needy families, and still she felt as if she'd failed completely. The strike was not declared officially over until November 20, and by then the old work force was almost entirely gone, replaced by new men brought in by Frick. Mae and her sons had disappeared with the others.

Lexy had left her address with Mae and had begged her to contact her if there was anything Lexy could do for her and her family, but even as Mae had thanked her for the offer, Lexy had known nothing would come of it.

The year had seen strikes in Western mines, on some railroads, in factories, and elsewhere, and there had been violence during many of them and injustice on both sides. There were union workers who did not want nonunion men to work; nonunion men who did not want union men to work; management that would not grant their workers' demands; and management that could not and stay in business. But for Lexy, the Homestead strike was the turning point, not only of the year, but of her career.

She had resumed covering the races from August to the end of the season in the fall, but she knew that more than ever before, the Abby Adams stories were taking precedence over the sporting news from Lexy, particularly because she had now worked openly as Abby Adams, as Elizabeth Cochrane did as Nellie Bly. But she didn't want either of her writing styles to suffer, nor did she want to cease writing about the races. Finally, though she hadn't made a decision, she decided she had to talk to Reid about her dilemma.

It was no more an easy decision for Reid than for Lexy. He had long believed that Lexy had the potential to be a serious journalist, but the work she did on the races was not be be lightly cast away. Most of the sporting news in the *Witness* was simply a listing of contest results in baseball, football, rowing, and various other amusements. Even trotting meetings, which were growing ever more popular, were given only cursory treatment in the *Witness*. Reid left detailed coverage to the specialized journals, with just enough sporting patter included in the *Witness* to attract those readers who were put off by the idea of a paper with no entertainment pieces.

But Lexy's columns were different. She had added hard work to her background and had developed a unique voice in the world of Thoroughbred racing, a voice heeded by thousands who bred, bought, trained, raced, rode, and watched the horses on the East Coast, and by many in other parts of the country as well. She was one of a very select group of English and American journalists who were specialists in the sport of kings.

"I don't want to lose the readers you attract," Reid told her frankly. "I understand how conscientious you are, and I don't want you to be in the position of feeling you are failing on both counts because you cannot give your full attention to either Lexy or Abby. But I would like to try a compromise. We haven't really got anyone on the staff who can or even wants to write about the races the way you do, but I will try to find someone who can at least write credibly about them. He or she," he smiled wryly at her in salute since both of them knew it was doubtful he would find another woman to take her place, "would be responsible for gathering the basic facts of the racing season and reporting racing results, and you could continue to write about the finer points, which horses to watch for, racing controversies, major sales, that sort of thing. That would free you from having to be at the tracks so much, but you would still keep your hand in. And God knows, it doesn't seem as if things are improving, but we can still hope that there won't be enough Homesteads to keep you busy."

It was better than Lexy had hoped for, allowing her a good deal of flexibility and sparing her the necessity of having to give up the racing world entirely.

Reid was blunt in his private conversation with Hawk. "Her columns from Homestead were superb. She made people who have never in their lives been dependent on a boss for wages know exactly how precarious that can be. She made the thousands of workers and their families into individuals who couldn't be ignored. And unless a sudden magic spell of peace and justice is cast over this land, she's going to be doing more of the same kind of work, running more of the same kind of risks. I need to know that the paper's not going to lose her because you can't handle that once you're completely in charge."

"I think I've already fought that battle, and I hope I've won," Hawk said. "And besides, I know as well as you do that Lexy's gotten to the point where the *Witness* needs her more than she needs the paper; there are any number of other papers that would like very much to hire her."

He shuddered at the thought of suffering that separation. Their marriage was difficult enough with the demanding schedules they often had with the *Witness*, but it was still enough of a family organization so that they managed their lives with a fair amount of harmony. If one of them were working for another paper, everything would surely be more difficult personally and professionally. He loathed the idea of their being competitors, unable to exchange ideas on stories as they often did.

That thought had enabled him to react calmly when Lexy had told him about her intention to speak to Reid and about the results. But though she did not remark on it directly, respecting it as private territory, he knew she had seen his apprehension because she told him, "I do not think I could be a married woman were you not my husband. Too many wives are prisoners, not partners, and I could not bear that."

It made him think again about what it would be like to be married to a more conventional woman. It made him think about what it would be like to be married to Caroline, who had, when he had seen her, seemed to be completely content as the social appendage of her husband. He thought of years and years of boredom.

"We're even, then," he said, "because I would not want to be married at all were you not my wife."

She did not know how much she had needed his reassurance until he gave it, and it made it much easier than it would have been otherwise to discuss the shift in her work with her parents when the family gathered for Christmas.

She realized as soon as she talked to them that they had anticipated her.

"We'd be lyin' if we told you we'll ever feel easy with knowin' you're in danger," Travis said, "but we'll just have to trust you to take good care. We'll miss seein' as much of you at the races, but the other work you're doin', it's important. We're very proud of you."

"And we're not the only ones," Gincie told her. She showed her a note from Frank Faber that said, "Your daughter's Abby Adams pieces about Homestead were eloquent. You must be very proud."

The praise meant a lot because Frank Faber had been a highly respected newspaperman for so long and because Frank's friendship with the family went clear back to the days before the war. But the note also reminded Lexy that her parents had met when both had been risking their lives for a just cause, which went a long way toward explaining why they had never been able to condemn any of their offspring for commitment to principle.

The strikes and politics in general were the main topics of conversation this year at the family gathering. Grover Cleveland would be back in the White House in March, having defeated Harrison in the election, and there was little doubt that the complications and cruelties of the Homestead strike had been an embarrassment to the Republicans, helping to insure Harrison's loss.

More than a million votes had been cast for the Populist candidate, James B. Weaver of Iowa, but neither the Democrats nor the Republicans were ready to incorporate Populist planks in their platforms. Hawk, observing the Populists' nominating convention and their campaigning, had been impressed by the order and dedication that had been in sharp contrast to accusations in the Eastern press that the Populists were "lawless, irresponsible, incendiary."

"On their own, or in an alliance with a major party, they are going to make a difference before too long," Hawk said.

"Not in time," Dermot countered flatly. "Cleveland was voted in because the Republicans have managed to solve the problem of the Treasury surplus by overspending. Some of it has gone for worthy projects—for veterans' pensions, for coastal defenses, and for schools—but a lot of it has gone down the drain of special interests. And the McKinley Tariff has insured the highest rates we've ever had on farm and industrial products. Workers think the tariffs protect them from foreign competition, and the initial idea was to do just that, but now the tariffs protect and enlarge the monopolies and increase the price of everything imported, from woolen cloth, to tinware, to salt—things even the poorest worker uses. Cleveland got in because he's frugal and conservative, and people believe he can take the country back to the common sense of his last administration, but I don't think he can."

Dermot and Jilly inhabited the world of the most privileged financiers and industrialists, a world the Republicans, with their sympathies for big business, had favored. There was a small chorus of doomsayers coming forward from Congress, the press, and the public, but it was astonishing and sobering to discover that Dermot was one of the voices. And Jilly had joined wholeheartedly in his defection.

"Do you remember that dinner party where the jewels were buried in the sand?" she asked. Her eyes searched Lexy's, and before Lexy could make any response, Jilly nodded and said, "I see that you do," and Lexy knew that her lasting distaste showed plainly.

"Well, I used to be amused by such gestures, even when I felt guilty about it," Jilly confessed. "It used to be exciting to see what extravagance would be offered next—hundred-dollar bills to wrap little favors, oysters served with pearls for the guests, jeweled collars for pet dogs and monkeys—it goes on and on. And finally it is sickening, like eating so much chocolate that you cannot swallow. There is something wrong about such displays when so many people have so little. I've learned I don't much care to be one of the Four Hundred."

She looked down the table at her parents. "You raised me better than to be seduced by such glitter. I'm embarrassed it has taken me so long to see through it."

"A lot of people never do see through it," Reid reminded his daughter, and Jilly answered his smile with one of her own.

Lexy was gratified by Jilly's new attitude, but she wasn't surprised; she had seen Jilly changing ever since the blizzard four years before.

She had also seen changes in another cousin, in Joseph, since he had gone south with her and Hawk. But the change this Christmas was profound enough to have the family making an elaborate pretense that nothing was out of the ordinary. For the first time, he had invited a young woman to be his guest at some of the celebrations.

Matilda Brunnell, known as Mattie, was tall, flaxen-haired, handsome rather than beautiful, and so warm and outgoing in contrast to Joseph's reserved nature that it was impossible not to like her.

Lexy was, in fact, prepared to love her because Joseph had never looked so happy. And the match had every chance of succeeding professionally as well as personally because Mattie was determined to be in the first class of medical students that would be admitted when Johns Hopkins University Medical School opened.

Anthea couldn't help wearing a cat-with-the-cream expression when the proposed medical school was discussed, and she brought further news of it to the holiday.

"Not only will women be admitted equally with men," she said, "but if Mary Garrett has her way, the school will be graduate level only, with entrance requiring study in biology, chemistry, and physics, and a reading knowledge of French and German. Mattie will be fine because of the rigorous study she has already done in college, but some of those who fancy themselves as suitable for faculty are going to find they don't even measure up to what entering students are required to know."

"Have the trustees then agreed to Miss Garrett's latest demands?" Lexy asked.

"No," Anthea said, not the least daunted, "but they will because they want that five hundred thousand dollar endowment on hand before they open the school, and Mary has offered them the three hundred and six thousand, nine hundred and seventy-seven dollars," she rolled the figure out with relish, "that are still needed to make up the total."

"Surely you deserve some of the credit, too," Mattie said. "Joseph has told me all about your activities on behalf of the school."

"Joseph flatters me," Anthea protested, and Lexy was amused to see that the usually forthright woman was actually blushing at the praise, but it was deserved.

Though Mary Elizabeth Garrett had had no formal higher education, she was a staunch campaigner for the right of women to be educated as well as men, and to that end, she with four other Baltimore women had founded the Bryn Mawr School for Girls in the city in 1885, setting a high new standard for women's secondary education. In order to graduate, the students of the Bryn Mawr School had to pass entrance examinations for a college of the first rank.

Miss Garrett was descended from prominent mercantile families, and at less than forty years old, she was a force to be reckoned with. When she set her mind, her money, and her friends to a project, it got done. Anthea was not equal in financial status, but she was greatly respected by Mary and the others for her practice of medicine, and she had been consulted often regarding plans for the medical school and had helped with the fund-raising.

The medical school of Johns Hopkins University had been planned for years but delayed over and over, so a few years previously, a group of women had offered to raise one hundred thousand dollars toward the project on the condition that women be admitted on the same terms as men. Miss Garrett had become the secretary of the local committee and the highest contributor to the more than hundred thousand dollars that had been raised at that time.

"Not only do I think that the trustees will agree to Mary's latest stipulations, but I think they will finally consider the funds on hand to be sufficient, if for no other reason than to stave off further demands for equality and excellence," Anthea said.

Her face looked soft and young as she contemplated this vision of medical training made so much more accessible to young women than when, despite all her experience in treating the war's wounded, she had had to go to Europe to complete her own education. But her smile was wry when she added, "You see, things can be improved, even if it requires a fortune to insure equality."

Though the family gatherings could be exhausting with so much going on at once, Lexy loved them not only for the emotional security they gave her, but also for the sheer vitality that radiated from the different generations coming together to exchange viewpoints and information. They were people capable of dreaming and of acting to make their visions into reality. Lexy liked the practicality as much as the dreaming, and she knew her great-grandmother Alex had possessed the same combination and would approve of the way her descendants continued to live her legacy.

Lexy felt it particularly when she was with her brothers. It had become a tradition for them to ride out on the land together during Christmas. Part of the tradition was that Hawk always found that he had something else to do, and now Georgie followed his lead, both of them feeling it was important for the brothers and sister to have this time together.

Kace was full of the past racing season and the hope of foals to be born in the new year. "It was a much better season for us this year than last; we've got a solid stable of top performers, but before long, we'll also be able to see how Pharaoh's get will run. If he breeds true, he could be the leading sire in four or five years. Moonraker's already up there."

"That's a big if," Lexy pointed out genially. "Don't you think you ought to wait a bit, see how his first foals do before getting your hopes up? If I had a dollar for each of the progeny that have proved inferior to a champion sire, I would be a rich woman."

"Ah, but I have faith, sister mine," Kace insisted, unfazed by her logic. "I'm more worried about the antibetting movement than I am about our bloodlines. For the first time, Papa is talking seriously about eventually having to race in England just to keep the breed at its peak, though it hasn't come to that yet."

"I hope it never does," Lexy said. "Aside from all the problems of shipping and training horses there, I can't imagine it working on a grand scale. American horses would flood the English races. I can't believe the English racing authorities would allow that. And even if they did, what a loss it would be for this country!"

"Well, there's more talk of a truly national jockey club, to replace the Board of Control, and maybe if that's done, maybe if the excesses in the sport are curbed, there won't be so much pressure against the gambling," Kace suggested.

"I hope you're right, but the reformers don't seem interested in any half measures. At least, Wild Swan and Sunrise produce horses for purposes other than racing, and there's other livestock and the crops. The farms wouldn't be forced out of business if racing fell apart." But as she said it, Lexy thought how impossible it was to imagine Wild Swan without the racehorses. And then it occurred to her that despite how vital the subjects they had been discussing were to the farms, Tay hadn't said anything for most of the ride.

He was trailing a little behind, and she turned in her saddle, meaning to tease him for his inattention, but the words died before she could say them.

He looked so alone and distant, and so intense. He was staring at the winterscape around them as if he had never seen it before—or as if he would never see it again.

Lexy felt guilty. She had been so taken up with her own life, she hadn't noticed the changes in Tay, but they were obvious now. He had been quiet during most of this holiday, when he had been here at all; much of the time he had been out treating ailing animals. She suspected he had arranged to be away more than necessary.

And she realized that the constraint wasn't Tay's alone. Kace and Georgie were young and very much in love; when they were together, they showed their affection in myriad ways, in how they looked at each other, in how they bantered with words shaded with multiple meanings, in the ways they reassured each other with a touch. But when Tay was there, they were more restrained with each other, anxious that they not exclude him.

Tay looked up at the pressure of Lexy's gaze and smiled automatically, but it didn't reach his eyes.

"Look!" Kace exclaimed, pointing skyward. "It's a good omen for us!"

The three of them watched the flight of swans pass overhead, and for an instant, it was as if they were children again and together as they had been then. But when the ride was over, Lexy waylaid Tay and asked, "What is it?"

He hesitated, and then he shrugged. "I meant to wait until the new year to tell anyone, but keeping things from you has never been easy, and you might as well be the first to know. I'm going to California as soon as I can. I know Mama and Papa will agree. It's high time one of us managed the property there. Papa has enough to do here without having to travel clear across the country. And there'll be no lack of veterinary work, either. California is full of horses, cattle, and other beasts."

Lexy's eyes filled with tears, and she gathered herself to protest, but Tay shook his head. "Don't, please don't! What would you do if you had to see Hawk every day, married to another woman and very happily so?"

She didn't want to admit it, but honesty compelled her. "I would go mad, or I would go away, far, far away."

"And don't blame Georgie," Tay said. "She loved Kace from the first, and she never led me on, never pretended any different."

"What are you going to say to them, to Kace and Georgie?" Lexy asked, brushing at her tears.

"They are the ones who will require the least explanation," he answered. "But Georgie will feel it is her fault, and I won't be able to convince her it isn't. Maybe you can. She loves me like a brother; she loves you like a sister; and I don't want her to feel that becoming part of our family was a mistake."

There was a small, dark part of Lexy that did wish Georgie had never come into their lives, but it had no strength against the truth of Georgie herself, who was everything Lexy could have wanted in a sister or in a wife to either of her brothers.

"I'll do my best," she promised. "But the thing that will convince her most of all is if you are happy. Don't worry too much about her. After all, she has proved herself very strong indeed. She not only stayed close during Kace's marriage, she was a most patient friend to Rosalind. Anyone who could do that with such grace can survive this."

This time Tay's smile was genuine as he gave her a quick hug. "I'm glad you helped to raise me and Kace; you've always been as sensible as our mother."

They stood for a moment, listening to the sounds of livestock and people; Wild Swan bustled even in winter.

"You were born here," Tay reminded her softly. "Kace and I were born in California, but Kace belongs here much more than I do now. Maybe I was always meant to go back."

The pain in Lexy's heart eased as she saw his eyes light with anticipation, and she clung to that image when she watched him leave on the train in January.

Everyone in the family was trying to behave as if this were no different from all the times when Tay had left for school, but the smiles were too fixed, the eyes too bright. Gincie and Travis busied themselves by giving him last-minute instructions and messages for the family in California, and the one thing that kept Gincie from breaking down was her desire to spare Tay extra pain. No matter how set he was on this new course, no matter even how much he might be looking forward to it, she knew how hard it was for him to say good-bye. She noticed how slow and drawling Travis's voice had become in his effort to keep it from breaking, and she held on to his hand very hard.

Kace and Tay embraced, and Kace managed a muffled, "Good luck; don't stay away too long." But for all their height and strength, they looked more like two disconsolate children than like grown men.

Georgie was the most controlled. She said little, and her normally animated face was curiously blank, but her eyes betrayed the deepest misery of all of them, just as Tay had predicted.

As they watched the train pull out of the station and exchanged last waves with Tay, Lexy whispered to Georgie, "It's not your fault. Tay made this decision himself, and he'll be all right. You and Kace have gone through enough to be together without taking the blame for this. There is only one question to ask: do you think it would be better if you and Kace were not married, not going to spend the rest of your days together?"

What little color there was left drained from Georgie's face as she considered life without Kace. She had seen how tentative and unhappy he had grown with Rosalind; daily she saw how contented he was now, and honesty demanded that she acknowledge it was because of their marriage. She was committed to Kace and he to her. Nothing but death could change that, and to add her guilt to her husband's burden would benefit neither him nor his brother. She knew that Kace had his own guilt in addition to the sorrow of seeing his twin go so far away.

"Thank you," she murmured to Lexy. "You are a good sister to all three of us."

Of all the accolades Lexy had ever received, none had meant more than this one, and it reminded her that wherever any of them were, they were still bound together by love.

She thought again of Alex, who had seen her beloved brother, Boston, leave to go west when the journey had been long and arduous, completely different from the speed and luxury of modern train travel, and yet, Alex and Boston had remained close to each other as long as both had lived.

For decades upon decades, Alex had set patterns for dealing with life's vagaries; it was vastly reassuring to find that the patterns still held true, as if Alex had charted the course of the heart as surely as the swans sought sanctuary in the South in winter and in the North in summer. It made Lexy believe that maybe Tay was right, that he had always been destined to go back to California, that it was just another part of the pattern.

Chapter 52

Letters began to come from Tay shortly after he arrived in California, and they were so relentlessly cheerful, Lexy questioned their veracity. But after a time, it was impossible to doubt the genuine excitement Tay was experiencing, particularly in one passage he wrote to Lexy:

It truly is as if there is some inner recognition between me and this land. The fog of the coast, the bright, harsh light of the interior valleys, the endless contrasts of the state—all of it delights me and makes me feel as if I have come home after a long exile. It is so different, knowing that I am not here just for a visit but to live . . .

She showed the letter to Hawk, and she asked, "Do you ever long for the Far West, for California in particular?"

"No," he answered, "because you are here and your family has become my family. And beyond that, my work is better done here than there."

It was as close as he could come to explaining that he was not land-connected as Lexy and her family were, and before Lexy he could not have imagined being so centered in a family. Even when he had thought to claim Jared, he had pictured being alone with his son, or possibly having Caroline with them if she insisted on being with the child. He had wanted to offer Jared more than that, but he hadn't known how he was going to manage it. Now he could not imagine being without the confusion and security of family he had acquired by marriage.

As usual, Lexy and Hawk were pulled apart by the varied demands of their jobs, so they were glad to be able to go together to the Columbian Exposition in Chicago. The fair was named for the four hundredth anniversary of the discovery of America, and it featured exhibits and people from all over the world. It had already been in operation for some months, but May 1, 1893, was the official day for President Cleveland to open it.

The fair offered such a variety of structures and exhibits, it was impossible not to be entranced. Buildings as large as palaces recalled the glories of ancient civilizations and housed offerings of everything from the fine arts to the latest examples of machinery and scientific advances.

Among other things, Lexy reported the details of the Woman's Building. It had been made possible by legislation in Congress, giving women a magnificent structure in which to hold their councils, the program controlled by the Board of Lady Managers. Much of the interior statuary, decorations, and paintings had been created by women. It was, in all, the first complete recognition by the government of women as part of the body politic.

It was more difficult to cover the living exhibits, the natives from various parts of the globe who were presented in models of their own villages. They varied from Laplanders with dirt-covered huts, neck comforters, felt boots, and other defenses against the cold, to a Moorish girl purported to be the sultan's favorite, fresh from the Seraglio, to Dahomeans from West Africa. The Dahomeans were touted as strong, intelligent, and preferring death to slavery, and the women were said to be particularly valorous beings, who, in the tradition of Amazons, formed King Behazin's army. These traits were all to the good, but the Dahomeans were also supposed to practice ritual cannibalism with an abandon not in the least tempered by the swift approach of the twentieth century.

"Do you think they really do eat people?" Lexy asked as she and Hawk left the exhibit. "They have such a pleasant aspect, faces of such strength and serenity for all that they are in a strange place so far from home."

"I don't know how people who eat people should look. Maybe they only slaver when they're crunching down on someone's fingers or other body parts," Hawk teased, making a horrible face. But then he sobered. "No, I don't think they eat other human beings. I remember hearing things like that said about Indians. It's the ultimate savagery, isn't it? And double-edged; the legend of it can be used to frighten one's enemies or it can be used by one's enemies as a charge of the worst moral degradation."

Lexy stopped walking, stood on tiptoe, and kissed Hawk, ignoring the stares of those around them. "I do love you," she said.

Her eyes were so wide and hurt for his pain at the memory of bigotry that he kissed her back and then added irreverently, "Besides, I doubt very much that humans are palatable."

She laughed as he had intended and said, "Then we are agreed that the more lurid claims for human exhibits need not be recorded in the *Witness?*"

"Agreed. But I think we need a personal experience of the Ferris Wheel to do it justice in print. Are you game?"

"Of course!" She hoped he didn't hear the wobble in her voice.

The Ferris Wheel was located in the Midway Plaisance. It had been designed and the construction directed by G. W. Ferris, who was the superintendent of a large bridge company. The steel towers holding it in place were one hundred thirty-seven feet high, and the derrick required to lift the wheel into place had been the largest ever made. The wheel was two hundred and sixty-four feet in diameter, and between the rims, at twenty-eight and a half feet apart, were suspended thirty-six cars, each capable of carrying sixty passengers.

Lexy busily jotted down all the statistics while waiting for a turn on the wheel. She hoped she would be able to read the shaky scrawl later.

"Have I ever mentioned to you that I don't like being on anything higher than a horse?" she muttered as they entered the car, and she held Hawk's arm in a death grip. But once the ride started, she was enchanted.

"Oh, Hawk! It's like flying!" She stared at the tiny human figures below them, at the tops of buildings, at everything made to look like toys by the giant wheel. It was even better than the sensation she had experienced at the top of the Statue of Liberty.

When they left the fair, Hawk presented her with a little model of the wheel, and Lexy kept it on her desk at the *Witness*.

The little wheel soon became a symbol of happier times that seemed to have happened a long while ago rather than just short weeks before. Everything Dermot had predicted was coming true, and also as he had judged, it was already too late by the time of Cleveland's inauguration for the new president to do anything to avert the disaster. But even Hawk and Reid, who had anticipated another financial panic sometime soon due to historical precedent and because they had been monitoring the business news closely enough to detect the ingredients for disaster, were stunned by the swift-moving ferocity of this one.

The first sign of trouble ahead had come as far back as February, when the Philadelphia and Reading Railroad was relinquished to receivers due to debts of more than $125,000,000. Other railroads and many banks began to sway and topple in the financial wind.

In April the gold reserve had fallen below the $100,000,000 mark that was in many people's minds the line between fiscal soundness and ruin.

On May 5, while the Mackennas were on their way back from Chicago, securities on the New York Stock Exchange plummeted. But most people still thought recovery could come without great damage.

On June 27, Hawk was writing an article about Illinois governor John P. Altgeld pardoning the last three anarchists in jail for the Haymarket Square riot of 1886. He was thinking that it didn't seem like seven years since he had come here and met Lexy; it seemed a far shorter time than that. He wished Lexy were not north at the races because memories of their first meeting made him miss her even more than usual.

He smiled, remembering how disheveled she had looked from getting caught in the rain at the Washington races, remembering how beautiful she was.

And then all thoughts of his personal life fled as first one voice and then another swore at the news coming in over the paper's wire. The New York stock market wasn't just dropping this time; it was crashing to the ground, taking with it the hopes of thousands of small investors as well as those of the wealthy.

President Cleveland's first action was to call a special session of Congress in order to repeal the Silver Purchase Act which had, since

1890, authorized the Treasury to issue notes redeemable in gold or silver coin with the provision for more silver than had been permitted by previous legislation. The act had been a compromise between those who wanted only gold as the standard and those who wanted free coinage, mainly the farmers of the South and West and the Western miners who believed that the purchase of silver by the government would not only help the mining interests by shoring up the sagging price of silver, but would also expand the money supply, helping hard-pressed farmers to pay their debts.

In fact, the price of silver had continued to fall, the purchase of it had drained gold from the Treasury, and since redemption in gold of the Treasury notes was allowed and preferred by foreign investors in particular, more gold had flowed out that way, too. Most of the major governments of the world considered gold the standard of exchange and were not impressed by the arbitrary value Congress assigned to silver in relation to gold as part of the bimetallic system.

Though dealing with the Treasury problem was surely vitally important, there was a month's delay between the call for the special session and the session itself, and Reid and Hawk chased rumors that the delay was caused by a personal need of the president, perhaps a health problem, but they could find no proof.

"I suspect there really is something going on," Reid said. "Our normal contacts are so, so silent. They're not even offering decent excuses."

The president was out of view for much of July, but the arguments over the Silver Purchase Act began in earnest in August, and by late October the act had been repealed. President Cleveland seemed to have lost weight from his heavy frame as well as appearing to be less vigorous, but that was understandable under the circumstances of the country's being in such trouble, so the cause for the delay in the summer remained a mystery.

The president's next target was the McKinley Tariff, but it appeared that he was going to have a long fight to gain any tariff reform. The repeal of the Silver Purchase Act had cost him political ground within his own Democratic Party and with the agrarian element in the country in general when the gold in the Treasury continued to dwindle and the financial crisis to deepen, despite the repeal of the Silver Purchase Act.

Lexy spent most of the summer and early fall covering the races and training Dan O'Rourke to take over basic coverage for the *Witness*. Dan was thirty, the son of Irish immigrants, and a sporting enthusiast. He didn't have Lexy's specialized knowledge, but he liked the races and the horses, and he was willing to work hard to be on the staff of the *Witness*, a job he considered a good step above the free-lance assignments he had done for various sporting journals. He also had the advantage of being a native New Yorker, which put him close to the major racetracks, though he would be expected to travel to Kentucky and to Chicago, where several race meetings were beginning to attract major stables.

Dan was familiar with Lexy's work and treated her with the utmost respect, not at all troubled by the fact that she was a woman. His attitude made it much more congenial than it would have been otherwise for Lexy to work with him, but still, she felt a pull of regret at relinquishing any of her responsibilities.

It was a negative impetus, but the worsening situation in the country also made it easier for her to share the sporting columns with Dan. With railroads, factories, banks, and other businesses going under, the human toll was going to be increasingly high, and Lexy wanted to write those stories.

But there were important developments in the racing world which Lexy covered herself. In December, Travis took part in a meeting in New York that was organized by James R. Keene. He, along with other prominent horse owners, protested the recent reduction of the value of sweepstakes and purses by racing associations which claimed the drop was due to a falling off of revenues. At last, plans were made to form a jockey club patterned on the English version. It would oversee all aspects of racing, and it would be dominated by owners of race horses, who were men more interested in the sport in general than in particular race meetings. Thus, track owners would have less to say about the sport than they had had with the Board of Control, which would be merged with the jockey club.

Lexy was proud that her father was respected enough to be a member of the Board of Control and to have been included in the select group of men who were founding the jockey club. She had every intention of writing columns giving strong support to the new body; it was a job she would not consider delegating to Dan.

At Christmas, they celebrated Travis's success in the racing world, success which he insisted was as much Gincie's as his own. And they toasted other family victories, including the news that Jilly was pregnant again. While Dermot allowed that he would welcome a boy or a girl, he confessed he would really like a daughter this time. Jilly vowed she was doing her best to oblige him.

Dermot was a good provider. He had heeded his own misgivings and had rearranged his whole portfolio before the crash in order that his family would not suffer. His holdings were so extensive, he had not escaped without damage, but he was still a very rich man, and substantial sums now rested in Maryland banks because they had remained solvent during all the ups and downs of many past decades.

But being solvent themselves did not blind Dermot and Jilly to what was going on around them. Every day in New York they were seeing more and more misery.

"So many out of work! They're cold and hungry now that winter has come. And though President Cleveland may be a sensible man, he is not a sensitive one. He believes people owe duty to their government, but not that the government has any duty to relieve suffering in times like these. It is hard enough to see the adults, but the children—it is unbearable to see them suffer!" Jilly said, her hands going unconsciously to her stomach.

With quiet pride, Dermot explained that Jilly had been organizing benefits using her own singing and any talents she could coax from their friends to raise money to feed the poor, turning the proceeds over to various charitable groups and churches.

"It's very little." Jilly's protest was genuine, but with a gleam of mischief, she added, "I must admit, though, that I enjoy maneuvering some of our more complacent friends into doing something. Before now, I would never have suspected how many people harbor theatrical ambitions. If I asked them directly for money, they might give once and reluctantly, but offered a chance to recite poetry, or play an instrument, or sing, all in the name of charity, of course, they will work extraordinarily hard and shame any number of friends into buying tickets for the performances.

"It is nothing compared to what Dermot has given and has persuaded his business cronies to donate, but maybe it will make a few people think about how serious the situation is, people who wouldn't normally consider it at all," Jilly finished, ignoring her husband's flush of embarrassment at her mention of his efforts.

"See, all your patience with our cousin has been amply rewarded," Tay whispered in Lexy's ear, and they exchanged smiles of perfect understanding.

Tay's presence at Wild Swan was the best gift Lexy could have wished for Christmas. Gincie and Travis had kept his plan secret, so his arrival had been a surprise to both of his siblings and everyone else.

Lexy no longer had the slightest doubt about the wisdom of his move to California. He was bronzed and fit, and his eyes glowed with excitement every time he talked about his life in the Far West. He was more alive, more forceful, than Lexy had ever seen him, and though he spoke of no special woman in his life, he was now at ease with Kace and Georgie.

It made Lexy understand that perhaps this wider separation of the twins would have been necessary for Tay to come into his own even had the twins never loved the same woman.

In addition to the benefits to Tay, Travis and Gincie discovered that he had lifted a heavy burden from them. Travis had grown accustomed to making the trip across the country to check on the California properties, as Gincie had grown accustomed to having him gone and to feeling the anxiety that thoughts of California still brought to her, despite her efforts to put away the old nightmare. Neither of them had wanted wholly to forsake what they had started in the Far West; to both of them it would have meant a final victory for Mark, though he was long dead. So they had continued the annual disruption of their lives. But now Tay carried the responsibility effortlessly.

For Gincie and Travis, having their son loving the life on the other coast as they once had, drawing strength and joy from that distant land was vindication for holding on to the acres and investments there for so long.

But even in California, imagined as a paradise before it had even been seen by white men, the problems of the present day intruded. The Geary Act of the previous year had been declared constitutional by the Supreme Court this year, and so Chinese laborers were prohibited from entering the United States for another ten years, as they had first been excluded in 1882. The Chinese Exclusion Acts were a direct result of West Coast fears of having the Chinese take jobs from white men. It didn't matter that the Chinese had helped to build everything from houses to railroads in the early days; once the transcontinental railroad had brought in multitudes of white workers, to be followed by yet more legions of whites seeking jobs and new lives, the Chinese were perceived not only as too alien, but also as willing to work for too little.

"It's an ugly business," Tay said. "There are gangs of bullies who think nothing of attacking the Chinese on the streets or driving them out of their little settlements. If they had their way, all the Chinese already there would be forced to leave. But nonetheless, the Chinese go on working and running their lives according to their own customs. It is a lesson in survival, and I would predict that they will still be flourishing in California a hundred years from now."

It was a relief to hear someone speculating about a time so many years away, but basically, they were all intent on taking each day as it came because the immediate future was so uncertain.

They could celebrate the fact that the medical school of Johns Hopkins University had finally opened this October and that Joseph's Mattie had been accepted in the first class. Still, Anthea, Max, Nigel, and their colleagues at the clinic were treating more and more patients for free, patients who were worn down and ill from lack of enough money to purchase even the most basic essentials of life.

The family's businesses were all run with such meticulous, conservative care, going under was unlikely for any of them, but Adam would have to exercise all his skill to keep his ships full of cargo and passengers as the depression deepened. And all of them suffered from seeing an increasing flow of unemployed workers of all sorts and from knowing they could help only a few.

The toasts to health, peace, prosperity, and remembrance on New Year's Eve had the fervor of prayers this year.

It was hard not to dread what 1894 might bring, and the fire that swept the grounds of the Columbian Exposition and destroyed most of the buildings on January 8 seemed a prophetic beginning, as if the prosperity and progress shown at the world's fair had been nothing more than an illusion easily swept away by the flames.

Early in April, rioting broke out among striking miners in Connellsville, Pennsylvania, and when 136,000 miners struck over wages at Columbus, Ohio, the country seemed to be approaching civil war.

Mining for coal had little in common with the romantic picture of placer mining such as had characterized the California gold rush. Commercial coal mining meant sending men down to work in deep, hot, airless, and endlessly dangerous shafts where cave-ins and gas explosions regularly killed miners.

Lexy went to Connellsville, and she listened to the workers describe the conditions underground, and she thought that she would not be able to go down there every day and work even if the mining company made all the improvements the miners wanted. She listened to the women describe what it was like to wait after an accident to see if their fathers or husbands or brothers or other relatives had been killed. She looked at the drab houses they lived in, and she thought that living and working here must be like residence in hell. But the miners were proud of their ability to work beneath the earth, proud of their skills and endurance. They didn't want mining to end; they wanted to be paid adequate wages for it and to have safety insured as much as it could be in an endeavor that would forever be hazardous.

She could not understand how greed could so overcome practicality. Even if the mine owners wanted to regard their workers as no more than beasts, still they should know that better care gained better work. The grim difference seemed to be that the owners considered the workers easily and cheaply replaced, unlike cattle or horses, which required an immediate outlay of cash.

At the end of April, "Coxey's Army" arrived in Washington, having traveled from Massillon, Ohio, on foot, by canal boat, and by rail to protest unemployment and the government's willingness to pass laws favorable to large corporations while voting down laws that would help the workers. Specifically, Coxey was asking Congress to finance a public works program for the unemployed.

Jacob Sechler Coxey, nicknamed "General" Coxey, was a well-to-do businessman who had joined the Populists, and despite some ridicule in the press, his band of marchers were orderly and earnest. Coxey's chief aide, Carl Browne, was said to be behind the idea for the march. But whoever was in charge, the marchers behaved better than most real armies and committed no violence on the way, despite the fear of revolution that had been felt in some quarters.

A large crowd greeted their arrival with cheers, but then everything went wrong for the men. Police prevented Coxey from delivering a speech in front of the Capitol, though he complained eloquently that "the lobbyists of trusts and corporations have passed unchallenged on their way to the committee rooms, access to which we, the representatives of the toiling wealth producers, have been denied."

Lexy took down the full text of his protest, and it was printed in the paper, but it was of little use. Coxey and his aides were arrested for walking on the grass surrounding the Capitol. This spurious charge allowed the authorities to remove them from the scene, and the army disbanded.

Some news reports had labeled the men disreputable tramps, but when Lexy moved among them, speaking to many, she found that the great majority, painstakingly neat in their threadbare garments, were deferential in attitude and desirous only of the chance to support themselves and their families.

Lexy was growing obsessed with the faces of the workers she met. She saw them in her dreams—people from Homestead, from Connellsville, and from the ranks of Coxey's Army—and she began to have nightmares about Mae and Jake, hearing Mae scream over and over, seeing Jake's blood bright-splashed on Mae's dress.

Hawk awakened her and held her when she cried out in the night, and he continually schooled himself to patience, but it grew harder every day. He could not deny the rightness of the work she was doing or her right to do it, but he hated the toll it was taking on her. She was too thin, and her eyes were always shadowed now.

On May 11, the workers at the Pullman Palace Car Company called a strike in protest against the reduction in wages that had come without a reduction in the rents and other fees they paid to the company for their housing, gas, water, and food, even for the use of church and library facilities.

George M. Pullman was proud of the model town he had built just south of Chicago for his workers. His press agent had described it as a place "where all that is ugly and discordant and demoralizing is eliminated and all that inspires self-respect is generously provided."

But the town called Pullman did not seem like such a beneficent place when one considered that workers who lived there had no say in the prices and fees charged. With wages slashed, most men were only bringing home six dollars a week after all the deductions, and one employee had received a check for two cents. Yet when a committee of workers met with Mr. Pullman to air their grievances, they were told that no connection existed between wages and rent, between employer and landlord. And though the committee had been promised they would not be harmed for protesting, its leaders were promptly fired.

Infuriated by Pullman's actions since the depression had started, workers had been joining the American Railway Union, which was led by Eugene Debs, a fiery idealist who was promoting a unionism among railroad men that would include all the workers in the industry, not just those who actually worked on the rolling stock.

When Pullman refused to consider the committee's complaints and fired the leaders, the strike was called.

Arbitration was out of the question because Pullman would not discuss the matter. His answer was to close the plant. Economically, it was easier for him to do this now than it would have been before the depression, when there had been generous orders for Pullman cars to fill the demand for train travel to the Columbian Exposition. Now orders were down in all parts of the industry.

On June 26, Eugene Debs and the American Railway Union called a sympathetic boycott of all Pullman cars, asking that union members refuse to handle the Pullman cars on trains across the nation.

By then, Lexy was in Chicago. She had made an honest attempt to fix her attention on the races, but she had followed every item of news about the Pullman strike, and she had realized that the impasse was not going to last much longer. She had left Dan to cover the Coney Island Jockey Club Meeting; she had told her parents where she was going; and she had sent a telegram to Hawk, not trying to reach him by telephone because she did not want to speak to him directly, for fear his objections might sway her this time.

Every time she thought of the reason she might falter in her course, she denied it. She wanted to cover the strike, not listen to the strange signals she was receiving from her body.

Once she reached Chicago, she immersed herself in the story. She talked to everyone she could. She used the prestige of the

Witness, her own reputation as Abby Adams, and whatever charm she could muster. She talked to labor leaders, to workers and their wives, and to an agent for Pullman who informed her that Mr. Pullman was personally hurt by the ingratitude his workers were showing him after he had done so much for them.

She listened patiently, and then she asked, "Does he really believe that? When he cuts their wages, but will not similarly cut rents and fees? Where does he think they are to get the money to survive?"

The interview ended abruptly with the man turning an unhealthy shade of red and muttering about petticoats and politics.

Mr. Debs was another matter. Tired and harried though he was, he knew the benefits of favorable press and answered her questions patiently.

Born in Indiana of immigrant parents from Alsace, he would turn thirty-nine this year. He had begun work at the age of fourteen in the railroad shops of Terre Haute and had then become a locomotive fireman. He quit railroading in 1874, but had been working toward strengthening the collective bargaining power of the various craft brotherhoods connected with railroading until last year when, having failed to make the progress he desired, he had formed his American Railway Union, open to anyone who worked in any facet of the industry.

Even in so short a time, his union had had some success in several labor contests, but there was no doubt that this dispute with Pullman was of major importance.

Lexy could feel the intensity of the man and found it both exhilarating and frightening. "How far are you prepared to go for the Pullman workers?" she asked, and his answer was as direct as her question: "As far as we must until there is justice."

The boycott Debs called on the twenty-sixth did not surprise Lexy, but the swiftness and scope of the official response did.

Chicago was the hub of twenty-four different rail lines, and their top men belonged to the General Managers Association. Within two days, the boycott was stopping traffic on the Western railroads, and in response, the managers brought in several hundred strikebreakers from Canada. It took Lexy precious time to discover that one of the main jobs assigned to the strikebreakers was to connect Pullman cars to mail cars. The significance was obvious: interfering with the movement of the mail was a federal offense.

If Debs was going to widen the conflict far beyond the Pullman Company, then his opposition was going to make sure they had government forces to supplement their private ones.

In just a few days, both sides had gone beyond the point where civilized negotiation was possible. The inevitability of open conflict had a horrible familiarity for Lexy.

With exquisitely ironic timing, on June 28 Congress declared Labor Day a national holiday. Lexy wondered if Congress was still on the same planet.

The railroads persuaded U.S. Attorney General Richard Olney to swear in as special deputies over three thousand men hired by the railroads to keep the trains moving. Lexy was sure the persuasion had been easy; Olney had been a railroad director and a member of the Managers Association, and was, according to various sources, still a lawyer for several railroads.

The deputies were match to powder, and Lexy followed the trail of violence with the reporters from other newspapers as the strikers began to clash with the special deputies. In one altercation, she saw men clubbing each other, blood spurting from numerous gashes; she heard the growling of their voices that was more bestial than human; and she watched it all as if she were a great distance away from it rather than close enough to see the sweat beading on the men's faces.

What she wanted more than anything was to be at home. Her body had finally caught up with her. She could no longer deny the symptoms. Her cycle had not been regular for nearly three months. For weeks she had been feeling vaguely sick when she awakened in the morning, and she could not bear the smell of coffee at all, though just a short time ago she had thought it a wonderful fragrance. And in the middle of a story that was rapidly moving from an isolated incident to a countrywide disaster, all she wanted to do was curl up and sleep.

She had, without acknowledging it, given up the idea of having children. She had even begun to believe that she could not conceive, particularly when there had been no issue from the wild lovemaking at Homestead or from other times when neither she nor Hawk had taken precautions.

Jilly had produced a healthy baby girl at the end of May, and Lexy was happy for her, for Mercy's joy in her offspring, and for Sally's delight in her children. But she herself did not feel any great pull of maternal yearning when she held a baby. In fact, she felt something akin to panic at their helplessness, at the endless needing.

She loved Hawk, and she loved her work. Both of them were demanding passions, and she did not want the balance to change. She flinched from the truth, but it was there nonetheless. And her worst fear was already coming true; the tiny being inside of her was shifting her attention away from her work, centering it on the changes in her body, centering it on itself.

When she dragged herself back to the hotel room that night, Hawk was waiting for her.

After the first moment of shock had passed, she continued to stand frozen, not knowing whether to run into his arms or to shriek at him for once again not trusting her to manage a story on her own, despite the truce they had made.

He put up his hands in surrender. "I wasn't going to come; I swear it! But Reid sent me, and he's still the boss. As soon as the mail was mentioned, he figured the railroads were going to use that as an argument to bring in the government. He didn't want you covering this alone. It's a good thing he sent me off when he did; with railroads closing down all over the country, it's difficult to travel."

His voice was calm, but his eyes grew more anxious as he realized how worn she looked, and then his control slipped. "Ah, hell, Lexy! I probably would have come anyway! I don't want to take this story away from you. I just want to help and keep you from getting hurt."

The fight went out of her so suddenly, she swayed on her feet, and Hawk crossed the distance between them to take her in his arms. He sat down on the bed with her cradled against him, and she murmured, "I am glad you're here."

Hawk unpinned her hat and cast it aside. He loosened her clothing, let her hair down, and massaged her scalp and the tight muscles of her neck. And all the while, he wondered what was going on. He had expected a stiff fight, not this swift surrender. And she had not said a word yet about a highly charged situation that had been absorbing her attention for weeks.

"Has it been very rough?" he asked, thinking that was a stupid question, but wanting her to explain.

The scent and warmth of him were making her dizzy; she wanted to renounce all responsibility for herself and let him shelter her. But she didn't want to tell him what was really bothering her, not yet, so she gathered her energy and recounted the latest details of the strike.

"It doesn't seem to matter if bodies are battered, but property damage is cause for serious alarm. The rioting has been sporadic, mostly a matter of strikers and the special deputies staging battles here and there, but now they've begun to attack railroad property and anything else in reach." She hesitated and then went on, "I'm not sure it's true, but I was told today that some of the men setting fire to railroad cars were employed by the railroads. I'm not saying that the strikers are blameless, because they're not. It's turning ugly on both sides, but if the rumor is true, then it means the railroads are inciting to riot, which is surely as serious a crime as interfering with the mail."

"And it's a damned effective way to gain more government support," Hawk said.

Lexy nodded against him. "Governor Altgeld has insisted that Illinois does not need outside forces to control the trouble, but the railroads want more. And they might be trying to get it by having their own men pose as strikers. Except that I can't prove it, and I admit, my two informants are union men, or at least, I think they are."

"Did either of them give you names or specifics?"

"Not yet, but I'm to meet them tomorrow. When I told them I couldn't write such a story without proof, they said they'd get it for me."

Hawk could not repress the shudder that ran through him at the idea of her going to the meeting by herself, as she had planned to do.

"It's all right," she said slipping out of his arms and sitting beside him. "I trust them. The puzzle is why they trust me. They did not ask for money or for any other reward, just that the story be printed. I promised I would do my best."

"Have you had any trouble with the authorities or with management's men?"

"No, not really. I've been followed a couple of times," she answered honestly, "but no one has interfered with me."

"No one will tomorrow, either, because I'm going with you." He stated it as a fact, but nonetheless, he was surprised when she raised no objection.

They went to supper together, but Lexy could hardly keep her eyes open through the meal, and she would have fallen asleep in her clothes had Hawk not helped her to undress.

He listened to the even rhythm of her breathing, felt the reassuring press of her body along the length of his own, and yet, it was as if she were miles away from him. He thought he had accepted her deep involvment in the economic wars being fought between workers and business owners, but this gulf between himself and Lexy was wider than ever before, and he sensed there were currents he didn't understand running beneath the surface. It made him feel more lonely than when he had been in Washington and she here.

In the morning, she looked so wan, he tried to persuade her to tarry long enough to have breakfast, but she refused, if anything growing paler at the mention of food.

"Are you ill?" he asked sharply.

By sheer effort of will, she kept her stomach from winning the contest; this was the worst wave of morning sickness she'd suffered so far. She managed to answer, "No, I'm just very tired. It's difficult to watch the violence increasing each day when it seems to me a little reason in the beginning could have prevented it."

The cab they hired would not take them all the way to their destination, and Hawk could understand why. As soon as they were in sight of the rail yards, they saw knots of men prowling, and the trains themselves were guarded by armed men on the roofs. The remnants of many freight cars that had been attacked and burned on the previous day still smoldered.

"Jesus! What a place for a meeting!" Hawk growled, and then his eyes widened as he realized that there were a few top-hatted gentlemen of obvious means who were there to support the strikers.

"What better place? There're so many people milling around at the main railheads, it would be hard to keep account of what everyone is doing. In any case, we don't have to go any closer to the crowd. I am to meet the men just along here."

Hawk did not bother to point out that while there might be scores of men and a few strikers' wives in the crowd, beautiful women like Lexy were not in evidence. She was dressed very plainly, but to him she still shone like a beacon in the drab surroundings.

She felt his tension as they waited for the men to come, and she tried to explain more fully what she had seen in the past days.

"The town of Pullman really is a nice place. The houses are much better than most workers elsewhere inhabit. When I first arrived, I spent quite a bit of time there. It is so sad that such a good idea could have gone so wrong. If only Mr. Pullman could have gone one step further, could have been able to see that he could not separate being the landlord from being the employer. And the unionists, they must see that tying up most of the railroads in the country will never be tolerated. They . . . Oh, at last! Here they come." Relief quickened her voice as she caught sight of two men.

She checked at the sight of Hawk, and Lexy said, "Wait here, please," and went forward.

He made himself obey her, but his muscles were bunched with tension and his eyes measured the distance he would have to run if the men made an untoward gesture toward Lexy.

He could not hear what they said, but Lexy had reassured them enough so that they came with her. She introduced Hawk but did not give the men's names because she did not know them.

"Some of the names is writ down here," one man mumbled as he pulled a paper from his pocket and handed it to Lexy. "I know it ain't much, but they helped set fire to some cars two days ago, pretendin' to be with us. But they ain't! They ain't union men."

"I seed 'em talkin' with some of the guards, real friendly like," the other man said.

"How did you get their names?" Lexy asked.

"We got 'em drunk t'other night," the first man answered with some pride. "We got 'em drunk, an' then we got 'em talkin', an' we pretended we was on the railroad side, too." As he spoke his eyes shifted around constantly.

"Why didn't you just take care of them yourselves?" Hawk asked.

The leader of the two pulled himself up very straight. "We ain't bully boys, don't want to kill nobody. All we want is decent wages."

"Fair enough," Hawk conceded, and then they all started at a yelp from the other man.

The knot of men seemed to come out of nowhere, and Hawk saw instantly that they were outnumbered two to one even if Lexy were counted.

"Run!" he hissed at her, but as she moved to obey him, the men were on them, flailing viciously with fists and short, stout clubs. "The paper, get the paper, get the names," someone was shouting.

Though he hadn't been involved in a brawl for years, Hawk still remembered the tricks, but they weren't magic enough to overcome the odds, particularly when the attackers seemed as intent on getting to Lexy as to him and the two other men.

He threw all his energy into protecting her, pulling her behind him when one of the thugs reached for her, taking blows that would have hit her as well as the ones aimed at disabling him because his sheer size and strength made him a lethal threat as long as he was conscious.

Lexy felt the impact on his body. She had never felt so helpless in her life. She did the only thing she could think of. She opened her mouth and screamed, shrill, loud shrieks that were like no other sounds she had ever made in her life before.

She felt Hawk's body jolt and then slump against her as one of the men mouthed a filthy oath. Rough hands pulled at her as she tried to hold Hawk upright, and then she was sinking to the ground under his weight. And it was just like Mae and Jake because Hawk's eyes were closed, his head was cradled in her lap, and his blood was flowing over her hands and her clothes.

His bleeding head was resting over the place where his son or daughter was growing inside of her, and he didn't know the beginning was there.

She howled the denial aloud and then started the litany, "You can't, you won't die!" She said it over and over and over again; she could not stop saying it.

Chapter 53

Lexy remembered little of what happened next. But as Dr. Blakeman explained, bits and pieces came back to her.

The attackers had fled from the strike sympathizers who had come in response to her screams, and it was Mr. Morton, one of the top-hatted gentlemen Hawk had noticed, who had taken charge and gotten the Mackennas to Dr. Blakeman. The two men who had been with them had been injured, too, but had refused any help, melting into the crowd. The list was gone; the thugs had gotten what they wanted, and the two informants would surely not come forward again.

It didn't matter. It didn't matter that President Cleveland had, in spite of Governor Altgeld's demur, called out federal troops to guard the trains and to stop the trouble in Chicago. It didn't matter that a widespread injunction had been issued against the union under the provisions of the Sherman Anti-Trust Act, an act designed, though little used, to curb the excesses of big business, but now turned handily against laborers. It didn't matter that Debs would undoubtedly be arrested, nor that his union had lost the battle.

Nothing on earth mattered to Lexy except Hawk. His broken shoulder and his various bruises would heal, but there was no way to know whether or not his brain ever would. The left side of his face was horribly swollen and discolored, and there was a huge lump where a club had hit him near his temple. He had not regained consciousness since the attack. He lay so still, Lexy had to keep reassuring herself that he breathed.

This was vastly different from when he had returned from South Dakota. He had been ill then, but this time his life was in danger, and it was because of her story, not his.

Dr. Blakeman was a caring and competent physician. His office was in his house, and he and his wife had immediately set about making the Mackennas as comfortable as possible, banishing any question of where they were to stay. But though the doctor tried to be reassuring, his apprehension and pity showed in his eyes.

"Your husband received a severe blow to his head. Head injuries are a tricky business. We just don't know much about how the brain works. It's a bad sign that he hasn't regained consciousness, but that doesn't mean that he won't. His pulse and breathing are satisfactory, and that's something to be thankful for. And he swallows the liquids we give him, which is all to the good. When you're with him, keep talking to him as you have, as if he can hear you. Patients who are unconscious often can, you see. When they awaken, they can recite much of what was said in the sickroom."

Lexy didn't need his admonition. She needed to keep talking to Hawk for her own sanity. She was afraid he would slip away in silence. She was afraid his bright mind had already fled.

"I've been afraid of so many things," she told him. "I've been afraid of losing myself, my work, like so many women do. I'm still afraid. I don't want to vanish into the cages society approves for women—someone's wife, someone's mother, but not someone valuable and separate for her own sake. I've been afraid to admit even to myself that I carry your child, our child. And I'm still afraid I won't be a good mother." She held his hand to her mouth, tracing the hard, capable structure of it with her lips. There was no response to her touch. "But I've learned an awful lesson. All those other fears, they are nothing to the terror of losing you. My work, my separateness, the things that make me unique, they would go on in some fashion, but more of me would vanish with you than would survive without you. I need you to live for me, for our child, if not for yourself. Without you, I and the child might have been killed."

Talking about it made the child more and more real to her. "I wonder how she or he will look, what color eyes, hair, how much of me, how much of you, will be visible. But, of course, the child will be its own self, someone unique in the world."

Because she was so focused on Hawk, it took her a while to realize that her resistance and reluctance about the pregnancy was being transmuted into hope and a kind of euphoria she had never felt before. It swept through her at odd intervals, and she clung to it fiercely against the darkness that lay in wait too close to Hawk.

When her parents and Nigel arrived, she found she had yet more cause to thank Mr. Morton. He had asked her if anyone should be notified, and she had given him Reid's name because Reid would be easy to reach through the newspaper, but she had not thought about it since. Reid had immediately contacted the Culhanes, as well as Nigel.

When Lexy saw her parents, she burst into tears and allowed herself to be enveloped in the comfort they offered, allowed herself to give voice to her deepest terror.

"What if he never wakes up; what if he's already gone?"

"Hawk is a strong man who loves you very much. He has everything to live for. Trust him to stay with you," Gincie said, her voice betraying no uncertainty.

None of the new arrivals shared their own doubts with Lexy, but they were appalled by Hawk's condition, though Nigel confirmed that Dr. Blakeman was taking excellent care of the patient.

"What do you think his chances are?" Travis asked bluntly, but Nigel had no easy answer.

"The longer it goes, the more dangerous it is, but he might yet wake up to full consciousness and no permanent damage. Or he might awaken with some impairment to his brain. Or he might never wake up at all."

Gincie thought of how clever her son-in-law was, and she thought if he could not awaken to the full use of his brain, it might be better if he did not ever regain consciousness. She didn't say the words aloud, but Travis understood because he was thinking the same thing.

"For now, one of the best things we can do is to make Lexy rest; she looks almost as bad as Hawk, though she assures me she is just tired," Nigel said. Because of the circumstances, they did not suspect the truth of Lexy's condition.

They did not want to inconvenience the Blakemans any more than necessary, so they rented rooms in a nearby hotel but took turns, making sure one of them was always with Lexy and Hawk or within easy call.

Lexy was glad of their support, but she would not leave Hawk for more than the short periods required to bathe and take care of her other personal needs. At least she was able to sleep, curled up on a cot in Hawk's room, confident that if there was any change at all in his condition, whoever was watching over him would alert her immediately. The sound of another voice speaking to him as if he could hear was particularly reassuring, making the belief in his recovery wider than her own faith.

But she talked to him about the baby only when the two of them were alone. She didn't want anyone else to know before he did.

"Of course, I hope you're hearing everything I tell you, but until I'm sure, I'm going to keep it a secret. It's strange, but I'm not sure how you're going to feel about being a father again. You've been so kind. You've never pressured me to have a child, and you never talk about Jared, though I know you must wonder about him sometimes. I'm not really worried about it, though. You are a very loving man, even if you don't think yourself so. You'll make a marvelous father."

On the tenth morning after he'd been hurt, Hawk's eyes opened briefly, and he murmured something unintelligible, but he slipped away again despite Lexy's urgent pleas that he wake up.

In the evening, his eyes opened again. But this time it was different. He blinked several times, struggling to focus, and then he looked directly into her eyes.

"I think the baby ought to be born at Wild Swan, don't you?" he said. Though his voice was faint and rasping, she heard every word.

It was the most he could manage for now, but when he closed his eyes again, he pressed his hand against hers in response to her touch, and it was sleep that claimed him, not the unnatural twilight of the coma.

Lexy heard her mother's gasp and smiled at her through her tears. "His mind isn't wandering. We're going to have a baby. It should arrive in January."

"A fine birth date for a Thoroughbred," Gincie said, and then she hugged her daughter, and both of them were laughing and crying at the same time.

It was going to take time for Hawk to recover fully, for his shoulder to knit, the headaches to cease, and his strength to return, but the pain was proof that he was alive, and he willed himself to patience.

"It was a strange place where I was, but you were always there with me, calling me back," he told Lexy.

He was dazzled when he looked at her now, knowing she carried their child. He had known she was not eager to have children, though he had not known the depth of her fears before, and he had not felt any burning desire to persuade her to change her mind. A part of him had accepted that Jared would be the only child he would father. But now everything was changed, and because Lexy had come to the joy of it, he could rejoice as well.

When Hawk had improved enough so that Nigel and Dr. Blakeman judged it safe, the family traveled home with him to Maryland in a private car hired by Travis.

The irony of traveling in such a way was inescapable, but Lexy admitted she would have done so even during the strike in order to take Hawk home safely. She was learning her own kind of patience to match Hawk's. The baby would take precedence for a while, but Hawk did not expect her to raise their child alone or to give up the profession they both loved.

The things she cared about most deeply—the battle for women's rights and for the rights of blacks and others who had yet to be recognized as equal members of the human race; the fight for decent hours and wages for workers—these wars would not have sudden or easy victories. But Hawk expected her to continue to bear witness to these last tumultuous years of the nineteenth century and as much of the twentieth century as she would see.

Somehow, she would learn, as had Alex and Gincie and the other women of the family, to find a way to balance motherhood, her career, and being Hawk's wife. It all seemed possible now, and infinitely easier than going on without him.

The people who loved them were waiting to give thanks for Hawk's escape from death and for the new life Lexy carried.

Della, ancient and enduring witness to all the years since the family had first come to Wild Swan, greeted the news of Lexy's pregnancy with approval and recognition.

"From Alex to Gincie, from Gincie to you, from you to your daughter, from generation to generation, from one to the next so that nothing is lost." Her words were prophecy and blessing.

Lexy and Hawk came home to Wild Swan to heal as the family had for decades, as Gincie and Travis had come home nearly twenty-five years before. The land was lush green in the heat of August. It enfolded them instantly in the steady beat of its own heart.